SARAH

He sighed, feeling a new burden upon him. This was a problem that he could scarcely bear to contemplate. Of course people would want to meet her. Unmarried men like Sir Nicholas could hardly fail to want to meet her. She would be pursued by suitors and in the eyes of the world it was his responsibility to see that she married as well as possible. Yet now, how could he face such an event?

Those two occasions of love-making had been so disturbing to him that he had not attempted either to justify them or even assimilate them into his conscious thoughts. Temporarily, he had felt it was something beyond his control. His relationships had always been not perhaps secondary but separate from his public life. The sea, his voyages, the estate had assumed the reason for his existence; his private life was his religion, his Catholic faith, his duty to his God. Somewhere between the two, his family occupied an assured and permanent place in his thoughts and affections, but never obtrusively so. Although he knew his concern for Sarah had gone beyond those rational bounds, he was still determined that his passion should be controlled, his lustful behaviour not repeated. But now the thought of her marriage to another seemed to lay waste all else in his life, his fame and fortune a mockery.

About the author

Renée Huggett was born in Devon in the home of her maternal grandparents. Many of her relatives came from Dartmouth and from early childhood she was taken on frequent visits to the town, hearing stories about life there in centuries past. The place has held a permanent fascination for her.

Renée Huggett now lives with her husband in Somerset, and makes frequent visits to Devon for research and inspiration. She is a lecturer and writer who has had several other works of fiction and non-fiction published.

SARAH

Renée Huggett

CORONET BOOKS
Hodder and Stoughton

'If men could learn from history, what lessons it might teach us! But passion and party blind our eyes, and the light which experience gives is a lantern on the stern, which shines only on the waves behind us.'

SAMUEL TAYLOR COLERIDGE

1

It was a golden morning in the year of our Lord, sixteen hundred and ten. As the July sun rose above the Estuary and glinted through the tiny windows of St Petrox Church at the mouth of the harbour, in the town the citizens of Dartmouth began to make their way up the wooded slopes of Jawbones Hill.

Earlier that morning, as the first shafts of ice-blue light cut across the black night sky, Sir Gabriel Hooper Humphreys had ridden his horse through the silent streets to be clear of the town before the rabble started their journey. He had left his horse at the stables in Bayards Cove, climbed the steep narrow steps behind the old castle and in half an hour had clambered to the peak of the hill.

As one of the Commissioners of Peace, it was his job to inspect the gallows and later to ensure that the execution was carried out properly. He had pushed at the hastily constructed posts of the gallows and they had swayed slightly. The cross bar was a heavy plank of wood which looked as though it had come from a ship's timbers. Would the supporting posts hold it? He had frowned. A mishap in these unpleasant circumstances was the last thing he wanted. Then he had reflected that the old woman was hardly any weight at all, even less after the torture and starvation she'd have been subjected to in the gaol. But the hangman would be leaning his ladder against the bar; that would cause further strain on the posts. He would get two of the stewards to hold the posts at each end – it was only a brief affair, after all.

Then he had waited, looking across the harbour at the boats moving slowly up the river and then to the sea beyond, and thinking of his next voyage.

Gabriel, a tall majestic figure against the vivid blue skyline, now looked down distastefully upon the ascending multitude. The steep stone steps between the narrow houses leading up from the quay were now crowded with fishermen, labourers and vagrants. Housewives with their reed baskets and excited children plodded up the narrow flags of Crowthers Hill and Slippery Causeway. From the market square, stall-holders and their customers pushed and jostled each other as they wound their way through the alleys behind St Saviour's Church, joining those who emerged from the old timbered houses in St Saviour's Court. From around Bayards Cove, the smiths and boat repairers climbed the steep ascent behind the old fort and up the soaring rise to Jawbones.

Gabriel reflected that only seven years earlier, upon the death of Elizabeth, James VI of Scotland had travelled triumphantly south to become the invited James I of England. He had found himself a foreigner amongst an ambitious and pleasure-loving people and this day was to bear witness to one of his few points of contact with the common people. He shared with them a morbid belief in the devil and witchcraft, exaggerated by them into a fear of witches. Only a year after his succession, he had made a first offence of witchcraft punishable by hanging. A year later there was the trial of the Abingdon witches and only a couple of years ago even a ninety-year-old friar had been accused and had cut his throat to avoid being burnt as a witch.

Yet their common belief in witchcraft had failed to bind the English people to their King. His views arose from a philosophical belief; theirs came from the resentments of a submerged population of the poor and destitute.

England was revelling in a new period of prosperity and the people of Dartmouth in particular were more interested

2

in exploiting the opportunities arising from the great new era of exploration. Large amounts of capital were invested in developing the cod fishing off Newfoundland and importing salt to process fish to sell at home or in markets overseas. Spain no longer appeared to be a threat and trade had been resumed with their old Armada enemies. The Iberian ports were re-opened in 1604, giving the English vessels access to the Mediterranean and a great boost to their overseas trade.

Most of them gathered here today were more interested in the excitement of the execution than in preoccupations with witchcraft. That merely served as an excuse rather than a compelling reason. Though, Gabriel reflected, there was much superstition amongst the common people.

The sun rose higher in the sky, pouring down on the excited mass as they plodded up the hills. Although it had been a hot summer, with cloudless blue skies for weeks on end, Gabriel knew they would interpret today's sunshine as a particularly happy omen. The Lord was blessing the events of this day. Gabriel did not share their enthusiasm.

He turned with revulsion from the surging mob to contemplate the harbour far below, at the water sparkling in the brilliant sunshine and the hundreds of small ships anchored round the Bight.

Periodically a vivid red light flashed and twinkled, which he knew from experience was simply the effect of the sun's rays on one of the windows of St Petrox Church. Some pilot vessels, minute from this height, were leading in a brig, returning with its cargo from Newfoundland. Because of the steep slope of the hill he could not see Bayard's Cove, but he knew that the brig would moor there to unload its cargo.

In his mind he could imagine the smell of the wet ropes and tarred decks of the fishing boats, the lingering smell of fish as it lay in the blazing sun awaiting collection by the market men, and his thoughts moved briefly to

3

his own vessels, expected that day, bringing fish from Newfoundland and fruit from the Azores. At least James had protected their fishing rights. The Dutch were now forbidden to fish round the coasts of Britain without the payment of an annual sum.

The spectators below him were spreading themselves across the hill. There was no shelter from the sun and they threw themselves on the grass to await the event. There was a carnival atmosphere, as there always was on these occasions; one small group began dancing, having already drunk too much beer. They fell over, rolling down the hill, shrieking with laughter and crashing into the climbers below. There was a brief, light-hearted shoving and jostling and then they all slowly resumed their climb. A man dressed in a mock jester's outfit was selling baubles from a tray suspended by a rope round his neck and everywhere people had baskets of bread and fruit from the market.

At 9 o'clock the bell of St Saviour's Church boomed and the devout who attended church on weekdays streamed out through the ancient carved wooden doors. Then they also turned along the Shambles in the direction of Jawbones Hill.

The officials coming up the other side of the hill could see Gabriel at the top. Gabriel knew that to the citizens of Dartmouth he was their great explorer and adventurer, a Devon man – and Catholic at that – who had risen by his own courage and cleverness to become Lord of the Manor, Deputy Lieutenant and the richest man in the west country.

His clothes reflected his position in society. His high-waisted purple doublet was made of an expensive velvet with a short skirt over wide padded breeches which were attached to the doublet with laces. His yellow knitted stockings were made of silk, with clocks of gold thread on the sides. A gold satin embroidered semi-circular cloak, lined with silk taffeta which showed through the slashed satin, hung fashionably from one shoulder. His

4

short brown leather boots had wide turnovers trimmed with lace, matching the white lace ruff which turned down from the high-standing collar beneath his doublet. The wide feathers on his tall black hat flapped lightly in the summer breeze and his fine leather gloves were decorated with gold thread and the fringe was perfumed with aromatic herbs.

Gabriel, although forty years old, was one of the new Englishmen. His attitude was coloured by his youthful experiences of a great Elizabethan age. The privileged among the population had begun to see visions and have dreams which had turned out to be realizable.

The sudden dynamic expansion of the English language had found its counterpart in incredible adventures across the unknown world. What Shakespeare had achieved in the metaphor and paradox of the illusionary theatre, he and his fellow merchant adventurers had found in the reality of wealth and power.

Only Drake and Raleigh had equalled Gabriel's success and opulence and they had started with greater advantages.

His rise had been so spectacular, his exploits so impressive, that none of the common people envied him. Gabriel knew that no-one envies a legend; it is something to be shared, something which adds to people's lives, to be built upon, dreamed about. His journeys to Newfoundland, Russia, China, were a permanent topic of conversation in the taverns and inns of Dartmouth, the humble homes of Kingswear.

The seamen who had sailed with him enjoyed a position of distinction in the community and it was they who were often envied. The fishermen, the boatmakers and quayworkers, the merchantmen who plied round the coasts were jealous that they had not sailed upon those magical journeys. They were not daunted by the sufferings, the hardships, the loss of lives. The sea had been their enemy for so long, had dominated their lives, heralded their deaths, provided hunger or plenty for them according to its mood, that no traveller's tale could intimidate them.

For the townspeople, the hardship and suffering were as essential a part of the legend as the discovery of strange countries and people, and the acquisition of amazing treasures. Hardship, violence, and sudden death, were a part of their own lives and provided a link between the known and the unknown. To have overcome these obstacles with such magnificence as Gabriel had done was something they could dimly understand.

The envy, where there was any, he found amongst the aristocracy, who had seen him rise to power and feted by the Queen although she had known of his religious affiliations. Not that Elizabeth had been much concerned with the Protestant and Catholic issue, as long as it did not intrude upon security. Loyalty to herself, the safety of the realm, was all that mattered. She had tried to bring peace and unity to her country and it was only when beliefs became flagrant, as in the case of Mary, that she had felt forced to act. Only three hundred Catholics had been executed during her long reign.

Coming out of his reverie, Gabriel noticed a tiny figure riding along high on the hill above Kingswear, unrecognizable at that distance but who he knew was Francis Carew, the Lord Lieutenant of Devon. He came every day to check on the arrival of his ships, as Gabriel did. Like Gabriel, he had grown rich on the spoils of foreign countries and pirated ships. The only difference was that Francis had been richer to start with, his family had joined the ranks of the wealthy when Henry VIII was disposing of the monasteries to the deserving and tolerant amongst his citizens.

Their children had grown up together, they attended each other's banquets and weddings and funerals and had often shared each other's successful voyages. It was through Carew that Gabriel had been appointed Deputy Lieutenant. Yet, looking at him in the distance, Gabriel felt uneasy, the more so because of today's event. James had changed the even temper of society which Elizabeth had tried to create. Meretricious people were promoted, his debts had reached massive proportions through dispensing favours, entertaining, and maintaining Salisbury's 19,000 strong army in Ireland. His hatred of Catholics had led him to introduce a ban on all recusants coming within ten miles of the Court. James's suspicions were unaccompanied by Elizabeth's astuteness. Even worse, he had brought a perverted form of Protestantism, which not only condemned Catholicism but challenged the moderate if ambivalent English church, creating suspicion and fear.

More and more Gabriel felt that he was living on the edge of an abyss, uncertain of anyone beyond his immediate family. Gabriel could never forget his own vulnerable position and that of his family, as acknowledged Catholics and practising recusants. If he were not to be seen upholding the law about witchcraft, his family might suffer later.

Gabriel turned as the group of officials who had come up the other side of the hill to avoid the crowds came towards him. They were led by the town-crier, who was riding on horseback and was flourishing a brass bell high above his head like a banner of victory. Behind him came the other Justices of the Peace, also on horseback, with their capes flowing out behind them. They were followed by yeomen carrying staves and by other petty officials and informers. The clergyman walked between them, stumbling already, not from the burden of his duties, Gabriel reflected, but from his over-consumption of wine. There had been complaints from his parishioners about Mr Hamford's behaviour. Eventually he would have to be deprived of his living.

As a member of the Sunday congregation of St Saviour's and as the Deputy Lieutenant, Gabriel, requested by the church wardens to deal with the situation, had threatened him with fines and dismissal. There had been no

7

improvement in Mr Hamford's behaviour as a result, but his sermons now usually included a reference to the dangers of recusancy and the Guy Fawkeses in their midst. Gabriel suspected that he was spreading rumours also about his contacts with Catholics abroad.

Behind them came the prisoner, flanked by three warders and followed by two or three women and a young girl. Gabriel had seen this girl in the courtroom when he sat on the Grand Jury which decided whether there was a prima facie case against the accused. Then, as now, her face was almost covered by her long gold-coloured unkempt hair, which reached down to her waist. There was something mysterious about her. Although he could scarcely see her face, there was an atmosphere of composure about her, a strange calmness unusual in a young person in her position. Usually anyone in such a situation looked terrified or distraught.

Gabriel moved towards them. It was his job to conduct the prisoner to the gallows, to see that there was an opportunity for confession and that there was no interference with the proper administration of justice. He reflected that his private deliberations with the circuit judge had already invalidated that aim. His own experiences of the persecution of Catholics and the lies told about them had long ago made him critical of the absurd claims made against alleged witches. Gabriel had pleaded with the judge to declare against the conviction of this old, ignorant woman against whom the only real evidence seemed to be that she kept toads and a cat and that people alleged they had seen her during a thunderstorm hidden behind a hedge in the shape of a calf. Their superstitions were so extreme that they were prepared to swear to any falsehood, exaggerate any imagining into fact.

In Elizabeth's time, she might have been imprisoned for a year but as the judge pointed out, in the present climate of opinion, this was not possible.

'If I declare against it,' the judge said, 'and say that it

8

is the devil himself who kills innocent children, it is the devil himself who will give them disease, ruin their crops, then the accusers will cry, "This judge hath no religion, for he doth not believe in witches. And that is the law of the country." So the poor creature must be hanged.'

As soon as Gabriel moved, the spectators knew it was the signal for action. A great shout went up from the crowd, from which isolated words floated up to him, 'devil', 'witch', 'curse'.

They surged further up the hill, screaming with anticipation, eager and excited and only the solid row of yeomen with staves pointing towards them prevented the leaders from entering the little area which had been cordoned off. Gabriel reached the prisoner. She looked even smaller than in the courtroom, a little old woman with a black woollen hood over her head revealing only the bottom part of her face, a small toothless mouth.

The hangman placed the rope, which was suspended from the crossbar, loosely round her neck in preparation and stepped on the lower rungs of the ladder before her. The clergyman asked her if she confessed to a compact with Satan. Most prisoners not only confessed, but repeated a catalogue of fantastic associations with the devil – fornication, nightly visitations, sucking of private parts, at which the crowd would scream in hysterical abuse. Gabriel frowned but he knew that the confession was part of the essential ritual in which accusers and accused fulfilled their allotted roles. It was the compact with the devil which excited the populace, permitted the accused to enter an illusory world where fear and logic had no place and gave James I's six-year-old law an added strength.

This old woman, however, failed to comply.

'No!' she screamed.

The clergyman seemed to sway, then asked if she confessed her guilt. In a voice incongruously loud and clear, she declared her innocence.

'I have never consorted with the devil, never pricked

9

images, nor cast the evil eye, and never harmed anyone or made them sick.'

The rest of her words were lost beneath the roaring of the crowd. The clergyman haltingly led her to the bottom of the ladder. The hangman now waited, high above.

Suddenly, the old woman turned, the crowd whistled and shouted and someone threw some fruit at her but this individual was instantly set upon by one of the yeomen and knocked to the ground. The rabble were not to be allowed to get out of hand.

The old woman was looking anxiously at the group around her. Suddenly, the young, golden-haired girl dashed forward, wailing incoherently. 'Don't go. Don't leave me,' she cried, flinging her arms round the crumpling body, and they both began to cry uncontrollably.

For one brief second silence fell on the crowd. Gabriel knew that momentarily even they were penetrated by this naked human suffering, touched by their own over-whelming inhumanity, but also by their own helplessness in the face of trivial fears, gossipings, paltry imaginings which were yet somehow linked with that vast super-natural which had to be placated and which demanded retribution. The moment passed and they began to jeer and shout at the girl also. Her hair fell further over her face. Gabriel was becoming curious and irritated because he could not see the features behind the tangled hair. Her sobs changed to screams and then to a dismal wailing which was echoed by the old woman. She was unceremoniously dragged away from the old woman by one of the yeomen. The clergyman advanced to the foot of the ladder and began reading the forti-eth psalm.

I waited patiently for the Lord; and he inclined unto me and heard my cry.

   He brought me up also out of an horrible pit, out of the miry clay and set my feet upon a rock and established my goings.

> And he hath put a new song in my mouth, even praise
> unto our God: many shall see it and fear and shall trust in
> the Lord.

The words were drowned in shouts from the crowd to demand a confession. The clergyman cut the psalm short and read the final verse. Then he turned to the old woman, pointing to the Bible. It was customary to ask the prisoner what words from the Scripture she wished to hear. Mr Hamford turned the pages and tried to raise his voice above the bellowing of the crowd.

> All that hate me whisper against me: against me do they devise
> my hurt.
>   By this I know that thou favourest me, because mine enemy
> doth not triumph over me.
> Blessed be the Lord God of Israel.

His voice was drowned by screams of abuse. She had not chosen a text of repentance and they were furious at her effrontery.

Gabriel waved abruptly to the hangman. It was time to make an end of it. Slowly she began to climb, higher and higher, her long, bedraggled skirts impeding her progress on the narrow rungs. A yeoman half-helped, half-shoved her up the rest of the ladder while the hangman waited at the top. He fixed the end of the rope round the bar, knotting it firmly. There was so much noise from the crowd that Gabriel could not hear the old woman's final words as she turned and looked at them malevolently. Her arms jerked backwards and forwards like a puppet as she shouted soundlessly. But they recognized her gestures of defiance and screamed even louder. She cast one last agonized glance at the girl, who was now kneeling on the grass, staring up at her, waiting. The hangman carefully descended the ladder, the yeoman snatched it away, and a great cheer went up.

As the body swung out above her, the girl let out a

shrill scream which momentarily rose above the shouts, jeers, laughter and obscenities of the crowd. One of the yeomen advanced towards the body dangling above him, reached up and sharply pulled at the feet. Often, with a lightweight body such as this old woman's, the neck did not break instantly and death was caused by slow strangulation. This might appeal to the crowd but the officials turned away impatiently, wishing to get the task done. The girl sank from her knees flat on the ground, burying her face in the grass, her hair covering her, above her waist, like a protective shawl.

Gabriel strode over to the town-crier. 'Lead off,' he said peremptorily.

The bell clanged and the procession began to move slowly off down the hill.

'Off with you,' Gabriel shouted at the people nearest to him. 'It's a working day, not a Holy Day. Go back to your labours.'

The people turned away slowly; you didn't argue with the gentry, particulary a Commissioner of the Peace, although they wanted to stay, to contemplate the body hanging from the bar, to revel in those feelings of revenge against a cruel world which could never find expression in their own lives.

The girl was still lying on the ground. He touched her lightly with his foot and said quietly, 'Go home now.'

The women who had been with her had gone and it suddenly occurred to Gabriel that she must have lived with the old woman. Her grandmother? Perhaps she now had nowhere to go.

He looked up to observe the orderly dispersal of the crowd and then realized that one rowdy group had not moved. He heard one of them muttering rebelliously, 'Should be lynched.'

Gabriel stood irresolute for one moment, wondering how many of that mob were vagrants, with no right to be in this town in any case.

12

The small group stood immobile. But they knew who he was; they had no wish to defy him, it was only the girl who was in danger and ultimately all Gabriel wanted was to keep the peace. These people had to live with their fears, they had to blame someone for their ill luck, strange misfortunes, unaccountable illnesses, they were merely trying to give coherence to pointless lives. But he could not leave the girl to this mob.

He advanced towards them, his hand on his sword.

Immediately, they began to move away, hiding their faces that he might not recognize them at some future date. His powers were so immense, from that of arrest and imprisonment to allowing them the liberty of earning their meagre bread and the peaceful occupation of their shacks and hovels. Yet still, from the departing group, moving quickly now down the hill, he heard one rebellious voice calling 'strumpet'.

Impulsively, Gabriel strode back to the prone body of the girl and lifted her up in his arms. She began to fight and he said angrily, 'Keep still' and started to stride down the hill. The crowd separated, leaving a path for him, but it was so steep that he began to stumble and he put her down again and said sharply, 'Follow me.' He grabbed her hand and dragged her along behind him to the level of the narrow road called Above Town, briskly crossed that and went on down the steps between the tall, narrow houses banked up the side of the hill. Pushing through the crowds, they reached South Town, then on down to Lower Street, until they finally reached sea level at the harbour. He turned and looked at her. What should he do with her now?

She sat herself wretchedly on the low flint harbour wall, her face still hidden behind her hair. All he could see was the outline of a small nose and her pale lips and the bony arms and legs which protruded through her ragged clothing.

'You can't stay here. Where do you live?'

'With Granny Lott. In the hut.'

13

'Well . . .' He looked back impatiently at the crowds still pouring down the hill all around them. 'You'll come with me today.' He grabbed her dirty hand again and pulled her along towards Bayards Cove. She squealed and exclaimed as she struggled barefoot over the flinty road and Gabriel snatched her up again, trying not to breathe in the acrid smell of her body.

'Push your hair back.'

The girl tossed her head and he frowned irritably as it swept across his face. People stepped aside staring at them as Gabriel strode along.

By the time he reached the quay, word had gone ahead of him as he knew it would, and his coach was awaiting him. He put the girl down. Joseph, his head stableman, looked expressionlessly at Gabriel as he approached. Gabriel pushed the girl abruptly into the open carriage and climbed in beside her on the leather cushion.

'Home,' he said briefly to Joseph and the journey began through the thronging streets, past the inner quay, along Smith Street and Fairfax and Fosse Street to Clarence Hill and Tunstall and up the long steep hill towards Vinelands. His estate lay beyond the town, high up overlooking the wooded part above the harbour. It had been an ancient priory and castle bought by his father from the proceeds of his expeditions to Newfoundland and the West Indies.

His father, a prosperous landowner with large estates in North Devon, had quickly seen the opportunities offered by the expanding trade off the Newfoundland coast. He had brought his family to Dartmouth when Gabriel was a young boy, bought the priory and built up a flourishing trade in cod fishing. By the 1580s, with 400 brigs, Dartmouth had the largest fleet of Newfoundlanders in the west and Gabriel's father was one of its best-known generals. With a convoy of ships under his command, each 200 ton brig carrying a crew of 60 men and 20 guns, he explored the Newfoundland coast, returning at the end of the season with cod and salted fish, which was then sold on the continent.

When John Davis, the explorer, told Gabriel's father of his plan to search for a north-west passage to Cathay and the East Indies, it was agreed that fifteen-year-old Gabriel should go with him as a cabin boy.

They sailed in two ships and reached the south west of Greenland, 'the land of desolation'. They bought leather suits and kayaks from the Eskimaux, fished and hunted for seals, whales and bears and returned to Dartmouth with their hauls of cod. They did not find a north-west passage to China, but by the time he was twenty Gabriel was commanding his own ship and had been three times to the West Indies with his father.

He grew rich on spices and sugar and gold from plundered Spanish vessels; he had sailed to Iceland and Ireland and south to the Caribbean. When his father died, as the eldest son he had inherited the estate and most of his father's wealth. He had gradually expanded the estate over the years, and it now covered hundreds of acres.

The sun was pouring down directly above and when they reached the last inn on the outskirts of the town, Gabriel told Joseph to go in and get some ale. He knew that by now not only his servants and household but his wife, Frances, and his family would have been alerted to his approach. Looking at the girl, her face still buried in the cushions, he realized he must decide what he intended to do with her.

When he had impulsively picked her up on the hillside, it had been a straightforward gesture of humanity. But now, what should he do? Presumably she was a pauper, dependent on the parish. It would have been simple enough, in ordinary circumstances, to get her a position in some large house, but none of the common people working there would wish to be in contact with the relative of a witch. She was, indeed, in danger of being accused herself. That would apply equally to his servants. None of them would rebel if he installed her in their midst because no other landowner

15

would employ a disaffected servant. But their real fears and superstitions could not be ignored. Hysteria could not be controlled by autocracy, as this trial had proved. He glanced distastefully at her dirty dress; it was scarcely a garment but a piece of cotton material covering her body. A small cloth bag like that in which the field labourers carried their victuals was tied by cord round her waist. There was earth in her hair from lying on the ground. He moved away slightly. When the tankard of ale was brought, he pushed her and said sharply, 'Here. Sit up. Drink.'

Slowly, she sat up, her hair still enveloping her.

'Is your face so ugly that you must permanently cover it with hair?' He held out the tankard and she took it in her grubby hands. She pushed her hair back sufficiently to drink and at last she looked at him. He was silenced. She had vivid green eyes and a smooth, pale skin unusual in a girl of her class and the small, straight nose above a beautiful wide mouth was contoured by a perfectly oval face. Her high cheek bones made her face look as though it had been sculptured in porcelain.

But it was her expression which silenced him and which sent the chilling thought through his mind that perhaps that old woman had been a witch, perhaps this girl had inherited her skills, perhaps those eyes did have some mysterious power. Her expression was not fearful, or respectful, nor even resentful, but a mixture of reflection and contempt, as though she were looking into some great, distant space – in time? – in imagination? – and seeing in this present situation only a trivial event not to be measured against that other secret yardstick.

'You're not ugly,' he said slowly.

She gulped the ale. 'Where are you taking me?'

She spoke with the intonations of the Devonshire accent but she had a thick, guttural voice as though she were speaking with a sore throat.

He frowned and hesitated. 'To my home,' then added involuntarily, 'they said you were a whore.'

She looked at him with the same distant expression but said nothing.

'That's not the reason I'm taking you home.' He frowned again at his own absurd remark.

'There is no reason why you should speak to me so,' she said coldly. Her green eyes looked into his appraisingly.

Instead of anger at her impertinence, Gabriel had a sudden acute feeling of anxiety, as though he were entering a bleak unknown world, but quite unlike the excitement he felt when entering those real, dangerous worlds of his explorations.

She was suddenly smiling at him distantly and then he felt a mounting anger at her cool treatment of him – a peasant, a pauper, how dare she.

'What is your name?' he asked abruptly.

'Sarah. Sarah Darby. I know yours,' she added without interest. 'You were at the trial.'

'Yes . . . Yours is a yeoman's name. Where is your father?'

'I have none.'

'Then perhaps you were a bastard. Your mother?'

'She died in the epidemic when I was eight. She was on the Parish. Granny Lott took me in.' The epidemic, Gabriel reflected, the last severe outbreak of plague, was in the year of James's accession. Sarah must be fifteen.

They continued the bumpy journey up the steep, rugged track in silence and shortly afterwards they passed through the great gates of Vinelands Priory. The road wound through rolling fields and then there was another long climb through a great avenue of trees.

Beyond this, the gardens opened out before them. The girl's expression was remote as she looked around her at the clipped yew hedges, the old fish pond with trout flashing in the sunlit water, the flower beds vivid with the perfume of sweet peas in a walled garden. As they turned a corner, the Priory lay before them, the magnificent stone building which had become to Gabriel a part of his identity. It was

17

an image of himself, of what he had devoted so much of his life to, his life's work.

'It's like a church,' Sarah said.

'It was at one time – a priory. Over there are the ruins of the castle.'

'Where is your home?'

'This is my home.'

'All of it?'

'Yes.'

Her green eyes seemed to look through him again; was she appraising, critical, assessing him? But what about? What views could a fifteen-year-old vagrant have about anything? It occurred to him that perhaps she was more than fifteen. The poor and illiterate were often unaware of their exact age; it was usually merely hearsay evidence, based on inaccurate calculations, particularly when parents had died.

Gabriel looked at her with a feeling of disapproval. His life had for so long been concentrated upon external events, that he had no wish for any other complications. His journeys to foreign countries, the enormous responsibility of a fleet of ships, of men and treasure; the political pressures to which he had been constantly subjected through his religion; his religion itself, which made demands upon his time and thoughts, and most important his involvement with the priests and recusants who were in need of help. Hiding them, making plans for their escape, his own permanent danger, all left little time for attending to more domestic affairs. His family had become a kind of backdrop to his life, themselves part of the greater problem of survival.

'I could live here,' Sarah said.

Gabriel looked at her in astonishment but she was looking out across the hills. He asked her to repeat it. Did he imagine it? Had she spoken? She said nothing. He shook his head. Perhaps the heat . . . the hanging . . . Yet he had the distinct impression that she was challenging him.

He felt himself faced suddenly with an individual who was making demands upon him, not in any external fashion, endangering his person, but as someone who was assessing him as a person himself. Yet why did he feel this? She had scarcely spoken. Was it some feminine guile? He had entered into no real relationship with a woman, indeed, since his marriage. Not because of any great morality on his part, although his religion was a driving force in his life, but because he had had no inclination towards any great debauchery, as so many of his friends had had during the previous reign; nor any tendency towards the sodomy practised so freely by the king and his minions.

They crossed the bridge over the moat and the coach drew up in front of the wide steps. Peacocks were strutting along the elevated paved-way which stretched the entire length of the house.

Sarah followed Gabriel up the steps and the great doors were opened by a man in livery. Beyond, a wide stone staircase led to a gallery which extended all around the first floor looking down to the great hall below. The stone stairs were covered with rush matting and great tapestries hung round the walls. The huge entrance hall was filled not with people but with marble statues and carved chairs and cupboards from the continent.

Sarah stood in the doorway looking suspicious.

Gabriel waved to her to enter and the great carved doors closed behind them.

'Call the mistress,' Gabriel said. The man disappeared along a corridor by the side of the hall.

Sarah was looking at the paintings which decorated the walls of the galleries and the tapestries on the walls of the staircase.

'Why are those covers on the walls?'

'They are tapestries,' Gabriel said. 'Come.'

He removed his cloak and sword which were taken by a steward who hovered in the shadows. At the top of the staircase, velvet-covered stools and settles were placed along the wooden-floored gallery. Sarah followed him up the stairs but when Gabriel told her to sit down on a vivid green velvet couch, she shook her head. At the same moment, Frances appeared at the top of the next staircase at the end of the gallery. She was tall and amply proportioned. Slowly she descended the stairs and came towards them. Her skirt rustled as she walked along the gallery, down a few steps, up a few steps on the other side. Her auburn hair was worn in a bun and she was wearing a plain blue gown with a starched ruff.

'Ah, Frances,' Gabriel went towards her. 'I am just returned from that unpleasant business.' He kissed her lightly and put his arm around her shoulder. She smiled at him.

'It happens but rarely,' she said soothingly.

'Yes.' Gabriel was about to continue but she let out a little cry when she saw Sarah more closely. 'What is this?'

'It is a sad thing, she is alone . . . The old woman . . . cared for her. She would not be safe in the town at the moment.'

'They will feed her, wash her, in the kitchens.'

Gabriel took his wife's arm and led her to a couch. They sat down together, facing Sarah, who stood perfectly still.

'The child needs a meal.' It was quite normal for the poor and destitute to come for food, Frances reflected. Gabriel, like all the rich landowners, was expected to, and did, make provision, daily, weekly and yearly for those in need. Elizabeth had encouraged a greater social awareness, because she believed that it would create a more stable and safer society. Frances found nothing strange in this. 'She will be supported by the parish,' she added. There was provision enough for the poor; the girl would be found a place somewhere.

'No. I wish to take her in,' Gabriel said.

'She is not unbecoming,' Frances studied her thoughtfully. 'She might even make a boudoir maid with training. The housekeeper will see to her.'

She did not ask why Gabriel had brought her into the house. Why did he not send her to the servants' quarters? She wondered if this great adventurer who had constantly invaded foreign soil, endured storm and shipwreck – and he had attended enough executions in recent years of Catholic priests – was he acting strangely simply because of the death of an old woman? Then Frances heard him saying, 'She will be one of the family.'

'One of the . . .' Frances' voice trailed into silence. Then she looked at Gabriel with suspicion and distaste. 'Where did she come from?'

'I don't know where she came from,' Gabriel said irritably.

'What are you thinking of,' Frances suddenly shouted. 'How dare you bring this . . . bastard . . . into my home. One of your family! What do you mean?'

'I shall be her guardian. She will live here.'

'She will not,' Frances shouted back. 'She will go to the servants' quarters if she goes anywhere.'

'I wish to take her in,' Gabriel repeated. For one moment he hesitated, overwhelmed by the absurdity of what he was saying. Frances was right. It was no concern of his. If she was on the parish, she would be given food and some sort of shelter. He could tell the vicar to keep an eye on her, find her some sort of occupation. Why should he feel responsible?

He glanced again at the dejected figure by the stool, at her wretched dress tied round with cord, at the little cloth bag dangling from her waist, at her knotted hair, dirty scratched feet and the sullen expression on her face and suddenly he knew what was in his mind. It was a vision of a fourteen-year-old boy – about her age – years ago. About sixty years ago, in fact. His father, Sir Robert Humphreys, had been involved in the Prayer-book rebellion and as a child Gabriel and his brothers and sisters had heard his stories of the massacre. In fact, it seemed to have dominated his childhood until it became family folklore.

He was conscious now that when this morning he snatched the girl up and dragged her down the hill, he had actually been thinking of that long-ago event.

On that occasion, his grandmother had taken a boy in; that boy, Edmund, he knew, had grown up with his father as one of the family and been educated and provided for. His father had told him how he had returned home after the massacre and his father's death and there on the steps had been a strange boy, dressed in a blue velvet suit. They had grown up together as brothers. It was as though his actions now had been dictated by obligations created in the past, the behaviour expected of him by his ancestors.

Sarah began to walk down the staircase. Gabriel bounded after her, snatched her by the arm and dragged her back.

'You will not go. Stay here. I will not be disarmed by female stupidity. Frances, call your woman.'

Frances did not move and Gabriel himself shouted a name. A servant appeared at the head of the staircase beyond and came quickly towards them.

Gabriel nodded towards Sarah. 'See that she is given food and water to wash,' he shouted angrily and strode along the gallery, down the great staircase and towards the front entrance. 'When that is done, tell the children I want to speak with them in the library. I will explain to them.'

Frances said coldly to the woman, 'Take her to wash herself. Find suitable clothes . . . Burn what she is wearing. Katherine's will fit her – a gown and mantle. When you are done, bring her to my chamber.'

Then Frances, without a glance at Sarah, swept down the stairs, up the other side and along the gallery, sending servants scurrying hither and thither to summon the rest of the family to listen to their father.

*   *   *

When Frances returned to her bedchamber, she slammed her door angrily and strode across the room. She felt

22

overwhelmed at the depth of her feeling, as though all the hidden resentment and bitterness she must have felt had suddenly come to the surface. Trembling all over, she marched round the room, picking up objects and then throwing them down again. Then she burst into tears, bewildered by her own frustration and fury.

'What's wrong with me? Why do I feel like this?'

Adopting or sheltering a poor or deserving child was not unusual, after all. Such events were sufficiently common amongst the gentry and nobility to excite little rebuke.

Only a few months ago, the Earl of Chevey had adopted a two-month-old boy whose mother had died in childbirth and Lord Lecom had suddenly presented the world with an eighteen-year-old female 'cousin' of great charm and beauty. It had seemed commendable to Frances that Sir John Pipley had given his illegitimate son a house when he came of age.

She sat down, painfully aware of the meaning of those acts of public benefaction. The gossip which these events led to and which she and her family and friends indulged in took no account of the private conflicts which must have gone on behind the closed doors of those homes. Because at the bottom of it all was the implication of deception, of a secret immoral life that men – and, she had to admit, women – participated in. The action was so uncharacteristic of Gabriel that she felt suspicious. Where had this girl come from?

Earlier this morning, she had caught sight of the coach coming up the drive as she stood by the open window of her chamber, looking out across the fields. She had watched the slow progress of the coach up the long rough road through the park, the dry red dust thrown up by the horses' hooves and the brass attachments shining in the mid-morning sun. The heat haze seemed to suspend it in time. She realized now that she had felt an unaccountable reluctance to go to greet Gabriel in the Great Hall as usual.

Two garden boys were weeding the flower borders in the parterre beneath. July was hot. The whole summer had been too hot. Her native Suffolk had always had a cool breeze, even on the hottest day, a thought which occupied her mind every year when the sun poured down on these rolling hills.

She rarely went there now. John, like many an eldest brother, had little time for his siblings since he had inherited the family home. But in her mind, looking out across the hills and wooded slopes, she saw still the flat fields and open expanses of her native county.

These people of the west country were very different from her friends and family of East Anglia. Their laughter and camaraderie made her suspicious; she never knew whether they were making fun of her or actually sharing their humour with her. They even made fun of their own misfortunes which seemed to Frances almost sacrilegious, an affront to the Almighty.

The inhabitants of Dartmouth had a tough, outgoing atmosphere about them, they greeted each other with enthusiasm rather than warmth, with a certain sharp abruptness as though they were entitled to speak to whom they chose and to say precisely what they thought. The prosperity of many of the inhabitants over the past few years had added to their habit of speaking their minds because self-confidence in their skills and success made them even more certain of their own rectitude. Always confident of the rightness of their own opinions, they now had ample proof of their superiority.

In her native town of Eye, her family's contact with the villagers had been remote and formalized. As one of the largest landowners in the county, her father's presence, when he passed through the village, had been marked with the doffing of caps and a general obeisance and respect. But here she always had the feeling that their obedience to Gabriel's demands was based on fear of his power rather than a real belief in his authority.

24

Her thoughts returned abruptly to Gabriel, incoherent images of past events, never actually thought about, but always there, submerged beneath the events of daily living. The agonies of childbirth, the last painful time when the physician had pronounced that after the birth of Adam, no further children must be conceived. It would mean her death. Gabriel's quiet, almost good-humoured removal to another bedchamber – perhaps it had been no sacrifice for him anyhow. Yet, it seemed impossible that he could have been deceiving her. Their relationship had seemed so even and trusting. But what did she know about his activities when he was not at home? She stood up and walked over to the window, frowning in bewilderment.

'Adam,' she called. He was sitting on the wall in the garden beneath, reading one of his endless tomes. He looked up. 'Your father wishes to speak to you in the library.'

'Me?'

'All of you.'

'Is it important?'

'You will discover. Go now.'

There was a light knock on the door.

'One moment.'

She turned to the mirror, straightened her hair and picked up the objects she had thrown to the floor. Then she walked to the door and opened it quietly.

'Come in, Cicely.'

'Why does Papa wish to see us? Is he in trouble?'

'No, dear,' Frances spoke in her usual calm manner, 'he has a small matter he wishes to discuss with you. Dear, why don't you put some rouge on your cheeks. You are so pale.' Frances looked at the dowdy girl before her. She looked much older than her nineteen years in her plain grey robe and with her hair tied tightly back. 'And why can't you wear your lovely auburn hair loose?'

'Mama. Surely we've discussed this often enough before.'

'You're not made more holy by looking unattractive.'

'You know I still want to be a nun.'

Frances gave a snort of exasperation. 'Cicely, you know it's not possible in these difficult times.'

'I could go to France.'

'It's too dangerous. Your father would never allow it.'

'Father would . . .'

They were interrupted by a knock on the door. At Frances' bidding, a servant entered and announced, 'The girl is ready.'

'Take her to the library when the children are all there,' Frances said curtly to the maid and flounced briskly along the top gallery to the library.

Gabriel was standing beneath a portrait of his mother and father when Frances and Cicely entered. He had rebuilt the library ten years earlier to accommodate his growing collection of books. Leatherbound volumes lined the high walls and the vaulted ceiling had been painted with murals by artists he had commissioned from Italy. He walked silently across the carpeted floor and sat down at the ornately carved desk brought back from one of his excursions. It was here that he wrote his journals and planned and charted his voyages. A huge chart lay on the desk marked with circles and asterisks in preparation for his next voyage to Newfoundland.

'Frances,' he said in a conciliatory voice, 'your behaviour is quite inappropriate. It is not the girl's fault that she is homeless. It is our laws which make her a vagrant.'

'Why adopt her? Put her in the servants' quarters.'

'I take other persecuted people into my home.'

Frances glanced at the open window and said in a whisper, 'That has nothing to do with it.'

'It is but a few years. She will marry.'

'And have some claim on the estate,' Frances said angrily. 'She could be a criminal for all you know.'

'Nonsense. You can see that she is harmless. She will simply be provided for like the other girls. Ah, come in.'

Gabriel looked thoughtfully at his offspring as they came

into the room. Katherine, his younger daughter, would be married in a few months' time; John would go with him on his next voyage and as the eldest son would one day inherit the estate. Gilbert, with a malignant and indefinable creeping disease, would probably not survive to manhood and clever and ambitious Adam, though only twelve, already seemed to embody all the virtues, opportunities and potential of the new age. Gabriel wondered, looking at him now, whether too much was being done for this youngest child. He had had a series of private tutors to further his studies and intellect. Gabriel had then despatched him to Merchant Taylor's School. Founded during Elizabeth's reign, it had in forty years achieved a remarkable reputation for the furtherance of the arts and culture. Adam was already fluent in Greek, Latin and Hebrew and was familiar with the works of Aristotle. He had written a play which the boys had acted at Court during the summer celebrations. Although in one way Gabriel was sorry that Adam had become a Protestant, he was aware that it would ensure his progress in life. England would never return to the Church of Rome. Mary's brief reign had been but a retrogressive interlude; her fierce hatred and persecution of Protestants, albeit only a limited number of them, had left a hateful impression on the Protestant majority, and still served as a justification for James's treatment of the Catholics.

'I want to speak with you all. I wish you to welcome another member of the family.'

They all looked round in astonishment.

'You will meet her soon,' Frances looked belligerent. 'She looks like an Egyptian.'

Gabriel looked irritated at this colloquial expression for gypsies, who were treated as vagrants and were sent from one parish to the next.

Katherine looked excited. 'Where is she?'

Katherine, like Gabriel, had black hair and dark eyes, and she had inherited his adventurous disposition which sometimes manifested itself in arrogance and rebellion. She was Gabriel's favourite child, it was her laughter which echoed through the halls and corridors of the house, her ideas and schemes and suggestions which constantly brought new activities, new people, new aims, into the lives of his children.

'She would have become a vagrant. She had been taken in by the old woman whose execution I attended this morning.'

Cicely gasped. 'A witch! Father . . .'

'She is not a witch any more than the old woman was.'

Cicely frowned.

Gabriel went on, 'These trials have no more connection with the truth than the trial of a priest has with treason.'

'She admitted at the trial . . .' Frances began.

'What do the fevered ramblings of an old woman matter?'

Suddenly Gabriel sprang to his feet, staring. They all turned. Sarah was standing in the open doorway. They looked in astonishment at the beautiful girl before them, her golden hair washed now and curling to her waist, green eyes in a pale face enhanced by the pale green woollen gown she was wearing.

'Egyptian,' Gilbert muttered scornfully, echoing his mother's unsuitable word. Gabriel was himself momentarily overcome by the dignified girl before him, at the slight smile which now played round her lips, at her unexpected composure. Doubt again assailed him; even to the enlightened, the mysterious superstitions of an age could not be cast off totally. How could a vagrant of two hours ago be transformed so easily into this creature? How was it possible? Then her smile disappeared and she said angrily to Gabriel, 'When can I leave?'

Gabriel was so astonished at the question that he could only mutter incoherently, 'What do you mean? There's no question . . . I haven't thought . . .'

'I want to go back.'

Frances interrupted sharply. 'How dare you speak thus. You will go when you are told. You have no right to . . .'

'She will not go back,' Gabriel said firmly. He strode towards Sarah. 'You will stay here. I have decided to adopt you. Give you a home.'

'I don't want a home.'

Frances turned to Gabriel. 'Here's the gratitude you get for all your fine gestures,' she said sarcastically. 'What sort of creature is she?'

'Sarah!' Gabriel grasped her by the shoulders. 'You can't leave. You have nowhere to go, you wouldn't be safe. In any case,' he added quietly, 'you said you could live here.'

'What do you mean?' Frances turned on him. 'Have you already discussed it with her?'

'No . . . She just said . . .'

'She will go,' Frances shouted, 'the courts will decide what is to happen to her.'

'The courts! I've been there before. Long ago. They sent my mother and me to the poorhouse. They . . .' Sarah stopped abruptly, walked slowly across the room and then looked calculatingly around, at the books and carpets, at the furnishings and through the long windows to the gardens beyond. Then at each member of the family until her eyes rested on Gabriel.

'Very well,' she said in a condescending voice, 'I'll stay.'

They all waited for a heated rebuke from Gabriel at her insolence. But instead, Gabriel said sharply, 'See that she is given a room', and he walked briskly from the library.

Frances hurried after him.

'Gabriel, I will not countenance this creature. And there's one other thing. I have something to show you.'

'Now? I have business to attend to.'

'It is important.'

He followed her up the stairs and along the labyrinth of

corridors to her chamber. Her bedchamber was adjacent and beyond that was his own.

'This is hers,' she said briefly.

She handed him a small wooden doll, roughly carved in chestnut, its face crudely painted with some sort of herbal dye. He took it and shuddered because of its associations. These dolls and carved images had become more and more associated in the ignorant mind with witchcraft.

'I have no belief in such things.'

'You may not.' Frances looked impatient. 'Other people have.'

'Yes.' Gabriel suddenly felt tired with all the unusual and absurd turmoil of the past hours. 'I'll speak with her.'

He took the wooden object, went into his room and put it in a bureau.

Joseph drove him back into town. He felt disturbed and excited by the morning's events and leaving Joseph near the quay he went up the Shambles to a whorehouse. It was filled with tradesmen, who receded into the shadows as he entered. Even the girls did not come to molest him.

'Who runs this place?'

A fat woman appeared from an alcove. 'I do, sir. There's no rowdiness here,' she added, fearing that there had been complaints to the Justices.

'I'm here on business.'

Her face lit up.

'I want information,' he said curtly. 'The girl . . . this morning . . .' Gabriel paused. There was no need to explain. He knew that by now the whole town would have heard of the events. 'Is she a whore?'

'Oh, no.'

Gabriel grabbed her by the arm. 'I want the truth! Has she been here or in any of the brothels?'

'No. Never. But she's strange.'

'Strange? In what way?'

'She lived with Granny Lott in the woods. She learnt to read.'

'How?'

'Granny Lott.'

'Where did she get the books?'

'Stole them.'

'Are these just stupid rumours? Where are the books?'

'In her hut. Send, see for yourself.'

'It is good that people read,' he said, puzzled.

'She walks along the beach alone, watching the ships. Always alone. She sings on the hills. She and Granny Lott made potions with herbs. On a still, hot day it is said you can smell the scent, floating across the hills.'

'Potions can cure,' he said shortly. 'The ignorant abuse what they cannot understand.'

'And who was her father?' the woman asked insinuatingly. 'There have been many rumours.'

'No more of these ramblings,' Gabriel said threateningly, 'or I'll have your place closed down.'

He knew that this information would likewise be relayed to the citizens in the town. They would know now that Sarah was under his protection, that to offend her was to offend him, with all the dangers that such indiscretion might entail.

He walked down to the Quay to check on the progress of his ships. One from the Azores was already three days later than expected. There had been reports from homecoming ships about storms and squalls. The cargo was worth a lot . . . but even more important, the thought of the loss of men's lives halted him, looking down to the harbour mouth. The smooth deceptive water of the harbour. But the captain, John Smithson, was a good Master, had lost only one ship in his long career. Anyhow, soon he would be going again himself.

He went back to Joseph waiting with the coach. 'I'll take a horse. Go on home.'

He took a horse from the Bayard's Cove stables, returned through the town and began his round of the estate; the barns, dairy, cattle sheds, the nursery gardens and smithies. The estate was the size of a small town; when he was not at sea, it occupied his entire day, as well as that of Frances and his eldest son John.

Joseph awaited him at the house. Gabriel sent him to seek out the old woman's hut, to collect its contents and then burn it down. Those contents belonged by law to the state but the officials would not bother to collect such meagre possessions and the other vagrants would be too superstitious to steal the belongings of a witch.

Even Joseph had to be placated; for months, even years, that part of the hill would be avoided, a place of ghosts, evil spirits, mystery.

'Take my crucifix, Joseph, and half a dozen men. You will be safe.'

Two hours later, Gabriel saw smoke rising from the next hill over the valley and waited impatiently for Joseph's return. When he finally saw the horses and cart trundling along the avenue, he went round to the stables to meet them.

'Job's done, sir,' Joseph said. His peasant face had an air of mystery.

'Well, what did you encounter?'

'A mob, sir.'

'Stealing?' Gabriel sounded astonished that they would risk contact with such malevolent powers.

'No, sir. Waiting.'

'What for?'

'They thought the . . . girl . . . would return. They say she has bewitched them. I fear they are carried away, sir.'

'Why? What's wrong with them?'

'They like a confession, sir. The old woman, she spoilt it for them, saying she was innocent.'

'Yes.' Gabriel could see that for them, justice had not been done. By denying her guilt, she had deprived them of the expiation of the evil spirits which were currently haunting their lives. They would be driven now by the need to find another victim.

'She's still on the gallows.'

'Yes. You will take a message that she's to be removed to the pit.'

'I brought what was in the hut.'

Joseph tipped the contents of his leather bag on the floor of the stable. Gabriel pushed them with his foot – a dilapidated bible, an earthenware bowl, a rush basket containing herbs which looked withered and dried and another carved wooden doll.

'Burn it all,'. he said.

Gabriel walked back towards the house. Having satisfied himself about the suitability of Sarah as a member of the household, he put the question out of his mind. There would be problems about it, he knew, but he was accustomed to dealing with so many dramatic situations, from concealing recusants to condemning people to death that he had taught himself to deal with problems only as they arose. He planned ahead only for activities, not for possible disasters. The disasters were never what one had expected, and life now was too uncertain to waste time on incoherent fears.

He had business to do with the steward; a marquetry cabinet, arriving from Germany, was to be delivered that day. Made over a century ago, it was a precious object and infinite care would be needed to transport it to the long gallery.

At five o'clock the supper bell rang and he went immediately to the dining hall. Punctuality at this meal was one of the few rigid rules which Gabriel enforced upon the household. He did not attend the midday meal as he was rarely in the house at that hour; there were too many preoccupations on the estate and it was left to the other members of the family to eat if they wished. But Gabriel believed that the formality of the evening meal gave the family a certain cohesion, acknowledged its existence as a unifying force. He tried to encourage intelligent conversation and an interest in affairs of state.

33

Gabriel sat at the head of the table in a tall, high-backed carved chair and Frances sat, far away, at the other end of the huge dining table. The children sat on either side of the table on benches and Sarah was placed between Cicely and Katherine. The servants stood behind them, waiting for Gabriel to nod his head for them to serve the food which was placed on large silver salvers on an oak table. Gabriel watched Sarah as she took the plate she was offered. Although he had put her out of his mind for the rest of the day, confronted with her now he felt again the same anxiety she had provoked in the carriage. She looked at him now, half insolently, he thought, although there was still a half-smile on her lips.

The two younger boys were looking at her with curiosity although in the fashion of young boys, they turned a strange situation which they could not understand into a source of humour, poking each other under the table every time she moved.

When Sarah picked up her two-pronged fork and looked at it with incomprehension they both began to giggle.

'It's for gardening,' Adam said to her. 'Digging up herbs.'

At this, Gilbert exploded in mirth, his faced turned red, and they both began to laugh uncontrollably.

'Gilbert,' Frances said sharply, 'you'll make yourself ill. Will you both try to be polite.'

Sarah only looked at them distantly.

Frances did not look at Sarah but helped herself from the salvers of food which were now placed on the table; a plate of oysters, portions of stewed rabbit, boiled mutton and roast chicken, with spinach, potatoes, artichoke and broad beans, until her plate was piled high.

Cicely took great chunks of lamb and portions of pigeon while Katherine contented herself with a whole lobster.

'What do you want?' she asked Sarah.

Sarah pointed to three carp nestling beneath carrots, parsnips and herbs. Katherine held the plate towards her and Sarah snatched one and placed it on her plate.

The boys sniggered again and when they saw their elder brother smile, they took this to be a sign of approval. Giggling, they began to pick up the vegetables from the dish with their fingers.

Gabriel said coldly, 'Boys, leave the room. You are too ill-mannered to remain.'

Gilbert began to whine, 'I shall be ill if I don't eat.'

'Go,' Gabriel reiterated.

They swung their legs over the long bench and crept out, still half-giggling and muttering.

Gabriel looked at them sternly. He knew that his treatment of his children did not adhere to the general parental pattern. They knew he would never strike them or treat them in the violent manner which most of their friends suffered. He frequently criticized the fact that children had few rights of protection from their parents. But they knew that he did expect courtesy and obedience.

Sarah ate in silence, picking up the food with her fingers, or cutting pieces off with her knife and thrusting it into her mouth. Then she watched the others eating and began to experiment with her fork.

'These forks came from Italy,' Cicely said. 'They're a new idea. It's easier for eating.'

Katherine gave her a Devon pie of gooseberries and redcurrants, followed by strawberries and cream. Then there were sweetmeats and pastries and wine was poured from a large silver tankard, though only Gabriel and John partook of this. Gabriel was discussing the balustrades which were being erected round the knot garden, and a stone temple which was to be placed at the end of the avenue. Frances and Cicely talked about the arrangement of Sarah's chamber. Gabriel noticed that Frances ignored Sarah, talking about her as though she were not there.

'She can have the small four-poster bed and the walnut chest. And a bowl and water jug, now that she's learnt to

35

wash herself. Then there's the settle and couch Gabriel brought from Italy.'

He wondered whether Frances would accept the situation. It was quite within her powers to protest. Women in her position had recourse to the courts in marital disputes – but would she contemplate such a course? If she did, it would probably be suggested that he abandon the idea, and simply relegate Sarah to the servants' quarters.

Looking at Sarah's pale, delicate face and her halo of golden hair, it occurred to him that apart from Katherine, his own children weren't particularly handsome or attractive. Was he just carried away by her beauty?

Earlier, he had told himself it was a simple act of charity, a quick solution to a minor, unexpected problem. Now it seemed a bit rash. Gabriel ran his hands through his hair. Frances noticed the rare, defensive gesture of his when he was uncertain, anxious. She looked at Sarah. There was indeed a strange atmosphere about her, yet not threatening, as though she herself was unaware of her current situation. There was a kind of raw insensitivity about what Gabriel was doing. A few hours earlier Sarah had left a shack on the hills and attended the old woman's execution. Then she had been almost kidnapped, placed in this palatial home and now dressed in a silk gown, when she had never entered such a place, never seen such food, never even touched the material of the dress she was wearing. What was his motive behind it all? Then, suddenly, Sarah spoke, addressing Cicely.

'Is that chamber to be mine?'

'What chamber?'

'The one with the four-poster bed.'

'Well, yes. It will be yours.'

'Granny Lott said everything in big houses is plunder.' She turned to Gabriel. 'What is that?'

Once again, Gabriel found himself silenced by what seemed her audacity, but Frances interposed angrily, 'It's the reward for bravery and self-sacrifice. Perhaps one day you'll go on a boat to foreign parts. Then you'll see.'

She stood up in fury and turned to Gabriel.

'This girl can't stay here. I won't have her,' she stated and marched from the room.

'I know why I'm here,' Sarah said to Gabriel. 'You thought they shouldn't have done that to Granny Lott.'

Gabriel sighed. 'Sarah, I don't know why. I only know that if you try to make trouble, I may change my mind.'

'Trouble?' Sarah looked mystified.

It was genuine mystification, Gabriel thought. She was only asking questions, perhaps they were not meant to be provocative. 'You will become accustomed to this life. Tomorrow, you will start lessons with Gilbert and his tutor.' Then he added, 'Rich or poor, people all have many problems.'

2

Charles Smithson was exceptionally lean and at thirty-seven his pale brown hair had thinned to a few strands. Soon he would be bald all over his head, as a result of the poor diet he had suffered as a child and the scurvy he had contracted when working in a reformatory. That was before he had had the good fortune to meet Sir Jonathon Fortescue and to be given through his influence this job with the Hooper Humphreys household. It was social progress beyond his wildest dreams.

He blessed the day, seven years ago, when he had been riding through the countryside on a hired black mare and had come upon Sir Jonathon lying in a ditch, blood pouring down his face from a gash in his head.

Instantly Charles, noting the clothes in which the man was dressed, the black silk coat, the lace collar, the long leather boots and the gold rings on his hand, had raised the man's head in his arms and wiped the blood from his face. He saw a middle-aged man whom he recognized as one of the Justices and a gentleman to King James' bedchamber. Charles's concern became more pronounced.

'Sir, I will place you on my horse and lead you to your home.'

The man beside him groaned. 'I can't move. I was attacked by some scoundrel who robbed me of my purse and my sword. My leg is injured, too.' But somehow Charles managed to raise him up and get him on to his horse and lead him back through the lanes to his great estate beyond the outskirts of Dartmouth. A physician was called who pronounced that only the good fortune of Charles's discovery had saved Sir Jonathon's life. His wounds were treated with dock leaf and comfrey, he was given a drink of borage to cure his giddiness and Charles was bidden to remain below in the kitchens until he was called for. He looked round at the huge scrubbed tables and watched a servant girl cleaning the copper pans. Sitting quietly in a corner was a young girl, playing with a wooden doll. Her golden hair shone in the light of the fire and when she glanced at him, he noticed the vivid green of her eyes.

When he was summoned, he was taken up to the bedchamber where Sir Jonathon was propped up in a large four-poster bed, his head swathed in bandages.

It was then that Charles had told him about his hard life as a young scholar of poor parents, of his wish to become a tutor, of his patient and commendable determination to pursue a life of study and sobriety. Sir Jonathon was noticeably impressed and promised him that only good would come of his efforts and his altruism in rescuing him from further assault. Sir Jonathon revealed that the scoundrel had run off when he heard Charles approaching on his horse. Charles privately panicked at the danger he had himself been running in arriving at such a moment but he bowed his head silently.

'It would be better for your own safety,' Sir Jonathon said, 'if you revealed to no-one that you have assisted me. Until the criminal is caught.'

Charles returned to his humble dwelling, awaiting a call. No word came and he began to despair and then to feel a wild and uncontrollable anger that he had received no reward, not even a financial acknowledgment. He began to plan a ridiculous revenge, imagining himself in the same position as the previous scoundrel, attacking Sir Jonathon at dead of night in the bleak countryside, only this time he would not survive.

Then, suddenly, the call came. From his dingy hovel he was transported in a coach, sent to collect him, through the iron gates of the ancestral home.

He waited, as he had done previously, in the kitchens until he was sent for and then he was escorted by a steward up the wide marble staircase to an imposing library, lined on every wall with leather-bound books. Momentarily, he did not notice the tall figure of Sir Jonathon leaning nonchalantly before the white stone fireplace. His eyes rested instead on the incredible spectacle of those hundreds of volumes, Latin, Greek, French, Italian – he recognized the titles because his grammar-school education had given him a smattering of all those languages. He noticed, too, that there were even folios of Shakespeare's works. Then Sir Jonathon's voice boomed him back to reality.

'Don't read 'em much myself. More interested in the outdoor life. But if you have a library you have to have books.'

'A wonderful sight.' Charles spoke in a voice of awe. He surprised himself at the depth of his feelings; he was not merely flattering Sir Jonathon.

'Well, young man, I haven't forgotten you. Have a jar of mulled wine.' He walked to a large, elaborately carved cabinet, his blue silk breeches rustling as he moved.

'No. No thank you.' Charles had never tasted such a beverage. He had heard that it might have drastic and unexpected results.

'Well, in gratitude for your service to me in saving my life, I've managed to find you a position which I hope will further your career.' He gulped some port from his tankard. 'It's with the Hooper Humphreys household.'

Charles gulped in his turn. He had certainly had hopes about advancement, but nothing as exalted as this.

'You will visit when you are summoned by Sir Gabriel. He has your address.'

Sir Jonathon went on to tell Charles that a man, almost certainly the one who had attacked him, had appeared at the Assize in Exeter, charged with the crime. Suddenly Sir Jonathon chuckled, his wide red face creased like a shrivelled tomato. 'He wasn't able to say much. Had a taste of his own medicine in gaol. Seemed a bit tongue-tied.'

Charles felt a sudden violent upsurge of fear and then revulsion against this man, against the power that all such people as he could wield. He should never have saved him. Cruelty, torture, false evidence. Charles blinked

'Thank you, sir, for your kind help.'

He was returned in the coach, watched suspiciously by the townspeople as he rode through the streets of Dartmouth.

But back in his tenement, Charles brushed his black blouse and knickerbockers and then went down to the cobbler in Smith Street to see if something could be done with his worn black patent shoes, the only decent article he had ever managed to acquire.

A few weeks later he had been installed in the Hooper Humphreys household. The two girls had been eleven and twelve at the time, and he had taught them not only the elementary skills of reading and writing and calculations, but also other accomplishments. They could speak French, had a smattering of Latin, knew much about the English poets and dramatists and both of them could play the lute. The two elder boys had been less satisfying to educate but Adam had started his lessons when he was six and outshone them all. Charles had hoped that in a few years' time, or even less in view of Gilbert's uncertain health, he might make even more dramatic progress. Perhaps he would be called to court, educating the young princes or their offspring. His progress to the Hooper Humphreys establishment had seemed to be a certain promise of his eventual arrival at the very top of the social ladder.

But now Charles was an unhappy man. Things had changed. A future full of promise had suddenly clouded over and three great shadows loomed over him. To begin with, he had always had a disturbing fear of his master's religious affinities. Gabriel was seen every Sunday at the Church of St Saviour's as was required by law. But of his family, only Katherine accompanied him which could mean only one thing – Charles was living in a known recusant household. In Elizabeth's time, mixing with Catholics was not a dangerous occupation, but nowadays no-one knew what the Court would decide.

Charles was aware that no other family in the west was more respected, more prosperous or more powerful. But who would defend them, who would risk their own skin, if things got worse? And as a willing member of that household, where would he stand?

Recently, his master's involvement with Catholic priests had begun to assume dangerous proportions. Charles had always known that a Catholic family like Gabriel's was in a suspect position but until recently their wealth and power made them unlikely victims unless they embarked upon unacceptable activities. Charles had also known of the hidden priest, whiling his time away in the dark corners of the house and administering communion and mass to the family. But now he had heard of the arrival of two

41

priests from France and their concealment in the chambers upstairs. He had no wish to leave his job unless it meant greater social progress, but he did wish to ensure that he would not be implicated in any illegal activities.

Secondly there had been the arrival of Sarah. At the beginning he had feared that he might be involved in helping to conceal a witch but Gabriel had made no secret of his adoption of the girl. It was known throughout Dartmouth that she had been taken in, housed and clothed and was evidently to remain. As far as officialdom was concerned, Gabriel had performed an act of charity and Charles had been able to breathe again. But in the present climate of opinion he was worried that he could in the future be incriminated for having dealings with the girl. Suppose she were accused of being a witch, where would he stand? He knew that it was a remote possibility that he would be involved, he could indeed make accusations himself, but the fear still lurked in the back of his mind.

Thirdly, it was the girl herself who compounded the problem for Charles. It was her atmosphere of superiority which made his life a misery. How was it possible for someone like her to learn so quickly, to have that quick and knowing understanding of everything he mentioned, and even to anticipate and know unexplained ideas? It had taken him years of hard work to reach a stage which she would be at in a few months. She seemed to remember everything he said, and he put this down not to natural intelligence but to some supernatural power.

Charles was alone with her today for her lessons. Gilbert was feeling unwell and remained in his room. Sarah was reading slowly from a pamphlet of Shakespeare's poems which Gabriel had bought her. She was wearing yet another new dress, a pale blue silk gown embroidered at the neck with lace. She glanced up at him as he questioned her – 'What does jennet mean?'

She smiled. 'A horse. A mare.'

Charles nodded curtly to her to go on.

'It's time to finish,' she said at the end of the poem. He frowned with irritation at her commanding manner.

'It's my lordship's wish that you should continue till supper.'

Sarah smiled. 'I'll speak to him. He's very pleased with my progress. I am sure he will commend you.'

Charles blushed at her implicit reading of his mind.

'You see,' she added, 'I want to see Gilbert. I am sure I can cure him.'

'The physicians have been unable to.'

'But they don't know about the secret herbs and potions that I can make.'

Charles shuddered inwardly; was she provoking him or was she really unaware of the implications of her words?

'Such activities may be misinterpreted,' he said shortly.

'Curing someone?'

'You may make him worse.'

She shook her head. 'No. I know what to do. But I shall have to go up the hill to get some leaves and roots. Would you accompany me?'

'I have no authority to do such a thing. You are not supposed to leave the estate. You must ask your guardian.'

Charles briskly packed up the books they had been using and waited for her to precede him through the door. Sarah tossed her head and walked out. Watching her as she flounced down the long, stone corridor, through the wide entrance hall and the iron gates and across the moat, his mind reverted to that visit, long ago, to Sir Jonathon's home, when he had been rewarded with the position in this household. Because he remembered, waiting then in the kitchens, the young girl he had seen playing with a wooden doll. Although that was seven years ago, he was sure that this was the girl he now watched crossing the moat. She clearly did not remember him: a mere child, she had barely glanced at him at the time but the golden hair and strange green eyes convinced him that she was the same person. Charles tried to work out how she came to be connected with these two exalted households in such different circumstances. Of course, Sir Gabriel had rescued her after the witch trial, but what had she been doing in the Fortescue home? If her mother had been a servant there how had she become connected with the witch?

Deep down in the recesses of his mind was the conviction that if only he knew the answer to that question, there might be some further advantage in it for him.

*　　*　　*

Although Gabriel had tried to present Sarah's adoption as a simple act of charity, the views of the other members of the family were more diverse. An uneasy silence fell over the household. The older girls knew that they would be little affected by the addition. Cicely saw another potential convert to her religion. As the possibility of becoming a nun had been denied her, she knew it would be her duty to marry. She had no illusions that the men who wished to marry her were influenced by the knowledge of the family into which they would be marrying and the dowry they might expect. The disadvantages of having a Catholic background were outweighed by the wealth into which they would come as members of the Hooper Humphreys family. But perhaps Sarah would share with her a life of devotion.

Katherine, already planning her Christmas wedding to Sir William Greenhayes, a wealthy barrister and a Protestant with influence in royal circles, saw Sarah merely as a new interest in her already varied life. Although younger, Sarah seemed to be a kindred spirit, had a strange, remote quality which appeared to separate her from the other human beings she met. Katherine interpreted her dreamlike quality as being the same as her own rebellion, her deliberate flouting of normal conventions.

For John, Sarah's arrival raised only one question. He knew that he would inherit the estate, that one day he would have a wife and children to support, that he might have to help that future wife's family. He did not want the complications of providing a dowry for Sarah. He intended to raise the matter with his father at some suitable time in the future. At the moment, his father seemed to be acting so much out of character, so compulsively, that he could only wait until he came to his senses.

Frances continued her opposition to the adoption, arguing with Gabriel every time she saw him. She rarely attended the family meals, having food sent up to her chamber.

But it was Gabriel's behaviour which affected everyone and this seemed to be dictated entirely by Sarah's. Because she vacillated between two extremes. At one moment she was delighted with her good fortune, her new clothes, her own bedchamber, the house and gardens. She would walk round the house, picking up precious vases, inspecting them as though she were a purchaser looking for flaws. Walking through the long gallery, she would touch the old bullion chest Gabriel had brought back years ago from a Spanish ship, or gaze in wonder at the Bruges tapestries on the wall, or sit silently in the French walnut armchair in one of the drawing rooms. She helped Katherine weed the bowers and arbours, or sat on the stone seat in the walled garden, looking into the fishpond.

Then, suddenly, her mood would change and she would declare to Gabriel that she was in prison, that she wanted to return home and when Gabriel told her that her house – as he called it – had been burnt down, she implored him to take her to see the ruins, to let her go back to the fields where she said she could live under the hedges.

Then she would dash from the house, fleeing across the fields of the estate, flinging off her new leather shoes and her satin dress, running along in her silk petticoats. And Gabriel would dash after her, catching and shaking her like a puppy. He would drag her back to the house, both of them exhausted and angry, still shouting at each other.

Frances would sit in her chamber, watching their antics through the window. She was worried that perhaps Gabriel was becoming demented, that something had happened to unbalance his mind. His outbursts had become more frequent than in the past and they were different in intention. Shouting, commanding, sweeping through the house, declaiming, had merely been his method of dealing with difficulties. A man did not waste time discussing, arguing; he seemed to think it was more effective to shout. But now his behaviour was uncontrolled: he shouted now in spite of himself, as though he could not hear what was going on in his mind. The absurdity of his behaviour did not seem to occur to him and when Frances approached him about it, he simply said it was their responsibility to protect Sarah.

One night, Frances sat in the darkness of her chamber, listening to the midnight booming of the church clock. She put on a light ermine robe and crept from her room. Tapers glowed along the corridor and she went along the gallery and down the marble staircase. Silently, she swept along the stone-flagged floor and past the kitchens to an alcove where steps led down to a closed door, shaped like a church window with a curved top.

She went into the chapel and knelt beneath the statue of the Virgin. Candles glowed on the little altar and the smell of incense filled the air. Then she realized she was not alone. Father Pierre was kneeling in the shadows, his white hair flowing almost to his waist. Frances felt an overwhelming pity for this solitary man who had devoted his life to silent prayer. Why should he need to hide? The world beyond seemed a vile place, the terrible persecution and violence a mockery of the Lord.

Father Pierre smiled and then began to prepare the bread and wine.

'Father,' she said, 'what can I do?'

She did not need to explain her question.

Father Pierre turned. 'Gabriel does no harm,' he replied.

'But his behaviour. The girl. The whole house is in turmoil.'

'Perhaps it is God's will that she should come here.'

'Is everything explained by God's will?' she challenged. 'Perhaps it's God's will that I should have her removed.'

Normally he referred such questions to the speaker's own conscience but unexpectedly he replied, 'No. Something tells me that she should be here.'

Were they all carried away by this girl? Could no-one see the effect she was having on the household? Or was it her own jealousy?

She bowed her head. At that moment, the door burst open and Sarah stood there, clutching a candle. Frances almost called out, it was as though she had overheard their conversation.

'What is it, child?' Father Pierre shuffled over to her.

'I thought I heard music. Chanting.'

'No. Perhaps you are hearing the voices of the generations of monks who were here before us.'

'What are you doing?' Sarah gazed round at the little altar and flickering candles. 'It's too small for a church.' She looked at the small white marble statue of the Virgin Mary, mystified.

She had never been in a church although it was compulsory for everyone in the land to go to church on Sunday morning. The absence of the dispossessed, the vagrants, tended to be ignored. The ordinary populace were happy enough for them to stay away. They might be diseased, there was always the chance they would cause trouble.

Frances looked irritated. 'What are you doing here? Go back to bed.'

Father Pierre placed his hand lightly on Frances's shoulder. 'Let her come in,' he said, 'she should know. It's our chapel,' he said to Sarah. 'We shouldn't be here, either. As you know, the law of the land says we must not celebrate mass or high communion.'

Sarah frowned. 'I don't know,' she said.

47

'This is Father Pierre,' Frances said curtly. 'He lives in the house and helps Gabriel with his accounts and books.'

He was standing now in front of the statue, before a small table which held little glasses and a tray with tiny pieces of bread on it. Sarah looked in wonder. 'Are you having another meal?'

'This is our spiritual meal,' Father Pierre said. 'Stay, you may listen. Sit in the little chair.'

Sarah sat down and watched as they each took a tiny piece of bread and a small sip of wine and then returned to the little stools to kneel down again.

'This is the altar,' Father Pierre said to her. 'This is the flesh and blood of our Saviour; and above,' he said, pointing to the statue, 'is the Virgin Mary who protects us.'

He began speaking in a foreign language. Then he said to Sarah, 'Come, child. We have finished now. Go to bed.' He led her up the steps and Frances followed. She forced herself to speak to the girl.

'Sarah, we are worshipping in a church which is not acknowledged by the religion of this country. If we were discovered, we might be in a dangerous situation. Our King doesn't believe in what we do. It is better if you don't come any more.'

'Why?'

'At the moment, it's accepted that we have these beliefs as long as we do nothing about them. But it's not legal to encourage someone else to accept them.'

'I can keep a secret,' Sarah said, looking at Frances with her strange green eyes. 'If I'm one of the family,' she added softly.

Frances frowned, controlling her anger, and returned to her chamber. There was a new danger now. If Sarah were evicted from the house, she could take revenge by exposing Father Pierre and all of them. Frances knew that she would have to make her peace with Sarah, to accept her into the home as though she were welcome and even entitled to be there – or she would have to find a safe way of getting rid of her which would not endanger the rest of the family.

3

The journey to London to return Adam to his school would be accomplished in about eight days. It was the first time that Sarah would leave the estate since her arrival over two months before and Gabriel felt apprehensive for her safety. When he went into Dartmouth on his daily business he still felt an undercurrent of resentment, not against himself but against a world which committed so many of its inhabitants to a life of poverty. They were too poor and abject to think of rebellion; they would only turn on someone weaker than themselves. Because of his concern, Gabriel had decided to take the girl with him to London. He knew that his fears for her were exaggerated but also that Frances would not exercise the same vigilance over her activities as he did. He felt resentful also towards Frances that he was compelled to take the girl with him. But Frances, still angry at the presence of Sarah in the house, had insisted that she would not accept responsibility for the girl in his absence. It was up to him to make arrangements for her.

The coach rumbled through the outer courtyard and the great iron gates opened for them to pass through. As they crossed the bridge over the moat and, skirting the gardens, entered the deer park, she asked about the great plantation of young trees, planted on the slopes.

Gabriel said, 'They're mulberry trees for the silkworms.'

He looked at her thoughtfully. Her attitude had changed in the past few weeks. She seemed to have accepted her situation and no longer talked about leaving. Not that he had taken her protests very seriously. Gabriel was of the opinion that there was not a great deal to know about young girls of fifteen. They were simply females growing up, interested in domestic activities and marriage. Once she had recovered from the experiences of the trial and its aftermath, she would settle down and see the opportunities she had luckily been presented with.

Sarah continued to ask about the silkworms.

'We need them to produce silk. For the dress you're wearing. They feed on mulberry. The white mulberry is too delicate for this climate, so we've imported the black species. Joseph, wait.'

The horses came to a halt and Gabriel jumped down, holding out his hand to Sarah. 'Come and look.'

He showed her the furry caterpillars amongst the leaves of the trees which would eventually spin the threads of silk.

'The trees grow very slowly. The climate's not really suitable. The best silk comes from China.'

He knew that she would inevitably question 'China?'

After her first few days of silence, and the rows and arguments which followed, her questioning had become inexhaustible. She seemed to have a natural intelligence and a quest for knowledge which he had found only in the educated classes.

They passed St Clements on the hill and clattered down the steep and narrow track of the Tunstal to the river, crossing at Hardness. Gabriel had some calls to make in the town and Sarah walked with young Adam down to the New Quay to watch a Newfoundlander being unloaded. Then the coach slowly climbed the steep hill up old Mill Lane towards Dittisham and Totnes, to begin their long journey to London.

The early September countryside was still a blaze of flowers and blossom and the coach was constantly stopped for Sarah to collect flowers and blackberries. Adam expostulated with her. He was trying to teach her the Greek alphabet as they trundled along.

They left the coach road and that evening reached the bustling city of Exeter, spending the night at Coldeney Prior, the home of Gabriel's sister, Julia.

The next night they stayed at Sherborne and the following day reached the outskirts of Salisbury. Sarah looked in astonishment at the great spire of the cathedral in the distance, rising high above all the other buildings. They spent that night at Bingley Manor, the home of Frances's brother, Charles. Charles had married a wealthy widow and, like Frances, rarely visited East Anglia. But he found the west country people, including Gabriel, as unsympathetic as she did and Gabriel found him a dour and gloomy man who ruled his household with characteristic autocracy. Gabriel only stayed there out of deference to Frances who seemed to find these tenuous connections with her past of some comfort. Charles expressed his disapproval of the adoption of Sarah, pointing out that these sort of people should be kept in their place, which Gabriel gathered would be the House of Correction. They left early the next morning and spent that night at Winchester. Two days later, they put up at an inn within the shadows of the great Palace of Windsor. Sarah's excitement mounted when, the following morning, Gabriel announced that this was the final day of their journey. 'Tonight,' he said, 'we reach our destination.'

Then they were in the streets of London, amongst swirling masses of shouting people, horses, houses on every side and the smell.

'The smell,' Sarah said. 'It's so awful.'

She had become accustomed to the perfume of aromatic herbs which, at Vinelands, were scattered on those floors which were uncarpeted.

'So many people,' Gabriel said. 'Horses, filth, everywhere. People are supposed to burn it, but . . .' He waved his hand deprecatingly.

But young Adam came to life as he entered the city. He had been silent on the long journey. Brought up in the comfort of his palatial home, he did not care for the rigours of the countryside and the uncomfortable coach with its iron wheels rumbling over the rutted roads.

'Wait till you see my school,' he said eagerly to Sarah.

But when they reached Threadneedle Street she said she could see little difference between that and the timbered buildings in all the other narrow streets. And the smells persisted. They went through the iron gateway and Gabriel was taken by a porter to the headmaster's room. Adam took Sarah to see the schoolroom, with its wooden benches and heavy wooden desks arranged in rows on three sides of the room.

'What do you do?' Sarah asked.

'We learn,' Adam said proudly, 'Greek, Latin.'

'Why?'

'When I leave here I shall go to Cambridge and then I shall go to visit foreign places – Rome and Florence.'

'And then?'

'I intend to be a writer, great romances and poesy.'

And then a group of boys rushed into the schoolroom and fell upon Adam, laughing, pushing, punching and falling on each other.

After a few minutes, they all got up and Adam said calmly, 'This is my sister, Sarah.'

The boys turned to the corner where she had retreated and muttered greetings in an embarrassed way. They were not yet old enough to have acquired the graces and gallantries of chivalrous gentlemen.

'Adam said you work in here,' Sarah said questioningly. The boys shuffled, taking this as a rebuke at their silly behaviour, but one tall blond boy stepped forward and said laughing, 'I'm James Marston. May I escort you to the refectory?' He offered his arm and Sarah walked beside him across the quadrangle, while the others giggled and danced behind them.

After five o'clock supper, Gabriel and Sarah said good-bye to Adam. Gabriel told Sarah that they had to visit a friend of his in the City. They would walk there. Dusk was not yet falling but Sarah clutched his cloak in order not to get lost in the throng of people in the congested, narrow streets. They were constantly forced to jump aside to avoid being trampled under the feet of horses or crushed by the carts which almost touched the houses on each side. Sarah was holding up her skirts to avoid the rubbish on the footpaths and the dirty running water in the gutters. Every time a coach or horse and cart clattered past, they were splashed with filth. The houses here were narrower and dingier than around Merchant Taylor's and beggars constantly came up to Gabriel asking for money. She had heard about the pickpockets and footpads and murders in dark alleys but Gabriel showed no fear nor even interest. He was peering up at the houses, evidently looking for some distinguishing sign that would tell him which of these identical buildings was the right one.

Then a face appeared at a dark window, Gabriel stopped and they went through the open doorway at the side.

They walked down a dark alley to a courtyard and a side door of the house was opened to admit them. The narrow room was filled with sick people, lying on the floor or on rush mats, all silent or moaning quietly to themselves.

They went on through to another side room and in the shadows were the outlines of two men in priests' clothes. One of them was lying on the floor, breathing heavily. The other knelt beside him, wiping his forehead with the loose sleeve of his gown.

Another man appeared from a dark recess. 'We've been expecting you,' he said quietly. 'They arrived last night.' He nodded his head in the direction of the two men. 'Father Matthew is very sick. It's hard to believe he will recover.'

'If he dies, he must be buried at night,' Gabriel said. 'No-one must know they're here. Can you arrange that?'

The man nodded. 'Usual procedure. Strip him, take him to the river.'

Gabriel took a pouch from his doublet.

'When they are recovered – if they do – send word and I will have them despatched to Devon.'

'There are more arriving. It is a dangerous venture.'

'Yes.' Gabriel knew that the man was not referring to his own position but to that of these priests. They continued to come from the seminaries of Douai and Rouen, to enter upon their mission in England, arriving by boat in the darkness of the night. Their capture would mean imprisonment or even death, preceded by hours of stretching on the rack, or other tortures like forcing prongs between the nail and the quick. The spirit of Topcliffe, the torturer and prosecutor of Catholics, was still alive amongst the warders and judiciary. There were enough wealthy Catholic families in the country to shelter them, but many of the priests preferred to stay in London and carry on their work amongst the poor and destitute.

When they left, Sarah wanted to see the Palace of Westminster. She had been told by Charles, the tutor, about the fire of 1512, when it had ceased to be a royal palace, and how Henry VIII had later taken over Wolsey's York House.

They walked along by the side of the river Thames. In the growing darkness, Gabriel pointed out White Hall, where the Lords met, and the Jewel Tower with the moat around it, where the King's jewels were kept. The houses around Westminster were inhabited by members of James's court and by knights and burgesses of the city. There they met, as representatives of local communities and had done so, Gabriel told her, for nearly three hundred years. It was called the House of Commons.

Then they went to the nearby inn at which they were to stay for the night.

Gabriel took Sarah up to her room where she took off her clothes that were splashed with dirty water from the streets and washed herself in a large basin by the log fire. A room was reserved for travellers in which to eat in privacy, away from the common people in the beer parlour.

They had a supper of game pie and roast pork, followed by blackberry pudding, in the company of two other gentlemen who were also returning their boys to Merchant Taylor's.

'We must retire early,' Gabriel said. 'Tomorrow we will have an early start and hope to make Windsor before dark.'

As they pushed through the crowded parlour, Sarah stopped to listen to the ribald song which was being delivered by an Egyptian-looking sailor. Gabriel noticed with irritation the obscene leers directed at the golden-haired girl beside him and heard the lewd comments about her green eyes, her pale skin and the soft curves which her blue taffeta dress made all too apparent. He put his arm round her protectively in order to shield her from contact with the crowd around them. He felt even more irritated when he saw that Sarah was smiling. Then one drunkenly bold youth bent forward and put his hand on her breast.

In one furious gesture, Gabriel leapt forward and had him by the throat. 'Scum,' he shouted.

Immediately, there were screams and shouts as Gabriel shook him like a dog killing a rat and arms were flung out to restrain him.

At the same moment, Sarah said, 'Gabriel. Don't. It is nothing.'

Gabriel glanced at her, gave the man a final shake and threw him to the floor. Silence ensued as she said, 'Come,' and they walked through the crowd and up the staircase.

Outside her door, Gabriel put his hands on her shoulders and looked at her in bewilderment. He had intended to reprimand her for her interference, but he simply shook his head and said, 'Sarah.'

She turned. 'Goodnight Gabriel.'

'Bolt your door.'

Gabriel sat in his candlelit room, looking down on the crowded street and at the timbered houses opposite which seemed so close that you could step across. He was overwhelmed at the violence which had welled up inside him, at his totally disproportionate response to the youth's behaviour. He knew that he could have killed him. He knew also that his passion for this girl had begun on the morning of the execution, when he had seen her kneeling on the grass in the sunshine. The anxiety he had felt the first time he had talked to her in the coach was simply the result of his own unacknowledged desires. His determination to take her into his home, in spite of his doubts, had not been one of charity. For the first time in his life, he had been so attracted to a female that he felt he would stop at nothing to have her with him. He knew, too, that for him his religion made his thoughts and feelings totally unacceptable. Whores were one thing: this girl, in his care, a ward in his household, was another. If he had listened to Frances and sent her to the servants' quarters, or to his own common sense and sent her to a House of Correction or to the Poor House – or – he could even have taken her to Brixham where she would not have been recognized and settled her in some respectable merchant's house or on one of the farms. Even placed her in one of the convenient houses of Dartmouth. So many solutions now presented themselves that he felt a growing anger and impatience at his own folly. Sitting now in the darkness he knew that his feelings were completely inappropriate. His position could not accommodate absurd romantic involvements. The parameters of his life were clear and unequivocal. But he had obstinately put himself in the situation and he would deal with it as with all other problems. Sarah was his responsibility. She would be brought up in his household in the correct fashion. His private feelings were his own concern and would remain so. They would have

56

no influence on his conduct. He blew out his candle and climbed into bed.

4

Frances watched the coach go slowly away down the avenue as she had watched it approach a few months earlier.

The presence of Sarah in the household still caused her deep resentment. At the back of her mind was still a question of why Gabriel had taken her in; she was also suspicious of Sarah's motives. When she was not at her lessons with Gilbert, Sarah spent much of her time in the grounds. It was here that each member of the family seemed to go and talk to her, as though she had some strange attraction which compelled them to follow her round the knot garden or sit with her in the rose garden or in the privacy of one of the bowers.

For a time, Gabriel had appeared to watch her anxiously every time she went out of the house, as though he were fearful always that she would escape. There had been one occasion when Sarah had secretly taken Gilbert across the hills to see the remains of her old hut. When they returned, Gilbert had collapsed with exhaustion and had promptly complained bitterly to Gabriel that they had been chased by some village boys, shouting abuse at Sarah and attacking them with stones.

Gabriel had turned on Sarah angrily.

'I asked you not to go out alone.'

'I didn't,' Sarah retorted. 'I went with Gilbert.'

'You mustn't leave the estate without me.'

'Why is it so dangerous?'

'You know perfectly well why it's so dangerous. They believe you're a witch. While this mood goes on in the town, they'll be after you.'

'It's all right. I can deal with them.'

Gabriel sighed. 'That makes it worse. If you can silence them, they'll believe you are a witch.'

Sarah laughed. 'Perhaps I am.'

'Sarah, it's not a matter of fun. It's a serious thing. We're all in a vulnerable situation here.'

Cicely pointed out that it was ridiculous, that there was no reason for going out, the estate was so large that if she walked round all day she would never cover it all. Since then, Sarah seemed to have accepted the situation.

Frances turned from the window. Today she was beginning the final preparations for Katherine's wedding in a few months' time and when she saw her in the garden beneath the chamber, she called to her.

'Katherine, come. We must discuss the final guest list.'

Plans were now well advanced. Adam would still be at home on the Christmas vacation for the celebrations early in January and for two days there would be great feasts and dancing and drinking. Katherine had discussed it endlessly, how she would have a new beautiful home nearby and Frances could come and visit her whenever she liked. She pictured herself as the lady in a great household indulging her passion for fine clothes and expensive jewellery and Frances knew that Katherine had little appreciation of the sacramental aspect of marriage. But for Frances, there were other problems besides the wedding. She had hoped that with her betrothal, there would be changes in Katherine's behaviour. Even as a young girl, she had behaved in what Frances felt to be a wanton fashion, flirting with the stable-boys as well as with guests staying in the house. Frances had often said, 'If you were a common village girl, you'd be put in the stocks.'

Then she had met Richard, young and attractive, but an adventurer, an explorer, who clearly had few thoughts of marriage or domestic ties. Katherine had fallen wildly in love, responding with her whole being to this dashing young man. Then, when he was away on one of his long voyages, Sir William Greenhayes, whom she scarcely knew and who was ten years her senior, had unexpectedly proposed marriage. Even more incredibly, Katherine had accepted.

When Frances had asked her about her attachment to Richard, Katherine had frowned.

'It would never work. He's not rich. He's away so often.'

Reflecting upon it now, Frances had to admit to herself that it was she who had persuaded Gabriel to agree. Although, at eighteen, Katherine was really too young for marriage, Frances had hoped that she might settle down, that the attractions of an opulent life would be sufficient. Yet her flippant behaviour had not changed. When Frances confronted her about it, Katherine laughed. 'Don't worry, Mama. I shall be a married lady soon.'

In fact, Frances feared that Katherine was still in love with Richard, even that they were still meeting secretly. Did she believe that she could carry on that relationship after her marriage?

Katherine had said once, 'William spends half his life in the courts. He is frequently in London. And Richard is not always away on the high seas.'

Frances watched as the seamstresses helped Katherine try on her new dresses. It was strange that Sir William appeared to know nothing of that attachment, had no suspicions. He seemed, indeed, singularly unperturbed by Katherine's irresponsible attitudes. Then, a few weeks before the wedding, Katherine suddenly became attentive and polite when William called upon her and she frequently went to inspect her new home with him.

Her wedding day arrived. The evening before, Katherine said she was going out for a walk with Sarah. She and Sarah had become friends since Sarah's return from London. She found the little waif, as she called her, a new and interesting element in her life. Sarah would sit and listen with a smile on her lips to Katherine's plans and hopes and dreams and finally she had told her about Richard. And she had promised that Sarah would meet him before the wedding.

They walked through the gardens and around the lake to her arbour. It was a cold, damp January evening and they pulled their cloaks around them and sat on a stone seat sheltered by a high brick wall.

Katherine said suddenly, 'This is the last time for Richard and me. In our present situation.'

'What do you mean', Sarah asked, 'your present situation?'

Katherine laughed. 'Well, he probably won't be able to visit me at night any more, will he?'

'Does Richard come to see you at night?' Sarah's green eyes were wide with surprise.

'When else would he see me? But tonight he's coming to sit with us in the garden.'

Then Richard suddenly appeared, walking casually through the trees.

'Where's your horse?' Katherine asked.

'I walked. I wanted to have a last stroll through the gardens . . . the fields.'

Katherine looked at the handsome man before her, at his usually smiling face which was today tense and anxious.

'What else can we do?' she said, as though in answer to a question.

Sarah stood up and started to walk back through the garden.

'Don't go,' Richard said. 'You're the beautiful Egyptian I've heard so much about. Stay and talk with us.' Sarah turned. 'What will become of us, Sarah?'

'Don't bother the child. She doesn't understand such things.'

'Yes. I do,' Sarah said.

'How is that?'

'I would only marry for love,' Sarah said firmly.

'I think my mother will have some influence on that,' Katherine said. 'She'd disapprove of your marrying a pauper.'

Sarah said nothing and left them in the garden.

Katherine did not appear that night for the evening meal but no-one commented on it. Even Gilbert, who usually commented on everything, was silent. Frances hoped that by ignoring the situation, no trouble might arise.

And sure enough the next morning Katherine appeared in her sparkling white wedding dress and arrived in her decorated coach at St Petrox Church. She and Sir William exchanged marriage vows and the vicar blessed their marriage and then they returned in a great fleet of coaches to the celebrations at Vinelands.

Gabriel had laid on a great feast and for two days the dining hall was the scene of a perpetual banquet attended by all the gentry and nobility for miles around. Silk ribbons and scarves decorated the shoulders of the ladies, gifts from the bride, and on the final evening a masked ball was held in the ballroom and quieter music echoed from the library for the older guests. In the music room, little groups of lovers sang madrigals and lute songs and groups of men played cards in the games room.

In the early hours of the morning, Katherine and William bade farewell to their guests and began the short coach ride to his home, Greenhayes Manor, four miles away.

Exhausted from the celebrations, Katherine had a feeling of dissatisfaction as they approached the house in the grey dawn light. She knew that it was smaller than the home she had left; it had no moat or drawbridge, only iron gates in a high stone wall, leading into a courtyard. The stone house was gaunt, the gabled, leaded windows looked dark in the shadows and the only sound was their coach rumbling over the cobbled stones.

William stepped down and held out his hand. For a second she sat still, feeling desolate and then panic-stricken as she seemed to see before her a long vista of years, stretching endlessly away in an interminable silence. Alone with him, she would live in this great gloomy building that looked to her now like a prison and not that beautiful sunlit acquisition that had meant wealth and power when she visited it.

He smiled, she choked back a sob and stepped down beside him. Then the oak doors were opened by the steward and she followed William into the brightly-lit hall. A huge fire was blazing at the other end, servants were coming and going, taking her cloak, carrying casks of wine and beer to the kitchens, lighting candles and tapers up the wide staircase. She nodded to them as she walked slowly down the hall and sat on the settle by the fire while William poured her some hot mulled wine.

She smiled briefly. He was looking at her thoughtfully, his blue eyes seeming to look into her soul. She turned away. It was not a look of passion, not an erotic glance of desire – that she could cope with – but this look of concern, this probing intimacy, was unwelcome. It would invade her privacy, make demands upon her quite beyond the simple requirements of the marriage bed.

'You are very quiet, Katherine.'

'The celebrations have been very long.'

William nodded.

Does he think I'm frightened, shy, she thought? The absurdity of it.

'Let's go to bed,' she said briefly.

She stood up and took his arm. William instructed the steward to keep the fires burning.

'It's a lovely staircase.' Katherine looked at the tapestries as they mounted the stairs. 'These will always give me pleasure.'

'I hope everything here will do that.'

Katherine nodded, thinking firmly of the purely physical

benefits of her new life. She was rich, she would have jewels and carriages, parties and travel. She would have all the lovely clothes she wanted. She was Lady Katherine Greenhayes. When she reached her bedchamber, she looked with approval at the rich blue velvet curtains around the bed and the huge oak cupboard in which she would hang her clothes.

Her serving maid had laid out her nightgown on a small velvet chair and it was only when she glanced at the enormous four-poster bed that desolation swept over her again.

William left them while the maid helped her to remove her shoes, unlace her gown, and take off her petticoats and bodice. Then she abruptly dismissed the serving maid and stood calmly by the bed, awaiting William's return.

She turned. He stood quietly in the doorway. Suddenly, she tore off the remaining petticoat and stood naked for a second and then grabbed her nightgown and pulled it over her head.

She turned and glanced at William, who was watching her still with that concerned expression as she pulled back the covers.

'Come on, then.' The impatience in her voice suggested no joy or excitement. It was a command.

William walked round to where she sat on the edge of the bed and put his hands on her shoulders.

'Katherine,' he said firmly, 'this is not a penance nor even a duty. You are tired, dear.'

He pulled back the covers, smiled at her and lifted her legs on to the bed.

'We have the whole future before us,' he said softly.

He turned away, undressed, and climbed in beside her. He wiped the tears from her face.

'It is sad, you know, leaving your childhood home, but I will make you happy, Katherine.'

His kindness made her feel even more desolate but he held her in his arms, stroking her hair.

'Let us rest now,' he said gently.

Before Katherine fell asleep from exhaustion, she realized that this man could not be dealt with as easily as she had believed. He would not be content with a dutiful semblance of marriage.

She saw for the first time that William was someone to be reckoned with.

5

In the New Year, Gabriel planned with his eldest son, John, the annual expedition to Newfoundland. They would leave in early February, reaching the fishing fields for the beginning of the cod season and for the sealing around Grand Bank, then wait for the salmon to gather in early summer. He was always meticulous in his preparations for the forty fishing vessels under his control. Supplies, equipment, fishermen, safety of the boats were all checked and noted in detail. His reputation for being a great captain had spread throughout the west country. But for the first time in his life, he had a feeling of anxiety as he made his lists, inspected the boats, ordered repairs and renewal of sails, removed one boat from the fleet altogether. There was even a suspicion in the back of his mind that he should not go at all. This fear was not connected with the journey but about what might happen while he was away.

He had never had this apprehension before. The house was well enough protected; the servants could be relied upon. His own bodyguard could deal with any unexpected attack. He had inspected the armoury and talked to his steward, who looked astonished at Gabriel's sudden questions about the weaponry. 'It's all in order. The men are well-trained. But attacks, m'lord. From what source?'

'No, of course not.' Gabriel frowned at his own incoherent fears.

Frances, too, discussed his anxieties.

'We're not living in Crusader times,' she protested. 'Neither are there any Wat Tylers in Dartmouth.'

'There are too many vagrants.'

'Vagrants! They do no harm.' Frances added thoughtfully, 'Your fears go back to the hanging, I think.'

'The poor are still in an uncertain state. See that Sarah doesn't leave the estate alone.'

'Sarah is all right here,' Frances said irritably. 'All that trouble was half a year ago.'

'The people aren't to be relied on,' he replied angrily, 'she must be protected.'

'She will be.' Frances closed her accounts book. She had matters to attend to with the household. She looked at Gabriel coldly. 'Your preoccupation is excessive.'

Gabriel strode from the room and down the staircase to inspect the latest work being executed in the house – the raising of the ceilings in the Great Hall, the intricate plastering being carried out by some Italian craftsmen.

He went round to the stables, told one of the half-dozen stable boys to saddle his black horse and rode down into town. The harbour was crowded with fishermen, navvies, boat repairers, all preparing for the journey to the fishing fields.

Gabriel went up the gangway to the deck of his own ship. The animals which would be slaughtered on the journey to keep food supplies going were being coaxed up the gangplank. All the food necessary for at least six months had to be stored in the hold. Seamen were loading great barrels of salt and large earthen pots containing legs of mutton minced and stewed and close-packed with butter, sides of gammon, pork and roast beef preserved in vinegar, dried fish and salted meat. The cooks were supervising the loading of sacks of wheat flour, oatmeal, rice, sugar, butter and cheese. Large casks of wine, wine vinegar, casked waters and oil were carried below and spices such as ginger, cinnamon, mustard and pepper which might be needed to improve or disguise the taste of the food in the future. There was a plentiful supply of lemons and prunes, rumoured to be an antidote to scurvy. Two of the women were complaining that barrels of almonds and currants had disappeared and boxes of biscuits and marmalade had been broken open. The purser was checking the boxes of gifts; cheap jewellery and baubles, woollen blankets, tobacco, pieces of crockery, which might be needed in hostile situations.

Gabriel knew every seaman and fisherman in his whole fleet, although there were over six hundred men and women.

The fisherwomen who would accompany them on the expedition, to salt the fish, get it ready to bring home, and be responsible for the preparation of meals, stood giving orders. They were a rough and coarse lot and their language was no different from the men's, but they worked hard and were indispensable to the success of the trip.

Gabriel said goodbye to his family on a cold February afternoon. It was always a formal occasion; the perils for ships sailing in the North Atlantic were too well-known to permit of cheerfulness or the display of emotion.

He walked along Bayards Cove to his waiting ship. Hundreds of figures hustled about in the fading light. The masts of ships moved gently backwards and forwards in the gentle tide of the harbour. He stopped for a moment to look at the notice boards outside the Customs house.

WRECKS AND CASUALTIES

The barque, *White Lily*, bound from Falmouth for St John's, Newfoundland, having left at midday on the first day of the year, last spoken at sea on 21st day of January in the year of Our Lord 1611, is now overdue.

The brig, *Mermaid*, bound from Horta port, Azores, with a cargo of pineapple and spices for Brixham, having left in first week of December, last spoken at sea on 18th day of that month and never having been heard of since, was posted today as missing.

Gabriel read the chilling messages without emotion. No sailor ever considered that it would happen to him. Fear in a way was diluted by the variety of dangers that might arise – rocks, wind, squalls, storms, icebergs, pirates. He took a horse from the stables and made his customary ride along the lane and up the hill to the harbour mouth. The sea was quiet and smooth for February and there was only a light easterly breeze as he hoped. He walked down by the side of the castle into St Petrox Church. This was always looked upon as the mariners' church. It was the last building they saw as they ventured out to the open sea; it was the first they viewed when they returned to Dartmouth.

It looked bare to him now – the candles and images and the statue of the Virgin had been removed from all churches – but he knelt beneath the cross and prayed to his God. He asked for protection and safety in their expedition; he accepted that if it were not to be, then God's will would prevail.

Yet he knew that his faith required more than acquiescence because one day he might be called upon actually to offer his life and not just to lose it. He stood looking thoughtfully for a few minutes at the plain altar, feeling infinite loneliness and solitude, and then he walked briskly back to the Cove. All the boats were now loaded and lanterns flickered on the decks. Gabriel climbed the ladder of his ship and looked back to the quay. The wind was rocking the small boats moored to the side, sails flapped in the wind and his gaze took in the rows of workers moving about in the shadows of the harbour, the familiar shapes of the buildings, the wooded hills behind.

Then he went quickly down the steps of the galley, pulled on his working clothes and went back to help the men. Everyone worked on his ships; it was another reason why men always wanted to accompany him on his voyages. That, and the fact that they were always more successful than anyone else's.

They waited till dawn, pulled anchor and set sail for Newfoundland. He intended this time not only to get the catch of fish but also to try to get further up Baffin's Bay where he had sailed years ago as a young lad with John Davis. No seaman had given up hope that there might be a north-west or north-east passage to China although expeditions had become less frequent in recent years.

As they left the sheltering hills of the harbour a cold easterly breeze told them they were approaching the open sea. The pilot boat led them out, away from the coast until they reached the end of land at Start Point. As they rounded the Point south of Mounts Bay the full force of the east wind in the Channel attacked them from behind and Gabriel turned to ensure the fishing fleet were close together.

Stretching behind him, the great sails billowed in the wind, moving like a team of dancers on the tossing waves. For Gabriel, it was the most beautiful sight in the world. Beyond all the joys of gain and possession, beyond marriage, friendship, children, the home he had built up over the years, above his love of Dartmouth and its rolling countryside, beyond even the excitement of new worlds, new people, was this simple, overwhelming delight in the spectacle of white sails in the murky yellow light of a February morning. He looked behind to the faraway horizon and ahead to the open sea. He knew when they had passed Lizard Head their last sight of land would be the Isles of Scilly, the last shallow waters, and then there was only the deepening Atlantic Ocean before them. The great desolate expanses of the North Atlantic. Three thousand miles to St John's. It was not until no land could be seen that the journey had really begun.

He went down to the gun deck. It was important to see that the general standards which were to be maintained throughout the voyage were established immediately. Spaces had to be allocated for the men so that there would be no disputes and resentments later in the journey. It was important, too, that the men should know he was concerned for their welfare and that any problems should be referred to him. After many days at sea, men began to build up grudges, to imagine insults and abuse which did not exist. The space on the ship was so confined, the work so arduous, that the atmosphere could become aggressive. Once they reached Newfoundland it would be all right. They left the ship frequently then, fishing from boats, going up country hunting. But the difficult time was the journey there and back. In the dimness of the hold, stuffy and congested, with only a few fisherwomen, mostly their wives and daughters, to relieve the boredom, organization was all important.

They all tried to stand up as he came in, awkwardly, because the ceiling was too low for any of them to be erect. The wooden boards creaked as he jumped down and the air was heavy with the smell of oiled ropes.

'Sit down. Don't forget. Eat the fruit in the kitchens. It's to protect you against disease. Anyone drunk will be put on the mast, and if there are any fights – overboard.' Gabriel flung his arm meaningfully towards the side of the ship.

He glanced at the cannons projecting through the mullion-shaped windows and the iron pikes stacked neatly in the corner. Nowadays, fishing vessels were fitted out like warships. At the end of the deck was the Great Cabin, about six feet wide, where he slept and had his meals, and the small Capstan where armour or ammunition could quickly be handed out to the crew. Below this was the hold where the men slept;

although it was dark, there was at least room for them to stand up.

As the days passed, the winds became stronger and snow began to fall. Further north, they entered the belt of almost permanent fog and mist and the little ships kept close together. Gabriel spent his time teaching John to use the compasses and astrolabes. He was a quiet and reliable boy who got on well with the fishermen, seeming to get their cooperation by his pleasant, easy manner. It was a comfort that he, as the eldest son, would inherit everything.

The weather gradually deteriorated. They had constantly to shorten the sails in the violent winds. Gabriel spent hours on deck, looking out across the desolate wastes of the sea and listening to the staccato clapping of the sails. The first days at sea always had a sobering effect on him and the men, too. The vast spaces, the seemingly endless distances, the meeting of water and sky reflecting each other's image, reminded them of how trivial life was compared with this eternity. Faced with their own vulnerability the crew worked purposefully as though their human actions gave them validity against that great power which held them up, carried the ship, but which could capriciously destroy them.

Gabriel watched the white foam spraying higher as they went north, looking gloomily into the whirls of mist turning gradually into fog, observing the surge of the waves rolling monotonously towards them. He never made peace with that despotic ocean, wondering about its depth, its real extent. He always experienced a feeling of inertia as though his life were flowing by like a dream. The melancholy was exacerbated by his sense of responsibility to the men and ships and his knowledge of his ultimate helplessness. He knew there were captains who disappeared into their cabins for the first days at sea, speaking to no-one, not eating, drinking alone. Yet he knew the sea was the reason for his existence, as he felt in the end it might be his death.

He was also still preoccupied with Sarah. He wondered

if he had been sufficiently firm about her not going into the town alone, whether Frances would look after her while he was away, whether she would be molested . . . His mind would never go beyond this thought, he would break out in a sweat and spring from his bunk and walk about in the blackness of the night, muttering to himself. He knew that the men were commenting on his behaviour, that it was making them feel agitated also. The superstitious sailor needed a calm and confident captain. They feared he was worried about the weather or pirates or disease. His motto had always been 'The only danger is today.' Was he suddenly becoming anxious and thus endangering their lives? He dismissed his anxiety and forced himself into action, keeping the crew and fishermen busy, mending nets, adjusting the rigging, washing the deck, because he knew from long experience that they, too, had a morbid fear of the sea. The isolation, even in a fleet of forty fishing vessels, gave birth to superstitions and fears; fights and arguments tended to break out in the confined area of the gun deck, events which Gabriel dealt with as he had warned, having the culprits thrown overboard into the icy sea, to be picked up, if they were fortunate, by one of the other vessels.

But at last, at the end of the third week, they sighted land and preparations for the expedition began in earnest. There were many more fishing vessels around the coast of all nationalities but particularly Portuguese and Dutch, Gabriel noted. Every year, these Newfoundland waters became more and more crowded with ships. On the rocky coast, small settlements were being set up. But they never lasted.

He had intended to take the fleet straight on past St John's to Francis and Conception Bay but a violent gale forced them into Ferrylands. The hazard here was the great whales that inhabited the waters beyond the harbour. Although they were not aggressive, it was their enormous bulk which made them a danger to the fishing fleets. Long

71

before they reached the harbour, Gabriel could see the
breakers and the white spots that seemed to indicate a
rock which he knew was really the moving flesh of a whale.
He watched sea swallows and petrels hovering over the
great, grey hump about two hundred feet long, covered
with limpets and shells, and then the grey mass moved
and two huge jets of water shot thirty feet into the air,
instantly changing into mist in the freezing temperature.
The whale disappeared beneath the ocean, the great tail
beating the water to propel it smoothly away and a few
minutes later the grey mountain emerged again, far away
out to sea, preceded by fountains of rising water.

Gabriel turned. The crew were all standing on the deck,
watching. Their first sighting of these great creatures of the
sea always silenced them. Perhaps it was their size that
made their peaceful nature almost inconceivable.

The next day they passed St John's, the safest harbour
on this coast, but becoming too crowded already. The
entrance to the harbour was protected by rocky hills on
either side but, further in, the land flattened out on each
side of the inlet and all along there were now fishing
stations and hundreds of sailing boats moored alongside.

They went on round the coast to Conception Bay and
dropped anchor between two rocky promontories. In order
to retain control of the fishing stages and protect the
property, it was becoming necessary to stay throughout
the winter. So far, Gabriel had managed to retain control
by superiority of force, but it was becoming increasingly
difficult. Last year, a small group of Englishmen had
started the first small English settlement here and had
surprisingly survived a whole year. But the men were
already talking about going home when the season was
over. No-one would remain in this inhospitable land
permanently.

Gabriel's fleet spread itself along the inlets and the
building and repair of the stages began in heavy rain
and incessant fog. The stages were enormous timber

72

constructions built on the sea's edge. Wooden scaffolding at the base led up to a platform to which the fish would be carried, to be cleaned, cured, dried and salted, and the oil extracted and poured into wooden casks. The catch began immediately, with groups of men fishing inshore from the sides of the boats. Great shoals of cod were caught each day. They were split and boned, then washed and salted by the women. They complained constantly about the difficulty of salting fish in the damp conditions, and about the biting east wind which froze their fingers, but Gabriel knew that this was merely their bitterness about the harshness of life generally.

The cod were then washed again and dried in the sun which, as the spring came, cast a blinding light on the water during periods when the rain and fog were mercifully absent. It was a skilled job, drying fish. Either rain or over-exposure to sudden sunshine could ruin them and they had to be constantly moved, covered and turned.

A few weeks after their arrival, a captain of another group of fishing vessels came to see Gabriel. He was arranging a trading expedition up the coast. As well as the fishermen from the European countries there were still the indigenous Indians to trade with. There were Indians further south around Trinity Bay who were peaceful and willing to trade with the white man but the Boethuck Indians, who inhabited Notre Dame Bay about three hundred miles to the north, were reputed still to use stone tools, fight with bows and arrows and wear furs and sealskins.

'All Indians are peaceful,' Gabriel said.

The captain looked sceptical. 'I haven't had any dealings myself. Only hearsay.'

Gabriel agreed to accompany him, leaving John in charge of the fishing fleet and taking with him half a dozen reliable men. He also took his own ship and armour. This fellow John Farthing from Bristol seemed honest but in the lawless conditions at sea, motives were always questioned.

73

Gabriel had been at sea too long to trust anyone. On the other hand, the opportunity to trade with the Indians for furs such as sealskins and bearskins could not be missed.

The small group of vessels sailed up the coast and into Trinity Bay. There were few fishing boats here and forty miles up the west side of the bay it seemed completely deserted.

But it was here that they expected to trade because they knew that the coastal Indians would have observed their arrival. Rays of spring sunshine glinted on the icy water and across the snow-covered cliffs. The boats anchored, waiting.

John Farthing shouted over to Gabriel. 'They'll know we're here. Been watching for days, no doubt. We just wait.'

Gabriel knew that this inexperienced merchant was anxious, uncertain of what would happen, what to do, how to behave.

Two days passed, then they came, out of the forest, small, brown-skinned, black-haired, the skins they were wearing decorated in vivid colours. They came dancing down the beach, their faces masked by brightly coloured dyes, moving into the water in a great horde.

Gabriel frowned. To the uninitiated it looked like a war dance but he knew that they carried no weapons. It was their form of greeting. The Indians and Eskimaux were deadly enemies who fought each other with unbelievable ferocity. But to the white man they seemed to have only peaceful intentions. They shouted, a strange, whooping call that had made his blood curdle when he had first heard it. Suddenly, a deafening sound of gunfire struck the icy air from the other ships. Presumably in panic, John Farthing had ordered his men to open fire.

The Indians stopped, those who had been hit vanished beneath the water and the survivors fled back into the forest. Here and there a trail of blood floated across the water, and two bodies came to the surface.

A few of them, presumably injured, floundered helplessly.

'Idiot!' Gabriel shouted. 'What's wrong with the man?
Put a boat down. I'll go and see him.'

He boarded Farthing's boat.

'They were just greeting you! Why did you open fire?'

Farthing said coldly, 'That's the way I intend to trade.
You can't bargain with savages.'

'This isn't the high seas!' Gabriel exploded. 'Piracy is one
thing. You can win. You get treasure. But we don't want
enemies here. We shall never be able to fish in peace!'

'The men need recreation,' Farthing said. 'You can't
keep them here, make them work in this frozen hell if
they don't get some relaxation.'

Gabriel looked at him with contempt, not because of
his attitude towards the Indians but because he couldn't
control his own fleet. He deplored the fact that Indian
hunting had become a common sport, that expeditions
were organized into the woods, with guns and axes,
and there was a prize for the man who could get the
greatest 'head of Indians'. It was this kind of behaviour
that had given the English the reputation of being pirates
and savages themselves. Gabriel had never permitted these
activities. Killing was not a sport, only on occasion a
necessity, but it had to involve real gain, or be the answer
to real danger. There would be no trade with these Indians;
it was a wasted expedition. But they were about a hundred
and fifty miles from base. He had to calculate whether he
could risk his men and ship by returning alone.

'My men will remain on board,' he said shortly. 'We'll
return with you.'

He returned to his ship. His own men knew his views on
the situation. They had no great feeling about the sport
either way, but they knew that their captain could be relied
on and his views were usually right. So they stayed on the
ship, watching Farthing's men. Boatloads of them went
into the woods and in the afternoon, about a hundred

Indians were driven out from the trees on to the ice. Small children ran in front, shouting and crying. As they ran, the Englishmen shot them in the legs, laughing delightedly as they were thrown into the air or were twirled around with the violence of the assault. Then they lined up the men and shot them, their bloody bodies falling silently from the ice floes into the sea. Suddenly huge yellow flames shot up from the forest; the sailors had set fire to the camp.

Gabriel's men watched as though it were a scene from hell, the unearthly orange light rising up in the arctic mists; the red-stained ice floes, the children writhing in agony. The Indian women watched, huddled together on the ice. Not a sound came from their lips. The sailors looked at them, uncertainly. The women remained still, without fear or anticipation, as though they had become part of the ice on which they stood. Then they walked in a slow file towards the children. They picked up the bleeding bodies, a few tiny corpses, and carried them without any display of emotion back into the woods. Gabriel turned away in disgust.

In the silence that followed, Gabriel knew that suddenly the sailors were afraid, their minds filled with superstitious fears of spells and evil spirits which the Indians were believed to control. They sprang into their boats and returned to the ships. The next day they returned to base.

His few days' absence confirmed Gabriel's suspicion that the cod fishing was turning out to be less profitable than usual. The increasing number of fishing fleets all around the shores meant that next year he would need to go further north to less populated areas. This was why it was important to establish friendly relations with the indigenous Indians. He sent some of the fishermen up country for the salmon season which began in the early summer, while he took some of the ships on the more dangerous mission south, around St John's and west beyond Placentia for the spring sealing around Grand Bank.

It was on that dismal journey that his thoughts turned to home, to the family, the estate, and to Sarah. He thought about her constantly, longing to see her, speak to her and, although it might never be possible, hold her in his arms.

6

On a clear spring morning a few months after Gabriel's departure to Newfoundland, Charles entered the library. Sarah was already there, studying a large map which Sir Gabriel had placed on the wall, outlining his journey to Newfoundland. Her thick golden hair was plaited into a long rope at the back, which revealed her bare white shoulders beneath a delicate pink silk gown which fitted tightly at the waist.

She turned when Charles entered.

'Oh, I wish I could go, Charles. Grand Bank, Ferrylands, Greenland, such lovely names.'

'It is scarcely a suitable venture for a lady,' Charles said severely.

'Uh,' Sarah scoffed. 'Before I came here, I lived a rough life. I slept on the hills, often out in the open. Granny Lott's hut was cold and bare.'

'The Dartmouth hills can hardly be compared with the Atlantic Ocean. You don't understand what it is like.'

Charles always felt a glow of satisfaction when he could point to some deficiency in her knowledge. She was so sure of herself, she learnt so quickly, that it was a relief when he found some simple fact of which she was unaware. It showed that there were great gaps in her knowledge of the world; he was still necessary.

But she dismissed his superior knowledge with a shrug. 'That's not important. You learn to adapt to those conditions. Perhaps one day I shall go with Sir Gabriel.'

Charles placed his books on the great oak desk.

'In the meantime, let us proceed with our studies.' He opened the first book. 'Did you complete your conjugation of verbs in the French passage?'

'Oh, it's too boring. So I transposed this into French instead, just to see what it sounds like. Listen.'

She read a verse of a Shakespeare sonnet, first in English and then in her version in French. Charles frowned, torn between anger at her disobedience and admiration for her skill, but there was no point in disagreeing with Sarah. The whole morning would be lost in argument because she seemed to delight in twisting her mind around any point that could be made into a dispute. She never seemed to accept anything as fact.

He corrected the French sonnet with her; when she was convinced of his accuracy, she re-read it. 'Isn't it a nice sound,' she said. 'Nicer than English. Sir Gabriel says he will meet Indians and Innuits in Newfoundland who speak strange tongues never heard in this country.'

'All countries speak in different tongues. The Italian you are learning . . . that is the speech in some countries.'

'Yes.' She paused as though this had not occurred to her before.

'Now. Shall we proceed with our arithmetic?'

They worked through some arithmetic and Greek until the bell rang for the midday meal.

The spring sunshine moved slowly across the desk and Charles felt himself bathed in a temporary luxury. He preferred working in the library, as Sarah did, but for different reasons. While she found it suitable to her mental activity, Charles was more aware of its social implications. Briefly, he could imagine himself as the owner of a great library, he could immerse himself in the surroundings of wealth and power, he could identify with that world above him as though it were truly his own. In the back of his mind was always the suspicion, indeed the conviction, that he should have been sharing in that prestige. Since Sarah's arrival last summer, Charles had found himself paying more attention to his attire. It would not have been appropriate or even permissible to dress in the clothes of a gentleman but he had recognized that he was still wearing the fashions of twenty years ago.

He abandoned the old style of cloth stockings and now wore knitted hose, though he did not aspire to the brightly coloured silks worn by his masters. His breeches reached to the knee with his stockings drawn over them. Although there was no ruff over the highstanding collar of his doublet, he now wore a sleeveless, double-breasted jacket laced at the front with linen thread and a short skirt with overlapping tabs. He had acquired a pair of the newly fashionable leather shoes which had heels instead of being completely flat, and a new pair of pumps for indoors. Finally he had had his long cloak shortened to resemble the modern fashion and recently he had acquired a linen handkerchief.

He had even convinced himself that their temporary promotion to the library from the schoolroom had been to some extent the result of his more desirable appearance.

'This afternoon I have my music lessons. And then my dancing,' Sarah said. 'Shall we have our painting and drawing before supper?'

Charles agreed. They walked along the long gallery where Sarah left him to go to her chamber.

Frances smiled at him briefly as she passed and then turned.

'Gilbert will not be attending lessons, Charles. He is very sick.'

Charles expressed his regrets. 'Has the physician called?'

'Yes. He's been bled again but I fear it does no good.'

79

Frances hesitated and then added thoughtfully, 'Perhaps it would be better for Gilbert to abandon lessons altogether. When he is well enough, it would be more beneficial for him to rest in the garden.'

'As you wish, m'lady.'

'I'll consider it,' Frances said as she turned into the dining hall.

Charles went on, down the marble stairs towards the servants' hall. He sat at the top table with the steward and the housekeeper and Joseph, the head stableman. The plates of meats and vegetables were placed on the tables by the kitchen maids, who ate at long trestle tables running the length of the hall. The babble of voices mingled with the sharp clonk of the housemaids' wooden heels as they darted back and forth over the stone floor. Charles always felt slightly out of place; he felt that he and Mr Weaver the steward should have their meals in the family dining hall upstairs. He knew that this happened in some of the large houses. But although Sir Gabriel treated the whole household as one large, cohesive family, he had never permitted this development. It was made even more unacceptable to Charles because Father Pierre, who was not even supposed to be there, often shared his meals with the family.

Admittedly, the same food was served here as upstairs. But Charles felt the indignity of being categorized with ignorant people when he had had the benefit of a grammar school education and had been involved in the education of all the children of the family who were accepted in the world as cultured ladies and gentlemen.

But now his mind was on more immediate problems. When Frances spoke about Gilbert he had been too fearful to reply. The implications of her words were too devastating. Now, sick with apprehension, his mind crept round to the real situation.

If he were no longer required as a tutor for Gilbert, there was only Sarah left. She had only arrived by chance, and he was unsure if she constituted one of the 'members of the family' for whose education he had been employed. In any case, she was likely to take more and more interest in her drawing and music and feminine accomplishments rather than in scholastic studies.

He looked back now with sadness to the beginning of his employment here, when all the children were young and his career had seemed full of promise. He remembered how his hopes had been directed to a position in the royal household and realized now that those dreams had always been absurd illusions. All opportunities seemed to have disappeared and his life was whittling away.

Charles pushed the plate of rabbit away from him uneaten, gulped his mug of ale and stood up.

'Are you sick, Mr Smithson?' Mistress Dodds the house-keeper asked anxiously. She always had the dread that sudden sickness in the household might herald the beginning of an epidemic.

'No, Mistress Dodds, I have many matters to attend to.'

Charles had established long ago that the mental activities in which he was employed were beyond the comprehension of servants and were of infinitely more importance than their concerns.

He mounted the stairs to the library. It was one of the benefits of his job that he could always go there for study and research when it was unoccupied.

This afternoon Sarah would be in the music room and Lady Frances was in the dairy. He stood at the windows, trying to concentrate his mind on the current problem. It was always difficult for him to consider any situation which must inevitably lead to a decision – and action. So he contemplated first the mystery of social advancement. Many people less worthy than himself had made spectacular progress. To begin with, there were all the intimates of King James. Of course, it was well-known how they established themselves in palatial homes, enjoying extravagant living – but how did they get into suitable contact in the first place? How had they made that leap from anonymity to prominence?

It was clear that somehow you had to get noticed, to get on intimate terms with people.

Charles thought about Sir Gabriel. You would never get on intimate terms with him. In many ways, he was the most approachable gentleman he had ever known. He had such real concern about the lower classes. Yet his life separated him from the common people, he seemed as remote as Shakespeare and the Greek writers, as though he inhabited a different, greater, almost sublime world.

At that moment, Cicely quietly entered the library.

'Good day, sir.'

Charles picked up his books.

'Pray, do not leave on my account. I have come merely to collect a volume.'

Charles bowed. 'I must leave, m'lady. I have affairs to attend to.'

Cicely frowned. Charles noticed that her bright auburn hair was tied back even more severely than usual.

'Gilbert is not well,' she said slowly. 'We must pray for him.'

'Yes, m'lady.'

He waited fearfully. Was she about to tell him that his services would no longer be needed? Is that what they were both hinting at? But she turned away and Charles left the chamber. Then, suddenly, he thought of Sir Jonathon Fortescue. It was he who had got him this situation, he who had helped him. Of course, he could have made more progress with Sir Jonathon who, in a way, must still be indebted to him for saving his life!

Charles realized now that that was the opportunity he had neglected. It was Sir Jonathon whom he should have continued to cultivate; he could have been the entrance, the magic path to a better life.

In his chamber, Charles told himself that it was not too

late, that even now he could make use of that valuable contact. Tomorrow, he would pay him a visit, tell him of his progress, his gratitude, his current indeterminate circumstances.

His stomach fluttered as he rode through the Fortescue estate next morning. He constantly cleared his throat as he alighted at the stables and walked round to the kitchen entrance.

The housekeeper greeted him enquiringly.

'Good day, Mr Smithson. Have you come to see the steward?'

'Good day, Mistress Taylor. No, I've no appointment.'

As he spoke, he remembered suddenly the mystery of Sarah. Mistress Taylor had been here on that day years ago when he thought he saw Sarah in these kitchens. She would know the answer to that question.

'Oh.' She folded her arms across her large bosom. 'You haven't come calling?' She glanced round at the kitchen maids questioningly.

'Oh, no. I've come to make an appointment to see Sir Jonathon.'

She nodded and offered him a cup of ale. He sat on a bench by the great open fireplace surrounded by girls washing plates, cleaning silver, polishing the furniture and the housekeeper sat opposite grasping a large jug.

'How's the boy Gilbert?'

Charles hesitated. He never discussed anything with anyone. There was always the fear that anything he said might later incriminate him. He cleared his throat.

'Not well, spends a lot of time in his bed. The physick doesn't seem to cure him.'

'There's no physick for his sickness. Even for the rich. And how's our Lady Katherine?'

'She visits Vinelands frequently.'

'And how about Lady Katherine's other pursuits?'

Charles blinked. What were they talking about? A housemaid laughed.

'No better than she ought to be,' the housekeeper commented. 'What's happened to the great lover? Does he still visit?'

Charles wanted to jump up and escape, it was getting out of his depth. He restrained himself and cleared his throat.

'I don't know.' he said.

The housekeeper leaned over. 'And what happens to our Lady Sarah while his lordship's away?' She emphasized the word 'lady' and the girls giggled.

'She attends lessons.'

'And who teaches her?'

'I do,' Charles said. 'She learns well.'

'You!' They all exploded with laughter. 'I warrant you find her an eager student.'

Charles blushed. He realized that instead of getting information, he was simply providing it. Suddenly he raised his voice.

'There's something strange about her,' he said.

They all gathered round.

'Strange?' The housekeeper looked interested.

'I've seen her before, long ago,' Charles said firmly. 'I wonder where she came from.'

They looked round at each other. Charles said challengingly, 'I think I saw her here once in the past.'

'Here!' The housekeeper turned away but Charles knew by the tone of her voice that his suspicions were right. 'Yes,' he persisted. 'What was she doing?'

Abruptly, Mistress Taylor turned to the staff.

'Get on with your work,' she said sharply. Then she turned to Charles, motioned to him with her head, led him into the pantry and closed the door.

'Now,' she said, 'what are you hinting at?'

Charles knew that he would have to offer some real information in order to obtain any from her.

'You see,' he said, 'I think his lordship is infatuated with her.'

'Infatuated? What happens?'

'Well . . . nothing. But he does whatever she says. He is a strong man. His orders are obeyed. But with Mistress Sarah – she does as she likes. He is much concerned for her safety. He has become very demanding of everyone else. My lady Frances spends much time in her bedchamber. Sarah is very beautiful. She went with his lordship to London. Is she a witch?'

Charles broke off. He had never spoken so freely in his life; he had not intended to say all that. Instantly, he regretted his foolhardiness.

Then Mistress Taylor said, 'No. She's not a witch.'

Charles realized they had reached a new level of communication. He said seriously, 'Then who is she?'

'Perhaps she belongs here,' the housekeeper said.

'Here?'

The housekeeper glanced at the closed door and said softly, 'In a just world, this should be her home by rights.'

Charles frowned. What did she mean?

Mistress Taylor said, 'Our Sarah's mother was employed here at one time. She found much favour with the master.'

Charles gulped. Why had he been so stupid, never even thought . . . He cleared his throat.

'Her mother was beautiful, too, but not like your Lady Sarah. When I last saw her, she had the golden hair of her father. But her mother was a black-haired beauty,' the housekeeper said. 'Chambermaid.'

'Died in the plague?' Charles said.

'Yes. Destitute. But what did she expect?' The housekeeper stood up. 'Strange though, Sir Gabriel taking the girl in like that.'

Charles was so overwhelmed by the burden of this new knowledge that he almost forgot the purpose of his visit. He stood up.

'Come,' Mistress Taylor said. 'We'll find the steward.'

'Oh, yes.' Charles followed her to the steward's quarters.

At Vinelands, he treated Mr Weaver, the steward, with respect. He was, after all, responsible under Sir Gabriel and Lady Frances for the running of the estate; an important person. But Mistress Taylor showed no such deference.

'Godfrey, Mr Smithson wants to see the master.'

'Well,' Charles said. 'An appointment. If that's possible. When it's convenient.'

The steward returned a few moments later. 'He can see you now,' he said. 'He's not occupied.'

Charles followed a footman up the wide staircase to the library. Since his sojourn at Vinelands, it did not seem as impressive as it had the first time he had come here. He remembered how magnificent all those books had appeared then. Sir Jonathon had changed, too, in the ensuing seven or eight years. He had put on even more weight and his face was red and blotched. He had a glass in one hand and a half-full bottle stood on the table.

'Good day, sir.' Sir Jonathon beckoned him in. 'I understand you wish to speak with me.'

Charles walked towards him. 'Yes. I'm Charles Smithson.'

Sir Jonathon inclined his head questioningly.

'You found me a situation with Sir Gabriel Hooper Humphreys some years ago.'

'Oh, yes. Yes. I recollect. I presume it has been to your liking.'

'Yes, sir. Thank you, sir.'

'Sir Gabriel's a good fellow. Away on the high seas at the moment, I believe.'

'Yes, sir.'

'Well, Smithson, I must say I didn't remember you. Look a lot older,' he said bluntly.

'Yes, sir. Well, sir, at the moment I am rather troubled.'

Sir Jonathon looked at him quizzically. Charles had

the feeling that he would not welcome other people's problems.

'Not money?'

'Oh, no, sir. But, if you recollect, you were kind enough to advise me before. In fact, you were instrumental in establishing me in my present position. Well, the boy Gilbert is sick, and can no longer continue his studies. And I fear that soon Mistress Sarah, the young lady he adopted, will no longer have need of my instruction. I wonder if it would be possible for you to suggest some further employment; whether amongst your acquaintances you know of anyone in need of a tutor.'

Sir Jonathon frowned. 'Well, can't say I do. Most of my acquaintances, their families are grown up. Can't Sir Gabriel help?'

'He's absent at the moment. Newfoundland.'

'Ah, yes. Any case, aren't you getting a bit beyond it?'

Charles blanched. He felt wounded, as though a sword had cut him down. He conjectured that both Sir Jonathon and Sir Gabriel were older than he. It was an unjust world.

'Oh, I hope not, sir.'

'Nonsense, my good fellow. Your master will offer you some other position. You won't be destitute.'

'I was hoping,' Charles said bleakly, 'for further advancement.'

Fortescue shook his head. Charles observed an expression of pity struggling with impatience.

'Well,' he said dismissively, 'if I hear of anything suitable, I'll bear you in mind.'

Charles bowed his way out and went down the wide staircase, slinking past the kitchens so that he would not have to confront the women again and into the stable yard.

As he plodded home on his pony, a wild and incoherent anger possessed him. He had been insulted, ridiculed, written off. His grammar school education, his respect for

87

learning, all dismissed, not even considered. He wished he had never met Fortescue, wished that he had left him to die all those years ago. Without him, he might have made real progress. And what of Fortescue? What about his secret life? What about Sarah?

The next morning, he looked thoughtfully at Sarah as she entered the library. He had spent the night wondering whether he should tell her. What would she think, what would she do, if she knew she was the daughter of Sir Jonathon Fortescue? It was because he could not answer these questions that he hesitated. Did she even remember being taken to that house as a young child? Or was she living there? He had not asked about that.

This morning he had heard Sarah in one of her heated arguments with Lady Frances. Her ladyship had complained that Sarah spent too much time attending to her toilet. Vanity was not an attractive quality, she said. Sarah retorted that she was merely admiring a new gown which Katherine had given her. Katherine, she said, was very kind.

Lady Frances had looked angry and reminded her that she was fortunate to be in this household to which she did not belong.

Sarah replied provocatively, 'Ah, I thank dear Sir Gabriel for that,' and flounced from the dining hall.

Charles longed for the day when Sir Gabriel would return. These outbursts always unnerved him, because Sarah was always in a bad mood afterwards.

Today she was subdued and silent. They were reading *The Faerie Queene*. Normally Sarah would read it to him, 'to show its meaning' as she said, but now she listened apathetically to his comments. Then she stood up and said belligerently, 'I don't want to do this today. I'm going out in the garden.'

Still hesitating with the burden of his knowledge, Charles said quietly, 'Are you not happy, Mistress Sarah?'

She turned in astonishment. Normally Charles protested

if she wished to abandon her lessons, fearful, as they both knew, that he might be accused of failing to teach her properly.

'Well,' she said, 'that's the first civil remark you've ever made to me.'

'I hope not,' Charles said defensively, then added, 'perhaps you may have a happier future about which you as yet know nothing.'

'Well!' Sarah looked genuinely puzzled. 'What do you mean by that? I am surprised that you think of me at all.'

'Sarah.' He almost began to speak, then he was silent, overwhelmed suddenly by the enormity of what he was about to say. Because if she knew, of course she would act immediately; she would march up to Fortescue's and confront him. Fortescue would find out where she got her information and then what would happen to him? Whatever was he thinking of?

'Sarah,' he said feebly, 'I am only concerned for your welfare.'

'Charles, you are keeping a secret,' she said instantly. 'What is it? Tell me.'

'Mistress Sarah, there is no secret. I merely thought . . .'

Sarah looked at him quietly.

'Yes. There is a secret. But I'll find out, Charles. You'll tell me in the end.'

She smiled. Charles shuffled his books together, his hands shaking. There would be no peace now. She would cajole, plead, persist, rage at him until he told her. There would be no escape. In the end, he knew he would tell her. All he could do now was prevaricate, delay, so that he could work out what he would do if she ever exposed the source of her information.

7

When she left the library, Sarah did not go in for the midday meal but walked through the knot garden to Katherine's little arbour. She sat on the stone seat and looked across the rose garden and the park beyond to the hills sloping down to the harbour.

Almost a year had passed since Sir Gabriel brought her to this place but she felt at times as though she were taking part in a masquerade. It was like one of the entertainments that Adam had told her about, which he took part in at Court.

There were girls in lovely clothes, dancing about on a stage but they were really boys. People were dressed like kings and queens but they were only actors. Sometimes, she feared she would wake up one morning and find that she, too, had only been acting in a drama, that this house, her lovely clothes, would all vanish.

Of course, it was the spring that disturbed her. Sarah knew that. There was a moment always, walking out into the sunshine, when the light seemed to have changed and she became aware once again of the physical world around her.

It was as though she and the flowers and fields, the very air she breathed, had all come out of a long sleep, had been awakened by that light in the sky. She saw vividly now, although they must have been there days ago, the primroses scattered across the fields, the buds on the lilac trees and in the garden the opening blossom, carpeted beneath with pink and purple primulas.

It had been the same with Granny Lott up on the hills. There had been few flowers high above Stoke Cliff and the Ridges, she reflected, where Granny Lott's hut had been, yet they were still bathed in that enveloping light. The wooded hills across the valley seemed to cast a shadow in the brilliant sunshine. One great flank of trees on the north side was black like a shroud, sweeping down from the house, down and down to the lake at the bottom, but the top of the trees shimmered, flashing bright where the sun touched them.

Sarah stood up and danced suddenly across the lawn, the wide yellow frills of her silk gown twirling around her and then she sat down again. It's not only the spring, she thought. That's exciting. But there are other things disturbing me.

To begin with, there was silly Charles with his silly secret. What could Charles possibly know that would affect her? But he had spoken of her future, and it was the future that worried her. Because whenever something had happened in the past, it had always been a change for something worse. She could only remember isolated events with her mother. A room shared with another woman and some small children, down in the town somewhere; sitting somewhere in a big kitchen, talking to the servants; her mother's death and Granny Lott coming to fetch her, saying she was her grandmother and would take care of her.

Until now. Sir Gabriel and Vinelands had been different. It was the only good change which had ever happened. She didn't want any more changes; the future could go on like this. So did she even want to know Charles's secret? She made a face at herself knowing that she would pester poor Charles until he told her, because her sense of power, her curiosity, were stronger than her fears. And, indeed, what did she have to fear? Her new home had given her some sense of security and belonging. The discovery of the chapel and the mass had become a new mystery

91

for her, a compelling experience, so that she frequently went to the little chapel and sat in the single light of the candle and looked with curiosity at the statue of our Lady.

She enjoyed the constant activity of the household. Before Sir Gabriel left, she went frequently round the estate with him; she had her lessons with Gilbert, visited Katherine and tried on all the clothes in her enormous wardrobe, walking the length of the long gallery towards the mirrors which reflected her image at either end. Cicely dressed her hair and told her stories about the life of this curious Christ person and his holy mother and the travels of St Paul. Sometimes she went with Lady Frances to the kitchens and the dairy and the great wash rooms, where all the clothes and household linen were washed in huge vats and dried in a great stone area.

She watched the women cleaning the rooms, polishing and dusting the priceless furniture which Sir Gabriel had brought home from his travels in France and Italy and China. There seemed to be endless conversation and talking and laughter, as though she were taking part in a perpetual carnival.

One day they all went to the annual fair in Exeter, travelling in the coach which had taken her and Sir Gabriel and Adam to London. It was a slow, uncomfortable journey and they spent the night once again at Coldeney Prior.

She had been to fairs with Granny Lott when they had sold the corn dollies which they made in their little hut. Sometimes Granny Lott erected a little stall and told fortunes, looking into a large piece of glass which she called her crystal ball. But in her new life everything was different. She and Katherine had wandered round the booths in their silk dresses and leather boots, buying little souvenirs and baubles and scarcely noticing the people who were offering their wares.

Of course, everything depended on Sir Gabriel, he was her protector. She looked down the long avenue, wishing that he would come riding up in his flowing cape and thinking of his handsome face and curling black hair. He was the most beautiful man she had ever seen.

She had said that in the Great Hall one day when he came in wearing a new blue velvet doublet and silk breeches and Lady Frances had rebuked her sharply.

Of course, Lady Frances didn't like her. Sarah suspected it was because she had believed all those stories about Granny Lott and thought that Sarah was a witch also. But Sarah had also realized that Sir Gabriel was not influenced by the animosity of Lady Frances.

Yet, at the back of it all, Sarah still had a feeling of anxiety which she could scarcely even recognize. She knew only that beneath all this apparently regulated life, its certainty and security, something threatened. It had nothing to do with the things that Sir Gabriel talked about at meal times – the way Catholics were treated, the behaviour of the king and his court, although these things seemed to be terribly important to Sir Gabriel and Lady Frances. They seemed always to feel insecure because of things the King had done. Yet they were so rich and had so much that Sarah could not understand their anxiety. How could anyone take all that away?

No. Sarah's anxiety was something more intangible. It was at night, lying in her goose feather bed that she was most aware of it. The dark and bitter side of life seemed more real to her than this outer covering. There was a world where people could be hanged, where there was no-one to whom you could turn for help, no safety or escape. She knew that. But it was even more, it was something connected with herself. Some deep fear. And then, lying in the darkness one night, she was suddenly overcome by the unavoidable revelation that really she did not exist at all. All that existed was a body, as though that were really herself. A cold fear came over her that it was only by chance that she was here, she was not really alive in any permanent way, it was only an accident. As she lay there, she felt more and more terrified that her existence was so insecure and transient. She sat upright in bed, staring into the darkness, looking in her mind into the sky, down into the sea, across the hills and the moors and it all seemed a remote and dangerous mystery and that she only happened to be here. A chance event. She felt as though she were sinking down, down into a dark abyss. In my beginning is my end, Father Pierre said, but what was the beginning?

When Gabriel left, she had felt even more insecure. His strong body, his commanding manner, his apparent ability to deal with any situation, had given an illusion of permanence but without him she longed to find the answer to her nagging question which arose every night in the darkness, where did I come from?

She began to long for her open life with Granny Lott. Somehow, the solution to her problem seemed closer out there than it did within these protective walls. The warm touch of the wind round her ears, the wet grass in the early morning dew, the smell of dandelions and blackberries and seaweed; the proximity of stars in a silent night, Granny Lott's laughter and busyness and walking, walking always over the moors, up the hills, sitting amongst the heather. And where did the toad go, and the gull with one leg who came to feed every day?

Then when the morning came, she would spring out of bed, welcoming the new day in the lovely house on the hills, amazed at her good fortune. For the next few days, Sarah persisted in her questioning of Charles. Was it a nice secret, did anyone else know, when would it happen?

Charles declared that there was no secret until one day when he stood up briefly to walk to the window, she put down her books, stood in front of him and put her hands firmly on his shoulders.

'Now, Charles,' she said. 'I shall do no more lessons until you tell me.'

Charles felt his body stiffen. He averted his eyes from the white curves of her breasts hardly concealed by her low-cut bodice and from her laughing eyes which seemed to mock him.

Then Sarah realized that his fear was genuine, that he was not merely being cautious. Her voice changed. She put an arm around his shoulders.

'Charles,' she said softly. 'You can trust me. It will be a secret between us. I'll never tell.'

Charles tried to move away. He realized now that there was absolutely no benefit to him in telling Sarah the absurd secret. There never could have been. He knew it had simply been his anger and resentment that had prompted him to hint at the information. Yet he felt trapped by this girl; the look in her green eyes made him feel as though he were in her power.

'Sarah, you put me in a grave situation.'

'Oh, Charles, please. Tell me. It would be such fun to share a secret.'

Charles sat down. Sarah moved her chair to sit and face him. He turned away from her compelling green eyes.

'It's just a rumour, Sarah,' he said slowly.

'Well, just tell me a little bit of the rumour.'

'It's about your father.'

'My father? I haven't got a father.'

'It seems you have.'

'Well, who is he?'

Charles stood up again.

'It's rumoured that he's a gentleman. A nobleman from these parts.'

'Is that all, Charles?' she said impatiently. 'You must know more than that. Who is he?'

Charles shook his head. 'I can't . . .'

'Charles, I shall have to ask Lady Frances about the noblemen in the area.'

'Sarah, you promised it was a secret.'

'But you haven't told me! How can I know what . . .'

'Very well.' Charles paused. He was beginning to enjoy what was for him an intimate personal conversation. No-one had ever listened so attentively to his words.

'I think it is not someone with whom you are yet acquainted.'

'Who, Charles?'

'He is well-known to Sir Gabriel and Lady Frances.'

'Charles!'

'His estate lies over the hill on the Totnes Road.'

Sarah considered.

'I know. Let me guess! It's Branwell Hall. Sir Jonathon Fortescue.'

'Sarah. It is but a rumour.'

Sarah paused and then shrugged her shoulders. 'Charles, it is of small account. It is a secret easy to keep because it is of little interest.'

Charles looked at her in amazement. She had clearly not understood the implications of his statement. Apparently had no conception of what it could mean to be the daughter of a baronet.

He breathed a sigh of relief. It would obviously not occur to her to make an issue of it, she would not have any interest in telling anyone.

'You see,' he said. 'I told you it was an insignificant secret.'

'Yes.' Sarah looked disappointed. 'But it was kind of you to share it. Come, Charles. The bell has rung. I wish you good day.'

Charles followed her along the gallery and she smiled at him as she passed into the dining hall.

That afternoon, Sarah went to her stone seat in the knot garden. What a fool Charles was. He really seemed to believe that she found his secret of no interest. Of course, that was what she meant him to think; she did not intend to share her feelings with him. But it was more than that. He did not realize that in reality his words had stunned her, frightened her, it was as though a part of her life, dim memories, anxieties, vague impressions were suddenly aroused, exposed. It seemed to be part of the answer to her secret fears. It occurred to her that if only she knew who her father was, it would be the beginning of the discovery of where she came from. She must belong somewhere, to someone. Someone who could tell her who she really was. Not just a lost creature who had been taken in and dressed up like a lady as though a real Sarah had never existed. But first, she had to be practical. Supposing it were true that Sir Jonathon was her father? What difference would it make? Would she be entitled to an inheritance as his bastard? Did he know of her existence even? Would he wish to? Did he have a wife, children? Was he rich? Sarah recognized that there were too many questions for her to form any opinion.

If only Sir Gabriel were here. Should she consult Lady Frances? Her promise to Charles did not even cross her mind. But, no. If Lady Frances heard such a rumour, she might try to remove her from Vinelands without even bothering to find out if that was her rightful home. Should she speak to Father Pierre – but what would an old priest know about such things? She could discuss it with Katherine. Katherine might know what to do.

She walked through the knot garden and into the park, looking out across the rolling hills until she came to a stile, and suddenly it all came flooding back; another stile, other fields, an early summer's day such as this.

She was with her mother. She could see her clearly; a thin body, her kind face, but mostly she remembered her curling black hair. Her mother had said, 'It's too far to walk all the way.'

They were down in the town. A stableboy lent them a horse, down by the quay. It had all been very secret. Somewhere, they had reached great iron gates which were locked and her mother had tied the horse to a tree. 'Come. We'll get through the hedge.'

With great difficulty, she had pushed Sarah through the

dense, prickly hedge and then they walked through a park, over a stile somewhere to a large house.

She remembered being hustled into a huge high-ceilinged kitchen, with what seemed like many people in aprons coming and going. At one point she was placed on a stool by the fire and her mother disappeared. It was very hot because outside the sun was shining. The servants all came and talked to her and said what a pretty little girl she was and how she deserved better.

After what seemed a long time, her mother reappeared and they all sat down around the long scrubbed table while her mother talked to them all in undertones, so that Sarah only caught words and phrases here and there. Then they went back through the park and rode down into Dartmouth. But as they squeezed through the hedge her mother had peered through the iron gates, dragging Sarah beside her.

'This is all yours by rights,' she said. 'You'll never get it, but that's the way of the world.'

Sarah did not understand what this meant, but she had asked no questions and her mother had not alluded to it again. Except that just before she died, her mother had said, 'If I go, Sarah, go and see him if you're in need.'

Sarah was too overcome with grief and fear to listen to her words because she knew her mother was leaving her, alone, for ever. She had screamed in panic, clinging to that flimsy body until she was dragged away and she saw her mother no more. Then Granny Lott came and took her to the hut. But now she knew that her mother had said a name. Was it Fortescue? She couldn't remember. All she could see was a big grey house like a castle and that stile and the bramble hedge.

She turned back towards the house. It stood in the distance like a great powerful giant protecting her from the world. She realized with a kind of shock that she actually thought of this as her home, as though she belonged here. Gabriel had told her so much about its history; the life of

98

the priory, the cloisters and the chapter house; the castle, built earlier than the priory, he had said. The strange fact, he said, of having a moat and a drawbridge around a religious house.

But now, Charles's information told her that this was not her home, she did not belong here. She belonged at Branwell Hall, where it seemed no-one wanted her. Yet how did she know that? If only she could remember more clearly what her mother had said.

As she mounted the stairs to the library that afternoon, she decided that she would mention the information to no-one, not even Katherine. It seemed to be something she needed to work out first for herself. So she said casually to Charles, 'I think we should put your secret from our minds, Charles.'

She smiled at his obvious relief, his whimpering, 'Yes, Mistress Sarah. I am much relieved that you take such a view.'

Then something happened which shattered her plans to consider the matter in a quiet fashion. To begin with, she found that having opened her mind to those painful memories of the past, she could not close it again. Yet there were no specific memories, only isolated pictures which floated constantly across her mind. All she knew was a feeling of anxiety, of something dreadful about to happen. But the pictures were mostly of Granny Lott, the trial, the body hanging on the cross bar. Sometimes, lying in her bed at night, looking through the latticed windows at the moonlit sky, listening to the wind blowing, to the waves breaking distantly around the harbour, she could actually think without pain about Granny Lott. She could look straight at her and smile. She would feel that they were floating into their little shed, watching the spiral of smoke rising up from the tallow candle, and Sarah would nod and listen to those strange words that Granny Lott had spoken. We can see into the future by looking at the past. You are never alone, the world is infinite. The future is now.

She would have a sense of peace, but it was only momentary, because she knew she would never see Granny Lott again. Before Sir Gabriel went away she had almost forgotten her but now she began to wallow in self-pity as her thoughts went on to her own insecurity, to the strange mystery of who she was and where she came from.

Then one night, it happened. She crept down the stairs to the chapel and sat before the little altar. When the door opened she turned, expecting to see Father Pierre. But it was Lady Frances in her ermine robe. She smiled briefly at Sarah and then said quietly, 'Sarah. Come with me to my chamber. I wish to talk with you.'

She followed Frances up the stairs. Frances rarely talked with her, merely exchanging brief remarks when they met.

'Sit down, Sarah. I think we should discuss your future here.'

'My future? But I live here. Sir Gabriel has said this.'

Frances looked solemn.

'He did not realize that your presence here might endanger the whole family.'

'Endanger! In what way? I do nothing untoward.'

'Events have occurred since Sir Gabriel left. It has become more dangerous to harbour people, particularly young people, who have been converted by us to the true faith.'

'But no-one knows. I have spoken to no-one about it.'

'That may be. But there are many spies and informers. I have had news that a rumour is abroad that we are forcing you to become a convert to the faith.'

'But what are you suggesting?'

Frances sighed as though she had come to an unwelcome decision. 'It would be better for you to go into a religious house.'

'A religious house! But that is not possible! Cicely has told me that it is against the law of the land. There are no religious houses.'

100

'Ah, not in this country. But in France . . .'

'France! Lady Frances, I cannot go to France. I know no-one, I live here.'

'You do not need to know anyone. You will be taken care of.'

'Sir Gabriel would not wish it. He wanted me to stay here.'

'I will explain to him on his return. He will understand. Now, child, return to your bed. Tomorrow we will discuss it further.'

'Why can't I live with Katherine?'

'That would be just as difficult. Do you wish to subject us all to such dangers, to possible death? Surely you could not be so selfish?'

'But the priests. They are concealed here. That must be dangerous.'

'It is possible they may have to leave also,' Frances said. Then she added in a tone of finality, 'I'm sorry. It is an unhappy situation.'

She opened the door and Sarah walked from the chamber and slowly back to her own apartment. Her world that had seemed so safe was on the edge of disaster. She had no way of knowing whether Frances was telling the truth. Was there real danger, or did she just want to be rid of her? Her life was bounded by the periphery of the estate, the protecting walls of the house. She knew little of what was going on in Dartmouth, let alone the rest of the country. Without Sir Gabriel and John there was little political conversation at meal times as there used to be; Sir Gabriel always seemed to know what was happening in London and at court.

But France! It was a foreign country; how could she go there? Panic seized her. She would not go there.

The next day no reference was made to their conversation but when Sarah was passing the stables in the afternoon, on her way to the dairy, she came upon Frances talking to Joseph. They were quietly making arrangements for his trip to London; Sarah knew that these trips were for one purpose only, to bring priests who had arrived from France back to Vinelands. She called Sarah over.

'Sarah,' she said, 'you will accompany Joseph to London on the morrow. Arrangements have been made for your safe passage to the Continent.'

'Tomorrow!' Sarah froze. It had not occurred to her that it would be so soon; Frances must have been planning it for a long time. She had always meant to do this.

And then, she felt a sense of peace and calm which always seemed to come upon her in the face of disaster. She looked at Frances, looked through her, far into the distance, the way she had looked at Gabriel when he rescued her on Jawbones Hill. She smiled. She saw Frances turn pale as though she felt some power in her that she could not counteract. Sarah did feel, indeed, a strange power inside her, as though she were merged into a great universe of which this little event was only an insignificant part. The words she spoke seemed to come from that universe.

'It will not save you, Lady Frances,' she said. 'The world is an infinite place.'

She scarcely knew what she meant herself, except that events seemed quite separate from herself, that her existence was beyond the vagaries of chance.

Frances frowned and then quickly turned away.

'A servant will assist you in packing your trunk,' she said. 'You will inform no-one of your departure.'

That evening, Frances came to her bedchamber and bade her farewell.

'You can, of course, communicate,' she said, 'and with Katherine, if you wish, but please be circumspect in your information.'

Sarah smiled distantly. 'Have no fear, Lady Frances. You will have intelligence of me again.'

Sarah retired to her chamber early and waited anxiously until the house was silent. Then she dressed quickly in her white petticoats and red velvet dress, pulled on her high leather boots and took her fur cloak from the closet.

Opening the door gently, she crept along the corridor with the one great candle burning high above at the end and went silently down the wide marble staircase, confronting briefly the memory of the day she had arrived, coming up that staircase in her ragged clothes.

She knew that although the great oak doors were bolted and the gates beyond them chained, if she went through the kitchens, there was a small back door into the herb garden. The iron bolts moved back slowly and the scraping noise they made against the hinges seemed to be deafening. She listened for any sound that might indicate she had been heard and then crept along by the hedge, through the lych gate and into the field. Running down the hill, she realized that there was no need to run. She had all night to reach her destination.

As she went down across the fields of the estate, she could see the sea glimmering far away to the horizon and on the other side, far below, the curve of the harbour, although the hill was too steep to see the Bight. She walked along through the trees smiling to herself. She had almost forgotten the feeling of safety she had known with Granny Lott which emanated from the darkness of the woods and she listened to the sound of the toads croaking and a solitary gull screeching unaccountably in the dark. A fox was barking far away in the distance and nearer she recognized the call of the barn owl – it must be the one they used to listen to.

When she finally reached the end of the estate, she branched out into the lane and began to walk more quickly. She had to go down into the town to get her bearings. That was the way she had gone with her mother. It was only by retracing their steps that she could remember how to get there.

The moon had now emerged through the clouds. It was a sandy lane, soft to walk on like the beach, and she breathed in the night air. At last. Freedom again. She thought briefly of the house she had left, of Sir Gabriel. It was like a curious dream, an interlude that might never have happened. But even as she walked along, she knew that this was not the end of the dream. It was going to follow her.

She reached the Tunstall, passed St Clements and went down into the silent town. When she reached Crowthers Hill she knew where she was, this was where she and her mother had begun that journey long ago and she started the long ascent up Waterpool Lane towards Totnes. After a few miles she could see the dim outline of the house across the moors and sheep on the horizon, standing and looking without purpose into the distance. Then she reached the iron gates and the place where they had climbed through the hedge, and then the little stile, and she knew that this was the place. The sun was just rising, still low in the eastern sky. She stopped. For the first time, she thought about her plans. Running away had seemed such a major step that she had thought no further. All she knew was that she would not go to France. After Frances's words, she had feared to go to Katherine. Perhaps she would also feel that France was the best solution. Then, suddenly, last night in the silence of her chamber, she thought of her mother's words, 'If you are in need, go and see him.' She thought of Charles's recent revelation; it was almost as though her mother had spoken through him, as though some mysterious providence had given Charles this message for her.

She crept up behind the stables to avoid the boys already turning out the hay and around the milking sheds where the girls were seated beside the cows on their little milking stools and then she reached the kitchen door. A smell of cooking hams and damp, blazing logs greeted her as she stepped inside. She remembered that heat, the kitchens at Vinelands were like this; even on the hottest summer's day, the fires had to be stoked for cooking all the meals.

A woman came towards her, looking in bewilderment at Sarah's velvet gown.

'My lady,' she said, 'are you lost?'

'I've come to see Sir Jonathon Fortescue,' Sarah said firmly.

She noticed that all the maids had stopped work and were also looking at her red gown and her leather boots.

'I fear you've come to the wrong door, my lady,' Mistress Taylor frowned. 'Why did not the coachman take you to the Great Hall?'

'Oh, no,' Sarah said quickly. 'I came across the fields. Through the hedge.'

'Through the hedge?'

'I don't know that Sir Jonathon will wish to see me.'

'Is he not expecting you?'

'No. I think I may need your help,' Sarah blurted out. 'I think a long time ago you helped my mother. I think she brought me here. I am in trouble.'

The maidservants all crowded round. Mistress Taylor rebuked them sharply. 'Girls, back to your labours. There is work to do. Emily, build up the fire.' She turned to Sarah. Her expression was a mixture of curiosity and suspicion. 'My lady, are you quite well?'

'I'm Sarah Darby,' Sarah cut in. 'Did you not know my mother?'

The girls stopped work again. Mistress Taylor put her hands on her hips. 'Great heavens! Sarah Darby!'

'Yes. My mother told me to come here if I were ever in trouble. To see Sir Jonathon.'

'Well!' Mistress Taylor seemed for a moment completely overwhelmed. She kept repeating 'Sarah Darby. Well!' until Sarah became anxious. What would happen if they turned her out, if Sir Jonathon would not see her? But she said coolly, 'Madam, were you not here when my mother brought me as a child?'

The housekeeper took Sarah to a quiet corner of the huge kitchen and said slowly, as though reluctant to answer, 'Sit down, Sarah. You have changed so much. I could not have known you.'

Sarah sat on a bench by the kitchen door. The heat was becoming unbearable.

'Yes, I was here when your mother came.'

'But why did she come here? What was she doing?'

'She came for my help,' Mistress Taylor said slowly. 'She was once employed here.'

'But how could you help her?'

'She was my sister.'

'Sister! Then you're my aunt! Why didn't . . .'

She stopped. An initial feeling of joy that perhaps she had some family in the world was instantly followed by another doubt. Did she really want to be related to this woman when she might have the opportunity of becoming a lady in this household? Indeed, if this Fortescue discovered about such a relationship, he might decide she did not need his help.

'Yes, I may be your aunt,' Mistress Taylor said defensively, 'but when your mother . . . went . . . I couldn't take you in. Where could I have hidden an eight-year-old child? Sir Jonathon would have evicted me.'

Sarah was silent.

'I arranged for you to go with Granny Lott. That was the extent of my duties.'

'Yes, of course.'

'Well, it's worked out all right for you. With your fine clothes, living in that great house.'

Sarah looked thoughtfully at Mistress Taylor. She felt the woman's resentment at her good fortune; perhaps she wouldn't help her. Perhaps she didn't even know about Sir Jonathon.

'Is not Sir Jonathon also related to me?' she asked quietly.

Mistress Taylor glanced around. 'It is possible,' she said slowly.

'My mother said . . .'

'It was a long time ago,' the housekeeper interrupted. 'Sir Jonathon never admitted any responsibility. But why do you wish to see him?'

Sarah told her briefly of her life at the big house, of Sir Gabriel's absence, of Lady Frances and her decision to send her to France.

'I have run away. I intend to confront Sir Jonathon.'

Mistress Taylor folded her arms across her bosom.

'No,' she said firmly. 'You would be hounded from the parish. It would be better to go to France.'

'No! I cannot go. Aunt, can I not be concealed here?'

When Sarah spoke the word 'aunt' again, Mistress Taylor opened her eyes wide and frowned. Perhaps, Sarah thought, she suddenly remembered her sister, had some feeling of responsibility towards her.

'Surely,' Sarah went on, 'as your sister's child, you must help me.'

Mistress Taylor sighed. 'Your mother rested under too many sheets. She was ever a wild one,' she said in an irritated way. 'It was merely her belief that Sir Jonathon had fathered you.'

'Tell me about her,' Sarah entreated. She could see that her aunt could be cajoled into some kind of action. 'What was she like? I can scarcely remember.'

'There is no time now,' Mistres Taylor said curtly. She stood up, looked around the kitchen and summoned the maids around her.

'Girls, Sarah will join us as a kitchen maid.'

The maids all looked at Sarah in astonishment but Mistress Taylor went on firmly, 'She will work as the rest of you. No-one will discuss her. Her name will be Sarah . . . Miller. Sarah, your clothes are . . . not suitable. You must remove them. I will find you a more fitting gown.'

Sarah was taken to the long hall behind the kitchens where the maids slept. Mistress Taylor gave her a straight grey gown and tied her hair back with black ribbon.

'Now,' she said, 'you will mention nothing to Sir

Jonathon. He takes little interest in the servants. It is my job, and the steward's, to appoint and dismiss staff. You will perform your duties as instructed.'

'Aunt . . .'

'You will call me Mistress Taylor, as the other maids do.'

'Mistress Taylor, they must not be informed of my presence at Vinelands.'

'No-one visits here from Vinelands,' Mistress Taylor began and then stopped.

'Except perhaps Charles, the tutor?' Sarah said questioningly.

'Ah! So that's where you got your information. Of course!'

'Yes . . . Perhaps he is not to be trusted.'

'No-one is to be trusted. No-one,' Mistress Taylor retorted.

Sarah followed her back to the kitchens. Mistress Taylor summoned the whole staff around her once more. 'Remember, girls, no-one is to speak Sarah's real name. If anyone should think of revealing it to Sir Jonathon, I shall see that you are all held responsible for concealing her.'

Sarah looked around at the eyes focused on her.

'I shall cause no trouble,' she said. 'I will work.'

After her leisured life at Vinelands, she found the cleaning and scrubbing and carrying and early rising more exhausting than she expected, but she made no complaints and the girls soon accepted her. She began to feel secure again. They asked her about life at Vinelands as though she had come from another world and told her about Sir Jonathon and Lady Margaret and of their three children who were now grown up and of the two who had died, and the hunting parties and the evening balls.

Sarah felt as though she were looking always in a mirror, because for a year at Vinelands she had looked from the remoteness of her chamber, her privileged life with Sir Gabriel and the family, at the activities of the servants around her as though they were creatures with whom she had no real connection, except for the benefit of her own happiness. Now she was looking from the other end of life, from the kitchens and dairies and stables, towards that life in which she now played no part. Yet where did she really belong? Was she a part of neither?

Then one day, Mistress Taylor told her to go and clean one of the upstairs bedchambers.

'My lady may notice that you are a new servant. You will politely tell her your name, Sarah Miller, should she enquire.'

Sarah did indeed see the mistress, who glanced at her briefly but did not enquire anything of her and Sarah made the bed and polished the furniture and said nothing. After that, she was sent often to the upstairs rooms until one day, she was sent to the library to clean the carpets. It was then that she first saw Sir Jonathon. He was standing by the window, holding a glass in his hand and when she came in he turned. Sarah hesitated as he looked her up and down. 'I have been sent to clean the carpets,' she said uncertainly. Mistress Taylor had not told her how to deal with this situation. At Vinelands, servants continued their work whoever was in the room.

'That's right, m'girl. Get on with it.'

Sarah moved across the room with her brushes while he watched her reflectively. Her heart beat faster; she felt a curious churning in her stomach, an unexpected excitement at meeting this man who might be her father. She had had a similar feeling when Mistress Taylor had said she was her aunt. A sudden sense of actually belonging, having some real connection with someone. But Mistress Taylor had appeared to dismiss it as unimportant. Would Sir Jonathon do the same if he knew? Mistress Taylor had warned her of the likely consequences.

'Haven't noticed you before. Are you newly engaged?'

'Yes, sir. A few months.'

She tried to avert her eyes, unable to rid herself of the

stupid fear that he might recognize her, might suspect something. But curiosity overcame her and she looked straight at him; at the red face, the tall, once well-proportioned figure that had now become gross. Only his golden, almost auburn curly hair suggested the handsome man he might once have been. And a strange, piercing expression in his vivid blue eyes, which were now looking directly into hers.

'Well, you're a comely wench,' he said. 'Who are your family?'

'I . . . I don't know, sir.'

Sir Jonathon looked at her appraisingly as she had seen Gabriel look at a horse.

'Huh.' He nodded his head briefly, then turned away as though he had lost interest in the conversation.

She began to brush the carpet and he paid no more attention to her.

Back in the kitchens, she told Mistress Taylor of her encounter.

'Well, you watch your tongue,' she said, 'now he's seen you, he won't have any more interest. You're just a servant. And don't offend anyone,' she added, nodding around at the other maids, 'You never know.'

That afternoon she was sent to the dairy to help with cream-making and then to the wash-house and after supper she had to help bring logs into the upstairs rooms.

She longed to be alone, she wanted time to think about these disturbed feelings inside her. It was only when she was in bed at night, surrounded by the sleeping girls in their wooden cots, that she had any semblance of privacy. She longed for her life at Vinelands and thought with bitter regret of the world she had lost, the life that Frances had snatched away from her; her own chamber, her lovely clothes, even her lessons with Charles. Although she had helped Frances in the dairy and the estate office, or checked the laundry with Cicely, she had never been required to do all the hard physical chores which now dominated her life. And she realized that she might have married a rich man, had a beautiful home of her own. She remembered Katherine's words, 'My mother wouldn't allow you to marry a pauper.'

Now, meeting Sir Jonathon, she felt an even greater sense of injustice. If he was her father, she should be living here, not as a servant but as a lady with her own chamber upstairs, eating in their dining hall, going out in the carriage. This house was not as beautiful as Vinelands. It was small in comparison. But she thought she had the same rights to it as his other daughters.

Then she thought about Sir Jonathon himself. Apart from Sir Gabriel, she had never actually considered men in an individual way. Of course, he was old, like all fathers. Lots of people had no fathers; they had died. Lots of people had no mothers either, she reflected. Many of the girls around her had either no mother or no father and some had neither. Many of them didn't know where their parents were in any case. It didn't seem to be important to them. Yet she still clung to the belief that if Sir Jonathon knew who she was, he would take her in. Gabriel had taken her in – but then, he wasn't her father. In any case, there was no-one like Gabriel that she had ever met. She felt as though he were the only person in the world that she really knew, well, he and Katherine. She longed to talk to Katherine but she knew that she could never reveal her whereabouts. If Frances found out, she would be sent to France.

A few days later she was sent to clean the sleeping chambers. She was polishing the silverware when, reflected in the mirror before her, she saw Sir Jonathon standing in the doorway. He was wearing vivid green satin breeches and a pale green velvet doublet. She turned. His face was red; a sapphire ring glittered on his smooth white hands; he came slowly towards her. She moved backwards. Had he discovered who she was; was he going to evict her, hound her from the parish?

111

'Well, miss. What are we doing here?'

'I've been instructed to clean the sleeping apartments.'

He stood before her. He was so close that she could feel the contours of his fat belly touching her.

'And what are we doing with the silver mirror?'

'It must be polished.'

He put his hands on her shoulders, she could smell the beer on his breath, his piercing blue eyes seemed to sink into her body.

'Then desist from your labours, wench.'

He suddenly pulled her closer, enveloping her in his arms, bringing his large face down towards her, his lips forcing a kiss on hers. His hands grasped at her bodice, trying to untie the laces.

'No!' Sarah shouted. 'Stop! You don't know what you do!'

'Quiet, girl,' he hissed as he tore her bodice open. He looked at her white breasts, picked her up roughly and carried her to the large four-poster bed.

'No,' she shouted. 'Let me go.'

She tried to fight against his grasping fingers groping down her body. He held her tight with one hand, clutching at her skirts with the other to tear them from her. His face came down towards her again and with a great effort she pulled one arm free, brought her hands up to his face and dug her nails into his cheeks, scratching down to his neck.

He screamed in pain and anger and as he struck her across the face, she sprang up and kicked him violently with her wooden shoes.

He fell back on the bed and she ran from the room clutching her bodice over her breasts and dashed down the back stairs to the servants' sleeping hall. There was no-one there at this time of day. She sat on her bed, trembling with anger and fear. What would happen; what would he do? She must leave before he found her. But where could she go now? It didn't matter. She flung her coarse woollen cloak over her shoulders.

No-one questioned her in the stable yard when she said she was going on an errand for Mistress Taylor. She went through the gate and when she was hidden bv the hedge she began to run, down through the lane, across the fields, over the stile, never stopping until she was through the bramble hedge at the edge of the estate.

Then, once again, she walked down through the streets of Dartmouth, along Foss Street, up Brown's Hill and the Tunstall to head for the only place left for her to go.

8

When they reached Grand Bank, Gabriel had little opportunity to dwell on thoughts of home. This area was the worst in the world for fog and icebergs. It was also the only place in the world where the great ocean itself seemed to Gabriel a secondary factor. The power of gigantic waves, of fathoms of water, was reduced, almost ignored, in the face of those other two imminent dangers. As summer approached the fog became denser and the crew lived in a perpetual state of apprehension.

The icebergs were an even greater threat and Gabriel had been told they were more numerous this year than usual. Great mountains of ice drifted south with the current from Labrador, all carved into weird, monolithic shapes where they had collided with other ice-fields and where the sea had hollowed out enormous holes in the base. The problem was that at night the half-submerged icebergs could be seen only from a short distance, even when there was no fog. It was then that Gabriel's ship was always ahead, as he stood peering into the darkness, assailed by the endless sound of the crashing and grinding of the bergs against each other, sounds that echoed thunderously around them and rumbled away in the distance.

The perils were enhanced by the increase in shipping and when they reached Grand Bank fleets of fishing vessels were already anchored in the misty bays and amongst the grey rocks.

During the breeding season great shoals of seals came into the coast from the deep seas and for six weeks the men hunted them from the ice floes. It was a cold and hazardous occupation, although they were easy to catch in such plentiful supply. The men skinned them, extracting the valuable oil, cutting out the meat and drying the skins, after which the remains of the carcasses were cast into the ocean for the sharks. At night, the mahogany-coloured meat was cooked on the ship, but it was at this stage that the fishermen were always reminded of England because the rich lean meat tasted like wild duck and they began to yearn for the safety and warmth of their homes. Gabriel listened to them in the hold beneath, talking sentimentally about their wives and children and their childhood experiences in the waters of Dartmouth. Then someone would start to boast about his fishing achievements, and then his sexual prowess, and the talk always degenerated into ribaldry.

For Gabriel, these weeks were the most difficult period of the whole enterprise. The dense fog made every movement dangerous both on the ice and in the ships. His eyes ached with constantly staring across the glinting water for icebergs and he was glad when the season was over and they emerged from the dense fog to return to Conception Bay.

On the journey they came upon a lone sailing ship signalling for help. The apparent leader of the nine men on board turned out to be a rough, barely-clad individual, his face marked and blotched with frost-bite. He requested food and safe passage and told Gabriel of a dangerous expedition that they had undertaken far away to the west in a barren sea of icebergs and a land of dense forests. They had sailed south, through a gigantic bay where the ship was frozen in for weeks. He talked about the ice, the black bears, the shrieking east wind. When the ice broke in the spring they had taken many weeks to navigate the dangerous journey back.

Gabriel was puzzled. 'Who financed the expedition?'

The man shook his head. 'Merchants in the city of London.'

'What happened to your captain?'

The man hesitated, then said, 'He was mad. Wanted us to continue up to the north . . . The crew mutinied.'

'Well, where is he?'

'He was put in a small boat with his son and two seamen who sided with him and there were five sick seamen . . . We had very little food.'

'And then?'

'They were cast adrift. It was us or them.'

'You savages. Get back to your ship,' Gabriel shouted. Then, to his crew, 'No provisions.'

He watched the man return to his own ship. He considered sinking it but the idea of mutiny was a delicate subject. Extreme fear had uncertain effects upon seamen, particularly in the remoteness and solitude of the arctic regions where the rule of law had a more fragile influence on the affairs of men. Gabriel believed that the idea of mutiny lurked somewhere in the back of every sailor's mind. A captain's authority lay ultimately in his personality, his ability to enforce his will on other men. Sailors and fishermen were not youngsters just released from their mother's apron strings. They were tough, experienced adventurers who had suffered every danger known to the high seas. They understood risk and accepted emergencies; what they would not tolerate was foolhardiness. Ironically, by mutiny they would risk their lives to support the principle that they would not throw their lives away.

He considered this factor in relation to his own crew

when, at the end of the summer, the fishing was complete. He had set his heart on making one further attempt to find a north west passage up beyond the Davis Straits to Cathay. Logic told him that there must be one; if it were all land, why had men never traversed it?

But for once, Gabriel listened to the remarks of the first mate, who was concerned that stocks of food might not last and that scurvy had broken out amongst some of the seamen. Some of the men were muttering that they wanted to return, not to go in for exploration unless there was profit to be made. He knew that if he went north, they would not return to England before Christmas and perhaps later. They had received messages from home from other ships arriving at the base and some of the men were worried about sick wives or children and other domestic problems.

He had word from Frances that all was well at Vinelands. More workmen had arrived from Italy and the estate had had a prosperous season. She also mentioned that two more visitors had arrived, a reference to the growing number of priests who were concealed in the house. Everyone wished him a safe journey and a speedy return. She did not mention Sarah.

So, issuing no orders, he asked for volunteers to sail with him up the east coast of Labrador beyond Davis Bay to explore the coasts of Greenland. Some fishermen had opted to brave the fogs and easterly wind and remain at Conception for the caplin scull. In summer, these small silver fish came into the bays in their billions, so many that the water in the cove seemed to turn black from their shadows. They were followed by sharks and whales and shoals of squid which ate millions of the caplins. A small contingent agreed that when this maritime carnival was over, they would remain at the base over the winter, to retain control of the fishing stages. Only six ships were to go north with Gabriel and the remainder left for the journey home.

116

They sailed up the coast of Labrador, a journey of twelve hundred miles, past mountains of sheer rock rising three thousand feet out of the sea, where hurricane force gales battered the little ships and they were swept into the comparative safety of Hudson Strait, into a world ever colder and more ice-bound. It was not the great mountains and pinnacles and pyramids of ice around them which caused their anxiety; it was that as their little ships sailed precariously between them, these gigantic masses were moving, like menacing primeval giants.

There was also the painful effect on their eyes, the endless searching and watching on the glaring expanses of icy water which had the effect of throwing dark patches on the clouds, giving the feeling to the crew that they were standing upside down.

Further north, they reached land, rocky coasts behind which were dense coniferous forests where they traded with the Innuits for furs and sealskins and beyond that with the Indians, until the ships were loaded to capacity.

Gabriel wanted to go on but he knew that the ships might be frozen in. The men had been away too long to accept that possibility. They were satisfied enough with the huge profits he would make from the journey because he rewarded them well for their enterprise, but one incident with a tribe of warring Indians, who had crept up to the ship at night to retrieve the goods they had traded during the day, told them that it was time to return. He decided it was the last time he would go in search of a north-west passage. It could never be successful while there were conflicting motives. Exploration demanded a total commitment to searching for that uncharted sea. It was not an aim which could be shared with trading.

He had not lost that sense of foreboding which had been at the back of his mind throughout the expedition. He never allowed his thoughts to dwell upon possible disasters and when one did come it was something he would never have anticipated in any case.

117

Weeks later, they reached St John's where Gabriel checked that all was well with the contingent who were remaining for the winter. Then Gabriel's six ships left St John's, joining another small fleet for mutual protection and he sensed a feeling of euphoria amongst the men. At last, they were sailing towards safer seas. Unless there were sudden storms or unmanageable gales, they would soon be home. It was when they were five days out into the Atlantic that the catastrophe occurred.

He went down into the hold to check on the diminishing supplies when one of the seamen barred his way.

'Sir, they're cleaning up in the . . .'

'It's all right. I only want to check the rations,' he said cheerfully.

The man moved back reluctantly and Gabriel went down the steps. Lying on the floor were two men. He went towards them.

'John! What is it? Are you sick?'

John did not reply. The man beside him was asleep.

'John,' Gabriel shouted angrily. 'You're drunk.'

'No . . . I just have difficulty . . . in speaking clearly.'

Gabriel dragged him to his feet. 'How dare you! You know the penalty for this.'

He turned to the men who had gathered at the other end of the hold.

'Bring them up on deck.'

Gabriel climbed up the gangway. An icy wind was blowing. In the growing darkness, he could dimly see the sails of the other vessels around them. His mind was filled with the implications of what he was about to do. If they were put on the mast, they could die in this temperature. But how would the men react if he absolved these two from the penalty just because John was his son? And Frances, her favourite son . . . the family . . . John was only a youth. About his own age when he first went to sea with John Davis. Yet even as the thoughts flashed through his mind, he knew he had no intention of changing the rules; they were not thoughts of indecision but merely of things he would have to deal with after the event. He turned as the crew clambered up behind him. The other man remained insensible but John revived in the bitter cold. He released himself from the men supporting him and walked unsteadily across the deck. Then he turned and looked challengingly at Gabriel. Gabriel could see only a small portion of his face because the men had wrapped thick clothing around them both. Neither of them spoke. Gabriel walked over to the lower mast.

'Tie them up.'

The crew and fishermen followed. Three fisherwomen stood on one side, their cloaks wrapped around them, their arms folded.

Then the mate came over to Gabriel. 'The crew refuse, sir.'

Gabriel frowned. Did they think they were pleasing him or did they mean it?

He looked round at their sullen faces.

'These are the rules,' he shouted at them.

No-one moved. Towering above them, he said violently, 'The rules are for the safety of the ship. I am a just man. There are no floggings, no bilboes, no duckings. I treat you like men. Behave like that.'

All the men looked at each other uncertainly. One of the fisherwomen strode forward.

'It happened to my son,' she shouted. 'Why not them?' She pointed aggressively at the two drunken figures.

Slowly the fishermen turned away. Four members of the crew went on towards the mast.

'Eight hours,' Gabriel said.

He did not wait to see his orders carried out, but went down to his cabin and closed the door. In spite of the sorrow in his heart, he had a feeling of exultation that he was still a great commander, that he could control not only his own crew, but also his own personal feelings. Justice was more important than any individual.

During the night the older man died of exposure. He was cast into the sea in the early hours of the morning.

Gabriel waited for the barber surgeon to come down to report on John.

'Well?'

The surgeon looked at him coldly.

'By a miracle, he survived. Minor frostbite. But you know what I think of these punishments.'

'It is not your job to think about that. I run the ship.'

'He wishes to transfer to another ship. He is not returning home with you.'

'Not returning!' Gabriel sprang to his feet.

'He says he renounces all title to the estate.'

'Let him go. He's not fit to be a sailor,' Gabriel shouted. 'Does he think I shall come begging for his return? Despatch him immediately.'

He did not attempt to see John before he left the ship but watched with tears in his eyes as he was rowed to a vessel from the other fleet. Although he might never see him again he felt admiration that such a fragile figure, a mere boy, could make such a gesture. He was proud that John was his son; one day he would get his inheritance. But how would he explain the event to Frances; how could she understand the need for his behaviour? How would anything justify the loss of John? She would never forgive him.

The trip north had lasted for six months and they reached England in late January, almost a year after they had left. Although it was a grey January morning, the safe little harbour looked to Gabriel and the hundreds of returning fishermen like the entrance to heaven. He watched the mooring of the boats at Bayards Cove, sniffing the air. After months at sea he was always conscious when he reached the quay of the smell of filthy drains, animal dung, the mounds of rubbish, rotting food. Then, finally, passing through the gates of Vinelands, the pungent smell of earth and grass, the first signs of early spring blossom and at the end of the avenue, passing into the fields, the smell of cows and stables.

After a brief word with Joseph, he walked through the kitchen gardens at the back of the house and then round to the front. Turning the corner, he smiled with satisfaction at the yellow bushes of jasmin. He pushed open the oak doors and went into the Great Hall. A red glow from the watery sun shone through the windows on to the tapestries along the upper gallery. He threw off his wet cape. All the clothes he had been wearing throughout the trip would be cast away or given to the poor.

Gabriel frowned, aware as always of the noise and bustle of endless servants coming and going around him. The congestion in the confined spaces of the ship seemed far less than this stream of boys and girls, men and women dashing hither and thither carrying every kind of commodity under the sun. Brooms, jars, dusters, timber, coal, dishes, barrels of herbs, up and down the great staircase, along the passages, into the chambers and halls. He climbed the staircase to the dining hall looking at the familiar treasured possessions that he had forgotten about.

The family were at their midday meal and sprang up as he entered. He embraced them all with real warmth. At last to be away from the sea, the cold, the danger, the desolate silences, the painful brightness of ice and water, the anxious darkness, the moaning of the wind, the depressing fog, the endless, endless sound of that great moving treacherous ocean. Cicely and Frances embraced him, Adam pulled out his chair for him; even Gilbert laughed.

'We were expecting you a week ago.' Frances put a plate in front of him and filled a tankard with beer.

'We were delayed by a storm. No boats lost,' he added hastily, seeing her anxious expression.

'It's been so long. Although we have had news of you.'

'Everything went well.' Gabriel smiled bleakly. 'It's my last attempt to find a north-west passage.'

Frances shook her head in disbelief.

'Was the fishing successful?'

'They're good men. But it's becoming more and more crowded. Portuguese, French, even the Spanish are becoming a nuisance. That pirate, Easton, is planning to build himself a mansion at Ferrylands using labourers from the continent. Must be one of the richest men in the world. He's just captured a Spanish galleon filled with treasure. It's rumoured he won't return here; won't share his booty with the King, he says.'

Frances asked where John was and Gabriel indicated that he would be coming up from the Quay later. For once he had evaded a confrontation, feeling he needed to gather strength for the onslaught that would result. He looked with pain at Gilbert's thin body, his emaciated face; he seemed now to have difficulty walking, as though his legs were too heavy for him.

Then he said abruptly, 'Where's Sarah?' Was she in one of her capricious moods, was she waiting for him to go and find her? Then he reflected that her moods had ended long ago. But he felt irritated, disappointed that she had not been there to greet him. Then he realized that they were looking at him apprehensively. They were all silent.

'Well, where is she?'

'She's not here, Gabriel,' Frances spoke quietly.

'I can see that. Where is she?'

It was Gilbert who said complainingly, 'Gone. Went off and left us.'

'What do you mean, gone?'

Frances said quietly, 'She just disappeared one . . .'

'Disappeared! When?'

'Months ago.' Frances began to sound truculent.

'Why didn't you find her?' Gabriel's voice grew louder each time he spoke. His trembling anger sent him pacing round the room, glaring, blaming. Who? What?

'We tried to,' Cicely said quickly. 'We made enquiries.'

'Enquiries! No-one would dare to hide her.'

'That's so,' Frances agreed. 'So, perhaps she's dead.'

'Dead! Dead. No.' Gabriel sat down, shaking his head. 'No. How?'

What trick were they trying to play on him? A stupid joke. They were all looking at him. What was this chasm they were opening up before him? Why would she go? Where? 'Is it something you did?' he asked Frances accusingly.

Gabriel sprang up, strode from the room and down and out again through the main doors.

When he had ridden through every field and wood and coppice on the estate, he galloped down the avenue and through the gates and down into the town. He asked in the shops and at the stalls, in the taverns and at the harbour, he looked in the churches, in the castle keep and then he rode to where her hut had once been. In the growing darkness, he stumbled up the steep hill, breathless in his anxiety. It was the first time that he had been to the summit, where the charred remains were now hidden by the grass which had grown through the ashes.

He thought he saw something move in the hedge beyond. 'Sarah.' His voice hung on the air. 'Sarah!' The shadow moved again and he jumped over to it. Behind the hedge an emaciated cow was quietly nibbling at the short, stubbly grass. She raised her eyes briefly and looked at him, then continued her chewing. Gabriel sighed, aware of the acute anxiety which once more possessed him.

Turning, striding down the hill, he realized he was holding out his arms as though he were carrying something, as he had held them when he carried Sarah down the hill, away from the mob.

Hours later, Frances heard a horse galloping across the fields, the hooves clopping across the bridge and round the house to the stables. She went along to Gabriel's chamber when she heard him mounting the stairs.

'Well?'

'Nothing.'

He looked haggard and threw his cloak down wearily.

'Perhaps it's better for you, Gabriel. She could have caused many problems.'

She looked almost sympathetic and he wished he did not have to tell her about John. But he could delay no longer. He made it as brief as possible. She listened in silence, her hands clutched together in her lap. She sat for a long time, her head bowed, until Gabriel thought she must be in a trance. Then said simply, 'At least he is alive. But as far as I am concerned, you are dead,' and she left the room.

He blew out the candle and lay on his bed. His world was falling apart. Yet he knew that all that mattered was to find Sarah. Only she could give meaning to his life. Life was so intensely personal and isolated. The barren wastes of the arctic, the great loneliness of the sea, those endless nights of silence, always made return seem strange. Yet, in the end, it was this warm domestic life which had always seemed unreal. Human contact was so fleeting and unsure, intimacy so marginal.

But Sarah had altered all that. Yet what had she ever said? Ever done? She was barely more than a child. He closed his eyes. Where in God's name was she?

The following days passed in silence. Frances waited for news of John, convinced that he must contact her eventually. Gabriel organized his bodyguard to scour the countryside in search of Sarah and when they had covered the parish they were told to go on to Cornwall and then north to the other Devon parishes. Somehow they must find her and bring her back. Alive.

9

Gabriel waited impatiently for the return of his men from Devon and Cornwall in search of Sarah. Without John there was much to do on the estate. Frances and Cicely continued to run the dairies and laundry, to supervise the staff and the wardrobes. But in John's absence it now fell to Gabriel to collect the rents and supervise the stables, as well as deal with all his trading commitments. There was also the business relating to the disposal of the catches from Newfoundland and of vast quantities of furs and skins.

When the men returned with the news that nothing had been seen or heard of Sarah, he went to see Father Pierre. There were now four priests concealed in secret chambers in the house and Gabriel knew that the old man would be happy to conceal every priest in the kingdom. He was reliving those long past days of life in a community devoted to prayer and contemplation.

Gabriel told him that he was going to London on business and then he said, 'Lady Frances is much disturbed about John.'

'Yes. It is very hard for her.'

'I had to do it,' Gabriel said defensively. It was only to Father Pierre that he would condescend to give any explanations. He always felt as though he were making excuses for his own weaknesses. 'It was my duty.'

'Every man's conscience is his own. We can only depend on our Lord's mercy.'

'Yes . . . and Sarah. She cannot be found.' Gabriel spoke

half-questioningly, as though Father Pierre in his spiritual capacity might have some answer.

'Perhaps it is better, Gabriel.'

They were the very words that Frances had used. Of course, Father Pierre must have discussed it with her as well but Gabriel knew that he could never reveal the private conversations of another.

'It is my responsibility.' Gabriel spoke more formally. 'I wish to protect her.'

Father Pierre looked at him thoughtfully.

'Perhaps we do not always recognize our motives. We can only ask for guidance.'

'I do ask for guidance. But there are many problems. John . . . Sarah . . . even our own religion.'

'And Frances . . . and you,' Father Pierre said, 'and the sacrament of marriage.'

'Yes.'

He felt as though Father Pierre had looked into his soul. He had thought little about his marriage since his return. The former easy relationship seemed to have evaporated. With a house full of servants, with separate chambers and diverse activities, he and Frances were rarely alone together and Frances seemed to have withdrawn more and more into a private world.

He knew that in his heart he blamed her for allowing Sarah to go; there was still the suspicion that Frances had had some part in her departure. Just as she blamed him, he reflected, for John's departure.

Then Father Pierre smiled suddenly and put his hand affectionately on Gabriel's arm.

'Take heart. We all create our own hell and then expect the Lord to save us from the results. But he supports us in our hour of weakness.'

In the early spring, Gabriel went to London to arrange the sales of spices, fruit and wines from the Azores and to organize a new enterprise importing marble from Italy.

It was over a year since he had been to the capital and

126

after the quiet of Dartmouth, the population seemed to have doubled. He heard a great deal of gross and derisive talk in the taverns about the court of James I. While Gabriel was in Newfoundland, Robert Carr had become Viscount Rochester and there were many stories about the young upstart. A burlesque performed in one of the inns in Chepeside was very popular, mimicking a young man in white silk underwear who when stripped turned out to be a female. Gabriel realized that to the citizens of London, the only activity at court was sodomy.

The hiding place for the priests had moved to a house near the Tower – 'it means a shorter last journey' one priest said cheerfully to Gabriel, but it was here that he saw the more sinister aspects of James's policies. He heard stories of new and ghastly tortures which were perpetrated on Catholics in the name of Christianity, though how far the king was the instigator it was impossible to say. Gabriel knew that there were some in power who simply used the opportunity to fulfil their own private desires for revenge.

It was a warm April day when he returned to Vinelands, the primulas and daffodils made a splash of colour in the gardens and primroses carpeted the lawn in Katherine's bower. He must visit her; the baby must be due soon.

Frances greeted him coldly as he entered the Great Hall. He realized that he was beginning to hate coming back to this place. When he entered its doors he was instantly reminded of Sarah, of her absence, of his continuing anxiety about her and yet he still had the same absurd expectation that perhaps she would be there to greet him. At the beginning, after a brief absence, he had asked hopefully if there were any news. But Frances had looked at him contemptuously, made no reply and walked from the room. Now the topic was no longer mentioned. But he knew it was really John that separated them. Sometimes, Frances seemed to look through him as though he did not exist. She discussed matters relating to the estate in a flat and detached manner and also Cicely's unexpected, forthcoming marriage to Stephen Kerswill, a Court barrister, but indulged in no other conversation. Cicely, too, seemed more distant, no doubt influenced by her mother's attitude. It was only when Adam returned on vacation that the house acquired any semblance of its former liveliness.

'Frances,' Gabriel said sharply one day, 'there is nothing to be gained by your unfriendly attitude. Cannot you return to your normal equable behaviour?'

'You have made it thus by your actions,' she replied.

'What is done is done. The past is over. We can only live now.'

She looked at him coldly.

'The past is not over,' she said. 'It is following us.' She turned and walked from the room.

He went up to the library to deal with his correspondence. An envelope containing no seal lay on his bureau.

'I don't know where that came from,' Mr Weaver, the steward, said. 'It was delivered in my absence.'

Gabriel opened it. It was written in a somewhat shaky hand.

'My lord out of the love I bear for you and your family I have a care to preserve and further your peace of mind. I hope it will do you no harm if I give you certain information which has come to my notice. I believe that you have some concern as to the whereabouts of the Lady Sarah who was lately resident in this place. Although I cannot help you in this respect, it has come to my intelligence that there is a certain noble establishment not far from here in which she has a certain right to be resident. I fear to mention the name of this place because of the evil that may befall me. But insofar as the responsibilities of paternity confer certain rights on the offspring, she would be entitled according to a higher justice which may not operate in this world, to better treatment than she has received. The estate to which I refer is close by, of lesser size than your lordship's but of greater distance from the town of Dartmouth. May it please your lordship to burn this letter and by the grace of God may you make good use of it.'

Gabriel's first impulse was to tear the letter into shreds. What cowardly idiot would write such a missive without declaring himself? Then he read it again and threw the letter across the desk to his steward.

'What do you make of that?'

Mr Weaver read it slowly, forming the words with his lips as he read. Then he frowned and shook his head.

'What advantage is there for him if he does not reveal himself? Perhaps, my lord, he acts for someone else . . . Perhaps he seeks revenge on someone.'

'But upon whom?'

The steward shook his head. 'He may be a lunatic.'

'Burn it,' Gabriel said, then added, 'no, return it to me.' He placed it in his doublet.

After his men had returned with no news of Sarah, Gabriel had outwardly appeared to abandon all interest in her. She lived only in the secret chambers of his mind. Now he felt a growing anger at the writer of the letter for opening so decisively the wound that she had left. If it were true, there were only two houses in the vicinity even vaguely approaching his own. Carew's, along the Brixham Road, and Fortescue's, up on the hill further along the coast. It couldn't be Carew. He had known him and the family too long and intimately not to have some information about his private life and activities. It was Carew, too, who had furthered his official advancement.

As the anxiety about Sarah grew once more in his mind, he decided that he would either act upon the letter or put the whole absurd episode out of his mind. He decided and that afternoon rode across the hill and along the coast to Fortescue's residence. The man was not an intimate acquaintance of his – Gabriel did not share his notorious passion for bear-baiting and cock-fighting. But he appeared to take no part in political

129

intrigue and had no violent antipathy towards the Catholic community.

He greeted Gabriel in the library, offering him a tankard of claret. Gabriel noted the huge family portrait which now rested above the marble fireplace.

'How went the Newfoundland expedition?' Fortescue asked amiably.

'Well enough. But the seas are becoming well crowded with Spanish and French.'

'I thought we'd subdued the Spanish tribes.'

'Yes, we have. But they still cause trouble.'

'And your household. Are they well?'

'Thank you, sir. Yes.'

'Pray be seated, sir,' Fortescue said, pouring more claret. 'How's that tutor fellow of yours – Smithson, was it?'

'Still with us.' Gabriel looked puzzled at the question, then remembered that it was Fortescue who had introduced him years ago. 'Performs his job adequately.'

'Curious fellow. Came to see me some moons ago when you were on the high seas.'

Gabriel nodded uninterestedly.

'Seemed to fear dismissal,' Fortescue went on. 'Appealing for my protection, I warrant.'

'Dismissal! Protection!' Gabriel looked astonished. 'Why did he fear such an event?'

Fortescue laughed. 'Thought you might not require his services much longer. Suppose you won't. But I assured him you wouldn't evict him. How about that lass you adopted? Didn't she make off in your absence?'

Gabriel forgot about Charles.

'That's one of the reasons I'm here. I wondered if you might know anything.'

Sir Jonathon looked puzzled in his turn. 'That old witch's offspring? Know nothing about her.'

Gabriel felt irritated at the man's reference to a witch but he said evenly, 'I have made many enquiries. It is not possible for her to have vanished completely.'

Sir Jonathon's steely blue eyes rested on him.

'Perhaps it is foolhardy, Sir Gabriel, to concern oneself with such a miss.'

'That is my concern,' Gabriel replied, pleasantly enough.

'Yes, indeed, sir.' Sir Jonathon grinned. 'The only female I've noticed of late was a newly arrived kitchen maid.'

Gabriel controlled the anger inside him that Sir Jonathon was equating his feelings about Sarah with his own lecherous feelings about a kitchen maid. But was it possible that Sarah had become a servant somewhere?

'Yes?' he said.

'A brazen minx. Caught her in my sleeping chamber. About to steal a silver mirror.'

Would Sarah do that? Perhaps she needed money.

'What does she look like?'

Sir Jonathon smacked his lips. 'A buxom maid. Could have bedded her m'self. Yellow hair, green eyes, like a cat. Still, should have been sent to the whipping post.'

Gabriel gulped his wine.

'Sarah has green eyes.'

'Can't be your miss,' Fortescue said. 'What would she be doing here?'

Gabriel began to feel a plot weaving around him – Sarah, the anonymous letter, Charles coming here.

'I had a strange communication', Gabriel said, 'which led me to your abode.'

Fortescue raised his thick brows.

'What I can only call a slanderous despatch.' Gabriel extracted the letter from inside his doublet and handed it to Fortescue.

Fortescue read it slowly. Reading was clearly not one of his normal activities.

Gabriel frowned. Perhaps the sense of anxiety that Sarah always created was clouding his judgment, yet he was beginning to think that the letter did refer to the man before him.

'Slanderous indeed,' Sir Jonathon said. 'No mark identifies it. But why, sir, does it bring you to this establishment?

'Merely in the description of the house, sir.'

'Sir, you do not impute that this missive refers to me?'

'Sir Jonathon, I do not impute it. I merely suspected that this communication may do so.'

'Then, sir, I think you would be advised to destroy it or see that the miscreant is brought to justice.'

'If I can apprehend him.'

'There is much dangerous false witness, as you know. Sneaks and informers trying to make some profit.'

'My enquiries are concerned only with the whereabouts of the girl,' Gabriel said.

'These scoundrels must be dealt with. They do much harm. Must be got rid of.'

'Yes,' said Gabriel, rising. 'I intrude upon your time.' Then he added suddenly, 'Where is this maid that you apprehended?'

'Dismissed, I presume, by the housekeeper.'

'Could we enquire in that area?'

Sir Jonathon shrugged his shoulders. Gabriel knew that he was tired of the conversation, perhaps thought him absurd, but courtesy compelled him to summon Mistress Taylor to the library.

Mistress Taylor said that the servant had been employed as a casual worker, she knew nothing about her; she had left suddenly. Nothing had been heard of her since.

'Do not your servants have contact with my household at Vinelands, Mistress Taylor?'

'But little, Sir Gabriel. It is some distance from here.'

'Yes, of course.'

After she had gone, Gabriel bowed his thanks to his host.

'Well, I shall be pleased to accept the invitation to Cicely's wedding. She seems to have made a felicitous choice,' Fortescue said.

132

Gabriel assented.

'I hear that Stephen Kerswill has some influence at court. Something we can all do with in these curious days.'

Gabriel smiled. He knew that this merely indicated Fortescue's implicit support for his situation. Then Fortescue added, 'A wench isn't worth worrying about, Sir Gabriel. Too much at stake.'

They bowed to each other as Gabriel passed through the hall doors.

Sir Jonathon turned back into the house and summoned Mistress Taylor once more to his presence. He suspected that she had been lying about that wench.

Gabriel rode across the estate and over the hills into Dartmouth. He was convinced now that they were both lying, but what about?

It made little difference whether Fortescue was Sarah's father or not. A bastard had no claims on anything. He would scarcely be harbouring her, much less indulging in any secret plot with his housekeeper. Yet he still had the suspicion that they knew something about Sarah; why would they not inform him?

Then his thoughts turned to Charles. Why had he made those statements about his position? How had this insignificant creature had the temerity to visit Sir Jonathon?

When he reached the house, he sent for Charles to come to the library. Charles had been transferred to the task of cataloguing the books, now that his duties as a tutor had come to an end.

Contemplating the thin faded person standing before him, the bald head and yellowing skin, Gabriel realized that he had scarcely noticed him for years.

'Good day, Mr Smithson. Be seated.'

Charles bowed his head and sat on the high-backed chair that Gabriel indicated.

'Are you well, Mr Smithson?'

'Yes, sir. Well,' Charles said anxiously.

133

'I understand you have concerns which you have failed to communicate to me.'

'Concerns? No, sir.'

'Yes, sir. I have recently visited Sir Jonathon Fortescue. He has informed me . . .'

'That was some time past,' Charles interrupted. 'You were absent.'

'When?'

'Perhaps a year, sir. In the spring.'

'Would you convey them to me now.'

Charles sighed. His thin hands rested nervously on the arms of the chair.

'Sir, I feared that my presence would no longer be necessary in this household.'

'Did you speak with Lady Frances?'

'No, sir.'

'Well,' Gabriel went on. 'On what grounds?'

'Gilbert, sir, can no longer pursue his lessons and Mistress Sarah, she is no longer here.'

'Was she still here when you visited Sir Jonathon?' Gabriel said suspiciously.

'Yes, sir.'

'Did you have some knowledge that she would depart?'

'Oh, no, sir. Certainly not.'

'Are you acquainted with the servants at Branwell Hall?'

Charles moved his hands uncertainly. 'No, sir.'

'Not Mistress Taylor?'

'I have made her acquaintance on the occasions when I have visited Branwell Hall. When I visited Sir Jonathon.'

Gabriel stood up suddenly.

'Of course. You wrote that letter!'

'Letter, sir?'

Charles stood up also. His hands went to his collar, as though he were about to choke.

'Sit! Yes, letter. Tell me the truth or I'll have you clapped in gaol.'

134

Charles tried to speak but his voice disappeared. He had a vision of a damp dungeon, chains around his ankles, intolerable tortures, hanging . . .

'Where did that information come from?'

Gabriel stood over him, waiting. Finally Charles cleared his throat and told him of Mistress Taylor's information.

'Idiot!' Gabriel said coldly. 'Why didn't you inform me when I questioned all the servants about Lady Sarah's disappearance?'

'I don't know, sir.'

'And that letter. Sir Jonathon's no fool. He'll discover the author of such a calumny. What benefit was there in writing such a communication, based on servants' gossip?'

Charles shook his head. 'He made me look stupid. He had no appreciation of my worth.'

Gabriel looked in astonishment.

'Revenge, was it? Well, you must beware. Fortescue will not take kindly to your accusation.'

'No, sir.' Charles stood up uncertainly. 'Life is difficult, sir.'

Momentarily, Gabriel's pity overcame his contempt.

'You are not in danger here, Charles. Although you may be a fool. You will remain here and continue to occupy your apartment. No doubt, there are other small duties you can perform.'

Charles experienced once again the bitterness of rejection; he would never get that promotion, never reach the heights to which his qualifications entitled him. He said slowly, 'My apologies, sir, but could you return the letter to me that I may destroy it.'

Gabriel felt in his doublet and sighed.

'Regretfully, no,' he said. 'I recollect that I left it with Sir Jonathon.'

Charles walked slowly along the gallery, feeling desolate. Now he was in imminent danger. What would happen if Sir Jonathon found out that he was responsible?

As he returned to his chamber, the conviction grew that

Sir Gabriel would not protect him. They were all against him, probably at this moment all plotting his downfall. Sir Gabriel's words had constituted a threat, not a warning. He was no longer safe in this vicinity at all.

A few days later, Frances told Gabriel that Charles was nowhere to be found. The next day a letter was delivered saying that he had decided to go north and would not return. Gabriel reflected briefly that Smithson could be of little danger to him. He would know of the priests hidden in the house but Gabriel was aware that there was an inherent distaste amongst the upper classes for underlings who betrayed their masters. They would only make use of Smithson if the need arose; they would not allow him to be an instigator. He put the man out of his mind. The next afternoon, Gabriel went to see Katherine. Her baby was expected in a couple of months. Frances had briefly informed him that last time she visited, Katherine looked ill and seemed to be losing weight rather than gaining it. Sir William appeared to treat her well, but Gabriel wondered if she were regretting her youthful marriage.

She greeted him as he walked across the garden. 'You look well,' Gabriel said with relief. 'Your mother feared you were ailing.'

'I was, Papa, at the beginning. But now, I have a nurse who cares for me.' She hesitated, looking assessingly at her father, then turned towards the house. 'Come, Papa, you must partake of the midday meal with us.'

Gabriel followed her to the dining hall. He noted the rich velvet draperies she had chosen for the long windows and the vivid displays of flowers arranged around the room.

'It is not yet time,' she said. 'Come to the library. I must talk with you.'

As she closed the door behind them, she pulled the bell rope.

'Sit down, Papa.'

'What's the mystery, Katherine? Have you some matter for concern?'

'Well,' Katherine hesitated. 'I fear you will not be pleased.'

'Katherine, what is it, what is wrong?'

'Sarah is here, Papa.'

Gabriel sprang to his feet.

'Here! What do you mean? How could I not be pleased? How did you find her?'

'I have sheltered her for many months.'

'Sheltered her! Katherine, why did you not inform me? What sort of treachery is this?'

'Papa, Sarah begged me not to reveal her presence. She fears . . .'

'Fears what?' Gabriel shouted angrily. 'You knew of my concern. Has everyone taken leave of their senses? There is deception everywhere.'

He sat down, overwhelmed that Katherine, his favourite daughter, should treat him thus.

'Where is she?'

Katherine stood before him, about to speak, when there was a gentle knock. Gabriel turned. Sarah stood in the open doorway. She was wearing a cream embroidered gown with a low-cut bodice and her hair was tied back with a velvet ribbon.

Gabriel sprang to his feet. 'Sarah!'

She closed the door behind her and walked slowly across the room.

'Good day, Gabriel.'

He looked in anger and incomprehension at the mature young woman before him. She seemed slightly taller, more dignified. Or was it just her cool attitude as she smiled at him? His gaze moved from the calm expression in her eyes to the golden hair curling down behind her ears, to her smooth white neck and then to the softly-rounded, barely concealed breasts. The Sarah he had left behind had been still a child, a pretty little girl taking lessons with Gilbert.

'Sarah! What are you doing here? Where have you been? Why did you leave? I've been looking for you.' His voice rose in his confused emotions of anger, indignation and relief.

She smiled. 'I know.'

Gabriel's face flushed. 'What do you mean, you know? Why did you do it? And Katherine, why did you not tell me? You knew of my concern.'

'It was my wish. I asked her not to,' Sarah said.

'Why?' Gabriel demanded.

'I was in danger,' Sarah said quietly.

'Danger. What danger?'

Sarah looked at Katherine uncertainly.

'We had not intended to speak of it,' Katherine said. 'It can do no good.'

'Speak of what?' Gabriel said angrily.

Sarah shrugged.

'It will give you no satisfaction. I ran away because Frances intended to despatch me to France.'

'France! What do you mean?'

'She said my presence endangered the household. I must leave.'

'Katherine, is this true?'

Gabriel sat down feeling totally confused. Even his own wife could not be trusted. They had all betrayed him.

'Papa,' Katherine said. 'Perhaps you cannot be surprised. It must have been difficult for Mama to accept the situation.'

'Accept what? Adopting Sarah?'

'She may not have seen it as you do.'

Gabriel stood up again.

'Sarah,' he said, controlling his emotions, 'if what you say is true, the matter will be settled. I want you to return with me to Vinelands.'

'No. I cannot return.'

'Why not?' Gabriel felt his anger returning. 'I have adopted you. You have no right to leave my establishment without my consent. If you had cause for fear, that is no longer so. Why did you not turn to me for protection when I returned?' he demanded.

Katherine walked over to him.

'Papa,' she said quietly. 'I am much in need of Sarah at this moment. I dread this impending birth.'

She put her hands on his shoulders. Gabriel sighed.

'Why did you not tell me, Katherine?' he said more quietly.

'Sir,' Sarah said. 'Do you not understand my fear?'

Gabriel looked at her. She looked so beautiful he had a sudden impulse to take her in his arms, but he said curtly, 'You may remain here till the birth of the child. Then you will return to Vinelands.'

'Katherine needs me after that,' Sarah said quietly. 'If the baby is fostered out it will die. They're not looked after properly.'

'All babies are fostered. And how about Gilbert? He needs you.'

Sarah shook her head. 'I can't help him.'

'What do you mean?'

'Gilbert can't get better,' she said slowly.

Gabriel frowned. Sarah spoke with a chilling certainty, as though she had looked into a known and inevitable future.

Perhaps she had not wished to deceive him. If she were really fearful, it was Frances who had caused the problem. Yet why she left, where she had been were irrelevant. She was here. He felt a sudden reluctance to make her come back against her will. He had brought her to Vinelands against her will in the first place. Now it was different. He was not doing it simply to protect her; he knew now it would also be to fulfil his own need.

His anger disappeared. He walked over to the window, looking across the lawns to the sea sparkling far away in the sunlight of the harbour. Then he knew that he could no longer force her to do anything. She had become more important even than his own desires. He turned away.

139

'What do you wish to do after the baby, Sarah?' he said in a different tone.

She looked at him thoughtfully, a smile on her lips, but she did not reply.

'Wouldn't you come and see Gilbert? Perhaps it would cheer him.'

There was a moment's silence. Then she came over and put a hand on his arm. He felt no surprise when she said, 'If you wish.'

He was accustomed to her flippancy, her changing attitudes, at one moment hard and aggressive and the next agreeable and malleable. 'I'll come home, if you like. After the baby is born.'

He felt a sudden exultant joy at her words. A terrible anxiety seemed to have been lifted from his mind. For the first time, the expression in her eyes was no longer challenging but as they looked at each other, he felt a great peace, as though he had finally come home.

'It is for you to decide, Sarah.'

'Yes,' she said. 'I know. I have.' She stretched up and kissed him lightly on the cheek. 'Dear Gabriel,' she said.

'Come,' Katherine said briskly, 'the meal is prepared.'

10

Cicely decided that her wedding should take place at St Clements on the Hill. Her Catholic convictions did not allow her to attend the obligatory Sunday service which Gabriel attended at St Saviour's with Katherine and her husband but last year she had visited St Clements when the marble portrait of Robert Holland was unveiled. The church seemed cold and bare but she preferred it to the parish church.

Stephen had little connection with this part of the country and after their marriage they would repair to his property, Hewell Grange near Lincoln. As he was a judge of the King's Bench, he would spend much time at court and Cicely realized that she would rarely have an opportunity to visit her parents.

She had met Stephen at Katherine's home. Sir William and he had been pupils at Sherborne School and their family connections had kept them in constant touch. Stephen was a startlingly handsome bachelor who appeared to have had no intimate female associates and both Katherine and William were delighted when he began to pay attention to Cicely. For her part, Cicely, who had thought of marriage only as a necessary duty, now found herself wildly in love with this dashing man. He was charming and attentive. It astonished her, indeed, that someone so attractive and agreeable was not already betrothed. But from the moment he met her, he made it clear that marriage was in his mind. So within six months, the dowry had been agreed between Gabriel and Stephen's father and the marriage banns had been called.

She had visited once his modest home at Hewell Grange and was happy to think that her dowry, ten times greater than the value of the property, would significantly improve Stephen's position.

When Cicely shared this delight with her mother, Frances had replied caustically that dowries were becoming absurdly inflated. Although she had constantly encouraged Cicely to improve her appearance in the hope that she would acquire a husband, Frances seemed to have no appreciation of the change in her daughter. Cicely, advised by Katherine, now wore the fashionable low-cut gowns of silk and taffeta with wide puffed sleeves and she even used rouge upon her cheeks.

Adam, now fourteen years old, had gone to university and would not return until Christmas. Gilbert was too sick and weak to leave his chamber for any length of time and a nurse was in constant attendance to administer poultices. John would also be absent. Since his disappearance, Frances had withdrawn even more into her own world. Nothing had been heard of him and she had received no communication. She spent more and more time in the chapel attending to the needs of the hidden priests.

So, of Cicely's siblings, only Katherine would be at the celebrations although she had been ailing since she was delivered of a daughter, Elizabeth, a month or so ago. The services of Mrs Reed, her midwife, had not been available at the birth because she herself was ill with fever. Joan Verity, the woman who had been engaged in her stead, believed in helping forward the course of nature. When Katherine felt the first violent pains in her back, Mistress Verity bade her lie upon the couch to see if she could extract 'the little monster'.

Sarah protested that Katherine was not yet in labour and demanded that nature should take its course. But it was a long and difficult birth and for two days Katherine moaned and tossed in her boudoir while Sarah insisted that Mistress Verity should not use the instruments designed by the local blacksmith to drag the child from its mother.

When, with one final agonized scream from Katherine, Sarah dragged out the little blue body, she allowed the midwife to exercise her professional skill in cutting the cord. The baby was struck on the back and when it let forth its first faint cry, it was wrapped in thick woollen blankets and carried off by a nurse. For two days, Katherine alternated between delirium and depression while her torn body was left to heal itself.

Sarah gave her medicinal herbs to reduce the fever and when Sir William came to see his wife he thanked her. 'You saved her life, Sarah. You will be rewarded.'

Sarah smiled. 'There is no need. You and Katherine, you also saved mine.'

Then she hustled Sir William from the chamber. 'Katherine must be quiet,' she said as he left the room. But her concern was to protect him from Katherine's delirious cries, when she called constantly for Richard, her lover, reliving the hours of joy before her marriage. She rarely saw him now; the life of secret rendezvous and assignments which she had planned had been difficult to achieve. Sir William was rarely absent and when he went on a journey to the capital, he insisted on taking Katherine with him.

Katherine had discovered that her infatuation with Richard was deeper than she had realized. It was not only the exciting relationship she had enjoyed; she found that her need to be with him could not be satisfied by a few illicit and haphazard encounters.

Sarah, living in the household, had become involved in these secret meetings. Katherine confided all her feelings to Sarah and when Richard came it was she who kept a lookout for them in anticipation of Sir William's unexpected return.

But when the baby was taken, in spite of Sarah's concern, to live with a wet nurse in Dartmouth and Katherine had risen from her sick bed, Sarah said she must return to Vinelands. She had promised Sir Gabriel that she would look after Gilbert.

Katherine demurred. 'It is so lonely without you, Sarah. This great, gaunt house.'

'Sir William is a good husband. Are you not content?'

'It is unfortunate. I dream only of Richard. I am tortured by the thought that he must find someone else.'

'He thinks only of you,' Sarah said.

'Perhaps you should marry him, Sarah. I could countenance that.'

'Me!' Sarah laughed. 'I have no intention . . .'

143

'If you return to Vinelands, my mother will see that you are betrothed. She does not desire you in the house.'

Sarah frowned. 'I will not go to France.'

'She won't mention that again, now that Papa is here.'

'Will he permit me to marry?'

Katherine laughed. 'I think it will be difficult to find someone whom he finds suitable for you.'

Sarah frowned again. 'I wish only to be at Vinelands. It is the only home I want.'

'Sarah, you cannot be there for ever. You must be found a suitable husband; perhaps not yet,' she added, seeing Sarah's distressed expression. 'In a few years, when you are ready.'

'I may not find anyone I like well enough.'

'Papa will not force you to marry against your will. He will give you a generous portion. You may marry whom you please.'

'You seem to find marriage of small account.'

'Ah, but it is preferable to spinsterhood. Indeed,' she added thoughtfully, 'perhaps your words will remind me of my good fortune.'

A few days before Cicely's wedding, Gabriel had told Frances that Sarah would be present at the wedding and would then remain at Vinelands. He had already told her that she had been discovered at Katherine's some months ago. Frances said angrily that if Sarah attended, she herself would not be there.

'It was her own choice that she left,' Frances said. 'It makes you look a weak and foolish idiot, permitting her to return.'

'She has told me of her reason for leaving,' Gabriel said coldly, 'I fear you may have had some hand in it.'

He looked at Frances quietly. His anger at what she had done had evaporated now that Sarah was returning. He felt, indeed, compassion for this solitary woman; he was aware that it was he who had faced her with the problem.

'I know of no reason,' Frances retorted. 'She is a wild creature.'

'Frances, you intimidated her in my absence. You wished to be rid of her.'

'Yes. I did,' she said, suddenly turning on him. 'She has no right here.'

Gabriel sighed.

'We have been through all this long ago. Sarah will tend Gilbert. She has cared well for Katherine during her pregnancy.'

'Only evil will come of this,' Frances retorted. 'It will be on your head.' So saying she retreated to her chamber.

The day before the wedding, Gabriel went to Frances's chamber in an attempt to reconcile her to Sarah's presence on the morrow.

'It is exceeding hot in here, Frances.' He turned. 'Sarah returns to Vinelands tomorrow. Let us enjoy domestic harmony.'

Frances looked at him.

'Your relationship with Sarah is of small concern to me,' she said curtly.

'You allow your suspicions to get the better of you.'

'And perhaps you are endangering us,' she said briefly. 'It must be your responsibility.'

On the day of the marriage, Katherine felt too weak to make the short journey to Vinelands and Sarah went in the carriage alone, promising to visit her frequently. She was wearing an ice-blue silk gown, richly embroidered with jewels and gold thread. The deep-cut neckline left her shoulders bare and Katherine had given her a diamond choker which fitted tightly around her white neck.

After the marriage ceremony at St Clements, Gabriel and Frances returned to Vinelands and stood at the doors of the festooned and decorated Great Hall to receive their guests.

Gabriel noted that Frances and Sarah briefly inclined their heads to each other in greeting. The eyes of all

145

the guests were on Sarah as she unclasped her vivid blue velvet cloak and handed it to a servant and then she swept across the hall to greet Cicely and her new bridegroom, Stephen, her dress and jewels sparkling, her golden hair flowing down to her waist.

Gabriel turned back to the guests. The steward was announcing, 'Sir Jonathon Fortescue and Lady Margaret.'

The two men bowed; the women curtsied and, at a convenient opportunity, Sir Jonathon muttered to him, 'I shall be interested to see your Lady Sarah. It has not yet been my pleasure.'

'She is settled again at Vinelands,' Gabriel replied. 'Some misunderstanding must have prompted her strange action.'

He saw Sir Jonathon's eyes glance around the crowded hall and then come to rest on Sarah. His face went red. 'That is the wench,' he said, as though in disbelief.

'She is now under my protection,' Gabriel said quietly.

Sir Jonathon smiled dismissively. 'Have no fear, sir. I shall proffer no charges. It is of no concern.'

Gabriel watched him as he walked across the hall towards Sarah. He saw her turn and look at him coldly, with that chilling expression in her eyes. She acknowledged his greeting but Gabriel could not hear their words.

Then Frances took his arm as he led the way to the dining hall for the wedding feast. He stood at the top of the staircase and watched as Sarah and Sir Jonathon slowly mounted the stairs amongst the guests. They were engrossed in conversation, Sarah looked composed and there was a slight smile on her lips as she listened to her companion.

Gabriel felt a mounting anger which almost became hatred. The man was a scoundrel. He had probably accused her of theft to hide his own guilt. He must have doubts about whether he was her father or not. If he were, why did he not admit his responsibility, at least privately to him. If he were not, what was he doing talking in this intimate fashion? Gabriel was about to walk towards him, when he felt a restraining hand on his arm.

'Sarah is too forward,' Frances said. 'But do not become involved. We want no trouble. This is Cicely's wedding celebration. Kindly consider her.'

Gabriel nodded curtly and signalled to the minstrels in the gallery above. The music heralded the beginning of the feast. The bride and groom at the head of the table held up their goblets to the guests and the merriment began.

When Gabriel looked again, Sarah had left Fortescue and was seated beside Carew and his wife. She smiled across at him coolly and he turned his eyes and his attention to Cicely. The change in her had been so dramatic that he could scarcely believe that this was the same girl who had only recently wished to enter a nunnery. She smiled fondly at Stephen, listening intently to his words, and indeed Stephen seemed to be as intoxicated with her. But he had heard ugly rumours about Stephen, admittedly from Catholics who tended to exaggerate any scandals about their Protestant brethren. He wondered briefly how Cicely had reconciled her deeply held convictions with marriage to a non-believer but it seemed not to be a matter of great concern to women. She could keep her religion, as long as she was circumspect. But it seemed Stephen's aberrations extended beyond religious belief. His name had been linked with people at Court, undesirables cultivated and promoted by the King, the ever-growing band of sycophants. Not that it mattered to Cicely. If he fell from favour, it would be unlikely to involve her. But it could reveal to her the sordid realities of life, for which Gabriel felt she was manifestly unprepared.

As the afternoon wore on, people began to rise from their seats, walking around the dining hall, pouring more drink, snatching at pieces of meat, chicken legs, quails, duck eggs, sweetmeats as they passed up and down. The music and the conversation grew louder. Couches were occupied by young men who had miscalculated their capacity for wine; ladies rested by the open windows and Gabriel stood up and suggested that guests might like to wander in the gardens or rest in the drawing rooms while the tables were cleared and replenished for the evening celebrations.

He went slowly with the crowd along the gallery and down the staircase. They poured into the gardens and he saw Sarah disappearing through the music room. He followed her to a room on the other side of the house. She was seated on a couch, looking out across the knot gardens.

'It is a great celebration, sir.'

'I hope for Cicely's happiness,' Gabriel replied. 'And have you now returned to Vinelands permanently, Sarah?'

'If it is your wish, sir.'

'It is as it should be, Sarah.'

'I would wish to stay here for ever.'

'That Fortescue fellow,' Gabriel said abruptly. 'I notice he engaged you in conversation.'

'Yes.' Sarah stood up and then hesitated again.

'Sarah, I have had no opportunity of conversation with you since I discovered you at Katherine's. When you ran away from Vinelands, did you immediately repair to her house?'

'No. I went to Branwell Hall.'

'Branwell Hall! Then Sir Jonathon was correct about . . . !'

'Not about stealing,' she interposed. Then she added challengingly, 'He is the liar. I have just told him so.'

'Then what is the truth?'

'He attempted to seduce me.'

'And did you resist him?' he asked angrily.

Sarah said slowly, 'Naturally,' and then added with satisfaction. 'He still bears the scar upon his cheek.'

'Sarah, why did you go there?'

'Sir Jonathon is my father.'

Gabriel sighed.

'Did you obtain this rumour from Mr Smithson?'

148

'No. My mother told me.'

Sarah related the whole story of the visit with her mother, of her death, of her aunt, Mistress Taylor. Finally, Gabriel said, 'It is of little consequence, Sarah, if you are his bastard. He has no need in law to acknowledge you. Your mother, indeed, could have been subject to the law herself. It is advisable that you think no more of this matter.'

Sarah was silent.

'And what was Sir Jonathon's conversation with you today?'

'I informed him of the situation. He said he would not acknowledge me publicly but that he would henceforth give me annual recompense.'

'Sarah! How did you manipulate such an undertaking?'

Sarah smiled. 'I said I would inform his wife of his behaviour in the bedchamber. He seems singularly anxious not to disturb her.'

'Sarah, such behaviour demeans you. How could you parley with such a man?'

'It is my right.'

'You have no rights with him,' Gabriel repeated irritably. 'You are too obstinate. I fear he has been persuaded against his judgment. He must surely come to resentment of this.'

'Gabriel, have no fear.'

'It is not fear, Sarah. I dislike such ignoble actions on your part.'

'You think of honour,' Sarah replied coolly. 'I think of justice.'

'You have no proof, Sarah. It is perhaps mere speculation, idle servants' gossip.'

Sarah turned away and said abruptly, 'Come, enough of this. Let us repair to the garden. It is hot in here.'

They walked amongst the roses, in the shadow of the tall yew hedges. Guests were lying on the grass, in shady bowers, while children danced in the sun. Then there was a sudden violent clap of thunder overhead that echoed across the hills, vivid flashes of lightning, great black clouds gathered and the rain poured down.

The guests rushed towards the house, laughing and shrieking, and they all assembled in the Great Hall, wet and cold. Instantly, the servants lit fires while the ladies removed their outer gowns which were whisked away to be dried in the washrooms.

'Pray go and change your clothes,' Gabriel said to Sarah, 'you will get a distemper.'

Frances stood behind them. She had not been in the garden.

'With your permission,' Sarah said quietly, 'it is Sir Gabriel's wish that I return to this house.'

Frances looked at her coldly. 'It is my wish that you bring no further misfortune to this house,' she said as she walked away.

Gabriel followed Sarah up the stairs. His own doublet and breeches were wringing wet and his hair dripped down his back. His leather pumps squelched water as his feet touched the marble stairs. Crowds of people were going up to the public rooms to repair the damage to their hair styles and rouges.

When Gabriel had put on dry attire, he went along to Sarah's chamber. The peace of mind he had felt when he found her, his joy at her return, were tempered now by reality. The presence of two antagonistic women in a house was not conducive to peace of mind. He intended to request Sarah to treat Frances with courtesy. It was not seemly that a young woman should appear to treat an elder with contempt. Sarah did not understand such matters but she had learnt to conduct herself well enough in society. She must learn also the requirements of personal contacts.

He knocked lightly on her door and at her bidding went in. The draperies were half-drawn to reduce the rays of the sun and when his eyes became accustomed to the shadows

150

he saw that Sarah was standing before her looking-glass. She was naked. When she turned towards him, she made no move to clothe herself.

Gabriel snatched up a robe from her sleeping couch and threw it across to her.

She smiled at him lightly, draping it around her shoulders.

'Sarah.'

'I was expecting you,' she said quietly.

'Sarah. Clothe yourself. Do not behave so.'

She walked slowly towards him.

'Gabriel, I have returned to Vinelands for you.'

'Sarah, you have misunderstood,' he said firmly. 'It was not with this intention. You have returned for Gilbert.'

She raised her arms around his neck, and gently drew his head down towards her.

'No,' she said softly. 'I have not misunderstood but it is only now that I have come to realize.'

Slowly, deliberately, she pressed her lips against his. The thought flashed through his mind that it was like the kiss of a naughty child seeking a favour.

He gently released her arms from around his neck and said severely, 'Sarah, you don't understood what . . .'

She clasped him again, looking into his eyes.

'Yes. I do. I do.'

She smiled and as he attempted to push her away his fingers touched her breasts. A wild excitement swept through him. He snatched her into his arms and kissed her passionately. He felt her small waist, the curve of her hips. His hands moved up to her shoulders and then down her back to her thighs.

'Gabriel,' she murmured. 'I don't know . . . I've never . . .'

But now the acknowledgment of his desire for her was released, the pretence was over. The joy of touching her, holding her, was a dream he knew had always been in his mind; all he had ever wanted was to possess her.

151

'Sarah,' he said hoarsely. 'Oh, Sarah, what longings you have awakened in me.'

He kissed her hair, her eyes, her throat, then he kissed her on the lips, long and tenderly.

'Gabriel, take off your clothes.'

She slipped from his arms. Pulling off his doublet and breeches, his long leather boots, he looked at her lovely golden body as she closed the draperies across the window and pulled the bolt across the door of her chamber.

Then she turned and smiled, but now it was no longer provocative or childlike. It was the smile of a woman who knew she was entering a world, who knew what she was doing. Yet, did she know, Gabriel thought, did she realize? Then she came over to him and began to touch his naked body, exploring, tentative. Gabriel picked her up and carried her to the bed. She lay in his arms and he felt her move towards him, her hands caressing him, her lips on his, on his neck, his body.

He touched her all over, until at last his hands came to her buttocks and finally between her legs.

Then she looked at him and he could see desire and excitement awaken in her, her lips parted, her cheeks flushed, her body trembling. She began to writhe in delight and he flung his body across her, forcing her legs open. Then she cried out but now his passion was beyond any control and he sank into her. Looking into those appealing green eyes, he felt as though he were descending into a cool, green sea, enveloped in a remote, timeless space.

At that moment, his mind seemed simultaneously to carry images of the altar in the chapel, Father Pierre's flowing white hair, Frances looking at him coldly in the crowded hall, John climbing down into the boat in the icy Atlantic, Fortescue's red face, the hanging of Granny Lott, the folding hills above Dartmouth, like a drowning man seeing before him the brief, sorrowful sequence of his life. But there were other images, too, of a general standing at the mast of his ship, leading his fleet through icebergs and storms; the firing of guns, capture of booty, the sounds of battle, the exhilaration of victory.

They lay in each other's arms, silent, while music drifted up from the hall below.

*　　　*　　　*

Many hours later, after they had shared breakfast with their guests, Cicely and Stephen set forth upon their long journey to Lincoln. Cicely went first to Gilbert's chamber to say that she would pray for him daily; that he must trust in God and the blessed Virgin. Gilbert, lying quietly on his bed, did not reply.

With all the other members of the family dispersed, only her parents were there on the steps of the house, to bid her farewell. She said goodbye to them tearfully, aware of the great distance, the travelling days, that would separate them. Frances betrayed no emotion, but her father took her in his arms and said she would ever be in his thoughts. But as soon as they were on the road, her joy returned at being with the beautiful man beside her. They took the bumpy coast track which Stephen had expected to be shorter than the main route to Exeter. He exclaimed irritably when he found that it was slow and uncomfortable, the hills long and winding. Cicely drew his attention to the beautiful countryside, the cliffs dropping down to the sea, the moorland and heather.

'The joys of rural life are not something in which I share. Pray, awaken me when we reach Exeter,' Stephen said and he rested his head on the velvet headpiece and fell asleep.

Cicely watched him fondly. Perhaps he did not have a strong constitution. He would need much attention and care. She gently took his delicate white hands in her own. The jewelled rings sparkled on his fingers but the most beautiful ring was the sapphire she had given him as a keepsake. Once again, she felt elated that, through her father, she had been able to change Stephen's situation dramatically. Almost overnight, he had become a wealthy man. She thanked the Virgin that it was she who had been instrumental in his good fortune.

When they reached Exeter, the solicitude he had previously afforded her returned. He was full of concern and apology that, on their nuptial night, they could not share the same bedchamber. It was too small and unsuitable.

'It is better', Cicely said, 'that such a solemn occasion is deferred until we are in more propitious circumstances.'

'In six nights, we shall be resting at Theobalds.'

'That is a palace. By what means do we remain there?'

Stephen smiled. 'It is by the King's dispensation. He has some regard for me.'

'Then we are fortunate.' Cicely spoke thankfully.

Stephen nodded and walked to the door. 'Tomorrow we leave early. Pray rest now.'

Five nights later, having made good time, they reached Theobalds. She knew that the King sometimes stayed here, but was relieved to find only the staff of servants in residence. They all seemed to know Stephen well and greeted him as though he were the master of the house. As such, they treated her also with great deference and consideration. She was taken up to a large, highly decorated chamber. The huge four-poster bed was hung with silk draperies; cream satin covers on the bed matched the rich cream floor coverings.

Her night clothes were laid out neatly on a couch and then she was taken to a small parlour where a table had been set for their evening meal. Stephen had gone to the library, saying that he had a few correspondence matters to attend to, but he arrived very shortly.

'Forgive me, Cicely, for the delay.' He smiled gently. 'The steward has placed us in here, fearing that the great dining hall is somewhat unwelcoming.'

'It is so kind of them, Stephen,' Cicely said, 'and I am

pleased to see you smile again. I fear the journey is very wearisome for you.'

'Yes,' Stephen assented. 'I am unaccustomed to such rigours. But soon we shall be in Lincolnshire. We have perhaps another day only to travel.'

Cicely had little appetite for the great display of food which was now brought to the table. She had only a few stewed oysters, a little of the rabbit pie with marrows, artichokes and raisins and a small gooseberry tart. Stephen ate voraciously and also drank a large quantity of syrup of tobacco, a present, he said, from the king.

Cicely saw that it affected his senses; he became highly excited and then sank slowly into silence. She watched anxiously. No-one in her parental home had partaken of much wine, and tobacco was held to be particularly potent. 'Come, dear husband,' she said, 'let us repair to the bedchamber.'

She helped him gently up the stairs to the bedchamber and pulled back the draperies around the bed. He lay down, fully clothed, and instantly fell into a deep sleep. Cicely watched him anxiously. Was he ill, or was it simply the effect of the syrup? He was breathing normally. Should she remove his clothes? She frowned, hesitating over the intricacy of the laces and ribbons and buttons. And what did a man wear beneath the doublet and pantaloons? She had seen clothes often enough in the wash-house when she had been supervising the servants, but now she could not remember. She turned away. Should she undress herself? She pulled the bell-rope. When a servant appeared, she said, 'Kindly take me to another bedchamber. His lordship is sleeping. Please cover him with some bed-linen.'

The servant nodded in understanding. 'I will request the steward,' she said. 'Please follow me, your ladyship.'

Cicely's night attire was carried along the corridor to an adjacent chamber.

She was brusquely awakened in the first light of dawn by Stephen, who burst into her room, trembling with anger.

'Why', he demanded, 'are you in this chamber? Why did you leave me?'

'Stephen,' Cicely said in horror, 'I did not leave you. I thought only of you, you . . .'

'Me! Do you make me look a fool, rejected by his wife?'

'Forgive me. You were sleeping.'

'Sleeping! Is that a reason for your going to another room? Am I to be reckoned incapable, stupid, spurned by my wife of a few days?'

'Stephen, I meant nothing.' Cicely burst into tears, clutching helplessly at his arm. He pushed her away.

'Leaving me to be undressed by the steward! As though I were some uncouth, drunken young nincompoop.'

Cicely fell on her knees, clutching his legs desperately. 'No! Forgive me. I meant nothing. They cannot think that.'

'Dress yourself. We shall leave immediately,' and Stephen hurried from the room.

He sat in irritated silence for the remainder of their journey while Cicely wept and protested. When they reached Hewell Grange, he alighted from the carriage and offered her his hand.

'Kindly compose yourself and at least behave correctly in my home,' he said coldly.

Cicely followed him across the courtyard and walked with dignity through the row of servants lined up to receive them, smiling at them distantly. Then she entered her new home. Stephen escorted her to her chamber and said that the midday meal would be partaken of in half an hour.

'Let us forget this unfortunate event,' he said. 'I hope you may be happy in your new abode.'

Cicely flung her arms round his neck and kissed him.

'Oh, you are my dear husband. May I bring you happiness, also.'

Stephen kissed her lightly and then disengaged her arms.

'I am sure that will be so. Now I must speak briefly with the steward.'

They sat one at each end of the long dining table. Stephen seemed to have quite recovered from her absurd error; her own folly now seemed to her incomprehensible, she had acted in a truly insensitive fashion. At least, she would never make such a mistake again.

She looked round the dining hall; new draperies were needed and there seemed to be insufficient tableware, too few bowls and plates.

'Now that I am here,' she said, 'I will see to the furnishings. We must purchase curtains, a new bureau is needed, a side cupboard for the food.'

Stephen frowned. 'We must not incur too many financial obligations.'

Cicely smiled. 'Ah, but now that you have my portion, it will be possible to . . .'

'Cicely, I trust that you will not constantly remind me that the betterment of my life is dependent upon you.'

'Oh, Stephen, that is not my intention!'

'Then perhaps I may have some say in my financial affairs.'

'I do not wish . . . I merely want to help you.'

'Then I must tell you that currently I have many commitments. We must use some caution.'

'Of course. It is as you wish. But I am sure Papa . . .'

'I do not wish to be constantly beholden to your father, either.' Then he added more gently, 'Unless, of course, it is quite necessary.'

Cicely looked at him with affection. She knew that, although in the past she had expected otherwise, it was not her father's wealth but Stephen's love for her that was the basis of their marriage. It was an unexpected joy.

'I know my fortune is only a detail, dear Stephen.'

'Today, we will inspect the house. You will meet all the servants. And you are not familiar with all the rooms. Let us go together.'

He offered her his hand and they inspected the servants' quarters, the kitchens and laundry, the upstairs chambers and parlours, Stephen's bedchamber and her own adjacent one, the small library and the public rooms.

'It is strange to think I am now mistress of all this.'

'Perhaps,' Stephen said slowly, 'you may be permitted to enhance the dining hall. I think we can possibly afford that.'

'It is as you wish,' Cicely said with delight. 'Tomorrow, I will start to plan. I will be very circumspect.'

'Unfortunately, tomorrow I must go to London.'

'Oh! So soon. I had not expected.'

'I have been away for many days because of our marriage. I cannot delay now that we are returned.'

'No. Of course not.'

That evening, Cicely retired early to her chamber and changed into the gown which had been made for her wedding night. She knew that it was her duty somehow to help Stephen overcome his shyness.

When he did not appear, she crept along the corridor to his chamber. He was not yet there. She returned to her bed intending to wait till she heard him retire. But she fell asleep and when she opened her eyes, the sun was casting shafts of light through the curtains.

She rang the bell and Mary, her new personal maid, appeared.

'I think I slept long,' Cicely said. 'What hour is it?'

'Almost noon, madam. It was a long journey.'

'Yes. Has the master risen?'

'Yes. He has departed, madam, at an early hour.'

'Departed!'

'He left a message that you must not be disturbed. That he has had to repair to the capital but would return in a few days.'

'A few days!'

Mary nodded her head in a matter-of-fact fashion.

'Does madam wish to dress?'

'Just put out a gown. I will ring if I need you.'

'Shall the midday meal be at noon?'

'Yes, if that is the usual practice. Leave me now.'

Mary nodded politely and left the room.

Cicely stepped from her bed and sat at the table by the window, her face cupped in her hands. She realized at last that Stephen's behaviour had nothing to do with shyness. She had a cold feeling in her heart. It was actually there, where it beat under her small breasts, that she felt a pain that told her that Stephen did not love her at all, that perhaps he never had.

She began to remember incidents that she had ignored at the time. All those occasions when he had failed to arrive as promised; periods of gloom and depression when he seemed to find her presence unwelcome and tiresome. Cruel remarks he had made about her plainness, then laughing them off as his own sense of humour. His sudden, heightened interest and attentiveness when he had discovered how truly wealthy her father was. Yet she still could not understand his behaviour. If only she had some greater knowledge of the world, of men. If only she could talk to someone, Katherine, even her mother. There was nowhere to turn, no-one here who could help her. Yet why would he have pretended, made all those professions of love? Was it for her portion? But there had been no need for those extravagant gestures, those wild protestations.

Had they been true, had he been sincere? Had she in some unknowable way destroyed those feelings, by her words, her actions?

For the next two days she scarcely left her room, alternating between feelings of inertia and anguish. Mary brought her meals to the little sitting room adjacent to her chamber and forecast that soon madam would settle down and forget her family. When the master returned the colour would return to her cheeks. And, indeed, when she saw his coach coming slowly up the drive, she could not conceal her joy. Mary hastily dressed her hair and suggested she should change into one of her new silk gowns, and then she rushed down the stairs to greet him. Stephen looked surprised at her smiling face and welcoming kiss.

'I feared you might be perplexed at my absence,' he said, smiling doubtfully. 'That perhaps I might expect wifely remonstrations.'

'It is so good to see you,' she said feelingly. 'I have been quite desolate.'

Stephen put an arm round her. 'Come. Let us partake of our meal.'

'What did you in London?'

'I have spent some time with the King. He is much pleased with my work.'

'It is well,' Cicely said admiringly.

'I shall get preferment, dear one. I now perform much law work for him. Perhaps we shall not need your father's assistance.' He smiled.

Cicely felt that he had forgiven her for her conduct.

Instead of sitting at the end of the dining table, he sat this time beside her. When Cicely ate voraciously, Stephen laughed.

'I have had but little appetite in your absence,' she said.

'You must not fret over me, dear one. I must frequently be at court and in London. I cannot ignore the demands of my legal profession.'

'No.' Cicely could not conceal her thoughts. 'But I feared you were no longer pleased with me. That perhaps you did not love me.'

'Are you to suppose that, every time I depart for the city?'

Cicely smiled uncertainly. 'I feared that, perhaps, you did not wish to consummate our marriage. It is, I believe, a sacrament, the joining of two souls in mind – and flesh.'

Stephen smiled quietly and drank the remainder of the wine in his glass. Then he took her arm.

'Come, then, dear wife. Let us waste no more time.'
Then he added enigmatically, 'It was only in London that
I was made to recognize the error of my behaviour.'

Cicely frowned, still feeling mystified by his words, his
actions. But this time, she decided to keep her doubts to
herself. She realized she would have to learn to understand
Stephen, his moods and strange reactions. She knew so
little about men, about the world.

11

When Sarah saw Gilbert after over a year's absence, she
was surprised at his rapid decline. He was standing in
the little study room looking out of the window to the
rose garden below and the evening light cast a shadow
across his face. But she could see that it was more than
shadows which were reflected there. His skin had turned
a pale yellow, there were blue circles under his eyes which
accentuated their size, his lips were as pale as his face and
there was a red spot above his cheek bones as though he
had a permanent temperature. He was very emaciated; a
wasting disease was eating away at his flesh until she could
almost see his bones.

'Gilbert,' she said falteringly, 'I've come back.'

Gilbert did not turn his head. 'I know. Father said you
were coming.' He spoke listlessly but there was still the old
tone of resentment in his voice, the irredeemable self-pity.

'I'm going to give you some new medicines.'

'You just left me,' Gilbert said petulantly. 'It's too
late now.'

'I'll get you some new herbs.'

'They won't work.'

'Do you still do your lessons?'

'When I feel like it. Mama says it is not necessary. Charles has left us, too.'

Sarah looked at him thoughtfully. Death, she knew, was always a frequent visitor but Gilbert was different from the others. Her mother and Granny Lott had fought the intruder, her mother making arrangements for her, giving instructions, making demands to the end. Granny Lott had gone shouting to the gallows. Yet it was Gilbert who disturbed her most with his pathetic acquiesence.

'Let us walk in the garden, Gilbert, while it is yet light.'

She was surprised that he did not argue, as though even that were too much effort now.

They went down to the knot garden and then to the little bower where she used to sit with Katherine. Sarah noticed that his legs were now curved outwards from the knee as though he had received a violent blow. She held his arm and felt the bones jutting from his elbows and the thin, scraggy wrists.

'You must make an effort, Gilbert,' she said firmly. 'And I'll get you some medicine. Come, let us return.'

Suddenly, he turned and looked at her. 'No, Sarah, it's no good.'

Sarah did not reply.

They walked slowly back to the house. Far away in the distance she could see the hills which rose above the estuary and a flock of gulls poised over the farmyard. She was struck again by the great, imposing edifice of this house, its aura of safety and strength and that outer world of freedom and exposure. But, in the end, there was no safety here either. Gilbert would not get better.

But when he had gone quietly to bed, Sarah's whole being reacted against his feeble submission to fate. The very next day, she began to ply him with herbs and potions.

162

He drank mixtures of borage and bugloss with the juice of pippins; she gave him a camomile infusion to induce sleep; he had spoonfuls of syrup of gilliflower and mixtures of hot spices. She gave him rosewater to drink and for his evening meal, a mixture of beaten eggs, comfrey and milk.

For the first time in her life, Sarah became totally involved with another person. She thought of nothing but finding a cure for Gilbert's sickness. She collected sprigs from the hedgerows and identified them from the herbal manuals in the library. She took claret from the wine cellar and cherries from the kitchens and boiled them together. When she found that this mixture had an exhilarating effect on Gilbert she decreed he should drink this liberally morning and evening. It was only when Frances protested that he was simply drunk that she reduced the quantity. But Gabriel remarked sagely that perhaps it was a desirable remedy; laughter and jollity were something Gilbert had not experienced for so long, they could do him no ill.

Frances had treated Sarah with total reserve and disdain after her return. The suspicion she had felt from the day that Gabriel first brought her to the house did not disappear. She had scarcely believed Gabriel's assertion that Sarah intended to care for Gilbert until she perceived Sarah's apparent total devotion to him. Her initial suspicion changed to relief and as the months passed to reluctant gratitude that Sarah had removed this burden from her own shoulders. She found it difficult to deal with the demands of the sick bed; it was beyond her patience to listen to his constant demands and she found the physical aspects of nursing repellent.

Adam's return from Cambridge at Christmas brought a little of the old joy to the now quiet household. He and Sarah greeted each other like bewildered strangers; he found her as beautiful as ever and her old remote attitude had developed into a serene self-confidence. When she was silent now, he felt it was because of certainty, not doubt. Sarah found that the rather priggish, bookish boy of the Merchant Taylor's days had developed into a young Cambridge gentleman, with his auburn curls reaching to his shoulders and with his elegant velvet cape and wide breeches.

'My enjoyment of learning has not decreased,' he said. 'I have merely added enjoyment of life.'

He told her about the balls and festivities he enjoyed at Cambridge, about tennis parties and boating trips and theatrical entertainments, while he strutted up and down the room in demonstration. Sarah would clap her hands, laughing, while Gilbert watched sullenly because Sarah was not concentrating upon his requirements.

He was clearly pleased when Adam departed. His younger brother would not be home again until the summer vacation.

Sarah returned with renewed vigour to her herbal mixtures. She remembered there had been a mixture Granny Lott used to make for fevers. What was it that Granny Lott used to add? Some fresh milk straight from the cow . . . but there had been something else. She lingered along the paths in the gardens, trying to recall. Then she saw a toad crouched amongst the tall grasses, its throat rising and falling, and suddenly she remembered. It wasn't what she put in it. It was the incantation she had used that was important. Sarah closed her eyes and the words came back to her. She ran back to the house and rushed up to Gilbert's room.

'Gilbert. I know what to do.'

Gilbert turned at her excited voice, his pale face reflecting a momentary feeling of hope.

'How do you know?'

'Granny Lott used to sell it at the fairs, a medicine to cure people, but it's the words that went with it that were important.'

She mixed up her herbs in a saucepan, heated them over the log fire and then she put the mixture in a bowl.

'Now, when it's cool, you must drink this and I'll say my prayer.'

Gilbert looked distastefully at the green and yellow shiny substance.

'I can't drink that.'

'You always say that. You know it tastes nice really.'

He held the bowl in his small hands and Sarah said, 'Now, drink it slowly.'

She closed her eyes and raised her arms in the air, her hair falling across her face like a curtain, repeating the incantation. Gilbert sat watching her, his large eyes expressionless.

Then she stopped, looking at him hopefully.

'How do you feel, Gilbert?'

He did not reply.

'But you don't have pain?'

'I rarely have pain,' he said.

For a few days, she repeated the incantation. Then she looked round for a new remedy but as the months passed she began to lose hope.

She had moved to a chamber next to Gilbert's to be close if he needed her. Her nights were increasingly disturbed because she feared that if she slept, she might not hear his call. She became pale and tired and Gabriel reported to her that even Frances had suggested she should go to Katherine's for a few days' rest.

'No,' Sarah said. 'I cannot leave now.'

Now she lay in bed, thinking of Gabriel. Dear Gabriel. She thought once again of those beautiful moments in his arms, of all those exciting feelings, and she had a continuing sense of incredulity that it had happened at all. Her behaviour on that occasion had been prompted by a conversation she had heard amongst the servant girls in the kitchens at Branwell Hall.

'Just take off your clothes,' one of them said, 'and any man's yours.'

Then they exchanged information about things they had

165

done and things that had been done to them. Kissing and touching and licking as well as all sorts of violent actions and strange positions.

She had listened in fascination, amazed that the human body, her body, could offer such strange experiences. Even at that time, her thoughts had turned to Gabriel. Did he do things like that? What would it be like, was it as exciting as these girls said?

Well, they'd been right about taking off your clothes; and they'd been right about the passion that seemed to consume a man. But they hadn't said about the pain and the blood so perhaps that didn't last for ever. And they didn't seem to have known about the lovely, gentle caresses; the soft words, words of love, the peace of lying in his arms. Afterwards, Gabriel had said, 'This mustn't happen again, dear Sarah. But I do not regret it. I love you.' Then, looking into her eyes, 'And you, Sarah?'

'I think I have always loved you, Gabriel.' She laughed with joy. 'You are so beautiful. I wish to be with you for ever.'

'We cannot anticipate God's will,' he said, 'but love can remain in our hearts.'

Now, mingled with that happy memory, was a growing discontent because Gabriel still behaved towards her, as he did everyone, with a certain formality. He gave no secret, intimate signs, made no attempt to find her alone. In fact, she thought, he still treats me as a daughter. When he was not engaged on the estate he was on one of his trips to London and she knew he was planning another foreign journey. She was simply left at home as another member of the family with no special demands upon his attention.

Was he content with that one encounter? Had he simply put her from his mind? Had he really meant that love could remain in his heart? Would he be satisfied with that?

And what were her feelings? He knew it had been the truth when she said she loved him. But what did that mean? Was love just that wild excitement, the thrill of his body, the passion he felt for her? Was her love for him any deeper than that which she felt for poor little Gilbert or even for Katherine? Or that which she felt for Adam? Or was it simply that the certainty of Gabriel's love seemed to remove the fear that one day she might be turned away from this house, that she might have to leave Vinelands?

Then, another night, turning restlessly in her bed, she began to wonder if Gabriel went to Frances's bedchamber at night. After all, she was his wife. Did he make love to Frances as he had to her? She had never even thought about it before and the idea suddenly filled her with a wild jealousy that perhaps at this very moment she was in his arms.

She sprang out of bed. If she went along to his bedchamber she would know. When she returned to Vinelands, she had found that Frances had moved to a chamber at the other end of the house. But perhaps Gabriel went to her there.

She pulled a robe around her and then stopped. What about Gilbert? Supposing he needed her. She hesitated. It would take only a few minutes.

She crept along the corridor to his chamber, gently opened the door and went in. The moon cast a pale light across the curtains around the bed. Silently, she pulled the drapery back a little. The bed was empty. She almost cried out, feeling a violent anger and desolation. Then she ran quietly along the corridors to Frances's chamber. She listened outside; there was no sound. She could scarcely bear to peep through as she opened the door but there was Frances, sleeping peacefully, alone. After looking into Gilbert's chamber to see that he was all right, she sat down on her bed, wondering now where Gabriel could be. Suspicion began to grow in her mind. Was that isolated experience with her merely a recurring event with him? Was he at this moment in some other bed? She crept out again into the corridor and along to the library. When she opened the door, he was sitting before his desk, reading a document.

'Sarah!' He sprang up anxiously. 'Is it Gilbert?'

'No, dear,' she said quietly. 'It's you.'

'What is it, Sarah?' he asked, looking at her distraught expression.

'Gabriel, do you make love to Frances?'

'Sarah!' He looked so astonished at the question that she said defensively, 'I have a right to ask.'

'It is not a question of right, Sarah. You must not occupy yourself with such matters.'

'Do you?' she shouted, ignoring his words.

He came over to her and rested his hands on her shoulders.

'No,' he said.

'Because of me?'

'No, Sarah. Not because of you. It is some years since we shared a marriage bed.'

'Why?'

'After Adam's birth, the physician said that any further pregnancy would be highly dangerous to Frances.'

Sarah remembered other conversations amongst the servants at Branwell Hall, how repeated childbirth made marital intimacy unwelcome. 'You might find all that romping desirable now,' one of the older women had said to them, 'but one day you'll be glad enough when he finds some trollop and leaves you alone.'

'And what do you do?' Sarah said.

Gabriel looked at her silently, knowing her suspicions.

'Nothing,' he said. Then he sighed. 'Sarah, what happened between us has nothing to do with all that. Although it was a sin, it was because of my love for you.'

Sarah put her arms round his neck.

'Then no-one suffers because of it. We can . . .'

'Sarah,' Gabriel interrupted, but she opened his robe and pulled him down to the couch.

'Last time', she whispered, moving her hands over his body, 'it was a painful experience for me. Perhaps this time.'

She kissed him, stroking his hair, her hands caressing his neck. Gabriel shuddered with the joy of feeling her body again. He took off her robe and nightdress and kissed her breasts. He felt all over her body in a wild ecstasy and now she began timidly to touch him, embrace him, until she, too, was gasping with delight, until tears of passion were running down her face.

'Oh, it's lovely,' she said at last. 'Go on.'

They lay, locked together, until light began to appear in the sky. Sarah opened her eyes. 'This cannot be a sin,' she murmured. 'Gabriel is going to belong to me. One day.'

Gilbert was still sleeping quietly when she returned to her chamber.

*   *   *

Word came that Cicely was pregnant and in the autumn Katherine announced that she was expecting her second child.

Gabriel commissioned Nicholas Hilliard to make a miniature of Gilbert; and Sarah, too had her portrait painted. She was seated at a virginal, wearing a blue gown richly decorated with jewels and around her white neck she wore the diamond necklace which Katherine had given her. The portrait was hung in the library by the side of those of Frances and Gabriel.

In that autumn Gabriel made a trip to the West Indies and, when he returned in the new year, it seemed that Gilbert had wasted almost to a shadow.

He commented upon this to Frances, saying she must prepare herself.

'I have already commended him to our dear Lady.'

Gabriel knew that she had already distanced herself from Gilbert, perhaps to save herself the pain of the inevitable.

'It cannot be long.'

'We have to thank Sarah that he has been preserved so

long,' she said quietly and then said as though she were forcing the words from her mouth, 'I was mistaken about her. She has been marvellously devoted.'

'Yes. But you have behaved with much dignity. It was not easy for you. Let us visit him now.'

When they entered the room, Sarah was pointing out to him the first early spring flowers pushing up in the garden below.

'Sarah,' Gabriel said. 'Pray take some fresh air yourself. I will talk with Gilbert for a while.'

Frances greeted him briefly and then with Sarah left the chamber. Gabriel sat beside the boy and took his hand. 'Are you comfortable, Gilbert?'

'Yes, Papa. I would that I could have gone with you on your voyage.'

'Shall I tell you of it?'

'No, Papa. I wish to hear of the Newfoundland journeys.'

He had heard Gabriel's tales of adventure many times, but he never tired of hearing about the Indians and the wild animals, the black bears and lynx, the reindeers and caribou. He knew about the moose, eagles and hawks and the horned larks and about the Innuits with their dog sledges and skin boats, their sealskin tents and trousers; their deerskin shirts and hoods and their stone igloos covered with moss and backed up with snow that could house forty or fifty people.

But today he wanted to hear once again about Gabriel's first journey with Davis when he was but a boy.

'We were looking for a route to China and India. We sailed out of Dartmouth harbour in June on a vessel called Sunshine and as we passed St Petrox I remember your grandfather standing there, waving proudly. About six weeks after leaving England we were approaching the coast of Greenland when we heard a terrible noise like a great lion roaring. When we checked the depth of the ocean we reached to three hundred fathoms but still it was deeper than that.'

Gabriel glanced at Gilbert. He had slipped down in his bed and was sleeping quietly. He pulled up the bedcover and crept from the chamber.

When Sarah returned, Gilbert awakened.

'Sarah, soon I am going on a journey, like Father went across the Atlantic Ocean.'

Sarah put an arm around him. 'Do not speak so, dear.'

'I wish you could come with me, Sarah.'

Sarah hugged him closer, tears running down her cheeks.

'Do you think it will be cold, like the icebergs, where I am going?'

'No. No. There you will not be ill, Gilbert. And one day, I will be with you again.'

She tried to imagine what that world would be like but all she could feel was anguish that this fragile body was being taken from her.

'Let us lie down together, dear,' she said in a choking voice. He moved over. She lay beside him on the bed.

'Don't weep, Sarah. I've been so happy with you.'

He rested his head on her breast and quietly entered his final sleep.

The little body was embalmed and laid out in a coffin in the Great Hall. There it was inspected by all the gentry and nobility from miles around and then by the citizens of Dartmouth, who filed silently past the coffin to pay their respects. The whole house was draped in black and two weeks later, on the night before the funeral, a memorial service for the family was conducted by Father Pierre in the little chapel.

The funeral itself was to be at St Petrox where Gilbert had requested to be interred. Sarah had taken him there one day before he was too ill to walk and they had gone over to the castle and watched the waves breaking against the rocks jutting out of the sea.

The family collected in the Great Hall. Cicely had journeyed south from Lincoln for the funeral and Katherine and William were staying at the house. Frances had covered her head with a black veil and Cicely stood beside her, swathed in a voluminous black gown, her hands moving restlessly, adjusting her cloak. Then they collected in the courtyard and the coaches lined up for the journey to St Petrox.

Sarah was wearing a black gown with a black shawl draped over her shoulders. Her golden hair was tied back with a black ribbon and above this was a black veil.

The coffin was placed on an open carriage and the cortege began to move slowly down the drive to the priory gates. As they went down into Dartmouth, the streets were lined with spectators.

The procession trundled through the narrow streets to the church. The stewards tried to maintain the correct order of precedence for the coaches, and as they alighted Gabriel observed the rustling of skirts, adjusting of hats, the running hither and thither of servants in the cold February air, contrasted with the real solemnity of the situation.

When they reached the church door, the vicar came forward to greet Gabriel. Gabriel noticed that he was quite sober on this occasion, more out of fear of the consequences than deference to the dead.

The church was crowded with the local gentry who would be returning after the funeral to the feast at Vinelands. The church was draped in black from the rafters to the stone floor so that no walls could be seen. As the breeze came through the open door, the huge drapes moved like billowing sails, as though the church were a ghostly vessel on its journey of death. Gabriel followed the family down the aisle to the front rows and the long funeral service began.

He stood beside Frances, who was wearing the stoical expression of someone who intended to conceal her emotions, not to succumb to the sorrow within her. But it was probably Sarah who was most disturbed by the event.

It was only when the music began that people reacted,

such was the strange effect that music had on the emotions. Then he noticed that Sarah was not with them and realized that she was standing on the other side of the aisle, near the coffin. She was staring fixedly at it, as though she were willing Gilbert to come alive again.

She looked up suddenly, feeling Gabriel's eyes on her, and smiled at him bleakly. He looked away and when he glanced again, she was listening attentively to the vicar's words.

'This child, taken into the arms of our Lord, where there will be no more suffering.'

Then the procession moved out from the church, back along the lane to the burial place. The coffin was lowered into the ground, Gabriel cast earth upon it and the family began to move slowly away, back along the little church path to the waiting coaches. Immediately, they all began to talk again, softly, as though the tiresome event over, they could begin to get back to normal.

It was only then that Gabriel allowed himself to think about Gilbert, the brief, unhappy life that was now lost for ever. He could let them talk and no-one would notice that he was not participating.

He thought about Gilbert as a child, running in the gardens in the front of the house, but always slower than the others, always more prone to falling over, being stung by bees, always complaining that he had been hurt, knocked, didn't feel well. He felt suddenly an overwhelming sorrow for that lost and lonely child, a guilt that he had paid so little attention to his needs.

He knew an overwhelming sense of loss. Gilbert's hold on life had seemed so fragile, as though he had scarcely even existed. But he remembered one particular incident, when he had watched, through a window, Gilbert and Sarah in the garden. They were walking along in the sun, it was a hot day, and he could smell the roses and herbs on the floor where they were always scattered in greater profusion in the hot weather. Although he could not hear

173

it, he imagined the sound of the sea beating against the rocks at the Castle, the entrance to the harbour. Sarah had started to run, and turned to Gilbert to encourage him to follow her. He saw Gilbert try to run after her and watched the spindly legs move forward and then stop, as though they could not propel him. Gabriel felt irritated with Sarah, at her asking Gilbert to do something which she knew he was incapable of doing, as though drawing attention to his infirmity. Then he watched her walk slowly back to Gilbert and put her arm round his shoulders, and they moved towards the seat in the arbour. She had pulled up the legs of his velvet trousers and massaged the calves of his legs, while Gilbert sat in silence.

It was only a few months ago but Gabriel had known then that Gilbert could not survive much longer.

When they reached the gates, their coach went ahead, crossed the drawbridge and stopped in the courtyard. He and Frances stood at the great oak doors, waiting to receive the guests and lead them into the Great Hall.

He had little taste for this kind of thing. He realized that he was in a minority in this age because he treated his home as a private residence for his family rather than regarding it as predominantly a setting for social occasions.

But it was also necessary to conform, to ensure that there were no grounds for accusing him of unkind or arrogant behaviour. He acknowledged all the guests as they arrived, Frances's brother Charles, her sisters, his own brothers, even Francis Carew and his family although he had seen little of them of late, the Fortescues. Then he noticed the coach of Sir Nicholas Maddick, a particularly spectacular model with gold silk curtains. Sir Nicholas was a wealthy landowner whose estate lay to the north of Dartmouth, encompassing great acreage south of Dartmoor; his family were wool merchants of high reputation.

He was a tall, overweight man in his thirties. His tunic and cloak were made of heavy black silk, the only colour being in the gold clocks which adorned the sides of his stockings. He had obviously ensured that everything was correct. He bowed to Gabriel and expressed his condolences. Gabriel nodded in acknowledgment.

'It was inevitable,' he said, 'although I think we have Sarah to thank that he lived so long.'

'How so?'

'She has cared for him for the past year or so. Tried to find cures.' Gabriel looked straight at him. He was determined that everyone should acknowledge her existence, he felt compelled always to issue this challenge, to confront people with it, so that he could assess their attitude.

Sir Nicholas said, 'I haven't met your Sarah. Perhaps I could have the opportunity today.'

Gabriel smiled. 'She's only a child,' he said.

'I understand that she is almost eighteen and very becoming.'

'Yes.'

'Perhaps more than a child,' Sir Nicholas said lightly.

Gabriel turned towards Sarah.

'I'll introduce you,' he said curtly to Sir Nicholas.

He sighed, feeling a new burden upon him. This was a problem that he could scarcely bear to contemplate. Of course people would want to meet her. Unmarried men like Sir Nicholas could hardly fail to want to meet her. She would be pursued by suitors and in the eyes of the world it was his responsibility to see that she married as well as possible. Yet now, how could he face such an event?

Those two occasions of love-making had been so disturbing to him that he had not attempted either to justify them or even assimilate them into his conscious thoughts. Temporarily, he had felt it was something beyond his control. His relationships had always been not perhaps secondary but separate from his public life. The sea, his voyages, the estate had assumed the reason for his existence; his private life was his religion, his Catholic faith, his duty to his God. Somewhere between the two, his family occupied an assured and permanent place in his

175

thoughts and affections, but never obtrusively so. Although he knew his concern for Sarah had gone beyond those rational bounds, he was still determined that his passion should be controlled, his lustful behaviour not repeated. But now the thought of her marriage to another seemed to lay waste all else in his life, his fame and fortune a mockery.

He called Sarah over. She walked slowly towards them. The velvet bow which had tied back her hair had slipped off and her hair now fell across her shoulders in long ringlets. She had removed her cloak because she had been standing before the blazing log fire at the other end of the hall. She had flung a black lace shawl over her bare shoulders.

'Sir, this is my adoptive daughter, Sarah. Sarah, this is Sir Nicholas Maddick. I don't think you have met.'

Sarah curtsied and smiled. Sir Nicholas took her hand and looked admiringly into her green eyes.

'I hope we shall meet many times,' he said.

Gabriel looked at the red, round face, at the thick lips moving loosely as he spoke.

Frances came up behind her and said sweetly, 'I'm sure Sarah would be pleased to offer you her company.'

Sarah glanced coolly at Gabriel and said, 'I don't know if Sir Nicholas and I would have much in common.'

'How could that be possible? I'm sure I would find your company most gratifying.' Then he added to Gabriel, 'Perhaps I could call. Take her to the entertainments next week.'

'I'm afraid no-one will be going to entertainments next week,' Gabriel said shortly. 'We are all in mourning.'

'Of course. I forgot.' Sir Nicholas blushed at his blunder. 'Perhaps I might just visit.'

'With Sarah's agreement.' Gabriel began to walk away to attend to his other guests when he saw what seemed a familiar figure standing at the doors of the Great Hall. He stared uncertainly, frowning and blinking in disbelief. It was John. His heart beat more quickly. He looked

176

taller and it was difficult to see his face under his black wide-brimmed hat curving up around the brim. Was it really him? Gabriel felt a surge of happiness, an elation that at this moment of loss another greater joy could come. He could see from the tight-fitting leather boots, reaching to his thighs, that John had acquired more manly proportions. He noted also that his black silk doublet had the fashionable wide sleeves and the short white ruff had clearly been starched.

Gabriel strode hastily across the hall, trembling with excitement.

'John, even in this time of sorrow, it is a great joy that you have come.' He flung his arms around him and embraced him and then turned, looking around the assembled guests. 'Frances, where is Lady Frances? Oh, John, we have long prayed for this day.'

Frances emerged from the crowd and ran excitedly towards him and tearfully clasped John to her bosom. There were great shouts and glasses were raised as the guests offered congratulations to John and Gabriel and a silver tankard was put into John's hand. He did not speak, but embraced his mother and raised his tankard to his father, smiling. When the guests had returned to their feasting Gabriel said again, 'Ah, son, how good it is to see you. It has been a sorry time without you. And how fare you?'

John did not reply but a man beside him, who appeared to be his companion, said to Gabriel, 'Sir, I must reply on John's behalf. He does not have the gift of speech.'

'What mean you, good sir?' Gabriel asked in astonishment.

'Sir, some moons ago he lost that gift which God bestows on most men.'

'Lost! When? How? And who are you?' Gabriel suddenly asked suspiciously. There were many impostors and quacks who tried to persuade innocent victims that they had some sickness which only they could cure.

177

'Sir, I was taken into your son's employment when the affliction descended upon him.'

Gabriel looked at John.

'What is this affliction, John? How is this possible? Pray, attempt to address me.'

John moved his lips but no sound emerged. His companion stared intently at his face.

'He says he would willingly speak with you if he were able,' he finally explained when John had finished.

Frances put a hand on John's arm. She had recovered her normal composure but now she looked at him anxiously.

'John, when did this happen?'

Gabriel scarcely waited for the reply. He knew what the answer would be. Was John pretending this, to exact some ghastly revenge for events in the Atlantic, or was it the hand of God, was it a punishment for his own arrogance and inhumanity?

'He has merely informed me that it occurred after an unnatural exposure to the elements,' the young man said.

Gabriel saw the stony expression on Frances's face but John displayed no anger or animosity.

'This cannot be,' Gabriel said. 'We will repair to London. Surgeons, physicians will understand such sickness. It will be cured.'

Gabriel did not see, in his preoccupation, Sarah sitting with Sir Jonathon Fortescue at the other end of the hall, engaged in a heated conversation.

12

A bitterly cold wind blew in from the sea as Gabriel descended the steep cliff road into Dover. It had been a long, slow journey, returning Cicely, pregnant and anxious, to her home in Lincoln after the funeral and then coming across country to this desolate place. These eastern ports were known for their lack of hospitality and Gabriel had no wish to linger here longer than necessary. But it was only early evening. The boat could not beach until dark and in the meantime Joseph must attend to the horses for the return journey while he must find the exact location of the boat's arrival further along the coast.

As they rounded the bend at the foot of the hill, Joseph halted the coach. A rowdy crowd was gathered in the square, shouting in delight. Gabriel stood up in the coach. A large bundle, sewn up in a bearskin, had been tossed into the centre of the square. A pack of mongrels were yapping excitedly as they tore and bit at the bundle. Gabriel thought at first that it was an organized dogfight, popular in some parts of the country, because the animals constantly turned on each other in their efforts to get to the sack. But the crowd were inciting the dogs to get at the contents, not at each other, to maul it, savage it.

Finally they ripped open the skin. The torn and bloody head of a man appeared, his arms trying to shield his white face. The crowd shouted even more vociferously, a man dashed forward and kicked the body violently. But he withdrew hastily as the animals turned on him for interfering with their sport. They growled with excitement and tore even more viciously at the sack until it disintegrated. The victim's shouts were silenced. He was bitten to death.

'In God's name,' Gabriel shouted. 'What is this? Where is the law in this God-forsaken place?'

A man standing near the coach said cheerfully, 'It's all right, your lordship.' He winked at Gabriel. 'The magistrates know what's up.'

'What is it?'

'One of them heretics, sir. Some popish priest, landed in a boat.' He laughed. 'That's what they all deserve.' He walked away towards the centre of the entertainment.

Gabriel felt sick with horror. The boat must have arrived early, been forced in by the gale. These Kentish ports had an evil reputation for their brutality to Catholics; the man would have been arrested instantly. This was their idea of summary justice.

'Perhaps, sir, we should depart with all haste.' Joseph was at his side. Gabriel knew that Joseph feared that he would draw his sword and attack the crowd. He did not reply but climbed back into the coach. Joseph turned the horses and they climbed slowly back up the hill. Gabriel looked gloomily out across the cliffs. There was nothing to be done. For the Catholics, life was permanently dangerous and unfulfilled. He had come to wonder recently whether the continuing importation of priests from France was advisable. They went to Douai, trained in seminaries, frequently donating their own inheritance to the monasteries on the Continent, only too often to be arrested the instant they reached English soil. Or they lived permanently in hiding, in fear, poverty, but to what end? There were reputed to be about fifty Jesuits in England now, was their sacrifice too great, was it a pointless suffering? He knew that they were willing to proclaim their faith in this way, to hear witness, but was there a sufficient reason for their refusing the oath of allegiance?

Furthermore, there was the state of the country itself.

The King's behaviour did nothing to stabilize the country. Although Salisbury had done little, after his elevation to the Lords, to solve the problems between the King and the Commons, since his death a couple of years ago the situation had deteriorated even further.

James had then come to rely more and more on the advice of the Howard family and his minion, the Earl of Somerset. He had not summoned Parliament for four years and now that he had, they were still as adamant about refusing the monies he demanded. In his anger, James said Parliament was addled and recently he had sent four members of the Commons to the Tower. Of course, such behaviour could only cause further resentment, yet Gabriel felt that in his own way, James was attempting to bring about an amicable solution. Unfortunately, his intelligence was inhibited by his personality, his human weaknesses.

Now he appeared to be attending to people like Ellesmere, and the Earl of Pembroke and Archbishop Abbot, who were all violently opposed to the Catholics. As such they would doubtless try to discourage James's plan to get his son Charles married to a Spanish princess because although she would bring an enormous dowry, she was also a Catholic. Gabriel reflected that it was only a move of that nature that could help the Catholics in this country but there was a faction in the Commons who clearly still preferred the idea of war with Spain.

His thoughts returned to the priests. Their demands upon his time and energy, as well as his protection, were increasing just at the moment when there were many other equally pressing demands. Perhaps at forty-four he was getting old.

No time for speculations of that nature, he thought abruptly. His expansion into new business interests in the silk trade and the broadcloth produced widely in Devon had meant that he had been unable to journey to Newfoundland for the past two seasons. As the two masters he had appointed seemed to do the job equally satisfactorily, he was now turning his attention to developing trade with Russia and along the Baltic coast. His civic duties as Commissioner of the Peace, his attendance at Assizes, his visits to Exeter, had increased with the growth of population in the west. He had bought more land, more manors, and his wealth had probably doubled in the past few years. Although he paid heavy taxes to the crown, gave much money to the poor and had made many donations to schools, there were few people who could equal his wealth. Indeed, his thoughts were prompted, as he knew, by a conversation with Stephen, Cicely's husband. He did not like the man, it was perfectly clear to anyone, except fortunately, it seemed, Cicely, that he was part of that inner group of sycophants for whom James would do anything. His thoughts rested briefly with Cicely. He had found her previous excessive piety unacceptable. She had seemed to wrap her religion in a kind of safe velvet case of small compartments, each one marked Right or Wrong. Sin was sin, virtue always virtue, with no room for tolerance or understanding. Gabriel felt it was merely a mirror of Protestant intolerance. But now she seemed to be mellowing somewhat, her demeanour less acerb. Marriage, it seemed, had forced her to accommodate a world beyond her chapel walls. Stephen had hinted that in view of Gabriel's public service, his contribution to the wealth of the country, the King would be pleased to raise him to the rank of a viscount. 'It would be on the assumption,' Stephen had said, 'that you would not espouse the Catholic cause in public.'

Gabriel had thanked his son-in-law for the information.

'He would also require a gift of perhaps fifty thousand pounds,' Stephen added.

Gabriel smiled. 'I had a notion that there must be some twist to the tale.'

'He is sorely pressed,' Stephen said. 'He gets little sympathy from parliament.'

'So be it,' Gabriel said, 'and have you an interest in the matter?'

Stephen blushed.

'Sir, I would not . . .'

'No. Of course not. It is merely my humour. But do you and Cicely manage satisfactorily?'

'Yes, sir.' But Stephen looked at Gabriel with anticipation.

'I would not care to think you had any anxieties,' Gabriel said.

'No, sir, and I shall, of course, do all I am able to advance your cause. If we may presume upon your discretion.'

That night, when they reached Arundel, Gabriel talked long and earnestly with Thomas Howard, who had received an earldom ten years earlier. There was indeed a compelling reason why the great Catholic families of England should survive – they were the only hope of ensuring that the true faith was not obliterated. If this involved collaborating, making concessions, this was a small price to pay in order to retain the wealth and influence which these families commanded.

Gabriel knew that he could not forsake the priests, could not deny them assistance, but he decided that night that he would undertake no new assignments, that he would take no further unintelligent risks, that in future his greatest help would be financial.

'It is not beyond possibility that you become Lord High Admiral,' Howard said. 'It is essential that we have trustworthy representatives in high places. Conduct your affairs circumspectly, my dear Humphreys.'

By the time he reached Vinelands, Gabriel felt that he had been on a voyage of discovery. He knew that the idea of a viscountcy appealed to him because it represented a different kind of power from that which money and his successful career had engendered. For the first time in his life, there seemed to be a possibility of entering the mainstream of political activity from which, because of

183

his religion, he had always felt himself excluded. God and mammon are not mutually exclusive, he thought. By the position he had attained through his own endeavours, he could serve God and King with equal fervour.

Gabriel gave his news to the family at the evening meal. Frances received his hopes of preferment with indifference, as he expected. Although she was conscious of her dignity as the lady of the manor, her real concern was with her faith. Her duty to her home and family, her affection for her children, were always secondary to her devotion to that higher world and Gabriel suspected she would be willing to make greater sacrifices for the priests than she would for any of them.

John smiled at the information and said, through his companion, that he was pleased at such a possibility. Only Sarah seemed delighted at his news. Her eyes sparkled with delight at the thought that he might become a viscount.

'Now I have business to attend to,' Gabriel said, rising.

He bowed and walked across the dining hall. Afterwards, he remembered the expression on Sarah's face as he left. The same distant look in her eyes which he knew so well, yet this time tinged with an anxiety he had not seen before. But when he turned at the door her face was hidden by her golden hair, just as it had been that first day on Jawbones.

But at that moment his mind was on the letter which had been on his bureau when he returned. A letter from Sir Jonathon Fortescue, requesting his attendance at Branwell Hall at his earliest convenience; to be conducted, with his lordship's indulgence, in secrecy. Gabriel took a horse from the stables and galloped across the fields. The evenings had lengthened, the air was mellow, and he felt exhilarated with the promise of his future progress.

He was taken up to Sir Jonathon's sumptuously furnished apartments. There seemed to be a surfeit of purple silks and red velvets, a harpsichord stood by the side of the marble fireplace, the ceilings were now decorated with plaster ornament, brightly painted, and the walls

184

were covered with the new wood panelling. Clearly, Sir Jonathon had increased in prosperity.

He bowed and indicated a settle.

'I have acquired some excellent brandy, sir.'

Gabriel accepted the glass and a plate of sweetmeats. Sir Jonathon placed himself opposite on a high brocade-padded chair.

'Sir, let us come to the matter instantly. I regret we still have problems with your Sarah.'

Gabriel frowned. 'Sir, I cannot see . . .'

'No. I feared you may not be cognisant of the fact.'

'To what fact do you allude?'

Sir Jonathon stood up. Gabriel realized that beneath the bluff, aggressive exterior there was a real anxiety.

'That creature is resorting to blackmail, sir.'

'Blackmail!' Gabriel felt his anger rising. 'That is surely too strong a word for what may be an admittance of your own responsibility.'

'She demands money. Does she have need?'

'Sir Jonathon, I forbade that. I think you will not hear of this again.'

'Then, sir, I fear you are in error.' He paused. 'She now also seeks more than money.'

'Sir, what do you imply?'

'She now lays claim to part of the estate.'

Gabriel suddenly burst out laughing.

'The situation is without humour, Sir Gabriel.'

'It is merely the absurdity of the situation which provoked the outburst. Clearly, an illegitimate would have no claim. But, Sir Jonathon, if we are to discuss this matter, we must be in possession of the facts. Is she your offspring?'

Sir Jonathon sat down again. 'I know not. It was many moons ago. Yet I fear she carries much conviction.'

'It seems,' Gabriel said, 'that she is in great need of knowing who her father was. I think she is less concerned with yourself than in establishing your paternity.'

'This can only be conjecture. There is no proof.'

'Sir, would it not be possible to make some settlement? Some token.'

'Lady Margaret would not countenance such an event.'

'She need not be aware.'

Sir Jonathon said slowly, 'All my property came through my wife's dower.'

'But that is now yours.'

'Ah, it is tied up in legal limitations, powers of attorney, such an action would be unsafe. I can make few private dispensations.' He poured Gabriel more brandy. 'It is possible, sir, for you to silence the wench.'

'Sir?'

'You are her guardian. Perhaps you should consider what manner of person you have taken in.'

Gabriel frowned.

'Sir?' he said again.

Sir Jonathon looked at him pointedly.

'You could remove such a dangerous creature from your household altogether.'

'Sir Jonathon!'

'She is a witch. She could be committed, tried, burnt if you like. Hanged.'

'How dare you, sir.' Gabriel sprang up. His voice trembled with indignation. 'She is my ward.'

Sir Jonathon did not move. 'I fear her mother, if so she be, was a common whore. I was deceived, as you are, Sir Gabriel.'

'No!'

'She is a whore, a strumpet, like her mother.'

Gabriel strode across the room to the door. 'Sir, I will leave before I do harm to you. Be assured, you will hear no more from Sarah.'

Sir Jonathon stood up. 'Sir Gabriel, if you do not deal with her, I shall myself do so.'

Gabriel turned. 'By what means?'

'She will be arrested as a thief, as a witch, as a common prostitute. I will see that she gets no mercy.'

At his words, Gabriel turned and sprang at him, knocking the glass from his hands.

'No-one will threaten Sarah,' he hissed.

He grabbed Sir Jonathon by the throat and struck a violent blow at his head that sent him reeling across the room. He knocked his head against the settle but Gabriel pursued him and hit him again.

Sir Jonathon fell against the marble fireplace, hitting his head on the iron firedogs. He did not move and uttered not a sound. Gabriel bent down and dragged him by the feet from the heat of the fire. He took the bloody head on his arms.

Instantly, his anger was gone. He looked in anguish at the prostrate figure. It was as though he had suddenly closed a great drawbridge, as though he had locked himself out from his whole past life, shut every gate against himself. He did not touch Sir Jonathon again. Gabriel knew that he was dead. There had been many deaths but he had the cold certainty that this was the only one which would devastate him. All the others had been for self-preservation; this one now put his own life in danger. He stood by the marble fireplace, deciding upon his course of action. A brief idea of escaping to France flashed through his mind but he dismissed it without further thought. Escape was associated only with battle, political situations where you escaped only to fight again. This situation, a result of his own action, would have to be faced. He would ride home, alert Frances, and then surrender himself to the Justices. Without a further glance at Sir Jonathon, he went down the stairs, saddled his horse and rode back across the hills in the darkness.

Anger swept through him again as he remembered Fortescue's words – whore, strumpet, words he had heard first that day on Jawbones. Well, he had settled it then; the brothel-keepers in the town had said 'No.' He knew only that his life was inextricably bound with Sarah's; that somehow there would be a future which was theirs.

Perhaps, now, he thought grimly, only in Heaven. He tried to pin down in his mind all the emotions, fears, doubts, suspicions, that represented Sarah. But all he knew was the totality of his desire, her all-embracing attraction, his all-embracing need. He must see her once more.

He crept up the marble staircase to her chamber. She was waiting for him, sitting by the open window in the darkness, in a white gown, her hair covering her to her waist.

Gabriel told her briefly what had happened.

'It is as it should be,' she said, 'he was a dishonourable man.'

'I fear that will not help me, Sarah. I fear you do not understand.'

Sarah said slowly, 'I understand, Gabriel. I belong here, with you.'

Gabriel shook his head. 'Sarah, we may not meet again. But remember, I have no regret. My thoughts are with you.'

'And mine with you, dear Gabriel.' Then she looked into his eyes. 'It will be all right, Gabriel. You will not be harmed.'

Gabriel sighed. He felt a deep and bitter pain that she appeared to have no appreciation of the danger in which he had placed himself on her behalf. No anxiety about the outcome. Yet, he could not concern her with the truth of his situation; she was too naive, too inexperienced to know about the dangers, the ultimate cruelties of that world beyond.

'Gabriel,' she said. 'Whenever anything bad happens, I always have a strange feeling.'

He looked at her, suddenly feeling exhausted.

'I always feel some power inside me that is greater than the event,' she went on.

The thought passed through his mind that she had not been able to save Gilbert, but he only said, 'I do not fear the consequences, Sarah. I fear only for you.'

He took her into his arms. 'It may be a long time, Sarah.'

Only then did she seem to realize the situation. She unfastened his doublet with trembling fingers, kissing his neck.

'Oh, Gabriel, I could not live without you.'

He removed his clothes and lay with her in his arms.

'Let us think of nothing,' he said. 'We cannot know the future.'

After they had dressed again, he went slowly along the corridor to Frances and then he sent for the magistrates.

13

Early on a June morning Gabriel stood with the Lieutenant of the Tower outside the side entrance into Westminster Hall. Although he was not a peer, his trial had been transferred to Westminster because of the importance of his position in society and the fact that he was a deputy lieutenant of the county of Devon.

After over six silent months of confinement in the Tower, the hubbub emanating from the throng inside momentarily bewildered him. Then the Sergeant at Arms shouted, 'Oyez. My Lord High Steward of England proposes this day to the trial of Gabriel Humphreys, Commissioner of the Peace, Deputy Lieutenant of the County of Devon. Any who have indictments in this case, now publicly give them in.'

Gabriel watched through the open door as the Lord Chief Justice passed the parchment sheet to the High

Steward. Then silence fell as the Sergeant Cryer shouted, 'Oyez. I call for those members of the jury who have been warned to be here this day.'

Gabriel looked round at the spectators, many of the peers of England who were to attend his trial. Bossiney, Courtenay, Petheridge, Darcy, Killigrew, Holland, Bonnalack, Carey . . . Then the Lord High Steward commanded, 'Bring the prisoner to the Bar' and Gabriel bowed to the High Steward and the jury as he was led in to his position behind the lawyers. He listened as though from a great distance as the High Steward, in his raised seat in a gallery above the jury who were ranged on either side of him, explained the purpose of the proceedings.

'That you, Gabriel Hooper Humphreys, stand indicted of wilful murder and that this jury shall decide upon your guilt or innocence. Hold up your hand. Do you plead guilty or not guilty?'

Gabriel raised his hand and said in an indifferent tone, 'Not guilty.'

He listened while the Attorney General, seated at the lower end of the Hall with the King's Counsel, then read the long indictment. 'That the prisoner, Gabriel Hooper Humphreys, did on the 12 December 1614 wilfully murder Sir Jonathon Fortescue at his home at Branwell Hall by a violent and vicious attack on an unarmed man; an unprovoked attack; then callously leaving him to bleed to death, to die in agony. Evidence will be given . . .'

At this point, Gabriel ceased to listen. For months, he had been subjected to questioning and investigation. Under oath, he had been direct and unequivocal in his statements, but apart from the inconveniences of a damp, stone cell and the constant company of rats, he had been subjected to none of the refined tortures normally meted out in the Tower to prisoners. He knew that it was all those written examinations, taken in secret, which would establish his guilt. Because only the incriminating parts would be read in court and the jury of his peers would have been chosen with the certain knowledge of what their verdict had to be. Later, it was only the Crown which would publish its own account of the trial, omitting anything which might have been in his favour.

Gabriel raised his eyes for the first time to study those around him. The peers, in their high hats and silk robes, were talking quietly amongst themselves, as though the event were of little importance. In a row below them, the judges sat in their scarlet robes and collars; two of them were already asleep. Near the High Steward, an usher sat with his long white rod, with what seemed like a whole regiment of sergeants at arms behind him.

The Attorney General was saying, 'May it please Your Grace, my Lord High Steward of England and you my lords the peers, to hear now the examinations made by the prisoner', and Gabriel listened to abbreviated extracts from his statements and items from letters he had written and then long excerpts from his diary.

He had always known that the true object of his trial was not simply to find him guilty of murder but to answer to the more heinous accusations of his Catholicism and aiding popishness. His secret diary, containing information about the concealment of priests, was sufficiently damning evidence against him. There was no need for the court to manipulate the examinations; there was scarcely need for a trial, the diary would establish his guilt. Yet he knew there would still be false witnesses brought to court to testify against him, a fervent display of rectitude and indignation against a treacherous and despicable traitor.

Gabriel wondered why men in power needed to give the semblance of truth and legality to all their deceptions. Everyone assembled knew that the evidence was either totally false or had been manipulated. Yet they behaved with the propriety and dignity of conviction; as though the observance of ritual somehow changed outright and petty deceit into truth. The truth was that many men resented the fact that although a Catholic, he had found favour with

the King. In the end, it was James who would decide his fate; only his version of the trial would ever be presented to the eyes of men.

There was silence again as the Lord High Steward called imperiously: 'Bring the first witness.'

It was now that the whole assembly settled down to enjoy the amusing display of rhetoric, insinuation, false testimony and, they would hope, intimate and erotic details of private lives. But the first witnesses were merely the domestic staff at Branwell Hall, who falsely alleged they had seen him on the night of the crime and then elaborated their evidence into wild statements about his lunatic and violent behaviour towards them.

But their remarks took him back again to that fatal night. In the darkness and solitude of his rat-infested cell in the Tower, he had re-enacted the event until it had become a drama almost separate from himself. Images of his past life had become merged with the event, as a dying man may in a delirium confuse one happening with another, one moment with another far removed in time.

As the days passed, the images became more and more violent; a murdered man on a dung heap; a child he had seen mangled on a plough; the massacre of the Indians in Newfoundland – events which had made only a fleeting impression at the time. They were mingled with his own recent action; he saw the blood flowing through Fortescue's short golden beard, the glazed, rolling eyes, the crunch of bone.

Then, suddenly, Gabriel was brought back to reality. The Sergeant Cryer called out: 'Charles Smithson' and the tutor was brought into the Hall, swore the oath and stood uncertainly facing the Lord Chief Justice. Gabriel's first thought was that the man had been apprehended and then compelled to make false allegations about his previous master. Either bribed or tortured. But he bore no signs of physical maltreatment and his shabby grey cloak suggested he had received no favours.

As soon as he began to speak, Gabriel knew that neither was the case and that Charles was contributing his testament voluntarily.

The Lord Chief Justice addressed him with the abrupt disdain he afforded all witnesses.

'Mr Smithson, pray make your statement.'

Charles was pale with fear as he unfolded his document. It consisted of a vituperative list of ills he had suffered at the hands of his master which Gabriel knew would be of no consequence to the judges. They were little concerned with personal grudges and complaints advanced by servants. But he went on to divulge details about the priests hidden at Vinelands; about the secret chapel, about Gabriel's connections with other prominent Catholics. Yet Gabriel knew he could not have been called for this; all this information was too well-known. Charles must have some other dubious evidence. Then, suddenly, his voice rose and he said querulously, 'There was also the witchcraft of his adopted daughter, Sarah.'

A murmur went round the Hall. This was an unexpected contribution. Gabriel felt his muscles tense.

'She made strange mixtures. Cast spells on people. It is my belief she consorted with the Devil.'

'Did you observe this?' the Chief Justice enquired.

'Yes, my lord. She tended the boy Gilbert.'

'The boy who died?'

'She mixed potions for him. It is likely that he was poisoned.'

Gabriel sprang to his feet.

'How dare you, you scoundrel. You lie.'

'Will the prisoner pray be seated,' the Lord High Steward interposed. 'It is for the jury to decide upon the man's testimony.'

Gabriel sat down. He knew that outbursts of that kind were merely intended to give the judge further proof of his guilt. But now Sarah would be implicated also and perhaps other members of his family. Charles went into greater detail about Sarah's activities and was then dismissed.

It was only when, some time later, that the Lord High Steward announced, 'Our final witnesses are members of the Hooper Humphreys family,' that Gabriel sat upright in his seat. What more would they think of? He waited.

The Sergeant Cryer announced 'Mistress Sarah Hooper Humphreys.'

Gabriel wiped a hand across his eyes. There was silence as she walked slowly through the door and was led to her position before the judges. Instead of her usual low-cut gowns she was wearing a plain grey silk dress with a high lace ruff around her neck and her golden hair was tied back with ribbon. A gasp of approval went round the court and the peers muttered amongst themselves.

Then she looked straight at Gabriel, smiled quietly, bowed slightly and said to him, 'Sir Gabriel.'

Gabriel felt a moment of terror that he had never experienced before. Tears came to his eyes; he knew it was not death he feared but being separated for ever from her. Then he stood up, bowed to her and sat down again.

'Mistress Sarah,' the High Steward said sharply, 'you will address only My Lord Chief Justice.'

She acknowledged his remark with a slight inclination of her head and turned to the judges.

'What is your testimony?' the Lord Chief Justice asked.

'My lord, I deal with the matter in hand. I do not detain you with the scandal and gossip presented to you by inferior and impertinent persons.'

'The witness will not comment upon the evidence of other witnesses.'

'There is no need, my lord. There has as yet been no evidence.' She raised her voice slightly. 'Slander and hearsay are not evidence.'

Gabriel watched the jury stir in their seats. After the tedious and drably predictable performances of the previous witnesses, here was someone who promised to provide some real entertainment. They all liked a spirited

194

woman and this beautiful and delicate-looking creature was turning out to be a surprise.

The Lord Chief Justice leaned forward.

'Mistress, proceed with your testimony.' He spoke firmly but his usual contemptuous tone had changed, as though he actually wanted to hear what she was about to say.

Gabriel longed to shout out, to silence her, knowing that anything said in his defence would simply involve her in his crime. He thought of the desolate girl he had picked up on Jawbones five years ago and of the arrogant way, even in her vulnerable state then, in which she had treated him. Watching her now, he felt the same overwhelming desire for her but six months of silence had wrought changes in him. For the first time, he saw her as a person in her own right. He realized that from the moment he met her, she had seemed to be a part of himself, a projection of his own dreams and an object of his desires. Bewildering, provocative, mysterious. Now she stood before him and when she spoke, he was listening to a complete, separate individual.

As she began to speak, Sarah half-turned towards the jury.

'I am come to testify that Sir Gabriel Humphreys cannot be guilty of wilful murder. He merely wished to protect my honour which I know your lordships would commend.'

The Chief Justice interrupted her.

'Madam, where is your evidence?'

'Sir Gabriel was summoned to my father's house, in connection with . . .'

'Your father?'

'Sir Jonathon Fortescue was my father,' Sarah said coolly.

The judges momentarily forgot their alleged role of impartiality and listened expectantly. The jury exclaimed and commented amongst themselves. It was clear that this was a piece of evidence which had not been known of nor manipulated. In his own examinations, Gabriel had not mentioned it, from some incoherent fear that Sarah would become implicated.

'There is no record of this. No intimation,' the Chief Justice said severely. 'By what circumstance do you make such an allegation?'

'By the circumstance, my lord, that he seduced my mother.'

'Proceed, madam.'

Sarah briefly and in a matter-of-fact voice told them her story; the visit to Branwell Hall with her mother; her mother's death; her life with Granny Lott; 'she was hanged as a witch' Sarah commented contemptuously; the generosity of Sir Gabriel in taking her into his home. When one of the jury smiled knowingly at this, Sarah interrupted her testimony to turn on him and say sharply, 'I see, my lord, you would not manifest the same benevolence,' and was severely reprimanded by the Chief Justice.

'Where is your evidence that the murdered man was your father?'

'That I bore an identical birthmark to Sir Jonathon.'

'Madam?'

Sarah glanced briefly round the court and then addressed the jury.

'May it please your lordships.'

She cast off her velvet cloak, neatly unbuttoned the white lace ruff and drew the bodice of her dress down to expose her bare white shoulders. The peers leaned forward expectantly. She paused.

Gabriel knew now the reason for her lace ruff; she had planned this effect.

'You will observe,' she said, pointing, 'upon my left shoulder, a birthmark of an oak leaf.'

It was a small brown mark that he had noticed when she first wore a low-cut gown. Yet it was so small that it had never called forth any comment from any member of the family, though they must at some time have noticed it also.

'What knowledge have you that Sir Jonathon Fortescue bore the same mark upon his shoulder?'

'I observed it,' Sarah said, 'when I tore myself from his advances. He tried to seduce me, also. Me, his offspring. In the struggle, his doublet and blouse were pulled back from his shoulder.'

Once again, judges and jury leaned forward, as though fearful of missing her words.

'Pray, explain,' the Lord Chief Justice said.

Sarah related the incident in a cold, expressionless voice. Gabriel noted that she employed here no feminine guile, no hint of a weak or hysterical female appealing for sympathy. He could see that to the jury it appeared to be a simple relation of an event and as such, they believed her. But he found her evidence distasteful. He equated suspicions about identical birthmarks as absurd as allegations about witches.

'Sir Jonathon accused me of being a whore to conceal his own guilt. It was for this reason that Sir Gabriel defended me. He had no alternative.'

The Lord Justice said quietly, 'How can we know that you speak the truth?'

'There must be members of Sir Jonathon's family who can point to the truth of my observation,' Sarah replied.

The Lord Chief Justice asked if she had more evidence to give and then said sharply, 'You may depart.'

Sarah turned to the jury.

'My lords, I desire mercy for Sir Gabriel Humphreys and that you will intercede for him to the king.'

This time, she did not glance at Gabriel as she walked from the court.

A buzz of conversation and speculation went round the Hall. The Sergeant Cryer called, 'Pray, silence. The Lady Frances Hooper Humphreys.'

Gabriel sighed. The Hall was stifling in the June heat. The day was wearing on; slowly, inexorably, all this evidence would be turned and twisted to prove his guilt.

It was normal enough for a wife to plead in defence of her husband. Would Frances do that or would she wish to take revenge upon him for his involvement with Sarah? He could tell nothing from her composed expression as she took her seat near the judges and read the oath, but he knew it was only her evidence which might produce some element of mitigation or of total condemnation.

'I come only,' she said, 'to ask for mercy for my husband. He has been a great and loyal citizen of this country. He has defended the crown, succoured the poor and acted honourably. He adopted Sarah as an act of charity.' She looked sternly at the Lord Chief Justice. 'I have no complaint.'

'Madam, what of his religious beliefs? Is he not a Catholic supporter?'

'My lord will answer for his own conscience. As we all do before God.'

The jury and the spectators were becoming restless. The evidence of a wife, one way or the other, was of small concern to them. Gabriel feared that perhaps her loyalty might condemn him even more in their eyes. She made a dignified withdrawal, and further evidence was then presented of his association with well-known Catholics and of his conversations with Raleigh over the past six months, the traitor also imprisoned in the Tower.

At last, as darkness began to fall, Gabriel was summoned to make his defence. He rose and looked coldly and imperiously around the Hall. He had worn his raised-heeled shoes deliberately. The silver buckles on his black satin suit sparkled and his black velvet cloak hung elegantly from one shoulder. His beard had grown long in gaol and was neatly combed.

As he began to speak, the flares of hundreds of torches lit the Hall, flickering on the vaulted ceilings, lighting up the faces of judges and peers and casting a black shadow behind Gabriel.

He had almost decided to change his plea to guilty but

some superstitious caution made him continue to behave as though the court would act legally. Results were finally unpredictable, it was always possible that some strange event, some false evidence, might lead to his being found not guilty. But he could think of nothing.

He looked down upon his judges.

'My lords, I treat only with the facts of this case. That Sir Jonathon Fortescue was killed by my hand there is no dispute. I submit that my action was prompted by a desire only to defend the honour of my ward, Sarah. I submit no other defence.'

He paused. The jury moved uncomfortably, fearing he would say no more. Gabriel knew that they would wish for some further evidence on his part so that they might at least appear to have considered his submission. But he went on. 'It is a matter of common knowledge that there can be only one outcome. My fate will depend on the altruism of my lord, King James, after my guilt has been established.'

The Lord Chief Justice interrupted.

'Sir, the sentence cannot be discussed by you. Do you impugn that this court acts not judiciously?'

Gabriel paused. 'Judiciously, perhaps. But immorally.'

There were murmurs of indignation.

'I do not propose to deal with that situation, however. I merely select a few irrelevant items of evidence to establish items of truth. I question the accuracy of Charles Smithson's evidence. As to allegations about my religious beliefs, I am a believer in the Catholic faith. I will testify to no other. This does not impair my loyalty to the sovereign. I have never plotted or schemed against the Crown; I have little interest in political intrigue. I apologize for nothing. I commend myself to your lordships.'

He looked at the jury challengingly and sat down as abruptly as he had risen.

While Gabriel awaited the sentence of his peers, he knew that even now he still harboured hope in his breast. But by the time they returned with their verdict he had already resigned himself.

The Attorney General passed the verdict to the Lord High Steward. Guilty.

The Lord High Steward turned to Gabriel.

'Have you any reason why death should not be pronounced against you?'

Gabriel waved a hand, sweeping the question aside.

Then the Steward took the long white staff from the usher.

'Whereas you have been indicted, arraigned and found guilty, you are therefore to be carried from hence to the Tower and from thence to the place of execution where you are to be hanged till you be dead. And the Lord have mercy upon you.'

Then he broke the staff and the jury stood in silence as the Lieutenant of the Tower led Gabriel away.

He returned to the silence of his cell in the Tower almost with relief. The trial had lasted for fourteen hours but now at least the verdict had been given, his fate settled. There was no indication of when the sentence would be carried out. It might be tomorrow; next week; or he could be left to rot in the Tower for years as Raleigh had been until by some whim of the King his life would be ended. Or remain a prisoner as Arabella Stuart was, had been for four years now, while her husband had escaped. Gabriel had seen her in her solitary walks around the ramparts, frail and lonely.

As the days passed, Gabriel himself began to contemplate methods of escape. Death had no fears for him; he had faced it too often. But to passively await its arrival was totally foreign to his experience. He found it difficult to spend time contemplating a past which was now over or a future in which he would have no part.

Stephen paid one of his visits to say that he was still interceding on his behalf with the King.

'My lord is concerned that in spite of his intention to

raise you to the peerage, he fears you have still much contact with recusants. It much disturbs my lord. He is little concerned with the death of Fortescue.'

Stephen gave him news of Cicely who had been delivered of a son last Christmastide and of Katherine whose second-born had died after only a few months; of Adam's progress at Cambridge and of John's departure to a surgeon in the Low Countries who had developed an iced-water cure for people struck with speech defects. Gabriel listened as though it were news from a foreign country, of people and events in which he now had no part.

But he said, 'I am much indebted to you, Stephen, for your support, your continued allegiance.'

His view of Stephen had changed over the months. This man whom he had looked upon simply as a minion of the King had proved to have qualities which led Gabriel to think that perhaps James was more perspicacious in his choice of associates than he had supposed. It was Stephen who had undertaken to see that, if his estate was not impounded by the King, it would be administered in the manner which Gabriel had stipulated.

Stephen rose from the stone seat and bade farewell.

'Sir, be not disheartened. There are many efforts afoot on your behalf. Do not despair.'

The next morning, Gabriel awoke early as the first rays of the sun penetrated through the grid of his cell. He tapped the grid and the yeoman guard opened the iron door to accompany him for his short walk along the walls to the chapel of St Peter ad Vincula. As he crossed the green, Gabriel felt an air of anticipation and he sat down in the sun, with the conviction that today, here on this spot where executions took place, his fate would be sealed. A great weight seemed to have been lifted from his mind, as though at last all the cares of the world no longer troubled him.

When he returned to his cell, Frances was waiting in silence at the entrance. He embraced her briefly and said instantly, 'You are permitted, I presume, your final visit.'

201

Yet he had heard no sounds of preparation outside, no voices of a gathering crowd. Her sudden presence unnerved him, beckoning him back to that beautiful, sunlit world which, at the end of this day, he would have left for ever.

But another tall figure appeared in the doorway and Sir Nicholas Maddick stood before him. His plump white hands were clutching a document.

'Sir Gabriel, I come from the King,' he said in a formal manner.

A slight ironic smile touched Gabriel's lips.

'Sir, many efforts have been made on your behalf. There has been much demand for your release.'

'I am grateful, indeed,' Gabriel replied.

'At last, the King has been persuaded,' Sir Nicholas said quietly.

Gabriel did not move, suddenly suspecting a trap, as though they had been sent to ensure his quiescent departure to his execution. Then he thought that perhaps it was an escape plan, that they would carry him away secretly, that the guards had been paid.

'How can this be, sir?'

Sir Nicholas came towards him.

'Sir Gabriel, I come only with good news. I have here your pardon from the King.'

'Pardon?'

'It is, of course, dependent upon certain vital conditions. Sir, he would make some negotiation with you.'

Gabriel looked at him calculatingly. What was he speaking of?

'He would desire the payment of seventy thousand pounds and the relinquishment of two of your vessels to His Majesty's use.'

'Nothing else?' Gabriel asked quietly.

'Sir, he requires that you give him also some assistance in Ireland.'

'Ireland?'

'In view of your public admittance of your Catholicism at your trial, he believes that you must have some influence with those Irish rebels who would cause trouble.'

Gabriel frowned.

'If your beliefs could be seen to operate in the King's favour, you will gain his support.'

'What does he require?'

'That you go to Ireland to quell those Catholic insurgents. And also that you start a plantation in the south, where few have yet been attempted.'

Gabriel did not reply. He stood looking through the window of his cell, thinking of the implications of those words. Would he be required to lead an army against the Irish, to persecute them for their religion? No. The King could not be anticipating that. All he wanted was someone who could somehow keep them quiet, so that he could reduce the impossible costs of his campaigns.

'Very well. I will negotiate.'

Frances sighed with relief. She placed a hand on his arm. 'Come. Let us depart forthwith.'

Gabriel glanced round his cell. Just as, a short time ago, he seemed to have relinquished this world for ever, he now looked round its stone walls as though they represented a strange and repulsive experience from the past.

He turned to Sir Nicholas. 'Sir, I know not by what means . . . How can one thank a man for his life?'

'My lord, let us depart. We must explain later,' Sir Nicholas replied.

They went down the stone steps to the waiting coach.

14

My dear Sister Katherine

We are duly arrived at this place after a noisome journey from Albion through the northern parts of this country.

The crossing to Calais was undertaken in an extreme gale which confined me to my cabin and even rendered some of the mariners inactive. The sound of the sails was like great booms of thunder and methought at one moment that the guns had been fired.

Our landing at the port was completed in torrents of rain and I reflected upon whether the discomforts of travel were not greater than the benefits to be enjoyed. But the next day, having spent the night in an inn, and having enjoyed a most excellent meal, the sun shone as we took carriage for Paris.

The countryside is drab, having much of the flatness of the environs of Cambridge, and the farms and villages seem in much need of care and attention. I saw nowhere any signs of that prosperity and diligent activity in trading matters which is so apparent in our English towns and villages but the other travellers were loquacious persons who were much impressed that we conversed so easily with them in their own tongue. They appeared to have little knowledge of our ways and customs and could comment only upon the English treatment of the Catholics. They are, of course, a popish nation and would have our Prince Charles marry their Princess Henrietta in order to exercise influence upon our Protestant bishops.

Paris is but a small city compared with London but there are great palaces and other constructions which I shall see anon and which, knowing your interest in such matters, I will report to you in my next communication. My mind has been occupied with matters at home and I have felt much concern about Papa since his release last month. It is to be expected that nine months confinement in the Tower must have adverse effects, yet I found him strangely aloof and remote upon my latest visit. My sojourn at Cambridge has increased my lack of intimacy with him but it seemed to me that he has other preoccupations of which I am not cognisant.

I have felt only much admiration for dear mama in her fortitude and support of Papa during the trial. I fear that perhaps Sarah has unwittingly brought misfortune upon our household. Dear Katherine, I should much appreciate your correspondence with me. I hope you are now recovered from the untimely death of your little infant. Although I much look forward to these travels abroad, it is my dearest wish that all the members of our family shall proceed in happiness and safety.

With fond greetings, Adam

Greenhayes Manor   *November 1615*
Dartmouth
County of Devon

Dear Brother
    Your letter, delivered by a carter from London, was most welcome and I trust you will find your tours abroad truly rewarding. The joys of seeing the great art treasures and noble buildings are not, I fear, sufficiently compelling to

brave the discomforts of the coach for any great distance. I wish that even my trips to London might be less frequent and I understand that foreign travel is even more hazardous. Is it not the case in France that one must frequently travel in a cart or wagon?

Yet I enjoy our life in London and find confinement to this great house in Dartmouth tedious. But William is a dear husband and supplies me with more than my needs. I have only to express a whim, some fleeting fancy and it is instantly satisfied. He has, I fear, suffered more than I at the death of little Jane, in anticipation that it has disturbed me. But I am quite recovered from this loss, for I think I expected such a result. She was a weakly child from birth and showed little aptitude for survival. It is perhaps preferable to the lingering sickness which Gilbert suffered. We must thank dear William, also, for his efforts in promoting Papa's release. Both he and Stephen took all opportunities to influence the decision and it was William who conceived the notion that Sir Nicholas Maddick might have some interest in deserving Papa's gratitude. If, as I suppose, he intends to press his suit with Sarah, Papa could now raise little objection to such a marriage.

I have to say that Cicely is once again with child and is feeling very sickly. But with her first-born she suffered only for the first few months and one must hope that this will be repeated. For myself, I have no desire for more of it. The pains of pregnancy, the terrors of childbirth, are but little compensated. No sooner is the infant dragged painfully from the womb than it is snatched away, to be deposited with a wet nurse, rarely to be seen for perhaps two years, subject to all the ills of disease, then to return to the parental home to be cared for by nurses and governesses. Would that I should enjoy instead the visits of friends, the company of entertainers and musicians, the pleasure of writing to you.

My only other news is that John has not yet returned from the Low Countries although many months have passed since he went for the cure. His behaviour fills me with unease and I know of no similar instance of the disease from which he suffers. I wonder if it is not merely a device for exacting revenge upon dear Papa. But Mama will hear none of this. She still passes her time awaiting his return. Dear Adam, I commend this letter to you and hope it will reach you as you pass on through France.

Your affectionate sister, Katherine.

Still in Paris   *Christmas 1615*

Dearest Katherine

May I wish you joy and peace on this nativity. As you will see I have delayed longer in this city than anticipated. It is a city of much interest and is not without its own culture. A sennight ago, I visited the great palace of the Louvre and the Palace of the Tuileries. The gardens are truly spectacular and I have seen nothing of its kind in our own domain. There are fountains sparkling in the sunshine, a grotto decorated with terra cotta figures by one Bernard Palissy and great lawns and walkways. I went also to the festivities in the Place Royale, a vast, newly completed square surrounded by beautiful and elegant houses. The Jesuits occupy one part of this square, and many nobles and courtiers have built houses designed by great artists and architects. It is also becoming the home of great intellectuals and philosophers, and persons who spend their time conducting conversations of wit and sophistry. In the square itself, one may see parades of fashion and ladies of elegance perambulating along the streets.

When there I fell in with a nobleman who had in the past spent some time at Cambridge and who invited me on a hunting expedition to a small village called Versailles. It is surrounded by marsh and woodland, but the area finds favour with the King on account of the wide variety of game there to be pursued.

This gentleman took me also to the Luxembourg mansion which Queen Marie de' Medici has acquired and where her architect is planning a great palace. The queen is of Tuscany origin and wishes her palace to resemble the Pitti Palace of Florence, which I shall hope to visit as I pass to Rome.

But now I must thank you for your letter. I observe that you give no news of Papa or Sarah. I must hope that this is because nothing untoward or of sufficient interest has occurred to call forth comment. Yet I have wondered constantly about certain allegations made at the trial, slanderous statements which I dismissed at the time as of no account. In making the absurd suggestion of his wild and amorous behaviour, was there thus no truth in the insinuations about his conduct with Sarah? I mention this because of a communication received from Mama in which she states that it is her hope that Sir Nicholas and Sarah are likely to be betrothed. Is Papa cognisant of this; is he prepared to help the marriage forward? It must be of benefit to all; Sir Nicholas does not embrace the true faith and must therefore be a further bastion of protection for the family.

I have heard from Mama about the visitors remaining in the house. May one hope that Papa is circumspect in his dealings with the Court. After recent events, I do not yet understand his position. I find here much criticism about the Catholic situation in England. The Frenchmen with whom I have conversed appear to have respect for the English explorers and adventurers, although they find them piratical, and all Catholics in England have their support. Yet I question whether Papa is wise to continue his crusade. As priests can live in peace and safety in Europe, why do they find it necessary to go to England? The King and the Protestants must surely find this merely provocative. As for myself, I become more and more immersed in literature and the great works of art with which I am constantly confronted. I have little taste for religion or politics, although at one time I felt I was committed to the Protestant ethic.

After the festive season, I depart south for Italy. Adieu.

Your affectionate brother, Adam

Greenhayes Manor   *30 January 1616*
Dartmouth
Devon County.

Dear Adam,

Your letter delivered by a gentleman who resides at Exeter. First, I must reprimand you about Papa. He has shown naught but courage in his religious behaviour and although he may appear to achieve little in this respect, I prefer that he shall be as he is, and bow to no man. For myself, I have no interest in politics and would leave these matters to all those self-interested and ambitious persons desirous of raising their rank and fortune. Papa has been engaged in trying to exact the release of Walter Raleigh who has today been permitted to leave the Tower. The King has authorized him to conduct an expedition to Orinoco in search of a goldmine. May he be successful or I fear he will once again fall from favour with the King, at his peril. I believe that Papa would have accompanied him, were it not for his own impending commitment in relation to Ireland. I think he regrets the neglect of his foreign travels and intends to repair the deficiency at the earliest opportunity.

Sir Nicholas continues to visit Sarah with increasing frequency and apparent ardour. I am much reminded of my own youthful dreams. You were too young to know about Richard, perhaps, and of our long attachment. But a marriage settlement was not possible and I decided upon a union with William. Richard continues to visit in William's absence, but these occasions are less and less frequent. William is always attentive yet I wonder that he knows nothing of my love for Richard. It would be of much convenience to me if the whole affair were ended, yet as time passes, he becomes more and more necessary to my comfort. I find it not possible to forget him; it is as though my life must end without him. Now I question whether Sarah can find happiness with Sir Nicholas.

As you know, I am privy to her most intimate thoughts. I find her a person of infinite charm and since the trial, it seems, she has blossomed and grown into a strong and determined woman.

Yet she and Papa have a most curious relationship – or so it seems to me. To answer your question, he has, of course, known her most intimately though I believe only on rare occasions, as though it were an aberration neither of them could countenance. Why this is, I know not. Mama appears little concerned with these matters; I believe she renounced the marriage bed after you, dear Adam, her fifth child, arrived, and would find no insecurity now in the situation. I believe since the trial they have a better understanding of each other; Papa is grateful for her support, Mama is perhaps proud of his defence of Catholics and for the risk he took in stating so.

As to Sir Nicholas, I have it from Sarah that it was her influence which led him to act on Papa's behalf. He had no great interest in Papa's release. But she intimated to Sir Nicholas that she would be betrothed to him only on that condition. As he fulfilled that obligation, she now intends to fulfil hers. She says she is fearful that if she did not, Sir Nicholas might retract and Papa would be in danger. In these dangerous and treacherous times, I fear this may be so. Papa, of course, knows nothing of this and believes that she wishes to marry Sir Nicholas. As he is concerned for her future and for her happiness, he has supported the proposal. Yet in spite of his conduct, I cannot feel that Sir Nicholas is an honourable man. I think he acted only in self interest and he is singularly unattractive. I wonder that Sarah can contemplate such a union, or that Papa can accept her profession of love of the man. It must be bewildering for Papa. But he at least is an honourable man. We are truly fortunate in our parentage.

Yet I must confess there are aspects of Sarah I do not comprehend. I know that she loves Papa, yet she has variable moods when I feel she is prompted only by ambition. She also has that strange, compelling power which we have all observed. I have watched people in her presence who were clearly completely captivated by her, fascinated by her cold green eyes. Yet the only true devotion I have observed was in her attention to Gilbert during his sickness. I am constrained to think that she must truly love Gabriel to think of sacrificing herself to marriage with Sir Nicholas. But is that the reason? Is it not a simple matter of social advancement? Of this, she seems frequently to be indifferent. And yet . . . and yet.

Ever your devoted sister, Katherine

At the abode of Signor Pietro Zapelli   25 March 1616
Via Giulia
In sight of Piazza del Campidoglio
Rome, Italy

Dear Sister

Your missive has been delivered to me here. My three months' silence has been filled with such activity that I know not where to begin.

Our journey through France must call forth many observations and comment. The countryside as we proceeded south gained somewhat in charm and is more akin to our own southern areas. But the landscape is much different from ours in that the disposition of land and farming property does not follow the English pattern.

It would seem that the nobility and gentry in these parts are of a different character from that of their English counterparts. Although they have great châteaux which were once enclosed in magnificent and capacious grounds, their chiefest interest lies in living the life of a nobleman.

Their days are spent in the hunt, their wealth goes upon extravagant living and fine wardrobes; their profits disappear at the king's card tables. As a result, they must dispose of part of their ancestral estates to maintain their lives of pleasure.

The peasant in these parts has by diligence gained plots of land from this source. Most of the peasants are freemen, though I have been informed that there are still serfs in this country held in mortmain. So everywhere there are plots lovingly cultivated for the benefit they afford their owners. Yet, although the King's power is absolute, and he can pass laws and impose taxes as he wishes, the nobles here have for many decades paid no royal taxes and the whole burden falls upon these labouring peasants. In addition, they must pay ground-rent to their lord who, though he has sold them land, retains permanent rights over their possession. They must pay also tithes to the church, perform statute labour for the Crown, and support the passage of troops through their farms. Yet constantly they add to their possessions of land.

A gentleman who travelled with us (in a kind of horse wain, there being no other kind of transport available) conjectured that the peasant is able to do this owing to his great greed for gain, his perspicacity in relation to concealing the extent of his profits and his ability to save. 1 know not whether this be the case, though I told him with pride of the English system, where the nobility and the commoner alike are united in their antipathy to royal despotism. He said that he had heard that in England the peasants are protected by the landowners, and expressed surprise that the English lord worked on his own estates and spent little time in the environs of the court.

We proceeded by way of the ancient town of Lyons to the tiny hamlet of Briancon, where we remained for the night in the shadow of the Alps. The air is so cold that we donned fur coats and two pairs of breeches. A guide took us on the morrow by mule up the mountain paths and

I must confess to no small fear as we rose ever upwards and gazed down at the gaping ravines on either side of us and to the great stark peaks rising above. An awesome silence surrounds the place as though emphasizing the feeble insignificance of man. When we halted for refreshment I was filled with a strange inertia at the spectacle of that vast inhospitable world of white rock. Our guide affirmed that many people are overcome with awe and suffer an impulse to cast themselves down into the abyss.

But when we had passed through this landscape the countryside mellowed into the softer Apennines. After much journeying, we arrived three weeks later in Firenze. Its art treasures are of much magnificence but as we intend to visit this city upon our return journey, we did not delay but passed on to Rome.

The air grew ever warmer as we travelled south and the vegetation more lush but I was scarcely prepared for the spectacle of Rome itself. It is truly like stepping back into the Roman world of long ago.

On every street corner there are the red brick buildings of centuries past, many still in fine condition. Even the ruins are spectacular. We went first to the Colosseum which stands at the confluence of three hills and where gladiatorial shows were held in antique times. It is constructed of great curved stone tiers which could seat up to fifty thousand spectators, with tall curved apertures all round the exterior which serve as entrances to the arena.

It is a most fearful experience to stand high upon the stone walls and look down upon the central maze of alleys and dungeon-like cells and to reflect that here the first Christian martyrs met most violent and repulsive deaths. And here, hills and woods were constructed in the huge central area, where slaves were hunted and torn to pieces by wild animals. After these disagreeable reflections, I was pleased enough to return to observation of the many magnificent buildings for which the Romans were responsible.

Their churches have a magnificence incomprehensible to English eyes. The ornate interiors, filled with gold decoration and incredible paintings, confirm one in one's view that the English Protestant is a poor creature if he fears that our churches represent idolatry. In comparison with these edifices they must appear as bare as a vagrant's hovel. But of this, more anon.

Your recent letter may seem to pose more mysteries than it solves. I see not the intricacies of Sarah. I found her to be vivid, intelligent with a mind much concerned with justice. It is this, I hazard, which informs her attitude to Papa. I feel she suspects him of acquiring his wealth at the expense of others, but of whom, I know not. I know little about Sir Nicholas beyond his wealth. But may the marriage succeed.

Farewell, dear Katherine.

Write to me soon. Adam

Greenhayes Manor   *25 May 1616*
Dartmouth
Devon County

My dear Adam

Your correspondences begin almost to give me the desire for foreign travel. I speculate now whether the inconveniences are of a trivial nature compared with the joys one may experience.

My silence has been due to many domestic preoccupations, the chief of which is the early death of Cicely's second born. The poor infant lived long enough to involve Stephen and Cicely in all the expenses and paraphernalia of the christening ceremony, though I know not how Cicely managed to drag herself to the church. She is now confined to her bed.

I have been reading of late of the many cures against conception; for many months I have taken much interest in the herb garden, which should surely be the married woman's favourite sanctuary. I am now trying to persuade Cicely that such sweet herbs as marjoram, thyme and parsley must be important elements in her diet. It is my hope that by these means I shall avoid any further experience of the disgusting horrors of pregnancy. Even Mama shows no disapproval of my suggestions to Cicely; I fear a further pregnancy may destroy her.

Sarah departed to Lincoln to attend Cicely in her illness. She displays the same forbearance and devotion as when Gilbert was ill. It is a strange virtue; I find the sickroom repellent yet it seems to be her wish to attend people in such a state.

Mama awaits always John's return and is reluctant to venture far abroad in case she should miss him but occupies herself with the running of the estate in his absence. Papa has become much involved in activities to which heretofore he appeared indifferent. He pays as much attention to his many domestic and civic responsibilities but he now entertains persons previously not seen at Vinelands. Protestants, bishops, associates at court. I believe he may yet get the royal favours which were lost to him at the trial.

Yet I think it is the trial which has strengthened him in that resolve. It was a great chance he took in openly declaring his faith and as it has succeeded, he has seen that the outcome of all events is arbitrary and unpredictable.

He observed to me recently, 'All roads may be traversed. There is nothing to fear but death and that is but a simple and brief event in a man's life.' I fear his equanimity is something I cannot emulate.

He favours also many of the prominent Catholics who have perhaps persuaded him that their cause may better be furthered by other means than secrecy. But the visitors remain, scattered about the house like beetles hidden in the woodwork.

The wedding plans proceed, Sir Nicholas continues the

preparations with Mama. Yet he cannot be unaware of his good fortune in marrying someone such as Sarah.

Dear Adam, I must end this gossip.

With fond love, Katherine

Greenhayes Manor   *12 June 1616*
Dartmouth
Devon

My dear brother

Now I must tell you of the nuptial celebrations. On the eve of the marriage, when Sarah and Papa returned from a visit into Dartmouth, I was with Mama at Vinelands. We watched their coach come up the avenue. When they alighted, it was as though they bore the sun in their arms; the world seemed suddenly irradiated by their mutual presence. I think Mama experienced the same impression that a halo of joy surrounded them because she observed to me as we looked through the window, 'They look like the birth of the world. Perhaps that is what is meant by "God gave light."' It is unlike Mama to make such observations although she spoke in a somewhat sardonic fashion.

Papa was instrumental in the wedding preparations and neither of them seemed to view the event with any distaste. They appeared to have entered a new understanding and he discussed the settlement and other pertinent details with Mama.

St Saviour's was decorated with flowers, the streets of Dartmouth were lined with people and Sarah arrived looking even more beautiful than the gown she was wearing. Music filled the church, the sun shone through the stained-glass windows and only then I realized that papa was absent. He did not attend the celebrations and it was revealed that he had been called away on urgent business. You will have heard by now from Mama that he had repaired to Court, where the King bestowed upon him

216

the accolade of a viscountcy. The King mentioned Papa's services to the nation and particularly his anticipated services in Ireland and the fortunate marriage of Sarah and Sir Nicholas Maddick and also Cicely's marriage to Stephen who is, of course, well-known to His Majesty. At the celebrations, Sarah was composed and offered a toast to Papa and Mama for their long and continued happiness. I still find Sir Nicholas singularly distasteful. In fact, he seems to me to have sinister properties. Rather I would have a crude and vulgar kind of person than this overweight, smug and opinionated creature whose paltry observations are equalled only by his total lack of graciousness. Yet his very blockheadedness seems to me a potential danger.

But perhaps I exaggerate. He seems to me so inferior to his bride. The only fortune is that she will be close at hand, the Maddick household being not many miles distant.

After the celebrations, when she was bidding me farewell in her chamber, she observed quietly, 'I wonder. Shall I continue to feel about Gabriel as you do about Richard? If so, Katherine, I shall not endure it as you have. I shall make other arrangements.'

And she smiled and kissed me but she looked suddenly very sad. She is a dear, strange creature.

Goodbye, dear brother. I have had no communication and fear that you may be indisposed.

With dear love, Katherine

Italia   *26 August 1616*

Dear Katherine

Greetings! After two weeks in the company of the beautiful Sarah, the world has been transformed into a place of hope. But now she has departed and I write to tell you of her sojourn here.

You mentioned not in your latest letter that she was to travel to Italy so when I received information that she was to arrive I knew not on what pretext. But it seems that she had prevailed upon Sir Nicholas that such a journey was to be one of the conditions of the marriage. And so they arrived. I have to say that the heat in Rome at this time of year is without parallel and Sir Nicholas felt it difficult to bear. For me, this was good fortune because it meant that he was frequently confined to his room or to the coolness of the walled courtyard here while I accompanied Sarah on visits to famous buildings and galleries of art.

When she saw the paintings in the Senator's Palace on the Capitoline Hill she was transported, although I must say that few of these beauties of the past could equal her own. Yet she displays a charming indifference to this. It is almost as though she fails to believe that this is so. I have taken to dabbling in the art of painting since I have been here, and attempted to transfer her to canvas, but with signal lack of success. I have more regard now for the portrait of her which hangs in the library at home. At the time, I thought little of it, but I see now that such a task is more than difficult and that the portrait does bear a passable likeness.

During one of the afternoons when Sir Nicholas was indisposed, Sarah came with me along the Appian way, an ancient thoroughfare which appears to be famous amongst the citizens here.

As you may recollect, I am not much devoted to the rigours of the countryside and would have taken a horse or coach. But Sarah finds much delight in going on foot and I was persuaded. The road passes through many ruins, red brick edifices and monuments of a bygone era and it is a beautiful vista with the yellow sandy soil, the vivid green of the grass and the blue halo of the heavens. It is a singular experience to walk along this ancient paving which is yet superior to any road to be discovered in England.

It is hard to describe the great warmth of this climate; the sun appears to make the shadows darker than in our own milder climes and the certainty of daily sunshine is not without its attraction.

218

We walked some distance and Sarah would have continued but when we came to the Catacombs I persuaded her to descend into its cool environs. Below we found a world of winding corridors, rooms and sepulchres.

It was here that the early Christians lived and died, a secret Rome built beneath the great and powerful city above. It is marvellously constructed of galleries and crypts, artistically carved and designed.

Yet one finds here also many fine examples of the artistry of present day Rome. In one lovely park, the Villa Borghese, a casino is almost completed which is to house famous paintings and sculptures. Truly, the magnificence of their art and sculpture is nowhere to be found elsewhere.

On the last afternoon of their visit, we went to St Peter's Basilica. Sir Nicholas once again declined to accompany us, not wishing to observe popish idolatry. This was fortunate, since Sarah became quite intimate in her conversation and told me much of her feelings which she is rarely wont to do. She is, as you have observed, a strange and complex creature and I feel perhaps she does not forget the freedom of spirit found by being a childish vagrant. As to Sir Nicholas, I find him an oaf and would that Sarah was not tied to such a person. Still I question, did she do this for prestige or sacrifice? Or were both influences at work? I know not. But soon you will see her yourself. They have already begun their journey home. No doubt she will tell you of the Vatican and the Pantheon and the Baths of Caracalla. I shall pursue my way, intending to take some months to pass through Spain and France and thence to England where I shall repair to Cambridge to take my Master of Arts.

My fond regards to Sarah upon her return and to yourself, dear sister,

Adam

15

As soon as Sarah was awakened by the sun's rays shining upon her bed through the leaded lights of her windows, and by Nicholas moving around in his chamber, she knew that this was to be a sun day.

She looked with satisfaction at the long formal gardens, neatly laid out in lawns and flowerbeds with straight pathways running between them, and beyond at the smoothly rounded lake with the swans moving slowly across the water like orderly sailing ships. In the distance she could hear the grinding sound of the cider mill as it slowly traversed its circular journey and, from the farm buildings, the muffled lowing of cattle in the sheds.

She did not wish to think of yesterday, one of the dead days, but her mind insisted on questioning where those moods came from. Why was it that suddenly the world would darken, she would feel trapped in an unending series of pointless activities, while out there, somewhere, where? was some sort of freedom which eluded her.

Yet she had to admit that, unexpectedly, those black days had become less and less frequent since her marriage. At Vinelands, she had mentally divided her days into sun days and dead days. Her presence at Vinelands had seemed to create a strange kind of turbulence which had heightened her sense both of infinite possibilities and of disaster. But she reflected that now those days were so infrequent that it would be more sensible to refer to normal days and abnormal days. Except that those rare, dark, abnormal days now seemed more devastating in contrast to what seemed the normal sun of her life.

Here, life seemed even and sure. No ideas were discussed in this household, Nicholas went along with the smug assurance that what he planned he would achieve. Sarah saw that with his limited objectives – expanding his business interests and his possessions, his implicit acceptance of the Protestant ethic, his friends at court who were yet never intimate – success was assured.

As she jumped from her bed and searched around for the new white calf shoes which Nicholas had brought her from London, the midwife entered the room. 'Pray, Mistress, do not behave so. Care must be taken.'

'It is nonsense, Lucy,' Sarah said impatiently. 'I am but a few months with child.'

'As you know, my lady, Sir Nicholas has required me to visit daily.'

'Pray do not bother yourself while Sir Nicholas is away. He is to go to London for three days.'

She selected a rose pink silk robe from her cabinet and then summoned the sewing maid.

'I must have new, loose robes,' Sarah said. 'Soon this deformity will become apparent. You can cut up my old robes for the infant's wardrobe.'

But she smiled as she swept down the wide staircase to the dining hall. She had felt none of the unpleasant consequences of pregnancy, soon it would be over and in the meantime she did not intend to allow it to interfere with her life.

Sir Nicholas awaited her in the dining hall and rose and bowed as she entered. She had found his behaviour comic at first, but she also found it gave her a feeling of power. She was the lady of Trevayne Abbey.

He kissed her on the cheek she offered and asked his usual question.

'Are you well, Sarah?'

She nodded briefly. In spite of his absurd formal behaviour she knew that his concern was genuine. It still astonished her that he had never appreciated the true terms upon which she had married him. When she had stipulated that it depended entirely on Gabriel's release and reprieve, he seemed to have taken it as an expression of extreme concern for her adoptive father. He discussed now his visit to London.

'I shall take horse to Exeter. It is quicker so.'

'Then I may use the coach. I shall visit Katherine.'

'Pray, do not tire yourself.'

She smiled at him. His doublet had become too tight. Between its high collar, almost concealed by a vivid yellow starched ruff and his wide-brimmed hat with a blue plume, his round pink face looked like a doll's.

'Do not fear, Nicholas. I must attend also to the builders. And the new plantings in the garden.'

Since her arrival the library had been redesigned at her request, a great new wing had been added on the east side that she might have more accommodation in which to house guests, and the gardens had been replenished with many trees and shrubs.

As she bade him farewell on the steps of the house, she looked around with satisfaction.

Trevayne Abbey, with its ancient walls, the old cloisters and chapter house, the refectory which had been converted into the dining hall, had the same properties as Vinelands, although it lacked the moat and drawbridge and the castle ruins which Gabriel had repaired. But now, as Nicholas's wife, all of this belonged to her.

She returned to her boudoir, had her hair dressed in long ringlets, and then went down to speak to the builders and gardeners. Then she took a light velvet cloak and walked down the avenue and through the gates. She would walk to Katherine's, it was only a few miles. She had all day to do as she wished and could return in William's coach.

Even in early summer there was always a blackberry

smell in the lanes. In the woods on her right a great blue sea of bluebells led up to the hills. At the end of the lane, she turned on to the moor and sat down on the grass, looking back at the house, nestling in the valley. Then she moved to a higher mound; it was uncomfortable to sit on the flat grass with this protuberance in her belly. The moors sloped away down to the sea and sheep raised their heads, looking at her uncertainly as they dithered past on their spindly legs.

She felt a sense of peace and serenity. Her mind flitted lightly over the events of her life, each name – mother, Granny Lott, Vinelands, Fortescue, Charles, Frances, Gilbert, Nicholas – setting off a train of thoughts that culminated in her marriage, her possession of Trevayne. Now that it had happened, it all appeared simple and inevitable.

Then her thoughts turned to Gabriel. Whenever she thought of him, it seemed like entering a different world. She never connected him with any other person or events; outside circumstances had nothing to do with them. It was not her mind but her whole being which mused now on those occasions when they had made love. How lovely it had been the first time when he had seemed quite bewildered at being overcome by desire for her, except that she had then also been bewildered at how it hurt and all the blood.

And then the last time on the terrible night of his arrest. It had seemed then like the end of the world, as though they had been acting out the final scene of their lives and she knew that at the time, Gabriel had not understood how calm she felt, how he thought her uncaring. Yet as he lay in her arms, she was already scheming about how she could help him and marriage to Nicholas had then seemed a small sacrifice. As indeed it had turned out to be. She found his embraces neither attractive nor repulsive. They were irrelevant.

Now, for the next few months until the child was born,

she was even relieved of that obligation. Prompted by Sarah, the midwife had persuaded Nicholas that any kind of intimate activity might be dangerous to both child and mother. Beyond that, he was simply a part of those outside forces which were providing for her needs and desires. She walked unhurriedly across the moor until the grey stone walls of Greenhayes Manor appeared in the distance. She could understand why Katherine found the castle-like exterior gloomy. There seemed to be too few windows for the size of the thick walls. Sarah found her planning the arrangement of pictures with William in the long gallery.

'They are gifts from Adam,' Katherine said, 'brought back from Italy. How good it is to see you, dear Sarah. But I did not hear your coach.'

'I walked.'

'Walked! How did Nicholas countenance that?' William smiled.

'He has gone to London.' Sarah sat down. 'Perhaps it is a long excursion,' she conceded, 'but it is as I wish.'

'Ah,' William said, 'as he is away, perhaps you could remain here for a few days. Dear Katherine has not been herself. You always give her such happiness.'

Sarah looked reflectively at Katherine's pale face, the lines of unhappiness around her eyes and mouth.

'Yes, of course,' she said. 'What is it, Katherine?'

Katherine shook her head but her eyes filled with tears.

'I think you must know the source of this, Sarah,' William said slowly. 'I believe you have Katherine's confidence.'

Sarah frowned. 'I do not know, sir . . .'

'Do not be troubled, Sarah,' William said. 'You betray nothing.'

'No,' Katherine addressed William, 'Sarah knows of the circumstance but not of this particular event.' She turned to Sarah. 'I could not bear this alone,' she said. 'I have perforce to ask my husband's help.'

'But Katherine, what has happened?'

Katherine shook her head once again and it was William who said, 'Katherine has had word that Richard has become betrothed to a lady in the northern parts of the country. She has been much distressed.'

Sarah turned to William. 'But how did you . . . ?'

William raised his eyebrows as though puzzled at his own behaviour.

'I have always known, Sarah. It has always been my hope that this involvement would cease, that perhaps one day Katherine might come to care for me.'

'Well,' Sarah said, 'you have certainly, sir, behaved most admirably. And it is my belief that Katherine cares much for you. But this other . . .'

'Speak not of it,' Katherine interposed.

'Come, Katherine,' Sarah said impatiently. 'It is not a desperate situation. Let us walk in the garden.'

William looked relieved. 'Yes. The steward will complete the pictures with me. Go, Katherine.'

As Sarah and Katherine departed, he added, 'It is good to have you here, Sarah. Your advice may be better than mine.'

Sarah turned and smiled. 'Not better, William, but perhaps different. You are too kind.'

Katherine led her along the garden paths. She had constructed another arbour like the one at Vinelands, surrounded by rose hedges, with a stone seat and a thyme lawn scattered now with primulas and lilies of the valley.

As they sat down, Sarah said severely, 'Katherine, you have no need to behave so. It is without dignity.'

'Sarah, I do not wish to live. Richard has betrayed me. I have lost him.'

'Katherine, you made your decision long ago. Did you expect him always to live in celibacy because you had married another?'

'It was a mutual agreement.'

'How so? Then Richard must have been too weak to

225

resist your decision or too selfish to make any effort to retain you. Perhaps he welcomed that easy solution.'

'Sarah, do not speak of him so.'

Sarah observed the anxious girl before her.

'Katherine, you were so pretty. You still are. Yet your haunted look detracts.' Then she added thoughtfully, 'You were so full of life. It was you who showed me how joyful life is. Don't take that away. You are not just a shadow of Richard.'

Katherine sighed but she said reluctantly, 'No. That is so.'

'Your life with William can be so – delightful, Katherine. He displays much tolerance. You can take your love for Richard along with you, like a little treasure chest you carry. It need not intrude.'

Suddenly Katherine smiled. 'Little witch. Yes. You are right, Sarah. I will not decline into an embittered old lady. Yet you are stronger than I, Sarah. But I will try.'

Sarah sprang up. 'Let us go to your chamber, dress your lovely black hair, find a new gown, as we used to.'

'Yes. I must show you the lovely mother of pearl casket, mounted in silver, that William gave me yesterday.'

As they climbed the stairs to her chamber, Sarah said slowly, 'If I considered the matter, I might feel I could not live without Gabriel. Perhaps one day it will come to that.'

'Let us forget this . . . nonsense,' Katherine said suddenly. 'We both have so much to be thankful for. But what of you, Sarah? How are you?'

It had been Sarah's intention to discuss with her those strange, black days of her life, like yesterday, to try to isolate the cause. But she knew that this moment was inauspicious and she said instead, 'My pregnancy is without event so far. But I do not welcome it.'

'As you were present at my lying-in, I cannot conceal the distasteful aspects,' Katherine said. 'For myself, I shall see that it does not occur again.'

226

'How so?'

'I drink each morning hot mixtures – herbs, honey-suckles, and if I fear conception, I have taken to fierce exercise.'

Sarah frowned questioningly.

'I have found that violent exercise encourages the flow of blood. It must therefore induce it in the first place.'

'What sort of exercise?'

'Well, I have taken to jumping off the steps, first one, then two, then three . . . I have even jumped from the balustrade.'

They both laughed. 'Katherine, you must injure yourself. You are quite wild.'

'Perhaps, but it has been successful these three years.'

'Then I shall take note of that advice.'

'And Nicholas. Do you find happiness there, Sarah?'

'I behave as I advise,' Sarah replied. 'But Gabriel is ever in my heart.'

'Then Nicholas shows the same strength of purpose as William has.'

Sarah laughed.

'It's not strength. He is quite unaware. Nicholas displays but little imagination. I feel always that nothing could destroy him. Not because he is strong, but because he has an overweening sense of his own rectitude.'

'But he has much devotion to you.'

'Yes. But in a way it's because I am an ordinary event in his life, something he would have expected to occur. I think his late marriage merely signifies that he awaited the most suitable person to share his domain. He is now satisfied of that circumstance.'

Katherine laughed. 'Adam writes that he will soon be visiting and sends you his dear love.'

'He is well at Cambridge?'

'Yes. Writing romances and studying the art of the Roman world.'

'And Frances?'

227

'She has repaired to Lincoln. Cicely is pregnant again. I know not why she finds herself in this state for a third time.'

Sarah shook her head. 'I know not how it is to be avoided. I think yours may merely be good fortune.'

When she returned to Trevayne Abbey two days later, she received news that Nicholas was delayed in London and could not return for some days. A wild and passionate longing had come over her. Suddenly she saw herself not as the lady of Trevayne Abbey but as someone who had made a great and unacknowledged sacrifice. Well, briefly, she would get her reward. Sarah went to her chamber to change her gown and dress her hair and then ordered the coach.

The head stableman looked anxious as he assisted her up the high step.

'Do not concern yourself,' Sarah said cheerfully, 'I have seen the midwife. It is but a short journey.'

'Where go you, my lady?'

Sarah paused. 'To Vinelands. Do not delay.'

As the coach trundled up the long avenue, she looked hopefully for signs of Gabriel. She passed through the great oak doors and Mistress Dodds greeted her.

'Is his lordship within?'

'He is in the library, my lady.'

Sarah's heart beat faster as she quietly climbed the marble stairs, crept along the gallery and flung open the library door. Gabriel was sitting at his large desk, studying a document and some coloured maps.

He stood up, his face lit up with joy as she rushed towards him and kissed him jubilantly.

'Gabriel, we are alone. The first time since my marriage. Oh, it has been so long.'

She stepped back a little, her arms still raised around his neck, and smiled into his face.

'We have behaved with such forbearance and now we are rewarded,' she said. Gabriel frowned as he looked down at her.

'Oh, Sarah, this must not be. We have long ago agreed.'

'Katherine informs me that Frances has departed for Lincoln,' she interrupted gleefully, 'and Nicholas is detained in the capital.' She stopped and added slowly, 'But you look much saddened, dear Gabriel. Are you not pleased to see me?'

Gabriel smiled. 'How do you ask? But it has been very hard without you.' He pushed back her long golden hair, falling about her face, and looked into her eyes. 'You become more beautiful. But you are content, Sarah?'

She stroked his face, her fingers moved down his neck to unfasten the top button of his doublet.

'Sarah. No. We must be resigned to the situation, to your marriage.'

'Last time we were together, you did not speak thus. You were distraught. I see your love had little meaning,' she suddenly said angrily.

'We have decided, Sarah,' Gabriel said wearily.

'I should have been your wife. I should be your viscountess.'

'Sarah, how can you speak so. It was you who decided, you who then persuaded me. I was willing then to change the situation. Now it is too late.'

It had been about this time a year ago that she had been preparing for her marriage. At the time it had seemed that they had worked out a total mutual philosophy of life. Between their love-making they had talked as Gabriel had never talked to anyone, about the meaning of love, of life, of past worlds and future hopes, of Vinelands and her impending marriage, of his religion and the Catholic cause. He had even offered to divorce Frances but Sarah had pointed out that this might be impossible and in any case was unwise.

'After that trial, your fortunes might be endangered by such an act. And in any case,' she had added sagely, 'our own happiness might be endangered by your awareness of living in perpetual sin. And even if you found it easy to sell your soul, you might find it more difficult to live in the world.'

He had thought about her words frequently in the ensuing months. His viscountcy had involved commitment to many social and business activities which put an increasing strain on his religious activities. He recognized that while the wealthy and aristocratic Catholics such as himself were accepted by the King as part of the establishment, this acceptance rested entirely on the presumption that they took part in no subversive or secret acts against the state.

Sarah changed her tone.

'Dear Gabriel,' she said softly. 'I married Nicholas for your protection.'

'What mean you, Sarah?'

'I thought at the time he was not to be trusted. Perhaps it is still so. In spite of his assistance at the trial, I feared he might betray you. I had made it clear that I would marry him on the condition only of your release.'

Gabriel grabbed her by the arms.

'Sarah, is this true? You told me nothing of this. I was to believe that you wished to marry this man.'

'I could not tell you. You might have prohibited the marriage. But I think it is so. That I have no regard for him is certain. Yet now I think perhaps I welcomed the security Nicholas offered.'

'Security! Did you not find that at Vinelands?'

'No. There I was just a chance arrival.'

'But you returned there of your own volition. And I needed you, wanted you there.'

'Yes. But by marrying Nicholas I became free of doubt.'

'Doubt?'

'I did not know, but I have freedom now. No-one can command me.'

Gabriel looked down the avenue in silence. He wished in the end only for her happiness and if it had worked out thus, he was content. Yet he felt also a great joy that she had been willing to make this sacrifice for him. For the first time, he believed in that love between them which she had said could never change, never be damaged by any external event.

'Yet,' Sarah said, 'perhaps I cannot sustain this life. Unless,' she added, 'we can be together thus.'

'It cannot help, Sarah.'

She smiled, her eyes searched into his.

'It must surely be a reward for the sacrifice I have made.'

He took her in his arms. An indifference to all consequences, even to his religion, came over him.

'Come, Sarah, let us talk no more.'

He took her hand and led her along the gallery to his chamber. It was cool and dark but he opened the curtains because Sarah liked always to see the sun, streaming across the bed.

For three days, they shared the old life at Vinelands, attending to the running of the estate, riding down into Dartmouth to check on ships and cargoes, visiting Katherine and calling once at Trevayne Abbey to see if Nicholas had yet returned. There Sarah left a message for him in case he should return, to say that she was visiting Vinelands.

On the third day, the steward arrived from Trevayne to inform her that word had come; Nicholas would return on the morrow.

She and Gabriel had their evening meal in the dining hall while musicians played softly in the minstrels' gallery. Then they walked through the gardens to Katherine's bower.

'Why are you silent?' Sarah asked. 'It may be some time before this occurs again, but it is of small matter. We are always close in spirit and indeed in fact.'

They sat down on the stone seat.

'Sarah,' Gabriel said. 'I have delayed telling you until now in case it should have interfered with our happiness, but . . .'

Sarah looked at him with apprehension. Ever since the

231

night he had appeared in her chamber with his terrible account of the death of Fortescue, she had feared the arrival of any news.

'What?'

'Be not concerned, dear heart,' Gabriel said gently. 'It is of no disaster.'

'Then tell me. How could it affect our happiness?'

'I must soon fulfil my promise to the King to go to Ireland. My mission is to start a plantation and to see that the Irish come to an accommodation with the English community.'

Sarah laughed with relief.

'But that is of no concern. A few days, weeks.'

'No,' Gabriel said. 'I must remain for one or even two years, though of course I shall return regularly to Vinelands.'

'Two years! But for what purpose, Gabriel?'

'Sarah, for centuries the Irish have suffered at the hands of the English. My Catholic faith demands that I must go to their assistance.'

'How do you know that they desire it? And surely you go on the King's behalf. How could you help them without endangering yourself?' she said angrily.

'I know not until I reach there. Yet I am certain this must be my decision. Sarah, we have said our love surpasses all separation.'

Sarah turned away. She knew he was not leaving her in the way Richard had left Katherine. She was certain of Gabriel's love but, like Katherine, it was she who had chosen to marry. Yet here she was, almost behaving in the undignified fashion for which she had admonished her friend. Her anger disappeared and the old distant look came into her eyes. Would the black, dead days return? It did not matter. She could deal with it.

'Yes,' she said, turning back to him at last. 'Everything can be contained. But I fear for your safety.'

'Do not distress yourself. I will send word regularly.'

'Tell me of Ireland. What is the problem that you speak of?'

He told her of the disturbed history of that little country of Ireland, which from the fifth century onwards had been divided into small tribes, each with its own king.

'At any time there might be one hundred and fifty chiefs ruling in that little land,' Gabriel said, 'and in just the same way that the Normans invaded and conquered England, the English have taken advantage of all those divisions in Ireland.'

'But why should they not have many kings if they wish? Must the English tell the world how to live?'

Gabriel laughed. 'I fear the English have a capacity for gain. Yet perhaps this is not reprehensible.'

'But why must you remain there?'

'There are many English – and also Irish – landowners who take over great estates and have no interest beyond the profit they bring. They but rarely visit.'

'But what is the concern in that?'

'The development of the plantations should be for the benefit also of the inhabitants. They are but poorly provided for.'

Sarah smiled.

'You have no concern for such matters in other foreign parts. Newfoundland, Greenland.'

'Ah, there are few attempts at settlement there, the north is mainly uninhabited – Indians and Innuits merely.'

'And what is your concern for the Catholics in Ireland?'

'I fear they show but little true concern for their religion, for centuries they have been reputed to be dissolute, corrupted from the true faith. It is my belief I should assist in these matters.'

'Oh, Gabriel, are you to involve yourself in these dangerous activities? You act now on behalf of the King. Are you to reward him thus?'

Gabriel put his hands on her shoulders and looked into her enquiring eyes.

233

'Sarah, I hope by my influence and intervention that no more lands shall be taken from the Irish in the south. I have the King's support because he fears that the Protestant behaviour in Ireland at large may lead to greater trouble. He fears also the intervention of Spain and France whose coasts are so adjacent.'

Sarah shrugged. 'I know naught of this, Gabriel. I find it all but a mystery. I do not understand risking your life for such a cause.' She spoke the word ominously as though he had already been condemned.

'It will not come to that, dear. Ireland is a different place.'

'And yet,' Sarah said, 'treachery is surely everywhere. But come, you are decided. My heart goes with you. Let us spend our last night in peace.'

'I will bring you word when I am to depart,' Gabriel said as she stepped into her coach the next morning.

During the summer, they met occasionally in the company of the rest of the family but it was not until a grey November morning that a message came that he had boarded his vessel that very day for the shores of Ireland. At the same instant, Sarah felt the first sharp pangs of labour. A violent pain stripped through her back and she shouted for the midwife.

'It is coming,' Sarah said.

The midwife laughed. 'I fear not, my lady. These pangs are but warning signs. At first, the pains will come every hour, then fifty minutes, then forty minutes; it is only when it is persistent that we can anticipate the birth.'

'Cannot we aid it, Lucy?'

'No, my lady. We await its proper arrival. Here, this potion will soothe your fears.'

Sarah drank.

'Please send for Lady Katherine. She promises to stay with me.'

Nicholas came and held her hand anxiously and then was dismissed by the midwife.

Then Katherine arrived, her green gown and mantle splashed with mud.

'It is a foul day. A great wind blows and yet there is a dreary fog over the sea.'

'And the Irish Channel. How will it be there?'

'Concern yourself not with Gabriel, dear girl. He has weathered many storms. I think he finds it of small account.'

'And yet I am fearful, Katherine.'

'It is only your condition.'

Sarah's face creased with pain.

'Remove your gown. I will apply a poultice.'

'I think Lucy will permit no interferences.'

'A poultice is not an interference. It is simply a comfort.'

Sarah relaxed on the bed as the warm poultice was applied to her back, then sprang up again.

'It is no good. The pain returns.'

Katherine said soothingly, 'As it must do.'

'It is easier standing up. Let us walk up and down the chamber.'

The day wore on. Nicholas hovered constantly beyond the door, waiting. The storm increased and the wind howled around the Abbey mournfully. One of the serving maids came in and whispered to Lucy, but Sarah heard her words.

'Katherine, she speaks of terrible storms at sea. Of a shipwreck. Katherine!'

Then she shouted out with the pain that had extended suddenly also to her belly.

'Katherine, it is everywhere. My body is on fire.'

Lucy hurried over.

'Lady Katherine, fetch hot water, linen. I think her time is upon us.'

She forced a tankard of hot brandy upon Sarah and bade her drink it. Sarah entered into a somnolent state, punctuated by violent moments of fearful awareness, of being pressed and pushed and exhorted until suddenly there was a final violent agony and the pain ceased.

She lay in a semi-conscious state and then she heard the cry of an infant. Katherine came over to her extended hand.

'Is he all right, Katherine?'

'It's a girl, Sarah.'

'Not her. I mean Gabriel. The storm still rages.'

'Sarah, there is no news. He will be safe.'

Katherine sat with her all night waiting to apprehend the first signs of fever. But Nicholas had ensured that the midwife he selected was more than proficient at her job. Sarah's temperature rose slightly but at last she slept peacefully and with the dawn Katherine crept from the bedchamber. Nicholas took her place at Sarah's bedside.

The wind had dropped and Katherine wanted to discover news of any disasters at sea before rumours might reach Sarah. She requested one of the stable lads to ride down to Bayards Cove and waited anxiously in the dining hall for his return.

Sarah smiled bleakly at Nicholas when she awoke.

'It is good that it is over,' Nicholas said softly.

'And the infant? Is she well?'

'Yes.' Nicholas smiled. 'A healthy little creature. And what shall be her name?'

'I wish it to be Catherine.'

'Then it is so. But now I must leave you to rest. Lucy will bring you succour.'

He bowed and quietly closed the door behind him.

Sarah fell again into a deep, exhausted sleep. Darkness was falling once again when she awoke.

Then Katherine came, walking slowly towards the bed. Sarah sat up.

'Katherine.'

Katherine sat down on the bed, her lips trembling.

'Is it bad news?'

Katherine put her arms around Sarah. 'No! He's all right, Sarah. He's all right.'

'Oh, Katherine.'

'But I hope never to suffer such a night again.'

For a moment, they wept silently, folded in each other's arms. Then Sarah said abruptly, 'Come, then, Katherine. Call for the infant. Let us see what she looks like.'

16

The wind dropped suddenly, although the rain continued to lash down upon the ship as it finally turned towards the coast. Gabriel shouted to the exhausted sailors to slacken sail as they entered the protection of the estuary and began slowly to wind along the wide, curving roadway to the harbour. The coast rose in great rocks above them until they finally reached the steep slopes of Kinsale.

As the boat docked, the wives on board looked in silence at the shacks along the quayside and the Irish labourers walking slowly across the cobbles. The seamen, aided now by the women, began to unload, watching the Irishmen suspiciously, knowing from hearsay that they were all thieves and vagabonds.

Gabriel had selected the twenty or so settlers to bring with him, most of whom came from the estate and were either Catholics or sympathizers. It was he who had suggested they should uproot themselves from their native land and accompany him. He had explained that if they helped to build a plantation with him in Ireland, they might enjoy few benefits but their safety would be more assured. No English monarch had yet managed to subdue the Catholic Irish and now with greater pressure from France and Spain the King was being forced to abandon the attempt. But when Gabriel returned to England he knew they would be remaining as settlers and while he was here he intended to make their future positions secure.

It was a tiny harbour; a few small sailing boats rocked lightly at anchor but there was no other sign of activity. The groups of Irishmen watched them impassively until one group wandered over.

'Are you for the plantation?'

Gabriel's men stopped, listening in fascination more to the Irish accent than at what the man had said.

'No.' Gabriel always spoke briefly and curtly in an uncertain situation.

'You're not?'

The Irish all looked astonished and suspicious. The other groups began to saunter over.

'No.'

'Well, one thing's for sure. You're not shipwrecked.'

Gabriel smiled.

'No. We haven't been forced in.'

'Just unloading supplies for the planters?'

'No.'

Gabriel smiled again. He was accustomed to landing at unknown ports and harbours; his life and that of his crew had often depended on his making a quick and correct assessment of a situation. Now he recognized the curious and friendly native who in spite of all good reasons for behaving to the contrary did not abandon his natural friendliness and goodwill.

'We have come to settle our own plantation,' Gabriel said.

'At Kinsale?'

'Perhaps a few miles north, inland. Where we can purchase land.'

'Purchase?'

'Yes.'

Gabriel knew that the Protestant English settlers did not purchase. They simply confiscated any Irish lands they wanted.

'You are English?'

Gabriel nodded, then added, 'We stay tonight at the house of Dominic Eliot. Know you that place?'

The group instantly responded that they did, discussing amongst themselves the distance, the easiest route.

'Two miles.'

'Nearer three.'

'The road over the hill.'

'Nah, the valley's quicker.'

'Dominic Eliot, eh?' one of them said thoughtfully.

Gabriel knew that he need explain no more. Dominic was one of the old Anglo-Irish as they were called, whose family had lived here since the time of Henry II, and who were devoted Catholics.

'Can transport be found to take these goods to that estate?'

Further conversation took place amongst the Irish, but nothing definite was suggested.

'Carts? Wagons? Horses, even.'

Finally, three or four of them went off to the village to get help. Gabriel's people finished unloading the ship, moored it securely and then sat down on the quayside. A watery sun filtered through the clouds and the women shivered in the damp November air, but the Irish did not seem to notice.

While they waited Gabriel walked up the steep, narrow street and looked out across the sea and behind to the softly rising hills. He had a strange feeling of safety that he was aware now he did not feel in England. But was it an illusion that the Catholics here enjoyed any greater religious liberty?

After a time a few more Irishmen went off and finally they all returned with a horse and wagon and an old mare.

The estate lay a few miles north and the settlers spent the day carting their goods to be deposited in the barns, while they were housed in a huge derelict mansion formerly the home of Dominic Eliot. This was to be their quarters while Gabriel conducted negotiations for the purchase of land, when the building of their houses could proceed. Eliot had suggested that Gabriel should stay with him in his great, newly-built home but Gabriel declined, saying that he would work with his people and live as they did. But in the evening, he presented himself at Eliot's home and was received with what he remembered as the old-world courtesy of the Elizabethan era. Gabriel realized that England seemed to have lost those desirable graces. Although the fare at the table resembled that of England, Gabriel noticed that the house was but sparsely furnished with little of the modern furniture which was being imported from the Continent into all wealthy English homes.

Eliot spoke with the same soft Irish accent as the workers had done. Gabriel remarked that they had seemed singularly pleasant, although only a few of them had actually assisted with the transport of the goods. Eliot smiled. He had a long, rather unkempt-looking beard and his clothes, although of the English style, were loose-fitting and seemed to give an air of casualness.

'I fear you may not appreciate the maelstrom into which you have precipitated yourself.'

'How so?'

'I think that perhaps where they shout in England, Ireland seethes beneath.'

'Perhaps that is why I come. I feared the Catholics may need some English support.'

'It is not perhaps your help that they want.'

'No?'

'I think they may prefer your absence. How can you help them?'

Gabriel accepted the strong whiskey which was passed to him.

'The situation is not without irony,' he said. 'But at the moment the King is in a mood to favour the more opulent Catholics in the realm.'

'We have seen variations in the King's mood before. It augurs no good.'

'No, but while he is set upon the Protestants settling the plantations, he is finding the project not without its problems.'

'My dear fellow, Ireland has always been a problem.'

'I think the King has found the Ulster settlement a fairly simple undertaking.'

'Much of that land was abandoned after the nobility fled some years ago. It was a simple event to take that over.'

'But he fears now for the rest of the country. I have come to endeavour to make the Catholic community more amenable to the English developments, in their own interests.'

Eliot laughed again. Gabriel realized that he saw his altruistic motives as not only arrogant but absurd. For the first time in his life, he found himself looking mentally back at England from the standpoint of the natives of those lands that the great English explorers and adventurers were attempting to exploit and requisition.

'The Irish have no wish to be joined with England. It must always be under duress.'

'But you. You are English.'

'I was. My family have been here for five hundred years. Ireland is my home. I accept the Irish way of life although I have some sympathy with the English. At least, the Catholic English.'

Gabriel asked quietly, 'But if it comes to a confrontation, whose side would you be on?'

Eliot repeated, 'Ireland is my home. There are many old English families here more extreme than myself, who have become totally Irish. There was no trouble between any of us. We co-existed amiably enough. The trouble comes from England.'

'And would you join an Irish insurrection?'

'I am Irish. Here, the talk is of liberation.'

'You are very frank,' Gabriel said.

'The Irish dissimulate only about personal matters, not about matters of conscience,' Eliot replied, laughing again. 'But of what assistance can I be to you?'

'I hope by my influence that no more lands shall be taken from the Irish in this area. I hope to settle some lands for those Catholics I have brought with me, not as occupiers but as legal tenants.'

'Your aims at least must have my full support. They must also commend themselves to the Irish lords.'

'I would that I might meet them.'

'That will, of course, be arranged. I will send word as soon as it can be done.'

He escorted Gabriel to the gates of the estate.

'We have few facilities here compared with England but you are welcome always to my hospitality. And may your mission be fruitful.'

He bowed, still smiling, and Gabriel returned to the little settlement. One of the settlers greeted him anxiously.

'What is it, William?'

'The provisions. Some of them have gone missing. While we were collecting the last loads from the ship, they must have been stolen.'

Gabriel frowned. He realized his sense of safety extended only to his political awareness. The need for ordinary physical protection was the same everywhere.

'We cannot act on this. At this stage, it would do no good. In future, we must leave always guards by the barns. Someone must also sleep within them.'

The old house had been arranged with their few belongings, mattresses for sleeping, basic cooking utensils, stools and tables. A separate room had been set aside for Gabriel with a wooden bed and even a chair and a chest for his clothes.

He wondered briefly whether it would not have been

simpler to remain with Dominic Eliot but instantly dismissed the thought. It was wiser to stay here with the settlers, even if trouble was unlikely.

A rota was drawn up for guarding the barns where the supplies and their tools and implements were housed.

'Tomorrow, I shall explore the area to find suitable land and then I visit some Irish lords to arrange its purchase,' he said. 'Then we can start upon the building.'

A damp, heavy mist hung over the countryside as he set forth. He went up the hill past St Mulrose's Church and the new little houses which had been built for the English settlers. The only impressive building seemed to be a three storey tower house but larger houses were being erected further up the hill. The Carmelite friary looked neglected although he could see monks working in the gardens. When he reached the top of the hill he looked down on the little town. It would have been simple to build here but Kinsale had become an English town fifteen or sixteen years before, closed to Irish residents, and Gabriel had no wish to be identified with the Protestant settlers.

He found the same situation further north at Bandon, where he was told by the proud English settlers that the great new Kilbrogan church was the first Protestant church to have been completed in Ireland. He studied the rough little map that Dominic Eliot had drawn for him. To the south lay Clonakilty, which the Earl of Cork had founded only three years before for the English plantation. Beyond Bandon the countryside became deserted. The houses appeared to be mere shacks and after passing a castle and, further along, the ruins of another, there seemed to be few signs of habitation. He decided that here might be the site for their settlement, the first English Catholic plantation, he thought ironically.

In pouring rain, he returned to Kinsale.

'The land round here is much occupied by the English,' he said. 'We must find a place where the Irish are not excluded. Tomorrow, I visit the Irish peers.'

'Tomorrow is the Sabbath,' one of his settlers replied.

'Ah, yes. Eliot informs me that St Mulrose's is taken over by the Protestants. But we may travel a few miles to Kilbrittain where mass is still celebrated.'

On the morrow, Gabriel accompanied them to church. He was surprised at the size of the congregation. Passing through sparsely populated country to reach the church, they had seen only a few shacks and houses with unkempt gardens and even the larger houses looked uncared for. It was as though the Irish were perversely allowing their buildings to decay in the face of the English onslaught. Yet the church was filled with peasants whose look of poverty seemed to astonish even his own settlers. Even the poor in England appeared to have some neatness compared with these wild-looking individuals. They all turned as Gabriel and his twenty settlers and their families entered the church and stood uncertainly at the back. The priest left his altar and walked slowly down the aisle towards them. Gabriel reflected that even his robes looked shabby and crumpled. Gabriel explained their presence to him quietly, the priest indicated some empty pews and returned to his rostrum.

'Today we welcome brethren from England,' he said to his flock. 'We are all equal in the eyes of God.'

It is as though he is apologizing for our presence, Gabriel thought. But perhaps it is also a warning. Why should they welcome us, when we take over their land?

Then he glanced at his own settlers. They were all looking overawed and apprehensive. Even the children were silent and some of them began to cry. He realized that although Father Pierre had held private services of mass in the dining hall at Vinelands, it was many years since they had attended mass in a public church.

They all seemed overwhelmed and although the service lasted a long time and the priest droned on in Latin, they still listened intently. Only the Irish, after an interval, began to wander out, crossing themselves and bowing. As Gabriel and his group left, the priest blessed them, promising to visit, and they stepped out into the sunshine. It was the first time the sun had shone since their arrival and the group walked back across the hills and valleys towards Kinsale.

'Yes,' one of them was saying, 'we will make a life here. It will be better for our children.'

Gabriel looked across the bright green of the slopes. It was not as beautiful as Devon, this countryside, yet freedom of worship was perhaps more important than one's homeland.

They were hailed suddenly by a group of Irishmen who were standing outside their small houses. The settlers stopped, half-smiling.

'Come. Would you care for a drink?' a soft Irish voice asked.

They all walked slowly up the garden path and sat down in the wintry sun.

'It's our own, home-brewed.'

The settlers accepted the tankard which was offered.

'Come, we must pay for this,' Gabriel said. 'There are too many to partake of your generosity.'

'No. This must be a celebration. We meet the first human English.'

The Irish all cheered, laughing. Tankards were passed round and Gabriel sipped the violent brew which was presented to them. Most of the settlers had tasted nothing but beer in England and soon they were as drunk as their Irish hosts. They all lay or sat in the sun and then the Irish women produced great dishes of hot onions and potatoes and gave the children jugs of hot milk from the cow.

Many hours later, the English staggered back to the house, having told the Irish they would return their hospitality on the morrow. But Gabriel had intervened, pointing out that tomorrow was a working day and that the invitation must apply to the following Sunday.

As he entered his barn, Gabriel remembered Eliot's words, how many of the Old English had become native and taken on the Irish way of life. He could see now how attractive that way of life might appear to people who had lived a restricted life in England, dominated by landlords, landowners, the church, the government, the King; by rents and extortions they could never afford, by religious intolerance they could never understand.

The next morning, a messenger arrived for Gabriel. He would take him that day to the home, between Enniskeen and Dunmanway, of The O'Connell, an Old Irish chief who had seen him at church and was desirous of meeting him. Gabriel knew that it was illegal for the Irish to give themselves these old titles. He knew also that it was these Old Irish landowners whom he needed to meet.

He mounted his horse, informing his settlers where he was going, and followed his guide up the slopes from Kinsale into the green valleys and ranges of hills leading to Bandon. They followed the river through forests and plains and he felt that Ireland was a place of abandoned castles and decaying priories and abbeys from the past, interspersed with hovels for the living. As they went along, the landscape became more fertile, the grass a vivid green, the air mellow even at this time of the year. They came to yet another grey castle and his guide indicated that here, on the outskirts of Ballineen, was their destination. They circled a lake and rode across the drooping, uncut grass which had now turned brown.

The guide took his horse and a servant met him at the castle gate and led him into a large stone-floored hall. Although a fire blazed in the huge fireplace far away at the other end, a cold dampness seemed to penetrate him. The only furniture was a long bare table with benches around it.

A handsome man came towards him, greeting him cheerfully, his footsteps echoing on the stone floor. He was dressed in the Irish style, with a long flowing red cape over his black doublet and breeches, and his black hair was loose.

246

'Greetings, Viscount,' he said cheerfully, 'I am The O'Connell.'

They bowed and Gabriel smiled. In England no-one used his title, addressing him simply as 'sir' or 'my lord' but he had heard that the Irish cherished their titles, even if they were unacknowledged or banned by the English.

'My lord, be seated.'

They sat facing each other at the table. The heat from the fire did not reach to this end of the hall and Gabriel felt cold and uncomfortable but servants appeared instantly with dishes of hot food and O'Connell poured from a steaming tankard. 'My special brew,' he said. 'This will warm you.'

It was the same burning liquid which they had been given on the previous day and which had left him this morning with a beating head. He sipped it carefully. O'Connell raised his glass.

'Welcome to our country,' he said, gulping. 'I have news that you are not a visitor of the ordinary sort.'

'I do not come to take your land,' Gabriel said instantly. 'But I have a mind to settle a plantation for my Catholic brethren. They have a need for protection.'

'Then call it not a plantation. That is for English Protestants.' He spoke the words with sudden vehemence. 'Your people become settlers – Irish settlers – or they are not wanted here.'

'Sir,' Gabriel said slowly. 'You appear to have little choice in the matter, while the English maintain their present policy.'

O'Connell's eyes flashed. 'Be not mistaken, Viscount. We are not defeated. The English will be banished in the end.'

'I come not to fight the Crown, sir. I come also on that behalf.'

'I know enough of you to speculate why the King now favours you.'

'Sir?'

Gabriel poured himself more liquid from the jug O'Connell

pushed over to him. The venison, cooked in beer, the wild duck, cheeses, the hot mulled drink all made him feel pleasantly mellow. He liked the man's direct, fearless conversation.

'The King knows that he has offended the Old English over here as much as he offends the Irish. He knows that the Protestant scum cannot control this country without our cooperation. So he sends you to act as a kind of solace to the Catholics and a brake upon the Protestants.'

'He did not only send me, sir. I desired to come. He merely supported my unspoken intent.'

'So?' O'Connell raised his eyebrows. 'I am surprised.' He thought for a moment.

Gabriel laughed. 'England is a country of manipulators.'

'As it always was,' O'Connell said, then added, laughing also, 'But then, so is Ireland. The world's a wicked place, dear Viscount.'

'But, sir, to business,' Gabriel said firmly. 'Is there land that I might purchase for my people?'

'I have much land. I could spare some small amount. There is some in the region of Skibbereen. Later, we will repair there for your inspection.'

'There will be also a grant from the King, if you are willing.'

O'Connell chuckled. 'Ah, that pleases me much. Let him pay for his marauding. But come, sir. I do not compromise you. Mean you to settle here also?'

'No,' Gabriel said truthfully. 'I shall give the land to my tenants when I depart.'

'Ah, as I said, you are not of the usual sort. But we will speak further at the conference.'

'Conference?'

'We meet in a few days' time – the other peers of my realm. It will be well if you should attend.'

'Indeed, I will.'

'Perhaps, sir, we might visit the site of your settlement on the morrow. Let us for today have another small drink.'

248

Gabriel rose, but the room now seemed warm and pleasant. He sat down again and they continued to drink until Gabriel finally called for his horse and O'Connell escorted him to the door.

'I care not for most English,' O'Connell said suddenly.

'You have reason,' Gabriel assented.

'I could kill you now, if I so wished.'

'That would scarcely further your cause.'

'We have plenty of instant action in these parts. We have learnt to live by present gain rather than future hope.'

'But I represent neither,' Gabriel said. 'Thank you for your hospitality, sir. I think we have drunk enough.'

O'Connell smiled again, walking unsteadily.

'What does your William Shakespeare say – "To be or not to be". Fair words, sir, outrageous fortune – Ah, I wonder, sir, if you will not find yourself in such a dilemma in this fair country of mine.'

Riding back across the hills, Gabriel began to understand the maelstrom which Eliot had mentioned. It was not only religion here that could never be ignored; it was a political situation which would never be solved, where it seemed impossible to be uninvolved. Yet the Old English here appeared to have succeeded in running a course where they neither sided with the Irish nor joined ranks with the English. Or was it like that? These Old English had lands here, had lived here for centuries, Ireland was their home. They thought of Ireland as their country. They would never fight against it.

Two days later, he went with O'Connell and six of his settlers to inspect the land above Skibbereen, in a green valley on the River Ilen with hills rising in the background. Gabriel knew that as they contemplated the little fishing harbour below his group were thinking of the flourishing Dartmouth they had left behind, yet they seemed already to be adapting to their new country.

'We shall find this suitable,' Gabriel said, after a brief consultation with his men.

'Then that is settled,' O'Connell said immediately.

'I shall arrange for immediate payment, though the grant from the King may take some time longer,' Gabriel said, smiling. 'We shall begin work forthwith.'

When they returned to Kinsale the following day, he held a meeting of all his tenants in the bare hall of the old house. Plans were worked out for the entire project. The land was to be divided into equal plots for the twenty families, to accommodate a house and a piece of land for growing vegetables and the keeping of a cow or pig. An area was also to be allowed for the building of a larger house for Gabriel, or any subsequent owner. When each family completed building, the property became their own.

'It is also necessary that we have here some kind of authority for when I am absent,' Gabriel said. 'You will choose by ballot who is to be my deputy, and also his deputy, and we must also have people responsible for the supplies and a wife who will oversee the cooking arrangements while we are all together.'

Gabriel smiled at the enthusiasm with which they responded to his plans. He knew that, accustomed as they were to the limitations imposed on them by the authorities at home, they would adhere at first to all the decisions. Yet it was very different here; they were creating their own authority. Would it work?

It was John Williams who was elected as the deputy. At home, he had been Gabriel's chief blacksmith.

He came over to Gabriel holding a piece of paper, from which he read slowly. 'We also wish to express, my lord, our undying gratitude and thanks to you for your infinite generosity. We are unable to find suitable words that we have been blessed with a master such as yourself. On behalf of the whole company.'

Gabriel cleared his throat. 'We must all act according to our conscience,' he said slowly. 'I hope only that our intentions succeed.'

Later in the day, a letter was brought to him from Cork

informing him that the English judges would be holding their Assizes around the country and requesting him, as a deputy lieutenant and high commissioner in England, to accompany them on the circuit. The English judges came at regular intervals to administer justice in the courts, forming a Grand Jury composed of the Lord Chancellor, Chief Justice and judges, for dealing with more serious crimes and appointing petty juries from amongst the population for lesser civil crimes.

Before departing, Gabriel supervised the removal of his settlers from Eliot's estate to their new land above Skibbereen. There they were to commence clearing the land and to start building during his absence.

He set out the next day and joined the judges in the walled city of Cork. He found a different atmosphere here from that of Kinsale and its surrounding areas. There were many English soldiers living in the garrison with a special contingent of fifty horse soldiers to accompany the judges on their passage round the country. When James came to the throne, the citizens of Cork had briefly shown their opposition to English rule by openly celebrating mass and besieging the English troops in Skiddy's Castle. Reinforcements arrived and their revolt quickly ended. But fifteen years later, Gabriel could still feel the vibrant opposition – 'the Irish seethe beneath' Eliot had said.

The Chief Justice admitted to Gabriel that the attempt to make them go to church could never succeed and the fines had been dropped.

'It is impossible to administer,' he said. 'Searches would be useless; every town, hamlet and house is a sanctuary. There are also many of the Old English here who do nothing to control the Irish. In fact, they have become Irish themselves.'

For the next six weeks, Gabriel travelled with the judges round the country, sitting with them on the Grand Jury. They proceeded from Mallow to Limerick and Tipperary and Gabriel began to see, as Eliot had hinted, that his mission was of a different nature from what he had anticipated. The Irish did not need his support for their Catholicism; they continued to practise it with varying degrees of secrecy or effrontery according to the situation. Priests and officials refused to sign the oath of supremacy; only the law officers would accede. The judges might scour the country as they wished, seeking out recusants, but as soon as they were gone, the people continued in their Catholic worship.

Gabriel had made his own position clear to the judges before they proceeded on the circuit.

'I am a known Catholic myself, therefore I believe in liberty of conscience. As you know, I am here also on the King's behalf to ameliorate the situation. Therefore, I sit upon the Grand Jury only in those capital cases such as murder and violence.'

He knew that the Chief Justice and his commissioners would have wished him elsewhere but they knew also that at the moment the King found more use in his services than in theirs.

As they travelled, they came upon ruined churches and shabby houses in some towns, while in others the buildings looked cared for and well-preserved. There were state clergymen who appeared as indifferent to the law as the Catholics.

At Waterford it seemed that all the families in the area were related because the lords had produced so many bastards that no-one would testify against anyone. They found Clonmel a stronghold for Jesuit priests and it was impossible to obtain any evidence about the recusants.

'Largely,' as the Chief Justice remarked, 'because they are all of that persuasion.'

Everywhere the petty juries found prisoners not guilty of theft and other minor crimes in spite of all evidence to the contrary, and it was known that most of their food supplies came from cattle stolen from the Protestant Pale. Gabriel felt a perverse pleasure that what they looked upon as these ignorant Irish were defeating the English system of justice – which in itself was as corrupt as their own manipulations.

When he returned to Skibbereen weeks later, he found the settlers had completed many of their houses and were already embarking on early spring planting. He detected a change in their attitude, not towards him but towards themselves. In spite of their hard work and industry, they seemed to have taken on something of that relaxed attitude of the Irish who appeared to have adopted them cheerfully into their midst. They spoke more directly, argued and disagreed with each other and the Sunday conviviality had evidently become a regular event. In a few years' time, would they be Irish, too?

He had been back at Skibbereen only a few weeks when he was visited by a Protestant landowner from Bandon. Already the settlement was taking shape, becoming a living community. Gabriel surveyed the man with indifference, realizing that he himself had found a new freedom in this little island. Here he was part of a Catholic majority, even if they were under attack, and he felt a new sense of power.

'Lovell Webster. I am come, my lord, on behalf of some others from Bandon. We hear that land is available just north of here.'

'That is not my understanding,' Gabriel replied. 'The land is that which I have purchased from The O'Connell to expand our settlement.'

He watched with satisfaction as the man frowned at his use of the title.

'We do not need to negotiate with the Irish,' the man said shortly. 'We will allow them some part of it.'

'That is not so,' Gabriel replied firmly. 'No land will be taken in this area without proper negotiation. And that is unlikely to succeed.'

His visitor flushed with anger.

'The Irish have no rights. It is English property, subject to the Crown. The Irish are lazy, uncouth trouble-makers.

The King has supported many Protestant settlers. He will not be thwarted.'

'The King will not support you in this area. The Protestants have also caused much trouble to him. I am here to try to redress that.'

'Then I shall have recourse to the King and council. You will hear further of this.'

Gabriel bowed. 'Sir, that is your prerogative,' and he waved him out.

He dismissed the episode from his mind until he received a command from the King that he should conduct a meeting of the clans with the Protestant planters. The King indicated that he should exert his influence in curbing the expansionism of the Protestants.

'They have my support,' the document read enigmatically, 'but they are in danger of turning the loyal Irish against us.'

The meeting was conducted in O'Connell's hall, the Irish chiefs bearing swords, the Protestants accompanied by a troop of soldiers. Gabriel bade them all be seated on the benches.

'I am here,' he said, 'to represent the King. Pray, let me have your submissions.'

He glanced at Webster and then quickly turned to the Irish.

'O'Connell, will you hear the English?'

O'Connell nodded impatiently.

'Webster, your submission.'

'We are desirous of acquiring land north of here. If the area of Skibbereen is bespoken, then we will accept further north, if it is fertile.'

Gabriel looked at O'Connell.

'No,' O'Connell said.

'We will purchase,' Webster said reluctantly. 'We will not confiscate.'

O'Connell laughed loudly.

'That is very true, sir. You will not confiscate.'

'I said purchase,' Webster said evenly.

O'Connell glanced briefly at his chiefs.

'No,' he said.

'If we do not,' Webster said, 'the Scots will simply take the land.'

'We have nothing to fear. We have our own armies.'

Gabriel turned to the Irish.

'You do not wish to sell. That is the verdict of you all?'

They all nodded.

'Then,' said Gabriel, 'that is an end of the matter. The land will remain with the clans.'

The Protestants stood up in anger.

'This is not mediation,' Webster shouted at Gabriel. 'You are simply an Irish lover. A popish traitor.'

Instantly, the Irish drew their swords and Gabriel sprang to his feet.

'No! We give them no cause for complaint. Sirs,' he turned to the English, 'the matter is closed. Pray consult with the King and council if you feel no satisfaction in my decision.'

As he watched them leave the hall, Gabriel realized that by identifying with the Irish, he had now cast his lot. He had declared open war on the Protestants and while he was safe at the moment, the day must surely come when he would be called to account.

O'Connell returned his sword to its scabbard.

'Sir,' he said to Gabriel, 'you will need protection now. They will not forgive you.'

As the months passed and he spent much time with the Irish lords, Gabriel knew that he was becoming more and more compromised. They talked openly in front of him about rebellion and revolution and although he did not join in the conversations he knew that his silence meant implicit assent. He spent long, solitary hours as he knew others before him had done for centuries, thinking about the situation in Ireland. Yet somehow his religion could not eliminate his loyalty. He was still English and the King continued to support him. He acquired more land, further Catholic settlers arrived from England – 'it is one way of ridding himself of troublesome recusants' – the Irish lords commented – but Gabriel knew that the King wanted to be rid of the problem. He could not afford, with his rising expenditure in England, to maintain an army in this country.

It was only after many months that Gabriel finally faced the real issue. That event was precipitated by the unexpected arrival of Adam for the Christmas celebrations.

Gabriel had corresponded regularly with Frances during the year he had been absent. She ran the estate with the help of his sons-in-law, William and Nicholas. Gabriel's fishing fleet had expanded under the direction of the two masters he had appointed and the broadcloth trade was being extended to the Continent.

Frances recorded the activities of each member of the family. John had returned recently from Holland. His long treatment there had produced amazing results. He could now speak almost as distinctly as before, though a bit more slowly, and had taken over the management of all their affairs. Katherine now spent more time in London with William and seemed to enjoy much entertainment in Court circles. Nicholas had bought another great priory near Exeter which Sarah was now engaged in renovating. Before reading Frances's letters, Gabriel always glanced through quickly until he found that name, avidly reading any brief information about her. He knew that he had told her that he would return regularly from Ireland, but his involvement had so far made that impossible.

Sarah had written to him only twice, yet in a way further letters had become unnecessary. What she had said was perennial and unchangeable. Her undying love, their real communion of spirit, the deep, silent, secret world which was theirs, which no-one could ever invade. She was with him always, as he was with her; her pleasant, easy, opulent – even exciting – life had its foundation always in their love.

When he read her words, he felt always complete certainty; it was only in the silence of the night that he would lie in the darkness longing to see her, feel her, knowing that life with her must always have been better.

Gabriel laughed when he saw Adam, tall, handsome, his auburn curls falling down his back, his flamboyant vivid clothes, his swirling gold-coloured cape in violent contrast to the drab Irish peasantry.

He walked across the little quay towards him as Adam left the ship and embraced him eagerly.

'I received word only this morning of your arrival. You appear no longer as a wild student.'

'Ah, Papa. I fear I become ever wilder beneath,' Adam replied, laughing.

'We must take horse to Skibbereen. The house is now finished.'

'I still have little taste for the rigours of country life,' Adam replied, 'but no doubt a horse is preferable to an old cart in these places.'

'You will find the house fairly furnished, though not perhaps with the facilities of Vinelands.'

Two days later they reached the settlement and Adam expressed his astonishment.

'It is inconceivable. So much completed in a year. It is like a small town.'

Adam did not accompany him on the morrow to the Christmas Mass, but later Gabriel took him to meet the Irish lords. They greeted him as though he were their own son, plying him with whiskey and other hot drinks. Gabriel was surprised at the amount that was poured into Adam's tankard which he quickly swallowed, only to have it replaced with more. A great banquet had been prepared to which the lords and their families came from miles around, and the great bare hall was filled with music and laughter. The wives and children appeared to drink as much as their lords and the celebrations continued into the night.

At one point, Gabriel was engaged in conversation and when he glanced again, Adam had disappeared. He looked around amongst the crowd to see if Adam were joining in the Irish dancing, then he wandered down the hall and through the oak doorway to an antechamber.

Adam was sitting at a trestle table talking to O'Connell and some other Irish lords.

'I cannot answer for my father,' Adam was saying. 'You are perhaps more cognisant of his opinions than I am.'

O'Connell stood up as Gabriel came in.

'Ah, Viscount. We find much to commend in your son.'

Gabriel smiled. 'He may perhaps be a wild talker like yourselves. But what do you commend?'

'We speak simply of Irish freedom,' Adam said.

'I have no love for the Protestants,' Gabriel replied.

O'Connell passed Gabriel a tankard.

'We all drink to that, sir. Pray be seated.'

'I speak of more than that, sir,' Adam persisted. 'The English have no rights here, except as immigrants.'

'My lords have been persuading you, I think,' Gabriel laughed.

'No, sir. I need no persuading. The English are invaders on this soil.'

Gabriel glanced round at the lords. He had been aware always of the dangerous nature of their conversations but now he felt a different anxiety.

'My lords,' he said. 'I have heard much talk between you and you know of the trust you may have in me. But my son is but immature, he cannot be implicated in matters which only the Irish can settle. It is a dangerous business.'

Adam sprang up.

'Father, it is not a matter for the Irish. The English must be led to see they are culpable, they take over rights which are not their own.'

'Adam, you commit yourself to a hopeless, nay, a deadly

path. The Irish cannot defeat their power; therefore, it is better to try to limit and diffuse it.'

'No! In that way, they can never be defeated. The only way is to raise armies, gain the help of Spain, fight them.'

He spoke the words like a battle cry and the Irish stood up and raised their glasses once more, laughing with delight.

'Adam,' Gabriel said bitterly, 'that has been attempted many times. The Irish are always defeated. They cannot raise sufficient armies.'

O'Connell said, 'There are always brave men who will suffer for the cause of justice. We shall finally conquer.'

Suddenly Adam said quietly, 'Gentlemen, but recently I attended the last hours of Walter Raleigh.'

O'Connell nodded slowly.

'You, my lords, may have but a poor impression of such an English adventurer but I think he may have been one after your own hearts. It was Lord Mayor's Day. The King had hoped that by having the execution at such a time, few people would care to leave the celebrations to witness this event.

'It was a cold grey morning as I went down to the Gatehouse to find a huge crowd already assembled. Raleigh stood on the scaffold, dressed in black, waistcoat, breeches, a black velvet cape, his long silver hair neatly dressed. He seemed to rise above all the nobles who stood with him, bidding farewell. The sheriff lit a fire that he might warm himself but Raleigh declined.

'Then he spoke at length of his innocence, of all the infamous treachery against him, the slanders and malice. He impressed all with his dignity and composure. Many in the crowd were weeping. Any who had desired his death were now turned to sorrow. The executioner placed his cloak upon the ground for Sir Walter to kneel upon. It was not possible to hear their words but it is reported that when asked if he would not rather lie towards the east, looking towards the promised land, he answered, "So the heart be right, it is no matter which way the head lieth."

'He was seen to examine the axe and smile, then he stretched his arms before him. When the fearful deed was done a solitary voice from the crowd shouted, "We have not in England another such head to be cut off."'

Adam stopped. Gabriel could see that he was clearly much disturbed at what he had witnessed.

O'Connell gulped his drink and put an arm round Adam's shoulder.

'It is a pretty story, boy. He was a brave man.' He stood up. 'But here in Ireland, it is but commonplace. No man expects justice.'

Gabriel stood up abruptly and walked to the tiny leaded window which looked out across the valley. It was completely deserted; everyone was inside celebrating Christmas.

'We are all compromised,' he said slowly. His thoughts had become hazy with the drink but somewhere in the back of his mind he could see the answer. 'We are all compromised,' he repeated. 'The King persecutes the Catholics yet he has Raleigh executed because the Spanish Catholics have told him to. As Catholics, can we support Spain in this action?'

'Or Raleigh either,' one of the Irish lords said, 'a Protestant, a great pirate against Spain, a man who did much against the Catholics – what think we of such a man?'

'I care for neither cause,' Adam said. 'It is freedom of the soul that I am speaking of.'

They all fell into a brooding silence, considering Adam's words.

Then Gabriel said, as though his mind had suddenly cleared, 'Gentlemen, the answer to the problem is evident.'

They all looked at him expectantly.

'Yes, my lords. The English belong here as tenants only. And the Protestants must be subdued.'

They all awoke at his words, cheered and shouted, raising their glasses and pouring the liquid into their mouths.

'We will draw up a document', Gabriel said, 'which I will present to the King forthwith.'

Paper and a quill were hastily brought and the document was written and signed by them all, demanding the return of confiscated lands to the Irish and the implementation of the old Irish laws.

On the morrow, when they had all slept off the effects of the food and drink, the Irish lords appeared in the chamber which Gabriel had been given to rest.

'My good lord,' O'Connell said, 'we do not expect your concurrence in the document we constructed last night. We were all much affected by the occasion.'

Gabriel rose. They all stood before him, waiting. He took the document.

'Allow me to re-read it. The words may not perhaps be entirely suitable.' He read it slowly, then he smiled.

'It is entirely as I wish unless you find some fault with it.'

O'Connell looked at him seriously. 'It is a hard matter,' he said. 'You put yourself in much danger.'

'Not in the instant,' Gabriel said. 'The King is in a mind to pacify the Catholics. But I fear it will be a long and difficult business.'

No reply was received to his document. Then in the summer, he had orders to return to England to attend upon the King.

He gave his settlers their homes and lands as he had agreed and said farewell to the Irish lords.

'In case of trouble,' O'Connell said, 'we will come to your defence.'

Gabriel smiled.

'I feel much at peace,' he said. 'All may yet be well.'

O'Connell shook his head gloomily. As the ship moved slowly out of the harbour, he saw O'Connell pull his sword from its scabbard and dash it against a wooden post, as though he were assuaging the centuries old rage of the whole Irish nation.

Gabriel turned his eyes once again towards England.

17

Frances sat at the end of the long gallery on a velvet couch. From there, she could look through the balustrades to the crowded Great Hall below and watch the guests as they wandered up and down the marble staircase. At the other end of the gallery she could see through the open doors of the library to the windows far away at the other end, to the trees and hills beyond.

From the minstrels' gallery just above her, she could faintly hear delicate sounds of a lute and harpsichord, almost drowned by the noise and chatter around her.

Somehow, John's wedding had made her feel old and she was very conscious that she was approaching her fiftieth birthday. Yet when she looked in the mirror that morning, she could see no signs of sudden age; her face was not made hideous by the pox marks which disfigured so many women. Even her hair, although slightly thinner than it had been, had not lost its auburn colour and her skin had not taken on the scragginess that seemed so common amongst her acquaintances.

No. The feeling of age came from another kind of awareness, that she had been born and bred in another era and that somehow she did not belong with this younger generation. Although she had never lived at a time when the Catholic faith had been admissible, yet she felt now that its importance had receded further and further into the background of English life. There seemed to be fewer believers, they seemed increasingly isolated and she feared that one day they might disappear from the land altogether. More and more she felt at rest only with Father Pierre and the priests residing in the quiet chambers of the house. There had been fewer priests coming of late. For the moment, the antagonism towards them seemed to have diminished; the King was following a policy of prudence and they were less in need of a hiding place.

She watched John slowly mounting the stairs with his bride, plump and pink-cheeked and already looking matronly. Mary Chappell was actually a second cousin from Frances's native Suffolk but John had met her only a year or so ago during his illness. He had been accommodated by Mary's parents when he was making his journeys to and from Holland.

As a result, the whole Suffolk branch of the family, Frances's brother John, his wife and children, as well as her other siblings, had all descended upon Vinelands and would now be remaining perhaps for a week. Frances smiled down at John fondly and he smiled back at her and then led his wife into the music room.

In a way, his marriage would remove for her some of the burden of running the estate during Gabriel's absence. He had rebuilt an old farm on the estate, converting it into a palatial house, and Mary would now take over with John many of Frances's duties. As it would be his inheritance, she and Gabriel had welcomed the arrangement.

Yet she felt an anxiety because since his stay in Holland he had developed an antipathy towards the Catholics. She realized that out of deference to her he spoke little of it, but she had heard him discussing with Mary his admiration of John Robinson and his dissenting church in Leyden. She was aware of an even deeper anxiety that somehow the aversion was connected with Gabriel, with Gabriel's devotion to the Catholic cause, to the event on the Newfoundland ship years ago, to John's illness. And what would become of Father Pierre and the priests when John possessed Vinelands?

She saw Gabriel, smiling at something Nicholas was saying, then he began to climb the stairs alone. In a way, Gabriel always appeared to be alone because to her he always stood out in any company.

Gabriel never changed, never seemed to age, was as erect and handsome as when she had met him with that sense he gave of power and dignity. She still worried about events in Ireland. When he returned, he insisted to the King and his council that the attempt to mollify the Irish while continuing to support Protestant invaders was doomed to disaster. Frances had yet again feared for his life and she knew he was only temporarily safe because of the modifying influence of Spain in the background.

He came along the gallery towards her, unbuttoning his blue velvet doublet.

'It is extremely warm for May.' He sat on the couch beside her.

'There are many people. But think you not the celebrations have had much success?'

'Indeed, yes.' Gabriel smiled at her. 'It gives me much pleasure that you have your eldest son now so close.'

'It is well,' Frances said. 'But I have some concern for Adam. He lives a precarious life in the capital.'

'Fear not, Frances. Young men become wiser with time.'

'But I hear that his writings, his romances, are of a seditious nature. Is he not in danger?'

Gabriel frowned. He did not wish to spoil her day, yet he could speak only the truth.

'Not at the moment.' he said. 'Such exercises are looked upon as the excesses of youth. But I fear he must learn to be circumspect.'

'As you are not,' Frances smiled.

264

'No,' Gabriel admitted, 'Yet in matters of belief perhaps one cannot be.'

Frances was about to reply when she saw Sarah coming up, arm in arm with Katherine. They were both dressed in flowing white gowns; jewels flashed around their necks and Sarah wore a small diamond tiara on her long golden hair. Katherine's black hair hung in ringlets to her shoulders.

Even Frances smiled. She had known always of Sarah's relationship with Gabriel; it was scarcely something that could be concealed from a wife, living in the same house. She had gone through all the emotions of anger, jealousy, contempt, resentment; it was Sarah's behaviour at the trial, even though she was the cause of it, which had somehow clothed Frances in the safety of indifference.

Frances had feared that after her marriage, Sarah might cause further trouble, yet she appeared to have no contact with Gabriel apart from those social and domestic events when other people were present. In fact, she had presented no problems at all.

With John's return, her own anger and resentment towards Gabriel had evaporated. Although their relationship would never return to its old, easy understanding, they could now speak civilly to each other. There was, indeed, a certain feeling of security between them now that perhaps had not existed before. Their relationship had survived so much, it was as though they could always rely on each other's support.

Frances brought her mind back to the present. Katherine and Sarah had reached the top of the stairs.

'They see but little of each other now; Katherine is so frequently in London and Sarah spends much time at Exeter. Yet I believe they both prefer these environs,' she observed.

'I think they will both settle here eventually,' Gabriel assented.

William followed behind with the children, holding

265

Elizabeth's hand. At seven, she looked like a tiny replica of her mother, with her laughing eyes and curling black hair.

'William proves to be as loving a father as he has been a loving husband to Katherine,' Frances said.

He was talking quietly to the little girl who suddenly laughed excitedly, just as Katherine used to do. At least, they presented no problems for her; it had turned out, at last, to be a happy marriage and after little Jane's death four years earlier, Katherine had avoided any further pregnancies.

Holding Elizabeth's other hand was two-year-old Catherine.

Frances could not understand why Sarah had brought such an infant to the wedding. It would have been more appropriate to leave her at home with the nursemaids. But Sarah seemed to have a curious attitude towards her children; even the two-month-old baby Nicholas she visited regularly at his nurse's home down in Dartmouth. It was not natural to be so obsessed with a child; if anything befell them, as was so usual in early childhood, she would only suffer more.

Frances remarked as much to Gabriel. She talked about Sarah dispassionately, as an offspring in whom they had some mutual concern. Whatever Gabriel's feelings, he always discussed Sarah in a cool and remote way.

'It is perhaps the result of her background and own early childhood. The poor are much with their children from birth,' Frances said.

'She had the same devoted attitude towards Gilbert during his illness,' Gabriel reminded her.

'Yes, yet she appeared to recover from that with some ease. Perhaps she can afford to be extravagant with her affections as she has the power to retrieve them should the worse befall.'

Gabriel smiled. He knew that Frances was making no veiled reference to himself yet he wondered if her words might not have equal application to him. Then he remembered the trial, Sarah's letters to him in Ireland; her feelings for him would never change.

Then the two children saw Frances and Gabriel and, dropping William's hand, Elizabeth dashed excitedly along the gallery followed by little Catherine. They sat on the couch beside them, chattering eagerly. Katherine and Sarah waved to them and turned away towards the library.

'William, dear,' Katherine said. 'Sarah and I will rest in the library a while. If you tire of the children, the nursemaids are below.'

William kissed her lightly on the head.

'I think perhaps I must rescue your parents,' he laughed.

Suddenly, there was a loud shout from halfway up the staircase.

'Stop!'

Everyone turned. There was silence. A little boy in a grey velvet suit who had been running up the stairs had halted abruptly.

'Philip,' Frances stood up. 'Dear child, how delightful to see you.'

This little five-year-old was the one grandchild who had roused some feeling in her; his delicate body and pale blond hair reminded her of her own dear Gilbert.

The child looked at her but did not move. Then behind him she saw the pregnant figure of Cicely, her face pale and anxious, clutching the hand of her other little child. But it was his father, Stephen, who had shouted the command. He was bounding up the stairs and when he reached Philip he hit him violently across the head and shouted, 'Do not run in front of your mother. Walk correctly.'

The child almost fell, then balanced himself, but he showed no emotion. Then Stephen looked up at the hundreds of eyes turned upon him, up the staircase, along the gallery. He blushed in the silence. It was not a silence of disapproval about his action, there was nothing strange in striking a child; it was simply the indignity of causing a disturbance on such an occasion.

Frances looked anxiously at Philip. Then Gabriel, standing beside her, strode to the edge of the balustrade. He looked down imperiously at Stephen.

'No-one will strike a child in this house,' he shouted violently. 'Either desist or leave.'

Frances was surprised at his anger. His voice seemed to thunder round the gallery; she feared he would dash down the stairs and strike the man.

Stephen's face was red with anger.

'Sir, I shall treat my child as I see fit. Your views, and those of all the rest of your family on the treatment of children, are no concern of mine.'

The guests continued to watch in fascination. Everyone knew about Gabriel's liberal views in relation to children. He had strange views about justice altogether. He had indeed taken great risks in relation to his beliefs, about Catholicism, about the corruption of court and crown, about Ireland and Irish freedom, and now he was humiliating his son-in-law, this Stephen who was so intimate with the King.

Stephen clutched the little child by the back of the collar but before he could act further, Sarah's voice rang out from the top of the stairs.

'Ah, Cicely, how lovely to see you.'

She ran quickly down the stairs, almost tripping over her long many-skirted gown, her hair flowing behind her, hastily embraced Cicely and then grabbed Philip.

'Ah, you are so much grown, child,' she said, and she turned and ran back up the stairs with him in her arms.

Everyone waited to see if Stephen would dash after her, but he turned to Cicely, said shortly, 'Come, wife. Collect the child. We shall depart forthwith,' and strode back down the stairs and through the door to the courtyard.

Music struck up loudly from the minstrels' gallery and the guests resumed their conversation. Frances watched

Cicely as she slowly came up the stairs towards them. This was her fourth pregnancy, in spite of the physician's warnings. It still seemed strange to her, in view of Stephen's suspected relationship with the King, that Cicely should continue to conceive with such regularity.

'You look very tired, dear,' Frances said, embracing her.

'I am well enough, mama. But I fear we must depart.' She took Philip's hand as Sarah put him down. The child had a red mark across his face where he had been struck.

'Are you well, Philip?' Frances asked.

'Yes, grandmother.' The little boy spoke quietly.

Elizabeth and Catherine stood by his side. 'Come with us,' Elizabeth said.

'Dear children, not now,' Cicely said. 'We shall meet at some future date.'

'I shall visit you in Lincoln,' Frances said.

'Dear Papa.' Cicely kissed her father but now her lips trembled.

'Remain a while. I will speak with Stephen,' Gabriel said. 'It is a great commotion about little,' and he strode down the stairs.

Cicely sat with Frances on the couch and Katherine and Sarah joined them. Some time later, Stephen and Gabriel reappeared through the great door, followed by William. Frances sighed with relief.

'Is it not strange,' Katherine said, 'this long friendship since schooldays between William and Stephen. They are so unlike.'

They were all silent, thinking of the difference between Katherine's husband, William, tolerant, generous, a great rock of strength, who could never be connected with the vile caprices of the King's set and Stephen. Then Cicely said unexpectedly, 'I think my dear husband is much in need of protection. I am sure he means so well.'

No-one replied.

Later, they all repaired to the Great Hall which had been

prepared for the evening's festivities. John and his bride began the dancing and the music floated up the staircase as Frances went quietly up towards the library.

Following her earlier thoughts that day about age, she wanted to look again at the new portrait of Gabriel which had just been hung there. The door was slightly ajar and the long windows at the other end, leading on to the balcony, were still open.

She stood before the portrait. It was true. Gabriel did not age. He was holding a silver goblet, given to him by his father, the stem of which was ornamented with oriental agate mounted in silver-gilt. On the dresser behind him stood a Chinese porcelain wine jug mounted in silver.

She passed over her own portrait to one of Sarah, painted when she was about eighteen. In a way, she had changed because she was even more beautiful now at twenty-four.

Frances looked at the clear, pale skin, at the strange, distant expression of her green eyes, at the way her hair hung round her face, curving down her back. Yes, it captured the essence of Sarah.

She reflected that these portraits would be there long after they were dead. Who would look at these in years, perhaps centuries to come? They would just be human figures in paint, but what would people know of them, the feelings, the misery and happiness of their living?

She turned away and then she heard a sound on the balcony. When she looked, she saw the profiles of Sarah and Gabriel silhouetted against the skyline. They did not see her; she was standing behind a central pillar. She realized they would not have seen her anyway, they were so engrossed in their conversation, though she could not hear their words.

Then Sarah raised her arms and put them round Gabriel's neck. Frances saw the expression on their faces, as though totally absorbed in their love for each other. Gabriel looking in a way he never looked at me, she thought. But Sarah looking, also, in a way she knew she had never looked. She felt a terrible pain and desolation; it was as though beneath all the layers of human contact they had reached a profound and ultimate level of which she was incapable.

A deep and violent rage swept through her, remembering her benign thoughts earlier that afternoon.

She had believed it was now all over between them, that they had given up their sinful behaviour. She felt suddenly convinced that they must still be meeting secretly. She had been deceiving herself that they would ever change; Gabriel could never be trusted again.

Frances crept from the library. She knew that the vision of those two, standing on the balcony, would be with her for ever.

18

Adam stood at the end of London Bridge. After being confined all day to his lodgings in the Strand, writing his latest masque, he had decided to walk to the tavern at Belins Gate to keep his appointment with Edward Greville. The bridge was excessively crowded at this time in the late afternoon, with horses and carts wending their way back and forth between the crowded shops on either side and busy merchants and tradesmen hurrying about their business. Housewives talked to each other from the first floors of the houses above; the balconies were so close that they almost touched across the narrow street and Adam watched two boys climbing across from one house to another.

Boats plied up and down the river laden with timber, fish and vegetables. The brown river was swollen with the November rains and he watched small boats approach the dangerous rapids beneath the bridge, created by the tall pointed arches jutting from the sides.

Adam found life in London more and more to his liking. He enjoyed the company of the many poets and painters who were beginning to congregate in the capital and the seething population of rich and poor were to form the subject of the new entertainment which he and Greville were to compose together. He knew that Greville had conceived of it as a comedy of manners, buffooning the life to be observed in the wealthy mansions of Westminster and also in the stinking slums of Cripplegate. 'A depiction of human folly and greed,' Greville had said. But observing the industrious activity on the bridge, Adam knew that for him the comedy must become a satire.

'It must present a moral view,' Adam said when he met Greville in the crowded tavern. 'You have but to pass between here and the Strand to observe that our original conception cannot be adequate.'

'How so?' Greville asked. 'It is but a light-hearted burlesque.'

'But I see a more important matter,' Adam replied. 'The whole population appears to be involved in a constant endeavour yet they are ever interrupted by unjust laws and the caprices of their betters. They must pay taxes for the extravagance of the King, they must provide protection for their towns and villages, they are drawn into armies to further his whimsical causes. In Ireland, they must help to support armies and planters who are merely marauders.'

'Ah,' Greville laughed. 'I see you are still involved with the Irish cause. You will do small good there.'

'But we can at least write of the King's extremes. There are many in parliament who support my views. They must constantly limit his avaricious ambitions.'

'You have changed much, Adam, since you went to

272

Ireland. You were previously but little involved in political themes. You wanted only poesy and romance.'

Adam shook his head. 'It is so. I found much there to cause disquiet and I cannot remove the memories from my mind.'

'Yet I cannot write of Ireland,' Greville said. 'I have but little enthusiasm for the Protestants, yet my father says the Irish are also of an indifferent kind and do little to further their own cause.'

'Then let us write of another matter,' Adam said. 'We will have a romance which disturbs neither of us.'

The two young men agreed and called for more ale.

'Let us write of the joys of love,' Edward said.

'And I will address my inflammatory verses to those who inspire them,' said Adam, laughing.

'I wonder whether you are not more devoted to the excitement than the cause,' Edward observed.

'Ah, my good friend, you must repair with me to Ireland. Then you will see for yourself the great injustice they suffer and the conviction with which they address their cause.'

As the evening wore on, the tavern became more and more crowded. A group of quay workers were singing lustily at one end of the room while another group were discussing the latest lampoons about the Court.

Adam and Edward joined another group of young men who were discussing Galileo.

'I studied at Padua,' one young man said, 'and attended his lectures on mathematics.'

'Is he not in some trouble at this time with the Roman church?'

'Yes. I fear they care not to believe that the sun is the centre of the universe.'

'What learnt you from Galileo?' Adam asked.

'At the time of my studies there, he was propounding the theorem that all falling bodies, both great and small, descend with equal velocity.'

The group pondered this statement.

273

'This surely cannot be so,' one young dilettante commented. 'If I drop a heavy object it must be drawn to the ground with greater speed than something of lesser weight. See.'

He held his tankard aloft and dropped it, half-filled with ale, on the stone floor.

'Now, a feather from my hat.'

It floated slowly down.

'It means not that,' Adam intervened. 'It is that each object falls at its own uniform speed.'

'Ho, ho,' someone laughed. 'Let us prove this theory.'

The group instantly began to drop any object they could seize upon, doublets, cloaks, ribbons, ruffs. The tavern owner shouted, but now they were carried away with enthusiasm and grabbed at jars, tankards, barrels, iron pokers, bellows, benches, finally raising their arms and pouring the beer and ale from their jars. Shouts and scuffles broke out as the liquid fell upon the other customers and when a ruffian produced a knife, fighting broke out in earnest.

Adam and Edward finally escaped through a side door and ran along the half-deserted alleys until they reached the comparative quiet of the bridge.

'I fear I have a gash upon my head,' Edward said.

'Let us return to my lodgings.' Adam examined his friend's head. 'I think it is but a graze.'

They walked along the almost deserted Strand. When they reached Adam's accommodation in one of the large new houses built by those desiring to escape from the now overcrowded conditions of the City, Adam was accosted by a black-cloaked individual wearing the old-fashioned funnel boots.

'Adam Hooper Humphreys?'

'I know you not, sir.'

'Sir,' he said softly, 'I am come from The O'Connell.'

'Ah! Then pray enter.'

The three men entered the house.

274

'It is most palatial,' Edward observed as they followed Adam into his room.

The Irishman pursed his lips.

'I find your air in London most fetid.'

Adam laughed. 'I fear it is not as the pure atmosphere of Ireland. But you have little of the trade and commerce which so characterizes this city. Take some ale and you will be refreshed.'

Adam put some more logs on the fire and passed to each of them a silver pipe.

'The tobacco is from my father's estate in Devon,' he said. 'I think you will find it of excellent quality.' They placed themselves on wooden settles before the log fire.

'How fares O'Connell and my other lords?'

Adam smiled at the Irishman. He was captivated by the people of that island, by their wild enthusiasm contrasting with their indolent ways, their irresistibly poetic way of thinking and talking.

'He sends me, sir, to seek your further assistance. He would that you would write for him a new treatise upon the cause of justice in my country.'

'That I will do willingly,' Adam said immediately, 'but I fear the English Protestants have much support here amongst the nobility and gentry and the common people are of no weighty concern.'

'My countrymen become increasingly resentful at the exploitation of their land and possessions. They have no rights in their own domain.'

'That I know.'

'If the King and parliament will not control it, there must be insurrection. They will not tolerate such an invader.'

'Yet I think the treatise must reach a wider public,' Adam said. 'It is of no benefit to address it to the King. We must enlist the support not only of the Catholics here but of all right-minded persons and we must renew our efforts to involve Spain and France.'

'We continue always in those areas,' the man said. He

glanced at Edward. 'And does your friend here enjoy your confidence?'

Adam laughed. 'Have no fear, sir.'

'Then I would say that we are yet enlisting an army which will be ready to rise at the right moment.'

They settled down to the composition of the treatise and Adam said he would attend to its printing. In the early hours of the morning the Irishman departed to return to Ireland.

'Your actions may be looked upon as seditious,' Edward said after he had gone. 'There are many people who would have you committed to the Tower for such writings.'

'I write only the truth,' Adam said, 'and it is a warning which any true lover of this country should attend to. In any case,' he added, 'I think I am not accustomed to act with caution. I learnt in my father's household that one's conscience is of greater concern than mere expediency.'

As the months passed, Adam found that all his energies were devoted to the writing of treatises dealing with the Irish cause and he requested Edward to complete the romance they had been writing together.

'My thoughts are ever with the Irish problem,' he said.

'It is as you desire,' Edward said, 'yet I fear more for your safety than for your peace of mind.'

Then one morning Adam received a letter from Sarah saying that she and Nicholas were visiting London and staying with Katherine. She would see him that very day. This was unexpected because although Adam saw Katherine and William frequently in their fine mansion in Westminster, Sarah rarely came to the capital and had never visited his lodgings. When she was not in Dartmouth she spent time on the estate at Exeter. She seemed always much preoccupied with her children, even taking the infant and nursemaid there with her.

He waited impatiently for her arrival. Although they saw little of each other now, ever since her visit to Rome they had enjoyed an easy intimacy which he found with no other woman except Katherine.

He saw her as she alighted from her coach and walked the remaining yards down the Strand, holding up the voluminous skirts of her long silk gown to avoid the filthy water swirling down the gutter beside her and looking with distaste at the rubbish piled in the roadway. She held her golden cloak around her and then stopped, looking up at houses to ascertain which was his.

Adam waved and ran into the street to meet her. All eyes were turned upon her, as much at the opulence of her attire as at the contemplation of her beauty.

He embraced her and led her into the house.

'It is a great delight to see you, Sarah.'

'And to see you, dear Adam. You visit Dartmouth too infrequently nowadays.'

She looked around the room. It contained only the desk upon which he wrote, a settle and bench, a small padded chair.

'It is rather dismal, Adam. You appear to have less interest in comfort than formerly.'

Adam smiled.

'Perhaps. Yet I think it is only the rigours of travel which I find tiresome.'

She studied his face.

'But what is that bruise upon your forehead?'

Adam glanced into the little looking-glass which hung on the wall.

'Oh, it is of no account. I contracted it last evening in an encounter at Belins Gate.'

He took her cloak and she seated herself on the padded chair.

'Will you have refreshment? Ale?'

She nodded.

'Are Nicholas and the children well?'

'I travelled here with Nicholas. He is engaged on business.'

Adam looked thoughtfully at her lovely face.

277

'Goes your marriage well, Sarah?'

'Nicholas has much respect for my wishes. He gives me no cause for complaint.'

'I have reports that you are much devoted to the children.'

Sarah smiled.

'I have a great attachment. I did not expect to feel thus. Yet it is as though they are a part of my being.'

'Children are fragile things. Their loss may cause you much distress if you feel so.'

'Yes, though I cannot be otherwise.'

'And your estate in Exeter? Spend you much time there?'

'We visit often. When you come to Dartmouth again, you must spend some time with me in Exeter.'

'I believed always that you were attached only to Dartmouth.'

Sarah said thoughtfully, 'I have of late had a strange presentiment. I have never wished to leave that place, yet when Nicholas proposed to buy the manor at Exeter, I felt a curious excitement, as though it were the beginning of a long journey.'

Adam laughed.

'Even Exeter must seem a long journey in the wretched coach.'

'I mean not that. It is as though it were the preparation for some more distant, unknown destination. As though I were weaning myself from what I hold most dear.'

Adam looked alarmed.

'Sarah, you mean not death? You are not ailing?'

Sarah laughed now.

'No. I anticipate no great tragedy. Yet I am perhaps restless. I find myself looking back to Dartmouth almost as though it were a completed episode in my life.'

'For me it has been ever thus. My despatch to Merchant Taylor's at an early age has made my home town less compelling.'

'Yet I care not for this London of yours.' Sarah made a face. 'This summer heat makes it even more noxious.'

'It is for me an exciting place,' Adam said. 'I spend much time conversing with poets and artists, who now seem to congregate here. People fear not to talk of philosophy and even religion is a favourite topic. And I find the intrigue and politicking of much fascination.'

Sarah frowned.

'Adam, it is of that which I had also come to see you.'

'How so?'

'Upon being informed that I was to come to London, Gabriel requested me to speak with you on this topic.'

'Ah, he is to repair again to Ireland,' Adam said eagerly.

'No. He negotiates still with the King. He attempts to persuade him that by some means the new English must be prevailed upon to leave.'

'That will be done only by the sword.'

'Adam, Gabriel refers to the series of publications which come from your pen.'

'But I recommend only what you have mentioned,' Adam protested.

'Yet not perhaps with a reasoned voice. Gabriel would inform you that the King sees your arguments as threats rather than loyal recommendations.'

'Sarah, the King cannot escape the consequences of his actions. He must be made to listen.'

Sarah shook her head.

'I fear the King begins to suspect that you and Gabriel intrigue with the Irish. You endanger your father as well as yourself.'

Adam was silent, then he said slowly, 'My father, as a practising Catholic, has for ever placed us in danger. I fight not for Catholics but for justice.'

Sarah said quietly, 'So be it. But there is another matter.' She looked upon his bruised brow. 'He receives news that you are frequently involved in brawls and tavern disturbances.'

Adam smiled.

'Report to him that there is nothing to fear. I make always a judicious escape.'

'Adam, London is a dangerous place. Thieves, murderers, informers. Your frivolous activities do nothing to further your cause and you put yourself at great risk.'

'It is but a game, Sarah, with friends. I come to no harm.'

Sarah shook her head and sighed.

'I also feel much anxiety for you, dear Adam. But now I must return to Westminster. Pray ponder upon my remarks.'

Adam walked with her along the Strand to White Hall where, being in sight of Katherine's house, he left her.

'Pray inform her that I will call on the morrow.'

Sarah walked slowly along the wider spaces of White Hall. The great new houses had a certain elegance and there were still green spaces along by the river but the roads were stinking with filth and the gutters flowed with the waste of the city. Tomorrow she and Nicholas would return to Dartmouth and the comparative cleanliness of the countryside. Even Exeter seemed cleaner than this place.

She was pleased to enter the coolness of Katherine's house and passed through into the shaded garden. There was no-one at home and she sat down, thinking still of Adam and wishing that she might enjoy his conversation more often. Then her thoughts turned again to her own anticipation of some approaching change. She was happy enough with her life, her relationship with Nicholas was cool and distant and caused her no distaste, and the children gave her constant pleasure. Indeed, she realized it was those very facts that made any thought of change unattractive.

So that when she heard footsteps on the garden path and turned to see Gabriel coming towards her, she sprang up and said, without delaying to greet him, 'What news have you, Gabriel?'

280

He came and put his hands on her shoulders and kissed her.

'Why do you look so anxious, dear one? I am in London unexpectedly on business and wished to see you.'

Sarah smiled as they sat down on the stone seat.

'It is a foolish fear I have,' she said, 'as though . . .'

Gabriel frowned.

'As though – what?'

'I know not. It is not of disaster, yet I fear some disturbance of my life. Perhaps it is simply anxiety about the children.'

'They are well, Sarah. They were with the nursemaids when I departed. I called in upon them, you have no worry there.'

'No. It is mere foolishness. I have visited Adam and told him of your concern, but I fear he will little heed your warnings.'

They began to walk slowly around the garden.

'Stay you long in London?' Sarah asked.

'I am here to make further arrangements for the journey to New England.'

Sarah laughed.

'I think this journey takes so long to arrange that it can never happen.'

'No. It is finally settled. We depart in a month.'

'It is not a long separation,' she said. 'The journey to New England, it is not long, is it?'

Gabriel led her back to the seat.

'Sarah, it is for that reason I wished to see you. When we arrive on that coast, I intend to remain for some time.'

Sarah frowned.

'Some time?'

'Perhaps two years, perhaps more.'

'Gabriel, why so long?'

'As in Ireland, I wish to found a Catholic settlement there. Yet it must be with my help and support.'

Sarah sighed. 'Gabriel, I cannot countenance such

another separation. Care you not that you see nothing of me, that you will know little of what may happen to me in such a time?'

Gabriel put an arm round her shoulder.

'Sarah, there is no other life but you. Yet we cannot be together always. We have designed our existence otherwise; the sea has always claimed much of my time and energy. It has always been so.'

'I cannot countenance it,' she repeated.

Gabriel looked puzzled.

'Sarah, I understand not your objection. You have never spoken thus. My business is with ships and exploration and trade with many countries.'

'Yes, yet your sojourn in Ireland and now this new endeavour are of a different nature. It is as though your real hopes and dreams had shifted; they are not of the trading kind, and I am excluded.'

'But I shall trade also and expect to develop further transactions in that new world. And you are never excluded from my thoughts, Sarah.'

Sarah shook her head.

'I must ponder these matters,' she said slowly. They were standing now by the sundial. She put her arms round his neck, looking into his eyes.

'Do you still love me?'

Gabriel felt the same excitement and anxiety that he always experienced, looking into the depths of her green eyes. They now had the old distant expression he had noticed on their first meeting when she was a child, the expression that always came when she was faced with some anticipation of change, a feeling of insecurity.

'Sarah, that question needs no answer. The longing for you is always there.'

He kissed her and then they heard Katherine's call as she came towards them across the lawn.

They returned to the house and Gabriel stayed for the evening meal, discussing with William his plans for going

282

to the New World. After he was gone Sarah led Katherine back to the stone seat in the garden.

'Katherine,' she said, 'I have a mind to effect a change in my situation.'

'Sarah, what are you planning?' Katherine looked interested. 'Can I share it?'

Sarah smiled. 'I must ask you to help me.'

'Oh, of course. But what is it?'

'It is about Gabriel's projected journey to the new territories.'

'Ah, you think of accompanying him,' Katherine said, laughing.

'Yes.'

Katherine stopped laughing. 'Sarah, what are you saying? I was merely being frivolous.'

'I think of accompanying him.'

'You cannot be serious. Such projects are not for persons such as yourself. My father would not consider it.'

'There will be other women, wives, going on the journey.'

'Sarah, they are not of your kind. They are poor persons, they are going for asylum, for a better life. For you, it would be grave deprivation.'

'Katherine, I feel as though my life must now be with Gabriel. My life here seems suddenly without merit or purpose.'

'Sarah, you cannot know what you say. Nicholas and the children – you could not lightly leave them.'

'No, yet I think I must.'

'And Mother, she knows of your strong attachment to my father, yet they have some regard for each other and I think neither of them would find your suggestion acceptable.'

Sarah turned to Katherine. 'Yet, if it should come about, could I rely upon you to take care of my little ones?'

Katherine stood up. 'Sarah, I cannot bear to hear you.

What would become of you? Your position in the world, it would be gravely affected.'

'I have no position in the world.'

'But you have!' Katherine protested. 'You must sacrifice it all for – a whim.'

'Katherine, would you care for my children?'

'Sarah, it would not be possible. Nicholas will maintain them at home; make no mistake, he will debar you from ever seeing them again.'

'Katherine, threaten me not with such unlikely ideas. He will be brought to understand.'

'Oh, Sarah,' Katherine replied impatiently, 'you must not persist in this nonsense. It is totally without reason. Pray, consider it longer.'

'Katherine, I will. When we have both returned to Dartmouth, we will discuss it again.'

They walked back to the house.

'I had also some slight news,' Katherine said.

'Oh, what is it, Katherine? I have been so concerned with my own little plans.'

'I am pregnant again, after so long.'

'Katherine, are you feeling well?' Sarah asked anxiously.

'Yes. It is strange. I have feared it so long, yet now I find it not distressing.'

'Ah, I think William takes such care of you.'

'Yes. I am fortunate.' Katherine laughed. 'So you see I shall be in need of your presence here.'

Sarah looked anxious. 'Yes. Yet, do not blame me if . . .'

'I shall not blame you, Sarah. It is only concern for your true happiness.'

The next day, Sarah and Nicholas returned to Dartmouth. He was concerned that she was so silent on the coach, fearing that she had overtired herself in the city. She closed her eyes that she might think in silence on the long journey to Dartmouth.

284

19

Sarah helped Catherine down from the high step of the coach and instructed the coachman to await them at the end of Bayards Cove.

'Take Emily with you also. I do not think she cares for vessels.'

The nursemaid looked relieved and remained in the coach.

'Come, Catherine, let us see the ships,' Sarah said, grasping the child's hand. Catherine ran along the quay by her side as they wove in and out of the great crowds of people who were making their way towards the boarding points.

The sails of the ten vessels preparing for the journey were motionless in the hot, breezeless afternoon. Sarah waved to Gabriel standing on the deck of *Triumph*, the largest vessel, his vivid blue, gold-braided doublet and pantaloons above his high leather boots standing out against the greys and brown and navy blue serge of the labourers and sailors. The ship looked to Sarah like a man of war with its brass guns protruding through the portholes. Gabriel stood on the gallery above the rudder post on which was mounted a carved and gilded dragon figurehead. Wooden carving, painted in red and gold, encircled the top deck of the ship. The four furled sails of the *Triumph* lay neatly across the spars and rigging, ready for the morrow's departure.

He came down the gangway towards them. The sailors

and labourers stepped back as Sarah led the child on to the ship.

Gabriel embraced her formally.

'It is good of you to come. But, the child?'

'I wished her to see the vessels. She will be no trouble.'

Gabriel looked down at the crowds of people on the quay, all clutching boxes, parcels, items of bedding.

'There is much confusion,' he said. 'You must be ruthless in your demand that each traveller may take only one item of luggage.'

He led her along to where the purser sat at a make-shift table of a plank of wood placed across two large barrels.

'Lady Maddick is come to assist you with the passenger lists.'

The man stood up, looking round uncertainly for a seat for her.

'Pray be seated.' Sarah nodded towards another barrel. 'That will suffice.'

It was moved before the table. She sat down with Catherine on her lap.

'I shall repair to the *Buttercup*,' Gabriel said. 'Frances is already on the *Starling*, John on *Devon Joy* and Mary on *Dominion*.'

'How do I proceed?'

'Guards are placed at the bottom of the gangway, but be diligent in your checking. This ship must carry only 180 persons.'

Sarah watched Gabriel as he strode across the deck and down the gangplank, instructing the guards that one family at a time might now be permitted to board. She could see why he had enlisted the help of his family. This project was unlike anything he had ever undertaken. To attempt to transport a thousand people on ten ships to a new world was very different from even forty ships of experienced sailors and fishermen. He had probably never seen children on a vessel before.

The previous evening, when the whole family had gathered at Vinelands for a farewell meal, Gabriel had talked about the journey and the growing number of expeditions to the New World.

He rarely mentioned the experiences of his voyages but last night he had seemed to be in a strange and reflective mood, as though he were aware of entering upon a new phase in his life.

'It becomes increasingly difficult to find people who will put up the money,' Gabriel had said. 'I feel it incumbent upon me to tell you of the risks we encounter.'

William and Nicholas had both contributed vast sums to the venture.

'We know the risks,' William replied. 'We can only wish you safe passage.'

'I can only wonder at your intrepid nature,' Nicholas said.

Sarah had looked at Nicholas almost with compassion. As a husband he had treated her always with such consideration, had lavished all his wealth upon her, that now she almost felt guilt at the deception she was planning. Yet in the back of her mind lay always the knowledge that her marriage had been the price she paid for his saving Gabriel's life after the trial. It had never been stated, never discussed between them. Yet the conviction remained that she was a prisoner of his emotional blackmail, that any evil consequences of what she was now planning would come from Nicholas.

'It carries a forbidding history,' Gabriel had said, 'our exploration of the New World.'

'I am grateful,' Frances said, 'that at least the long search for a northwest passage has been relinquished.'

'Ah, but it was along those Newfoundland coasts that we first tasted the joys of adventure.'

Gabriel looked pointedly at John. As far as Sarah knew, one fateful journey had never been mentioned but again she had had the impression that Gabriel was deliberately tying up his past life, leaving no untidy details, when he said to John, 'I fear the experience deterred you from further exploration.'

John blushed, then replied slowly. A slight stammer was all that remained of his earlier affliction.

'I did not believe, I do not believe now, that duty comes before love, parental or otherwise.'

There had been an astonished silence. It seemed totally foreign for John to express any feelings and Sarah looked round the table, aware of the effect those two elements of love and duty had had upon them all. Upon Katherine and William with her long attachment to Richard; upon her own feelings for Gabriel and her marriage to Nicholas. But what of Frances and Gabriel? Upon Frances there appeared to be little effect, she seemed content with her marriage, even if it yielded but little intimacy and even more with the certainty of her faith, though of late she had become increasingly distant. And Gabriel. He was the only one whose love for her, and for his family, had always appeared secondary to his beliefs. Although Gabriel was replying to John, he had looked at her, his eyes seeming to search into her soul as he said, 'I fear the ethics of my own youth were otherwise. It was commonplace, perhaps, that one would sacrifice personal desires for that which was honourable.'

Sarah remembered that Katherine had smiled as she said, 'The two are frequently interwoven.'

She watched now the first, neatly-attired couple climbing hesitantly up the narrow steps, followed by two children.

'John Carpenter, Emily Carpenter, Maria and Enoch.'

Mr Purser worked slowly down the lists.

'Mr Purser,' Sarah said. 'Allow me to check names while you determine that their baggage is as required.'

John Carpenter and his wife looked at her anxiously.

'All is in order,' he said, 'we were accepted.'

'Be not anxious. I find your names here.' Sarah nodded to him and turned to Mr Purser. 'But where are they to proceed? There must be confusion if all persons wander about the ship.'

Mr Purser frowned uncertainly.

'Then appoint sailors who will lead each family to an allotted space below,' Sarah said.

Mr Purser did as he was bid and slowly each family came before them for approval. Most of the families looked like the first, the men in grey jackets and dark breeches, the women in grey cotton gowns, some with white pinafores and dark serge capes and felt hats. Only the children had coloured gowns of indigo or blue. A few of them were dressed in silk or velvet gowns, obviously the cast-offs passed to them from some benevolent wealthy lady.

Sarah was searching in the lists for the names of the man and woman who now stood before her. Thomas Tucker, Rose Tucker of Dittisham. The woman was clearly pregnant in spite of the thick serge cape which she held around her in an attempt to conceal the fact.

'I fail to find your names,' Sarah said. 'Are you assigned to the right vessel?'

The man was silent.

'Pray, allow us, my lady,' the woman said. Her lips began to tremble. 'We have no hope in this town.'

Sarah looked up in astonishment.

'Have you not applied?'

'It is my wife's demand,' the man said belligerently. 'I have no employ. She believes we might start a new life in a new world.'

Mr Purser stood up, suddenly decisive.

'This cannot be. All places are allocated. Pray remove yourselves.'

The man roughly grasped his wife's arm.

'Come. We get no help here.'

The woman turned to Sarah.

'Please, my lady. If we are sent away, we have no place, no . . .'

'Pray, be gone,' Mr Purser interrupted. He waved to two

sailors, but the man was already dragging his wife back along the deck and down the steps. Mr Purser looked at Sarah's distressed face as she held Catherine in her arms.

'It is his lordship's command. The ship will become overladen. It would endanger all.'

Sarah was silent. Of course, he was right. It had to be regulated, otherwise you could get half the poor of Dartmouth surging on to the ship. Yet she felt unaccountably involved in the decision, as though she had been a party to some injustice.

She realized that she had never before been faced with a problem that did not directly involve herself. Her decision long ago to run away, her return, Gabriel's trial, her marriage to Nicholas, her love for Gabriel which was now leading her to an even more far-reaching decision, all revolved round her own desires.

As she watched the couple walking slowly along the quay, the man shaking his fist at the ship, the woman looking up hopelessly, memories came flooding back. She remembered how she had once called Gabriel a pirate. Even dimmer memories appeared – Granny Lott saying that the rich were thieves, living on the poor. It all seemed years ago, a lifetime away. But it was more than that. Because now she knew that Gabriel was not just a pirate. He helped the poor, was a great commander, sheltered the priests, had taken great risks about Ireland, saying always what he believed. He had also long ago rescued her.

Watching the next family coming towards them across the deck, thinking still of the events of the previous evening, she had a sudden awareness of what his religion meant, what it could be to have a belief beyond oneself, that dictated one's actions.

As the afternoon wore on into evening and the sun went down to be followed by a cool breeze, the last passengers climbed aboard.

Sarah led Catherine down the steep steps to the hold beneath. It was so crowded with people sitting and lying everywhere in the semi-darkness that Sarah thought they could surely not survive. She went on down to the hold below that, where more passengers would share the space with the crew. But in this hold there was just room to stand upright, which seemed in itself an enormous amenity.

Catherine clung to Sarah and she noticed the terror on the child's face.

'Come, my love, we return home now.'

Sarah stood at the top of the gangplank, looking at the crowded top deck. Gabriel could have no great desire to embark on this project. He would surely rather fish in Newfoundland or journey to the Azores, or explore the coasts of the New World rather than embark upon the hazards of founding a settlement for the poor, for the anxious Catholics, who had scarcely ventured beyond their own small hamlets.

She carried Catherine down the gangway to the quay. Gabriel awaited her at the bottom.

'It is complete,' she said. 'But I fear you may yet find persons hidden in the holds.'

Gabriel took her into his arms. 'Your coach?'

'It awaits at the Cove.'

He looked into her eyes.

'Farewell, my love. It is a long voyage, but our love transcends all separation.'

He kissed her and walked with them to the coach and Sarah smiled as he stood on the quay, waving to her as they passed into Lower Street. It was not until that moment, looking back at the tall, solitary figure, that she knew he expected never to return. She did not understand why, she could not at the moment dwell on the reason, she only knew that it could be the last time she would ever look upon that dear face, ever touch him.

She bade the coachman hurry, that it was late for the child to be abroad. When they reached Trevayne Abbey, the nursemaid took Catherine to her chamber and Sarah discovered Nicholas sitting in the library.

He rose and greeted her.

'Pray, be seated. I shall repair to my chamber. It has been a tiresome day.'

'I will send for food for you, dear.'

'No. I have no wish. Goodnight, Nicholas.'

She smiled at him, suddenly feeling a surge of gratitude towards this remote person with whom she had shared the last four years of her life. Spontaneously, she walked over and kissed him lightly.

'Thank you for your great . . . kindnesses.'

'It is as it should be,' Nicholas replied piously as he sat down.

Sarah sighed and walked from the room. Could he not, just once, step beyond his formal, boring behaviour? Her brief feeling of sympathy for him evaporated.

She went to the nursery to say goodnight to Catherine but she was already sleeping and she looked down at her silently. The baby Nicholas was with his wet nurse in Dartmouth; he would be all right.

Then she retired to her chamber.

It was a warm night and she sat by the open window, feeling a deep pain. She was faced with the decision now and whichever path she followed would mean only greater pain. Because she must choose between the two she loved, to stay with little Catherine or to go with Gabriel. It was not a question for her of love or duty; but of choosing between two loves. She had known, bidding Gabriel goodbye on the quay, that she had still not made up her mind. Ever since she discussed it with Katherine, she had intended to go, yet the thought of leaving Catherine had made her hesitate. Now she was convinced Gabriel would never return and the decision seemed even more terrible.

Last night, listening to Gabriel, she had been quite settled in her intention. He had talked of the early voyages to the New World and then of the great explorations of the previous reign, of how it all began as high adventure, small fleets of sailing ships, sometimes only three or four, braving storms, disease, shipwreck for the excitement of reaching unknown lands. But that period had quickly been followed by what Gabriel called the great era of people like Drake and Hawkins because although they had achieved notoriety because of their daring plunder of Spanish vessels, their massacre of Indians, their involvement in the slave trade, yet their exploits had been so spectacular, their invasions of Spanish towns so audacious that they had become the fear of the maritime world. There had also been many brave men who had sacrificed their lives in an attempt to claim foreign lands for their country. Many had been left behind along that New World coast to settle colonies, to try to build up trade, but when ships returned to these little settlements months or years later, the colonists had always disappeared, slaughtered by the Indians or carried off by hunger and disease.

The old seafaring gentry of the south west had turned their attention from Ireland to the New World. Merchants, wealthy landowners, had invested money in the expeditions in the hope of reaping a benefit from the trade that would ensue. But early attempts at settlement, organized by people with little knowledge of either the sea or of trade, interested only in profit, had been an almost unmitigated disaster. Many died on the journey, the remainder succumbed when they reached the promised land.

Now a new attempt was being made to settle the poor, to remove the people looking for freedom to worship their own God, to be rid of the unemployed and undesirables. But because of those earlier disasters, it was difficult to get sponsors for these endeavours. But Gabriel said he had only experienced and reliable captains to conduct his ships and intended to run the expedition as he would any voyage he commanded.

Sarah closed the window. She thought again of Catherine, of leaving her, and the pain returned. She thought of the children boarding the vessels that day, babies, infants . . . and suddenly she was astonished at her own stupidity. Of course, she would take the child with her! How could she have neglected to think of this before? She almost shouted with joy at the simplicity of the solution. Instantly, she packed a box with the only items of clothing she could find which seemed suitable, changing from her blue silk gown into the only dark, cotton garment she possessed. Then she crept along to the nursery and quietly touched the sleeping nursemaid's arm.

'Shush. Be not alarmed.' Sarah put down her candle. 'Emily. I believe you are alone in the world. It is my intention this night to depart with Catherine to voyage to the New World with Viscount Gabriel. I would that you accompany me.'

The girl looked so terrified that Sarah feared she would faint.

'My lady, how can that be? I have no passage, no money.'

'That will not be necessary. I will provide. You will care for Catherine.'

'Oh, my lady, I have never thought of such a thing. I know nothing of this New World. And ships!'

'I could not alert you before but I will see to your safety. My lord is a great commander.'

Emily rose from her bed, looking anxious.

'I will take a few of Catherine's garments,' Sarah persisted. 'Pray dress her and then find a few garments for yourself.'

Catherine opened her eyes but when she saw Sarah she smiled and slept again.

Emily dressed her nervously.

'My lady, how will we proceed undiscovered?'

'Speak no more. Follow me.'

They crept down the staircase and across the great stone dining hall. When they were outside in the courtyard, Sarah said, 'We must walk down into Dartmouth. We cannot take a horse and risk waking the stableboys. But the ships sail not till dawn.'

294

'I can carry Catherine upon my back. It is a simple matter.'

A dog barked as, creeping along the lane which skirted Vinelands, they passed John's farm and then they were descending the hill into Dartmouth. A guard still stood at the bottom of the Triumph's gangway.

'I must speak with his lordship,' Sarah said imperiously.

'My lady, I cannot leave my post.'

'There is no need. I will find him.' Sarah gestured him aside. 'Come, Emily.'

The deck of the ship was crowded and Sarah led them across the sleeping bodies and bade Emily lie down amongst them. Sarah sat beside her.

'We wait here till the ship has sailed,' Sarah whispered.

'But, my lady, where is his lordship?'

'Do not concern yourself. We must remain undiscovered. And do not look so alarmed. I have told you I will ensure your safety.'

They lay beneath the stars in the balmy night. Briefly, Sarah wondered what it was like on a ship. She glanced at Catherine who was folded in Emily's arms, and for the first time in her life she felt a deep and certain happiness, with no anxieties around the boundaries of her thoughts. At last she was free, she had Gabriel and Catherine and now she would find out what that other world of adventure was, that life that claimed Gabriel's soul.

As the sun began to rise, the ship came to life. Sarah had tied her hair back with ribbon and placed one of Emily's flat grey straw bonnets on her head. The high ruff round her neck partly concealed her face and as everyone packed their few belongings in neat parcels about them, she instructed Emily to speak to no-one. Sarah held Catherine in her arms and Emily accepted the bowls of porridge which were being distributed and they ate in silence.

Then, at last, Sarah watched the receding outlines of Bayards Cove as the pilot led the ships out from the harbour and the vivid light of the sun reflecting on the sea dazzled her eyes.

In spite of the crowded conditions, there was a great silence as the ships began to move across the water; most of the settlers had never been on a ship before and now the full significance of their decision overwhelmed them. They might never see these shores again; there might be perils they had never foreseen. Could the promise of a better life really be fulfilled?

As they rounded Start Point, Gabriel appeared on the platform above them and commanded them all to be silent. He looked down at the crowded bodies beneath him, at the anxious faces of the women, the children who had been instructed to be still, at the men uncertain about what actions they should perform.

'Passengers,' he said, 'we have before us a long and hazardous voyage. In the past, many of these adventures have foundered because of ineptitude on the part of the commanders, gentleman adventurers interested only in gain and profit. For your safety, it is necessary that all know the conditions under which these ships will operate. The captain's charge is to command all. All orders will be obeyed, on pain of death.'

Gabriel paused. As his eyes travelled round the deck, Sarah pulled her wide-brimmed hat further down on her head.

'The master directs the ship as the captain commands. He will decide the course, control the sailors, and trim the sails. The cape-merchant and purser are in charge of all merchandise and will take note of all that is received and delivered. There will be no theft of provisions. If a fight arises from foreign vessels, the master will direct the event with the master gunner in charge of shot, powder, arms, cartridges.'

Gabriel went through the duties of each member of the crew, while the passengers listened in silence. They knew now that they had entered upon a venture whose outcome must surely be unknown and Gabriel's words clearly had the effect of bracing them for disaster.

The sun was now high in the sky and Sarah became aware of the roll of the ship, and an unpleasant feeling in her stomach. She pushed back her hat and as she did so Gabriel looked across and she saw him frown in disbelief. Then Sarah smiled and her eyes assumed that expression which he knew so well. Gabriel turned and came down the stairs to the deck and strode across to her.

'Sarah,' he said without greeting, 'come with me.'

Sarah picked up the child.

'Leave the child here with the maid.'

Sarah hesitated. She remembered his recent words to the passengers. They all recognized her now and she did not wish to embarrass him. He must be seen to be obeyed.

'Emily, pray remain here. I will not leave you long and Catherine sleeps again.'

She followed Gabriel to the Great Cabin which he occupied alone. There was room only for a bunk and a small table on which lay his maps and astrolabe.

He closed the oak partition behind her and turned on her angrily.

'Sarah, what manner of action is this?'

'I can live without you no longer,' she said quietly. 'There is no need. I have but one life and perhaps much of that is already past.'

He placed his hands firmly on her shoulders. 'Sarah, you understand not what you do. The danger, disease, the risk to your own child. How can you behave so?'

'There is danger to all other children here. You protest not at that.'

'They are children of the poor who hope they may find a better life. Some of them come for profit. Some of them escape from criminal actions in England. You have no such need.'

'I have need only of you.'

'Sarah, what of the consequences upon yourself?'

297

'Gabriel, it is decided. Does it not fill you with joy?'

She smiled at him slowly. Gabriel was the one certainty in her life. She knew her actions were right.

'My joy is not the prime consideration,' Gabriel replied shortly.

They stood in silence. The ship rocked slightly as they began to leave the coast behind and head for the open sea.

'Sarah,' he said, 'you can be returned on a boat, back to Dartmouth. It is not too late.'

'No. I will not go back.'

'What of Nicholas? You could never return.'

'No,' she agreed.

She pushed him away and looked at him with a determined expression.

'If you should insist upon my return, I shall kill myself,' she said quietly.

'Sarah, do not speak thus! We have borne our previous separations with . . .'

'Gabriel,' she interrupted. 'I am decided.'

She put her arms round his neck. 'You never fear for the future. You believe in today.'

'Sit down, Sarah.' Gabriel pushed her gently to the bunk and sat down beside her. 'When we reach the New World, there is nothing there. We must build even the shelters over our heads, to protect us from the elements.'

'Yes,' Sarah replied calmly. 'I lived thus as a child.'

Gabriel half-smiled and shook his head.

'Perhaps. But this may be a more unwelcoming environment.'

'Gabriel, do you remember when I came to the ship to help you with the admissions of the passengers?'

Gabriel nodded briefly.

'When I left, I stood on the quay and looked back and you were standing on the gangway. I feared then that if I did not accompany you, I might never see you again.'

'Sarah, we cannot anticipate the will of God.'

Suddenly, she stood up and put her hands on his shoulders, looking into his eyes.

'Gabriel, I leave it then in your hands. It is your vessel. But I have never failed you. Do not fail me now.'

'I think only of your happiness, Sarah.'

'In that case, permit me to remain.'

Gabriel sat in silence, looking at her. Suddenly, she looked very small and fragile. She smiled.

'It is but a simple matter,' she said. 'You have made far more momentous decisions.'

Gabriel smiled. 'Such as bringing you to Vinelands in the first place.'

'Do you regret it, Gabriel?'

He stood up abruptly.

'Sarah! I cannot imagine the world without you. And perhaps I have thought too much of my own ambitions. You have made this decision and I must support it, as you would me.'

'Yes?'

'Yes,' Gabriel said firmly.

Suddenly, Sarah clutched the side of the bunk.

'I fear it is a storm brewing,' she said anxiously.

'It is calm,' Gabriel replied.

She sat down. 'I feel not well. My stomach turns over.'

Gabriel pulled her up firmly.

'It is a simple matter. Come.'

He dragged her up the steep wooden steps and across the bodies crowded together on the deck, to the rail.

'You do not hide from the sea. The cabin below is hot and putrid. The air here is more conducive to health.'

'Gabriel, I feel . . .'

'Look.' He pointed down into the lightly curving waves and the narrow ripples of foam. 'That gentle motion conceals the great and deadly power of the ocean. Observe it.'

'Gabriel, it makes me feel worse.'

'You must learn to go with that movement, Sarah. You cannot retreat from the Atlantic.'

She looked down and felt a pulse beating in her head. Then she looked up, beyond the now full sails of the other ships, across the immense mass of water to the remote horizon. The huge space of sea and sky made her feel giddy.

'It is a fearful sight.'

'The sea is fearful,' Gabriel replied. 'Yet it has a greatness denied to the land. It can never be exploited, modified as the earth can. It has its own total power, its tides and depths, its ebb and flow. Gales, hurricanes, earthquakes strike the earth low, but the sea responds with a fury that sucks men and ships into its own eternity.'

Sarah looked at him. For a moment her sickness had receded. This was the Gabriel she had never known. The land-locked man she loved had seemed above and indifferent to, even contemptuous of, all people and circumstance. He towered always above everyone she had ever met. But here, in acknowledging a power greater than himself, he seemed more heroic in his eagerness to confront it.

'I think you love the sea more than you fear it.'

'Ah, it is not thus, Sarah. The sea tells each man of his infinite solitude. Man confronts something he knows he can never conquer. Yet the disloyal sea, a friend to no-one, leading to all unknown coasts, also gives man total freedom. Man has no dominion here.'

Gabriel turned abruptly.

'Sarah, I must return to my duties. Remain here, or go below to the cabin. Do not wander around the ship.'

He had Catherine and the nursemaid installed in a small cupboardlike area next to his cabin and a mattress placed within the cabin for Sarah. Sarah had feared that the child would be unhappy in her new situation but she had been playing with other small children, appearing to be unconcerned at the great mass of water around her.

When she had seen that Catherine and Emily were safely accommodated, Sarah went to the cabin and sat at the tiny table, anticipating that the worst part of the journey would be the long inactivity which must ensue. Gabriel had told the passengers that the voyage might take twelve weeks and over that period of time these confined spaces must prove a terrible restriction to all.

When Gabriel came to the cabin that night many hours after she had retired, she was still sitting on his bunk.

He said instantly, 'I have considered your words this morning.'

Sarah did not reply.

'Even more, I have considered your actions. It requires great courage to do as you have done.'

Sarah looked astonished.

'Ah, but I am with the two I love in all the world. It is others I have sacrificed.'

Gabriel sighed. 'I think I would have wished to do thus, yet had not the fortitude to make that decision. And you have sacrificed much wealth and comfort.'

Sarah put her arms round his neck and smiled.

'Remember, you were reared on honour. I had no such disability in my early childhood.'

Sarah spent the next day walking unobtrusively round the crowded ship. She saw instantly that the initial problem for everyone would be boredom. All these people had made this dramatic decision to leave their homeland and travel to this unknown world. For weeks and months they must have been assailed by fears, anxieties, doubts as well as hope. Now at last they were here, with nothing to do but clean their tiny space and move as little as possible.

She knew it would be the same for her. Gabriel would be employed all day in running the ship and she would see little of him. Those vast expanses of water did not appeal to her as the views of the hills and fields of

Dartmouth did. Soon she would long for the sight of land.

That evening, awaiting Gabriel, Sarah saw that Catherine was attended to and then repaired to the cabin. To pass away the long, lonely hours, she resolved to keep a journal, a record for herself of this new experience. She took writing materials from a tiny cupboard and sat down at Gabriel's table.

Journal of the voyage from Dartmouth in the county of Devon, England, of the Triumph *with nine other vessels to a destination yet unknown, but in the environs of the New World.*

5 July 1620

Two days out to sea. It is my decision to keep a record of the strange and peculiar events which must present themselves to me upon this progress. Because already my past life appears a dream from which I have awakened.

Yet the spectacle of this great ocean surrounding me and which Gabriel conjectures must be in some areas four thousand fathoms, fills me with dread. One is encompassed not merely by a great circle of distant horizons but also by those awesome depths beneath.

It is as though, bereft of the familiar sights of terra firma, the gardens of Trevayne, cattle in farmsteads, tall chimneys rising from houses, kitchens and chambers, one can recognize nothing which appertains to human life. I am not sensible of any loss in what I have foregone, and Gabriel is happily reconciled to my presence here. At first, he appeared to treat of my arrival as he did many moons ago when I first approached Vinelands. He was as one bewildered by a mystery he could not unfold. But after admonishing me, we spoke of my feelings, and of his, and now he appears to welcome my presence.

10 July 1620

As we proceed to a more southerly firmament, the power of the sun increases. The crowded passengers on the top deck divest themselves of their garments and try to shelter themselves in the shadows of the great sails. But their cheer increases after being much subdued for the first days. They speak of the new life, of the chances of employment, although Gabriel has warned them that nothing yet exists except what they will create themselves. Some have heard that there is gold in Virginia and expect that they will acquire great wealth and will build great palaces. In the holds below, the discomfort is greater. The master commands the sailors to clean the decks of the foul matter deposited there and the passengers must wash their clothes and dry them in the sun. Daily, great mounds of rubbish are cast overboard and although all the other vessels perform the same action, it is soon left behind, floating away into the distance of the vast waters.

Each day, Gabriel places a cross on the white track chart to fix the position of our vessels. Frequently at night we go out on deck and he gazes ahead. If this wind continues well, he says we shall soon come upon the Azores.

14 July 1620

As the days pass, Gabriel becomes more and more restless. He constantly stands upon the front of the upper deck as though he feared we might miss the land we shall approach. Though it is scarce possible, because from the high bridge the horizon is a great circle of many miles around us and even a small ship can be clearly seen at a great distance.

Today, one of the passengers was stolen of his purse and by perseverance the sailors have apprehended the culprit.

Gabriel had the miserable creature placed before the main mast and bade all the ship's company to shout, 'A lyer, a lyer.' The call was taken up by those on the other vessels who heard our call and the unison of voices echoed across the waters like a terrible judgment. Now he is put to cleaning the beak-head and chains. Gabriel said that should such another incident occur, the perpetrator will be cast overboard.

18 July

Today we saw in the distance a great vessel which looked as though it were made of gold with much vivid decoration and fearsome guns protruding through the portholes. Gabriel observed that in the past that ship would have been captured but as a lone ship would retreat from our fleet, he would not risk the expedition by pursuing it. Gabriel gave orders to the other captains to this effect and laughed heartily when he reflected upon the astonishment the Spanish captain must experience at such a happy escape.

Indeed, two of the captains expressed dismay regretting the loss of a chance to obtain much booty, but they did not choose to thwart the determination of Gabriel, who governs all.

21 July 1620

We have come today to a strange situation. In this morning's increasing heat, the wind has reduced to a mere flutter and we spied at last the first land we have seen since we sailed into the north Atlantic. In the distance we saw steep grey mountains rising around the coast and there seemed to be no place accessible to man. But an even stranger sight was that of many sail becalmed some way off the breezeless coast as though they were held in some heavenly spell. Their white sails were spread wide to attract any slight air that might be moving and our passengers stood on the deck, looking fearfully at the eerie stillness. As we drifted slowly towards the harbour, our ships also lost their impetus and it seemed that we might wait there for ever in the breathless calm.

23 July 1620

We have lain here for almost three days. A curious gloom has descended upon the passengers. Small boats come out from the coast with fruit and other produce but no-one may leave our vessels as Gabriel decrees that instant advantage must be taken of any fair wind.

For the first time sickness has smitten some of the passengers and those in the holds below suffer from the putrid air and the inability to move around. This afternoon six Frenchmen were brought aboard and when I addressed them they expressed surprise that a woman could converse in their tongue. They revealed they had been cast away when their ship was captured in March 1619 by a Spanish pirateer. They had drifted to these islands where they had survived and were scarce aware that sixteen months had passed since that day.

24 July 1620

Last night ere darkness fell a sudden breeze seemed to sweep across the waters from northern parts and the sails shuddered.

This morning we have the spectacle of all those becalmed vessels moving in procession once more towards the open seas, like a great army of escaping prisoners. We must now reaccustom ourselves to the sudden movements, the rolling and rocking and dipping. More illness is reported and today an old man has died and been cast to his eternal resting place in the ocean. Gabriel commands that everyone must eat one lemon a day, however distasteful.

27 July 1620

I am distraught. Catherine has contracted a fever and lies motionless on her bunk as though death had already claimed her. For two days I have not moved from her side except at Gabriel's behest to walk upon the deck. Emily stays with her also and prays constantly by her bedside.

Yet I fear always that the Virgin pays but little attention to mortal needs.

28 July 1620

Catherine continues in her decline. For the first time I have looked back to England and questioned whether I should have left it. Yet how could I have known of these perils?

Gabriel comes with the news that eleven individuals have now died of this mysterious sickness with which the other vessels are similarly affected. The sea now appears a great and desolate place from which there is no escape. Can we never reach some cool land where perhaps the sickness would abate?

The chirurgeon comes almost hourly with physick for Catherine and I am painfully reminded of the last days of Gilbert.

Tonight Gabriel came to address my fears. He looked sadly upon Catherine, who has taken no refreshment for many hours. Then he turned to me. He said that every person must stand by his decisions. I said perhaps I would not have taken this step if I had known of the dangers. Gabriel replied that it is in the nature of living that human beings always operate with insufficient knowledge. Only God is immune from that peril. Then he said firmly though not severely, 'You have thrown in your lot with me, Sarah. Whatever befalls, we go forward together to a new world. Look not backward to England.'

His words revealed to me that I had apprehended always the possible consequences. I would have pursued this course in any event. The responsibility must be my own. I now feel much calm.

4 August 1620

As though she had understood my loss of anxiety, Catherine suddenly began to mend. Now she sits on deck in the sunshine, her spindly legs barely carrying her.

But much sickness has prevailed on the ship and the death toll has now risen to twenty-two. Gabriel has blamed the overcrowding and says that such conditions must not be permitted again.

7 August

This morning we were approached by some dozen Spanish vessels who feared we were heading for their settlements. But Gabriel quickly commanded our vessels to open fire. Great guns boomed and echoed across the sea and clouds of vapour temporarily hid the enemy from us. The distressed passengers hid beneath their scanty possessions, the children screaming, but when the smoke had cleared, the Spanish ships had moved already away and we experienced no more of them.

21 August

For many days, we have been overtaken by the lonely monotony of the sea. It is as though we are cast under a spell, sailing ever on towards our destination.

Now a gale is rising, and Gabriel stands upon the gallery, listening to gauge the force of the wind. He says it is the west wind that sends the Atlantic rollers and he observes the clouds and the violent waves.

The sun glares low in the sky and streaks of yellow lightning flash down and dive into the sea. The storm is upon us.

22 August

Last night, Gabriel commanded all passengers to lie low and to cling to their possessions. There was a terrible howling through the ship, great green waves stood up around us hissing menacingly and we thought we must surely be sucked into their ghostly embrace. Poor Emily hid below, praying to the Virgin. But Catherine danced on her thin legs at the spectacle of the white foam and showed no fear. Has she been blessed with that fortitude which seems also to have entered my soul?

Then the ship bent over in the squall, Gabriel shouted to the riggers above to shorten sail, the sailors below tied and battened, there was a fearful grating and shuddering and the wind howled and rumbled like thunder. The decks were full of water, there were articles falling everywhere. The sails were blowing loose, torn from their masts, the rigging flew helplessly in all directions, the ship lay over. We feared we were surely lost.

Now, it is still.

Last night, one ship was lost. A great wave was seen to pass over it and then we saw it no more. As the great storm subsided, I crept aloft to observe the devastation. The passengers on the top deck have lost what little they possessed. A man was taken off the poop by a huge wave, to be seen no more. As though in recompense for its violent assault, the waters now lie quiet and placid and the gale has reverted to a gentle breeze. We have been blown far off course and soon we approach the land of Bermuda. Gabriel has determined that we shall anchor there to prepare for our arrival upon the New World, there being no other convenient place in this vast ocean where necessary repairs may be effected.

25 August 1620

Now we rest in the harbour of this island which some call Somerset. The hills rise from pale sandy beaches and there are palm trees everywhere. From the ship we can see narrow paths leading across the slopes with forests of cedar trees beyond. The rocks are strange mixtures of pink and white and green covered with tiny holes and crevices which Gabriel says are formed by the coral insect.

He reports that ten years ago these islands were uninhabited when an English ship was wrecked here on a reef. The adventurers remained for nine months and then sailed away to a settlement in Virginia. But settlers from the following ships remained and small groups of them live here in little wooden structures with reed roofs. He says their chief occupation is piracy and the inhabitants grow rich upon the spoils they capture. But seeing our many guns, they did not approach but left us in peace.

8 September 1620

It was five hundred miles from the islands to the New World and after many days being engulfed once again by the sea, Gabriel conjectures that soon we shall come upon the coast of Carolina. We have suffered no more storms or inconveniences. The sickness has abated. In all, we have lost thirty one persons on the journey, the other vessels faring somewhat better, through carrying fewer passengers.

12 September

As the sun rose above the far horizon behind us we saw at last before us the land we have longed to see.

The passengers stood in silence on the deck and then a cheer went up that we had safely negotiated our passage. And then the master stood upon the gallery and shouted that we must thank not only the Lord but also our captain for his constant vigilance. There were more cheers and Gabriel bowed and said we must now have some further forbearance. For we were not to land here in Raleigh Bay but continue up the coast to form a new settlement further north and he bade us to observe the coast as we went, that we might begin to learn how people live in these parts.

I observed as we proceeded green lands and great forests and mountains at one place coming almost to the sea. Yet it seems of little habitation. The settlers live in small communities in houses of wood, but I saw not any sign of much diligence in their working.

22 September 1620

As we proceed, larger settlements appear. The shacks are often built around a central building and Gabriel said that these places are used for worship. There are areas planted with fruit and vegetables and always far away behind them are plains and hills and great forests.

The ship has become very quiet, observing these features. There seems a strange loneliness in this land, a plainness we had not foreseen.

30 September

Today, we were passing along the coast of a long island. As we were close inland, we could see people working in the fields beyond. Men, women and children were all black. We gazed in astonishment at this phenomenon more particularly because they were so scantily clad as to expose much of their bodies.

Shortly afterwards, we went briefly into Narragansett Bay and all were filled with hope that this was our destination. But Gabriel said that this was not the place for our settlement and we left the harbour and sailed on again, up the coast.

Everyone was much disappointed. We long now only to be on land.

20

Gabriel stood on the bridge of *Triumph* as the nine vessels moved slowly out of the harbour and headed north. He had visited this area only once some years earlier when the whole area above Narragansett had been completely uninhabited. There had been evidence then of attempts at settlement but the few houses were abandoned and where there had been the beginnings of cultivation of the land there was only weed and forest.

It had been his intention to land here to establish his colony, but now there were already small groups of English and Dutch settlers who must have prior claim. Although there were probably only a couple of hundred persons along this piece of coast, he knew that his company, although it had been reduced to something over eight hundred from the original thousand who had set out from England, would need a large area of land to ensure their prosperity. Also, he did not wish to be involved in disputes with other communities. Life would be hard in any case, without the further complications of competition. So they had not landed, but sailed on once again to look further north.

The settlers listened with dismay to his decision as they passed the lush green pastures, a coastline which was fertile almost to the water's edge. They had found comfort and sudden encouragement in seeing other people who already had experience of this new land and had expected to join them. Yet even when they had rounded the bay and come into the safety of Cape Cod, Gabriel was still dissatisfied and ordered the ships on. There were few habitations here but ships were anchored in the many natural harbours and he knew that this land was already claimed. As they sailed on up the coast the landscape changed. Great uncut forests rose above the cliffs and the high rocks and mountainous terrain, reaching almost to the sea, looked unwelcoming and almost impenetrable.

But at last, before a small area of cleared land, with one green hill rising gently from the shore and forests beyond, Gabriel bade the ships drop anchor. He stood on the gallery and looked down upon the settlers.

'We have reached our destination. This land is known as Sagadahok. Here we will make our plantation.'

The passengers all stood up and looked solemnly at the rocks and hills and the mountains in the distance.

'It is not as fair as that coast we have passed,' a voice came from the crowd.

'It is not,' Gabriel agreed, 'but this place will provide our needs. These very rocks and hills will give us protection. The forests will provide timber for our houses and buildings, the waters here are deep enough for our ships, the inlet provides a sheltered harbour, the summer climate will permit the growth of many crops, and the seas around supply fish better even than Newfoundland. We have also a river which will supply all our watering needs.' He spoke slowly that they might understand the advantages of this place. 'It is well, also,' he went on, 'that further up the coast there are craggy rocks and desolate, barren land. We shall not find other settlers infringing upon our territory.'

The occupants of the holds below had all come up on deck, some of the sailors were on the rigging and Gabriel sensed a feeling of hope pass through the ship as they all looked upon that uninviting coast.

'Now, we have heavy weeks ahead. We must first clear land and cut down trees to construct the houses. During that period we shall remain at night on the vessels, so that our supplies remain safe. And may the Lord bless your labours.'

It took only about a month to achieve Gabriel's objective. Accustomed to arriving on coasts such as those of Newfoundland or the West Indies, with experienced sailors and fishermen who fell about their tasks without supervision, he had feared that these inexperienced travellers would need constant instruction and encouragement. Gabriel was aware of all those plantations in Virginia which had failed because of the idleness of the settlers. Many of them had been unemployed in England, idleness and hunger were normal and they had subsisted on a few

312

sheep or cattle which they grazed on common land. In Virginia they frittered their time and energy, trading their few possessions with the Indians for corn and awaiting new supplies of men and provisions from England. When they failed to arrive they simply starved and, with the added hazards of sickness and disease, the settlements disappeared.

But here there were no Indians to trade with – they had been wiped out or forced inland by earlier settlement attempts or by traders or adventurers sailing up the coasts – and no new supplies would be arriving from England. The voyagers knew their survival depended on their own efforts and, learning from the experience of those past expeditions, Gabriel had been careful to select settlers with all those crafts and skills, building, fishing, husbandry, carpentry, blacksmithing, ploughing, farming, vital to their survival.

After months at sea, they exhibited signs of sickness and exhaustion when they first set foot on land. They sat on the sandy beach in the soft September sun, speaking little, eating little when they returned to the ship.

Then, after a few days, the clear air of their new land began to revive them and one morning the men from all the vessels collected apparently spontaneously upon the seashore and, at the bidding of the masters, began work.

Inland from the sandy shore and the high rocks, they found a green plain leading to the forests beyond and here the settlement was begun. Plots of land were allocated so that the passengers from each vessel remained in their community. For work, the whole company was divided into groups according to their many trades and overseen by the most senior and experienced amongst them. The timber houses were hewn from the forest and constructed along a single path, each house having a few acres around it and the houses were all built on a concentric plan, with a meeting house in the middle. All the houses were of a uniform size except that for each of the captains an extra

313

room had been added for the purpose of holding meetings and conducting business. The store buildings were erected separately at varying places on the plantation so that in the event of fire or attack not all would be lost and the ammunition shed had double walls.

Towards the end of October, Gabriel gathered them all together. The meeting house was as yet merely a circular construction of many upright poles, with a sloping thatched roof nearing completion. But the wooden houses were now adequate for occupation and Gabriel decreed that supplies would now be brought ashore and then there would be two days of rest before the next stages were embarked upon.

He then requested that the captains and masters of the other vessels should gather in the meeting house.

Gabriel surveyed the men now seated before him, landowners, merchants, gentlemen, aware that upon this meeting rested the success or failure of the whole endeavour. He had a clear conviction of how the plantation should be run and during the past weeks he had already seen signs that these men might not prove amenable to all his suggestions. Now he was determined to enforce his authority, in the interests of all those settlers whose lives were totally dependent upon its success.

They passed the ale amongst them. Gabriel joined in their self-congratulations.

'Much has been achieved, gentlemen, in these weeks. Our letters patent from King James, chartering us to establish a settlement, have been initiated. Our next interest must be to ensure that it becomes a success.'

'I am sure we all have that aim at heart,' one of the merchants, Godfrey Rufus, agreed. 'As well as the gains to be obtained from the fishing fields, we must hope for some profits from furs and into the interior we may yet find gold or silver.'

'And the fine veined stone of these rocks must find a market in Europe for building and tiling.'

'And these huge forests must provide a great trade

314

in timber, which is becoming a scarcer commodity in England.'

Gabriel assented.

'But first, gentlemen, I would have us review the purpose of our venture. Furthermore, we are over eight hundred persons and it is necessary that our mode of life be well regulated.'

'The laws of England must surely operate here.' Milton Sayer, gentleman, looked puzzled.

'Except that of worship,' Gabriel replied.

'Ah, but of course that is understood. We have two priests to attend to that matter. I think we are all of the same persuasion.'

'Yet I desire no coercion in this matter. I fear that some of the settlers were but poor persons, desirous of finding a better life. Let every man and woman attend to their own conscience.'

'No such freedom was vouchsafed to us in the old country,' Robert Payne, a Devonshire landowner, replied.

'That is why I wish it here,' Gabriel said firmly.

'Then so be it,' the merchant Godfrey Rufus agreed and each man nodded.

Gabriel turned now to the matters he knew would raise more opposition.

'It is necessary, also, that each man and woman cultivate their own plot, that they may provide for all their needs. All manner of fruit and vegetables may be grown here as in England.'

'They must surely find this of little hardship,' one of the captains said lightly.

'As I hope all of you will not,' Gabriel smiled.

'I had thought to employ such labour,' Milton Sayer said doubtfully, 'while I attend to matters of administration.'

'Ah,' Gabriel replied, 'those matters must be accomplished at other times. I had assumed that each of you will attend to any personal needs of the shipload you

315

brought with you. But that relates not to the labours we must perform.'

'What mean you?' Robert Payne looked indignant.

'There will be no employment of persons like that to which we are accustomed. Time must be designated that each person in the family shares as they agree the jobs of working the land, fulfilling domestic needs, preparing food, sewing and clothing, with the remainder of the time devoted to the betterment of the community – fishing, hunting, building, trading.' Gabriel paused and then added slowly, 'All and any profit to be returned to the community. There will be no private wealth and speculation.'

There was silence. They looked as though they could scarcely comprehend the enormity of his remarks.

'Let us address ourselves to these questions,' Gabriel said.

'I came here to start the settlement, true,' Godfrey Rufus blurted out, 'but I am a merchant. There can be no attraction in a venture which admits of no real gain.'

'The gain must be in a better life for all.'

'For me, it is not better,' Milton Sayer replied. 'I have sacrificed the peace and safety of my home, the civilized appurtenances to which I am accustomed, to make this venture.'

'Then as a free man, finding this not to your liking, you may return thence.'

'Ah, these are strong words, sir,' a captain interposed. 'We must reach here some accommodation.'

But Milton Sayer went on angrily, 'And what of those persons in England who have invested money in this enterprise?'

'Ah, our profits must first go to their recompense,' Gabriel agreed, 'and then to this settlement.'

'I am but little versed in the arts of digging and planting and my wife must surely tax my stomach if she ventures into the kitchen,' Robert Payne complained.

'No doubt you must both benefit from the instruction of those more experienced than yourselves,' Gabriel said curtly.

'It would seem a grave waste of skills that each man does not perform that to which he is best suited,' Payne persisted.

'I fear', Gabriel replied, 'that some gentlemen would have but little to offer, being skilled only in commanding others to work, or riding to the hunt, for which there is but little opportunity here. In any case, it is not so. Those skills which each man possesses will be employed in that time designated to the public good. Clearly, the fisherman will fish, the ploughman plough and you, gentlemen,' looking at the captains, 'will command those ships which go in search of trade and exploration.'

He glanced around at the now hesitating company and then suddenly stood up.

'Gentlemen, I have heard and read much of past endeavours of this nature. They have failed through idleness, through personal acquisitiveness, through diversion of aims. We may have much to combat in the environment, disease, many as yet unknown hazards. I beseech you, let us for one year proceed as I request. After that time, we will meet again to change that which you find without benefit. Pray confer.'

Gabriel stood, looking out between the wooden pillars to the large circle of houses around them. Beyond them he could see the sea and, far behind, the forests and the mountains. He believed that here, with all the centuries of experience of that old world, they could enter upon a new and better existence.

He turned as Robert Payne, the landowner, spoke.

'Very well. We agree to your proposals. Let a document be drawn up which shall be placed upon this meeting house for all to see.'

Gabriel smiled as they stepped out into the early autumn

sunshine. He walked along the path to the house designated for his use. Each house had been given a number but he noted that some of the occupants had already painted their names and trades on the wooden doors – George Chick, fowler; Charles Lock, fisherman – as though their identity were insufficient without a trade to accompany it.

As he contemplated the large, rough plot of land which was his responsibility he reflected that, having admonished the other captains, he himself might find this kind of labour demanding in spite of the rigours of seafaring and fishing to which he was accustomed.

He saw through the open shutters that Sarah was standing in her plain grey dress with her back towards him, looking through the open shutters on the other side of the room to the hills beyond. Her hair hung in a single thick, golden plait down her back. He was aware again of that strange mystery about her. She never changed, never seemed to get older, her pale skin and the soft contours of her body still looked as though she had been carved in delicate porcelain. Looking at her, he was aware of the old anxiety she had aroused in him. He knew she filled him with an absurd desire that they might live for ever. It was not that he feared death but that he felt an uncontrollable anguish that there could never be long enough, never enough time for them. He felt guilt, too, that this earth, with her, was more desirable than the hope of heaven.

Yet until this journey he had accepted their separations, seen them as a condition of their own desires and weaknesses. When they were apart, the knowledge that she walked this earth had sustained him. Now she had shattered all that. Although in the future he might embark upon journeys and expeditions, he knew that in future it must be Sarah he would return to.

He stood behind her and put his hands on her shoulders.

'We have seen but little of each other during these past weeks.'

Sarah turned. 'Yet more than we would otherwise have done.'

'Is Catherine well?'

Sarah smiled.

'You worry about her even more than I. She has grown already and it is difficult for Emily to coax her away from the other children to partake of her meals.'

'It is real freedom for them, I suppose.'

He put his arms round her.

'And what of you, Sarah?'

She looked at him thoughtfully.

'It is a strange thing but it is like coming home. Even when we looked first upon those barren rocks and the dark forests, I had this feeling.'

'There is great peace here,' Gabriel said.

'It is as though we belong here. Oh, I wish we could stay for ever.'

'We have no need to think of the future now. Let us be happy with the present,' Gabriel replied, but his face clouded. He knew that at the back of both their minds were all those unacknowledged problems which one day would have to be faced.

'Yes,' Sarah said. She turned abruptly and closed the shutters. 'We have had today distributed wooden bedsteads and straw mattresses. See.'

She took his hand and led him across the room.

Next day, Sarah penned the regulations as dictated by Gabriel and after inspection by the captains they were placed on the meeting house door and read to the assembled settlers.

Rules of the new settlement of lands north of Sagadahok and on the banks of the river Kennebec understood and agreed by all the company on this 30th Day of October in the year of Our Lord 1620

319

All persons shall work the land allotted to them, to grow their annual supply of food and will maintain and improve their dwellings

All persons shall spend six hours a day executing their trade or skill for the benefit of the community

There shall be no payment in cash or kind for any labours

No-one is a servant to any other but all must perform their own labours

Women with small children shall be directed to suitable employ in aid of the settlement

Children between the years of six and twelve shall attend each forenoon at the school house for instruction in reading, writing and calculations

When the hospital house is complete, any sick persons shall be removed thereto to avoid contamination, to be administered by the chirurgeon and persons trained to medicine

Profits of all expeditions of fishing, hunting and exploration to be devoted to the purchase of further supplies for the colony

The captains and masters will jointly settle any disputes arising in the colony of a financial nature

Each captain shall be responsible for the administration of justice in criminal offences of those who sailed upon his vessel. Juries will be appointed from those who sailed on other vessels

Mass and other church ceremonies will be administered daily by the priests

Attendance is voluntary

As they returned to their labours, the settlers looked content. Autumn saw great catches of herring and turbot and the fishermen predicted that the cod would be better than anything caught in the northern seas of Newfoundland. Although the whales proved to be of a strange species and could be caught only with difficulty, they soon became a part of the staple diet which was supplemented by the hunting of deer and the snaring of geese and ducks.

On one expedition further inland, the settlers returned in terror with stories of an abandoned village they had discovered, with fields of stubble, dwellings, burial sites and evidence of European goods. They had heard fearful tales in England of the Indians who inhabited these parts, that they were cannibals and that their favourite sport was removing the heads of white men. Gabriel said that there were few Indians remaining, because the friendly and hospitable tribes had been decimated either by other tribes or by the white man.

But a few days later, a small group of Indians were found on the outskirts of the settlement, obviously watching the activities of the inhabitants. They offered no resistance when they were surrounded by the sailors, but indicated by signs and gestures how their villages had been attacked and burned and how some of their number had been carried away, leaving them as the only survivors. Yet they seemed to harbour no resentment and showed the settlers how to plant winter maize on the hillsides, using ground-up fish for fertilizer.

They took groups into the interior where, with bows and arrows, the Indians hunted goats and bears. On another expedition the settlers returned with the pelts of about six thousand black fox. These they traded further down the coast for supplies of wool and cotton to make clothes and blankets for the approaching winter and for the fruits and vegetables they had not yet been able to plant themselves.

The school house had been constructed in a few weeks and Sarah conducted the lessons, aided by a number of those settlers who had received a grammar-school education.

Now the hospital was nearing completion and the chirurgeons from each of the vessels were demanding that more beds be provided.

'If all sick persons must be housed here, the winter may find a great demand.'

'It seems but autumn yet, the sun still shines,' Milton Sayer commented.

But as if to justify the surgeons' words, the Indians

321

appeared from the woods next morning clothed in bear-skins, and long woollen socks and tunics given them by the settlers.

The settlers stood in the sunshine, looking at them in astonishment. Then one of the Indians pointed to the north and said in his broken English, 'The evil spirit of winter approaches. Soon it will be like iceberg. Cold white everywhere. Not much fish or hunt.'

Two days later rain fell in a deluge such as they had never seen in England. It fell in sheets so that they could not see a yard before them, hailstones battered in the thatched roofs and the long paths leading to the meeting house flowed like rivers.

The torrents continued for a day and then ceased as suddenly as they had begun. But scarcely had the settlers begun to repair the damage, swept the muddy waters on to the beach and erected barriers around their homes for future protection than the temperature dropped and snow began to fall. It fell day and night in huge cascading flakes; the paths and roadways were covered, great drifts piled up around the houses and every man and woman on the settlement was devoted entirely to keeping the low-built houses from total submersion.

Timber had to be brought from the forests to maintain fires in all the homes and the Indians constructed a bonfire in the centre of the settlement which burned like a great funeral pyre. Then a gale arose, tearing down from the mountains and howling through the rooftops so that the thatched roofs, weakened already by the weight of snow, began to sag. Gabriel would have moved the settlers back to the ships anchored in the harbour but it would have been impossible to board them from the fragile boats. The fishermen had been unable to put to sea for over a week, instead cutting a path through the snow and fishing upon the snow-covered banks of the river because the current was too violent now to allow boats to enter. They came back with only paltry catches, their clothes frozen to their bodies, and the hospital became filled with frostbite victims.

Then one night the river Kennebec itself froze over and their pure water supply and last source of food was cut off. The vegetables they had planted were now buried beneath twenty feet of snow. The cattle and horses were sheltered in the meeting house and now it was necessary to slaughter them for food.

As the temperature continued to fall, people became sick with exhaustion, the children suffered from frozen hands and feet, older people could not breathe. The settlers developed a strange illness, alternating between high fevers and bouts of cold and shivering. Then the deaths began to increase and the burials had to be postponed because of the frozen earth. Gabriel summoned the captains together in his house. The Indians who accompanied them through the blizzard seated themselves on the floor.

'Gentlemen, I have consulted with our friends here about our serious situation,' Gabriel said, indicating the seated Indians. He noted the barely concealed supercilious expression of the gentlemen, knowing that they still tolerated them as savages whose knowledge might be of some use.

'And what is their solution?' one of them asked.

Gabriel smiled. 'All people sleep in same skins,' he said, imitating the Indians but without offence.

'How so?'

'It is obvious when brought to our attention. The heat generated by many bodies must be greater than that of the small family group. Therefore, half the settlers will move into the meeting house with the animals transferred to the houses, the other half will go to the schoolroom. Granbanico suggests we sleep in a circle, our feet towards the centre where the fire will be kept burning.'

'I'll take my luck in my own house,' Robert Payne remarked. 'And what of the disease that will be passed amongst us?'

Gabriel looked at him coldly. 'No. You will not. We will all go to those places. And the sick will all go to the hospital house, however crowded.' He paused and added, 'Gentlemen, until this adverse winter, we have achieved some progress. Let us continue in our resolution.'

Milton Sayer nodded. 'Aye, it will be as you suggest. We have agreed to your governance.'

The captains expressed their approval.

'There is another matter,' Gabriel said. 'I find our situation is not aided by the lethargy which has descended upon the settlers.'

Godfrey Rufus voiced the obvious astonishment of them all.

'Lethargy, my dear Gabriel! Our energies are absorbed ever clearing paths, bringing great timbers from the forest, slaughtering, carrying.'

'I know it,' Gabriel assented, 'yet much time is spent within each house, its occupants concerned only to keep warm.'

Sayer laughed.

'Would you have us attempt to build in the gale and blizzard? Or organize a game of stoolball?'

Gabriel sprang to his feet.

'Gentlemen, yes, that is the answer! Each of you will select teams of adults and children. The area by the meeting house will be cleared. A great tournament shall be held.'

In the months to come, they all looked back on that event as the turning point of that ominous winter. Although the terrors of the ice and snow were reduced dramatically when they all transferred to the communal shelters, finding in the end the heat within almost too great, it was agreed that those two days of sport were their saviour.

The laughter of children rang out through the snow storms, men and women who had not run for many years found themselves persuaded to behave like the Greek athletes of old, people fell about in the snow like infants and the final winning team were given extra rations of hot ale and roast meat. They felt they had conquered the elements.

After that, men spent their spare time in knock up games of stoolball and football, the Indians made toboggans for the children and they went sliding on the frozen river, while Gabriel prayed that the dwindling supplies of food might last till the spring.

Then, suddenly one night the snow and wind ceased and they awoke in the morning to an unaccustomed silence. An eerie ray of sun shone across the white wasteland and all the settlers stood momentarily outside the meeting house and the school house as though astonished to see clear skies again.

The Indians said to Gabriel, 'Now, much water.'

As the sun rose higher, the glare pained their eyes and they retreated into the buildings and the snow began to melt. It happened so quickly that within a day streams of water ran down the paths and then the waters rose as torrents poured down from the hills and forests and rushed through the settlement to the sea. The river burst its banks and cascaded across the areas they had dug for spring planting. Tree trunks they had sawn in the forest floated through the settlement and the settlers cursed and blasphemed as they tried to barricade the houses against the onslaught. After a week, the floods subsided, leaving only slush and filth and the settlers emerged again but now with a new and almost fanatical determination. They had survived.

The spring arrived with dramatic suddenness and they all worked with fury to clear the debris, plant their acres, repair their houses and continue with the building of the church. They planted spring maize and corn, tobacco and flax and in March the cod fishing began.

They found that the spring was not only swift but short. The trees were already beginning to leaf, the sun was higher in the sky and there was a feeling of summer.

In March, a ship departed for England. Sir William

Whatley, who had previously ventured no further than the Azores, feared that there would be little profit in the current venture. On the evening before his departure, Gabriel called the settlers together and said that any who now regretted their decision to settle in this new country were at liberty to return with Sir William and reminded them of the hazards of that journey. On the morrow about forty people left with him, most of them gentlemen who had found Gabriel's administration of the settlement inconsistent with their plans for personal profit.

Some months later, two vessels with over a hundred new settlers arrived from England. They were greeted with an excitement that overwhelmed them and every item of news from the old country was eagerly absorbed. Letters, parcels, presents, messages were distributed and the new arrivals listened in turn to the tales the settlers had to tell of their exciting and terrible experiences.

Gabriel and Sarah walked up the beach and through the settlement to their house, clutching the pile of letters they had received from home. Sarah looked at Gabriel apprehensively.

'I scarcely dare to open them,' she said. 'We have been gone so long, so many events may have occurred.'

'Yes,' Gabriel smiled. 'I am more accustomed to this experience than you. But you must anticipate that there may be good news also.'

Gabriel had letters from all the family and Sarah received communications from Katherine and Adam and Nicholas.

They learned that John's first child Thomas was born though Mary was still ailing from the birth. Katherine reported to Sarah that she and William were spending much time in London and Cicely saw little of Stephen, who was most of the time with the King at Windsor and elsewhere. She revealed that Cicely was much reduced in happiness and suffered from many strange palpitations and hot flushes.

Adam's letter was filled with stories of his life in London and of his frequent visits to Ireland.

'His letters are such a delight,' Sarah said, and she read it out to Gabriel.

She noticed that he had not yet opened Frances's letter. It lay in its package on the table and she had a feeling of dread as she anticipated its contents. She looked at Gabriel. He picked it up and opened it. He did not first read it himself, but read it straightaway to Sarah.

Frances spoke first of Vinelands, of affairs on the estate, of financial matters. She reported that the King appeared to be taking a more tolerant view of the Catholics, no doubt because of his wish to maintain peace between England and Catholic Spain. She expressed the hope that the Catholic community in the New World would flourish and that they would find opportunity to convert the heathen Indians to the true faith.

'The Indians do not have the same arrogance,' Sarah observed. 'They do not suppose that they should convert us to their faiths.'

'Ah, but their faiths are merely superstitions, magic cults without foundation.'

'As the Christian faith must be to them,' Sarah replied.

Gabriel smiled. 'You change not, Sarah. Even as the little waif I found upon the hills of Dartmouth, you experienced no difficulty in expressing adverse views.'

He returned to the letter. Frances said that the guests remaining in the house were safe and well and expressed her concern about the health of John's wife, Mary.

Sarah sat down; perhaps Frances would not allude to her own departure at all. Perhaps she was indifferent. Then Gabriel stopped and read on in silence.

'What is it, Gabriel?'

He finished reading the letter and looked at her and sighed.

'Gabriel, do not look so distressed. Does it concern me?'

327

He read it again and Sarah held out her hand. She read the final paragraphs.

'I regret I must refer to your vile deception. It is certain that Sarah has brought only tragedy and disgrace to this household. She was, perhaps, what many people have called her, though I foolishly believed that she had lately redeemed herself and that you had ceased to indulge in licentious behaviour.

'But I care not to involve myself with her misdemeanours nor with your own sins, which lie between you and your Maker. I would report only that Nicholas will not rest until he is revenged upon you both. Take heed. It would be better for Sarah if she never returns to England.'

The letter ended abruptly with a formal, 'May the Lord have mercy on your soul. Frances.'

Sarah sighed.

'Perhaps she is right. I have no wish to return except to see again my dear son.'

'But what is that other letter you hold?'

'It is from Nicholas,' Sarah said slowly. 'As Frances says, he will surely dearly love revenge upon me.' She passed it to him. 'It is filled with grossest slander and abuse.'

It was addressed to 'That vilest adultress, the once Lady Sarah Maddick, now returned to her natural state of witch, murderess, thief and abductor of the Honourable Catherine Maddick.'

Inside was a brief note.

'This woman is now disinherited from all lands and testamentary rights, banished from hearth and home and subject to the restraints of the law upon all those misdemeanours aforesaid.'

'Is there no further communication?' Gabriel asked.

Sarah examined the envelope.

'No.'

'He clearly plans further action. I will get intelligence from England. Be not concerned.'

Sarah looked at him calmly. 'I am not.'

328

Gabriel held her in his arms. There would be many matters for concern, but at this moment there was no need to worry her.

'Come,' he said, 'the building work for the new arrivals must be set in motion.'

The summer proved to be hot and long. The crops grew twice as fast as in England and they were surfeited with fruit and vegetables but now they ensured that supplies were laid down in preparation for that fearsome winter. Houses were reinforced, barricades constructed, and the fishing vessels traded their huge catches of cod, mullet and sturgeon in the Catholic countries of southern Europe.

They became accustomed to working in a great heat which could also drop by as much as forty degrees in the space of a day; to violent thunderstorms, deluges of rain, to hot and swirling winds.

The day came when Gabriel summoned the whole settlement to the large open space outside the meeting house. The captains stood in a row beside him. The crowd sat on the grass in the evening sun. Looking at them, he had a moment of doubt. He remembered the silent, anxious people who had landed upon this territory a year ago; the overall air of poverty and deprivation. Now they were made bronze and golden by the sun; they were healthy from the good air, their physical labour, the lack of disease resulting from healthier living conditions.

Yet were they ready to respond to his new plans?

'As we approach the last days of September,' Gabriel said slowly, 'we approach also the day of our arrival here. My governorship of this land, in the name of King James, has been confirmed. We have suffered much adversity and we have achieved much success. Now we go on to the next stage.

'There are here many advantages not to be found in the land of our birth. The land we occupy came to us free. The house you inhabit, the land you work, are yours by right and labour. It is now to be your own possession. You will

329.

pay no rents or dues; what you wish to sell will be for your own profit.'

For a moment they all looked uncomprehending, they had heard of no such thing before. Then their faces lit up with joy.

'In England,' Gabriel went on, 'the country is governed by those elected by only a few. We have all here contributed the same in labour and hope and suffering. All of us know equally of the perils. It is meet, therefore, that we shall all take part in the election of those persons.'

They looked at him without understanding.

'I mean,' he said, 'that all those who wish to take part in this government as burgesses shall offer their names. There will then be a day when every man and woman shall vote. It is suitable that for this year you shall remain for this process with those who travelled with you upon the vessels. From those persons you will select three to represent you. It may include your captain or some other. They will then be responsible for plans for the safety and security of this place, for the furtherance of your mutual desires and for the organization of development of the settlement. We shall all, of course, continue our free labour to the working of the settlement.'

He paused.

'What say you, settlers?'

They all rose in unison.

'Yes,' they shouted, 'may it be so.'

Gabriel turned to the captains, the remaining gentry and landowners and merchants. They were silent. Now he had to deal with them.

21

Sarah walked along the path beyond the schoolhouse as the children dispersed towards their houses. A light layer of snow covered the earth but the sun warmed the air and she pulled her cloak around her and went on beyond the houses towards the river and the hills.

A tall, gaunt man emerged from one of the houses armed with shovel and pickaxe.

'Good day, mistress.'

'Good day, Tom. It is a fine day and November already.'

'Aye and months of winter to come,' Tom said lugubriously. 'But this year the Council has ensured that we shall be prepared.'

He walked by her side, looking critically at each settler's plot of land as they passed.

Sarah smiled. Tom had been elected as one of the twenty-seven settlement representatives. When the settlers had voted for the first time in their lives, all of them had elected the captain of their vessel as one of their representatives, though Gabriel had observed that this was probably more from a habitual fear of their betters than from respect. But the new representatives had proved to be more restrictive and dictatorial than had been Gabriel and the captains, who now found themselves in the role of moderators.

'There are plots here that need more attention,' Tom observed. 'And the barriers around some of these houses are not sufficient against the blizzards.'

331

'Ah, much effort has gone into erecting the communal houses,' Sarah reminded him.

'Yes,' Tom said with satisfaction. 'They surely contain all that we will require.'

He turned away towards the river where an army of men and women were building barricades in preparation for spring flooding.

Sarah went back along the path. She could see now the vessels rocking in the harbour and from that angle it reminded her of Bayards Cove. With a sudden unexpected surge of emotion, she remembered that day when Gabriel carried her down the hill. She stood still, shocked by the violence of that memory, she could feel his arms around her skinny body, smell the aroma of the strange scent he was wearing. She put her hand on a fence, and looked with a mystified expression towards the harbour, remembering with absolute clarity the overwhelming attraction she had felt towards him and the even more overwhelming realization that he had felt the same about her. Looking at it now, with the November sun glancing across this harbour thousands of miles distant from that other place, she felt astonished that she, a fifteen-year-old urchin, had recognized instantly the feeling of power she had over him.

Yet, somehow, something was missing. She sighed and shook her head and began to walk on slowly. It had been her decision to come, in a way she was perfectly happy. But suddenly she found herself wondering whether that power she had over Gabriel was only an attraction he could not control rather than . . . what? Surely all love was merely an uncontrollable emotion. You could not decide to love or not to love.

When she entered the house, she was surprised to find Gabriel was there, playing with Catherine. He rarely had time to return to the house during the day and she said instantly, 'Is there something wrong?'

Gabriel stood up and smiled. 'No. I merely forgot some documents necessary for the Council this afternoon.'

'Oh.' Sarah frowned. 'It is strange.'

'What is it, Sarah? You look confused. The meeting is simply to confirm that the sailors remain under the command of the captains and not that of the Council.'

Sarah nodded vaguely.

When Emily had taken Catherine away to the washroom, Gabriel went on, 'Do you not find that decision welcome?'

Sarah removed her cloak. 'I was not concerned with that.' She looked into his eyes and said inconsequentially, 'I miss seeing you in your English silks and velvets.'

Gabriel smiled. 'They are scarce appropriate here. But is that what concerns you?'

Sarah shook her head. 'I wonder if your love for me is mere attraction. Am I most important to you?'

Gabriel looked surprised. 'How can you ask this, Sarah? Have I offended you?'

He put his hands on her shoulders and added, 'I must frequently be absent. There are many obligations, are there not?'

She shook her head again. 'I speak not of that. Do you remember when you picked me up on Jawbones? Do you still feel as you did then?'

'On that occasion, I think I felt nothing but an obligation towards you.'

'No,' Sarah said. 'That is when you fell in love with me.'

Gabriel smiled. 'Yes. Perhaps it was always so.'

'And now?'

Gabriel sighed. 'I would die for you, Sarah. I almost did once. Can I give more than my life?'

He held her in his arms and kissed her.

'No,' she said. 'There is no more.' Then she smiled. 'Perhaps I am merely talking of magic.'

When he was gone, she began to wonder conversely whether in gaining certainty, they had lost the mystery.

Then she shrugged her shoulders and went down to help

in the hospital, reflecting gratefully that those black days she had known in England had disappeared completely in the New World. Perhaps, she thought, it is simply that I can never be satisfied.

The snows grew heavier as winter closed in, but they did not suffer the extreme temperatures and the great blizzards of the first winter. Spring came early, the fields and plots were planted and then unexpectedly there were violent rainfalls. The young seedlings and crops were washed away in the floods and once again the settlement was reduced to emergency action. Then, almost before they could replant, the sun poured down and they were faced with the possibility of a drought. But the river was wide and deep and now they set about creating a permanent system of irrigation.

Two more ships arrived from England in the summer with more settlers, bringing news and letters, and when the ships left only a handful of people elected to go back to the old country. Among these were some of the gentry and landowners and merchants and of the original gentlemen the few who remained intended to settle permanently with their families.

Gabriel and Sarah had never discussed the future. Sarah knew that Gabriel's whole life operated within the circumference of each day. His energies were absorbed in the accomplishment of the day's activities and tomorrow arose from the opportunities he seized each day. She felt always that he never made decisions because every action and event in his life seemed to flow naturally from what had gone before.

She knew that one day he would return to England, he had never been absent for more than a couple of years. He was an adventurer, an explorer, not an exile. His purpose here had been to settle a Catholic community. When he felt that was accomplished, he would surely leave. She knew, too, that he considered every word Frances wrote in her letters about Vinelands and the estate. In spite of the problems of the Catholics or, Sarah reflected, perhaps because of them, he would never leave England.

Then, at the end of that summer and almost two years since their arrival, another ship arrived bringing supplies for the settlement and letters and parcels for the settlers.

Sarah stood with Gabriel on the quay, watching the ship unload, while Gabriel waited to greet the captain. He glanced through the letters handed to him by the master, read one slowly and then handed it to Sarah.

'A letter from Frances,' he said briefly. Sarah sat on the harbour wall to read it.

Frances reported that John's wife Mary and her second child had both died at its birth and as a result John had suffered a relapse into his speechless affliction. He could no longer manage the estate and Frances found the responsibility too onerous. Adam, who might have been expected to assist, was still in London, but his situation became more precarious. He constantly published dangerous and malicious pamphlets and propaganda and was known to be inciting insurrection in Ireland. Frances feared that at any moment he must be cast into the Tower.

Sarah passed the letter back to Gabriel in silence. She watched the forty or so settlers landing from the boats, plodding up the beach looking apprehensively around them at the wooden houses, the long paths leading to the meeting house, the new church, the schoolhouse and the hospital. Did they realize their good fortune, she wondered, in arriving upon this colony which two years ago had been desolate and empty? But even now there were many deaths, this new contingent was insufficient to replace those lost in the past year and she could see already who would be the survivors, who would succumb to the cold, the heat, the unending hardship. It continued to mystify her that although their poverty in England had been a factor, their main reason for venturing upon that dangerous voyage was to enable them to worship their own God in peace. How could one church, one God, be different from any other?

Then she turned to Gabriel.

'You will go, won't you?'

'I must ask the King to appoint another governor in my place. In the meantime, Milton Sayer will act as my deputy when I leave.'

He spoke as though the matter were already settled.

'And can you leave the settlement with so little concern? Have you no fear for its safety when you are gone?'

Gabriel frowned.

'Sarah, you know I had no intention to settle. Now it is established, they have no further need of me.'

'But the Catholic community?'

'There are two priests here now. They will safeguard the holy church. The King has granted the charter for this place. There will be no danger there.'

'And what of the Council? There are many disputes and disagreements now.'

Gabriel sighed.

'If they are to control their own governance, they alone must learn how to conduct it. If they do not, they will not survive.'

They had reached the house and as they entered through the portal, Catherine ran towards them and Gabriel picked her up in his arms.

'And what of Catherine and me?' Sarah suddenly said angrily. 'How can we go back?'

She had had no further communication from Nicholas after the threatening letter he had sent, but she feared what would happen when he heard of her return.

Gabriel put the child down and Emily took her away. He put his hands on her shoulders.

'Of course, you will return with me. We knew that some time this must end.'

'No. I do not know. We have made no plans. I would stay here with you for ever.'

She pushed him away and ran towards the door but he leapt after her and dragged her back.

'Sarah. Nothing will change. We will be together.'

'How can that be? What of Frances and Nicholas, and how about Catherine? He will take her from me. I shall be committed to the Tower. What . . .'

'Sarah,' Gabriel interrupted. 'Those matters can be settled. You do not need to fear.'

'I do not fear,' she shouted at him. 'I will not be treated so, like a detail in your life that must be dealt with. I will decide what I do. Not you.'

This time she walked from the room and he did not follow.

He watched her striding down the path in her rough grey gown, her golden hair swinging from side to side in a long plait. She turned along the track towards the river and he went out and slowly followed her, comprehending suddenly the deep sense of loss that he knew she must be feeling about leaving this place.

These two years now seemed like the beginning of the world, as though they and all the other settlers had joined together in the creation. It truly was the new world. In leaving here, they would be leaving their real lives behind. The memories of those two years, the snow storms, the burning sun, the hunger and drought and sufferings, the building and labour, the deaths and births, the great free community of worshippers, journeys into the interior, fishing around the coasts, trading in the Azores and always Sarah laughing, talking, dancing. Sarah teaching the children in the schoolroom, helping the physicians in the hospital, reading to Catherine, building with the other men and women, Sarah in his arms in bed.

Then he thought anxiously about what he would do if she decided to stay. They had been parted so often in the past, but this time it was different. They could never be parted again. Yet he would not force her to return. He halted. He was accustomed to the burden of guilt that he carried always with him. The fact of living in sin was something of which the priests reminded him every week.

337

He had cast himself upon the mercy of the Virgin Mary but ultimately he knew that he would risk hell and damnation for Sarah.

But would he now sacrifice his other earthly life for her? Vinelands, into which so much of his life had gone, his position in the world, his family, all the duties of his public life. He walked on to where Sarah was sitting on the river bank and sat down beside her.

'This peace, this freedom, it is much to lose.'

Sarah did not reply, looking away at the mountains in the distance.

'Sarah, it is my duty to return. I cannot leave Frances with these responsibilities which are really mine. And I must endeavour to persuade Adam of the danger in which he increasingly places himself.'

Sarah nodded her head slightly.

'I think you could not reside at Vinelands,' Gabriel went on. 'We will build another house, where we can live together and I can continue to attend to the estate affairs.'

'And where am I to go in the meantime?'

'You would be happy with Katherine, perhaps.'

Sarah pursed her lips in half agreement.

'And what of Frances? Will she tolerate such an arrangement?'

Gabriel frowned.

'Frances will know that it cannot be otherwise. But it is for me to deal with that situation.'

'And how would I deal with Nicholas? Perhaps he has a greater reason for resentment than Frances.'

'Sarah, I have thought about Nicholas. I believe you have nothing to fear. He will not act against you.'

Sarah laughed without humour.

'And why should he not? He has expressed that intention.'

'Yet you will find he will not,' Gabriel said firmly. 'And should he attempt to do so, I will deal with that. I would take you to some safe place.'

'Oh, Gabriel.' Sarah's voice sounded hopeless. She knew that what Gabriel said was inevitable. He would have to go back. Yet she knew also that it was possible to reject everything, relinquish everything, as she had done in coming. Gabriel could never be like that.

They sat for a long time in the setting sun.

'Perhaps the sun is setting for us for ever,' Sarah said gloomily.

Then Gabriel said quietly, 'Sarah, if you must remain, I will stay also.'

Sarah turned with tears in her eyes.

'It is not necessary. It was my decision to come. Sacrifice not everything for me.'

'It is no sacrifice, Sarah. It is my choice.'

She looked at him for a long time and then stroked his face gently. 'No,' she said. 'It could not be. You could never rest in the knowledge of what you had neglected.'

He put his arm round her shoulders.

'And will you come, Sarah?'

She sighed.

'I said I wished only to be with you. So,' she smiled slightly, 'perhaps England will have its compensations.'

She sprang up.

'Think no more of it. We will return to England together.'

'Sarah, I would stay . . .'

'Yes,' she said. 'I know. There is no need. It only saddens me that we will never return here.'

22

Stephen Kerswill watched critically as the coachman loaded the luggage on the back of the coach at Hewell Grange.

'Leave space on the platform. The boys will travel outside.'

The two children stood on either side of Cicely, shivering in the cold morning air.

'There is room in the coach,' she protested. 'The journey is long.'

Stephen waved his arms to the boys.

'Up here,' he said, ignoring Cicely's remark.

They climbed on to the wide back ledge outside the coach in silence.

'Hang on to the rail.'

'Philip is still weak from his recent illness,' Cicely went on.

'Then let him travel in the coach,' Stephen retorted. He turned to the child. 'Climb down.'

Philip blushed with fear.

'I will stay here with John,' he said.

'You will do as I command,' Stephen shouted at him. 'Perhaps you fear to be in the coach where I can observe your misdemeanours.'

Cicely began to tremble.

'Pray, Stephen, allow them to travel together.'

Stephen looked at her irritably.

'Let us not have one of your attacks,' he said brusquely. 'Leave them be. Come.'

He left the children and climbed into the coach. 'We waste time.'

Cicely followed him, pulling her wide skirts around her to negotiate the high step.

'Away,' Stephen shouted to the coachman and they began their long, bumpy journey down the Lincolnshire tracks.

'They are but young, dear Stephen,' Cicely persisted. 'I fear they may not survive such a journey.'

'Philip is nine years old,' he replied angrily, 'and John but three years less. You make them into weaklings.'

He glanced into the small looking-glass he carried in his doublet, patted his short curls and adjusted the long curl which hung down the left side of his face. Then he carefully brushed the powder from his starched yellow ruff and looked with satisfaction at the red silk rosettes on his new leather shoes.

'My father treated us as children with kindness,' Cicely said.

'And with what result,' Stephen shouted. 'John is but an inadequate who must surely end in Bedlam. Adam is a ne'er do well whose very life will be forfeit – and Gilbert is dead.'

'Speak not so,' Cicely said tearfully.

Stephen looked at her with distaste. She still wore her hair in the old-fashioned style with a roll of hair on either side of her head and a flat roll on top and her full dark red dress and high white collar hung loosely on her thin body. Ever since her last still birth three or four months ago, she seemed never to cease complaining.

'And what of your father,' he went on, 'taking a strumpet to the New World.'

'She is not that,' Cicely said falteringly, 'but I understand not what happened.'

'You understand nothing. You are a blight upon my existence.'

'As you are upon mine.' She suddenly sprang to life.

'You return to the marriage bed only when the King tires of you. Now you have lost your youthful charms, I think he has rejected you for ever.'

Stephen sprang up and struck her across the face.

'Speak not so, woman, or you will ride upon the platform with the boys.'

Cicely collapsed across the seat with a strange choking sound in her throat.

He hesitated for a second. Was it merely an act she was putting on to frighten him? Her eyes were closed. He propped her up roughly.

'Come. Enough of this nonsense.'

She did not move. He rubbed her hands, looking fearfully at the deep red mark on her face where he had struck her. Like the children, he had only to touch the stupid creature and she developed a bruise. He stopped the coach.

'Fetch ale from that inn. Her ladyship has fainted with the jogging of the coach.'

Cicely opened her eyes and Stephen said irritably, 'Sit up, woman. It is but a mild attack you have suffered.'

As he passed the ale, the coachman said to Stephen, 'The children will be safer in the coach, m'lord. We have a few hills to negotiate further south.'

Stephen was about to remonstrate angrily that there were no hills, that his unsought opinions were a grave impertinence. But the coachman was looking at him with a steely determination.

'They are permitted,' Stephen said curtly. 'Fetch them.'

They spent the night north of Huntingdon, where Philip developed a fever but nevertheless they continued on their journey next day towards London. Stephen was anxious to be back in the capital. Cicely and the children were travelling on to Vinelands and he welcomed the weeks of freedom ahead. Yet as he saw the coach depart down White Hall, he knew that his years in that palace were over. Indeed, the King had made it clear that he found his presence not only irksome but undesirable. Stephen had

342

the fear that some terrible accusation, some treasonable offence, would be levied against him if he continued to force himself into the palace confines. Yet he still nurtured the hope that he could do something to please the King, something that might ensure his return to royal circles, even if not to the King's intimacy.

As he walked along his spirits rose as he saw the envious looks of passersby. His clothes, the jewels on his hand, his air of nonchalance, identified him as a man of wealth and substance. He still had a flourishing legal practice, the King, not a malicious man, at least still used his services in that direction. Then he saw two noblemen of his acquaintance on the other side of the road. They had always been eager enough to cultivate his friendship, to entertain him in the past but now, as he prepared to cross the street, they bowed briefly and passed on. His spirits sank again, he felt a bitter desire for revenge that he knew would never be satisfied. He turned into a tavern off the Strand where the gentlemen from the City commonly congregated to execute business. Here he was received with civility and even warmth; his skills as an advocate were still in demand. The affairs of the Court were of less interest than financial gain. Then he saw a young man seated alone at a table. He was leaning back in his seat, impassively surveying the scene before him. His gaze settled on Stephen.

He had vivid blue eyes and his fair curls had clearly not been treated with honey or henna. A slight smile played round his lips and when he blinked, his eyelashes seemed to flicker provocatively. Stephen felt a surge of excitement inside him. It was the way, he remembered with sorrow, that he once used to look at the King.

He walked slowly over to him and said quietly, 'Will you partake of some wine with me, sir?'

The young man stood up. His green breeches fitted elegantly around his shapely legs; his pale green velvet doublet was unbuttoned at the neck to reveal beneath a gold-coloured ruff.

'I am honoured, m'lord.'

The rough tone of his voice did not match the dignity of his clothes. He had surely mixed little in noble society. So much the better. If this young man had arrived but lately in the capital, he would be unknown in Court circles. He would be a prize to offer to his majesty. Stephen anticipated already his certain reinstatement in royal favour.

'Pray, let us repair to my house at Westminster.'

The blue eyes smiled at him.

'I am acquainted, m'lord, with your identity. I have seen you with his majesty at the palace of Theobalds. Sir Stephen Kerswill.'

Stephen nodded affably, his vanity comforted. Clearly the young man could not know of his recent difficulties in that direction.

'And what is your name, good sir?'

'Sam Small. Lately from over the border at Chepstow.'

'I know not of that place,' Stephen admitted, reflecting that his name must be somewhat adapted before presenting him to the King.

As they entered the house, the steward took the visitor's cloak.

'Shall a room be prepared for you, my good sir?' Stephen asked.

'That would be most gracious.' The young man smiled at Stephen, who showed him into a panelled room hung with silk draperies and led him to the richly upholstered seats by the fireplace.

He brushed the young man's hand as he passed him a silver goblet and looked into the inviting blue eyes, at his clear, smooth skin, at the contours of that youthful body. As the evening softly passed, Stephen felt a growing excitement, but it was no longer connected with the King but with his own desires.

* * *

344

Frances stood in her chamber watching the gardeners erecting the maypole in preparation for the May Day celebrations on the morrow. She closed the window. There was still a chill air and Philip was still running a fever which the physician seemed powerless to reduce. He emerged from his delirium only when his mother sat beside him, though Cicely herself looked as if she must collapse at any moment.

Frances felt relieved only that Stephen had not come and that for a few weeks they would be freed of his monstrous presence. Although she prayed for his soul, Frances did indeed feel that he was a monster, an evil spirit who must surely go to everlasting damnation.

She adjusted her dress, feeling relieved that the high-waisted bodices were nowadays less stiff and boned than a few years ago and that the absurd farthingale had disappeared almost completely. She placed a neat black lace cap on her hair and pinned it on with a jewel.

Some servants were removing the rush matting from the top gallery and replacing it with a long strip of Turkish carpet which Gabriel had imported and women were washing the marble stairs as she descended to the Great Hall.

As she went along the corridor towards the chapel, she still had a sense of loss that Father Pierre was no longer there to receive her. Every day she lit a candle for him, experiencing a sense of inadequacy that she should be praying for that soul which was so much holier than her own. Yet she was fortunate that on his death the two other priests living in the house had taken over all the spiritual duties connected with the servants and tenants of the estate.

She prayed that John might be relieved of his present affliction; that Cicely be given the fortitude to bear the burden of her sorrowful marriage; that Adam be spared the consequences of his wild behaviour and then her mind encompassed all the other members of her family in a general prayer for the mercy of the Virgin.

As she rose from her knees, she heard a movement behind her. John was sitting in the shadows at the back of the tiny chapel. Was it possible that he might return to the true faith?

'Good day, John. May you find peace and comfort here.' She placed a hand on his head. 'You will come tomorrow to the celebrations?'

John nodded, yet he frequently gave her the impression that he did not understand what she said. She feared that perhaps not only his speech was affected, but also his mind. He spent much of his time riding over the hills to no purpose. What would happen to the house, to the estate, if he were unable to inherit it? Adam would surely be unable, and indeed showed no desire, to take on such a burden.

Walking back up the wide staircase, with the priceless tapestries, the beautiful chests and draperies and upholstered seats, the lacquered pots and silver bowls, the high carved and painted ceilings, the ornaments which adorned every nook and cranny, she had a vision of it all falling into decay, abandoned, rotting, a silent, uninhabited house. Yet all things must pass away, she reflected, true wealth lies not in this world.

Gabriel was at his desk as she entered the library. She walked briskly over to him.

'I noticed those maps on your desk when I passed here yesterday,' she said sharply.

'Yes,' Gabriel replied. 'It is a rough chart of a route to Russia, by the Baltic Ocean, Kurland, Livonia, Novgorod to Russia.'

'And what is your interest?'

'Much is developing there in trade. I intend to proceed there next year. First, ships must be refitted for the New World, further supplies must be sent, more settlers found.'

At the mention of the New World, Frances looked at him angrily. She knew there could be nothing more to say about that episode that had not been said in the three months since his return. The advice of Father Anthony that marriage was a sacred union that could not be abandoned because of one partner's frailty, and her own determination to cling to her social status and material possessions had combined against Gabriel's equal determination to protect Sarah and continue his illicit relationship. She had awaited their arrival on that bleak evening, prepared for a confrontation. But Sarah had not come. She had elected to stay with the child at Katherine's. Yet she could not prevent herself from endlessly returning to the topic.

She said sarcastically, 'And is Sarah to accompany you upon that voyage of discovery?'

'It is far ahead. I know not our plans.'

She felt an even greater rage at his calm reply. He always spoke about Sarah as though their relationship were a normal, acceptable phenomenon.

'And what of me?' she demanded.

Gabriel said wearily, 'It does not affect you, Frances.'

'It does not?' she shouted. 'You elope with our adopted daughter to the other side of the world and then return to our home as though nothing had occurred. What of our marriage? Am I of no consequence? What of the holy church which you profess? What of my position in society?'

Gabriel looked at her with a curious combination of resignation and mystery. The very thought of Sarah seemed to bring a light to his eyes.

'Yes,' he said. 'I would not burden you with this situation if it could be otherwise.'

'Then end it.'

'It would also be idle to give such an undertaking. It is beyond redemption.'

'And so is your soul,' she said vehemently.

'So be it. My soul is between myself and God.'

'Will you sacrifice everything for that . . . creature?'

'It is not a sacrifice, Frances.'

'No. It is an indulgence. A wanton profligacy. You are a vile adulterer.'

Gabriel said quietly, 'Frances, we have discussed this daily ever since my return. Pray let us discuss other matters.'

'But what will become of her? Her marriage is annulled. She is homeless.'

'Her marriage is not yet dissolved. Such petitions have been known to take ten years to succeed.'

'She will not come here.'

'She has not come here,' Gabriel said conclusively. He added, 'Sarah will probably not accompany me on that expedition.'

Frances said venomously, 'I have come to see that it is she and not you who has sacrificed everything by her wantonness. But I care not whether she accompanies you or not.'

Gabriel stood up.

'Frances, I am building a manor north of here in which Sarah and I shall reside.'

'A manor!' Her face went red. 'And am I to run this place alone?'

'No. I shall continue its administration.'

'You cannot do this. I shall apply to the courts.'

'Frances, you have relinquished nothing. I regret the situation but I cannot be deflected from that purpose.'

She looked at him helplessly. She knew there was nothing she could say that would alter the situation. It was irretrievable.

She turned and left the library and walked silently down to the chapel. Truly it was only within that quiet place that peace could be found.

*   *   *

'The horses are saddled,' William said as Katherine entered the hall.

'Are you ready, my love?'

'Yes.' She smiled. 'The children go in the wagon with Matilda, or we shall never reach Vinelands by noon.'

'You appear most charming,' he said, looking appreciatively at the gathered-up scarlet silk overskirt, revealing beneath a stiff taffeta petticoat and the tight decolleté bodice, laced in front to partially conceal her breasts, and the huge puffed sleeves slashed to reveal the white arms beneath. 'And this new hair dressing suits you.' He touched the thick curls hanging on either side of her face.

'Pray, do not handle them,' Katherine laughed. 'Or they must surely collapse.'

He kissed her lightly on the top of her head where the hair was flat.

'What becomes of Sarah today?'

'I believe she intends to go for a ride across the hills.'

'I still fear that Nicholas may yet exact revenge upon her,' William said. 'And I fear she can have no case in law to retain Catherine if Nicholas demands otherwise.'

'And Sarah? Can she be in danger?'

'I suppose a judge might find her actions of criminal proportions,' he said with a laugh, 'except myself.'

'But to what purpose would be her incarceration in gaol?'

'Perhaps it cannot come to that,' William said encouragingly. 'But do not concern yourself. In a few days we shall be travelling in Italy. She must be safe there.'

Katherine turned to him.

'William, I fear she has a wish to bring Catherine. She is anxious that Nicholas may snatch her away in her absence.'

William frowned.

'That would be a difficult matter, Katherine. It cannot be wise to take the child out of the country again, against her father's wishes.'

'But Nicholas has made no communication, taken no steps.'

As they cantered through the gates of Vinelands, she said suddenly, 'Come, I will race you to John's farm,' and she galloped ahead, her black hair fluttering in the wind, her curls forgotten.

William galloped after her, feeling delight that she still, at thirty-one, retained that youthful responsiveness that had attracted her to him and wondering at his good fortune that somehow she had come to love him after the turmoil of Richard.

She awaited him at the gates of the farm.

'I cannot see John. I will go to see if he is within.'

The steward reported that John had already left to go to Vinelands and Katherine and William rode on to the house.

*   *   *

Sarah watched Katherine and William ride down the drive to go to Vinelands, wishing she could have gone with them. She had thought that the new manor house Gabriel was building on the road to Stoke Fleming would have given her happiness. Yet the old walls of Vinelands, the feeling of the past, could not be recaptured. Even Trevayne Abbey seemed more attractive than the new, brick edifice which was being constructed.

Her thoughts turned once again to Nicholas. She had heard nothing from him since her return. His silence made her even more anxious than if he had taken some violent action. She knew of his petitions to parliament, yet of late, these seemed to have ceased. If only he were not there – if he were dead – she could still have Trevayne Abbey. She knew that this was a foolish thought. He was not dead and he had disinherited her anyway.

Yet the more she thought of him, the more strange it seemed that he had taken no action. What was he doing?

And was there no way by which she could regain Trevayne Abbey?

She went upstairs to her chamber and looked down at some children playing around a maypole near the stables.

Catherine was with them and Emily was watching her. Sarah had told her that Catherine must never be left alone.

She went downstairs again and out into the brilliant sunshine. It was a pity that they could not go to the maypole at Vinelands.

But Trevayne. Was there nothing she could do?

The more she thought about Nicholas, the more convinced she became that she could manipulate him even in this situation. Supposing that somehow she could persuade him that she would return if he abandoned all attempts at retribution. And then what? She could return as a widow, if only he were dead.

She sat thinking, the sun rose higher in the sky and then she went to the stables and had a horse saddled.

*   *   *

Nicholas tugged the laces of his doublet together as tightly as he could manage but he could no longer conceal the separation down the centre. He pulled his wide, gathered breeches up over his stomach; the points attaching his doublet to his breeches with hooks were still wide enough to conceal the gap occasioned by his expanding torso.

'I like not these tight silk stockings,' he said to the footman, 'Pray select some of larger proportions. And request the tailor to call at eleven of the clock on Wednesday forenoon. And why is this door ajar?' he asked sharply as the footman followed him along the gallery.

'I know not, m'lord. Doubtless the cleaning women . . .'

'I have commanded that this door be always closed.'

'Yes, m'lord.' The footman's hand was on the handle.

'Wait. Go on ahead. Pray have breakfast seven minutes early. I have an appointment.'

The footman hastily ran down the stairs. Nicholas opened the door of Sarah's chamber and went in. He noticed with irritation that the pink brocade gown lying on her couch had been moved slightly since yesterday and her silver jewel case had been shifted. There must be a new cleaning girl who had not been acquainted with procedures. He looked round the chamber. It looked strangely alive with the sun shining across the bright silk draperies and the polished furniture. Normally he came in only at night, when it was shrouded in darkness and shadow.

What was he going to do about it? Today, it seemed better to wait and see. Yesterday, he had decided to go to Vinelands and confront Gabriel. The day before, he had considered cancelling his application for annulment of their marriage, if that were possible. If it were not annulled, perhaps he could compel her to return.

It was a long time. Over two years of this daily questioning, decision, reassessment, anger, hatred, incredulity, waiting. He sat down on the bed; how could she have had the effrontery not only to leave, but also to return to Dartmouth? His now rising anger conflicted with his bewilderment. How could she ever be made to see the terrible iniquity of her ways? What would he do if she walked in now? Kill her? No, that would only save her from the enormity of her actions. That one letter he had written to her when she left, ignored; or had it made her too fearful to return? He stood up abruptly. It was clear that she just did not understand many things.

Walking down the stairs, he reflected on the day three months ago when the ship had docked in Bayards Cove. He had stood in the shadows of the quay on that drab day watching the passengers come slowly down the gangplank. Then he saw the tall figure of Gabriel, dressed in courtier clothes as though he had but recently left a palace. He had stood at the top of the steps, surveying the quay beneath him. Then he turned and held out his hand and Sarah appeared, similarly attired, holding Catherine by the hand. At the sight of Sarah, Nicholas had been so overcome with emotion that he had been compelled to sit down on the quayside to control the trembling of his body. He had intended to confront them but he watched them walk away across the quay to the waiting coach. Then he had ridden slowly home, deciding on the morrow to go to Vinelands and demand the return of the child. But on the morrow, he had spent the day in the library, picturing Sarah as she walked down the gangplank, and preparing another petition to parliament.

He ate his breakfast of baked fish, cold meat and potato and drank his cold beer while his mind continued to circle round the insoluble problem. He reminded himself that he was a Knight of the Most Noble Order of the Garter, a Knight Grand Cross, and a Gentleman of the Bedchamber, but without her his world had ended. Yet how could he permit himself to continue to think about such a creature?

For three months he had awaited some word, an apology, admission of guilt, some conciliatory gesture. None had come and he was suddenly faced this morning with the thought that for her he had ceased to exist. She never thought of him at all. It was something that had never occurred to him before.

He walked slowly from the dining room and went into the drawing room that looked out across the spring garden. It was May Day. The whole place was deserted. Everyone had been given the day off to attend the maypole down in Dartmouth. Then as he sat down on a bench, there was a movement behind him. He turned. Sarah was standing in the doorway, watching him, a bemused expression on her face.

He sprang up, frowning in disbelief, his heart beating faster, feeling a constriction in his throat as though he must choke.

He rushed towards her.

'What are you doing here? How dare you . . .'

Sarah stepped back slightly in case he should strike her.

'Good day, Nicholas.'

His eyes travelled from the long golden hair, tied back with blue ribbon, to the tight-waisted purple bodice threaded with lace, the soft folds of her full skirt, the wide lace collar clasped at her neck with a silver brooch.

The sound of her voice seemed to paralyse him. She advanced slowly into the room.

'How dare you enter this house,' he demanded. 'And where is the child?'

She looked at him with her wide green eyes.

He knew that if he did not turn away, he would strike her, kill her.

'Pray be seated. I fear I have perplexed you.'

He sat down on the bench, there was a strange tingling in his fingers, his arms suddenly ached and seemed too heavy to be supported. He felt bereft of any power to act, even to speak.

'You have gained weight,' Sarah observed calmly. 'Enforced bachelorhood must agree with you.'

Feelings of outrage, anger, indignation, swept through him. He began to tremble but he could not drag himself to his feet. A terrible anxiety swept through him. She stood, watching him.

At last, he spoke.

'You are thinner, Sarah,' he said stupidly.

'Yes,' Sarah said calmly, 'it was a hard life yet one which I regret to leave.'

Nicholas felt as though his mind, as well as his body, had ceased to function. He could not collect his thoughts. Then the speech which he had mentally rehearsed for two years came to his lips.

'How dare you treat me in this fashion,' he began, 'You are a wanton . . .'

She stepped back as he began to stand up.

'You have ruined my life, Sarah, by your treachery.'

'Our marriage was ever a mockery,' Sarah said coldly.

'You made it so!' He advanced towards her, finally controlling his shaking body. 'And what have you come for now?' he demanded.

He grasped her by the shoulders, prepared to drag her through the hall, to cast her out through the gates. But she sprang free and leapt towards the door.

'Catch me,' she said tauntingly.

He lunged towards her, beside himself now with rage.

She laughed, dancing through the doorway and along the corridor into the library.

'Would you not like me to return here, Nicholas?' she said provocatively.

He followed her, his face red, the muscles in his throat contracting as though he must suffocate.

'Do not mock me. You will suffer for this.'

She positioned herself on the opposite side of a table, her body alert. He was clearly still so besotted by her that in spite of his blustering remarks he still wished for her return. Old fool. Did he really believe that she would ever live with him again? But it would not be difficult to persuade him that she was filled with remorse and humility. Then, when he had signed the document she had brought with her, ensuring her inheritance, she would explain that she must return to Katherine's to collect Catherine. She had thought no further than that. Yet she knew that at that stage, she would think of some plan to be rid of him.

'Nicholas.' She suddenly became serious. 'I fear I made a terrible and fearsome error. I come to seek your forgiveness.'

He stopped, his eyes opening wider, and he glared at her suspiciously.

'What mean you?'

'Perhaps we may effect a reconciliation.'

'Reconciliation!' His face became tense, he clenched his

355

hands as though he were holding within them all his pent-up emotions. He looked at her and then he began to move towards her but she stepped back.

'Your expression shows no humility,' he said. 'It shows only hatred.'

Then Sarah laughed, a laugh of mockery and contempt. In spite of her plan, she longed only to humiliate him, and felt overwhelmed with revulsion. Unable to control herself, although she knew it would ruin her chance of success, she said, 'Nicholas, it would not, of course, be possible to resume a marital relationship.'

She looked at him, her eyes fixed in a cold stare. She watched the colour rise in his cheeks, watched him clutch the door for support and suddenly he fell, gasping for breath. There was a kind of gurgle in his throat and she crept around the table and looked down at him. Then he was silent. She bent down.

'Nicholas.'

His eyes were wide open but he was perfectly still. She touched his face lightly, but he did not move. She slowly bent her head closer and put a hand on his heart. There was no sound or movement.

Sarah stood up, feeling panic-stricken. He hadn't signed the document. She would lose the house. Then she looked round the library. She knew in precise detail where he kept everything, documents, papers, business communications. Everything had always been in its exact place. The key to the bureau was where it had always been, within a secret panel in the wall. In the bottom drawer of the bureau was his will, the deeds of the houses on the estate, information about rents.

With fumbling fingers, she opened the will. It was dated two days after their marriage. Everything was left to her. She looked again in disbelief. Her heart leapt with joy and relief. Then the thought occurred to her that there might be a later, altered copy. She went through all the drawers but there was nothing. 'It is strange,' she thought, 'perhaps he could never bring himself to that stage.'

She returned the papers to the bureau, locked the drawers and rehid the key behind the panel. Looking at Nicholas, she could scarcely control her excitement. He was dead. She had only to wait until the funeral, until the will was read, and she would be a wealthy woman in her own right. But she knew she would spend the next few days in an agony of suspense. Supposing . . . She crept away, unseen.

*   *   *

That May Day was a day of joy. The sun shone upon the vivid ribbons as the children and the young servants and tenants danced around the maypole, and feasts and picnics were shared upon the lawns.

Frances and Gabriel received all the family as they arrived, and even little Philip emerged from his boudoir, having recovered at last from the terrible fever.

Katherine took Cicely to enjoy the quiet of her old rose garden, William and Gabriel and even John joined in a stoolball match with the gardeners and stable boys, and Adam arrived on a black horse from William's stable. The young servants vanished into the bushes, their elders ate and drank and laughed and talked until the sun set and shadows fell across the lawns of Vinelands. Tomorrow was another day.

357

23

Sarah opened the golden locket and read the inscription inside. 'Sarah, for ever.' She could not remember Nicholas giving her this piece, though he had given her so much that it would have been impossible to remember them all. Ever since she returned to the house after his funeral a year ago, she had come upon objects she had forgotten, reminders of a marriage that seemed now completely remote. Even more strange was the evidence of his life after she had left, which seemed like sudden stark confrontations, as though he were still following her from the grave. Her chamber and clothes just as she had left them, as though awaiting her return; the furniture exactly as it had been placed, although she had had it moved around constantly during her residence. She had looked with distaste at the blooms she had arranged, still standing, dead, in their vases and at a drawing she had been executing, lying still on a table in the library.

Only once she had felt a touch of compassion when she glanced at his open journal on the library desk, dated 2 July 1620: 'Tonight Sarah bade me goodnight with a gentle expression upon her face. Perhaps all is not yet lost and she will come in time to care for me.' It was the night she had left to go with Gabriel to the New World. The journal remained open at that page and had never been added to. She had frowned with incomprehension at the curious inadequacy of this man, wealthy, influential in the world, yet who had harboured this uncontrollable attachment.

Later, she had had the whole house decorated and refurbished. With new curtains, new colours, new tapestries and floor coverings, and the furniture completely rearranged, Trevayne Abbey now belonged to her and her alone.

She put on the locket and walked along the gallery to examine the new drawing room which had been furnished in the French style with red and gold velvet draperies and upholstery and silk tassels tying back the curtains. Through the window she could see the garden boys erecting this year's maypole.

She waved to Katherine, who was riding up the drive accompanied by twelve-year-old Elizabeth on her pony.

'I did not expect you today,' she called. 'Elizabeth, you will find Catherine in the schoolroom. Pray inform Emily that you may all go to the gardens.'

Sarah ran down the stairs and embraced Katherine with delight. 'Come, let us go to the rose garden. It is warm enough to sit out.'

'Oh,' said Katherine, 'I have such news. You cannot imagine! John is betrothed to Urith Eliot. They are to wed in August.'

'John! Urith! But John is . . . ailing. And Urith comes from a Catholic family.' Sarah frowned. 'John seemed at one time opposed to the Catholic religion.'

'Yes, but that phase seems long past.'

'And why should she . . . ?'

'Ah,' Katherine laughed again. 'I know your thoughts. Why should the heiress to a great fortune contemplate John. Yet she has been tending him of late and seems to find his company agreeable. Also, she will one day inherit Vinelands, which cannot be a disincentive. They will be the richest people in England.'

'Well,' Sarah smiled, 'almost, perhaps.'

'But why do you look sad, Sarah? Do you think this marriage is not suitable?'

'No.' Sarah shook her head. 'It is not this marriage I think of.'

'Ah, I fear you miss Papa. But he is gone for only a few months.'

'No. It is not that either. I think it is really that I never belong anywhere. I am always on the outside. I feel somehow as though this new marriage puts me even further away.'

'But you belong here,' Katherine protested. 'This is your home, your children's.'

'It is not the home where I should belong.'

Katherine frowned.

'Sarah, you know that cannot be. You surely cannot protest at your situation. Mama has accepted the situation and Papa does not conceal his devotion.'

'You think I speak without reason, but I feel sometimes I am a mere appendage, a disposable item in life.'

'Oh, come, Sarah dear,' Katherine said encouragingly. 'This is a lovely house. You conduct your life as you wish. You have your children. You would perhaps never have been reunited with your son Nicholas if his father had survived.'

'Yes, he is a dear boy. Yet sometimes, Katherine, I hate it here. Perhaps I was fortunate to inherit it, yet it is filled with the presence of Nicholas.'

'But, Sarah, you have changed it all. It bears no resemblance to that which Nicholas planned.'

'No,' Sarah agreed. 'But his gloomy spirit still pervades the house. It is as though I cannot be released from his enchantment with me.'

'Sarah, he can have wished you no ill.'

'Come, let us walk upon the hills where we can look down upon the distant sea.' As they walked along, she said, 'Sometimes, I long for Sagadahok.'

'Surely life was very harsh.'

Sarah smiled. 'Yes. Perhaps I do not yearn for that part of it. But there I felt as though I belonged. Oh, Katherine, it was such a beautiful life. It flowed like the river. All we did had a purpose. It truly was a new world. Sometimes I feel that I will return there alone.'

'But you would not leave Papa.'

'No. I cannot do that.'

'Let us go and see if the maypole is prepared. Papa says that we should not worry about the morrow, does he not?'

Sarah laughed. 'Yes. But then, he is perplexed by nothing.'

'Except, perhaps, by you,' Katherine replied.

*   *   *

Gabriel stood on the bridge as the pilot led the four laden vessels into harbour. What he had intended as a brief journey to Russia had occupied a year. The old king had been buried and now Charles was on the throne. Gabriel sensed a new feeling of hope as he spoke to the officials on the quay. They told him that that very day the King was meeting his new bride at Dover. But, he reflected, there had been hope years ago when James had travelled down from Scotland. Would it be the same again?

As he rode through the streets of Dartmouth, he felt a growing excitement at the thought of seeing Sarah again. He went across the hills to Trevayne Abbey. Later that day he would have to visit Vinelands, but for the moment everything else could wait because mixed with the excitement was an anxiety that perhaps this time Sarah would have tired of his long absence. It was, he knew, a situation that would be with them for ever. His journeys would always be necessary. But Sarah had clearly become increasingly convinced that they were more than a necessity. She had come to believe that it was a part of his life that he could never relinquish, pointing out that there was no longer any need for him to embark upon these projects because he had so much wealth, so many diverse activities already. Gabriel knew that there was no answer to her protestations. It was simply that he could never lose that desire to journey, never be indifferent to the exhilaration of looking out across great expanses of ocean, barren landscapes, new worlds, the vast snow-covered steppes of Russia. He longed always to be with her, to return to her, but always he felt impelled to venture once more on one of his adventures.

He galloped up through the silent drive and entered the house. The steward was in the hall.

'Lady Sarah?'

The steward hesitated for a moment. Then he said, 'She is above, in her chamber, I believe.'

Gabriel climbed the stairs, still feeling uncertain. He walked along the gallery and opened the door.

Sarah was standing by the window and she turned and came eagerly towards him as he entered.

'Oh,' she said, 'you have been so long.' She kissed him. 'And I didn't even see you coming.'

Gabriel kissed her but his eyes were on a handsome young man on the other side of the room.

'Who is this, Sarah?'

She smiled.

'Oh, Gabriel. This is Lord Mannering. Viscount Humphreys.'

Gabriel bowed distantly, the anxiety about Sarah that he had been feeling ever since he reached Dartmouth reasserting itself. Perhaps he had had a presentiment that something would result from his absence.

The blond young man came towards him eagerly.

'My Lord, I am honoured to meet you. I have heard so much of your exploits that I feel I already know you.'

'I do not have the same advantage,' Gabriel said coldly.

'Ah, but you do,' Sarah said eagerly. 'Dominic is the son of a dear friend.'

Gabriel frowned at her intimate use of his Christian name.

362

'Who would that be?' Had he made an absurd misjudgment?

'The Earl of Bodnant, my lord,' the young man said, 'who contributed much to your New England venture.'

'Ah.'

Gabriel reassessed his thoughts as Dominic went on, 'He is much contented with progress there and has heard that another Catholic community has been settled just north of your own.'

'That is good news. And what do you do?'

Dominic smiled.

'I have lately been in the entourage of the Duke of Buckingham to bring the Princess Henrietta Maria from Paris. His majesty desired a few of our persuasion in view of the lady's religious affiliations.'

'Yes. I see. But it is a curious business because I hear that the new king excluded all Catholics from his father's funeral.'

'My lord, I think he finds this marriage desirable in that he would wish to align France with us against the Spanish threat. I think he accepts the Catholic connection.'

'The threat comes more from the English throne and the Protestant fear of Spain. I believe Charles is set upon war.'

'Well, my lord, I have hopes that this new reign may bring forth better results.'

'I fear you betray the enthusiasm of youth,' Gabriel said quietly. 'There is little evidence that Charles will reveal more discretion than his father.'

'My lord, this lady brings her own Catholic household and insists that mass shall be celebrated daily.'

'But that may only cause dissent among Charles's subjects. And Charles has already shown his dictatorial attitudes towards parliament. He had already made himself unpopular before he came to the throne with his absurd expedition to Walcharen when most of the sailors died of disease and starvation.'

'Yet at least the King shows a more serious disposition. He enjoys the country yet rides and hunts with but little enthusiasm and does not yet go in for that extravagance at court so loved by his father.'

'While he is so much influenced by Buckingham, we can hope for little progress.'

Gabriel turned to Sarah. She was listening in silence and she smiled at him and said, 'Dominic is such a thoughtful young man, is he not?'

Gabriel felt a doubt inside him.

'I hope so,' he replied stiffly. He addressed Dominic again and put the question that had been nagging at his mind since he first laid eyes on him.

'But what brings you here, sir?' It was his own question that made his fears concrete. Sarah was, after all, a wealthy widow, as well as being so attractive. There must be many men who would desire to marry her and his lengthy absences could only add to their interest.

'I have come with information about Adam,' Dominic said.

'Oh.' Gabriel feared that no news from Adam could be good.

'I know not whether it is good news or not,' Dominic said slowly.

'What is it? Are you acquainted with Adam?'

'Sir, we have spent time in Ireland together. We have combined in the production of verse and pamphlets of a satiric fashion.'

'Then perhaps I have little to thank you for. Your efforts are foolhardy and produce little. Though I doubt not,' he added truthfully, 'that Adam is more at variance with both parliament and King than you are.'

'My news is of a different nature, sir. He intends to marry.'

'Marry!' Gabriel smiled. 'My good sir, how can you doubt that this is good news? He has long lived a dissolute life in the taverns of London. This must surely cure that defect at least.'

'It is to be hoped so, sir. He is to marry The O'Connell's daughter.'

'O'Connell!' Gabriel spoke in astonishment, aware of a new view of Adam. He had always felt that his revolutionary zeal, his political activities had simply been for the joy and excitement of danger. Was he serious in his devotion to that concept of justice which Gabriel himself espoused or was this merely another gesture of defiance? 'And does he settle in Ireland?'

'That is his intention, sir. The plantation continues, though we know not whether Charles will countenance it.'

'It depends', said Gabriel, 'on whether Buckingham's influence is greater than that of Henrietta Maria.'

'Sir, I must depart.' The young man bowed and then smiled at Sarah.

'Your hospitality has been most gracious.'

'Give my fondest love to Adam,' she said eagerly, 'and I will welcome him soon. And always you will be most welcome.'

As Dominic departed, Sarah went on, 'Adam has requested to reside here for a period of time with his bride. Oh, it will be such a pleasure.'

Gabriel looked at her thoughtfully.

'Sarah, it is not suitable that you receive gentlemen in your chamber.'

Sarah laughed provocatively.

'I do not anticipate that Adam will wish to visit my chamber.'

'Sarah, you know of what I speak. This Mannering. Has he been here before?'

Sarah smiled. 'No.'

'Then how do you receive him so casually?'

'I met him in London with Adam.' Then she added reflectively, 'I believe he is in a mind to propose marriage.'

'Marriage! Sarah, what are you speaking of?'

Panic and anger engulfed him.

'You are married,' she said quietly.

'Sarah, that has nothing to do with it. My marriage was established long before I met you.'

'And that is indestructible.'

'We have always known that. It cannot be changed. And you know Frances and I do not live as man and wife.'

'How do I know?' Sarah tossed her head. 'And even if I do, of what benefit is that to me? I am but someone you visit at your convenience. You depart for great periods of time and I must be expected to wait patiently till you choose to return.'

Gabriel grasped her in his arms.

'Sarah, you know that is not so. I think only of returning to you.' He put his hand beneath her chin and kissed her. 'I have left the company in Russia that I might return to you earlier.'

She rested her head on his chest. 'It has been so long, Gabriel. I become discontented.'

He ran his fingers through her hair and unlaced the bodice of her gown. Then she flung her arms round his neck and kissed him passionately and his suspicions melted away.

'I wish I could come home with you to Vinelands,' she said when he was leaving.

'Sarah, we must think of this as our home. Vinelands, the estate, these are responsibilities I have accumulated.'

'Yet you love Vinelands.'

'Yes. And I would love it more if you could but share it with me. But let us be content. I will return this evening when I have dealt with the business.'

He rode over the hills and called upon John when he reached the farm. He found the newly-weds engaged in the library on their accounts and informed them of Adam's impending marriage. They received the news with delight. John smiled; he had not recovered his speech.

Then Gabriel went on to greet Frances.

She met him coldly and discussed the affairs of the estate with an icy civility as though he were a business associate whom she distrusted. Gabriel did not attempt to bridge the chasm between them. There was nothing more that could be said.

* * *

A few months later, Sarah informed him that she was pregnant.

'I fear it is the result of your returning after so long absence,' she said, laughing.

He put his arms around her.

'It is a strange feeling,' Gabriel said slowly. 'It is something I have not contemplated.'

Sarah smiled. 'It is always a possible consequence.'

'Yes, and one which fills me with joy. But you, Sarah, are you of the same mind?'

'Yes,' she said. 'How can I feel otherwise?'

'But I fear also the difficulties of childbirth.'

'Ah, do not worry, dear. I found it not very distressing. And he shall be called Andrew.'

Gabriel laughed. 'And if it be a girl?'

'No. It will be Andrew.'

'I go to London tomorrow for perhaps a week and had thought to take you with me. But there is plague in the city and your condition does not permit of the taking of such a risk.'

'Ah, my state does not preclude that. But on this occasion, I will remain here. I have matters to attend to.'

He said farewell to her reluctantly the next day; this creature in her womb seemed to make separation from her even more unwelcome and he resolved to return as soon as possible.

When he was gone, she changed into a new golden coloured gown, dressed her golden hair with amber combs and ordered the coach to take her to Vinelands. She had not visited the house since they returned from the New World.

She noted the new barns which had been erected, the extension of the house, trees which had been planted, a pond and waterfalls which had been installed. Crossing the bridge, she entered the Great Hall.

Servants were still dashing hither and thither and she recollected that first time when, as a child, she had been so bewildered by all the frantic activity.

The steward hesitated when she said she was going up to see Lady Frances but she brushed past him and went up and along the gallery to her chamber. She knocked on the door and entered. Frances was at the window, engaged in her tapestry, and she turned and said indignantly, 'Sarah! What are you doing here?'

'Good day, Frances. Forgive my sudden intrusion. I must talk with you.'

Frances blushed with anger.

'Get out,' she said. Yet the sight of this creature who had ruined her life seemed to release all her pent-up emotions. She wanted Sarah to be there, she longed to tell her of her anger, her hatred, to have at least the satisfaction of speaking her agonized thoughts.

'It is news, merely, Frances. I am with child.'

'And what is that to me? It is scarcely to be wondered at.'

'No, indeed, that is true. Yet you have some responsibility.'

'Me!' Frances shouted indignantly. 'Pray, take yourself off.'

'No, Frances. You will hear me. My child will be illegitimate as Gabriel and I cannot wed.'

'So be it. What did you expect from such a union? All children born out of wedlock are illegitimate. It is a common enough event in these days. Of what consequence is it to me?'

'Much, Frances. Because if Gabriel and I could wed, it would not be so.'

Frances looked bewildered.

'How could you wed? You know that that cannot be.'

'Yet if you were not here it would be possible.'

'But I am here.' Frances still spoke uncomprehendingly.

'If you cared for Gabriel you could surely solve this problem. He would dearly love me as his wife. Yet his conscience, the law of the land, makes this impossible.'

'Sarah, I cannot change the law, even if I would. And marriage is sacred.'

'Sacred!' Sarah replied contemptuously. 'You have no marriage. Your life with Gabriel is a lie.'

'And your life is a perpetual sin. Have you no care for what you do to Gabriel's soul? Do you call your liaison love?'

Sarah laughed ironically.

'Gabriel has no concern for his soul when he is with me. And I have no use for such superstitions.'

'You are a heathen. You come from the devil.'

Frances began to feel sick with anger and with her own words. It was as though this fiend were beginning to invade her soul as well.

'Pray, leave my chamber,' she said, trying to steady her voice.

'Very well. It is as you wish,' Sarah said suddenly and walked to the door. Then she turned and looked at Frances. To Frances, her green eyes seemed to shine unnaturally, as though they were lit by some inner power. She felt a deep anxiety inside her.

Sarah said quietly, 'If you were dead, Frances, Gabriel might achieve true happiness.' Then she left the room.

Frances sat down, trembling with anger. She clutched the missal which was lying on her dressing table, trying to control the thoughts almost of hatred towards Sarah. She was a wicked creature. Evil. She would do anything

369

to entice Gabriel to her. Yet it was his decision, too. He had no concern for anyone but Sarah.

She was right. She and Gabriel had no marriage. Gabriel surely longed to be free of her, that he might live a true marriage with Sarah. Frances went down the stairs and along to the chapel. Neither of the priests were there and she knelt down and prayed for guidance. The raised hand of the Virgin seemed to be beckoning her and she turned her head, looking in the direction of the raised fingers. Her eyes rested on the small painting hanging on the wall, of Christ carrying the cross to Golgotha.

She stumbled from the chapel and back up the stairs to her chamber. For two days, she remained there, haunted by that icy look from Sarah as she had stood finally in the doorway.

On the third afternoon, she looked through the windows to the garden beneath. She went out and walked in the herb garden, remembering how Sarah had come here years ago, collecting herbs for Gilbert, trying to cure him. In those days, she believed she had been mistaken about Sarah. There were times when she had almost believed that Sarah had been sent as a ministering angel.

The picture came into her mind of that last evening of Gilbert's life, when Frances had crept back into his chamber to find him lying in Sarah's arms. It was Sarah who had been his final comfort. Frances walked slowly round to the bower where Katherine and Sarah used to sit and talk. It was as though Sarah pervaded every part of Vinelands but she began to feel a strange sympathy for her. Her anger and resentment disappeared, yet she knew her own problem was more than that. A voice inside her was saying that she had no right to judge the actions of others, she had no jurisdiction over the soul of Sarah, nor of Gabriel's either, for that matter.

She became aware of her own lack of humility in condemning the behaviour of others. There were qualities that Sarah exhibited that she would never possess; her courage, for example. Would she herself have ventured to the New World to be with Gabriel?

Frances got up from the stone seat and walked along the path towards the house. She was filled with a sense of her own culpability. We are all in need of mercy, she thought, all but fragile beings. Christ said, 'Love one another.'

Like all human beings, she was a sinner herself. She had no right either to condemn nor even to forgive.

Frances smiled, quickening her step. Suddenly, she felt released from all the anger and fear that had haunted her. Truly, she could accept Sarah, feel concern for her and for Gabriel.

Those old, judgmental attitudes of hers had no relevance in the eyes of God. She would see Sarah. Frances began to run up the stone steps to the walkway round the house. Tell her that she bore her no malice. Her foot became entangled in her long, wide skirts and she tripped, falling to the ground and crashing her head against a stone balustrade. She rolled back, down the steps, and was still.

* * *

Through her tears, Katherine looked uncomprehendingly at her mother lying on her couch. She stood for a long time in silence, thinking.

A bitter pain engulfed her. It seemed to her that her mother had been the victim of terrible injustice and for the first time, she began to see her father's relationship with Sarah as an evil that should not be condoned. Katherine sighed. She would think about that later.

For a moment, she held her mother in her arms and gently kissed her pale face. Yet, she thought, she no longer has that expression of sadness. Then she left the chamber to await the arrival of her father.

24

The news of his mother's death reached Adam on the eve of his marriage to Margaret O'Connell. He was overwhelmed with sadness. Although he had spent so much of his life away from home, he had always looked upon her as a support. She had never criticized his behaviour, expressing only concern for his safety. But the preparations were now too far advanced to permit of delay and the wedding went forward as planned. The O'Connell had organized great celebrations and the wedding feast at Kinsale continued for two days. Adam found the wild behaviour that Margaret had inherited from her father as attractive as her blue eyes and soft blonde hair. The drinking and laughter and argument which had brought him into such disrepute in London were here a part of normal life and he had resolved never to return to England to live. He would spend his life here, supporting the Irish cause.

When the celebrations were over, they took the ship to England and arrived at Vinelands on the evening before the funeral.

'My father seems much subdued,' Adam confided to Margaret.

'Why, surely he must be,' Margaret replied.

'That is so. Yet, now he can marry Sarah, who is with child.'

'Oh, yes, he will do that. It's just remorse he's feeling.' Margaret grabbed his hand and pulled him towards the bed. 'Come. Let us have a romp. I did not enjoy it on that rocking ship.'

'You're a heartless girl,' Adam laughed.

'No. I knew not your mother so I cannot be sad and you know that in Ireland, the dead expect us to celebrate.'

'Oh, there will be a feast tomorrow but I think perhaps here in England it is more of a consolation.'

When they went down for five o'clock supper, they found that Cicely and Stephen had arrived with the two boys. A young fair-haired man stood beside Stephen, his elegant clothes enhancing his tall, well-proportioned figure. Cicely and Adam embraced eagerly.

'You are excessively thin,' Adam said to her. 'Does not Stephen care for you correctly?' he added, jokingly.

Stephen blushed but Cicely said hastily, 'Oh, he is a good husband.'

Adam bowed to Stephen and then turned to the two boys and embraced them both.

'Philip, you are becoming a handsome fellow. I can see that you will shortly be a recruit for the Irish cause.'

Philip smiled slightly. He was now almost as tall as Adam and his father, and his puny legs were beginning to develop muscles.

'I find Merchant Taylor's a sympathetic environment.'

'Yes,' Adam said. 'So did I. May your life be as eventful as mine has proved to be. But sir,' he said, turning to the man who stood by the side of Stephen, 'I think we have not yet met.'

'Samuel Delaney,' Stephen said. 'My brother-in-law, Adam.'

The two men bowed.

'Ah, yes, of course,' Adam said.

Stephen blushed again. He would have preferred to leave Sam at home at Lincoln but the latter would have looked upon that as an insult. Furthermore, Stephen felt increasingly apprehensive about the tenuous nature of Sam's attachment to him. With James's death, there was no longer the hope of advancement in Court circles and though Sam professed indifference to such preoccupations, he seemed to have a great facility for meeting noble gentlemen in the London taverns.

Even worse, he seemed to have developed a great regard for Cicely which Stephen found irritating and even disturbing. Admittedly, she complained about nothing and treated both Sam and Stephen with civility but she spent half her life in that stupid chapel and the remainder organizing relief for the poor in Lincoln.

Sam smiled at Adam, the smile which he bestowed indiscriminately on every man he met. 'Good day, Adam,' he said. 'I believe you are the Irish rebel.'

'He is no rebel,' Margaret interposed swiftly. 'He merely supports a just cause. The English are the rebels over there.'

Sam adroitly evaded the confrontation and said, laughing, 'And you must be the lovely Margaret. Felicitations to you both upon your wedding.'

Stephen sighed in exasperation and turned to the boys.

'Philip and John. Go and see what assistance you can offer to your grandfather. And Cicely, perhaps Margaret will need help with the arrangement of her wardrobe.'

Margaret laughed. 'Help! That's amusing. I have with me only two robes. But come, Cicely, show me around the house.'

She kissed Adam and Cicely followed her up the stairs.

When they arrived early on the following morning, William and Katherine found everyone subdued and solemn. It was William who had made all the arrangements for the funeral because Gabriel seemed to be in a state of shock. He had scarcely spoken since Frances died. Now William quietly organized the coaches while the family gathered in the Great Hall. He stood by the first coach and watched the tall, majestic figure of Gabriel, now robed in black, come slowly down the steps with John and Urith.

'Sir, will you three take the first coach. I have arranged for the children to travel together.'

Gabriel nodded and glanced briefly at the decorated coffin on the funeral cart in front.

The remainder of the family climbed into the following coaches. The tenants and servants would follow, some on horseback, the remainder on foot.

The cortege started on the slow journey, down the drive and along the lanes into Dartmouth. The streets were lined all the way to St Petrox by the citizens of Dartmouth. William knew that it was only curiosity and the warm September day which prompted their presence. Frances had been little-known in the town and had rarely left Vinelands. But the whole town knew of the life and activities of the people in the big house from the gossip of the servants, exaggerated and interpreted according to the extent of their imaginations. Frances had, indeed, been a shadowy figure to her family as well, William reflected. Her religion had been a remote and personal affair, a spiritual experience that had little connection with the practicalities of life. Probably her most intimate relationship had been with Father Pierre. After his death, she had become even more withdrawn.

The tiny church was full and many of the tenants were required to stand outside during the long service. Gabriel had elected to hold the funeral here in preference to St Saviour's because although Frances had never attended either church, he said that even if it no longer bore those sacred symbols of his Catholic faith, it was always looked upon as the sailor's church. It was the place to which he always came before setting out on his voyages, adding 'And this is a final journey.'

Then the vicar led the way down the aisle and out to the churchyard. The sea was crashing against the rocks beneath them and Gabriel stood for a moment looking beyond the harbour to the open sea. Then Katherine took his arm and conducted him to the graveside.

William frowned. She also had acted strangely since Frances' death. It seemed not to be a matter simply of grief or loss; Frances, after all, was fifty-five and had borne five children. Death at that age should not be such a shock. He had felt that somehow Katherine was controlling some feeling of anger, some curious resentment. Even when her dear daughter Elizabeth had asked whether she felt indisposed, Katherine had replied angrily, 'No, I am quite well. I simply have much to contend with, with the family.'

William contemplated the family gathered in silence around the grave. Did this family have any greater difficulties than any other in the land? John had not recovered from his affliction but Urith seemed a dutiful wife and his business activities had not suffered; Cicely had certainly suffered grave indignities with Stephen and now must have his latest amour in residence with her. He glanced at Samuel Delaney, standing with the children, his own two, Elizabeth and five-year-old Richard, Cicely's children, Philip and John, and little Thomas, John's child by his first wife. He found it distasteful that this Samuel should be present at all; even Sarah had elected that neither she nor the children should attend the funeral.

A slight smile of acknowledgment played round Adam's lips as he realized that William was looking at him. William smiled and turned his eyes away. Well, Adam and Margaret were gay enough at the moment, though his wild behaviour, his connections with the Irish rebels, could land him in dire trouble at any moment.

Earth was scattered on the coffin and the mourners turned away and walked back to the coaches. Gabriel's coach led the way back to the house for the funeral feast.

The house was decorated to receive the mourners, guests from all the big houses for miles around. Gabriel stood on the steps, bowing to them as they entered. He still looked bewildered, William thought, as though he had still not appreciated what had happened. Yet why should the event affect him so much; he had been absent so frequently, and his love for Sarah had appeared to dominate his whole life.

Then, as if by magic, his expression suddenly changed. William saw a gentle light in his eyes, his whole demeanour became relaxed, he smiled and raised a hand.

William looked at the coach which was arriving and watched Sarah alight, clothed in black velvet, her golden hair tied back with a black bow. She smiled at him through the crowd and then walked up the steps, her pregnancy barely visible.

In spite of the solemnity of the occasion, William felt a glow of joy inside him and smiled. Then he saw Katherine looking at him and he said, almost apologetically, 'I cannot help feeling glad that your father finds such solace in Sarah's presence.'

To his surprise, Katherine replied sharply, 'That may be. It is not suitable here.'

'Dear, it can cause no embarrassment. It is known to all,' William said, and then noticed that Katherine was wiping a tear from her eyes.

He put his arm around her.

'Come, dear, do not distress yourself. Let us take some nourishment.'

The feast continued for many hours, though neither Gabriel nor Sarah appeared to partake of much food or wine. William discovered her at one point standing in the library, contemplating the garden and the grounds fading away into the distance.

'Are you well, Sarah?' he asked.

'Indeed, yes. My condition seems to have little effect upon me. But how is Katherine? I have seen but little of her today and she appears very abrupt.'

'She is much distressed, I fear,' William said. 'It was Katherine who came upon the sad event. It may perhaps be the shock of that which has upset her so severely.'

Sarah nodded thoughtfully.

377

'Yes. It may be so.'

'I will ask her to visit you when she is recovered.'

When Sarah departed to return to Trevayne Abbey with the children, it was arranged that Adam and Margaret should join her on the morrow. She said that whenever they were in England, the Abbey should be at their disposal. She and Margaret explored the hills around Dartmouth while Adam, caring not for physical activity, remained in the library, writing pamphlets and corresponding with the Irish. Charles was agitating for war with Spain and Adam had had intelligence that he was also planning an expedition to attack Cadiz. 'An event doomed to failure,' he wrote, 'though in one way to be welcomed, because it must remove English soldiers from the Irish mainland.'

Sarah and Margaret visited John and Urith and had dinner with William and Katherine who, though still subdued, seemed to have somewhat recovered her composure. Gabriel had departed to supervise the contingent of fishermen who would overwinter on the Grand Banks, intending to return before the child's birth in January.

Then, one morning, Sarah said to Adam, 'I am planning to return to Vinelands before Gabriel comes back from Newfoundland.'

'But what of your home here?' Adam asked.

'It is appropriate that I shall bear Gabriel's child in his home,' Sarah said smoothly.

'Yes. Perhaps that is so.' Adam hesitated. 'Sarah, dear, is it not a hasty action? The bereavement is but recent.'

'But, no,' Margaret said. 'It is their child. It should be born in its own house.'

Adam smiled. 'I know Sarah will do as she has decided,' he said. 'Yet cannot you wait until Father returns?'

'He may not return in time,' Sarah said. 'You know his journeys are frequently delayed. But you may remain here as long as you wish, and always return at your pleasure.'

Her clothes were transported that day to Vinelands, Emily and the children were installed in the nurseries and schoolroom and Sarah summoned the steward and servants to the hall.

'In the absence of his lordship,' she said, 'I shall again be resident in this house though your affairs will, of course, continue to be conducted by Mr Weaver.'

Then she requested the housekeeper to accompany her to Frances's chamber.

'It will be a comfort to his lordship,' Sarah said, 'if all these things are removed before his return. It can cause him only distress to look upon this chamber. Pray arrange for the despatch of the furnishings and furniture to be stored in some suitable place. At some later date, it can be redone.'

'Yes, my lady. But what of the clothes, the jewels?'

'Pray, take the clothes. You may share them amongst those servants you find deserving.'

'Oh, thank you, m'lady.'

'The jewels must be consigned to the safe keeping of his lordship's coffer until he returns.'

Then Sarah went round the house, studying the layout, the furniture, the decorations, making a note of all those changes she intended to suggest to Gabriel.

When Katherine arrived one afternoon, she found Sarah in the dining hall, enquiring of the steward whether it would be possible to remove a wall in order to introduce more windows.

Katherine listened in silence.

'Oh, Katherine, I am so glad to see you. It has been so long. Are you now recovered?'

'I have not been ill,' Katherine replied.

'Ah, but you were much affected by the loss of your mother.'

'And were you?'

'Katherine, that is as you know a difficult question. I am sad at her loss, but we have not enjoyed much contact for a long time.'

'I think her loss must be to your advantage,' Katherine said slowly. Sarah looked irritated.

'It may be. But I have had much to bear in that situation.'

Katherine glanced round her at the servants passing to and fro.

'Come up to your chamber,' she said. 'I wish to talk with you.'

Once in the chamber, Katherine sat down on the settle.

'I suspect that my mother may not have died as a natural event,' she said.

Sarah frowned. 'What mean you, Katherine?'

'I have a terrible suspicion that you may have had some hand in her accident.'

'Katherine, how can you think so?' Sarah said, looking horrified.

'Sarah, did she not know of your pregnancy?'

Sarah looked at her thoughtfully.

'And what if she did?'

'Only you could have told her.'

'Perhaps Gabriel did.'

Katherine paused.

'Sarah, you went to Vinelands. Mr Weaver has confirmed so.'

'Katherine, are you spying on me? How dare you!'

Katherine sighed.

'No. I am not. I wish to know the truth for my own peace of mind.'

'How dare you!' Then Sarah added, more quietly, 'I did nothing, Katherine, I told her only the truth. And that was some days before.'

Katherine stood up. 'I begin to fear you are an evil person, Sarah. Would you stop at nothing in order to be with my father?'

'Perhaps you may reflect that I had no need to be rid of Frances in order to be with Gabriel.'

'Then what was it? Is it for the possession of this place? Is it that you might be the lady of Vinelands?'

Sarah spoke coldly. 'I have no wish to discuss your stupid suspicions. And what have you suggested to Gabriel?'

'I have suggested nothing. Yet I think that surely in the depths of his being he must know or suspect.'

'There is nothing to suspect,' Sarah said angrily. 'What could there be? Am I responsible that she fell down the stone steps? Are you suggesting that I pushed her? I was not even there.'

'No,' Katherine said. 'Yet what agitated state of mind was she in?'

'I know not. That was her concern. Pray be gone, Katherine.'

Katherine walked to the door and Sarah followed her down the stairs to the hall.

'Goodbye, Katherine. Let us assume that our primary concern is Gabriel's peace of mind, not yours.'

After Katherine had departed, Sarah went into the herb garden and sat on the stone seat, breathing in the soft scent of the herbs and looking far away over the hills towards the harbour. She thought of her final visit to Frances. Would she be held responsible in Gabriel's mind for Frances's death, if he knew of her visit? But how could falling and knocking her head be attributed to her? Frances might have fallen at any time.

After her meal with the children, she took a horse and rode down into Dartmouth and along the lane to St Petrox. A milky sun was shining through the stained glass windows above the altar and she sat quietly, wondering about that Virgin who had dominated Frances's life. There was no statue here, as in the chapel at home: they had all been removed. Yet surely, if she existed at all, her presence must be here also. She went out into the churchyard and quietly contemplated the grave. She had not visited it before but now she felt an impulse to visit it, as though to make sure it was really there.

She smiled. Life at last could become as she had dreamed of it in New England.

Gabriel returned unexpectedly, early in December. Sarah was sitting in her chamber, wishing that she should soon be delivered of the weight inside her, when the door opened and he was standing there. She ran across to him, laughing with delight, but when he had embraced her, he said, 'Sarah, why are you here?'

'Oh, I had thought we can now live that life for which we have always yearned. There will be no separations, except upon your journeys.'

Gabriel sighed.

'You look tired, Gabriel. Have you had a tiresome voyage?'

'No. It is not that. But it had been my intention to leave this house.'

'Leave it!' Sarah sat down in amazement. 'But how could that be possible?'

'I had intended for us to reside at Trevayne Abbey. The estate and my affairs can be administered as easily from there.'

'But Adam and Margaret are in residence there.'

'It is quite large enough for all of us and soon they will return to Ireland.'

Sarah stroked his beard and looked anxiously into his face. He smiled at her, yet there was a remote expression in his eyes.

'Gabriel, dear, do you now have some distaste for this place?'

She felt a sudden panic. Did he suspect that somehow she had been involved in Frances's death? No. It was impossible.

'No. It is not distaste yet I cannot but feel that I added little to Frances's happiness.'

Sarah thought of the ease and wealth which Frances had enjoyed, her position in society as his wife, her power to order the affairs of Vinelands. Was she herself now to be denied that? Was the spirit of that pious creature to shatter their happiness? A bitter anger and resentment welled up

382

inside her. But she said softly, 'Dear Gabriel, it must be as you wish. Yet I feel that it is only by being here that you can recover. Cannot we share your grief together?'

'My love, you must not be burdened with my distress.' She watched a different expression of guilt cross his face. 'This must be a time of joy for you. You must not suffer anxiety.'

'Ah, dearest, it is merely that I have longed always to share this place with you. Yet, if it is not to be . . .' Her voice trailed into silence.

'Yes. It is to be,' Gabriel said firmly. 'My foolish preoccupations become but selfishness. Come, my sweet, let us hear no more of my nonsense.'

Sarah kissed him.

'I think it would be seemly if we postponed our marriage for a little time. It shows more respect.'

Gabriel took her in his arms.

'My dear, I had almost overlooked that event. But we need not delay.'

'No,' Sarah said firmly, 'you shall not be troubled with those concerns at this moment. Come, let us look around the house. We will make it into a great palace, Gabriel.'

She smiled at the grateful expression on his face.

On the day of Charles' coronation, on the second of February sixteen hundred and twenty-six, Sarah was delivered of a healthy boy. For two days, her own life was in jeopardy as the midwife seemed unable to stem the flow of blood and a fever raged inside her. Gabriel did not move from her bedside. Through it all, Sarah felt inside her a determination to live and on the third day the bleeding ceased, the fever abated and she lay still and silent, assured now that her life would at last be as she desired.

25

Sarah took longer to recover than she expected. After the fever had subsided, she lay for days in a state alternating between delirium and apathy. Gabriel remained with her constantly and permitted Adam and Margaret to visit her briefly in the mornings and John and Urith in the afternoons.

A silence fell on the great house. Mr Weaver ensured that the servants spoke little in the upstairs chambers and even the physicians that Gabriel engaged were required to tread softly.

Sarah was aroused from her apathy only when the children, Catherine and Nicholas, were permitted to come in and bid her goodnight. Her anxiety about the baby, her determination to keep him by her side, resulted in a wet nurse being brought from Dartmouth to reside permanently at Vinelands. Yet during that month, Sarah had periods of llucidity in which she seemed to be looking at life as if she were disembodied.

It was as though time had suddenly stopped, as though the world were in a state of abeyance and she could observe it and herself without involvement. The people quietly coming and going around her each represented a single element, eternal and unchangeable. As though they were no longer human beings, each of them became an image in her mind so that sometimes their bodies faded away altogether.

Margaret was a song of freedom, echoing in Sarah's

brain; Adam was gunpowder and when Cicely came she was a shroud, a great winding sheet that made Sarah tremble with fear. Gabriel sitting by her side, or standing by the window as though awaiting her recovery, was a huge rock from which dazzling lights shone and attached to the rock was a heavy anchor which went far down into the depths of the ocean.

Then, as the warmer spring days came, she slowly began to recover. She walked with Gabriel in the garden, visited the children in the schoolroom and finally one day walked alone up the hill behind the house. A dim sun filtered through the clouds and she sat on a little wooden bench and pulled her cloak around her and looked out across the hills and wooden slopes to the harbour. It was a place she had visited many times; ever since childhood she and Katherine had come to this spot. But now the view had changed. In the past it had always seemed as though all those paths led back to her, the views to the bay, the sea beyond, were a part of her life, almost possessions which went with Vinelands and the estate. Now it seemed to lead away to an immovable universe beyond. I am so small, she thought, of no significance. The images that had haunted her during her illness returned; rocks, shrouds . . . but what was she? It was a long time since she had felt that apprehension about her identity, not since those nights when she had longed to know where she came from and the black days when she had felt lost and solitary.

Yet there could be nothing missing now. All her hopes had been realized. Her life with Gabriel, the love that flowed between them, the baby and, once she and Gabriel were married, ownership of Vinelands. That was her identity. She stood up and began to walk slowly back to the house. These doubts were simply the lingering effects of her illness. She would soon be recovered.

Gabriel was saddling a horse as she walked around by the stables. He smiled.

'Ah, Sarah, some rose is returning to your cheeks. I feared that I would never see this moment.'

'And I fear that I have wasted much time in that sick-bed. I must take up my duties again, dear.'

'There is no need, Sarah.'

She frowned. 'Am I not needed, Gabriel?'

He put an arm around her shoulders and looked at her thoughtfully.

'Yes, you are much needed and perhaps your recovery will be hastened if you do as you wish. It is better that you do as your heart dictates. But I will detain the physicians here some time longer, for my own peace.'

'I shall go to the dairy and then to the kitchens and . . . but where are you going?'

'I must go to Exeter to arrange transport for the broad-cloth and then to Southampton to arrange the chartering of ships. It will take but two days. You will not tire yourself, dear?'

By the time he returned, Sarah had designed a new nursery for baby Andrew and ordered silk cloth from a London merchant for the draperies. She said she was fit enough now to ride and could once again ensure that the tenants' cottages were in good repair.

'Yes,' Gabriel said. 'My mind has been much occupied of late and I have neglected their needs. Pray make lists of their requirements.'

'And will you be going on a voyage?'

'In a few months, I go to Swedish waters and the Baltic coasts, but there are more urgent matters at hand at home.'

He told her then of the currently worsening conditions of the Catholics in London and the north.

'King Charles appears to accept a wanton persecution of those priests in our midst.'

'But surely there has been much relaxation of that policy.'

'Ah, that is something of the past. Perhaps if he had

386

married the Spanish Infanta, that might have been so. Now we are warring with Spain.'

'But now he is married to a French princess, who is also a Catholic.'

Gabriel smiled.

'He has experienced little support in that direction. It was accepted by the House of Commons that Henrietta and her own household should practise her religion but I fear she behaves in an outrageous and flamboyant fashion in connection with it.'

'Only recently she made a devout expedition to Tyburn, to pray for those Catholic souls who had suffered death there. There seems to me to be little harm in that.'

'Sarah, that must appear only provocative to the English establishment. It was the final straw which has angered even Charles. Now he has demanded the removal of all her French retinue.'

'But why does Charles not defend her? He appears not to like those awful Puritans.'

'No. His support for the bishops does not endear him to parliament, where the Puritans enjoy much power. But it also does not imply his support of the Catholic cause.'

'Yet he affects to pay no attention to parliament. He rarely assembles them.'

'No. But he cannot continue in that policy for long. He needs money and they will not tolerate expenditures and taxes which they have not voted.'

'It seems there must be but a minority who favour him.'

'Yes, and it augurs no good for the country or for the Catholics.'

Sarah frowned. 'I see little evidence of this in these parts. It is surely known to all that this is a Catholic household. The tenants must know of the presence of the priests. But you suffer no danger.'

'It is always a delicate balance of discretion and determination. In this part of the country, the Catholics are few

387

and appear to offer no threat. But in the capital and the northern parts there is dissension.'

Sarah sighed.

'This means you will depart thence?' she asked.

'Perhaps, in the future. But for the moment, I send financial support where it is needed.'

'Gabriel, the summer is now advancing.'

'Yes.' He looked enquiring at her remark.

'We have made no preparations for our marriage.'

Sarah thought she sensed a hesitation on his part, but he replied, 'No. I have been concerned only with your recovery. But now there is no further cause for delay.'

Sarah brightened. 'When shall it be, then?'

'When would you wish, Sarah?'

'Perhaps in September, when Adam and Margaret will be returned from Ireland.'

So, on a mellow day in September, she stood with Gabriel on the steps of Vinelands to receive the guests for the wedding celebrations. She wore an ice-blue gown and her eyes shone with joy as she greeted each member of the family.

Margaret was pregnant and she intended to remain briefly at Trevayne Abbey while Adam was in London, dealing with the publication of his latest book. But Sarah had persuaded them to return from Ireland again before the baby was born so that she could supervise the confinement.

She saw with relief Katherine and William climbing the steps. Katherine had not visited her for many months and Sarah had feared that if she did not attend the wedding, Gabriel must surely wonder why she disapproved of the marriage. But Katherine was cold and withdrawn when she looked at her, though she embraced her father eagerly.

Then she saw Cicely and Stephen coming towards her, and Samuel behind with the two boys. Suddenly, looking at Cicely, Sarah remembered the images she had seen during her illness and momentarily it was as though a great white shroud encircled them all; she felt a strange faintness and Gabriel looked at her anxiously.

'Are you quite well, my love? You have gone so pale.'

'No. It is nothing. Sometimes, I become tired.'

'Come. Let us go inside and welcome the guests in the Hall.'

Sarah sat down, shutting out the images from her mind because she knew they always led to that question about herself and her identity.

Well, now she knew. She was the Viscountess Humphreys. No-one could take that from her.

She opened her eyes and saw William standing before her.

'I am happy for you both,' he was saying to Gabriel. 'May you have great happiness.'

Sarah stood up. 'Forgive me,' she said. 'I have been subject to these stupid attacks since my illness. But now I am recovered. Come, let us celebrate.'

The celebrations continued for two days and as the last coach departed down the path Gabriel smiled and said, 'Let us get some rest. It has been quite wearisome.'

As they walked together up the stairs, Gabriel went on, 'I am much concerned about Katherine. She rarely visits, does she not. She was your dearest friend before.'

'Before what?'

'I fear it is since you came here. As though she resents that which was always apparent.'

'It is of no concern,' Sarah said. 'Do not worry.'

'But it is, Sarah. I will speak with her.'

'Pray, do not do so,' Sarah said. 'I would that you leave the matter.'

Gabriel looked surprised. 'But I find her attitude towards you offensive. It should not be thus.'

Sarah smiled and said lightly, 'Dear Gabriel, perhaps it is hard for Katherine to see me take the place of her mother. We must allow her time to deal with this matter in her own way. I am sure she will come round. It is better so.'

'As you wish, dear. And all the other members of the family welcome you gladly. John and Urith, Cicely . . .'

'Yes,' Sarah replied. 'I am fortunate in that.'

Sarah looked at Gabriel thoughtfully. There was still an indefinable air of remoteness about him, as though there were one small area of his life she could never share. She had always known of his devotion to his Catholic faith but since Frances' death it seemed to have become stronger, as though he were trying to make up for her loss. He spent more time with the priests and had begun once again to organize safe havens and escapes for those in danger.

He looked into her eyes as he always did, as though he were spellbound.

'Gabriel, we will have a beautiful life.'

When she drew the curtains around them in the huge four-poster bed and lay in his arms, she felt that perhaps there was, after all, no matter for concern.

The whole family arrived for her first Christmas as mistress of Vinelands. Philip and John, Cicely's two boys, were now both at Merchant Taylor's and arrived before their parents and Katherine brought Elizabeth and Richard over from Greenhayes to entertain them. Katherine was the only shadow across Sarah's life. Although she treated her with politeness, she entered into no conversation. But it was more than that. She seemed to have become equally distant with William. His concern and tolerance appeared to meet with little response and Sarah had noticed a pained expression in his eyes that their happiness had unaccountably been shattered.

When the children had gone off to the stables, Sarah said firmly, 'Katherine, cannot we come to some accommodation? Is your distant behaviour to me of any benefit?'

She looked at her. Katherine still wore the same flamboyant gowns and jewels, but there were grey strands in her black hair and an anxious expression on her face.

'There can be nothing to say,' Katherine replied.

'You cause Gabriel distress with your attitude towards me.'

'And you?'

'I cause him only joy, I hope.'

'But my father knows not of your visit to my mother.'

'Katherine, how can that have caused her to fall, days later?'

'Sarah, I believe you threatened her in some way. I believe you tried to force her into some kind of action because you were pregnant.'

Sarah laughed derisively.

'If that were so, I clearly failed in my attempt. She performed no action on my behalf.'

'Perhaps. Yet I remain convinced that she was much disturbed.'

'Katherine,' Sarah said decisively. 'I had no part. She was clearly preoccupied. Yet we all are on occasion.'

Katherine hesitated as though Sarah's words had led her to different thoughts.

'I think your sadness comes from some other source,' Sarah said suddenly.

Katherine frowned.

'I should have known. What is it, Katherine?'

'I shall not discuss it with you.'

'Katherine, we have shared always our thoughts. Cannot we forget this . . . . misunderstanding? It serves no purpose.'

Katherine sighed. 'I cannot forget my doubts, but my concerns are indeed also with other matters.'

'Let us go to the drawing room; there is a great fire there and the day is cold.'

They walked in silence along the hall and sat by the fire while Sarah ordered hot drinks. She smiled at Katherine.

'Everything in my life would be perfect if we would be friends.'

'I suppose you charm me as you do all others,' Katherine said, but there was a slight smile on her face. 'It is those green eyes and that little smile you have.'

They took the hot mead which was offered to them.

'Tell me what bothers you, Katherine.'

Katherine pursed her lips.

'Richard,' she said.

'Richard! But that was many years ago. He is married. Lives far away. I thought Richard was forgotten,' Sarah said.

Katherine shook her head.

'No. He is not forgotten. He happened to be passing this way some months ago. He decided to call upon me.'

'And?'

'And then he left.'

'But, is that all?'

'I have heard no more.'

'Then what is the concern?'

'It is just as before. I cannot remove him from my mind and thoughts.'

'But have you not told William? He is of great understanding.'

'I fear to bring up such a topic again. It would be too painful for us both. It is an absurd preoccupation of mine.'

'But Katherine, William solved this before. It must surely be better than this silence. I have observed that William looks quite despairing.'

'But Sarah, it seems he did not solve it. I thought I had recovered yet my life now seems quite dead and without purpose.'

Sarah stood up and put her arms round Katherine's shoulders.

'Katherine, would it not be expedient if I should invite him and his wife here, to stay at Vinelands for a period after the Christmas festivities. Then you might see him in the company of William and find, perhaps, that your interest may evaporate.'

Katherine laughed.

'Well, Sarah, at least you can still make me laugh.'

'Then that is settled?

'Perhaps. But it may also cause more havoc in my heart.'

'Does William know of his visit?'

'No. I could not bear to speak of it.'

'Then leave it to me.'

When Gabriel returned from his day in Exeter, he found the two women laughing in the dining hall. Sarah smiled at the pleasure on his face.

'Dear heart,' she said. 'You have seen but little of Katherine of late, so we have decided to repair that deficiency.'

He kissed Katherine, who smiled and said nothing.

The remainder of the family, Cicely and Stephen and Samuel, John and Urith, arrived on Christmas Eve and on Christmas morning, Adam and Margaret came over from Trevayne Abbey which they had reached the previous night. Margaret was large with child but she and Adam were as ebullient as usual and Adam was full of the great revolution which must soon come in Ireland.

The Christmas celebrations lasted for a week. There were great feasts and parties and, one day, an entertainment was given by the children in the Great Hall to which the family and all the tenants were invited. At last, there appeared to be no problems, no anxieties, everyone seemed relaxed and Sarah felt that her happiness was complete.

Margaret was delivered of her boy child Edward early in January. Gabriel had engaged a retinue of physicians and a midwife of great repute from London but Margaret seemed to suffer little from the usual agonies of childbirth and within a few days had risen from her bed. Early in the spring, Adam was to go to London to supervise the production of a new play he had written and Margaret agreed to remain at Vinelands until his return rather than be alone at Trevayne Abbey. She would also provide welcome company for Sarah, since

Gabriel had said that he must also visit London and then York.

'There are grave problems in the north,' he told Sarah and although she suggested she should accompany him, he wished her to remain at Vinelands.

'I have no great desire to travel,' she said, 'except for the advantage of being with you.'

'I shall be there as briefly as possible,' he promised.

Sarah and Margaret stood on the steps of the house in the April sunshine and watched the coach crunching down the drive, bearing Adam and Gabriel to London.

26

Gabriel bade farewell to Adam in London at the end of May to begin his journey north. Adam had elected to stay at a tavern near the river where, he said, he might better observe the foibles and fancies of his fellow men.

'The environs of Westminster provide little entertainment,' he said. 'It is here, amongst the wharves and alleys and tenements, that I can witness the true state of England.'

He was spending his days at the theatre, rehearsing his new play, the hero of which was an Irish lord whose lands had been stolen from him by a marauding band of privateers from across the water.

Gabriel's route out of London took him past the Tower. He rode slowly and paused by the small enclosed garden where he had sat thirteen years earlier at the time of his trial. It seemed now almost a place of peace amidst the growing turmoil of London. The restrictions on further building in the city had resulted in the expanding population of the poor living in ever-increasing squalor and congestion, while the nobility and the rich merchants continued to build their large houses in fashionable Bow Street and were now extending to Bloomsbury.

In spite of that, they appeared to be even more discontented than the poor. They all supported parliament in its endless battles against the King. There was still bitter resentment about the gaoling of seventy members of parliament for refusing to pay the loans Charles had forced upon them and even more that the judges had sided with the King when five of them had demanded a writ of habeas corpus.

The merchants supported, too, the Petition of Right, demanding that the King should end his unconstitutional behaviour in arbitrarily imposing taxes. It was presented to the King during his third parliament and they were angered at his delaying tactics to avoid signing it. Now that he had finally done so a few days ago there were cynical doubts about his intention to adhere to it. As far as the merchants were concerned, they were disturbed about the effect the King was having upon their purses. His illegal collection of tonnage and poundage dues when parliament had not been called to permit such a practice; the war with Spain and now France which meant that he was constantly seeking loans which were wasted on military and maritime disasters. There was further friction between the King and the Livery Companies of the City.

Added to his continual demands for loans there was a growing dispute about the Protestant Ulster plantation. The Companies had invested large sums of money in the project from which they shared the profits. The King was complaining that the estates were not properly administered and hinting that their lands would be forfeited and their profits seized. Gabriel could appreciate Adam's anger at these two protagonists, fighting over something to which neither of them had any right. He also had little sympathy with a parliament which had agitated for a war with Spain, simply because of their antipathy to Catholics, and now complained because it must be paid for.

He rode along the Minories to Aldgate and then turned along St Bwttafs and Bishopsgate Street towards the open lands of the Spitel Fields. The deeply-rutted roads were filled with people and he reined in his horse as he approached herds of cattle and strings of horses heading for the market.

Rotten fruit was piled in great heaps on the edges of the road and ducks, geese and chickens were being hustled squawking towards the Fields. Two carters were fighting near the entrance, the market women were screaming abuse at a group of children who had stolen some fruit and a large, muzzled black dog was snarling at his horse's hooves.

Gabriel forced his way through the throng and headed towards the open country. He intended to visit Cicely on his way north. She would be able to give him news of conditions in the north as far as the Catholics were concerned.

He passed through the flat lands to Lincoln, briefly visiting the grave of Frances' brother, before reaching Hewell Grange.

Gabriel had visited Cicely only once before, early in her marriage. He was rarely in these parts. At that time, she had still been much infatuated with Stephen. Now she had returned to the pious behaviour of her early years which Gabriel always found to be a barrier between them. He was therefore surprised when he rode into the estate and along the lane to the house to find Cicely in the herb garden laughing delightedly at something Samuel was saying to her. She ran towards her father eagerly, still laughing, and said 'Ah, dear father. We have so looked forward to your visit.'

Gabriel embraced her and bowed to Samuel.

'It must be but brief, I fear. But you are much recovered, Cicely. You have not looked thus for a long time.'

'Ah, I think it is Samuel who has aided me,' she said immediately.

Gabriel raised his eyebrows. 'How so?'

He looked enquiringly at Samuel. His presence in the household had been an embarrassment and anxiety which Frances had found it hard to bear. Gabriel knew that Frances had believed that Stephen was the personification of evil and had almost felt that praying for his soul could yield but little result.

'He has become converted to our faith, Father. He helps me much in my endeavours.'

Gabriel frowned.

'I was not aware. But what of Stephen? Does he view this with equanimity?'

Samuel smiled. He was indeed a handsome man. Was it not simply a plot between him and Stephen to gain Cicely's acquiescence to their liaison? Yet that was not likely. Stephen appeared indifferent to her feelings.

'Stephen has but little interest in such matters,' Samuel said. 'But I must thank Cicely always for bringing me to the true faith.'

Gabriel felt a great unease, but he forbore to ask what relationship now existed between the three of them. Yet he had a sense of something sinister in the situation, something beyond the realms of mere sexual unconventionality.

'Then I hope you may both advise me on my journey to York,' he said as he followed them into the house. 'I have been requested thence by Father Cornell, who operates the safe houses in that city.'

'In view of your good services to the Crown and your great public services, you are perhaps in little danger,' Samuel remarked. 'But I fear you must be circumspect in your association with the papists in York.'

'I am always that,' Gabriel replied.

'But perhaps you do not appreciate the frenzy of hatred

there is in these parts for the Catholics. They are hunted like animals and treated as vermin. But on whose behalf do you come?' Stephen asked.

Gabriel hesitated for a second. It was possible that the man might be in a position to help him. Then he replied, 'I have been summoned by those who must remain anonymous but who are in great need.'

'Ah, I wish that I might assist,' Samuel said.

'Yes,' Gabriel said, 'I hope that Stephen may know officials in York who can assist me.'

'Stephen has no contact with the Catholic community.' Cicely looked mystified.

'No. But he may have friends in the courts who look with little favour upon the hounding of harmless recusants.' Samuel smiled.

'In view of his family connections, Stephen must favour those who are sympathetic to our cause.'

Gabriel nodded. 'When does Stephen return?'

'I expect it may be tomorrow,' Cicely said. 'But he is somewhat uncertain in his activities.'

'Then I must go forth without his help. I cannot delay.'

'My lord, perhaps I might accompany you,' Samuel said. 'It would give me much pleasure.'

Gabriel smiled.

'It is most gracious of you, sir, but my journey must be made alone.'

After they had eaten dinner, Samuel said he must make a brief visit into town where he had an appointment.

'Cicely,' Gabriel said after his departure, 'I like not the sojourn of this man in your house. It augurs no good.'

Cicely frowned.

'Perhaps it may seem strange, but he has offered me much solace, Papa. I fear it is my dear husband who finds little pleasure in my company.'

'It is not that I speak of. Perhaps this Samuel is not a good friend to either of you.'

'It is not for me to decide,' Cicely said, 'yet his presence no longer distresses me.'

Gabriel sighed.

'May I hope that you exercise the discretion that he advises.'

'Sometimes,' Cicely said slowly, 'I feel that Stephen would wish for Samuel's departure. They appear to converse but little now, though Samuel seems content enough to remain.'

Gabriel shook his head. 'I would that I could discuss this with Stephen when he returns.'

But Stephen did not return on the morrow and Gabriel set out for York, accompanied by one of the servants to direct him on his course. Before they reached the city, Gabriel decided that he would stop at an inn for the night. He bade the servant return to Lincoln as his services were no longer required and paid a handsome sum to the stableman to follow him and ensure his arrival. Gabriel was still suspicious of Samuel, who had arranged for the servant to accompany him.

When the man reported favourably in the morning, Gabriel set out on the last stage of his journey to York and at last he saw the city walls in the distance and the towers of the Minster. He stabled his horse at a tavern and walked along the walls and into the crowded city. He stood in the transept of the cathedral and gazed at the vivid colours of the rose window high above him. If only the union of the Yorks and Lancasters that that symbolized could be emulated now by the union of Catholic and Protestant. Then he sat in the Lady Chapel and waited. At length a priest came in and looked at him quietly and then nodded. Gabriel stood up and followed him along the nave and through the choir and down into the crypt. The priest led him into a small anteroom and closed the door.

'I have come each day at the appointed hour,' he said quietly. 'I feared that you were delayed.'

'I called upon my daughter on the journey,' Gabriel said. 'And many matters occupied me in London.'

'The situation has declined recently. There is turmoil throughout the city. We are much in need of assistance.'

'Yes. I have heard so. The further north one journeys, the greater seems to be the agitation. But what has occurred?'

'A boat put in to Newcastle from Amsterdam bearing upon it suspected priests from France. It appears they had come upon this route to avoid detection. They were betrayed by an apostate priest to the governor of York Castle.'

'And what was discovered?'

'The boat was detained and ordered to anchor. When it was boarded, it was found to carry two passengers who declared themselves to be Dutchmen with no knowledge of the English language though they had English names. They were questioned without success. But when their luggage was searched, it was found to contain all manner of incriminating evidence.'

Gabriel sighed.

'These missionaries take unwarrantable risks. Would that they would show some discretion.'

'They say their faith demands their commitment, regardless of the cost.'

'But what has become of them now? Have they been prevailed upon to speak?'

'Their trunks were found to contain books of devotion, handbooks for confessors, missals. They wore upon their persons beads and a crucifix. There was even a breviary concealed upon one of them. They were examined before the Mayor and aldermen, declaring in Dutch that they were traders and that in their country both Catholics and heretics were permitted. They were thrown into Newcastle gaol, where they were further examined and accused of being English priests who had recently left the seminary at Douai. To this, they finally admitted.'

'It is a difficult matter,' Gabriel said. 'Upon such evidence, their release would be almost impossible. Might escape be arranged?'

'It would involve yourself in much danger.'

'That is of no great relevance,' Gabriel replied.

'There have been an increasing number of such arrests of late, with boats being searched, and whole libraries discovered being transported into this country. As a result, the gaols are filled with Catholics. The increasing rewards for the arrest of priests has created a whole army of informers. Companies have been formed, with bands of hired ruffians who scour the countryside to find Catholics. The bishops also bring them before the ecclesiastical courts.'

Gabriel frowned.

'I do not find that the King is devoted to such a policy.'

'Ah, I fear the King is poorly advised. The government is divided. On the one hand, there are servants here appointed by members of the Privy Council who are concerned only with the profit to be obtained from these arrests. On the other hand, there are those who like himself support the high churchmen and who still recommend church ornament, ritual in services, the old kind of priests' vestments. They are suspected of being both pro-Spanish and pro-Catholic, as he himself is.'

Gabriel looked at the man before him in his plain brown robe.

'And where, sir, do you stand?'

'I am a papist who finds it more effective to operate within the established church.'

'And you have taken the oath of allegiance?'

The priest smiled. 'I have not yet been requested.'

'And what would be your reply?'

'If it enables me to continue my work, then it would be yes.'

Gabriel smiled.

'Thus conscience doth make cowards of us all,' he said.

'Perhaps,' the man replied. 'Yet you may shortly witness things that you had supposed human flesh could not endure.'

They left the Minster and Gabriel was led through the narrow lanes and alleys of York to the walls of the Castle.

They crossed the bridge over the moat in the company of crowds of people who had business at the prison. Newly-arriving prisoners were each accompanied by a couple of rascally-looking keepers, unkempt and filthy and distinguished only by the cruel and repulsive expressions on their faces. They pushed and kicked their charges to the great iron gates, open to receive them. At the gates stood soldiers deputed by the keeper of the gaol to collect the fees all prisoners were required to pay for entry. The crowds following them were their relatives, hysterical women and screaming children, barking stray dogs, spectators who revelled in the daily entertainment the prison provided.

Gabriel and the priest walked up to the entrance. An old man was pleading that he had no money, that it had been taken from him when he was transferred from Newgate gaol in Newcastle.

'Take him to the dungeons,' one guard said angrily, 'there's nothing free in this place.'

Gabriel stepped forward. 'I'll pay for him.'

The guard turned and observed the attire and bearing of a nobleman.

'Thank you, sir,' he said automatically. 'Five shillings.'

Gabriel passed him the money without comment and then gave a further amount to the old man.

'Thank you, m'lord.' Gabriel frowned as a leer came over the old depraved face. 'These are hard times. And I shall be in much need before I quit this godless place, m'lord.'

'Be gone,' the priest said. 'Take thought for your soul.'

The Catholic prisoners were admitted last as being

402

greater scum than the murderers, pickpockets, cattle thieves and coin clippers who preceded them.

The keeper had decreed that when the prisoners reached the prison gate they should be put in irons for which they must pay according to their station. Priests and suspected priests were charged twenty shillings and their survival depended upon the patronage of visitors from outside.

Gabriel and his companion followed them into the gaol, Gabriel finding it impossible to distinguish between the convicts and the visitors who had come bearing food or money to sustain them. They passed along the stone corridors, peering into the putrid, unlit cells where men and women were herded together and whose oaths, shouts of abuse, anger and despair reverberated deafeningly against the stone walls. Hands were extended towards them, begging for help.

'They must pay for everything, every bit of bread, every drop of milk. And whatever they buy, they must pay the keeper twice as much for the pleasure of buying it,' the priest said to Gabriel.

'I have been in many prisons,' Gabriel said, 'as a commissioner, a magistrate, yet conditions here are most foul.'

Finally they went down a stone staircase and reached a large, crowded cell which was partially flooded so that the inmates were walking always in water up to their ankles. The priest peered into the dimness and finally led Gabriel to two manacled men at the other end.

'Mr Robertson, Mr Williams, my lord Viscount Hooper Humphreys.'

'I am come to give what assistance is required,' Gabriel said quietly, 'but I find your condition worse than I feared.'

The older man, Mr Robertson, replied, 'We do not complain. This place gives us an opportunity to fulfil our mission.'

'Your attire is not adequate,' Gabriel said firmly. 'You need protection from this filthy water. Those flimsy shirts do not protect you from the cold.'

'Yes,' the young man admitted. 'It is not comfortable, yet already we have made converts amongst these lost souls.'

Gabriel sighed as the young man's face lit up with hope. 'Only yesterday, I went down to the inner dungeon where a man was in chains, awaiting his execution this day and cursing violently. Yet during the night, I brought this man to the true faith and the excited crowds, collected to enjoy the spectacle of this violent murderer's end, found only a devout and repentant Catholic, eager to meet his Maker.'

Gabriel looked at the two gaunt men in silence. Momentarily, he felt not inspired by their courage but overwhelmed by the weight of years. The struggle stretched back to his father and grandfather, and seemed to lead ever onwards into a hopeless future, an agony that would not end in his lifetime and perhaps not for generations to come.

Then Mr Robertson said, as though in answer to his thoughts, 'Our lives are not of importance, m'lord. It is the faith that can never be lost.'

'Yes,' Gabriel said. 'I will send clothes for you and food and I have arranged to be present when you come before the magistrates.'

When they appeared in court two days later, Gabriel sat on the bench and listened to the questioning. It was vital that they should not be convicted as priests, an occupation technically punishable by death, and Gabriel was there to ensure that the investigation was conducted correctly. He protested when the magistrate asked them if they had received the Anglican sacrament as required by law. When the magistrate asked them if they were Jesuits, Gabriel pointed out that the law did not require them to reply to such a question and the magistrate acquiesced. They were asked to reply to other questions on oath, but Gabriel vehemently declared that there was no statute which required them to answer on oath.

Finally, Gabriel asked that they should be allowed

while in prison to be at liberty to visit the town as they wished. The magistrate, uncertain of Gabriel's power and influence, agreed, while saying that they would be called for further questioning.

It was while they were returning to the gaol that Mr Robertson said softly to Gabriel, 'My lord, I would warn you that you should be careful of a dangerous person in your midst.'

Gabriel frowned. 'Of whom do you speak?'

'It has come to our certain knowledge that Sir Stephen Kerswill has many connections with the Bench both here and in London.'

'Stephen!'

'It seems he has turned informer and has revealed the whereabouts of many Catholic persons.'

Gabriel stood still, suddenly seeing the terrible truth. It was surely Samuel, the converted Catholic, upon whom Stephen wanted revenge. And Cicely?

'It is bad news,' he said. 'But I will deal with it.'

A week later, the prisoners appeared again before the magistrates. This time, the attempt to prove their priesthood was abandoned, and they were released but exiled to the Continent and commanded never to return. Gabriel watched the ship as it sailed from Newcastle.

When, in July, he returned to Dartmouth, he felt elation that at last he would see Sarah again, that with her he could find peace and strength to go on with the struggle he faced.

But when he walked into the house he was greeted instead by Margaret.

'Oh, Gabriel,' she said, 'it is a delight to see you.'

Gabriel embraced her.

'And to see you, dear Margaret. But where is Sarah?'

'Sadly, she is not here,' and then, seeing his alarmed expression, she quickly added, 'but she has kindly gone on an errand of mercy. She will soon return.'

'But where is she?'

405

'She has gone to Katherine's for a brief period, Gabriel dear. The child Richard is sick.'

'He was well enough when I departed to the north,' Gabriel said, frowning. 'But why did not you go with her?'

She laughed cheerfully.

'I find the journey tiresome in my condition. I think I am pregnant again, but last time, after the first few months, I was perfectly well. As soon as Adam returns from London, we shall go to Ireland.'

Gabriel put his arms round her, controlling his feeling of desolation. It was only Sarah who could give him any sense of stability in what seemed an increasingly chaotic world.

'I fear Ireland is in a doubtful state, also. Perhaps Adam would be better advised to remain here for the moment.'

'But we must continue to fight for our cause. As you do.'

Gabriel smiled. 'Yes. And I would not deny you.'

'And how fared you in York?'

'It is a turbulent scene. Corruption and violence.'

'And Cicely? Is she well?'

Gabriel frowned.

'Stephen is a traitor to our cause,' he said slowly.

He looked at Margaret with astonishment as she said, 'Yes. We have lately suspected so. He is being watched.'

'Watched! What mean you?'

'Information has been passed to our enemies which but a few could know,' she said casually. 'We are accustomed to such events.'

Gabriel frowned.

'You have the true Irish character,' he said, 'Come. Let us talk about this matter.'

27

Adam knew that he was being followed. In the dark, crowded alleys he could not determine whether it was one person only or a gang. If it were a pickpocket, a cutpurse, the man would be alone; if it were his enemies, there would be a group. In that case, he would have no chance. He pulled his cloak around him and walked along by the embankment until he reached the bridge. A group of fishermen were tying up their boats and he circled round them and went into the nearest tavern.

He shouted above the din for a glass of ale and sat down in a corner opposite a buxom woman who was seated on the knees of a sailor. From there he could see the door. No-one had followed him in but after a few minutes half a dozen gentlemen in elegant cloaks appeared from the other end of the room and sat down at a table near him. He studied their faces but recognized none of them. When they saw him looking, one of them bowed. Adam nodded his head slightly and then looked away.

Were they the ones? He knew he was right in his apprehensions. It had happened before but of late, it seemed, with increasing frequency. So far, he had always evaded them, though on occasion he had been in such a vulnerable situation that he wondered that they had allowed him to escape. Was it merely intimidation or were they really intent on doing away with him?

It was over two years ago, Adam reflected, that he had walked in this area with Sarah. He and Margaret had been in Ireland for nearly two years, after the birth of their second child, but whenever he came to London now, he always had this sense of impending danger. Perhaps it was the result of his father's letters, warning him that the Protestants in England with interests in Ireland were becoming increasingly aggressive. Their anger at the King, who had begun to criticize their poor administration of the Irish estates, and had become determined to fine them or exact monies from them, had made them even more opposed to the Irish who still tried to claim back their stolen lands. The English now identified this with their opposition to popery and combined it also with their criticism of the King, who was too weak in his prosecution of the Catholics.

Adam gulped down his drink and stood up. The men before him appeared not to notice and he pushed his way through the room and out of the door. Then, from the corner of his eye, he saw one of the men was already standing up and moving away from the table.

He walked along by the wharves, jumping across the filthy water in the gutters and weaving in and out between horses and carts being led along the narrow road, the begging children and harlots on corners shouting to women in the windows above. When he looked he could not see the men in the crowds behind him and he turned into the Three Cranes and went to an upstairs room. Here, in a room filled with writers and actors of his acquaintance, he could feel safe. He was hailed by a group across the room and he went over and sat down, accepting the tankard which was passed to him.

'And how fare you and your good wife?' a young actor asked.

'Well, thank you. She remains in Ireland while I gain publication of my pamphlet.'

'Then, let us drink to its success,' an Irish voice said.

As the evening passed, Adam began to feel relaxed. Perhaps he would take a room here for the night and avoid the shadows of the streets.

But between the conversations and ribald songs, he was wondering about Stephen. He had come upon him unexpectedly a couple of days ago in a low tavern near Westminster. They had not met for a couple of years, ever since Gabriel had accused Stephen of being an informer. Stephen had vociferously denied it and in spite of all the rumours and apparent evidence and persistent enquiries, they had never been able to prove it. But the rift between Stephen and the remainder of the family was total. Cicely now occupied a separate part of their house. Samuel, whom Stephen suspected of being responsible for the rumour, had been banished from Hewell Grange but had instantly managed to ingratiate himself in noble circles in London.

When Adam had seen Stephen he had scarcely recognized him. His silk cloak and blue pantaloons were splashed with mud, there was little hair remaining on his head, and his now blackened teeth meant that he was bereft of his old, charming smile.

Adam had walked over to him. 'Good day, Stephen. It is strange to find you in this place.'

Stephen had looked at him through blurred eyes but he did not reply.

'And is my sister well?' Adam asked.

'Your sister is a whore,' Stephen had said thickly.

Adam had felt anger rising in him, but the statement was so preposterous that he laughed instead.

'I see you have taken leave of your senses as well as your honour.'

'What know you of honour? You are an Irish traitor.'

'And what is an informer, a creature consorting with the dregs of humanity? A Catholic baiter.'

'I serve the King.'

Adam had laughed. 'Ah, is that why you did it? Did you think to regain favour in that way? Well, you were much mistaken were you not? Our lord the King cares not for such activity. He has appointed as Lord Treasurer a man who conceals not that he is pro-Spanish, pro-Catholic; probably even a secret Catholic,' he added sarcastically.

Stephen tried to stand up and then slumped back in his seat. Adam had walked out. He reflected now that perhaps if he had stayed he might have gained information from Stephen in his drunken state.

He accepted another tankard of ale and agreed to a game of chess with the young actor. At that moment, five of the men he had seen in the other tavern entered the crowded room, looking round quietly and then seating themselves at a table at the other end.

Adam knew from long experience that there was only one way to deal with the situation. 'There are undesirable persons in our midst,' he said quietly to the group around him. They looked in anticipation as Adam nodded to the men at the table. They always welcomed a cheerful scuffle. They all strolled quietly over to the table and stood looking down at the occupants.

'Sir,' the actor said to one of them. 'Perhaps I might examine your beverage, we fear there are poisoners in our midst.'

He snatched up the tankard and drank. The man stood up. 'Sir, kindly replace that which you have drunk.'

The group all laughed.

'Would you have him piss upon you?' one of them said.

Instantly, a fight broke out, cups and tankards were thrown, tables and chairs were taken up and crashed down and in the pandemonium Adam slipped through the door and into the street. Had those men really been following him or was he beginning to imagine things? Was it simply chance that they had appeared at the same taverns? In the second that he stood in the shadows, recovering his breath, a knife was stabbed into his neck and he fell senseless into the gutter.

The news reached Vinelands two days later. Sarah was with the children in the schoolroom and Gabriel was walking down the stairs to the Great Hall when the messenger arrived. He could see from the man's attire that he came from one of the courts and he took the document with a sense of foreboding.

He turned his back on the man as he opened the missive, as though entering already into some private world of his own. The communication was sent from the criminal court, informing him that his son Adam had been cruelly set upon and murdered two days previously, by a person or persons unknown and as yet not apprehended. He understood immediately, but he read it automatically two or three times, simply looking at the words. The fear had always been there, the knowledge that Adam always placed himself in danger, but now he felt as though a knife had been placed in his heart and that he must die of the terrible wound inflicted. Adam. How could that life, that wild, courageous Adam be gone? He broke into violent sobs that trembled through his whole body and then Sarah came along the gallery and down the stairs. She took the letter and read it, and then dismissed the messenger. The servants hurried away in silence, fearful that whatever disaster had fallen upon his lordship must surely rebound upon them.

Sarah led him up to the library and closed the door. He sat down on the couch and she stood behind him, her arms around his neck, her chin resting on his head. She said nothing. The pain of Adam's loss seared into her also; their mutual love for him had been a bond which had suddenly become a source of agony. No-one, nothing, could replace him. There must for ever be a permanent gap in their lives.

As though she had spoken her thoughts, she went on bitterly, 'It is for this reason, Gabriel, that I do not pray to the Virgin Mary. Those things most dear to our hearts are plucked away indiscriminately. Our prayers are not answered.'

She had spoken instinctively, yet she knew that her words would rouse him from his desperation, that he

411

would find comfort in those very things in which she would find no solace.

He stood up and drew her into his arms.

'It is not so, dear heart,' he said. 'It is only in that certainty of eternal love that we can find strength.'

'I would not deny you that comfort, dear. Yet the cruelty of mankind seems to be more powerful.'

'It is only by the grace of God that we can enjoy peace. It is not in this world that we shall find rest.'

Sarah looked at him thoughtfully. He was recovered now from his tears and she said quietly, 'Do you think this was simply an unfortunate brawl in which Adam was involved, or the act of enemies?'

'I know not. A messenger must be sent to Ireland to tell Margaret of the catastrophe. I shall go to London to see what enquiries are made. But first, I must inform John and Urith.'

'I will go,' Sarah said. 'And then I will go to Katherine. Pray, Gabriel, remain here and prepare for your journey.'

Sarah was unprepared for the result of her news when she reached John's farm. She briefly told them what had happened and, when she had finished, John suddenly shouted, 'I will go with Father. I will kill them.'

The two women looked at him in alarm.

'John! You have spoken,' Urith said. She went over to him. 'Are you recovered?'

John frowned. He began to tremble, his lips moving soundlessly. They waited anxiously, as though fearing they had imagined it. Then he said slowly, 'Yes. Suddenly my voice is there.'

'Then perhaps,' Urith said, 'this is a gift from the Almighty to help us in our calamity.'

Sarah said nothing, but she knew that Gabriel would also surely see it in such a light.

Then she went to Katherine and William. Katherine was still recovering from the abortion which she had induced over a year ago. Nothing more had been seen of Richard

412

since he returned to the north but William now treated her with a coldness that perhaps could never be penetrated. She had talked to Sarah constantly about Richard, unable ever to forget the longing she felt for him. Yet she yearned also for that happy intimacy she had shared with William.

They were partaking of their evening meal in the company of Elizabeth and Richard. Elizabeth at eighteen was as attractive and light-hearted as Katherine had once been and ten-year-old Richard had the serious expression and attitudes of his father.

They begged Sarah to join them and she sat down and ate with them, taking little food but drinking more than usual of the red wine. She chatted to Elizabeth about the new straight gowns and the curly hairstyles and asked Richard about his lessons. When the meal was finished the two children rose, but Sarah said, 'Pray, wait a little.' She turned to Katherine and William. 'I fear my visit brings bad news.'

'What, Sarah? What is it?' Katherine asked sharply.

Sarah found tears streaming down her own face now. Her voice trembled as she said, 'I could not bring myself to tell you before. Adam is dead.'

Elizabeth burst into tears and Katherine clutched Sarah's arm and said, 'How, Sarah? What happened?'

She told them the little she knew. William prepared to travel to London on the morrow with Gabriel and Sarah departed mournfully for Vinelands.

By the time Gabriel and William returned from London a few days later, with no assailants yet apprehended, a wild and angry Margaret had arrived from Ireland, vowing revenge and saying that whole Irish clans would descend upon the scum who had taken Adam from her.

After the funeral, Gabriel went alone across the hills and surveyed the sweeping English countryside around him. He saw suddenly that England was becoming a divided country. It was no longer a simple situation of the Protestant majority persecuting a Catholic minority.

There was a chaos of disloyalties, animosities, deceits, which must lead to ever increasing disunity.

There had been the absurd scenes in the House of Commons when the Speaker had been forcibly held in his seat that resolutions might be passed. The daily business of parliament consisted of bitter accusations, anger and resentment, with members leaving the chamber in indignation.

The House of Lords and the Court of High Commission were opposed to the Puritans, who were gaining increasing influence in the House of Commons. Judges were siding with the King against imprisoned members of parliament. The King himself was issuing manifestos and proclamations, which were rousing further sections of the populace against him. His attempts to get relief for the unemployed, his regulations of wages and the prices of victuals because of the rising cost of living, made farmers resentful and gained little sympathy from the merchants and burgesses who seemed to have so much say in parliament. The ridiculous system of knighting gentlemen and then trying to exact taxes and levies from the profits of their lands simply created another group of tax evaders. His attempts to control cloth manufacture made no economic sense.

The King's government, responsible for running the country, was seen to be composed of ministers who were sympathetic to Spain and who were known to hope for a reunion with Rome. Charles insisted on the clergy wearing surplices and still hankered after the ceremony and ritual of the Catholic church, aided and abetted by his Catholic wife Henrietta.

What had become of that hopeful England of Gabriel's childhood? Elizabeth's devotion to creating a united country had been replaced by an increasing number of wealthy merchants and traders and a House of Commons whose main aim was to control and benefit from that wealth in place of the King. They were little concerned with the common weal.

The sight of Catherine and Nicholas riding across the hills towards him brought Gabriel out of his musings. Perhaps the next generation would make some sense of all the turmoil.

When they reached him, he said, 'Come, let's go for a gallop across the top and down over the hill.'

When they reached a hedge and low stile, Catherine's horse leapt over but Gabriel waited while Nicholas came slowly along behind.

Gabriel smiled. 'I'll open the gate for you. I think you care not for riding.'

'I wish to sail with you,' Nicholas replied.

'Ah, we are still with that topic. Very well, you shall come with me in the new year when I go to the Indies.'

'Sir, is that true?' Nicholas shouted with joy. 'For the whole voyage?'

Gabriel nodded. 'The whole voyage.'

'But Mama. She will not wish this.'

'Then we must persuade her together, must we not?'

Gabriel closed the gate behind him and then stopped.

'Papa, what is it?' Catherine asked.

Gabriel looked before him, down the curve of the hill to the roofs of the houses beneath and on down to the harbour and the water lapping far below around Bayards Cove.

'This is where I met your mother,' he said slowly. He heard suddenly the shouts of the crowds, saw the parade of yeomen, the scraggy girl with the matted golden hair, the small black-clothed body hanging from the crossbar.

'Here!' Nicholas said in astonishment.

'Yes. She was ever a magical person.'

'Papa, tell us of this event,' Catherine said.

'It was a golden summer's morning. She was but a few years older than you, Catherine.'

'Than I, Papa?'

'Yes. It is hard now to believe that. A mere child. Yet . . .' Gabriel frowned.

'What, Papa?'

415

Gabriel moved forward slowly on his horse.

'She seemed never to be a child. But come, let us return. We shall tell you of that strange past, for it is part of your past also.'

He turned and they followed him as he galloped away.

That evening, in the privacy of their boudoir, Sarah said, 'Why are you looking at me so?'

'I took the children up to Jawbones today.'

Sarah stopped combing her hair.

'Why?'

'We have told them little of our lives. They should know of these events.'

Sarah sat down.

'It is still painful to remember. It is long ago. Perhaps much of it I do not recall, Gabriel. I was but a child. And confused. What did it mean to me?'

'It changed my life,' Gabriel said. He looked into her green eyes, stroked her golden hair. 'Ever since, I have lived in the consciousness of your existence.'

Sarah said thoughtfully, 'Yes. It is so. I would sacrifice all for you. But must we speak of that dismal past?'

She had closed her memory to those things, electing to remember only the happy parts of her life and eliminating the sad episodes from her consciousness. The black days she had suffered in her childhood, her marriage to Nicholas and his death, the period after their return from New England when Frances was still alive, even Frances' death, all forgotten.

'No, dear. We do not need to speak of matters which may distress you,' Gabriel said.

Then she smiled.

'But promise me, Gabriel, we shall never leave Vinelands.'

'No. We will remain.'

'It is so beautiful. It is your life's work. Are you not still happy here?'

He smiled and kissed her.

'Yes. I am happy.'

But the expression in his eyes told her that for him this house had died, had died perhaps with Frances. Perhaps it was now simply a huge monument to the past and all these possessions were merely relics.

She felt a momentary panic as though she must call out to him, that he had gone far away where she could never follow. But there was a determination within her that this house, the great estate, this power and wealth were hers, would remain hers until she died. She climbed quietly into bed.

In spite of the loss of Adam, in the following months Gabriel appeared to find a new happiness in their mutual lives. They became involved in the activities of the town in a way that Frances had never contemplated. The plague that had devastated Dartmouth two years earlier had made the inhabitants aware of the need for clean water. The conduits which formed gullies for the water flowing down between the houses from springs on the hillsides were now covered, so that clean water was piped to the collection places.

The churches, too, were in need of repair and Gabriel commissioned one of the smiths on the estate to design a new south door for St Saviour's Church. He also helped to finance new windows and the enlargement of the tower.

He set up a new shipyard at Hardness to give employment to the rising population and, with the merchants of Dartmouth, planned housing development to relieve the crowded conditions in which people lived. He built up a small fleet of armed vessels to combat the growing piracy around the coast. On one occasion he paid a large ransom for the return of a ship which had been captured with all its crew. Sarah visited the Poor House and took food and clothing for its inmates and tried to find them useful employment on the estate. She told the would-be emigrants to the New World about conditions there and instructed them on the techniques of survival.

When Sarah had moved into Vinelands, she had set out to convert it into a welcoming haven not only for the family but for the gentry and nobility for miles around. There were great parties which lasted for days and became the legend of the west country. Now that court life was quiet and subdued since Charles had become King, invitations were eagerly sought by those living in the capital. Her guests were charmed by this beautiful woman who treated them with such warmth and dignity and yet who had eyes for no-one but her beloved husband. The idea that she had been the beneficiary of the marriage was dissolved and Gabriel was frequently told of his good fortune.

She arranged entertainments for the children, organized musical evenings and theatricals and held exhibitions for artists. At the same time, she supervised the dairies and laundry, oversaw the accounts with Mr Weaver, controlled the household of servants and inspected the maintenance of the buildings.

The tenants had found her a sympathetic listener to their requests and a programme of repair and improvement had been introduced, which involved the full-time employment of thatchers and stonemasons.

Sarah knew that the unspoken resentment and suspicion the tenants and servants had felt towards her had changed to gratitude. A school had been erected on the estate where their children could receive education and, as time passed, Sarah had inaugurated a scholarship system whereby clever pupils could be sent to Merchant Taylor's, as Adam had been, to be financed by Gabriel. She had become a connoisseur of the arts, sending representatives on expeditions to the Continent to purchase paintings, porcelain and silverware and to bring back great carved chests and cupboards.

Sarah felt that she was now truly mistress of Vinelands. It was at one of her lavish parties, at the end of that year of sixteen hundred and thirty, that the disaster occurred.

A great celebration was taking place in preparation for

the new year. The whole house, packed with guests, was festooned and decorated. Music filled the air, there was an extravagant display of wine and food in the dining hall and in the transformed schoolroom games were organized for the children. Four-year-old Andrew was sitting on Sarah's knee watching the older children play hunt the thimble.

Katherine appeared at the door and called to her. 'Come, Sarah, come and dance. Papa will not commence without you.'

Sarah kissed the child.

'There, darling, play with the others. I'll soon return.'

She put him down and whirled from the room, her pink silk gown rustling as she danced along the gallery. As she went down the marble staircase, she heard the patter of footsteps and turned to find Andrew rushing after her.

'Ah, silly boy,' she said fondly and bent towards him. But when he reached the top of the stairs, unable to stop, he rushed on down, falling and falling. She tried to snatch him up but he fell past her, there were shouts from guests at the foot of the stairs, someone dashed forward but Andrew lay at the bottom, already still.

Sarah flung herself down the stairs and took him in her arms.

'Oh, baby, what are you doing?'

She held him close and then looked at him. There was a gash across his forehead and his face was white. He did not move. She sat down on the stairs and laid him in her lap. Someone brought water and bathed his head and then Gabriel came and said, 'Darling. Give him to me.'

He took the child and listened for his heartbeat and felt his pulse.

'Sarah, let us take him up to the nursery.'

She accompanied him back up the stairs, the guests following silently as though in a funeral cortege. Gabriel laid him on his cot and a physician came and examined him and shook his head. Then Sarah knew. She broke into a scream that echoed down the stairs. She knelt down and took Andrew into her arms, clutching him desperately.

'No! Andrew. Wake up! Wake up!'

Gabriel tried to pull her up but she cried agonizingly, 'No. Andrew, don't leave me. Oh, my baby!'

Katherine came and said to Gabriel, 'Send the guests away. I'll stay with her.'

She sat on a couch and said nothing, knowing no words.

Sarah shook the child, stroked his face, kissed him.

'Oh, Katherine. My heart will break. He will not wake, Katherine.'

'Sarah, dear,' Katherine said.

'Katherine, moments ago he was talking to me.'

'Sarah, let us lay him quietly in his bed.' Katherine gently took the child from her and laid him down. She put her arms round Sarah.

'Sarah,' she said, 'what cruel fate is it that brings us such unhappiness?'

But Sarah continued to look at the child. 'Oh, God. Please let it not be true. I cannot suffer this.'

When Gabriel came back, he found them weeping on the couch. He looked quietly at the little body in the cot, the small, peaceful face, the tiny hands that would never touch him again. After Adam, this. What more suffering could they endure?

Then he heard Sarah sobbing, 'It is my fault. I left him. I did not see that he followed.'

'No, Sarah. It is no fault. It must be the blessed Virgin's will to take him home to rest.'

Sarah sprang to her feet.

'Then I hate her!' she screamed.

Gabriel felt his stomach turn over.

'Sarah. No. You are distraught. Come, pray with me.'

'Pray! Pray!' She broke into tears again. 'Oh, Gabriel. There is no comfort for such a loss. I would rather suffer than console myself thus.'

Gabriel put his arms around her. He felt suddenly a strange, deep peace. There was a mystery beyond all human feeling; suffering was merely a part of this earthly living. Yet that lost child was somehow not lost, even as Adam was not. They were a part of that infinite mystery of living where pain and happiness were but two sides of the same coin. Man was never called upon to endure more than he could bear. The soul was always separate, inviolate against human frailty. Then he looked at Sarah. There was a wild look in her eyes.

'No,' she said. 'It is my fault. I have killed him.'

He and Katherine led her to the chamber and put her to bed but all night she moaned and cried, 'I have killed him.'

In the morning she became quiet, but there was still that wild, uncomprehending look in her eyes.

28

Gabriel stood up and smiled as Sarah entered the library. Today she was wearing a straight white gown and the weak rays of spring sunshine filtered through the coloured glass of the windows across her golden hair, piled on the top of her head and fixed in place with a diamond comb. She did not smile but looked at him anxiously. Was this to be simply one of her sad days or was it the beginning of another period of delusion and imaginings? The brief period of violence and anger after Andrew's death had never returned but he was fearful always that she might suddenly do some damage to herself.

'What season is it?'

Gabriel came towards her. 'It is spring, dear.'

He had become accustomed to their almost symbolic conversations. Her questions and comments dealt always with abstract concepts, her mind never seemed to deal with tangible realities.

'Why are you not at sea, Gabriel? Spring is the time for your voyages.'

'I do not plan any journeys at the moment.' He sighed. He had postponed his expedition to the Indies and had ventured only briefly to France and Spain, returning with wines for the home market. For the rest, he had concentrated on his ship-building activities and on building up the exports of cloth produced on the estate. 'Do you remember,' he asked hopefully, 'that we were planning some almshouses to be erected above Tunstall?'

Sarah smiled. 'It would make a pretty picture,' she said.

'Come,' Gabriel said. 'We are to sup this afternoon with John and Urith. I will call for your cloak.'

'No cloak can warm me,' she said. 'There is an icy wind from Russia. You were in Russia, Gabriel.'

'Yes. The ice and snow there are greater than that which we knew in the New World.'

Sarah frowned.

'How much longer will it be, Gabriel?'

'Not very long, Sarah.'

It was an apparently pointless and incoherent question she always asked and which he had answered in a thousand different ways but it was never the answer she needed. The question always remained when he had replied.

She turned to the door. 'Well, we shall see.'

Emily brought her cloak and said quietly, 'The children are well, m'lady.'

'Yes,' Sarah said and then added suddenly, 'Though Catherine gives me much pain.'

Emily hesitated and then replied, 'It is simply that she reminds you of the little one you have lost.'

Gabriel waited. He had ceased to mention the tragedy, yet perhaps Emily was right. Perhaps it would be better to force her to speak of it.

Sarah began to look around her, on the floor, down the stairs, but she merely said, 'I have lost nothing, Emily. Why are we searching?'

Gabriel shook his head.

'Emily, you will accompany us to the farm with Catherine and Nicholas. We shall all eat there.'

John was in the farmyard with his steward when they arrived and proudly displayed his new herd of cattle to Gabriel while Sarah went on into the house with the children. Urith greeted her cheerfully.

'Good day, Sarah. Come and help me with the flowers.'

Sarah took a great bunch in her arms and crushed them against her body.

'They hurt,' she said. 'I can feel a hot, wet prong piercing my body. They are meant for torture. Why do you have them, Urith?' She suddenly turned on her angrily.

'They are flowers,' Urith said calmly. 'They do not harm you. See.' She took a bloom and held it up to Sarah.

Sarah turned away sharply and hurried from the room.

'Do not despair,' Urith said to Catherine when she looked at the child's distraught face. 'John recovered from his affliction. Why should not the same occur to your dear mother?'

When Gabriel entered the house, Urith told him of a new physician they had heard of in Paris who could cure people who were sick in the mind. He was reputed to use a painless method of inducing people to sleep for long periods of time and when they awoke they were cured.

'I know not,' Gabriel said. 'We have tried many physicians and surgeons and soothsayers without success. Perhaps they may make matters worse.'

'But dear John was cured.'

'Not by doctors, though. It seems that the shock of Adam's death relieved his symptom.'

'Yes,' Urith replied. 'But it was a dreadful price to pay.'

Sarah sat during the meal eating little. She turned her gaze from one to the other, John and Urith, Catherine and Nicholas, her eyes resting finally upon Gabriel. Then she said quietly, 'Of course, Gabriel is a murderer. He would wish also to dispose of me.'

Gabriel closed his eyes and sighed.

'You are a horrid, horrid woman,' Catherine said fiercely. 'I would that you were not my mother.'

'Hush, child,' Gabriel said. 'Your mother does not mean these things.'

'Ah, but I do,' Sarah reiterated. 'I am no longer safe in this place.'

Urith said casually, 'Sarah, take more food. A guinea fowl, some lobster, perhaps. You have always enjoyed lobster.'

'It has a foul smell. I care for it no longer.'

John passed Gabriel a tankard of wine. He gulped it down, feeling the pain of her words. Of course, mad people always turned upon their loved ones, they did not know the meaning of what they said, but it made it no easier to bear.

As they were leaving, Gabriel took Urith aside.

'Urith, I must request your help. It has been planned that I accompany Margaret who is desirous of returning to Ireland. Then I must visit York once again and I have business to attend to in London which has been much neglected of late. While I am absent, would you reside in Vinelands to ensure that Sarah is safe?'

'She will be safe with me, sir,' Urith assured him. 'Pray have faith that one day she will be recovered.'

Katherine promised to visit her daily, nurses and doctors were also appointed to her care, but when he returned in

424

the autumn she still inhabited her dark dream world. She scarcely seemed to realize that he had been three or four months absent but continued to ask him how much longer it would be.

Then, as winter set in, a messenger arrived from Lincoln to say that Cicely was ill. She begged that her father would come to see her but he was reluctant to leave Sarah for a further period of time. Unexpectedly, Sarah understood the message and requested that she should go with him also.

Gabriel looked doubtful at her temporary lucidity. 'It is a long journey, dear. Perhaps you would find it tiring.'

'We cannot leave her,' Sarah protested. 'Perhaps she is in need.' So it was decided that they should travel in a few days' time and Sarah appeared to supervise the arrangements normally.

Then, the night before they were to depart, another messenger arrived to say that Cicely had suddenly taken a turn for the worse and had died on the previous day.

Gabriel received the information with a heavy heart yet he could not forget his reply to Urith a few months ago, 'It was the shock of Adam's death which cured John', and in the bitter loss of Cicely there was a desperate hope that perhaps it would have the same effect on Sarah. She had already retired to her chamber and he went in and stood before the bed, half-inclined to delay the information until the morning.

She was lying in the shadows of her candles, gazing up at the ceiling.

'Sarah, are you asleep?'

'No, Gabriel. I observe the stars.'

'Sarah, we shall not go tomorrow.'

She sat up in bed. 'Why not?'

'Cicely died yesterday. A messenger has just come.'

'Ah.' She lay in silence for a moment. Then she added, 'Shall we not go for her burial?'

'No,' Gabriel said. 'While she was alive, I would have

425

made the journey. But now . . . the roads are bad with snow and ice, and there are epidemics which make such a venture dangerous. Many places are affected by plague. I fear those parts of the country have taken little heed, as the citizens of Dartmouth have, of events three years or so ago. Little attempt has been made to clear their filthy streets.'

Gabriel stopped. Sarah was not listening to his words. He found himself hoping passionately that those few sensible words she had spoken would continue, that perhaps she would be cured.

She stepped from the bed.

'What is it, Sarah?'

'Well, I don't know about that.'

'About what, Sarah?'

'Cicely,' she said vaguely. 'Who was Cicely?'

'Don't worry about it, dear. You must rest now.'

'You speak of people I have not met,' she said irritably.

'Come, you are cold. I will have the fire made up and Emily will bring you a hot drink.'

She laughed.

'Every hot drink makes me colder.'

He pulled the covers over her.

'Look, Gabriel, they are all creased.'

He smoothed the counterpane.

'It is quite neat.'

'No. It is wrong, Gabriel. It is a long road. Bumpy. Look, there. Take it away,' she said agitatedly.

Gabriel sat on the bed where she was pointing.

'There. It's gone now.'

He looked into the wide green eyes staring up at him.

'Oh, Sarah,' he said. 'What can we do?'

But she continued to stare in silence.

When the fire was made up and she had sipped her hot drink, he put out her candle and crept back to his own adjacent chamber. For months he had not shared their huge four poster bed because every time he moved she had awakened and begun her incoherent ramblings. But it meant now that he rarely allowed himself to sleep, anxious always about what she might do.

After lying for a period on his bed, he heard the rustle of her gown. He got up quickly and found her standing at the beginning of the long gallery. She was sleepwalking again.

'Where is it?' she was muttering.

She crept along to the top of the staircase and began to descend. Gabriel went swiftly past her, walking down before her in case she should fall. But she went slowly down, peering around her, searching.

'Where did they put it?' There was a red glow in her cheeks as though she had a fever and he almost decided to awaken her and carry her back to bed. But there was a strange, unearthly aura about a sleepwalker; it was as though a spirit from another world inhabited the house. If only he knew what went on in her mind. It had begun after the child's death, with that burden of guilt; that was what she was retreating from. But it had meant that she had retreated from life altogether. Was her mind completely vacant?

Sometimes she walked round the house appearing to see things normally. There had even been one brief period when she had designed a new drawing room and supervised the installation of the furnishings. Then she relapsed into her illusory world, where her words were often meaningless, there was no sequence or connections between her thoughts and statements, no consistency in her conversation. For a short time, Gabriel had continued to invite guests to the house, hoping that she might have felt the impulse to behave normally in a social situation. But she had treated them in the same capricious fashion and now he invited no-one, unwilling to expose her to their pitying or fearful stares.

When she reached the Great Hall, she hesitated, then walked across to a long window and stood on a chair, feeling across the glass for an opening, as though trying to escape.

Then she began to moan, 'Oh, it is so rough, so hard. So hot. I shall choke in here.'

Gabriel lifted her off the chair, afraid that she might put her hand through the glass. He did not speak and she turned and went quickly back up the stairs.

'So hot. Can't breathe.' She sat on the bed and he laid her down and covered her over again.

He walked around in his chamber and absently opened a chest, touching the books and maps inside. Then his fingers felt something unfamiliar and he pulled out the old wooden doll that he had taken from Sarah as a child. He looked at it thoughtfully and on an impulse took it into her chamber and laid it by her side. Would that familiar object from the past restore her memory, her comprehension?

Hours later, he went in to awaken her. She was already dressed and standing by the window. She turned. 'Perhaps today we shall visit some place of peace,' she said.

Gabriel glanced across at the bed and then on the floor, where the doll lay, its legs and arms torn from its body, its face mutilated.

He sighed and took her down to breakfast.

He knew now that he had to face the probable truth that she would never be cured. After he had seen the steward to discuss the accounts, he went to the little chapel and sat in the dim light of the single candle. For the first time, he looked clearly into the reality of his situation. Mad people did not recover. The inhabitants of Bedlam testified to that. He thought with a bitter agony of the beautiful years, of that intense love they had shared, of the joy of their lives, and knew that he should thank God for that gift.

Yet he could feel only the desolation of his loss, and question the meaning of such an affliction. Then the thought came that perhaps she was possessed of an evil spirit who would lead him to question the human condition, try to destroy his faith.

428

He knelt down silently, feeling nothing. Was he briefly being granted a blessed respite from his suffering or was he losing his soul?

Sarah took no interest in the birth of Urith's child the following spring and paid even less attention to her own children, Catherine and Nicholas. In the summer, they had an unexpected guest. Gabriel was riding back across the estate one hot July afternoon and observed a coach bumping up the drive.

He dismounted from his horse and waited as the coach came across the drawbridge and a bald and stooping man carefully alighted. Gabriel walked towards him and then uttered in disbelief, 'Stephen!' His voice expressed incredulity rather than welcome and Stephen bowed briefly and said, 'M'lord.'

'Pray, enter,' Gabriel said distantly. 'I had no cognisance of your coming.'

He led Stephen up the steps and into the library. He had not seen him for some years and not since Adam's murder. The culprit had not been apprehended but he was certain that Stephen had had some hand in it. Stephen looked around him.

'I had not expected to visit this place again,' he said.

Gabriel led him to the settle by the fireplace.

'What brings you here, sir?'

Stephen frowned.

'It is but your welfare, sir.'

'I am glad to hear of it. I have fears that you attended to it but little in the past.'

Stephen scowled.

'My belief in the treatment of a wife or of offspring does not coincide with yours, sir.'

'I do not refer to that,' Gabriel said shortly, 'though I have no admiration for it.'

'I know of your suspicions in other matters,' Stephen retorted. 'It is about that I have come to see you.'

Gabriel studied the man before him. It was not just his

429

person that had deteriorated. The shock of his appearance had temporarily blinded him to the fact that Stephen's whole demeanour was that of a defeated man.

Gabriel's distaste for such a person made him say sharply, 'Then I hope you may explain that to my satisfaction.'

Stephen looked resentful at Gabriel's attitude but he said, 'There is no satisfaction to be had, sir.'

'Then what information do you bring?'

'There are people in high places who would do you harm.'

Gabriel pursed his lips.

'I doubt not that has always been the case. You do not travel thus far to give me such small advice.'

Stephen frowned uncertainly.

'Come, Stephen,' Gabriel said, 'let us not mince matters. I suspect that you had some part in Adam's murder.'

Stephen stood up.

'Sir, that is an attack upon my honour.'

'I fancy you will not wish for a duel to defend it,' Gabriel said contemptuously. 'Pray do not dissimulate. What is your purpose here?'

Stephen sat down again.

'Sir, it was a case of mistaken identity. The murder weapon was intended for me.'

'You, sir? How could that be?'

'It was Samuel who had manufactured the plot.'

'Pray explain.' Gabriel's old doubts returned. Which of the two men was really responsible? He recalled once again Frances's belief that Stephen was an evil man, yet was he implicated in this event?

'Samuel had for long plotted against me. He wanted to be rid of me.'

'That must surely have been an easy matter. He could simply have left long ago.'

'No,' Stephen said slowly. 'The benefits I offered made it difficult.'

'Then why would he be rid of you?'

'He became the tool of the anti-papists at Court. They conferred upon him even greater attractions.'

'But you are not a papist.'

'No. But by pretending allegiance to Cicely, he obtained much information about the priests, about the safe houses in York and the north.'

'So?'

'Many have been apprehended.'

'Yes. I know.'

'And then, because I had evicted him from my home, he hatched his own private plot to have me gone.'

Gabriel looked at Stephen with distaste – yet if he were not speaking the truth, why would he have come?

'And Adam?'

'I was there that night,' Stephen said.

'You were?' Gabriel said incredulously.

'I had met Adam on a previous occasion but that night he did not see me. There was a fight in the tavern. In the confusion, the assassins got the wrong man.'

'Why did you not come forward with this information?'

'Sir, I was fearful of my own life.'

'Yes, of course,' Gabriel said shortly. 'But what proof have you of your allegations?'

'I know only from informers.'

'And will they testify?'

'Sir,' Stephen said. 'They are anonymous persons.'

'Then of what value is their testimony? They merely seek you out for reward.'

But Gabriel believed, because of his very ineffectualness, that Stephen was telling the truth.

'But now, sir, I have further intelligence that I believe to be true. There are many jealous of the esteem you enjoy and watch is being kept upon your visits to the capital.'

'With what intention?'

'That you be apprehended in the company of those dissident priests.'

'My religion is no secret,' Gabriel said shortly.

'But they intend to prove treason against you.'

'Well, sir,' Gabriel said quietly, 'I thank you for your information. But for what purpose do you risk your own safety to come here?'

He sat down opposite Stephen, observing him carefully.

'Sir, for two years, ever since Adam's murder, I have lived in fear of my life.'

'You still practise at the courts. You are not a destitute person. You can pay for protection.'

'I am weary, sir, of the struggle.'

Gabriel sighed. 'Then I am afraid,' he said ironically, 'that you must seek a different world from this one.'

'Ah,' Stephen suddenly brightened. 'That is the other reason for my presence here. I would seek your good offices in assisting me to emigrate to the New World.'

'Emigrate!' Gabriel laughed loudly. 'Stephen, I do not think you would find that life more comfortable.'

Stephen reddened.

'I do not dally,' he said. 'I wish that you could find me admittance to the colony in Sagadahok.'

'But what of Philip and John? What of Hewell Grange?'

'Philip is eighteen now. He will learn, with the steward, to administer the estate. John is yet at Cambridge. They will be provided for and I have adequate funds for my own purposes.'

Gabriel stood up. The anxiety in Stephen's face convinced him that he had spoken the truth, though his information was of little value. Who am I to judge the weakness of man? he thought.

'I will arrange your passage on the next expedition,' he said shortly.

Then he looked up. Sarah was standing silently in the hall, hidden by a large court cupboard. He held out his hand and she came slowly towards them.

'Stephen,' she said quietly.

How did she remember this creature when she often

432

forgot people whom she saw daily? Could she leap more easily into the past?

Stephen bowed. 'Sarah,' he said.

It occurred to Gabriel that perhaps Stephen knew nothing of her illness.

'It was a long journey,' she said.

'The roads improve not,' Stephen said. 'Though more people occupy them.'

'Are you to remain here for some time?'

'With m'lord's permission for a day or two.'

'Then we shall go in to Dartmouth,' Sarah said.

Gabriel frowned. Stephen looked surprised but said, 'I shall be pleased to accompany you.'

'On the morrow then,' Sarah said as she turned away and walked from the hall.

'Sarah has been much troubled since the death of Andrew,' Gabriel said.

'Yes. I have heard,' Stephen replied.

'If she insists on the morrow, it must be necessary for me to accompany you also.'

'As you require, sir,' Stephen replied. 'But Sarah will be safe in my company. She appears to be in good health.'

'Yes, but prone to changes of mood, which require some understanding.'

But when, the next day, Sarah reminded Stephen of their visit, she insisted that Gabriel remain at home.

'You need not worry,' she said in a matter-of-fact way, 'I am quite well. I wish only to show Stephen of the changes.'

She looked at Gabriel calmly. Was she trying suddenly to prove to herself that she was recovering? He could not endanger that possibility. Yet did she know at all what she was doing?

'Very well,' he said reluctantly. 'Emily may accompany you in the coach.'

Gabriel almost went after them as he watched the coach trundling down the drive. Yet something held him back. He felt almost as though Sarah were consciously forcing herself back to normality but even as the thought went through his mind, he knew that it was an absurd and forlorn hope. But she would be safe enough with Stephen; he would not jeopardize his own safety by allowing any harm to come to her. He seemed, indeed, flattered by her wish to show him the town and had clearly had no experience of sickness of the mind. Anyhow, Emily was there and the head coachman, Hubert, old Joseph's son, was a reliable fellow. Gabriel turned towards the stables to inspect the new horses which had arrived yesterday.

When they came down into Dartmouth, Sarah stopped the coach.

'Emily, you and Hubert will await us at the Cove.'

'M'lady, his lordship has said I must accompany you.'

Sarah looked impatient.

'I merely show Sir Stephen the new buildings. Pray do as I bid,' and she waved imperiously to Stephen.

Emily looked anxious, but Hubert signalled her back into the coach.

'Be not disturbed. We will follow from a distance. No harm will come.'

Sarah led Stephen along Foss Street to the building works which were in progress. Stephen shuffled along by her side. He had no interest in developments in Dartmouth and cared not to walk at all but he had felt that her request last night could not be refused. It was necessary to please his lordship.

He followed Sarah to the beginning of Fairfax, where she turned and went briskly up the steep steps between the houses of Smith Street. At the Cherub, Stephen sat down breathlessly on a low wall. Sarah looked suddenly anxious.

'I must go there. Come.'

He dragged himself up and followed her into Higher Street. Cattle were being led along by the slaughterers and he glanced with distaste at the great carcasses hanging in Shambles House and the other butchers' shops.

434

Sarah swept on up Crowther's Hill until they came to Jawbones and then she stopped on the top of the hill and sat down on a stile. Stephen threw himself on the grass, panting for breath. Sarah was gazing around her and far away into the distance. For the first time, he began to be fearful. What was he doing here, with this mad creature? How could he deal with her? He stood up again, leaning on the gate.

Then she suddenly began to cry, her body shook with uncontrollable sobs, she rocked backwards and forwards as though she were possessed. Stephen said nothing, his fear growing. The sun was pouring down on his bald head; in the breezeless heat he began to feel faint. He looked again at Sarah.

Her grief began to affect him. In her sorrow, he saw his own misery; the youthful hopes, the wild ambitions, all mutilated and defiled. She was a lost, a kindred spirit.

For the first time in many years, perhaps ever, he felt a desire to help another human being. Yet what was there to say to a hysterical mad woman? He put his hand awkwardly on her shoulder, with an unfamiliar feeling of tenderness. But he could think of nothing comforting to say.

'Sarah,' he said finally, 'you do not need to go on any longer.'

She stopped crying and looked around her. He was afraid that she might suddenly strike him, become completely uncontrollable.

She stepped down from the stile. Then she blinked her eyes, as though she had suddenly begun to see again.

'No. I need not go on any longer.' She paused and looked at him. 'Why are you here, Stephen?'

He frowned uncertainly. Was she referring to this instant, or to his visit to Vinelands?

'You wished to walk up the hill,' he said.

Sarah nodded. 'It is of no consequence. Come, let us return.' Then she added, 'You are the sad one, Stephen. Perhaps for you it is too late.'

Gabriel was standing by the drawbridge, awaiting their return. Sarah alighted from the coach and walked towards him.

'You were a long time,' Gabriel said with relief.

Sarah half-smiled. 'But you could never say how much longer.'

Gabriel frowned. Her reply seemed almost sensible, as though she were actually referring to that past often-repeated phrase of hers. But it had happened so often, these brief periods of apparent lucidity.

He followed her into the Great Hall and she walked over and sat on the settle by the fireplace. She looked at him as she had looked so often in the past with that expression which seemed to penetrate his soul. Or was he just imagining that it held that old intimate awareness?

'I've come back, Gabriel,' she said quietly. 'It's all over.'

He pulled her up and held her in his arms, praying that it could be so.

'The pain has gone,' she said.

Gabriel was silent. He longed to ask her what had happened, to be certain, yet he feared that any word of his, any question might precipitate her back into her dark world.

She sat down again and pulled him to the settle beside her. He saw the familiar frown, but she simply said, 'It was that absurd Stephen. We went up the steps, up Smith Street and Higher Town and we got up to Jawbones. And suddenly, Gabriel, I heard Granny Lott.'

He looked at her, but he did not speak, his fears returning.

Then she said sensibly, 'Of course, it wasn't her voice. It was just my memory of her words.'

Gabriel said, 'Sarah, let us not speak of it any more. Now you are well, let us be content.'

'There is no need to talk of it further,' Sarah agreed. 'But there is just one thing I must speak of. When I felt the great

436

burden of Andrew's death, it was also the burden I felt for another.'

Gabriel frowned.

'What do you mean, Sarah?'

'For Frances.'

Gabriel hesitated. 'Yes. I know.'

Sarah looked at him suspiciously. 'What do you mean?'

Gabriel said slowly. 'Perhaps the love we had for each other caused her great unhappiness. Although I could not change it, it must ever be on my conscience.'

'But did you know . . .?'

Gabriel interrupted. 'Sarah, it makes no difference what I know or do not know. The past is past. We live now.'

Sarah looked at him reflectively in silence. Then she stood up.

'Yes. The past is buried. Dear Gabriel,' she said, 'I have wasted so much of our time. Let us start truly living again.'

29

Lady Sarah, Viscountess Hooper Humphreys: Her Journal

8 January 1633

Today Gabriel and Nicholas departed for the Indies and I am minded once again to commence a journal. Since my illness, I have felt this compulsion to commit my thoughts to paper. It is as though at that stage I left the world and I have never quite returned. There is a fence over which I must climb, a drapery that I must pass through, and it is only when I see my thoughts in words that I begin to approach understanding. I fear that Gabriel may construe that I am affected by those Puritan writers, who commit their soul-searching to paper in the belief that they might thus appear more pious.

They stood on the bridge, Gabriel and Nicholas, and looked down at us on the quay. Even as he bade me farewell, Nicholas could not conceal his excitement and anxiety to be off. He looked well in his new deep blue breeches and doublet, though Gabriel said these will soon be off and he will appear in his working attire. I reminded Gabriel that he is but a child, but Nicholas protested indignantly that he is to be a working man as the others. I felt thankful, in spite of my concern, that he has not inherited the prudence and numbness of his father and that he can have little memory of him. He is, indeed, somewhat as Gabriel must have been at his age, a combination of solemnity and rebellion.

Gabriel seemed, as he always does, to tower above even those larger than himself. He has the dignity of someone who cannot be compromised. The white streaks in his hair contribute in a strange way to his youthful appearance as though they were there by accident and he may defy for ever the sorcerers of age and infirmity.

Yet there is a sadness now about his smile; I fear my sickness has left a permanent mark upon his soul and he can never eradicate the fear that it may return.

Catherine was much distressed at his departure, though he has been on such voyages so frequently in the past. During my illness, they grew closer together and she came to rely much upon his comfort. But perhaps Catherine has taken more of her father than I could wish and not only in her physical appearance. Gabriel has observed the misfortune that though as a child she resembled me, she now tends towards Nicholas's heavy features.

John and Urith stood beside us at the Cove. In many ways, they appear of an earlier generation than Gabriel.

Sedate and plain. Urith favours the fashions of some years ago and John looks older than his father. Perhaps his recurring affliction has removed his youthfulness.

What has become of the huge dowry that Urith brought with her? They appear to benefit little from it and have acquired no great house or estate but content themselves with the farmhouse. They pursue a steady Catholic path, speaking nothing of it. John attends St Saviour's on Sundays, a practice which Gabriel abandoned long ago, preferring to pay the fines which such behaviour attracts.

Now, in my casual writings, a fear has entered my mind. Is John indifferent to improving the farmhouse because he expects one day to inherit Vinelands? Does he suppose he is the eldest son? Does he have claim over Nicholas?

Nicholas is my child, my eldest son. It is I who shall decide to whom this inheritance goes.

It was a strange event that Urith and John came to the quay. They have not done so before. But I think John was compelled there because Nicholas was also going upon the voyage. He recollected his own fateful childhood journey though he made no mention of this.

For myself, I reflected upon how Stephen was faring in the New World. Gabriel and I bade him farewell but a few months ago, seeing him on to the ship at night that he might not be apprehended. Though whether his fears of persecution are well-founded is hard to assess. Gabriel is plain that neither the King nor most of the noble lords would care to involve themselves in such a pursuit. Yet Adam's murder remains a mystery, though he was always wont to involve himself in brawls and argument and can have incurred the wrath of many persons.

3 February 1633

Margaret has returned to Trevayne. Now I must write of this because I do not recollect her departure. I know that she remained some time there after Adam's death and that she has been often to and from Ireland. But I must accept that vacant period of my life, a lost era that I cannot recall. Gabriel commands that I look not to the past nor to the future, that life is always today. Then we cannot fear. Yet there is a weird fascination in creeping back to that secret world.

As I waved goodbye to the ship, I had a feeling of release that I had never felt before. There was no joy in Gabriel's departure but as the ship began to move slowly from the harbour, I felt some excitement at my own free state. It was as though I were escaping, rather than Gabriel, and I began to turn away to hasten to the coach, then looked back again that I might dutifully observe the ship passing through the Mouth. But since his departure, I have felt an increasing discontent that he still finds it necessary to embark upon these voyages. There is a part of me which rebels against the certainty that for Gabriel I must always be of secondary importance.

Margaret has miraculously recovered from the loss of Adam, though she retains all the anger and hatred of the Protestant invaders. She has in her company a handsome gentleman, one Robert de Coursey, of the curly brown hair and blue eyes type we are wont to hear of. They are here to discover what support may be attracted from the Catholics in this country for the uprising they plan in the south.

They are much troubled in Ireland by the exploitation of the English and the sequestration of lands without compensation. There are even stories of the old English Catholics who have long resided in Ireland also losing their lands and property.

I am reminded that Margaret wants nine years upon my age, and her youthful appearance led me to reflect upon the inexorable passage of time. Gabriel has commissioned Mr Dobson to execute my portrait during his absence, to hang in the library beside that of Mr Hilliard's portrait of me when I was but eighteen. I sat before my looking-glass and my reflection gave me no displeasure. By what good fortune I acquired these features I know not when I consider my paternity. It has been many years since I thought about my father and his odious person but now it concerns me not. A few days ago I saw his son in Dartmouth, who has now inherited the estate, and is reputed to be a drunkard and wastrel who will quickly deplete the family fortune.

March 1633

A great collection of persons frequently visit Trevayne Abbey to attend upon Margaret. If they are plotting against the Protestants they appear to be without circumspection. Yet it is an attractive quality that they show no fear of their enemies and puts me in mind of Gabriel.

I am also much indebted to Margaret for bestowing upon me a volume executed by one Mary Ward which has not previously come into my hands though it was written some time since. The liturgical and pious writings of religious and Jesuitical persons have attracted me little but this Catholic person speaks of worlds I have not known and matters on which I have never pondered. Margaret seeks to gain her support and bids me read her works that I may be acquainted with events upon the Continent and understand that this country has many deficiencies.

10 April 1633

My time has been much occupied with this Mary Ward. It now appears to me a matter of much good fortune that I obtained the education I did in this household. It had previously seemed to me of little note that I should read French, Italian and Latin, Plato and Aristotle, the works of Thomas More, George Herbert and William Shakespeare as well as enjoy those feminine accomplishments of the music and dancing variety which are but a frivolity that enables a lady to exhibit her domestic felicity. It is apparent from the writings of all those worthy men who affect superiority over our sex, that learning is something that they would increasingly deny us except in so far as it

441

furthers their own comfort. It is to my liking that this Mary Ward is a nun who finds it insufficient that the religious should occupy themselves only with prayer within the closed confines of a convent. She is devoted to the cause of education for women and has written of her travels in the Low Countries, where women enjoy a greater freedom than in this country.

It is certain that the females in this household have not suffered from this deficiency. Indeed, we were free to pursue whatever course of learning we desired. But it shows a want in my own perspicacity that I had scarcely observed that it is not the usual lot of women in this country. They are perforce homely creatures, subject to the dictates of their fathers and the whims of their husbands. The many English girls who have received education in her convents in the Low Countries did so in the face of much danger. There was the excitement of escape, the flouting of the Protestant authorities, though I find they scarcely suffered the privations we encountered in the New World.

But doubts enter my mind for Mary Ward's purpose is not for women true freedom. She would render them equal with men only that they may be able better to propagate the holy words that both Protestant and Catholic subscribe to. They are released from one form of subjection for another.

I have passed the volume to Catherine who has of late shown more interest in this Catholic ethic, being perhaps somewhat influenced by Urith. But she seemed to find Margaret's robust attitude to the subject more difficult to comprehend.

'Ach,' Margaret said cheerfully. 'Either you become a nun and get on with it, or else you confess to the priest and get on with your living.'

15 May 1633
Catherine is to go to Mary Ward's establishment at St Omer to aid in her work there, though she has no intention as yet of entering the nunnery.

It is a sad time for me as we have never yet been parted. The anticipation of this event also preys heavily upon her. Yet she is determined to go and I would not deter her. She opines that she may be back before Gabriel and Nicholas are.

My time is much occupied with running the estate and the overseeing of the accounts with Mr Weaver. But there must be a gap in my life upon her departure.

19 June 1633

Today, my first letter from Gabriel since his departure. Has he seen so few returning vessels that he could not send earlier? Or is he too preoccupied with his own activities to devote time to me?

He speaks of the journey to Saldanna Bay, of Spanish ships being captured and returned as prizes to this country. Would that he might have accompanied them. Now he proceeds to Natal. He writes that he is disconsolate without me and regrets the length of time that we must be parted. Yet only he makes the decision to go. I begin to feel a weariness about the situation.

This forenoon I visited Margaret at Trevayne. When I ride up that long drive, I have always confused feelings of distaste and content. For I have no desire to recollect my previous marriage to Nicholas, yet I am sensible of the fact that it was here that I came to deal with that solitude of the spirit which had haunted me much at Vinelands. It was here I found it is not something to be dreaded but which is an inner strength.

Today, Margaret had another handsome visitor from Ireland, Sean Murray, whom she introduced as a colonel. His long black hair curls about his ears, his eyes are bluer than the sky at evening and he laughs as though the world were a joyous place. But his conversation is much like that of Adam; he speaks of great battles that will be fought in Ireland, of the total defeat of the English hordes. Yet he bears no animosity to the King, whom he appears to see as a silent partner.

We drank much of the brew he had brought with him in giant casks and when it was time for my departure I found my head quite heavy. Colonel Murray insisted upon accompanying me in the coach to Vinelands, though Margaret laughed heartily and said many ladies later regretted his charming attentions. But he made no impertinent advances in the coach and when we reached Vinelands escorted me up the steps and bade farewell, gallantly kissing my hand. Strangely I have met no-one of his character before.

30 July 1633
Now the preparations are proceeding for a farewell celebration which shall be held at Vinelands before Catherine's departure to the Low Countries. I wonder if it is not perverse of me to organize such an extravagance when she is entering upon convent work. Yet I wish her to be sensible of what she would sacrifice if she decided to become a nun. The house is gay with flowers and sweet herbs; a hundred candles will glow around the minstrels' gallery and up the staircase tall silver holders are placed, six feet high, to hold the rushes. Many noble persons will attend, also Katherine and William and Elizabeth, and John and Urith though I doubt that they will remain for long. Margaret is to bring Robert de Coursey and also Colonel Murray.

Word has come from Stephen in the New World. He appears in better heart than I anticipated. Yet I cannot expect that he can ever be relieved of his shabby personage.

21 August 1633
Another letter from Gabriel today strangely made him seem even more remote than the long silences. He speaks of violent storms and fearful gales, of sailing through distant seas to places of which I have no knowledge. Maxambique, Seilon. He tells of how the King of Maliapor

sent boats to bring him and his crew safely to land, of elephants and mountains and whirlpools.

Yet how can I share this with him? However, compared with previous journeys, he seems to find our separation more unwelcome. He speaks constantly of his love, his longing for me, that perhaps such travels are no longer attractive.

Yet I have waited so long, so often, his absences seem to trail through my life, creating voids which can never be filled. It is hard for me to believe that it will ever be different.

10 September 1633

Catherine left today, escorted by Lord Wilmott, a trusted friend of William, and also by Emily who will return under his protection. We both felt much sadness yet I find it better that she should discover her true wishes at this youthful age, though I wonder if that is ever accomplished. When she was gone, Margaret took me off to Trevayne where we were enlivened by the conversation of Robert and Colonel Murray and other visitors who seem to remain often with her. They made much merriment with charades and dancing but I was clear that I would return to Vinelands that night, fearing that on the morrow it would be even less attractive, with Catherine gone and Gabriel and Nicholas still absent.

My discontent with Gabriel seemed even more acute. Must he for ever continue upon these long voyages, forcing these separations upon us?

5 October

Yesterday, Katherine held a lively entertainment at Greenhayes mainly, I believe, to console me at the lonely state in which I find myself without Catherine, and also without Gabriel.

For the moment, I find little interest in the parties I continue to hold at Vinelands, but I think I must persevere.

Katherine wished me to stay at Greenhayes but once again I insisted that I must return to Vinelands. Colonel Murray elected once more to accompany me and we rode down through the silent streets of Dartmouth and along the starlit lanes and up the hill to the house. I felt somewhat weary, though his presence seemed to cheer me. I know not what persuaded me, but when he took my hand and kissed it, I said, 'Now, kiss my lips.'

He smiled in the moonlight and did as he was bid. Then, as I stood before him, he looked long into my eyes and took me in his arms and I did not dissuade him. He kissed me again and I know not whether it was the Irish liquor or the events of the day, but I felt a great excitement inside me. I turned to the door and entered the hall and he followed me. He followed me up the stairs to my chamber and I did not discourage him.

I sat upon my bed and he unlaced my bodice and when he touched my body my excitement appeared to increase. He removed his own garments and we were naked in the bed. It seemed to be like great waves of the sea crashing over us. He performed actions which Gabriel does not enact and we were both carried away with the ecstasy of it. It seemed like many hours before I awoke and he had already departed. My body is still filled with desire.

7 October
Ecstasy

8 October
Ecstasy

30 October
My journal is neglected. Now I sit at my desk, yet for the moment I have no desire to commit words to paper. Tomorrow Sean leaves for a brief visit to Ireland. I find myself longing that he may return before Gabriel does.

Christmas 1633

Once again, I glance into my journal. Sean returned after only a short absence and stays still at Trevayne with Margaret and Robert de Coursey. He visits me daily, though I do not permit him to reside here. The excitement I feel overwhelms me. Is it real love we feel or just ecstasy?

12 March 1633

Spring is almost upon us, though winter has been of little concern for me. It is not only my journal which has been neglected. The estate, my commitments in the town, even Vinelands itself, have all been overlooked. Sean has communicated to me his own light-heartedness and fun. I have never known this gay abandon, except perhaps a little with Katherine when we were young. Sean and I behave as though we were but eighteen, discovering the adult world and finding it of much amusement and joy.

Today, a letter from Gabriel.

My dearest love,

This strange, heavy climate inclines me to anxious thoughts. The nights are black and heavy and even in winter the heat hangs over the land in a sort of torpor. The Monsoon has changed direction and the violent thunderstorms and torrential rains have abated.

I sit often upon the deck, thinking of you and trying to imagine what you are doing at Vinelands, or with Margaret and Katherine.

Young Nicholas is delighted with the journey and I fear he has that same longing for adventure that has dominated my life.

But now, dear Sarah, I find the exigencies of this roaming life no longer desirable. Throughout this voyage, as we sailed through the Sea of the Indian Islands; when we suffered a great hurricane, with rivers flooding; when we were threatened by wild animals in Siam, I have realized that I am past my wandering days. This must be my last voyage.

I know now what loneliness you have endured, I long only to be with you. Today we left Bantam, heading towards the Road of Saldanna. It must be a slow journey owing to the great loading of our ships but already the excitement of being once more with you overcomes me.

We cannot reach Dartmouth until July but then we shall be apart no more. Soon you will be in my arms again and this time there will be no more partings, my beloved Sarah.

For ever, your devoted and adoring husband, Gabriel

15 March 1633

I have been much disturbed by Gabriel's letter because I cannot determine my feelings towards it. Perhaps he has decided to go on no more journeys because of his age, rather than for any great desire to be with me. Yet that must be an ungenerous thought. Then my thoughts turn to Sean. Has Gabriel decided too late? Is it all too late?

Sean is riding up the drive. I must go to meet him. Tonight, for the first time, he will remain here with me, Margaret and Robert being absent for a few days.

Yet as I reflect, another thought comes to my mind. What of Vinelands? I could never give that up, never leave this place that is mine, never abandon my life here, the life I have built up with Gabriel. Surely, that conviction must come before all other.

30

'It is a strange event,' Katherine said, 'that she is more beautiful now than when the previous portrait was executed so long ago.'

She glanced at her father as they looked thoughtfully at Sarah, smiling quietly down at them from the library wall.

'Yes, yet the painting does not exaggerate.'

He turned slowly to Katherine.

'I notice, indeed, some greater composure on her part as though she only continued to increase her being. It is as though in my absence she had found some new vitality.'

'You were gone eighteen months, Papa,' Katherine replied. 'I suppose there must be changes in all of us.'

'Yes, I have not been gone so long in recent years, yet I attribute it not to that cause.'

'Perhaps it was the fact of managing the estate alone. With Catherine gone to St Omer and Nicholas with you, she was much alone,' Katherine said.

'She has also become much involved with Margaret and the Irish cause, in which she had but little interest in the past,' Gabriel replied.

Katherine laughed.

'The Irish are persuasive people,' she said lightly. 'Indeed, Papa, you found so yourself when you were there.'

'Yes, I agree. But I wonder whether it is not their more youthful ways which attract her.'

Katherine looked at him.

'Papa, there is no cause for concern,' she said seriously. 'Sarah's devotion to you need not be doubted.'

'Ah, I do not complain. It is her happiness only I concern myself with.'

'Then perhaps you will go on no more voyages.' Katherine took his arm. 'I must away, Papa. William returns from London this evening.'

'Ah, yes. Are they all well?' He spoke absently, and then added, 'And this Colonel Murray of whom Sarah speaks.'

Katherine frowned. He had never discussed Sarah

449

before; she realized she had always viewed their relationship as though it were something which was for Gabriel totally private and unquestionable.

'He has stayed much at Trevayne with Margaret. A dashing colonel in the Irish movement. He has recently sailed with other Catholic settlers for Maryland, where they are setting up a Catholic community.'

'Sarah has told me that much.'

Katherine did not reply.

'Katherine, you have her confidence. Does she love this man?'

'You have her confidence also, Papa.'

Gabriel replied simply, 'I cannot ask her.'

They walked down the stairs in silence.

'Papa, you must do so. I do not prevaricate. I know not.'

She kissed him as she ascended the step of her coach.

'My love to Sarah. I had forgotten she was today in the courts. Tomorrow you will both come to Greenhayes to sup with us. And thank you for your gifts, dear Papa.'

Gabriel turned back into the house. The servants were employed in the Great Hall, decorating it with flowers and ribbons for the entertainments that Sarah was organizing to celebrate his return. When he remonstrated that it was unnecessary, that he had returned from many voyages, she had said, 'Dear Gabriel, you cannot know my delight at your return. You were so long away.'

By the warmth of her embraces, he did not doubt the truth of her words, yet he felt an agony of doubt about what had occurred during his absence. At times he regretted that he had delayed so long, though he knew he could never curtail an expedition on the grounds of personal concerns. And a deeper fear told him that there were other reasons for her interest in Colonel Murray apart from the length of his own absence. Gabriel reflected that he was twenty-five years her senior and it seemed to him now that as the years passed that fact must become increasingly significant. He did not feel old, yet how did he appear to her?

He looked through the window of the long gallery and watched her riding up the drive. She had never liked horses, looking always awkward and ill at ease, preferring, she said, to walk in freedom. But today she was galloping along the path, her hair flowing behind her, yet appearing to hold the reins with great casualness, as though she were completely confident. Had that colonel been instructing her?

He went down to meet her. Her cheeks were glowing and as a stableboy led the horse away, she said cheerfully, 'Gabriel, perhaps we shall ride across the hills today.'

Gabriel kissed her.

'I think you liked not horses previously.'

'No,' she said instantly. 'But I spent much time riding to Trevayne with Colonel Murray. He is an eager horseman and taught me much.'

They walked up the steps with his arm around her shoulders. Perhaps she wished him to ask; perhaps it was just as difficult for her to speak of what had passed, of her feelings for this person. Or did she have no feelings for him? But he only said, 'Well, let us ride tomorrow when we visit Katherine.'

He knew that the man was returning from New England and would be present when Margaret married Robert de Coursey in October. Gabriel had met that young man when he was in Ireland and could only approve of the match. He came of that same independent, proud stock as The O'Connell, men who towered above the inferior, invading English Protestants who could only conquer by superior force of arms and a greater dedication to power and wealth.

The heat of August gave way to a soft, mellow September and their time was occupied with installing in Vinelands the treasures Gabriel had brought back from the Indies. Sarah had a green life-size Buddha placed at the top of the staircase and was enthralled by carved Indian screens which now graced her chamber.

Then Gabriel went to London on business and when he returned Sarah was at Trevayne, helping Margaret with preparations for the wedding. Gabriel attended to the accounts with Mr Weaver then, as she had not returned by nightfall, had a horse saddled and rode over to Trevayne Abbey. Was that man already there? Had Sarah gone to see him? It was a crisp October night and as he rode over the cobbled paving stones to the stables, he felt as though the horse's hooves were acting as a warning of his arrival to the occupants of the house.

But when the iron doors were opened and he was admitted, he found Sarah and Margaret were alone in a chamber above, examining her wedding clothes.

'You look well, Margaret,' Gabriel said. 'I wish you great happiness.'

Unexpectedly, Margaret said seriously, 'I do not forget Adam, sir. He was my first love. He will ever be thus.'

Gabriel put an arm round her affectionately.

'I know, dear. There can be only one Adam.'

'But likewise,' Sarah said softly, 'there is only one Robert de Coursey.'

'Yes.' Margaret smiled. 'I am fortunate. He is a dear man. And tomorrow he will arrive with his Irish friends.'

Gabriel felt suddenly cold. He knew now that his anxiety came from fear of his own reactions; what might he do to this man, could he control his feelings if his suspicions turned out to be true?

'I was not expecting you tonight,' Sarah said to him guilelessly, 'and had arranged to stay here with Margaret.'

'But you will both remain,' Margaret said eagerly. 'You are already acquainted with Robert.'

'And have great respect for him,' Gabriel said. 'If it is Sarah's pleasure, we shall remain.'

When she lay in his arms that night, Gabriel tried to convince himself again that his anxiety was unfounded but now even her responsiveness made him doubt. Was not her delight at being with him greater than she normally expressed? Yet surely it was an absurdity to be suspicious of her simply because she declared her love. Certainly, the simplicity of her remarks when she mentioned that man gave no evidence of a secret passion.

On the morrow, word came that the party had been delayed on the Irish crossing and Sarah and Gabriel returned to Vinelands. So it was not until the wedding three days later that Gabriel first saw Colonel Murray. It was a chilly, damp day and they rode over from Vinelands in the coach. Sarah wore a deep rose-coloured gown of Chinese silk which Gabriel had brought back from his trading in the Indies. An intricately-worked gold necklace encircled her throat and her golden hair was coiled behind her ears.

The hall of Trevayne was crowded with Margaret's Irish kith and kin and Gabriel embraced The O'Connell with warmth.

'My dear sir,' O'Connell said. 'It has been too long since we met, yet I find you not a moment older.'

'It is indeed a delight,' Gabriel said. 'And Sarah, you have not met, I think.'

O'Connell smiled at her.

'Ah, dear lady. I find that even all I have heard about you is but a pale imitation. Even in this, dear Gabriel, you have been most fortunate.' He kissed Sarah's hand and she smiled.

'Gabriel speaks most warmly of you, also,' she said.

'It is a good thing you returned, Gabriel.' O'Connell laughed. 'That young Murray never ceases extolling her virtues and beauty.'

Gabriel felt a shiver inside him. He looked at Sarah but she merely smiled lightly and turned to greet Margaret.

Then her eyes fell on a tall, dark haired man on the other side of the hall. Gabriel looked at him. Colonel Murray was far more handsome than he had anticipated, he had a dazzling smile, yet there was no sign of impudence or familiarity as he looked at Sarah.

She ran across the room towards him, laughing with joy and he picked her up in his arms and swung her round in the air jubilantly.

Gabriel looked at the guests. No-one seemed to find anything incongruous in their behaviour. The Irish are not as other people, he reminded himself. They do not prevaricate. Yet what were his intentions?

'Dear Sean,' Sarah said, 'I feared you might not come. Pray, come and meet Gabriel.'

Sean put her down and kissed her formally on each cheek.

Gabriel frowned at her use of the man's Christian name. She always called him Colonel Murray in conversation.

Sarah took his hand and they came towards him. He had expected to feel a consuming anger, a bitter hatred when he met him, he had even feared he might kill him. But now as he looked at the young, eager face and at Sarah filled with enthusiasm, Gabriel felt only a deep loneliness of spirit. You could not contain the soul of another, feelings could not be controlled by dictate nor by the sword. Surely she loved this man.

'Gabriel,' Sarah was saying, 'this is Sean.'

She smiled at him as though she were presenting to him a piece of her handiwork, some achievement about which he should be delighted.

The two men bowed to each other.

'Sir,' Sean said. 'It is an honour to meet you.'

Gabriel frowned at the words which came into his mind. Yet they were not capricious or idle. He could not dissimulate.

'Sir, my pleasure is reduced in that I believe you love my wife.' He spoke quietly as though he were simply seeking clarity about a situation.

'Yes,' Sean said without hesitation, equally quietly. Then added, 'But then, I love many.'

454

For the first time, Gabriel felt anger.

'Then do you toy with her feelings?' he said indignantly. 'Is she but a passing amusement?'

'No. I am not,' Sarah interposed sharply. 'If you wish to consider these matters, it is perhaps I who should be accused of that.'

'Sarah, what mean you?'

She looked at him reflectively, but it was Sean who said, 'Sir, in your absence, I was pleased to amuse her. I love her truly, but there is no cause for concern.'

They were the words Katherine had used. Sarah touched his arm. 'Gabriel, dear, Sean's chief interest is the Irish movement.' Then she added, 'And my chief interest is you.'

Then O'Connell was pressing another tankard into his hand, Margaret and Robert led him to the dining hall and Sarah and Sean swirled away to the other end of the large hall amongst the dancers.

He knew that they had spoken the truth to him, yet there was also much left unsaid. He knew also that he could have forced that information from them but something had restrained him. Patience, he knew, was not one of his attributes. He liked immediate action, affairs to be settled. But some instinct told him that these matters could not be settled by words. In his heart, he knew there was the hope that the danger, whatever it was, would recede by not speaking the words that described it. One day, in her own time, Sarah would tell him. In the meantime, he could only bear the anguish of uncertainty alone.

The O'Connell took his arm and began to talk of the Irish situation in his usual caustic fashion.

'And what think you of this Wentworth,' he asked, 'and his devious ways?'

Gabriel smiled.

'It is unfortunate,' he said, 'though I believe the King had some honest motives in sending him.'

'Then they are much disguised,' O'Connell replied. 'He

has upset not only the old Anglo Irish, but also the new English settlers, though that gives me some pleasure.'

'And how do the Irish fare?'

'More taxes, more dispossession. Nothing changes.'

'At least Wentworth favours a form of worship more closely related to the Catholic version.'

'Ach, the Arminians bow to the bishops. The Protestants have no interest in the Catholic cause. They are now merely getting a little of their own medicine, because Wentworth is now recovering church lands, not for the benefit of the Protestant church but for the government.'

Gabriel laughed.

'Perhaps the situation will arise that we find Protestant and Catholic alike joining the Irish cause.'

The celebrations continued for two days, during which many plans were discussed with O'Connell and the other nobles for the uprising which must surely come in Ireland.

When they returned to Vinelands in the morning, they retired to bed and Sarah tenderly reiterated her love for him, laughingly accusing him of disloyalty in suspecting her. He held her in his arms, touched her soft, warm body and said the matter was at an end. They slept till the morrow and when he woke, Sarah was standing by his bedside with a document in her hand.

'It is a plan regarding the new merchant houses which are to be built in Duke Street.' She passed it to Gabriel.

'Mark Hawkings has paid for the eighty-year lease,' he said. 'He intends to build one of the houses for himself and has engaged woodworkers and stonemasons from St Malo who indulge in much ornamental carving.'

'Ah,' Sarah said instantly, 'perhaps we might have such carvings upon the pillars of the long gallery.'

Gabriel laughed.

'We expend much upon these extravagances, but if it pleases you I am content.'

'You wished some time past to leave Vinelands that we might live at Trevayne. Are you now reconciled?'

'That was but a brief interlude,' Gabriel said. 'I think I cannot now leave Vinelands.'

In the new year, Margaret and Robert returned to Ireland. Sean had departed some time ago and Sarah appeared to suffer nothing from his absence. She and Gabriel were occupied in running the vast estate. In addition, Gabriel's ship-building interests were steadily growing, causing him to leave the administration of the cod trade in Newfoundland to trusted captains, and Sarah was becoming more and more involved with the new buildings in Dartmouth.

Then, in March, a communication arrived from New England. Sarah received it from the messenger.

'It is about Stephen,' she said. 'He died in an epidemic which struck the settlement.'

Gabriel sighed.

'He was a sad person but I fear he will be little missed by his sons.'

'At least they are provided for.' Then Sarah added, 'We must be glad that his fears of assassination were not fulfilled.'

'John and Philip will have been informed but I must repair to Lincoln to see to the administration of their affairs. Philip is twenty-one but must be in need of assistance.'

'I shall stay with Katherine in your absence,' Sarah said. 'I have seen her little of late.'

Gabriel rode over with her to Greenhayes Manor, aware of the satisfaction he felt in the knowledge that she would not be alone at Vinelands, that she could have no intention of entertaining Colonel Murray. Then, as though she read his thoughts, she smiled and said cheerfully, 'I shall only be thinking of you, dear Gabriel.'

On the long journey north, Gabriel observed the increasing turmoil and dissatisfaction in the country.

The King's indifference to parliament, his autocratic behaviour, encouraged by his Catholic wife; the unpopularity of the men in his government and his imposition of ship money all contributed to this. In the taverns at which he put up, he found greater dissension between Protestants and Catholics because the Catholics were more numerous than further south. In spite of the laws against recusants, the pro-Spanish and pro-Catholic views of Lord Treasurer Weston seemed to have convinced the populace in these parts that Charles was a secret Catholic himself.

There was some justification for this view, Gabriel reflected, because there was an increasing persecution of Puritans. There had been trials of pamphleteers in the Star Chamber, trials at which Protestant bishops acted as judges. As a result, moderate Protestants were joining what had been a Puritan minority. The King was pleasing no-one. Even his peace with Catholic France and Spain caused suspicion.

When Gabriel reached Lincoln, he found Hewell Grange in much need of repair. The funds left by Stephen to maintain Philip and the estate had proved inadequate in the face of rising prices and Philip was concerned that the recent proclamation giving justices of the peace power to seize land to make salt petre might involve the unworked areas of the estate. He had dismissed many of the servants and had raised the rents of his tenants so that there was much discontent amongst them.

Gabriel studied the scrappy books of account.

'You are as yet inexperienced in these matters, Philip. Too little is being produced from the estate and even that is being sold at unsuitable prices. I shall send my steward, Mr Weaver, to help you organize affairs and then appoint a steward to manage.'

'I have few funds to pay for that,' Philip said.

Gabriel studied him thoughtfully. He was strikingly like Stephen had been in his youth, but lacking in that charm which his father had displayed before his marriage. It was as though the harsh treatment of his childhood had removed some element of hope and confidence. There was an apprehensive air about him, as though he were always awaiting disaster.

'I would that I had brought Sarah with me,' Gabriel said suddenly. 'She gives much support.'

Philip smiled.

'She was ever kind to me. But I must learn to deal with these matters.'

'And what of John?'

'Ah, he wishes to go to Italy and the Low Countries. He has an interest in the arts and would become an architect. Yet the funds are too low, I fear.'

Gabriel felt a pang, remembering the hopes with which Adam had set forth years ago on such a journey.

'Be not concerned about that, Philip. I can finance all that is necessary.'

He remained for a week and then departed again for Dartmouth. Spring was passing into early summer, leaves were appearing on the trees and as he proceeded south the air became warmer. He passed on the outskirts of the London villages, reflecting that in spite of all the protestations of exploitation by the King, new houses were being erected and there was a certain air of prosperity. The boats and barges along the river were loaded with imports coming from the ports; the large fields on the estates were planted with rye and barley and the strips of land of the cottagers were beginning to produce a plentiful supply of vegetables.

He spent the final night with his sister Julia at Coldeney Prior. Even Exeter was becoming a large town and she complained of the violent anti-Catholic feeling amongst its citizens, 'as though they had never recovered from the Rebellion', she said caustically.

As Gabriel rode the last miles to Dartmouth, he realized that his anxieties about Sarah had abated. His fears and suspicions seemed exaggerated. Everything would be all right.

Then, as he rode up the drive, he saw her standing on the steps of the house. By her side was Colonel Murray with his arm lightly round her shoulder. They did not see him until he had crossed the drawbridge and heard his horse's hooves on the cobbles.

He saw Sarah's face cloud in consternation. She ran down the steps towards him. Gabriel alighted from the horse.

'What is this?' he said sharply.

'Gabriel, have you heard that there is a plague on the Continent?' Sarah said anxiously.

Gabriel stopped in astonishment. What relevance did that have to the present situation?

'No. Yes. I have heard it rumoured.'

He glanced up at Colonel Murray, standing still on the steps.

'Sean has just come from those parts,' she said. 'He reports that it is already in Dunkerque and will surely spread.'

'But what of this matter?'

'Catherine. It is Catherine. She is at St Omer. I have great fears for her.'

'Ah.'

In his anxiety he had totally forgotten Catherine. He found Sarah's fears exaggerated in any case, but he also felt an inner absurdity at his own suspicions.

He put his arms around her and kissed her.

'Sarah, perhaps it is not a dangerous situation.' He turned to Colonel Murray. 'Good day, sir. Let us go into the house and discuss this matter.'

Colonel Murray said that the plague had already affected Flanders and had passed into Germany. Incidents had been reported as far south as Nuremberg and Cologne.

'Is it but a rumour?' Gabriel asked.

'I know not, sir. I saw no evidence, yet perhaps it is so.'

'Dear Sean has offered to go to St Omer to bring Catherine back,' Sarah said.

Gabriel frowned slightly at her use of the epithet, while feeling irritated at his own persistent fears.

'It is most gallant of you, sir,' he said.

Colonel Murray smiled.

'It is a small matter. If I go, I can see if it is desirable for her to return and if so I hope I can convince her of this.'

He departed the next day, bearing a long letter to Catherine from Sarah, having been given detailed instructions as to the best method of persuading Catherine to come home.

Even Gabriel had laughed.

'Sarah,' he had protested. 'Sean must bear himself as he thinks fit.'

'She has much affection for Catherine,' Sean said. 'I will do my best to fulfil her hopes.'

During the next few weeks, Sarah continued with her duties on the estate and, in spite of Gabriel's reassurances, was constantly preoccupied about Catherine's welfare.

At the end of June, Sean returned without Catherine. He told of how she was involved in the running of the convent, that she was considering taking holy vows and would not leave her charges. Sarah was dismayed by this information, her fears about the epidemic becoming even more acute.

'Can we not compel her to return, Gabriel?'

'She is most reluctant,' Sean said. 'It is not in my power to persuade someone against her will.'

'And would you wish that, Sarah?' Gabriel asked her.

Sarah sat down. They were in the library and Gabriel glanced up at the portrait behind her. Today, the sparkle in those eyes was not to be seen in those of the woman before him.

Then she said, 'No. I would not. It must be, if that is what she desires. But I find the loss of her company very arduous.'

'I know, dear,' Gabriel said. 'But no doubt she will return to this country at some time and we can visit when you wish.'

'The plague seems less in that area, though it is now virile in most parts of Germany and further south,' Sean observed.

'May we pray that it does not arrive here,' Gabriel said.

But in the autumn, the first case was reported in London. For some months, fears had been expressed that it must surely arrive, and demands had been made to prohibit vessels from the Continent arriving in English ports. The merchants had been reluctant to see such a ban and it was not until October that the prohibition was instituted. By then it was too late.

Each week a few more deaths were reported. A priest arrived at Vinelands, secretly landed at Gravesend off a boat from the Continent. He informed them that the plague had spread from St Giles in the Fields, with its alleyways of slum tenements, to Whitechapel, Stepney and Shoreditch. No-one had yet recognized it as another epidemic, but he had seen vast areas of Germany, whole towns and cities, decimated by the scourge.

Father Benedic, who had now taken over Father Anthony's pastoral duties at Vinelands, instantly elected to go to London to tend the sick. In times of emergency such as this, it was the Catholic community who suffered most. Their names did not appear on the parish registers of the Protestant churches and so they were entitled to no official relief. The poor, herded together in filthy and squalid accommodation, were forced to rely upon the charity of friends.

It was through the agency of Father Benedic that news of Colonel Murray's sickness was brought to Vinelands in February. The colonel had been passing through London recruiting aid for his Irish cause when he had been struck down by the plague. He was lying in a room at Westminster. When Gabriel received the information, Sarah was at Trevayne tending Margaret who was in the process of being delivered of her third child.

462

He found Robert hovering beyond the chamber in a panic of fear and uncertainty. The two men retreated.

'I have come upon another unfortunate business,' Gabriel said as they entered the dining hall.

Robert passed him a cup of Irish whiskey.

'It is about your compatriot, Colonel Murray.'

'He has not been apprehended in some illegal act?' Robert asked anxiously.

'No. I know not whether it is worse or better news than that but he is reported to have contracted the plague. The epidemic grows worse in London.'

'God forbid. That is bad news indeed.'

'I have to go to London and have a mind during that visit to go and assist him.'

'Sir, that cannot be. You endanger yourself.'

'Colonel Murray put himself at danger some time past when he went to the Continent on our behalf. He may, indeed, have contracted the disease there. I believe I must go with Sarah's blessing,' Gabriel said quietly.

Robert frowned.

'Sir, I fear that by introducing my friend to this house, I have added little to your happiness. I am responsible for that.'

'For what are you responsible?' Gabriel asked, turning away. He felt reluctant to discuss the matter.

'Sean is much enamoured of Sarah,' Robert replied. 'But I believe he is an honourable man.'

'Then that is why I must assist him.'

'Sir, it is correct that I should go.'

'No,' Gabriel said decisively. 'Margaret will need you here for some time.'

Robert's face clouded again with anxiety.

'I fear to lose her,' he said.

They shared a desultory meal, then crept up the stairs again to the bedchamber. There was an awesome silence. Then Emily opened the door and said peremptorily, 'More water. The child is delivered. It is a girl.'

They went into the room while a servant dashed down the stairs.

'It is a weakling child,' Sarah said quietly. 'But Margaret is well. I will bathe her and then she must rest.'

Margaret opened her eyes and murmured with a slight smile, 'But not for long.'

'You must rest yourself,' Gabriel said to Sarah.

Half an hour later, Sarah crept from the room. The baby was placed in the hands of a nurse and Sarah joined Gabriel and Robert where they waited in an adjacent chamber.

'Margaret has no fever now, but we must watch during the night.'

'I will remain there,' Robert said. 'You must sleep now, Sarah. Come, dear. Go to your chamber.'

Sarah sighed briefly and then smiled. 'No. I'm hungry. I feel as though I've been on a long journey.'

As she ate her meal, she seemed to recover from her weariness. Gabriel had decided to leave the news about Colonel Murray until tomorrow, but when she turned the conversation to Catherine and her concern about the epidemic, he felt constrained to say reluctantly, 'I fear I have other news in that connection.'

Sarah looked at him enquiringly.

'It concerns your friend, Colonel Murray.'

'Sean?'

'He has fallen ill with the sickness.'

He spoke slowly, fearing her reaction. He reminded himself that she had never expressed any overt feelings about the man. Yet he had anticipated that she would despair, that she might even return to her madness. She looked concerned, but she merely said, 'That is a regretful occurrence. Can we not assist him?'

'As I must go to London, I intend to see him and put him into the care of a reliable physician.'

'That is a hazardous proposition, Gabriel.'

She came over and stood behind him where he sat, her hands on his shoulders.

464

'I do not wish you to endanger yourself.'

He turned and she sat down on his knees.

'I could not live without you,' she said.

Gabriel held her in his arms. He looked through the windows at the cold February afternoon but it was to him as though the sun shone.

'I shall be gone only briefly,' he said. 'I must visit Father Benedic, who wishes to remain there, to ensure he has adequate help.'

The next day, Sarah bade him farewell on the steps of the house.

'Give my dear love to Sean,' she said, 'and be careful of your own health.'

As Gabriel approached London he met people already fleeing from the capital. With the warmer spring days the plague had begun to spread alarmingly and in the country-side around Hampton Court and Greenwich where the King kept house, Londoners were banned from entry.

He found Sean in a room in Westminster near the river. The Irish family who had admitted him had done so out of much charity because the sickness was so much feared that no-one would risk going near an infected person. But they did not enter his room, leaving food at the door for him to collect.

Then Father Benedic appeared and they entered Colonel Murray's chamber. He was sitting by the closed window. His face and hands were covered with sores and carbuncles and he shrank back into the shadows.

'You do not recognize me,' Father Benedic said. 'I have come with Viscount Hooper Humphreys to seek you out and remove you to a better place.'

'It cannot be,' Sean said. 'It is not permitted to move such persons as myself. The contagion is so great that we must infect others.'

'There is a house, beyond the city at Cheam, where priests will tend you. We shall go tonight under cover of darkness.'

Father Benedic dressed his sores and they promised to return. He commented to Gabriel that as Sean was so much weakened, they would have a difficult journey to the outlying village. Yet, by wrapping him in an encircling cloak, placing him upon a horse and riding either side of him, they managed to evade the searching eyes of inspectors and got him to the house at Cheam.

The priests placed him in an attic room, which they had perfumed with herbs, and said that they would tend to his needs.

Gabriel had spoken to him only briefly. The man was too weak to be taxed with conversation but Father Benedic said that he would recover.

'I have cared for many people with the plague,' he said. 'One learns to know those who can or cannot survive.'

A few days later, Father Benedic prepared to return to London. Already Sean had begun to breathe more easily, the vomiting which had racked him almost ceased, and Gabriel said, 'I have decided to accompany you back to London, Father, before I return to Dartmouth. It is my belief that soon many Catholics will be in need of support.'

Their return to London was delayed by the crowds of people along the country lanes. Anyone who could escape appeared to be doing so; horses were carrying their few domestic belongings; carts were loaded, bearing the burdens of whole households. Gabriel and Father Benedic were told that business dealings had collapsed and tradesmen had locked up their shops.

They rode through Westminster and up White Hall. Gabriel pulled up his horse and read the proclamation which was nailed to a post, issued by an Order in Council on the previous day 27 April. It stated that all houses visited by the plague must be bolted and barred. No-one could leave or enter.

Special inspectors had been appointed, who were now scouring the streets to ensure that the regulations were carried out.

'It is fortunate,' Gabriel said, 'that we removed Colonel Murray when we did. It is now an offence punishable by death for a plague victim to attempt to leave London.'

'You must also beware,' Father Benedic replied. 'There are those walking abroad who may carry the disease and those also who conceal it as long as they may.'

'I intend only to visit the home of one of the justices to offer financial assistance. Then I return to Dartmouth. I begin to find these journeys increasingly wearisome. But there are many able-bodied creatures locked in those houses deprived of earning a living. They will die of starvation if not of the plague.'

He was eagerly admitted to the home of the justice when he revealed the purpose of his visit. He was told a pesthouse was being constructed in Westminster near the river and that funds were desperately needed to pay for gravediggers, watchers and searchers, as well as the costs of medicines and medical aid. Although a tax had been imposed on each parish and the victims were also required to pay for such costs, many of them were bereft of money. Gabriel offered whatever sums were needed.

'There is another request I would make,' the justice said. 'I believe you have a priest travelling with you.'

Gabriel frowned. In his preoccupation he had forgotten the army of informers who infested the capital.

'What of it?' he said sharply.

'Sir, it is still an offence for a priest to be at liberty.'

'I know of no priest,' Gabriel replied. 'And if I did, it is my certain knowledge that these people do more to administer to the poor and sick than the Protestants ever do.'

'Sadly, sir, I know that to be true,' the justice replied. 'And the officials are instructed to take no action with such people. Yet there are many sneaks and informers and ruffians who would make a living from hunting them down. It is not in our power to ignore these creatures. They appeal to the law.'

'Yes,' Gabriel said slowly.

'These priests must not be seen to be attempting to make converts among the dying,' the justice said. 'It is that which angers the populace.'

Gabriel nodded but said no more. The man was trying to help, trying to warn him of the dangers; he would relay the information to Father Benedic but he knew that the warning would fall on deaf ears.

'Sir, there is one other thing. I would elicit your help in other than financial matters.'

'Of what kind?'

'The building of this pesthouse. It requires to be overseen. Most gentlemen, aldermen, many justices have fled the city, sir. There is no one to direct the labour. Also there are many thieves and vagabonds roaming the streets who steal and plunder whatever they can lay hands on. Sir, if you could remain some time here, you could attend to these matters.'

Gabriel sighed.

'I have much to attend to of my own affairs. I came but to assist a friend. I also begin to find these activities beyond my physical capacity. I am no longer a young man, sir.'

The justice nodded.

'It is a hard thing to ask,' he said. 'But you will, of course, be involved in no laborious tasks. I ask merely that you organize these builders.'

'You need authority in this city,' Gabriel said, 'to ensure the regulations are carried out.'

'You might provide some of that,' the justice said.

Gabriel sighed again.

'Perhaps I could remain until some control is established,' he said slowly.

'Sir, I will also ensure that the person who accompanied you is protected.' Then he went on quickly, as though fearful that Gabriel might change his mind, 'As the sections of the pesthouse are completed, you will call upon those barred houses in the vicinity. Anyone there suffering from the sickness will be transferred, that the other occupants who have not contracted the disease can burn the contents and then resume some form of work.'

'There appears to be little work left to be done of a normal kind,' Gabriel observed.

'And food becomes scarce. But they can be employed killing the cats and dogs and other animals who spread the disease,' the justice replied. He passed Gabriel a white rod. 'You will need this. Only people with this rod are permitted to gain entry to the houses.'

Gabriel walked around the great Abbey, which was surrounded by the slums of small courtyards and alleys edged by flowing ditches of filth. He knew it was here that the highest incidence of plague occurred. Watchers stood outside those doors which had been barred and bolted, to ensure that no-one entered and no-one escaped.

Gabriel walked along the embankment towards the Strand where the pesthouse was being built. In one alley, he came upon a group of people indulging in bear-baiting and he hastily commanded them to disperse. All communal activities had been banned, churches and schools were closed, it was illegal to sell wares in the streets. But those who had not contracted the disease and who were now bereft of employment hung about trying to find some amusement.

The pesthouse was simply a timber construction, hastily plastered over and encircled by a high fence whose purpose was to keep the occupants in, rather than shut people out. No-one would wish to visit that place. There was no kind of furniture. In that section which had been completed, piles of rags lay on the floor and a few bowls and other vessels were heaped in a corner.

Gabriel commanded that the rags be removed and burnt on the bonfire outside. Bonfires were one method devised to fumigate the streets. Rubbish and tar were piled up by the citizens and three times a week great clouds of smoke covered the city while the flames rose dangerously near to the thatched and timber roofs above.

Then he went down the road, weaving amongst the great piles of rubbish which lined the street. A herd of swine were snorting and pushing amongst the filth. He stopped at the first bolted house with the plague sign of a red cross on its door. Even the small windows had been covered with heavy board to ensure total proof against the emission of dangerous germs. He tapped the door with his white stick. At the same moment, the sound of a cannon reverberated through the city. It was fired regularly at the Tower in the belief that it would help to disperse the noxious fumes.

The inspector who accompanied Gabriel drew back the iron bolts on the door and shouted, 'Beware. The door is opened.'

Instantly, a man and woman rushed to the entrance, followed by some small children wailing dismally and all trying to push past.

'Stop!' the inspector shouted. 'Remain within.'

Gabriel covered his face with his kerchief. The stench emanating from the house almost made him reel. He peered into the dimness beyond. The room was half-filled with the smoke of burning sage and rue, but it was the even more violent stench of urine and vomit which assailed him.

'We must leave here,' the distraught woman shrieked. 'Our food is almost exhausted. We shall die of suffocation.'

'Retreat, woman,' the inspector said severely. 'Who is it here that is stricken?'

'We are eight, locked in here,' the man said, 'but only two lie with the disease. Yet we all must surely die.'

'We are come to transfer those persons to the pesthouse,' the inspector said. 'You will wrap them in these covers that they may touch no other person, and then the house will be locked again that you may burn all the contents. At the end of three days you will be released.'

470

But the woman screamed hysterically, 'No. You cannot take my children. Perhaps they may recover.'

Gabriel stepped into the room. The inspector pulled at his arm.

'Sir, it is an infectious place.'

'The infected children must go,' Gabriel said to the woman quietly. 'In the pesthouse they will receive attention. Your other children may then escape the disease.'

He looked at the two sufferers lying in dirty straw on the floor.

'Pray, wrap them in these robes.'

He looked down upon the pale face of a young girl, who lay so still she appeared to be dead already. Her golden hair mixed with the hay, her thin, almost naked body seemed paralysed and then momentarily she opened her eyes and looked at him.

He had a cold feeling of dread. Her eyes were green; it was almost as if he were reliving that first time when Sarah had looked at him. On that occasion he had been officiating at a hanging; on this occasion he was officiating at the removal of plague victims to a pesthouse. The difference was that he had been able to save Sarah; this child he could not save. He frowned at his thoughts. The same suffering amongst the poor went on; nothing had changed in all those years. Yet who but God could change it?

Then the girl closed her eyes and shuddered. The woman screamed again and rushed over to her.

'She is gone. Gone,' she wailed.

'She cannot be removed until nightfall,' the inspector instantly called from the doorway. 'The cart will come to transfer her to the pit when darkness falls. Prepare to cast the body out. Now we take the other child with us.'

'I must go with her to the burial ground,' the woman wailed.

'That is against the law,' the inspector shouted. 'Such an action will commit you to the gaol.'

Gabriel lifted up the other covered child and stepped

over the piles of rubbish, filthy bandages, decaying food piled up in the room.

'Sir,' the inspector protested, 'there are carriers for the child.'

'I will take her,' he said. 'It is but a few steps.'

He put the sweating child down on the floor of the pesthouse. Pus was oozing from the sores on her face, but here at least two nurses had been found to wipe the excrescences.

Gabriel felt increasingly tired as the days passed. The harrowing spectacles he observed daily contributed to his sense of a growing physical weakness.

Once the pesthouse was complete, he had intended to return to Dartmouth. But with the heat of the summer, the plague became even more rampant and he sent word once again to Sarah that he was still delayed.

He visited the sick with Father Benedic and distributed money amongst the poor Catholics who were bereft of any kind of government or parish assistance. The Queen contributed vast amounts of money for the relief of the Catholics and Gabriel visited Denmark House to report to her on the terrible sufferings of the Catholic community in the slums. He also tried to organize, with the few remaining justices, some semblance of administering the law against all the felons who had crept into London during the crisis.

It was not until the autumn that the epidemic began to subside and he decided to return to Dartmouth.

On the night before his departure, he rode through the City with Father Benedic to visit a Catholic enclave near Bunhill Fields where a great pit now housed many of the dead. Nightly, carts arrived to deposit more bodies and a constant fire burned around the perimeter. At the gates a man stood on a wooden box. 'Come and repent,' he shouted. 'This pestilence is caused by the devilish popery that has overtaken our land. Be rid of the evil Catholic souls that spring up in our midst.'

They stopped to observe the man.

'In the reign of our dear Queen,' he shouted, 'the bright light of the gospel had dispelled the thick cloud of popery. Now the clouds have gathered and thickened again.'

He waved his arms, embracing the whole of London in his vision. 'We are cursed with this dreaded popery which proceeds from the devil. We are all condemned by these followers of the Antichrist.'

Father Benedic smiled.

'He could as well blame the rats that run along our streets,' he said. As he spoke, a rat ran on to his foot and would not be moved. Gabriel pulled it up by the tail and cast it away into the air.

'They have grown fat with the rubbish they consume,' he said.

The next day, he left London and headed towards Cheam. He had resolved to take Sean with him, if he were still there and recovered sufficiently, but when he reached the house he was informed that Sean, completely recovered, had already departed.

'Know you whence?' he asked the priest.

'To Dartmouth,' the man replied.

Gabriel felt the old suspicion curdling inside him again. How long had Sean been in Dartmouth? What had been happening in his absence? He asked no further questions, but when the priest offered him bed and sustenance for the night, he declined.

'I must head for home forthwith,' he said.

He stopped for only five nights on the journey, in spite of the intense cold which descended and the wet conditions as he proceeded west. He felt suddenly weary and his mind was filled with anxiety which was slowly changing to anger at his predicament. At last, he decided he must confront Sarah with his suspicions, insist upon her honesty.

He arrived on a gloomy November afternoon and went up the steps to the iron door. He strode into the Great Hall. A huge fire burned in the fireplace and he walked towards it, telling the steward to fetch her ladyship. She came slowly down the stairs but she did not smile and when she reached him he said, 'Sarah, I must know the truth of this situation.'

Then, as she was about to reply, the room began to move around him, his head throbbed violently, he felt his legs weaken and he fell unconscious to the floor.

31

Sarah sat silently by the blazing fire in the overheated chamber. The doors and windows were firmly closed, candles burned constantly at the bedside, the fumes of sorrel and thyme filled the air. Although she knew that it was necessary, she felt herself at times almost overwhelmed. For three weeks she had been enclosed in the room while Gabriel lay in an almost permanent fevered delirium, interspersed with periods of violent shivering or desperate demands for water.

She stood up and gently smoothed the coverlet. He was sleeping briefly, his breathing seeming almost normal. But then she knew he would suddenly be gasping for breath, his body shaken by violent coughing, sweat pouring from his forehead, his limbs trembling uncontrollably.

The physician, who came reluctantly to tend his sores, had intimated that there could be no hope of recovery. He would slowly decline; perhaps he would simply waste away, perhaps the end would come in a fit of convulsions and paroxysms.

He had also warned Sarah that she could not hope to

evade the disease. Her constant proximity to Gabriel's person, her determination to remain always with him, guaranteed that she must surely succumb. Sarah had forbidden anyone else to enter the room. Food was placed outside the door and water was left in the adjacent chamber which was unoccupied.

Gabriel's face had become so thin and haggard that she seemed to be watching his gradual disintegration; it was as though the person she had known was slowly disappearing before her eyes.

She looked through the window at the snowflakes falling on the knot garden and the farm in the distance and the hills beyond. Soon it would be Christmas; could he last until then?

Slowly an inertia was beginning to descend upon her; the hope she had first entertained, the absolute determination that he should be cured, was turning into a frustrated desperation. There must be something that could be done, some cure to this terrible scourge that constantly struck people down.

She thought briefly of Gabriel's belief in his Catholic religion. She had discussed it long ago with Margaret, who had tried to explain the God whom they worshipped and the comfort and protection afforded by the Virgin Mary. When Sarah had asked Margaret about it, she had simply said, 'It's being brought up as a Catholic. You can never forget it. In Ireland, you're surrounded by it. It's just a part of your life.'

But now, what prayers would save Gabriel? It was quite apparent that none of the misfortunes and sorrows of this household had ever been reduced or evaded by some magnanimous power beyond.

It was the same with Gabriel as with Margaret; he had been subjected to Catholicism from childhood. She looked at him, lying quietly at the moment. He had devoted his life to his religion, he would be willing to die for it and she felt guilty about dismissing it so lightly. It could do no harm if she spoke to that Virgin, just a few words, because Gabriel could not speak for himself. Yet it was ridiculous; the Virgin must surely know of his plight; how could her own feeble request have any significance? She said softly, 'Please, let him live.' Then she said it again, passionately and fiercely, 'Please let him live.'

Tears rolled down her cheeks and she exclaimed angrily to herself, 'It simply creates weakness. I do not need this dependence.'

Gabriel had another fit of coughing and then he lay quiet.

Sarah built up the fire and sat down again. She thought of the day three weeks ago when he had returned and collapsed in the hall. In spite of her distress now, there was still a bitter anger inside her. His unnecessary absence for so long in London had finally convinced her that she was not a major preoccupation in his life, that she never had been.

She had reluctantly accepted his long journeys abroad as being an essential part of his life, his trading and adventuring and exploring were the inevitable activities of many men. He had said that these expeditions were over. But now she realized that all those Catholic poor in the city, all those plague victims, were of more consequence than herself. His religion would always be more important. He would risk his own life and indeed hers as well.

The matter was made worse in her mind because she was aware of the sacrifice she had made. When Sean had returned from Cheam in the summer, she had sent him away.

'Gabriel saved your life,' she said, 'and I shall find it difficult to deceive him further.'

Sean had put his hands on her shoulders and looked at her in puzzlement. 'But we have surely agreed that he need not be made aware. It could serve no purpose.'

Sarah had felt her body tingling at his touch, but she said, 'Yes. I think so still. It seems to me that if he is to be so long absent, I am not required to live as a nun.'

'Then why must we forego this delight now?'

'It is merely I feel he is devoting himself to the welfare of others and he will be but briefly absent,' she had said then. 'It would seem a kind of treachery.'

Sean had stroked her hair.

'Dear Sarah. We do him no harm.'

'Do not make it hard for me,' Sarah replied. 'Pray do not linger here.'

Sean had shaken his head, but he said, 'As you will, dear. But I shall return.'

After he had gone, she felt a torment of longing for his caresses, imagining other women in his arms, remembering the gay abandonment of his love-making.

Now she felt the injustice of her sacrifice, when Gabriel had merely been indulging his own need to satisfy his conscience.

She knew that she wanted him to recover because there seemed so much unfinished in their lives, that she must leap across this abyss which had opened before her. If he died now, she would feel for ever abandoned, for ever angry that these matters had not been resolved.

That night, she lay down before the fire on the straw mattress that she slept on, and fell into a deep exhausted sleep. When she awoke, it was already dawn and the fire had gone out.

She quickly began to coax the smouldering ashes, then stopped and went to the window. She felt a deep longing to escape from the putrid atmosphere of the sickroom and impulsively opened the window. The sudden gush of sweet, cold air almost overpowered her, she shuddered and was about to close it again, when Gabriel muttered almost inaudibly, 'The wind from the sea.'

She hurried over to him. If he were dying, it was the sea he would be thinking of.

For a moment he opened his eyes. 'It is good,' he said.

Sarah hesitated. He had not spoken for so long. Then she returned to the window and flung it wide open. The air seemed to come into the room in great waves and she felt she could almost see the repulsive fumes passing out.

Gabriel opened his eyes again. 'Water,' he said.

She propped him up and held the cup to his mouth. Then it suddenly occurred to her that it was that cold air which had revived him. Perhaps all those other prohibitions were also wrong; perhaps she should do the opposite of what the physicians said.

'Do you wish for food?' she asked softly.

A faint smile touched Gabriel's lips. He nodded.

She laid him back on the pillows, opened the door and called. A servant stood halfway up the staircase.

'We require hot stew, meats and fish, fruit pies, mulled wine. Quickly,' she added as the servant hesitated in astonishment.

She put out the candles and the smouldering bowls of herbs and when the food arrived demanded clean bed linen and covers and even required that new carpets and rugs be brought.

'The old stuff I will cast through the window,' she said. 'It must all be burnt.'

Gabriel ate but little of the meal, he had been starved for too long, but Sarah persisted with her new regime, constantly having meals prepared of oysters and guinea fowl, lobster and roast meats, sweetmeats and jams. Only a small fire burned in the grate, the windows remained slightly open and she stopped giving him the hot medicine which the doctor had prescribed. One day she remembered a herb that Granny Lott had used and sent a servant up to the hills to gather its leaves. Gabriel found it distasteful but drank it as he was bid.

Slowly, he started to recover. The sores began to heal and no more appeared. Only one night, he fell into the old delirium, speaking of a devilish presence which would consume them all.

At first, Sarah did not recognize his state, thinking that he was recovered and imagining that he was speaking of some actuality.

'Who is this person?' she asked.

Gabriel said, 'He is an Irishman. He must be removed.'

Then he fell into a coma and Sarah feared that the end had surely come. He frothed at the mouth and tossed restlessly in his bed. Sarah called for the priest to come but before he arrived, Gabriel suddenly sat up in bed and said sensibly, 'There are many stars tonight. Is it the equinox?'

'No,' Sarah said in surprise. 'It is but February.'

'I am much recovered, Sarah,' Gabriel said. 'It is somewhat cold in here.'

Sarah smiled. 'It is good that you feel so. It is cold for those who are not sick.'

A knock came upon the door.

'I think the priest visits,' Sarah said.

'For what purpose?' Gabriel asked.

'I know not,' Sarah replied, but when she opened the door, she said with delight, 'Oh, Catherine. Whence come you? You did not send word.'

She embraced her eagerly and then stepped back.

'Catherine, do not enter. I almost forgot. You must not subject yourself to the infection.'

Catherine smiled.

'Be not concerned, dear mother. If I were intended to get the disease, I would have contracted it long ago. I have been in daily contact with the victims for so many months.'

Sarah stepped back as Catherine entered the room. 'You have lost much weight, dear,' Sarah said. 'Yet you do not look ill.'

'No,' Catherine said. 'I have suffered nothing.' Then she looked at Gabriel, 'And you, dear Papa. You must surely be almost recovered.' She embraced him, looking with experienced eyes at the signs of the disease.

Gabriel's face lit up.

'Ah, it is good to see you. But pray do not endanger yourself.'

'Papa, I have enjoyed much protection from Our Lady. She will not fail me now.'

Sarah turned away. It was not the Virgin Mary who had saved Gabriel but her own care and a capricious fate which had led her to throw open the window.

But now Catherine insisted that they share the nursing duties and Sarah was able at last to leave the sick room. She went to her chamber and changed her robes, consigning all those she had worn to the bonfire. Then she took her cloak and walked out into the cold winter garden and along the paths to the sloping hills. She sat on a tree stump and looked down towards the distant harbour.

Now that he was recovered, she found all her anger had evaporated. A sense of peace invaded her. What had it all been about, that violence and frustration that had burned inside her? It was simply fear, she thought, that she was alone in the world, that Gabriel had this great sustaining belief which had no need of her, that in the last resort his religion would come first. But now it seemed a greater sacrifice that he would make, that he would not act for his own personal benefit.

She thought of Sean; the wild excitement he offered her now seemed remote and unattractive. All that mattered was that Gabriel had been spared, he was alive and all those emotions which had torn through her now seemed trivial.

She watched two buzzards hovering, almost motionless, high above her then circling swiftly down and up again, not touching the ground, sweeping away into space. That freedom, she thought, was shared also by human beings. Every living thing has the right to act as he is able, as he chooses. Just as I had the right to be with Sean.

There was no need to tell Gabriel. He could not understand, just as she had not understood his decision to risk his life in the plague city.

Gabriel recovered slowly but soon insisted that he would rise and leave his sick bed. His strength quickly returned when he began to move around and Sarah and Catherine walked with him in the gardens. As he improved, John and Urith began to visit again. Katherine had come daily to check upon his progress and all the grandchildren began to gather around him.

In a few weeks he was able to resume his estate duties and Catherine began to speak of returning to St Omer.

'It had been my hope,' Sarah said, 'that you would remain here.'

'There is much work to be done there,' Catherine said, 'but I think perhaps I shall not be there much longer.'

Sarah smiled with delight.

'Oh, I would that you come home again,' she said but she added, 'But only if that is your wish. Perhaps it is advisable to delay your return to the Continent. The plague is much reduced in London, it seems, but the ports are still a source of infection.'

'Yet I am needed at the school,' Catherine said doubtfully.

Later, in the privacy of their chamber, Gabriel commented to Sarah that Catherine appeared to be hesitant in her plan to take holy orders.

'We should not persuade her one way or the other,' he said wisely. 'Our persuasion might only strengthen her desire to go.'

'I find myself quite unsympathetic to the idea of life in a convent.'

Gabriel smiled. 'I think it would not suit you,' he replied.

'You begin to put flesh on your body again,' Sarah said as Gabriel undressed. She went over and put her arms around him. 'See, my arms no longer circle your waist as they did but a few days ago.'

'Yet mine circle yours,' he laughed. Then he said suddenly, when all such apprehensions had fled from her mind, 'Sarah, when I returned, so long ago it seems, I had in my mind to demand some indication of your feelings for Colonel Murray.'

Sarah sighed, trying now to drag her thoughts back to those episodes. Gabriel watched her, looking suddenly anxious.

'Gabriel, there are no feelings. There never were.'

'Then what occurred between you?'

In a moment of silence, Sarah contemplated both denial and affirmation. Now she could take that leap over the abyss that had haunted her before, or she could close the episode for ever. She looked at Gabriel thoughtfully.

'What you no doubt feared,' she said.

Gabriel turned away.

'Why?' he asked.

'I did not love him, Gabriel. Perhaps at the beginning it was quite capricious, but later it was the pain of your absence.'

'That could not be avoided.'

'It could. It was your choice. You will always put certain things in your life before me.'

Gabriel sighed.

'They are not before you, Sarah. You are my life. But I cannot deny the duty I have to a higher authority.'

'No. And I cannot deny that Sean reasserted my identity. When you appeared to have deserted me, he made me feel my life had some validity.'

'Oh, Sarah, surely you have your life here. You are mistress of Vinelands, you have your children, your manifold activities in Dartmouth. Is that not what you desire?'

'Yes,' she said, 'but I do not have your faith and through Sean I found my true person.'

'Can that be found only between the sheets?' Gabriel suddenly said angrily.

'No,' Sarah said coolly. 'But it established the freedom that you automatically assume for yourself.'

She went over to where he was sitting on the edge of the bed.

'Marriage is a sacrament,' Gabriel said.

'My actions make it no less, any more than yours do.'

'Sarah, I could not share you with another.'

Sarah smiled. 'There is no danger. I have no need of it now. Yet I cannot regret it.'

Gabriel shook his head.

'I cannot claim your soul,' he said. 'But I cannot entertain this man again in our home.'

'He will not come, I think,' Sarah said. 'But if he should, it is a matter of indifference.'

As they lay in bed, Sarah said, 'I have wished so long to speak of these matters. In a strange way, I have never felt as though I belonged in this world. Perhaps it was the manner of my coming here as a child.'

'Sarah, we are all part of God's creation.'

'It is your belief,' she said. 'But I long for us to have a deeper understanding, that the certainty of our love can never be challenged.' Though he assented, she did not know whether he had really understood her words. But she slept peacefully, thankful that at last no deception remained.

The question of Catherine's intended return was settled unexpectedly when Gabriel had news from London that one of the priests had been arrested. Father Henry Morse had been working amongst the Catholics since the outbreak of the plague and Gabriel had frequently come upon him in the slums and alleys of Westminster and St Giles in the Fields. In spite of illness, he had worked tirelessly to help the sick. But there were many malicious persons who had been intent upon his arrest, and although the justices and officials had no desire to apprehend him, there were powerful people, aided by sneaks and informers, who had the law on their side. He was committed for trial at the Old Bailey and Gabriel expressed his intention of attending it.

Sarah and Catherine instantly protested at the danger to which he would subject himself, fearing a return of his sickness.

'There is nothing you can do to aid him,' Sarah pointed out.

'I can see that he is provided with funds,' Gabriel said, 'otherwise he is likely to starve in Newgate. I can also prevail upon the Queen, through the agency of intermediaries, to petition for his release.'

'It would be more suitable if I went,' Catherine said. 'I seem to be immune from the plague and I can as well provide funds and through your influence perhaps gain an audience with the Queen.'

'It is as hard to see you go as Gabriel,' Sarah said. 'Can we not send a servant?'

'No,' Catherine said. 'I will but stay for the trial and then return.'

She set off the next day and reached the capital on the day of the trial. A week later, she returned. Father Morse had been found guilty of being a priest but first the Queen and now the King had promised to intercede on his behalf, and the King had promised that he would be released. Two months later, in June, he was a free man.

While Catherine was at the trial in London, the remainder of the family attended the marriage in Dartmouth of Katherine's eldest daughter, Elizabeth, to the Marquis of Belmont. Some time before leaving Vinelands, Catherine had visited the great mansion beyond Exeter which would be Elizabeth's new home. Although she regretted missing the wedding of her cousin, she felt she was rewarded for the loss because it was during that time in London that Catherine met Reginald Stephen Moses. He was a physician at Denmark House and one of the rare doctors who had come to London to work ceaselessly amongst the plague victims. He was also a devout Catholic and had done much to obtain funds from the Queen and her court to help their cause.

They met in the great bare entrance hall of the Bailey when she was introduced to him by one of the Queen's stewards. She told him about her life at the school of English Catholic girls at St Omer and he told her of his work in his parish of Richmond. Now he was building a hospital for its citizens.

When Catherine returned to Vinelands, she said she had decided to stay on in England for some time. She also revealed that Doctor Reginald Stephen Moses was to visit them in the coming days.

Gabriel had already met him in London. 'He is,' he told Sarah, 'a man of substance, but only in a moral sense. He is a second son and has little wealth at his command.'

'Ah,' Sarah said, 'there is a matter which I have long had on my mind.'

'Regarding Catherine?'

'Well, to a certain extent. I have long been concerned about the inheritance of this house and the estate.'

Gabriel frowned. 'But, of course, in the event of my death, it will be yours during your lifetime.'

'And what of your other descendants – Katherine, John, the grandchildren? And, of course, Catherine and Nicholas.'

Gabriel smiled. 'Do not be concerned. I have left substantial sums to provide for each of them.'

'But the estate,' Sarah persisted. 'What happens when I die?'

'Then the property naturally goes to John, as my eldest son. It is usually so.'

'But Nicholas is your eldest son now.'

Gabriel looked questioning.

'Only if John is dead.'

'Nicholas is the eldest son of our marriage.'

'Ah, that does not signify, Sarah. John is my first-born.'

'But John has no need. He has the farm and Urith brings much wealth with her. She has estates already from her family.'

'Yes.' Gabriel pondered. 'Yet I think it must be so. Also, you still have Trevayne Abbey. That will surely go to Nicholas.'

'No,' Sarah said firmly. 'I have in mind that should Catherine marry someone of little fortune, Trevayne shall be hers. And what becomes of Nicholas then?'

'Sarah, I will ensure that he is provided with one of the other houses – The Manor at Dittisham?'

'Gabriel, I wish him to have Vinelands.' A cold and unyielding expression came upon her face. 'I have already spoken to John on these matters.'

Gabriel looked astonished. 'Sarah, it is not for you to discuss these matters.'

'And why not? This property is also mine. Nicholas is my son.'

'But it can be dispensed only by me,' Gabriel said irritatedly.

'That is what we are discussing. I wish him to have Vinelands. Urith has agreed that they have no need of it.'

'Urith!'

'Yes. John has little head for such matters. Urith requires only a few items of furniture from here, a gold cup or two as sentimental mementoes.'

'Sarah, I like not this behaviour of yours.'

She ignored his protest but took a small document from the velvet purse attached to her waist.

'John has signed this, saying that he foregoes all claim to the estate. Though I agree', she added, 'that he should receive any financial benefits you may care to bestow.'

Gabriel looked at her in disbelief.

'I find these actions incredible.'

Sarah smiled at him softly.

'Dear Gabriel, I know you will be concerned for my happiness. Let us settle the matter thus.'

'But it means also that John's children are disinherited.'

'Ah, Urith has assured me that they are well provided

for in her family wills. Whereas,' she said plaintively, 'poor Nicholas would come to nothing. You could not wish for that.'

'Sarah, I must ponder this situation. It is a hard request.'

Sarah smiled again.

'Dear Nicholas already shows much enthusiasm for business matters. Also, you found him a worthy companion on your voyage to the Indies. He will not waste his inheritance.'

'I know that is so, dear.' Gabriel put his arm round her. 'I know you are concerned for your children's welfare. It should be so.'

'Then, that is settled,' Sarah said cheerfully.

And, indeed, everything proceeded to Sarah's satisfaction. When she met the quiet, bearded Dr Moses with his gentle manner and elegant voice, she knew that Catherine must surely abandon her religious aims. He became a frequent visitor and in a few months they announced their engagement.

Sarah was filled with delight that Catherine would be living at Trevayne. She found that their old, intimate relationship had not been reduced by their long separation and Catherine had developed that same independence of spirit which she possessed herself. For his part, Gabriel found Dr Moses a worthy companion with a real concern and regard for the welfare of the poor.

It was arranged that he would abandon his duties as a royal physician, and practise in Devon. A hospital was planned on the outskirts of Totnes. Catherine would attend to its administration and she intended also to build a school adjacent to Trevayne run on the model of the schools she had taught in on the Continent.

There was further domestic happiness for Katherine when Elizabeth bore her first son, Henry. But it was not only family affairs that made 1638 a happy year.

There was during that period a greater degree of tolerance towards the Catholic community. Owing to the

King's support of the High Church party, and his dislike of the Puritan ethic, Catholic belief and ritual seemed less extreme and in many parts of the country the persecution eased. No priest had been executed for ten years and there was an official distaste for their apprehension and arrest.

Margaret and Robert were once again at Trevayne and awaiting the birth of her fourth child, after which they planned to return to Ireland. Catherine and Reginald Stephens Moses decided to postpone their wedding until they were gone and they could move into the Abbey so it was not until the summer of 1639 that their wedding was solemnized. The guests began to arrive the evening before and the house was filled with laughter and confusion as they were escorted by the servants to the chambers which had been prepared for them.

But it was the arrival of priests from London who had worked with Reginald during the plague that seemed to please Catherine most. They reported that Henry Morse had now been assigned to work with the Jesuits in the south-west and was currently resident at Teignmouth. On the morrow, he would attend their wedding to express his thanks for their assistance at his trial. A coach was promptly despatched to carry him to Vinelands.

Sarah awaited his arrival with the old feeling of doubt assailing her. More and more, the household seemed to be involved in the Catholic cause. Their beliefs were assuming a life of their own, and because she did not share them, she had the old feeling of isolation. Yet Vinelands was hers, it was she who had revitalized it, it was she who had overseen the preparations for the wedding.

But when Father Morse arrived, she did not find him the pious and retreating man she had anticipated, but someone with a fiery belief in his cause who did not hesitate to say so. She could understand why he had made so many converts during the plague.

She smiled to herself. Perhaps, given the opportunity, he might even convince her.

Catherine and Reginald thanked her delightedly as they left for Trevayne at the end of the celebrations.

'Dear Mama,' Catherine said, flinging her arms around Sarah, 'it is a delight that we shall be so near at hand.'

When she and Gabriel had said farewell to all the guests and repaired to their chamber, Sarah looked anxiously at Gabriel as he sat on the bed.

'Dear, you look very pale. Are you quite well?'

'Ah, it is but the excitement, the eating and drinking,' he began. Then, suddenly, he collapsed as he had done once before; but this time, as she quickly rang the bell for the steward, Sarah had the agonizing fear that now it was much more serious.

32

Sarah knew that he was going to die. She had known from the moment that Reginald, summoned abruptly from his marriage bed, had said briefly, 'It is not a recurrence of the pox. It is the strain that sickness put upon him. His strength is gone, Sarah.'

'I will tend him. He only needs rest.'

'Sarah,' Reginald said quietly. 'It is perhaps beyond our powers. We must call the priest.'

Father Benedic came to administer the sacraments and extreme unction. Sarah stood in the shadows watching the priest as he touched Gabriel's eyes and lips and prayed for his soul. She was reluctant to leave the room and, indeed, the priest did not seem to require it, as though he welcomed her witness of a soul going to meet its Maker.

She stood now at the end of the bed, looking at him without hope. When he was ill with the plague, he had been tossed by a fever, or lay in a coma, or had brief periods of lucidity, yet it had always seemed that he was a living being, fighting against some fierce, external enemy.

Now it was different. He lay for the most part still and silent, to revive briefly now and then, as though he were barely attempting to struggle back to a world that was slipping away from him. She felt a cold and desperate agony that now there was nothing she could do. Dark, inexorable death would claim him, he would be gone for ever.

Reginald came again with Catherine.

'There must be something we can do. He recovered from the plague. Why should this illness be more deadly?' Sarah asked.

Reginald said quietly, 'Madam, I have seen it before. People who have suffered from the plague will suddenly feel its drastic effects many weeks or months later. I have known of no-one who recovered.'

Sarah did not reply. All she could do was sit by him, take his hands, cling to that dear life until it was snatched from her. But that also was denied her.

The room was invaded suddenly by John and Urith, Katherine and William and all the grandchildren who were currently at home, Katherine's Richard and John's sons Dominic and Thomas and daughter, Eleanor. Messages had already been sent to Elizabeth at Exeter and Margaret and Robert in Ireland.

The family filled the chamber with their hushed concern.

Sarah stood at the window, awaiting their departure, but they seemed disposed to remain. The urgency of her misery made her turn and say suddenly, 'Pray, leave us now. We wish to be alone.'

They looked at her in astonishment then Urith signalled them to depart and they all went silently from the room.

Sarah bolted the door behind them and returned to

490

the bedside. She bent over and kissed him gently on the forehead.

'Gabriel,' she said, 'what can I do without you?'

His eyelids flickered momentarily but he did not speak. He moved his hand slightly towards her and she grasped it passionately and put her face against his. She put her arms round him and held him close, feeling his warm head against her breast. How was it posssible that life could leave this living body, that he would cease to exist?

She lay there with him, longing for just a word, some sign, a miracle. The afternoon wore on into evening, the light began to fade and still they lay in silence.

As darkness fell there was a soft knock on the door. She gently laid Gabriel back on the pillows, kissed him and pulled back the bolt.

Reginald came in quietly and glanced briefly at Gabriel. He put an arm around Sarah.

'Come away now, dear.'

Sarah knelt down by the bed, looking at Gabriel now with disbelief.

'Reginald. Is he . . .?'

Reginald nodded in silence.

'Oh, what can I do? How I hate life!'

'We must all leave this life, Sarah.'

'It is so pointless.'

'No. It cannot be. Gabriel was a great man.'

'Ah, you speak of him as the past,' she said through her tears.

Reginald pulled her up from the bed and led her to the door. There were no words of comfort, nothing that could take away that first shock, indeed, it seemed to him an insult to try to pretend that death was not a human tragedy.

Sarah turned and looked at Gabriel once more, thinking already that only a few moments before he had still been with her and seeing time suddenly as an insuperable barrier between then and now.

In her mind, she repeated the word 'never' to herself, 'never', 'never', 'never' as though by its violent assault it might somehow link with the extremity of her pain. Oh, God, how long was never?

She went to her chamber. Soon they would all come pouring up the stairs, weeping, whispering, gazing in silence. Some of them would resort to prayer and the Virgin Mary.

She tried to visualize every moment of the past night, every second of the time before he left her for ever. The last words she had heard him say during the night had not been addressed to her. He spoke of ships he could see far away on the horizon as he stood on the bridge and of a great whale that had appeared through the mist blowing a fountain of water high into the sky.

She had put her arms closer around him and finally he whispered, 'The horizon is fading away.'

Now Katherine came into the room, her eyes red with crying.

'It is the end of an era,' she said. 'Our lives can never be the same again.'

Sarah shook her head in agreement and it was clear from the number of people who attended the funeral a week later and the silent crowds who lined the roads all the way through Dartmouth to St Petrox that Gabriel had been to all of them an important person.

William had made all the arrangements with the help of Mr Weaver and John and the whole family of children and grandchildren attended, apart from Nicholas. He was in China, having acquired from that first voyage with Gabriel when he was only fifteen that same love of the sea and adventure.

After the funeral feast at Vinelands, Gabriel's will and testament was read to the family. Gabriel had left large sums of money to Katherine and John, John received the farm and all its buildings and livestock and every grandchild was given one of the houses on the estate and a memento from Gabriel's foreign travels. Vinelands, the estate, the contents of the house and all his personal effects were left to Sarah. There was no mention of the disposal of the house after Sarah's death nor of John's document relinquishing all claim to the estate.

Sarah scarcely listened as the will was read. She felt at the moment a total disinterest in what became of the estate.

'It seemed to me so important that I should inherit Vinelands,' she confided to Katherine. 'Now, it is of no matter to me.'

'It cannot be now,' Katherine said. 'But when you have recovered, then you will think differently.'

'It is not for me I am concerned. It is the fact that when I die it must go to Nicholas.'

'Nicholas!' Katherine said in astonishment. 'But it must surely be John's.'

'No. As you saw from Gabriel's will, he has inherited the farm.'

'Yes, but that is not for the future.'

'It is strange,' Sarah said thoughtfully, 'that Gabriel did not change his will as he promised. But it is most likely that John will not long survive me, even if he does.'

'Then it will go to his firstborn, Thomas.'

'No,' Sarah said quietly. 'It is for Nicholas.'

Katherine frowned. She was about to argue, then she saw the anxious expression on Sarah's face. There was no need to debate it now, Sarah was suffering enough from her bereavement; these matters could be settled in the future.

'Sarah, dear,' she said, 'would you wish to come and stay for a while at Greenhayes?'

'No,' Sarah said, 'Catherine and Reginald will remain here for a day or two, but come and see me whenever you are able.'

Sarah knew that they were all watching her anxiously, fearful that she might lapse into madness as she had done after Andrew's death. But she knew that this time it was quite different.

493

That had been a violent, unexpected shock against which she had erected no defences. Her only solution had been to escape into a world of illusion and dream. This time, she had no desire to evade the consequences of her loss. She felt it would be an insult to Gabriel, to their love, to try to find any solace, any rationalization, any religious comfort.

She looked straight into the bleak and empty future without him; he could never be replaced, her life could never be the same again, it was a loss so total that she made no attempt at all to console herself. She would continue with the same activities that they had shared together, running the estate, involved with his ship-building activities, the houses being built in Dartmouth, the fishing trade off Newfoundland, the imports from the Indies, but now it would be with the simple aim of providing an inheritance for Nicholas. To Catherine and Reginald, she would leave Trevayne and sufficient money to last them for the rest of their lives.

The New Year passed and in the spring Catherine announced that she was pregnant. Sarah felt a pang of anxiety at the information, knowing that whenever such an event occurred she would for ever regret that Gabriel was no longer there to share it with her.

During the summer, Sarah became involved in the rebuilding of St Petrox, contributing sums of money for the materials and paying for stonemasons to execute the work.

When she returned to Vinelands one afternoon from the church, she walked through the rose garden and the little bower where she and Katherine used to sit and out along a path towards the fields beyond.

She reached the end of the path, walking slowly in the setting sun which cast a vivid orange glow on the smooth water, a shaft of gold light across the fields to the windows of a house far away. Once through the small turnstile, she turned absent-mindedly to the right and started along a path, her thoughts fully occupied with Catherine.

She had not walked here for years, although she frequently went along the path as far as the gate. The river flowed south here and this path seemed somehow beyond the estate and she had always turned automatically and followed the narrowing stream leading back to the farm and Vinelands. Catherine would have her baby any time now. Although she felt relieved that Catherine should suffer no complications with a doctor for a husband, Sarah dreaded that event. Fear always descended over a household as the fateful day drew near, in which husbands and families were as deeply involved as the mother. There was always a feeling of an impending loss, as though a last farewell were imminent, a sense of doom hanging over them, which they were powerless to influence. She knew it was fear that often created a chasm between a mother and child, because while the pains of childbirth could soon be forgotten, the physical damage remained for ever.

Sarah looked up, realizing that she was still walking along the path. The river had broadened and she automatically jumped across the stepping-stones where she had occasionally played with the children when they were young.

And stopped. Because another remoter memory was in her mind, of Gabriel and herself hand in hand on the other bank, walking. She looked up. Across the bumpy field to the hillock, surrounded by bushes and the gentle hills beyond.

She sat down on the bank, momentarily overwhelmed by the recollection of Gabriel making love to her. There were no thoughts or words in her mind, only a picture, of a tall, handsome man, grabbing her suddenly, passionately pulling her into his arms, kissing her hair, her eyes and finally her lips.

Then she closed her mind.

'Oh, Gabriel,' she cried to herself, overwhelmed once again by the finality of his loss.

She felt the old panic that she had thought she was beginning to recover from, the knowledge that she would never see Gabriel again, he was gone for ever. Overwhelmed once more by the loss she felt, as she stared bleakly across the field, remembering his arms around her, his lips on her cheeks, in her hair, on her lips, she broke into uncontrollable sobs, feeling alone and desolate. Life seemed utterly pointless, as though nothing she had ever done or achieved had any significance.

She recalled their journey to the great new world, their laughter and fears and fights and anger, their return, the birth of their son, their marriage, building they had undertaken in Dartmouth and it all seemed like a dream. Here she was, a piece of female flesh and blood with no significance.

As the shadows began to fall, she got up from the damp grass and walked wretchedly back along the path towards the house. Once she was inside she felt better. Just the protection of those great walls reduced the floating feeling she had had in the fields, but it was something that she knew would never change.

She recognized that the feeling she had had as a child, of being just a nothing that had appeared unaccountably on the earth, of having no importance or identity unless she had a past in some other existence, was an awareness that had remained with her always. It was as though even when she was happy, something always occurred to remind her of her own insignificance. But she could see now why death was so terrible. It was the one event which mocked that infinite capacity for hope which all human beings possessed.

Two hours later, a messenger arrived to say that Catherine was in labour, the midwife had been summoned and Catherine was asking for her. Sarah called the coach and was galloped across the hills to Trevayne Abbey. There she found the usual state of panic. Great pans of water were boiling on the open grate. Catherine's room was filled with steam from all the hot water and the midwife had covered Catherine with blankets and silk sheets to keep her warm. The windows were closed to protect the patient from draughts and fresh air.

Catherine was propped up on her couch, vomiting, and every minute or so her face screwed up in agony and the perspiration poured from her forehead. Sarah cupped Catherine's head in her arms and forced a tiny pitcher of brandy to her lips. The woman continued to drag on the little slimy body which gradually emerged but mercifully by that time Catherine had passed into unconsciousness. The midwife cut the umbilical cord, hit the infant on the back and when it screamed wrapped it in a blanket.

'Scraggy. Don't fancy his chances.'

Sarah glanced at the red, shrivelled object before her. What a mystery it was. Could it be simply explained by the Christian story, a legend of a Virgin and a son of God?

She took the child and began to wash him in the warm water. The midwife protested. 'Are you trying to kill him?'

'It is as I wish,' Sarah said coldly.

Reginald was summoned and quietly examined mother and child.

'All is well,' he said calmly to Sarah.

Sarah sighed with relief.

'Yes. Her labour was much easier than most I have known.' She smiled. 'Perhaps it is on account of all the exercise you insisted upon.'

'As birth is a natural event,' Reginald said, 'it is surely wise to continue natural activities.'

'The midwife does not approve of the natural activity of washing the child,' Sarah observed.

Reginald laughed.

'Be not disturbed, madam. She is somewhat brusque but she is a good woman and has lost no child at birth since I took her in my employ.'

Catherine quickly regained consciousness and asked if it were a boy or girl. Then Reginald ordered her a meal of boiled fish and eggs and when she made a face, added, 'and a few sweetmeats and confections which you so enjoy.' But he looked at her thoughtfully. 'And then, dear one, you will rest quietly.'

Sarah kissed Catherine and prepared to depart.

'And what of the child?' she asked Reginald.

'Catherine will feed him for a week or two,' he said. 'I find it reduces the danger of fever. Then,' he added, smiling, 'in view of your concern, it will not be sent down into Dartmouth, but the wet nurse will reside here, so that you can oversee events.'

'You mock me,' Sarah said mildly, 'but you are a great comfort, dear Reginald.'

She returned to Vinelands and that evening William came with the news that his daughter Elizabeth had also been delivered of her second child on that very day. It was to be called Isabella.

'Well, September 15 will always be a day of celebration,' Sarah said.

'I fear there are matters afoot which we may not celebrate,' William suddenly said seriously.

'What is it?' Sarah asked anxiously.

'I fear there is a turmoil in the country.'

'Oh,' Sarah said with relief. 'I imagined that you referred to some serious matter.'

'It is a serious matter, Sarah.'

Sarah frowned at the urgency in his tone. She had been accustomed all her life to Catholic persecution, it was something that seemed to rumble on without hope of resolution. Beyond that, she paid little heed to events beyond her own personal and domestic concerns. As far as she could see, there was always trouble somewhere in the country, it seemed inevitable. But William seemed to have apprehensions of some real danger.

'William, what are you speaking of?'

498

William shook his head.

'I know not what to speak of,' he said slowly. 'Strafford and Laud impeached by the new parliament, the aggressive stance towards the King, the Scots invading in the north, armies being raised in London.'

'But Archbishop Laud was instrumental in the arrest of Father Morse who had surely caused no harm. You must surely approve of that impeachment,' Sarah protested.

'Ah, dear lady, it is not as simple as that. The Archbishop acted merely to save his own skin. He could not be seen to show leniency towards the Catholics because it is that for which parliament condemns him.'

'But what do you fear, William?'

'I fear a divided nation turning to violence.'

'But Catholics and Protestants have ever been divided.'

'It is not merely religion any longer. It is what it represents. Catholicism represents the King – autocracy, high church, privileges to people in high places and taxes extracted without the approval of parliament. As for Protestantism, it stands for a parliament wanting an independent constitution not dominated by the King, determined that it shall govern the country.'

'I know little of these matters,' Sarah said slowly. 'But you have darkened my day.'

'Forgive me, dear lady,' William said quickly. 'This should be a happy day for you. Yet I find it hard to eradicate my fears.'

'You are rarely fearful, William,' she said, thoughtfully. She rode home trying to think of the impending visit of Philip, Cicely's son, who was arriving from Lincoln with his new bride, Lady Isobel Hobson. Yet she could not concentrate her mind upon that long-awaited event, nor upon the joy she had felt that Catherine's child was safely delivered. Her thoughts returned to her conversation with William. He was usually so calm and detached; even years ago, when he had been disturbed about Katherine, his anxiety had never been obvious. For the first time in her

499

life, she felt a cold fear, a great ignorance and a desperate anxiety to know what was happening beyond the safe walls of Vinelands.

33

It was only when Philip and Isobel finally arrived from Lincoln in the new year that Sarah began to understand fully the issues that were dividing the country. Ever since her conversation with William, she had been trying to find some evidence of the turmoil he seemed to perceive. Yet she could see no great change in people's attitudes or behaviour when she went down into Dartmouth. The tradespeople still plied their wares, vessels came into the harbour, disgorging their catches of fish from Newfoundland, unloading huge chests of goods brought from the Indies and the Orient; the large estates were still administered by their owners, the courts and justices still dealt with the criminals and petty thieves; indeed, there seemed to be a greater determination to administer the Poor Law and the wealthy merchants and landowners appeared to contribute willingly to such demands.

She realized now that since Gabriel's death, her contacts had been confined to her family and to the inhabitants of Dartmouth. Perhaps their views did not coincide with the world beyond.

Philip had become more assured since she last saw him. Sarah reflected that he was the same age as his father Stephen had been when Cicely had fallen in love with him. Although he was handsome, he still did not possess that brief, youthful charm of his father. That must be as well, Sarah thought, considering the unhappy person Stephen had become and the way he had intimidated his wife and sons.

It reminded her of the unhappy childhood that this boy had suffered and she said warmly, 'It is such a delight to see you, Philip.'

'And to see you, dear madam. You look as lovely as ever.'

Sarah smiled. 'You have had a tiring journey. Come to the fire.'

She embraced Lady Isobel, noting the pleasant silk gown she was wearing and the sapphire and emerald rings which sparkled on her white hands. Her pale blonde hair hung in elaborate ringlets on either side of her small, pretty face. Sarah recognized the elegant tones which were adopted by ladies at court.

'I have heard much of John's success in London,' Sarah observed to Philip. 'I believe he is at present designing a great new dwelling near Hampton Court. The nobility appear to approve his buildings. The King – and the Queen – appear to have many projects in hand.'

Philip's face clouded. 'It is not for his majesty that I would employ my talents,' he said caustically.

Sarah frowned.

'I thought you also were frequently at Court.'

'But rarely, madam, and then only if necessity demands. The noblemen with whom I mix have small time for the King.'

'I do not recollect that Gabriel found him wanting,' Sarah said thoughtfully.

'Ah, my lord had little interest in politics,' Philip said. 'But perhaps even he would now be drawn into the quandaries that exist.'

'Come, dear,' Sarah said suddenly turning to Isobel. 'Let us go to your chamber.'

'I notice the additions to the house, and the banqueting

501

house in the garden, though perhaps there is too much glass,' Philip said as he followed them up the stairs. 'And also the charming additions you have within, all this fine furniture.'

'I have Gabriel to thank for all that,' Sarah said. 'And recently, this Chinese chest has arrived from the Indies, sent from thence by dear Nicholas.'

Philip smiled. 'I think Nicholas has taken his love of exploring and the sea from my grandfather.' Then he added, as though the problem were for ever in his mind, 'I hope the King benefits not from any of his activities.'

'I think not,' Sarah said with amusement. 'I would not suppose that he has yet collected much treasure. But your concern with the King seems very great.'

'Indeed, yes,' Philip said instantly. 'Only this week, we hear of his interference in the trial of that Catholic priest, who should surely die.'

'Yes,' Sarah said quietly, 'Father Benedic has spoken of it to me.'

The priest had been condemned at the Old Bailey to be hanged, drawn and quartered and three days later Charles had reprieved him. It had been a brave decision on his part, knowing that already the population suspected him of being over-tolerant to the Catholics, at the least, and even a secret Roman Catholic at the worst.

But for Sarah, it was the more immediate awareness that no-one openly criticized the Catholics in this household. There was always an understanding of its affiliation. William, who was a Protestant, and Katherine, who had no great beliefs either way, had sympathy with the persecuted Catholics.

But Philip went on.

'Parliament will not accept this autocratic behaviour. The King becomes intolerable. There are many noble lords who have the same conviction as I.'

'I find your intolerance towards the Catholics distasteful,' Sarah said mildly.

502

'Then, my good lady, you must remember that only a few months ago, there were rumours of yet another popish plot. The Ten Mile Act had to be re-enacted, that his majesty might not be in danger from criminal elements. Yet he performs this foolish act.'

'I doubt if he is in any danger from the Catholics,' Sarah replied.

'A member of parliament has recently produced a list of all those Catholics resident within the city of London. One knows not what foolish and dangerous plot they may be enacting.'

Sarah sighed. Remembering William's words, she said, 'I fear that you protest about more than religion.'

She had arranged to hold a dance to celebrate Philip's visit, where all the family and their acquaintances could enjoy her extravagant hospitality. There had been no such event since Gabriel's death and she had welcomed it as a proof to herself that she had at last recovered. Now, as the day arrived and she watched the coaches coming up the drive and the ladies alight in their elaborate and expensive gowns and the men escort them gallantly up the steps to the Great Hall, she felt apprehensive. That outside world seemed to be intruding even into the security of Vinelands.

The guests flocked into the hall, up the wide staircase, along the gallery, into the dining hall and the library. The minstrels' gallery had been extended and the sound of music pealed through the house. They all exclaimed with delight when they saw the dining tables filled with a spectacular display of silver dishes, decorated with flowers and herbs, and filled with every kind of meat, fowl and fish. The wine was served to the men in large silver goblets and the ladies drank from delicate glasses, edged with gold.

But as the wine flowed, the conversation turned once more to the state of the country. Although many of the ladies continued to discuss the latest fashions and the new hairstyle from France, Sarah was drawn to listen to the disquieting remarks that were being made around her.

It was Philip who introduced the topic of the attempted impeachment of Strafford, of the man's corruption and influence upon the King.

'I hold no great brief for Strafford,' William said, 'but I fear the Commons did not act with much honesty either.'

'How so, my good sir?'

'Well, to begin with Strafford and Laud are both detained under an Act of Attainder because they knew that an impeachment must fail.'

'If that is the only way the rascals can be brought to book, so be it.' Philip said instantly.

'I like not to see the law abused,' William said.

'Huh,' Philip replied. 'What care has Strafford for the law? He persuaded the King to dispense with parliament, he has robbed from the English in Ireland, revoked the City's charter for colonizing Londonderry, fined its citizens, stolen from their coffers . . .' His voice trailed away in indignation.

It was Catherine who replied, 'He has dealt an even greater blow to the Catholics in Ireland. Robbed them of their land, established arbitrary government by Presbyterian individuals from Scotland and this country. But he has not succeeded in making them abandon their religion,' she added with satisfaction.

Sarah glanced at Katherine's daughter Elizabeth and her husband, Edward. It was well-known that he supported the King and was much opposed to the impeachment of Wentworth, Earl Strafford. She smiled at his eager and youthful expression – he looked much younger than his forty years – as he said, 'It is my belief that Wentworth has done a good job in Ireland. He has got a stable government there. He has recovered revenue from church lands, the parliament there has contributed generous grants to the exchequer, customs duties increase.'

'But from no good motives,' Philip interposed in sudden

anger. 'His aim is to establish the absolute rule of the King. At last, parliament has got hold of him. They will not let him go.'

'It appears that everything Wentworth has done harms the Irish community rather than the English,' Reginald observed.

'And look at the outcry because the King has reprieved that poor Father Goodman,' Urith added. 'I think everywhere it is the Catholics who suffer, not the English or the Protestants.'

'Well,' Philip said triumphantly, 'the King has certainly made an error there. Because now the City refuses absolutely to give him the loan which would pay for his war against the Scots.'

'It is not to be rejoiced upon,' William observed. 'These events have split the Lords and Commons. Such divisions are dangerous.'

Then Catherine said sharply to Philip, 'And that is because that priest, Father Goodman, had the courage and self-sacrifice to advise the King, in his own interests, to remit his reprieve. At least the Lords have the moral rectitude to understand the sacrifice he makes.'

'He will not be hanged,' Philip said dismissively. 'The King will recant and the priest will simply languish in gaol. Because the Commons have more important matters to deal with in ensuring that Strafford is strung up.'

Suddenly Sarah stood up.

'Pray let us dance,' she said firmly, 'or I shall imagine that parliament has set itself up at Vinelands.'

Instantly, the arguments ceased, there were mumbled apologies that such discordant tones had been introduced into the conversation, and Philip took Catherine's hand and said, 'Come, dear cousin, I am sure our agreements are greater than our disunities.'

Catherine smiled politely and followed him to the dance floor but Sarah felt confusion at the submerged emotions which had suddenly been revealed. Some members of the family seemed to be taking up sides against each other, viewing the same events in a radically different light.

There was Philip, all for a parliament which advocated the rule of the merchant classes and those of the aristocracy who did not favour the King and his government.

There was Elizabeth and Edward; they supported the King's party, which was unwilling to give too much power to parliament. Perhaps Edward supported them because he had been brought up at Court and found their high church philosophy more sympathetic.

But what about Catherine and Reginald? As Catholics, they could not support a Protestant parliament and although the King and his Archbishop Laud were suspected of supporting the Catholics and the Queen's household was obviously Catholic, Roman Catholics seemed to be persecuted more than ever. Sarah knew that the recusancy taxes paid by Catherine and Reginald and also by John and Urith were higher than ever.

As to John and Urith, they were just quiet and simple Catholics, rather as Frances had been, she reflected, never looking beyond the immediate walls of their religion.

Perhaps William was the only sensible person, regarding with a wise detachment the passions and ambitions of them all.

Sarah was joined later by Catherine when she sat briefly in the portrait gallery, observing the dancers on the floors below.

'I care not for Philip's views, Mama,' Catherine said. 'He is not even supporting the Protestant ethic but is concerned solely with a parliament that must govern our lives.'

'Yet the King appears to have little concern for the country.'

'Ach. What can he do without funds? But Mama, I have some other news. I am once again with child.'

'Catherine, baby John is but five months old. It is very soon.'

'Yes, Mama. And perhaps we would not have chosen thus. Yet I cannot but be glad.'

'I suppose with dear Reginald to ensure your welfare you need not fear,' Sarah said, smiling.

Then Sarah was whisked away to dance by one of the guests from a neighbouring manor. The family had been jokingly reminding her of late that she was a wealthy and desirable widow and that soon she would be persuaded by some handsome suitor into matrimony. Sarah had only smiled, saying that no such event would ever occur. She did not intend to risk Vinelands passing into other hands and it seemed unlikely that there could ever be another Gabriel to tempt her.

She felt no need for anyone beyond her family and was even more certain of this when Nicholas returned two months later from the East Indies. He had grown broader and more handsome, his face was brown from sun and wind and he bore no resemblance to his father. In fact, Sarah thought, he looks more like Gabriel, with his elegant clothes and his fine upright bearing. He spoke of his voyages to China and the coast of India, of storms and monsoons and whales and strange tribes of men, just as Gabriel had done and he spoke too of his sadness at Gabriel's death. He looked with concern at his mother.

'And are you well, Mama? Is this large house not lonely for you?'

Sarah laughed.

'It could scarcely be that. So many servants and everyone living so near at hand.'

'I hear rumours and reports of much trouble in the country,' Nicholas observed.

'I think it will come to naught,' Sarah replied. 'These rumours have circulated for so long.'

But when Strafford was executed in May, the country appeared to be thrown into a further period of turmoil.

Early that year, parliament had declared its determination to become a permanent force in the country. Now it could not be dissolved by the King but only on its own initiative. The King could not raise taxes without its consent and Ship Money, a tax which the King had tried to extract for the reconstruction of the Royal Navy, became illegal. The Courts of Star Chamber and the King's Councils were abolished and their victims were released and compensated.

A long list of complaints against Charles was presented to him and then published. The country was dividing into two separate camps and people began more and more to declare their allegiances.

But it was not until Margaret and Robert arrived from Ireland in the summer to stay at Vinelands that Sarah became involved in events.

They expressed joy at Strafford's demise and when Sarah protested that this had been a Protestant act, that they surely condoned little of what parliament did, Robert said, 'Ah, but we rejoice for a different reason. Wentworth was no comfort to Protestant or Catholic. His concern was only for the King.'

'And what happens in Ireland now?' Sarah asked.

Margaret's face lit up with enthusiasm.

'A great revolt is planned,' she said. 'We come to gain more support. But this time, the English will be demolished. They will be driven from the country they have plundered and exploited and the Irish will gain back their lands and rights.'

Sarah sighed. She had heard these conversations so frequently when they stayed at Trevayne that she found herself almost dismissing them as forlorn hopes. But for the first time, she began to consider what it was they were fighting for.

'Tell me', she said, 'about Ireland.'

'Ah,' said Robert, smiling, 'you are like many English, I suspect, who know little of what occurs there.' And he settled down instantly to tell her of the invasion of Ireland by English and Scots, of their determination to impose their Protestant and Presbyterian religions, of their confiscation of lands, of their starvation payment of wages to the Irish workers, of towns which had been taken over in the south where the Irish were not permitted to enter, of the imposition of their English laws upon a people who had nothing in common with them.

Sarah listened in silence. Gabriel had spoken little about Ireland after his sojourn there yet she knew he had defended the Irish position. He had been determined in his fearless protestations to King James that Ireland should not be an exploited territory.

Now she said, 'You fight for freedom, not for religion.'

Margaret smiled. 'Perhaps you will join us, Sarah. Dear Gabriel was a great defender.'

'I cannot fight for that,' Sarah said thoughtfully.

'Ah,' Robert said immediately, 'there is much you can do to assist. We need financial help, you could talk to all those influential persons you know who might sponsor our cause.'

'I have never embarked on such a course.'

A few days later, more friends of theirs arrived from Ireland and Vinelands was filled with the sound of Irish voices, all eagerly talking of the years of freedom ahead. The same afternoon, Colonel Murray arrived.

Sarah was standing at the top of the staircase when the hall door was opened and he was admitted. He saw her immediately and came bounding up the stairs.

'Sean,' she said. 'Margaret did not mention . . .'

'She does not know. It is unexpected.' He embraced her eagerly. 'Oh, it is a delight to see you, dear Sarah.'

'And you,' Sarah said, smiling. He was as handsome and vital as ever. But the old excitement had gone. The past seemed like a faraway dream.

Sean looked at her reflectively.

'You look well. Perhaps more composed.'

'More subdued, I think,' Sarah said.

Sean laughed.

'We shall soon eradicate that. You are in need of good Irish humour.'

'I have had much of that in the last days. But why come you?'

'I am here to raise an army, support for the rebellion. But this time we shall be circumspect.'

Sarah said quickly, 'Then do not discuss these matters on the open staircase.'

'Ah, I see you are concerned with our cause,' Sean said instantly.

'I have been persuaded to contribute financial assistance.'

'Persuaded?'

Sarah hesitated.

'No. I believe it is right, yet I wish to visit Ireland to observe its truth.'

'Then you shall return with me. You shall stay at my home at Carbery.'

So it was that a few weeks later Sarah stepped on to Irish soil in the harbour of Kinsale where Gabriel had first set foot years before. During those weeks she had found herself more and more embroiled in the cause of these Irish people who had to fight merely to occupy their own country.

The family had protested at her determination to enter such dangerous territory. But somehow the situation in England occupied her mind increasingly; it was as though she had suddenly emerged into a world of which she had scarcely been aware and it seemed necessary to discover for herself what all these antagonisms and troubles were about.

William had pointed out that the Irish troubles were only an offshoot of what was happening in England, that the real problems existed between the King and parliament, between the aristocracy and the poor, the Catholics and Protestants, the bishops and the Puritans, the merchants and the royal monopolists.

'Yet there are many English in Ireland. There are the plantations,' Sarah had pointed out.

'They are simply a continuation of the old English habit of claiming territory,' William had said. 'The fact that they are Protestants is merely an excuse to rob the Catholics of their lands.'

'I simply have a wish to visit this land of which Gabriel spoke so warmly.'

'Then take care,' William replied.

'Remember, Margaret and Robert will be with me. They have suffered no harm.'

'They are Irish. And also, the situation is becoming more uncertain.'

Sarah looked now across the harbour to the hills beyond, misty in the cold October air, wishing that she could have come here long ago with Gabriel. Then Sean procured horses and they set off across country, in the company of a band of men who had awaited his arrival. They had assembled to join his forces and to fight in his cause.

As they went along, he pointed out to her what he called the Protestant strongholds, towns such as Bandon in which Catholics were not allowed to reside; land and houses, castles and buildings, taken over by the settlers.

'The dwellings are in but poor repair,' Sarah observed.

'Many they take over and then allow to decline,' Sean said bitterly. 'Others are occupied by the old English Catholics, who have been here for generations and have been exploited as the Irish have been, so that they no longer have any funds for the repair of their homes.'

'And what will become of them?'

'They will rise with us,' Sean said confidently.

Margaret and Robert had returned to Ireland earlier and on a dark evening three days later Sean and Sarah reached O'Connell's castle overlooking Ballineen. It was here that the rebels were massing in preparation for the revolt. They were then going north in small groups and under cover of

511

darkness to gather at the appointed hour on the outskirts of Dublin.

That evening, they all assembled in the hall where Gabriel had first been entertained by The O'Connell. It was filled with people eagerly discussing the planned attack. Maps were laid out on the table in the long hall, a great fire burned in the grate, food was brought in on large platters and a hot brew was thrust into Sarah's hands.

Margaret's father, The O'Connell, greeted her.

'Ah, dear lady, you are welcome here. I would only that your gallant husband was still with us.'

He spoke with such warmth that Sarah was momentarily overcome with a sense of loss. Then Margaret threw her arms around her.

'Come, dear, the children await you in the nursery. Louise is so excited at your arrival.'

Sarah followed her up the stairs to see five year old Louise and baby Cavendish, now almost two. And then Margaret's two eldest boys, Edward and Robert, burst in and Sarah said spontaneously, 'Oh, they are so like Adam.'

Margaret smiled. 'Yes, I would that he could see them now.' Then she added, 'But Robert loves them dearly and is a most dutiful father. I am most fortunate.'

'Are you to take part in the rebellion?' Edward asked eagerly.

Sarah laughed.

'I fear not. But I am most anxious at its outcome.'

'Oh, we shall win,' Edward assured her.

Sarah spent the following days listening to the conversations of Robert and Margaret and their compatriots and one day Sean took her to his home in Carbery.

It was another cold, damp day and Sarah, looking down at the grey house in a valley and at Sean's eager face as he pointed out to her the various landmarks, felt a great tenderness towards him.

The house had been closed up in his absence and

as they walked round the deserted rooms she turned to him.

'The Irish,' she said, 'you, all of you, must make such sacrifices.'

Sean smiled. 'It is not all sadness,' he said. 'Perhaps we have a great capacity for enjoyment.'

'Oh, I wish I could help you.'

Sean put his hands on her shoulders and looked into her eyes.

'Sarah,' he said quietly, 'my feelings for you have not changed.'

Sarah smiled.

'Ah, Sean, I am sure you have had many since our brief romance.'

'No,' he said seriously. 'I don't know what you have done to me, Sarah, but I no longer have any taste for anyone but you.'

'I think you must soon recover.'

'It is not so. Do not mock me, Sarah. Have you no interest in me now? I would wish to be with you always. We had such joy together.'

He looked so solemn that Sarah said quietly, 'Sean, I am not being frivolous. Yet I could no longer feel that joy I once did.'

'Sarah, will you marry me?'

The thought of Vinelands, of her family, swept through her. She shook her head.

'Dear Sean, I love you dearly, but I could not marry you, nor even share our wild love-making any more.'

Sean held her in his arms in silence. Then he kissed her gently on the head.

'It is my loss,' he said. 'Come, my love, we must return.'

When they reached Ballineen that evening, Sarah found the castle transformed. The cheerful eating and drinking had ceased and all the men were now dressed for battle in cloaks and long gaiters and some were even in armour, their swords ready in their scabbards.

Sean came over to her.

'Tonight,' he said, 'we depart for Dublin Castle. It is the signal for all of Ireland to rise against the English.'

Sarah frowned. 'I have never seen men prepared for battle,' she said. 'It is a fearsome thing.'

'All will be well,' Sean said confidently. 'You will get news of our success.'

The women stood in silence on the steps of the house as the long line of horsemen went away across the hill. Then they turned back into the house.

'How long will it be?' Sarah asked.

'We shall get news on the morrow,' Margaret replied.

But they had scarcely repaired to the drawing room when they heard a horseman galloping across the field to the house and then someone banging on the great iron door.

'Pray, admit him,' Margaret said to a servant, and a young man entered, breathless and anxious.

'Madam,' he said to Margaret, 'we are betrayed.'

'Betrayed! What mean you?'

'Our plot is discovered,' he said in agitation. 'We cannot attack. They know of our plan.'

'Who has sent you?' Margaret asked sharply.

'I come from Lord Cottingham. Here, I have a document.'

He snatched a packet from his pocket.

'Then do not delay,' Margaret said quickly. 'The men have already left. You have missed them on the road to Dublin. Pray hasten. They must be intercepted before they reach the castle.'

The man turned instantly and was gone.

The women occupied themselves ensuring that the dining room was prepared in case of the men's early return.

'I do not like this waiting,' Sarah said. 'I would prefer that I were there amongst them.'

'Ah, it is ever so,' Margaret replied.

The two boys had not been permitted to accompany their stepfather and they sat in a sulky silence as though they had been denied some treat. The night passed but the men did not return and finally the women retired reluctantly to their chambers, fearful of their lonely thoughts. Then at dawn, a messenger arrived to say that plans for the attack had indeed been abandoned, but the rebellion had gone ahead in the north and the men were hurrying thither to take part in the uprising.

'It is good,' Margaret said quietly. 'May they succeed.'

'I find it a strange circumstance that you approve this battle,' Sarah said. 'Is not your anxiety greater?'

'Perhaps,' Margaret replied. 'But you do not understand what it is like to fight for your freedom. In England, it is not so for you.'

'But the Catholics suffer constantly there.'

'Yes, that is also an awful circumstance. Yet at least the persecution is performed by those who have a right to be in the country. Here, they have no rights.'

'I do not know if I would die for a cause,' Sarah said thoughtfully.

'People only do that of necessity,' Margaret said. 'We do not choose it. Yet I know that Gabriel would have done the same.'

'Yes,' Sarah agreed.

The day passed in a strange kind of inertia and it was not until the next morning that further news arrived that both Robert and Sean had gone to give their assistance to separate parties in Ulster.

As the days passed, stories of the Ulster massacres began to reach them. Then a message came from Robert that he was on the outskirts of Drogheda with his army and that on their journey north they had taken many castles and houses owned by the settlers. There had been little resistance; come upon by surprise, the settlers were unprepared and disorganized. Those who had resisted had been hastily despatched; the women and children had been unharmed and left to fend for themselves. He added triumphantly that most of the Old English had been prevailed upon, or were even eager, to join the forces of liberation.

Margaret and her father read the despatch with delight. The O'Connell had not gone north with them because he was to lead the rebellion in the south and when they received the news his forces began to gather.

Then another despatch arrived, this time from Sean. He gave a graphic account of their progress north. His army of two hundred men had gradually increased as the Irish peasants joined their ranks. Many carried only pickaxes and shovels as their weapons but their ardour in attacking and demolishing every English and Scottish property had been uncontrollable.

'My disciplined troops have tried to control them,' Sean reported, 'but their ardour is irrepressible. Yet we gain much benefit from their large numbers, albeit we may deplore their ruthlessness.'

But it was the second part of his report which made The O'Connell purse his lips. Sean's troops had met with an army of Scots near Augher. Outnumbered and hoping to save the sacking of their properties, the Scots had surrendered. Sean had commanded that they be taken prisoner and contained in one of the captured castles. The Scots laid down their weapons and lined up in a field. Suddenly, the Irish peasantry had rushed towards the now defenceless men and attacked them. Sean's soldiers tried to intercept them, but short of attacking them themselves, they could not stop them. The Irish had ruthlessly butchered the whole Scots army. 'It was a field of blood and mangled bodies,' Sean reported. 'The poor Irish Catholics are not in a mood for compromise,' he added laconically.

O'Connell shook his head in dismay.

'We might have won these Scots to our side,' he said slowly. 'But when news of this massacre gets abroad, we shall simply have more people to conquer.'

As the rebellion spread throughout Ulster, Irish hopes of victory began to grow. Although horrifying tales of violence and cruelty began to circulate in England, the English parliament was still reluctant to authorize money for an army which would be under the King's control. Only a few towns like Londonderry remained in the hands of the Protestants. Elsewhere, the Irish army dominated Ulster and their commander, Sir Phelim O'Neill, began to turn his attention to marching south.

There was a permanent air of excitement and expectation in the de Coursey household. Margaret and Sarah were involved in planning support with the other Irish rebels in Carbery, Kilkenny, Kilbrittain and even Kinsale and the surrounding areas when the armies came south.

But now Sarah began to worry about the family at home. What would happen in England? She remembered the conversations with William at Vinelands. Would this Irish rebellion have made the divisions there even greater? Was it possible that the English would take up arms against each other? Early in the new year, she boarded a vessel bound for England. By then, it seemed almost certain that the Irish would conquer and retrieve the governance of their own country.

34

Sarah walked into the herb garden and on through the bare trees of the avenue. A breeze shivered through the holly bushes and as she turned towards the rose bower a light rain began to fall. Although it was now April, there seemed to have been no sunshine since she returned to England; this dismal weather seemed to have settled in permanently. Not that the climate of Ireland had been much more felicitous, she reflected. Yet here life had begun to appear dull after the excitement of Irish life. There seemed also to be a more sinister atmosphere in England. The Puritans appeared to be more arrogant than before, more confident in their criticism of the King and his government.

Yesterday Catherine had told her that she was pregnant for a third time. Three babies in three years. Sarah knew the effect that it had on a woman's health, yet Catherine seemed unperturbed and even unaffected. Admittedly, the first two births had turned out to be unbelievably simple, as though Reginald had some magic formula which made birth a natural event. Yet she was worried now at the cumulative effect that it might have on Catherine.

The fine, misty rain became heavier and she turned back into the house. She would go to the library and make a note of the matters to be attended to. The gilded leather needed renewing on the library chairs, the pink damask hangings in one of the drawing rooms must be replaced to match the deep blue carpets and a new cabinet was needed in the dining room to accommodate the silver bowls Nicholas had brought back from India. Privies were also needed in the upstairs chambers. Reginald had already had these novel conveniences installed at Trevayne.

She thought for a moment of the great bare halls of Sean's home near Carbery and of The O'Connell's mansion at Ballineen. They were devoted to claiming back the lands and buildings taken from them by the English, determined to repossess the country of their birth and claim their possessions, yet they had little concern for the material things of life.

A servant came up to the library with a despatch from Margaret, informing her of the progress of the Irish rebellion. In February, the settlers had been evicted from Carbery, Kilkenny was an Irish stronghold, Kinsale and many parts of Limerick had risen and soon the

English invaders would be driven for ever from Irish soil.

But she mentioned also that a Scottish army had landed at Carrickfergus which many Ulstermen were joining; the King had sent another Protestant army; while a third group of Irish Protestants, under the banners of the lord justices in Dublin, supported the English parliament.

'No doubt,' Margaret observed, 'they will all shortly be fighting amongst themselves and we shall have no need to demolish them. We hear that many of the new English settlers have hurried to Dublin to report on the massacres and atrocities committed against them. Yet there is small evidence of this; I think the English have been treated too lightly.'

Sarah reread the document. There had been many rumours in England, not only about atrocities but also about a great army which was being assembled to invade Ireland. But parliament was unwilling to vote money to the King, not trusting him to lead an army in that country, and the rebels had thereby been enabled to make more progress than they had expected.

Yet, did they have any ultimate hope of success? As though in answer to her thoughts, Mr Weaver appeared at the door of the library to say that two gentlemen wished to speak with her on behalf of a Dartmouth member of parliament, Samuel Browne.

Sarah hesitated.

'M'lady,' Mr Weaver said quietly, 'you would be advised to reveal little of your thoughts.'

Sarah smiled.

'Don't worry, Mr Weaver. I am aware of their allegiances. Pray, bring them up. And bring up ale and some mead. And send a maid to make up the fire.'

She greeted them formally, extending her hand graciously to each of them. She noticed the plain nature of their cloaks and breeches and the sombre colours of their doublets beneath. 'Probably Puritans rather than Presbyterians,' she thought.

'M'lady, we are most honoured to be received,' the elder gentleman said ingratiatingly.

'Pray be seated, gentlemen. And draw your chairs closer to the warmth. I find the air chilly here, after the warmer climate of Ireland from which I have but lately returned.'

Both men stopped, holding their chairs in mid movement, discomfited by her remark.

'We heard some news of your travels,' the younger man replied. 'I am pleased that you escaped before the rebellion truly set in, making life dangerous to all our citizens.'

Sarah smiled.

'I felt no great danger,' she replied. 'The Irish appear to me to be of great hospitableness and warmth.'

'Ah, no doubt. No doubt,' the older man said, 'and of course there are many who support our cause and are loyal citizens.'

'Of the Crown, perhaps.'

The young man frowned. 'Perhaps, m'lady. But the Crown is not to be trusted. We fear the King is at sixes and sevens about what to do in Ireland.'

'Would you then supplant him, sir?' Sarah asked as though in horror.

'M'lady, we act for the good of the country.'

'Sir, this is seditious speech,' Sarah said indignantly. 'What would my dear husband, ever a loyal subject to the Crown, think of such a denunciation?'

'Madam,' the older man said. 'Pray do not disturb yourself. We mean no treachery or disloyalty. But perhaps if your revered husband lived in these disastrous times, he might be persuaded to act otherwise.'

Sarah sat in silence, looking perplexed, while a servant came and poured ale for the visitors and then departed.

'I think you cannot have come with the sole purpose of denouncing his majesty,' she said enquiringly.

The older man cleared his throat.

'No, indeed, madam. We have come on behalf of your member of parliament to beseech you perhaps to offer some funds towards the employment of an army which shall bring down the rebellion.'

'And for whom does this army act?'

'For parliament, madam. For the Commons and the citizens of this country.'

'It comes to my knowledge,' Sarah said blandly, 'that there are already three armies in Ireland.'

'Madam,' the older man said in surprise, 'you are much informed. Are not these secret matters?'

Sarah laughed cynically. 'Think you that they land under cover of darkness and so remain concealed? Are their dastardly acts not known by every person in Ireland?'

'The dastardly acts, ma'am, are performed by those rebels you appear to espouse,' the young man said heatedly.

'And how', Sarah said sharply, 'would you remove an invader from these shores?'

'We have a rightful occupation of that land,' the young man said indignantly.

'Pray, let us not argue upon these matters,' the older man interrupted. 'I am sure, madam, you would wish peace to return to that province. It is only an army of parliament that can restore it to that state. We have already received much aid from many of the citizens of Dartmouth and the surrounding areas.'

Sarah felt a wild anger inside her, at the smug assurance of these two individuals, at their pious certainty of their rightness. She wanted to face them with the injustice of that occupation, of the religious persecution, the loss of lands, the closed towns. But she said quietly, 'I do not think it is within your power to do such a thing. My allegiance is to the King and any support I gave would be to him.'

'Madam, he is perhaps as devoted to putting down the Irish as this parliament is.'

'Then I do not support him, either. It is merely the

case that he appears more tolerant than your Puritan parliament.'

The two men stood up.

'We will not detain your ladyship longer,' the older man said. 'Apart from Ireland, this country is in a parlous state, madam, and we wish only to persuade the King to act in a reasonable manner.'

Sarah looked at him coldly. 'I see no evidence of that behaviour anywhere,' she said.

As they waited for Mr Weaver to lead them down the stairs, the young man said to her quietly, 'I fear the time will come when your behaviour may appear to be sedition.'

'So be it,' Sarah said contemptuously. 'No doubt I have a greater concern for justice than you have, sir.'

But after they had gone she sat, trembling inside her, bewildered by the emotions the interview had aroused.

She was neither a Catholic nor a Protestant; neither a royalist nor a parliamentarian, yet her allegiance went to a country she scarcely knew and people with whom she had little in common. Had it been created by the attraction that Sean once held for her, or by the Irish behaviour and attitudes?

But it was more than that. She had a feeling with them that she belonged, as though her natural habitat were with outlaws and adventurers. It was that part of Gabriel that she had recognized in herself. Vinelands had been important because it would give her identity, a place in society. Yet she knew now that it was a security and certainty she had passed on to her children, that she had shared with Katherine and Urith and the others, yet had never been a real part of herself. Perhaps I can never escape from Granny Lott, she thought. Perhaps I am always really alone. She tried to think practically of what had occurred. Now she would be looked upon as a traitor, sneaks and informers would be watching her actions, observing the visitors who came to

Vinelands, trying to prove that she was a dangerous person in their midst.

Mr Weaver was instructed to ensure that the great walls of the house were in good repair, that the drawbridge worked properly in case of emergency, that the moat was filled and the tenants on the estate were trained in the elements of combat.

It occurred to her that perhaps the servants and tenants might also support parliament, but most of them were Catholics and had no stomach for a parliament devoted to the Protestant religion. The increasing number of Puritans made the Catholic population even more aware of their isolation. It was the Irish rebellion which had finally forced the members of parliament to declare their allegiance. Up to then, disagreement with the King had involved matters of taxation and economic freedom. Now the equipping of armies was involved, with their potential for fighting in other causes than that of Ireland.

Sarah heard rumours and observed the rather half-hearted preparations in Dartmouth with an increasing gloom. Although they were collecting money for the parliamentary army, there seemed no enthusiasm to fight for such a cause. There was indeed an air of incredulity that such an event could occur.

But in May, Margaret sent news that events in Ireland had taken a turn for the worse. Kilbrittain Castle had been attacked by an army of Protestant volunteers raised in Bandon and the Irish were defeated. Dundanion Castle was lost but now the rebels were regathering and soon another great offensive would begin.

As the months passed, the turmoil finally involved Sarah's own family. Katherine arrived at Vinelands one sunny afternoon in a state of agitation.

Sarah greeted her on the steps.

'Why, Katherine, you look as though you had seen an apparition.'

'Ah, I wish that it were something as trivial,' Katherine replied.

Sarah had become accustomed to Katherine's crises over the years but gradually she had become calmer and more self-contained and had appeared to settle down to a quiet and uneventful life. But over the past two years, she had suddenly seemed to come to life again. Greenhayes was the venue now for parties and frivolities; she had even involved herself in events and celebrations in the town and had become a leading figure in the rebuilding and refurbishment of St Saviour's. She had begun to accompany William once more in his expeditions to London and invited many of the leading parliamentarians to stay at her home.

'Are you not well?'

Katherine smiled. 'It is not me,' she said. 'Richard has gone to join the King somewhere in the north.'

Sarah frowned. 'But with what intention, Katherine?'

'Sarah, there must be a war. People will fight each other.'

'But the King has simply fled from the antagonism he finds in London. And although there are those in Dartmouth who support parliament, I know there are many who refuse to subscribe.'

'That is the problem, Sarah. There is terrible division. William says that though he has no stomach for it, if it comes to a debacle, he must support parliament.'

'Ah, yes.' For a moment, Sarah had forgotten that William must surely be on the other side. 'But it cannot affect William and Richard personally. Fathers and sons do not fight each other.'

'Sarah, it cannot be otherwise.'

'And what of you, Katherine?'

'In London, we speak much with those who support parliament. Yet I find the King not objectionable. I think in many ways, it is the Commons who are trying to force great changes upon the people.'

524

'Sometimes, I think I do not care for either,' Sarah said, half-smiling.

'I fear neither of them contemplate justice in Ireland,' Katherine replied.

'No. I hear from Margaret that after some defeats, the Irish are at last uniting against the enemy with the help of the Catholic bishops. They are setting up a government at Kilkenny and have summoned a general assembly for the whole kingdom of Ireland, with a supreme council to conduct the war. Yet they still swear allegiance to the King,' Sarah added in a mystified tone.

'I know not why that is so,' Katherine said, shaking her head. 'But everything is chaos and without logic. I find these matters entirely strange.'

'Be not concerned for William and Richard,' Sarah said. 'They have much regard for each other. Richard's allegiance is dictated perhaps by his occupation, acting as he does in the prerogative courts. He cannot but defend the King's position.'

But she knew that William had listened with more sympathy than she had to the requests from the two Dartmouth members of parliament and had given substantial amounts of money to the parliamentary cause. How far would their devotion to their causes extend?

'Elizabeth and Edward send you greetings from Exeter,' Katherine said. 'They also, of course, support the King's party.'

'Does the situation cause dissent between you and William?'

'Not yet. There is only concern on William's part. But if it comes to conflict, what will become of all of us?'

'I know not,' Sarah said. 'Dear Catherine and Reginald take no part in this, thank God. Reginald declares that a doctor cares for persons of any persuasion. And John and Urith say their only ally can be the Queen, and King and parliament are the preoccupations of others.'

'Many think it is the Queen who has encouraged her husband in those autocratic ways that they so detest.'

'Is it not strange,' Sarah said suddenly, 'that we now discuss these affairs of state so solemnly? In our youth, life seemed so much more joyful.'

'Yes,' Katherine agreed. 'Even my parties have become increasingly strained, as though the vital question is always which side you are on. They appear not to be relaxed occasions any more.'

A few days later, Sarah was at the farm with John and Urith when Thomas, John's son, now a thriving merchant in the City, arrived with the news that he would be joining the parliamentary forces in London. His father and stepmother received the information with dismay.

'I thought until now you had but little interest in the political scene,' John said in a puzzled voice.

'It is no longer possible to ignore events,' Thomas said. 'I have no taste for this dissent, but it is clear that matters have reached a head. The city is becoming more and more deserted, trade is interrupted and until the matter is resolved, little progress can be made.'

'But what is planned?' Urith asked anxiously.

'The King is marshalling support where he can. He has been refused entry to Hull and now is amassing an army on the outskirts of Nottingham.'

In October, news came of the first battle of the war at Edgehill, of the King's progress towards London, of his defeat there and his withdrawal to Oxford.

Throughout the next year, the King's forces began to gain ground. In Dartmouth, only a desultory attempt was made at building defences. Although soldiers of the parliamentary army were now billeted in the town, it was only the merchants who had either the interest or the money to build fortifications against a royalist attack and many of the population still supported the King.

Sarah was approached again by the parliamentarians. They requested that Vinelands, having a vantage point high on the hill, might be used as a fort from which to repulse an advancing army. But Margaret's letters from Ireland had confirmed her in her support of the royalists. She not only refused the parliamentary representatives admittance; she also despatched the vessels she owned in the harbour to the fishing banks in Newfoundland, that they might not be used against a royalist invasion.

The Roundheads, as the parliamentary supporters had begun to be called, attempted to fortify the churches and houses, Kingswear and Dartmouth castles were repaired and the guns mounted and overhauled.

In September, Nicholas returned from the West Indies and informed Sarah that he was departing to Holland before he set out on further voyages. He had no interest in a war which seemed to him pointless, serving the purpose of neither party.

'It is a strange thing,' Sarah told him, 'but I find your indifference disturbing.'

'Mama, it is not indifference. You cannot believe that citizens should fight against, even kill each other.'

'No. I do not. Yet I must remain here.' She smiled thoughtfully. 'Perhaps it is Vinelands that I would preserve.'

'The town is surrounded by the King's men. You will be safe, Mama. When they advance, you must raise the King's standard upon the house.'

Three weeks later, the royalists, under the leadership of Prince Maurice, a relative of the King, occupied Exeter amd began their advance on Dartmouth. Sarah, with Catherine and Reginald, John and Urith and all the children, waited in Vinelands.

The rain and cold caused much sickness in the royal army. The roads were unmade and treacherous and steep but slowly the guns were brought forward until they were high above the castle. From Vinelands, the family could see houses burning in the town and hear the sound of guns. It was then that Sarah raised the royal flag as Nicholas had instructed.

'If they hold out,' John said fearfully, 'the whole town will be destroyed.'

But the mayor knew that they had no hope of withstanding such an army and surrendered. The siege of Dartmouth lasted for only a month. But during that month, Sarah had realized how dear Vinelands was to her. Messengers came up from the town, speaking of the destruction that was being caused. She watched the fires and explosions with an increasing dread, but with a growing determination to preserve this house.

In the silence that followed the cessation of the gunfire, John and Urith departed to the farmhouse and Reginald said he must go down into Dartmouth to see if he were needed. He returned many hours later, reporting that many men had been killed, numerous houses had been damaged or destroyed and the leaders of the garrison had been taken off to Exeter gaol.

With Reginald was the Commander of the royalist forces in the area. He advanced into the room behind Reginald and bowed to Sarah.

'Commander Sir Geoffrey Madison. I see that you are a loyal supporter of the King, madam, and as such will receive my protection,' he said quietly.

'It may be more correct to say I do not support parliament,' Sarah retorted.

The commander smiled. He had white teeth and vivid blue eyes which now looked into hers with approval.

'I see you are a lady of spirit,' he said.

Sarah looked at him thoughtfully. There was only one matter which now occupied her. She would preserve Vinelands at all costs. This lovely house, the great estate, were hers by right. Gabriel had devoted so much of his life to this place and whatever happened she would never surrender it. She knew she had chosen the King's side because that was the one that would conquer in the end.

She would ensure that she gave his army all the support she could muster.

'Sir,' she said quietly. 'Pray be seated. I will call for succour for you and your men.'

35

Sarah walked quietly round the estate on a cold February day of sixteen hundred and forty-four. Since the arrival of the royalist army four months earlier the whole place had been transformed. Soldiers were housed in the barns and cottages on the estate, and tents had been erected as extra troops arrived. The commander and his second in command had been offered accommodation within the house which they had gratefully accepted. Sarah had protested at the wanton behaviour of the army when they occupied Dartmouth. Houses had been burned at Warfleet and there was looting and destruction in the town.

'I regret these events,' Sir Geoffrey had replied, 'but many of the soldiers are untrained and suffered much in waiting outside the town in rain and wind. It is only now that they can be brought to some semblance of military bearing.'

'Then I think it will be necessary that such a thing is executed, in order that they may be prepared if armies of the parliament descend upon us.'

Sir Geoffrey smiled.

'I believe, madam, that you would show little fear at such an event.'

'Indeed not. And I would that they also behave with decorum in the area of this estate,' she said firmly.

It was thus that Sir Geoffrey ensured that the soldiers not only caused no harm but were also employed in work on the estate. Barns and outhouses were repaired, fences mended, a road was made upon which the soldiers should walk, that the grass parts should not be made unsightly. The young girls on the estate, the daughters of the tenants and the servants in the house welcomed this change in their circumstances. Never before had so many young men roamed the streets of Dartmouth. They were to be found at the lookouts on the tops of all the surrounding hills and even the cold winter weather did not prevent the young ladies from suddenly developing an interest in walking and viewing the beauties of the winter countryside.

Now that the whole of the south west had been occupied by royalist troops, the temporary food shortage, caused by the occupation of the port's entrance by parliamentary ships, had been resolved and life in that sense had returned to normal. In fact, Sarah reflected, life had assumed an air once more of permanence, tradesmen still plied their wares in Dartmouth, vegetables still grew in their gardens, the farm people milked their cows and tended their animals and the civil war seemed far distant.

Throughout that year, Sarah had a certainty that the royalists would win. It seemed to her vital, that only by that course would she retain Vinelands and her property.

When news came of the battle of Marston Moor, where the parliamentary army gained a decisive victory, she suggested to Sir Geoffrey that his troops should build greater fortifications around Vinelands.

'It is but a small setback,' the commander replied. 'Soon you will see that our victories are even greater.'

During the summer, when reports reached Dartmouth that the Earl of Essex and his parliamentary troops had surrendered at Lostwithiel, losing the whole of his infantry, there were great celebrations in the town. Sarah rode over to see Catherine and Reginald to acquaint them with the news. They had converted part of the house into a hospital for soldiers in need of medical care. A garrison of about five hundred troops was now housed in Dartmouth and the tiny hospital that Gabriel had built was insufficient for such numbers.

'I find the townspeople pleased enough with the situation,' Catherine observed. 'They must do much trade with such an influx of persons.'

'I know not where they find their money,' Sarah replied. 'The commander often appears perplexed about how the troops shall be paid. I have found it necessary to contribute towards that need.'

'I have news also of cousin Elizabeth, who has safely produced her latest child. It is to be called Hubert.'

'Ah,' Sarah's face clouded. 'I wish that I might call upon Katherine when she returns from Elizabeth's, yet William cannot be pleased to receive me.'

'Dear madam,' Reginald said. 'I think William would not allow the situation to interfere with his feeling for you.'

'No. Perhaps I will go. But Richard's sojourn in the royalist ranks must cause him much sorrow.'

'Soon it will be over,' Catherine said comfortingly. 'I cannot see the parliamentary forces holding out.'

As they passed into a new year, Sarah's hopes began to waver. Parliament was still passing laws, still throwing people into gaol for their religious opinions or for any act which appeared to challenge its authority. There seemed to be increasing persecution by the more fanatical Puritans in parliament who constantly had people arrested for their allegedly seditious views. The Puritans were becoming more extreme. Churches were now sealed on weekdays, even the Anglicans were hated by the Puritans and found themselves increasingly in conflict with their views. Then in April, further bad news reached them. Parliament, concerned about its defeats, formed a New Model Army consisting of the radical puritans and headed by Colonel

Fairfax, and a second-in-command called Cromwell. It was to be professional, well-trained and modestly behaved. Two months later it fought the King's troops at Naseby and inflicted a decisive defeat.

Rumours about the King and his intentions circulated through the taverns of Dartmouth. The main parliamentarians had escaped before the town fell to the royalist army, but now there were rumblings of a change of heart and those who had not spoken before now began to espouse the Puritan cause. Reginald reported that the Catholics in the town told him that there were increasing complaints about the recusants and allegations that the King had been subverted to their cause.

Sarah felt a deep anxiety settle upon her. What intentions did these Puritans and parliamentary people have? Did they simply wish to rid themselves of the King or would they become even more restrictive and prejudiced than their predecessors in parliament?

Then she considered what she would do if the armies arrived. Well, what she would do was fight, she would not surrender to that Puritan army. And supposing Vinelands was destroyed?

Her mind turned away from the thought. Vinelands was hers. Somehow, she would retain it. She realized that it had become even more important to her since Gabriel's death, as though it still bound them together.

She rode over to Greenhayes to see Katherine and William. Although a supporter of parliament, William had been permitted to retain his house and lands but had taken no further part in the administration of Dartmouth. Much of his time was now spent in London where he could still work in the courts. Katherine had become increasingly concerned about Richard's welfare and he had reported that he was now encamped on the outskirts of Oxford.

'William,' Sarah said, 'what think you will occur if the royalist cause is defeated?'

William looked dispirited. He shook his head.

'There can be no victory in this war,' he said. 'We must all suffer loss.'

'But someone must win in the end,' Sarah persisted.

'I think the only ones who will win may be the extreme Puritan believers who want no joy for anyone. They are an immoderate and bigoted group and those moderate parliamentarians with whom I threw in my lot can have no further confidence.'

'Then you now support the King?'

William shook his head. 'I fear he is to be defeated. He also has behaved in an unacceptable way.'

'Cannot peace be declared?'

'There are too many warring factions on the parliament side. Who is to parley with the King?'

Now the Model Army turned its attention to capturing the royalist strongholds in the south-west. It was only then that the occupying forces began to strengthen the defences of Dartmouth and place reinforcements on the hills above the town. This time, the town would not surrender without a battle. Sarah vowed she would never relinquish Vinelands.

In the closing months of sixteen hundred and forty-five news came that the Model Army was advancing towards Exeter, led by the same Fairfax and Cromwell who had decimated the royalists at Naseby. Sarah warned the priests hidden in the house that they could no longer feel secure, that escape was still possible, and if they were captured by the Puritan army they stood no hope of getting justice. The ships in the harbour had been manned against invasion; they could still be got away under cover of darkness. But they chose to remain, saying that their work was amongst the tenants of the estate.

Nicholas was still far away on the high seas and word had come that he could not return until the summer. Sarah persuaded Catherine and Reginald to bring the children and stay with her at the house. John and Urith continued to work on the farm but now they and the children also slept at Vinelands until the emergency was past.

Early in January the Model Army reached the outskirts of Exeter. It could be only a matter of time before it reached Dartmouth.

A few days later, Mr Weaver reported that enemy ships lay at the harbour mouth and that there was no way for the royalist ships to escape.

Hourly reports were now brought back to Sir Geoffrey at Vinelands from the guards posted across the hills. An army of soldiers and artillery under Cromwell was marching towards Tavistock. Great contingents of infantrymen had been seen approaching Stoke Fleming. Whole regiments filled the lanes and paths around Dittisham. In Dartmouth, the citizens were commanded to go into their houses and bolt the doors and the shutters of the windows. All able-bodied men were posted to the defences.

From the windows of Vinelands, Sarah could see fires burning all around the hills where the Model Army had erected its tents in the snow and ice, preparing for the assault. She looked down on the white roofs of the town. Far away, across the harbour, she saw a fire burning beyond Kingswear where great stores of corn were being burnt that it might not be captured by the enemy.

The whole house was filled with the movement of people. Sarah had permitted those of the tenants who could be accommodated to move into Vinelands as their own homes provided flimsy defence against mortar attack. Catherine's children, five-year-old John and four-year-old Gabriel, looked with delight at the lights glowing in the sky and even little Nicholas clapped his hands gleefully when the sound of a great gun boomed across the icy air.

Sarah hurried to the commander.

'Has it begun?'

Sir Geoffrey shook his head.

'It was from one of the ships at sea. But it must be a signal to the general.'

'Can we hold out, sir, against that army? There are fires spread across all the hills for a great distance.'

'Madam, we have had much time to prepare. We have nigh on a thousand men here in Dartmouth to provide for our defence. They are well-trained, our guns are set upon the enemy and news comes that they have abandoned much of their artillery at the siege of Plymouth.'

'Sir,' Sarah said firmly. 'I do not intend to relinquish this house whatever may occur.'

Sir Geoffrey looked serious.

'I do not care to ponder such a possibility,' he said quietly. 'But should disaster befall, you would not be advised to stand out against them. You would risk the total destruction of the place.'

'I would not surrender,' Sarah said. Then she smiled. 'So we must ensure that such a situation does not occur.'

For three days the town waited. The harbour entrance was now totally blockaded by the enemy ships; guards were set upon every street and road leading from the town to ensure that no spies entered to gain intelligence of its preparedness. Small parties of men were observed high above Tunstall surveying the town below.

The weather became milder. When Sir Geoffrey left Vinelands to direct operations in the town, Sarah knew that the fate of the house now rested in her hands. It was only her determination that could save it.

Suddenly, in the darkness, great waves of soldiers swept down Crowther's Hill and Tunstall Hill and the royalists let forth a great barrage of musket and cannon. Sarah commanded that the drawbridge be raised, the iron gates bolted and all the interior doors sealed. She ordered the servants to prepare food for all those inside; calm should be maintained. Catherine and Reginald watched from the library windows and John and Urith looked through the windows at the other end of the gallery.

Guns continued to fire spasmodically and then ceased altogether. As Sarah summoned everyone to the Great

Hall, there was a loud hammering on the iron door. The people inside were silent.

'Observe who it is,' Sarah said.

The steward looked through the spyhole.

'It is one of the ranks of our infantry, m'lady. He is alone.'

'Admit him.'

The door was hastily unbolted.

'M'lady. I come from Sir Geoffrey Madison. The Model Army have captured all. Mount Boon, Tunstall, the Castle, Gallant's Bower, with all the guns and pieces of ordnance. The town is filled with them.'

There were gasps of horror and despair.

'I am to report to you, m'lady,' the man went on, 'that men-of-war now lie in the river and Sir Geoffrey Madison has surrendered.'

Sarah said in confusion, 'But what has become of the royalist army? Its numbers approached almost a thousand.'

The man did not reply, shaking his head.

'I cannot believe it,' Sarah said. 'And was there then much slaughter?'

'But little, m'lady. The enemy had no fire, they had lost all their guns at Plymouth.'

'Then how did they take this town?' Sarah asked angrily.

'Madam, great hordes descended upon the town. They captured our guns and turned them round upon us.'

'Oh, how can it be? And now what is to happen?'

'The commander advises that you permit the Model Army to enter and you will not be harmed.'

'No!' Sarah said violently. 'I will not.' She looked around the crowded hall. 'Those of you who wish to, depart to your homes. Behave peacefully and no harm will come. I shall barricade this place.'

Most of the tenants decided to depart to their own homes but as they were about to leave, Sarah said quietly, 'There is one small matter. Let no-one divulge the presence of the priests in this house. Remember, their lives must depend upon it.'

When they were gone, the doors were again bolted and those who remained settled down to await the arrival of the soldiers.

One day, two days passed quietly and nothing happened. Then they heard horses trotting up the drive. Suddenly, a shot was fired.

'There are two horsemen only,' Mr Weaver said. 'They must come from the occupying general in the town.'

'Allow them to enter,' Sarah said.

The two officers stood before her and bowed.

'Sir John Morris,' one of them said.

'What news have you, sir?'

'The General Fairfax requests that this house be now surrendered to the army of parliament. All occupants will then be allowed to depart peacefully to their homes and occupations.'

'Sir, they are already in their homes,' Sarah replied distantly. 'It is here my family and servants reside.'

'Madam, we must demand that the guns be forfeited and the soldiers within negotiate a proper surrender of this place.'

'There are no soldiers,' Sarah replied instantly. 'They have already departed into the town.'

Sir John Morris frowned.

'Then who would deploy these guns if need be?'

'Sir,' Sarah said instantly. 'I would.'

The other man smiled, but Sir John replied, 'Madam, you then place yourself and your ladies in much danger. It is only to non-combatants that the general can offer pity and commiseration.'

'I am in need of neither,' she said coldly.

'The general demands that this house be forfeited immediately.'

Suddenly Sarah sat down.

'Sir, I cannot but remind you of my position. I am the

widow of that great man whom the whole nation honours. I must request that courtesy and respect which should be afforded to a lady in need.'

'Madam,' Sir John said instantly. 'It is not the general's desire to treat you harshly nor to harm the structure of this house. If you will leave peaceably, then the matter is resolved.'

'Pray, consult further with your general,' Sarah said softly. 'I have no argument with him but to remain in my own home.'

The two men departed and Sarah turned to Catherine and Reginald and all the assembled servants.

'I do not intend to surrender,' she said. 'It is for each of you to go hence if you wish.'

She looked round at the steward and stableboys and cooks and kitchen maids and maidservants. They did not move.

'I would hope to negotiate our peaceful occupation of the house,' Sarah said reassuringly.

Sir John returned the following day, requesting her obedience, but this time she sent him away sharply, protesting that she would rather suffer violence and preserve her liberty than treat with such an enemy. Gradually, soldiers surrounded the house, kept at bay only by the wide water-filled moat and the uphill slope to the house.

Then they began to pound the walls with great stones from the mortar and cannon which had been carried through the estate. The servants and tenants placed themselves at their allotted posts at the windows and their guns returned fire. It was then that Reginald said to her, 'Dear madam, it may be that the house will be destroyed. If you came to terms with the general, perhaps it will be spared.'

'And I may not occupy it,' Sarah retorted. 'No. I have considered. I would rather it be demolished than hand it over to these ruffians.'

As the days passed, the towers began to crack, the

outer walls to crumble. But the men from the estate and her own maidservants helped to man her guns and even the grenades thrown at the house did not weaken their resolve.

Yet the soldiers did not storm the house and Sarah gained news that the general was unwilling to do harm to women, an action which would make future sieges more difficult to resolve.

The days passed, the water supply to the house had been reduced and Sarah and her servants began to cast bullets from lead which had been stored in the barns. The days passed into weeks. It was only when a shell entered one of the upstairs chambers and seriously wounded one of the maids that Sarah began to waver.

Then, by good fortune, another event engrossed the attention of the general. Part of the Model Army was approaching Oxford and the parliamentary forces were anxious to regain the city. The troops in the south-west were needed to meet the offensive. Suddenly, one morning, the soldiers besieging Vinelands packed up and marched away, leaving only a token force in Dartmouth. The occupants looked through the windows in disbelief, fearing some trap. Then they held a great celebration in which much thanks and gratitude were offered to Sarah for her courage and determination.

In June, Oxford surrendered. News came of the defeat from Richard, who arrived home and told Katherine and William his regiment had been disbanded. He spoke of the fierce and bloody fighting, unlike the capture of Dartmouth, in which many had been killed and said there had been much looting and violence towards the women.

Sarah set about the repair of the house. Dartmouth had suffered a decline during those years of conflict. Trade had been affected by the blockade of the port; the fishing vessels had to regain their fishing interests in Newfoundland and although there was little animosity felt between the two sides in Dartmouth, the turmoil between the supporters of the King and of parliament elsewhere left scars which would not be eradicated for generations.

It was only in the autumn that Sarah had some good news. Nicholas returned from China and informed her that he was to be wed before Christmas. Penelope Bosiney was the daughter of Sir Lewis Bosiney of Warminster, a great landowner and previously a prominent adviser to the King. In spite of this former allegiance, he had one great advantage. He was the brother of one of the leading parliamentarians.

'But let us hope,' Nicholas said, 'that there will soon be a period of peace, when we shall not need to consider such matters.'

'We will have a great celebration for your wedding,' Sarah said.

'Mama,' Nicholas said seriously, 'the conflict is not yet over, the King will yet try to repair his fortunes and Dartmouth is now in the hands of parliament.'

Sarah frowned.

'What mean you, Nicholas? The matter is settled here.'

'Mama, the King will try to raise those Scots to his defence, who now have him in their power. But I believe he cannot succeed. Most of the country south of the Border is in parliamentary hands. The royalist armies are disbanded, the troops have returned to their homes.'

'But Dartmouth is settled,' she persisted. 'It has returned to peace.'

'Mama, nothing can return to what it was before. If the enemy succeed, the Puritans will take control. They have wantonly destroyed all cathedrals and churches they have captured. They pillage all great houses, they requisition and mutilate all objects of beauty, all those houses who supported the royalist cause are taken or destroyed.'

'The people of Dartmouth appear to harbour little animosity towards each other. They are only relieved that it is over.'

'It is not the people of Dartmouth who will cause the

havoc. It is those fanatics from London, it is the leaders of the Model Army and their ruffianly troops who will ensure that every royalist shall forfeit his property.'

'You speak with much certainty,' Sarah said bleakly.

'I have seen it,' Nicholas replied ominously. 'We can only prepare for the day when those parliamentary soldiers return.'

36

Katherine went up to her chamber to examine her wardrobe. She studied the blue silk gown she had worn recently to Nicholas's wedding and then looked critically at all the other gowns and mantles. None of them were new. Since the war began, elegant materials had become increasingly difficult to acquire and she felt bored with the fashions. Perhaps, now that the war seemed to be over, life would return to normal. William appeared in the doorway.

'Ah, I thought to find you here.'

'It is a gloomy collection,' she said. 'Perhaps when you next repair to London I might accompany you, to find some new garments.'

'I fear that little of interest will be found in the capital,' William said. 'The mood there is quite otherwise. The styles and fashions of the past get little support. In fact, I feel that the ladies appearing in extravagant attire perhaps put themselves in danger.'

Katherine made a face.

'Then I will remain here and do my own adaptations. I know that Sarah will have inspiration.'

William put his hands on her shoulders.

'You have been much support, dear Katherine,' he said suddenly. 'It is hard for you, who can have but little time for the parliamentary group.'

Katherine shook her head.

'It is my son I am concerned about,' she said. 'Richard's whole employ was in the royal courts and now he can have but little chance of exercising his skills. These royal courts are all abolished.'

'Fortunately, I hope to find him some place in the Court of Common Pleas. I still have some influence there amongst those more moderate Presbyterians whom I support. They are, after all, still the largest party in parliament.'

'And where does that leave Elizabeth and Edward? He is so much for the King's party and has so well supported him that I fear he must lose house and home to the Puritan faction.'

'That is what I came to see you about,' William said.

Katherine looked alarmed at his anxious expression.

'William, no harm has come!'

'No, dear. But I have had a message from Edward that they are to leave for the Continent until matters are resolved.'

'Leave! But what of the three children? What of the house and estate?'

'The children will accompany them, of course. Many who supported the King have left, Katherine. They will not treat with the present parliament while the fate of the King is yet uncertain.'

'They will be robbed of their house,' Katherine said hopelessly.

'Edward is to leave it in the hands of the steward. But perhaps it is better to lose the house than risk their lives?'

'Does it come to that?'

William sighed.

'One cannot be sure. Perhaps. There appears to be but little control over elements of the army.'

'Is it not in the control of parliament?'

William smiled.

'Unfortunately the army behaves as though it were that body and now the King is in its hands.'

'William, I must visit Elizabeth before she departs.'

'My dear, it is too late for that. They will already have left. Let us hope she will not be long gone.' He put his arms around her. 'We must find her safety of most import.'

'This terrible war seems to have given no-one happiness, resolved nothing.'

'No. It is a dismal prospect.'

'I shall visit Sarah,' Katherine said. 'She persists still that should anything untoward occur, she will never relinquish Vinelands.'

'There is another matter,' William said solemnly. 'When I went down into Dartmouth, I heard rumours that give me some concern.'

'What rumours?'

'About witchcraft in our midst.'

'Witchcraft!'

'There has been an increasing tendency to this kind of prosecution of late. It is almost as if we had returned to that madness of James's reign.'

'But what has that to do with Sarah?'

'There are those who remember Granny Lott and that awful event.'

'But no-one in Dartmouth now bears any malice towards her. She has been a great benefactor to the town.'

'No. It is not the inhabitants. But since the recapture of Dartmouth, there are many Puritan elements who have infiltrated and look for some ready excuse to remove her from her house and estate.'

'But she is not a witch!'

'None of them ever were. But in the past years, these prosecutions have increased a hundredfold. It is a part

543

of Puritan superstition. Most of these persons come from Suffolk and Essex and thereabouts, where the Puritan ethic is most strong, but they will try to spread their influence to other parts.'

'Then it is important that I warn her of these undesirables,' Katherine said.

When she reached Vinelands, she found the iron gates still bolted and was admitted by a side gate into the kitchens. She went through into the Great Hall, where Sarah was overseeing the movement of bags and parcels to a waiting cart in the stables.

'What is happening?' Katherine asked.

'Pray, come to the chapel,' Sarah said quietly.

Katherine followed her in silence. The two priests were waiting in silence.

'Pray, don these cloaks,' Sarah said to them. 'Mr Weaver will accompany you and I will visit you later. But please remember, mass cannot be held at the farm or anywhere else at the moment.'

The two men walked down the corridors and into the waiting vehicle. Sarah turned back into the house.

'I am persuaded that it is no longer safe here,' she said. 'Their presence must endanger not only themselves but the whole household.'

'But where are they going?'

'They are to remain with John and Urith until a boat can be found to transport them to the Continent. They are unwilling to depart but I have prevailed upon them to consider also the safety of the large number of persons in this household.'

'From what William says, it is not only priests who are in danger. It would seem that persons of any persuasion who do not suit the Puritans will find no peace.'

'Katherine,' Sarah said, 'do not despair. It must end at some time.'

Katherine told her about William's fears, watching the dawning incredulity on her face.

'Witchcraft,' Sarah finally laughed sarcastically. 'I thought such accusations were long past.'

'William takes this threat seriously.'

'Then I will ensure that I have no toads, cats or obscene thoughts,' Sarah laughed again. 'Come, we were to try to redesign our wardrobes.'

Katherine followed her upstairs. Sarah had acquired a confidence and fearlessness in the past years which made her seem even more attractive and vital.

'You seem never to get older, Sarah.'

Sarah smiled. 'I know not why,' she said lightly.

During the summer, they spent their time having their houses and appurtenances decorated and improved. News came from Nicholas that Penelope had been delivered of her first child, Sarah Clare. They had acquired a manor house in Cornwall and had hopes that in that non-Puritan area they might enjoy comparative safety.

Sarah continued to take part in the building of almshouses that had been interrupted by the war. Repair of churches was not permitted, in fact, any decoration, anything of value was either removed or destroyed. But the citizens of Dartmouth were mainly concerned with reviving the trade which had been lost; those who had supported parliament now began to regret their folly and the extremists came mainly from other parts and gained but little support. As only a small garrison had been left to guard the town, these soldiers found it was in their own interests to be as accommodating as possible. The two members of parliament had no wish for confrontation.

In August, Sarah was visited by a man dressed in the plain robes of the Presbyterian brotherhood. He came with only one attendant and requested an audience of the lady of the house to whom he stated that he was related.

Mr Weaver sought his name.

'I am John Kerswill, brother of Philip and son of the late Stephen Kerswill who died in New England and of Cicely, the departed sister of the lady of this house.'

545

The doors were unbolted and he came in. Sarah met him in the hall, frowning, looking in disbelief at the tall, auburn-haired man before her.

'John,' she said slowly. 'It is many years since we met. Yet you do resemble your mother, Cicely.'

John bowed and took her hand.

'Madam, I am honoured that you receive me.'

'Come, I would have welcomed you better had I known of your arrival.'

A servant took his cloak, wine and ale were brought and John and Urith were summoned from the farm to greet him.

Sarah observed his attire questioningly.

'When I last heard of you, you were surely a thriving architect in London.'

John smiled. 'That time is long past. Even before this terrible war, I had abandoned that profession, preferring to devote my life to a more worthy cause.'

'And do you still live at Lincoln with Philip and Isobel?'

'I lived nearby until recently. I have there a small property and a large congregation.'

'Ah, yes,' Sarah said instantly. 'Is it not that part of the country which supports this wretched Army parliament?'

John sighed.

'Yes, madam. It is from that area that Cromwell and the Independents hail.'

'I am surprised that you visit here,' Sarah said. 'You know this was a royalist establishment – and still is,' she added.

'Madam,' John said. 'Parliament is no longer composed of agreeable persons who would be concerned for the good of the country.'

'But you would surely not support the King's party,' Sarah said. Then she added fearlessly, 'If you have come to spy on this domain, you will find little comfort here.'

John blushed. 'Madam, I regret that you hold such an opinion of me.'

546

'Then what is the purpose of your visit?'

'Madam, I have come to warn you. Recently, a general council of the army was set up which is mostly composed of those Independents who would be rid of the King for ever. A few days ago, they occupied London and have now ordered the removal of eleven Presbyterians, whom I support, from the Commons.'

Sarah listened but did not reply.

'I fear, madam, that anarchy reigns.'

'But what has this to do with me?'

'Madam, it has come to my knowledge that my brother, Philip, is one of those who would support the extreme radicals. He will have all form of episcopal worship effaced from the kingdom. He will even persecute those who wish a moderate church of England.'

'But I support neither,' Sarah said. 'My concern is only to retain Vinelands.'

'Ah, that is the point. My brother Philip has become so carried away with these Puritan ideals that he will remove anyone who supported the King and, even more, those who have supported the Catholics in the past.'

'And have you knowledge that he intends to take this house?'

'Madam, yes. He intends to send a force under that very commander who tried to deal with you when Dartmouth was recaptured.'

'Ah, Sir John Morris. Then the barricades must be set up instantly. And you, sir, what becomes of you?'

'I return to my flock at Lincoln.'

Sarah was silent for a moment. Could she trust this man? She had not seen him for years. Why had he come now? He was Stephen's son; perhaps he had inherited some of his undesirable traits. Then she said, 'No, sir. You will remain here until this business is past.'

'Here?'

'Yes, my good sir. Perhaps you are in good faith; perhaps you are a spy. But if you have my interests at heart you will

547

not object to staying; and should you be a spy, I shall have ensured your impotence in this matter.'

As she spoke, Sarah had rung the bell and Mr Weaver appeared instantly.

'Mr Weaver, pray search this gentleman's person and that of his attendant. They are to remain in this place until my further order. A guard will be placed upon them until that time.'

Mr Weaver smiled as he led John away.

'It is wise, m'lady. This visit appears strange.'

The months passed and no event occurred. John was permitted to take meals with her and to walk around the battlements in the company of half a dozen armed guards or to amuse himself with music or books in the library. He was not shown the small, now unused chapel, though Sarah assumed that he knew of its presence through his father Stephen, and his visits to Vinelands as a child.

During those months, John had almost convinced her that he was concerned only for her safety. He talked to her of his childhood, of the cold cruelty of his father Stephen, of the silent suffering of his mother.

'Our greatest delight was to visit Vinelands,' he said. 'Our dear grandparents were so kind and we always thought of you as a shining star.'

'And what of your brother Philip?' Sarah asked. 'He does not appear to retain such happy memories.'

'I fear that Philip was permanently damaged by our father's treatment of him. He harbours many grudges. There is a strange, cruel streak in him that I do not understand.'

In November, the King escaped from the hands of the Army and went to the Isle of Wight. There were now rumours of a renewed civil war and when it was revealed in December that Charles had signed an agreement with the Scots, the Model Army took fright.

Regulations and restrictions poured from parliament and any remaining remnants of the royalist army were hunted down and demolished. That same month, the commander, Sir John Morris, arrived with a horde of troops at the gates of the house. They had crossed the moat in the darkness of night with the aid of ropes and chains and were now poised ready to enter.

Sarah sent a message that she would speak with Sir John. He entered alone, a sword in his scabbard, a gun in his hand. He bowed to Sarah.

'Sir,' she said coldly, 'I see you are still engaged upon your plunder and destruction.'

'Madam, I ask you again, as I did many months ago, to surrender this house and estate. You will be permitted to go in peace.'

'And where would I go, pray?'

'To those of your family who have not acted in the King's behalf and who do not risk eviction.'

Sarah laughed scornfully.

'No-one is safe from your violence,' she said. 'But I fear you have come too late.'

'What mean you, madam?'

'The house has already been occupied by other of your army. Sir,' she turned to Mr Weaver, 'pray summon John Kerswill to our midst.'

The commander turned in bewilderment as into the hall came a man in his own kind of uniform but not of his acquaintance, followed by a small contingent of soldiers.

As he entered, John Kerswill called through the doorway to the corridor beyond, 'Leave the remainder of the infantry without, with their ammunition.'

'Sir,' John Morris said, 'What is this?'

'Sir,' John Kerswill replied, 'I fear you are not informed. We have already occupied this house and have no need of reinforcements.'

'Sir, when did this occur?'

'Some days hence. Pray return your men to Oxford whence you came. And offer thanks to my Lord Fairfax for his action.'

The commander frowned.

'This is a strange event,' he said slowly.

'Ah,' John Kerswill said lightly. 'I fear in the excitements of war information is often but slow to arrive.'

The commander turned to Sarah.

'Madam, I take my leave. May I hope that you have surrendered to those who would permit you the peace that I would have done.'

'Sir,' Sarah said quietly, 'when you have removed your men beyond the drawbridge and repaired any slight damage you have done, I will have ale sent out to your soldiers. Good day, sir.'

He bowed curtly and walked from the room.

When he had gone, Sarah smiled quietly to John Kerswill.

'Thank you, sir. You have done well. I regret my earlier suspicions of you. My concern was only for Vinelands. But when they have departed, you must be away. Soon our ruse must be discovered.'

John Kerswill smiled at Sarah.

'You have done well also,' he said. 'I must congratulate your bravery.'

'It is of no consequence,' she said coolly.

Sarah ensured now that the servants remained dressed in their battle attire, that the musket and small cannon were always ready and the moat was reinforced with outer chains.

The months passed and no army returned. Then came the final blow. The King had been recaptured and was imprisoned with his children in Hampton Court. The Queen had escaped to France.

This time, Cromwell's army would ensure that he did not escape.

37

Early in the year sixteen hundred and forty-nine, the King was brought from Hampton Court to stand trial, was condemned to death and was executed on the thirtieth day of January. A gloom settled over the country. In the provinces, the Army continued its plunder of churches and cathedrals. Sarah knew that the moment could not long be delayed when the army would return to Vinelands. Cromwell's men would surely have discovered her deception and only their commitments in the capital had saved her so far. There were few royalist strongholds which had not now been occupied by the Model Army and she knew that they were now proceeding through Dorset and Wiltshire.

Early in March word came that they had passed through Exeter. It could be only a day's march to Dartmouth, even allowing for the delay caused by their constant forays into churches and large houses to pillage, plunder and deface. Catherine and Reginald would have stayed at Vinelands with the children but Sarah insisted that they should go to Trevayne Abbey.

'You will not be harmed. You have taken no part in the conflicts.'

Catherine pleaded with Sarah to go with them and abandon the house.

'It is not worth the loss of your life,' Catherine said tearfully. 'And you still have the fleet of vessels on the Grand Banks and they surely cannot confiscate the whole estate.'

'I shall not lose my life,' Sarah said confidently. 'John and Urith are at the farm. I can escape there if required. And if need be, we could all go to Nicholas in Cornwall.'

After they had left, the gates were barred again, the iron doors bolted, the ordnance prepared.

It was two days later before they heard horses coming up the long drive and the ribald shouting of soldiers.

This time, Sarah did not admit any messenger from the commander, not risking the opening of the doors. No promise came that if they would submit no harm would come to them.

'On this occasion, we can expect no quarter,' she observed to Mr Weaver. 'These are rabble we have not previously come upon.'

'M'lady, you should repair to the chambers above with your maidservants.'

Sarah smiled.

'Mr Weaver, I think at your age the time is also long past when you should be troubled with these dangers. By now, we are as versed as you in the art of soldiery. But we will take the upper windows where we have a goodly collection of flares and great stones to meet the intruders.'

Sarah went up the staircase, looking at the tapestries on the walls; at the green velvet couch at the top gallery where Gabriel had told her to sit the day she arrived; at the brocaded chairs, the Spanish cupboards, the great ewers from Italy. She rarely studied these objects now, they were such a familiar part of her life that she scarcely saw them. It was only during this terrible war that she had realized how much this place was a part of her life; would she have any identity without it?

She looked through the high library windows in the fading light of the afternoon. She could see no-one across the gardens. Then she went to the chamber once occupied by Frances; from there she could see down the long drive towards the gates. Her heart sank as she saw rows of soldiers on horseback, looking expectantly towards the house. Anger consumed her but once again she tried to consider rationally whether it was not better to surrender. Yet, she told herself, these creatures will destroy the place whatever I do.

A multitude of servants were coming and going around her. She turned.

'What think you, Emily?'

Emily had been with her for so long, had shared all the perils and dangers of the New World, that she did not need to explain her question.

'Ma'am, let us fight on.' Then she added, 'We cannot win in any case. Let us not submit without a fight.'

Sarah smiled.

'You are all brave people,' she said to those around her. 'But I will not let you be harmed.'

The bombardment did not begin until darkness had fallen, when a cannonball violently struck the library end of the house. There was the sound of breaking glass and falling masonry and the women rushed to the library to find the windows fallen in and a gaping hole in the wall.

Sarah and the women rolled the huge stones they had placed along the walls up to the hole and pushed them through. There were screams as they landed on the soldiers below, to be swiftly followed by burning flares and boiling water.

At the same moment, Sarah heard her own muskets and cannon firing from the towers above and the ground floor beneath. There was a temporary silence from the soldiers outside and then their large artillery was brought up and a barrage of mortar fire and cannon shattered the air and the thick walls of the house trembled. There were crashes and explosions through the house, the air was filled with screams and curses. Finally, the ground floor was stormed, the soldiers climbed through the broken windows and the iron door was thrown open.

'Come,' Sarah said to Emily. 'Now I will deal with them. But first, let me remove this torn gown.'

She ran along to her chamber, hastily changed into a deep red satin gown, and cast a silk shawl across her bare shoulders.

'Pray, adjust your attire,' she said to the women. 'Let us meet these oafs with dignity.'

She walked slowly, followed by her retinue, and paused halfway down the stairs. In the Great Hall below, soldiers were knocking over the statues, tearing down the wall coverings, breaking an ancient settle with hammers.

'Rabble!' she shouted.

The soldiers turned and looked up in astonishment. There was a moment's silence. Then two of them came forward, up the stairs. One of them said sneeringly, 'What's this?' and grabbed at the gold rope around Sarah's neck. But before he could wrest it from her, she dug her teeth into his hand so violently that blood poured from him and he stepped back in agony.

'Savages,' she said. 'Where is your commander?'

'Ho, ho, madam,' the other soldier said. 'Think you that our commander will treat with a royalist whore?'

Sarah looked at him, seething with anger. Then she looked round at the waiting soldiers beneath. She suddenly remembered Katherine's warning, that this superstitious uncouth Puritan rabble believed in witchcraft. She stared at them with her penetrating green eyes. Then she said, 'You are all in danger here. This house is cursed.'

The two soldiers in front of her stepped back but she continued to look at them challengingly.

'There are those in the town of Dartmouth who will tell you that my grandmother was hanged as a witch. It is true.'

No-one spoke.

'I am also a witch,' she said. 'Anyone who touches me or any of my servants will die.'

The two soldiers retreated slowly backwards down the stairs.

'Anyone who defaces this house will be cursed by me.'

She spoke in a weird, ringing voice and as she began to descend the stairs, the soldiers all drew away from her as she approached.

'Now,' she said. 'Get out.'

But as they began to retreat through the open door a tall officer appeared suddenly from a rear corridor. He strode towards Sarah.

'Madam, Commander Welbeck. We now occupy this house and all its surrounding lands. We have searched this place but find none of those objects of idolatry that we know to be here.'

Sarah looked at him contemptuously. The chapel had been sealed up with a stone wall since the last attempted invasion of the house. She had no fear that any incriminating objects would be found.

'Sir, if you be the commander, you have but poor control over these ruffians you call an army.'

'And you, madam, have committed grievous harm upon the government's troops.'

'And you have invaded my privacy and allowed them to assault an unprotected lady.'

The commander frowned and looked round at the soldiers who were sneaking away through the door.

'What goes on here?'

One of the soldiers turned and mumbled, 'Sir, we fear to be in this place.'

Sarah smiled.

'They are an ignorant lot, yet they show some sense in not wishing to remain in a place to which they do not belong.'

'They will do as they are bid,' the commander said shortly. 'In the meantime, madam, this house will be sealed off from any visitors who do not belong here. It is now in the property of my Lord Cromwell.'

'And what of my servants, those who run the estate?'

'They will remain until it can be taken over by someone appointed by parliament.'

'And what of me?'

'Madam, you will accompany me to Exeter gaol where it shall be decided what manner of punishment you deserve.'

Emily said, 'I shall accompany my mistress. It is my right.'

Instantly, all the servants pressed forward, expressing the same intention. The commander looked perplexed.

'This cannot be,' he said. 'I must again summon my soldiers to ensure your cooperation.'

Sarah had heard recently that while the soldiers of the Model Army had often been recruited from the criminal and thieving classes, the officers had received much training in the arts not only of chivalrous warfare but also in diplomacy. Perhaps he would not attempt to force the issue.

'Before I depart, I must attend to my toilet,' Sarah said and turned to go to her chamber. But when she reached the top of the stairs, she went instead to Frances's chamber where, in the cold dawn light, she could see the soldiers below. They saw her silhouetted against the candlelight behind, looking down at them. She raised an arm above her head and then pointed down at them menacingly. They slunk further away into the shadows.

When she returned to the commander, she said smoothly, 'Now, we are all prepared.'

'You cannot all come,' the commander said firmly. 'I shall recall my troops.'

Sarah smiled.

He went to the door and looked. There was silence. He stepped outside. The men had vanished. The guns and ammunition lay abandoned around the house, across the fields and gardens. He looked back at Sarah in disbelief.

'Do we have another mutiny?' she asked caustically.

'You will accompany me, madam,' the commander said.

Sarah smiled as her own men came towards him.

'Sir, I think not,' she said. 'But I must offer you my hospitality.'

He turned as if to march from the house, but the way was barred against him.

'Pray, let me offer you some refreshment.'

Sarah began to walk towards the dining hall and the commander followed her indignantly.

'Madam, you have no hope of continuing this defiance,' he said.

'Perhaps not,' she replied. 'But then, it would be a simple matter to kill you. Your troops have deserted. It is common knowledge that many soldiers, tired of these battles, are returning home.'

He stood before her.

'I believe you would do such a thing,' he said half-admiringly.

'Be assured, sir, I would do it with my own hands. Your life is nothing to me.'

'I shall be relieved, madam. The soldiers will report on what has occurred. You will suffer death yourself for such infamy.'

'But I fear, sir,' Sarah said lightly as one of her servants handed him a tankard of ale, 'that you yourself have made a poor blunder.'

'What mean you, madam?'

'I mean that you have desecrated this place which has been made over to someone of high importance in your party.'

The commander glared.

'Madam, your speech is always provocative. Of whom do you speak?'

'Know you not that Sir Philip Kerswill of Lincoln is of my kith and kin?'

'No,' the man replied slowly. 'He has been in command of the General Cromwell's forces in the north.'

'And that he has lately been endowed this property by myself?'

'I knew not of this. I was commanded to take those great houses not yet surrendered to the state.'

'Then I fear you have not been kept informed. He will shortly be arriving', Sarah continued, 'with his wife, the Lady Isobel. They would have been here earlier, were it not for her confinement a few months past.'

The commander looked at her in disbelief.

'Madam, this is but subterfuge. I shall return to the general to ascertain its truth. If you lie, it will be the worse for you.'

'Sir,' Sarah said quietly, 'you will remain as my guest until my kin arrive.'

The commander turned towards the door. Her men came towards him.

'Madam, this is an outrage. Do you propose to keep me as a prisoner?'

'Indeed not,' Sarah replied. 'I offer you my hospitality. Though I fear,' she added, 'that Sir Philip Kerswill can scarcely congratulate you upon your actions here.'

The commander hesitated.

'Madam, if an error has been made, it is to be regretted.'

'Regretted! It is an infamy. Deliberate spoliation of Puritan property.'

Sarah realized that the commander had heard of the fanatical exploits of Philip and his utter devotion to the Puritan cause. Although the commander had been acting in the line of duty, there was little love lost between the different factions of this Model Army and he would get little sympathy for his action.

What he did not know was that she was speaking the truth. While reinforcing Vinelands in case of emergency, she had come upon the idea of offering the house and estate to Philip, 'realizing the error of her previous allegiance and anxious to make recompense, she hoped that as a great Puritan Commander in the Model Army, he would accept Vinelands for his own personal use and comfort'.

As she expected, Philip wasted little time pondering her offer and only that morning a messenger had arrived with

558

fond greetings to her ladyship and a welcome thanks for her generosity. He commended her change of heart and allegiance to the new government of the country. Now that his duties in the north were complete, he would hasten down, that Vinelands might be made a fair headquarters in the west of the country.

'Madam,' the commander was saying, 'I know only of your devotion to the royalist cause.'

Sarah deliberated. Was it better to let this man go? He could do little harm, his soldiers had deserted him and such creatures collected together at random would never be apprehended. But what story would he relate to his superiors – to Cromwell and the like? Would Philip be sufficient to protect her? On the other hand, how would it look if Philip arrived to find this Commander Welbeck imprisoned within?

'I am prepared to consider allowing you to depart,' she finally said quietly.

'What mean you?'

'I will not divulge your part in this event. In return, and should the matter ever unfortunately come to light, you will not reveal that any of my servants were involved in the battle.'

The commander looked thoughtfully across the deserted gardens.

'So be it,' he said.

'Of course,' Sarah added, 'should you fail to keep your part of the agreement, I shall feel conjoined to reveal that you committed this crime for your own gain, knowing the house to be already in parliamentary hands.'

'That is not true.'

Sarah smiled.

'I think cousin Philip will listen more readily to my assurances. And now, sir, my men will escort you to the gates to ensure that none of your rabble lurk around.'

When her men returned, assuring her that all was well, she requested Mr Weaver to call all the servants to the

Great Hall. They stood before her, grooms and stableboys, smiths and poulterers, cooks and parlourmaids, cattlemen and ladies of the boudoir.

'We have but a short time,' she said, 'perhaps only a day or two. Pray remove and conceal all the armoury and ordnance. Set about clearing the house of glass and rubble. Repair what you can of the walls. Clean the furnishings and carpets.'

'M'lady,' Mr Weaver said uncertainly, 'it is our intention always to defend you and this house but some are now fearful of what will occur.'

Sarah looked at the anxious faces around her. She remembered suddenly Gabriel standing on the bridge of the Triumph, speaking to the emigrants to the New World on that first day at sea. It was his firmness, his definite words, his appearance of total confidence, that had given them all hope. She smiled calmly.

'It is also my intention, Mr Weaver, never to part with this place. There may be disturbing times ahead but if you all behave as I request, no harm will come. My plan will not fail.'

They set about the tasks as she had stated.

'There is one further matter,' she said to Mr Weaver. 'Pray ensure that all the silver plate, the porcelain bowls, the portraits and decorations, anything of value, are removed. Place them in chests and bury them.'

Mr Weaver smiled. 'Yes, m'lady,' he said.

Philip and Isobel did not arrive for another week, riding up the drive in a wagon with the two older children and the baby in a wooden cot, accompanied by a small troop of soldiers. By that time, Sarah had alerted Catherine and Reginald, John and Urith, William and Katherine to her plan. They all agreed that in the circumstances it was the best that could be hoped for.

Sarah stood on the steps as Philip came towards her, his black cloak looking too large for his thin frame, his flat black hat too wide for his narrow face. He took her hand.

'Madam, greetings.' He gazed around him in dismay. 'But what has occurred here?'

'Ah,' Sarah said sadly. 'I fear this unprotected house was violently attacked.'

'But did you not think to raise the standard of the Army?'

Sarah shook her head dismally.

'No, sir. But we signalled our willingness to surrender, yet still cannon were fired upon us. Women and children.'

She led him into the house.

'And see, sir, what turmoil is created within.'

'But where are all your valuable accoutrements, the gold, the furnishings?'

'Looted, dear Philip. Broken, defaced.'

'But what regiment caused this havoc?'

'It was under the instructions of a Commander Welbeck. We told him of your interest in this place, but he merely laughed scornfully. He intimated that he felt no loyalty to you.'

Philip glowered.

'And where is he now?'

'His soldiers deserted, I fear, unwilling to take part in such a massacre. And he departed some time past, I know not whence.'

'He will soon be apprehended,' Philip said shortly.

'Yet I think fine decorations and valuable properties are no part of your Puritan aims,' Sarah said softly. 'I have heard that the Model Army is devoted to destroying such objects.'

'That should apply only to religious and church appurtenances,' Philip said shortly.

'Ah, I am glad,' Sarah said and she turned to Isobel, standing behind, clutching the baby.

'Come, Isobel,' she said. 'I have prepared a quiet and simple chamber for you both. You will perhaps find the house to your liking, now it is relieved of its extravagances.'

That evening, Sarah revealed over a simple meal that she was prepared to remain at Vinelands to assist with the administration of the estate. Now that it was in their possession, she could ensure that matters proceeded smoothly and to their satisfaction.

Philip greeted the suggestion with pleasure.

'I shall frequently be absent on parliament's business,' he said, 'and dear Isobel must need much help here.'

That night, Sarah looked round her bare chamber with distaste. She suddenly remembered how, in her childhood, Cicely's chamber had been like this in the days when she wished to become a nun, before she met Stephen. She remembered the silent, pale little boy that Philip had been, she could not remember that he had ever spoken. What thoughts had he harboured in that infant mind?

Now, here he was, indulging in the same kind of extreme behaviour as his father, even if it was for a different cause. All extremes become vicious, she thought. Piety always seems to inflict restrictions on other people.

She settled down to a quiet and uneventful life, intent on improving the fortunes and profits of the estate even if it was now mainly to the benefit of Philip and the Puritan cause.

During the summer, she went to visit Penelope in Cornwall when she gave birth to her second child. Sarah had seen little of her daughter-in-law during the war and she now felt a great desire to see her new grandchild. Nicholas had embarked on another journey to the East Indies. The trade of the whole nation had suffered during the Civil War and now everyone hoped that peace might lead to renewed prosperity.

But as Sarah travelled through the countryside, she heard rumours of increasing dissent between Puritans and the Anglican Church, of the greater and greater restrictions imposed by the Army and its parliamentary leaders. Everywhere, she found churches desecrated, houses ruined and an air of despair descending upon the population.

She sighed. Would that she were at this moment in that far land with Gabriel. Life, she thought, had truly never been the same without him.

She returned to Vinelands, to Philip and Isobel and the three children. As she rode up the drive, she looked with sadness at the walls which had not yet been repaired after the bombardment. The house had an air of gloom but she told herself that that would not last. She had managed to stay at Vinelands; one day it would be hers again. 'Live today,' Gabriel had said.

Isobel greeted her quietly. Sarah had little sympathy with this pretty but dreary woman with all her regulations about what the servants should wear, the way they should dress their hair and control the manner of their speech. They were not permitted to leave the estate nor even to walk in the gardens after dusk and any spontaneous behaviour was looked upon as lustful and irreverent.

Sarah frequently managed to speak with the servants, encouraging them to accept the present tiresome regime, promising that it could not last for ever.

But a few days later, news came that cast her into greater gloom. Philip wrote to Isobel that he was heading a regiment under the leadership of Cromwell which had landed in Dublin with an enormous army of twelve thousand men. The Model Army would at last crush the Irish rebels who had continued their revolt unchecked while the English soldiers had been involved in the Civil War.

Isobel read her the letter with pride, certain that the Puritan faith would soon conquer the evil popishness which dominated the Irish.

'It will be dear Philip's desire,' she said, 'to wipe this scourge of Catholicism from the face of the earth.'

'There are many Catholics in this country,' Sarah observed.

'I think they cannot be given the protection of the law for much longer,' Isobel said. 'It is sacrilege to allow them such freedom.'

'What of John and Urith?' Sarah said. 'They are Philip's kith and kin. Would he have them harmed?'

Isobel's face hardened.

'I would not wish them harm, but I think the time approaches when they must renounce their dangerous beliefs or forfeit all they own.'

Sarah restrained her anger. One day she would be revenged upon these two hated creatures; for the moment she would keep silence. Only in that way could she hope to protect Vinelands and the servants and also, it seemed, the rest of the family.

She waited with a morbid anxiety for news from Ireland. Cromwell and his men had advanced, relieving besieged towns, attacking Irish strongholds. Everywhere they went, they achieved victory against the poorly equipped and outnumbered Catholic rebels.

'We despatch the enemy with the utmost vigour,' Philip reported. 'We shall avenge every drop of blood spilled in the Ulster rising.'

Then they reached the Irish-held town of Drogheda. The rebels had a great army there which had previously been unassailable. Sarah knew that Margaret and Robert were within those walls, that English troops had besieged it, tried to storm it, but always without success. Now she waited in an agony of fear until Philip's next communication should arrive.

Rumours spread of the cruelty with which the rebels were being put down, being butchered and slaughtered without mercy, those who surrendered being treated in the same way as the combatants. Then the news came that Drogheda had fallen, defeated.

Isobel read out from Philip's letter. 'It was a long battle. The Irish rebels were determined not to surrender, even women were firing muskets and cannon. They fought with the men in the streets, and when the gates were opened, they continued to use swords alongside their men. A foolish attempt, for they were all slaughtered. Over two thousand men, the whole garrison, were put to the sword. We took no prisoners.'

For a moment, Sarah felt that she must kill this woman, reading the communication with such complacency. Her hatred welled up within her but she turned away, forcing her mind back to Margaret, hoping absurdly that she might have been spared.

'Supposing,' she said suddenly, 'your Philip is killed.'

Isobel shook her head sadly, 'I cannot think of it, yet if it be God's will, I am content. It is his duty to wipe out the heathen, the traitor to England.'

Sarah breathed deeply and walked from the room. It will not last, she told herself, one day you will be defeated.

It was only many months later that she had news from The O'Connell that he had miraculously escaped. Margaret had been murdered in the streets of Drogheda, butchered by the English rabble. Robert had not been found, no-one knew what had happened to him. Few had survived that fateful day and many bodies had been cast into the sea. As to him, he would fight to the end.

Sarah felt the old heartbreak of loss, despair at the finality of death. Dear, dear Margaret with her laughter and hope and enthusiasm. And Robert, lost. And what had happened to Adam's sons, Edward and Robert? Then she began to wonder about Sean. Was he still alive?

She wished that she could go there, to Ireland, to find out for herself what had happened. In her heart, she made a solemn vow that one day she would avenge them all.

38

When Sarah returned from a visit to Cornwall to help
Penelope through her third confinement in the spring of
sixteen hundred and fifty one, she brought the four-year-
old Sarah Clare with her.

On this occasion, Nicholas had ensured that he should
be at home for the birth of their third child. Sarah had
looked at her handsome son with pride and a feeling of
gratitude. In these turbulent times, he still retained that
air of gallantry and solicitude that Gabriel had displayed.
His love of the sea, his stories of his travels and experiences
and Penelope's mystified questioning had reminded her of
her own months of waiting for Gabriel's return from his
voyages.

But this birth had not gone well and the child was still-
born. Sarah said she would take Sarah Clare to Vinelands
with her until Penelope had recovered.

'Mama,' Nicholas said. 'Can you cope with the demands
of Sarah Clare?'

Sarah laughed.

'Dear Sarah Clare is a delightful companion. We shall
have a real holiday. We shall call upon Catherine and
Reginald and I shall take her to the fair at Exeter.'

'And I will see that Penelope rests as you bid.'

'She will have no duties to perform. The wet nurse in
Lostwithiel can bring the child Frances here to visit, to
save Penelope the need to call upon her.'

Penelope smiled.

'I can go in the coach with Nicholas when I am recovered, dear mother.'

Now, as Sarah travelled towards Dartmouth, she looked at the golden-haired child beside her. Of all the grandchildren, it was Sarah Clare who had stolen her heart.

'Perhaps it is because she is my namesake or because of those golden locks. But she does not possess my eye colour,' she thought as the child smiled up at her. Her eyes were dark brown but there were tiny flecks of yellow and green that gave a strange kind of depth to her expression.

'You are a pretty little girl,' Sarah said, holding her hand.

'Mama says perhaps I shall be beautiful like you.'

'Perhaps as I was. Long ago,' Sarah added ruefully.

'No. Mama says you are beautiful now.' The child reached up and stroked Sarah's face. 'Mama says you have smooth skin. And your hair is like mine, grandmama.'

Sarah nodded.

'Why are your eyes green? Oh, when you look at me like that it makes me feel all prickly.' Sarah Clare shivered with delight and cuddled closer to Sarah.

'Silly girl,' Sarah said, laughing.

Yet it was true. She still had the feeling that had been with her all her life, of looking far away into some vast and infinite world, beyond the parameters of this earth. It still had a strange effect on people, as though she were leading them into a dangerous unknown.

Her thoughts turned back to the other grandchildren, to Catherine's three boys. John and Gabriel, the oldest, were now at Blundell's School in Tiverton. Though their parents had a high regard for Merchant Taylor's, where Adam and other members of the family had gone, the dangers of the Civil War had made Reginald reluctant to send them to London. There was, Sarah knew, the even more compelling reason that London was dominated by that parliament of Puritans and extreme Presbyterians. The comparative calm of Devon was a safer place.

Eight-year-old Nicholas was still at home, in the hands of a tutor. He missed the company of his brothers and found the house lonely and silent without them. So it was that when he saw Sarah and her granddaughter arriving at Trevayne Abbey, he dashed from his schoolroom to greet them. Sarah frowned as she watched them dance away across the lawns.

Catherine came towards her and kissed her.

'Dear Mama.'

'Catherine,' Sarah said. 'Nicholas is very pale. And he walks strangely. Has he been injured?'

Catherine's face clouded.

'No. Reginald is bothered about this. His legs have become thin and he has little appetite for his food.'

A deep anxiety pierced Sarah. It was as though she saw the child Gilbert standing before her; the agony of those days and months when she had cared for him, longing for him to recover, flooded through her. It was so long ago, yet it was as though she must once again go through that fearsome experience.

'Do not be so anxious, Mama,' Catherine said, looking at her mother's expression. 'I think it is but a temporary event.'

'Yes, of course it is.' Sarah smiled briefly. 'He merely needs tonic, some herbal tonics.'

'Reginald is in the town,' Catherine said. 'There is some slight epidemic but he thinks it will be only brief.'

'I hope so. And have you visited Vinelands in my absence?'

'Briefly,' Catherine said. 'I find Isobel tedious. And she has made even more rules about the conduct of the servants.'

'What rules?' Sarah asked angrily.

'They are not to wear bodices which reveal any part of their neck or shoulders. And the grace to be uttered

568

before meals has been extended to almost five minutes.'

Sarah groaned.

'My God, I cannot stand this occupation longer. I shall despair.'

'No, Mama, you will not,' Catherine said reassuringly. 'Remember, you have saved the house from further demolition and occupation. One day, you will have it once again in your own administration.'

'I wait only for the time when they are defeated.'

'Mama, Prince Charles has been pronounced King of Scotland. There is still hope.'

'Then let us pray that the Scots invade shortly.'

Reginald entered as she was speaking.

'It is perhaps our only chance,' he said, 'though no-one could hope for yet another civil war. But there is some good news. I rode over to the farm today to see Urith. John informs me that son Thomas is to wed Lady Harriet Keverne. It is to take place in a few months.'

'Thomas is a Presbyterian,' Sarah replied dismissively.

'But of the milder sort,' Reginald said. 'He is not of the Independent persuasion.'

'Then he will also come to grief,' Sarah said cynically. 'And Lady Harriet was an erstwhile supporter of the royalist cause.'

'Then how do they accommodate?' Catherine asked.

'I know not.' Reginald shook his head.

Sarah pursed her lips in doubt.

'I must repair to Vinelands shortly. Would not young Nicholas like to accompany me? He appears to find Sarah Clare a ready companion. He must miss the company of his brothers.'

'Perhaps, for a few days,' Reginald said readily. 'While I am treating this epidemic in the town it will be better for him to be away.'

They returned to Vinelands the next day. The two children sat together in the coach, giggling excitedly.

'Perhaps it is simply loneliness that makes him so peaky,' Sarah thought hopefully but as she studied his face, she noticed the pink flush on his cheeks that she had observed with Gilbert.

When they reached Vinelands, Sarah found the servants lined up in the Great Hall, being inspected by Isobel.

'What goes on here?'

'I have found a lack of modesty amongst those younger members of the household,' Isobel said sharply.

Sarah looked, smiling quietly at each of them.

'I find nothing objectionable,' she said.

'You may go,' Isobel said curtly to the assembly, then she turned to Sarah. 'They must be kept under constant surveillance.'

'Madam, you demean yourself,' Sarah said coldly.

Isobel blushed. 'What mean you?'

'It is no part of a lady's duty to occupy herself with such details. I left such matters to the housekeeper. Do you not occupy yourself in prayer?'

Isobel blushed even redder.

'I chastise myself as much as I do them,' she said.

'Ah,' Sarah replied, 'I begin to wonder if you concern yourself as much with your own heinous sins.'

She looked at Isobel, deliberately staring into that pious and now doubting face.

'Sarah,' Isobel said, 'you cannot doubt my devotion.'

Sarah shrugged and began to walk away. Perhaps in the end she could demolish this creature.

Isobel followed her.

'It is of some import,' she said, 'that all the servants are well-trained. Philip is to bring his brother John and his wife Philippa back with him on the morrow. They are to stay here for some time.'

'But John is a Presbyterian minister. I thought such mild persons met not with your approval.'

'Ah, perhaps we would wish him to mend the errors of his ways. He has not yet achieved that grace that we could wish. But he comes for the purpose of officiating at the wedding of dear cousin Thomas. The wedding will be here and not at the farm which could scarcely accommodate such an event.'

'And do John and Urith agree to this arrangement?'

'Philip has persuaded them that it is in the best interests of all.'

Sarah breathed deeply. Those two quiet Catholics would attend the celebrations, they would conceal their disappointment that Thomas was not and never had been a Catholic. And indeed cousin John, the Presbyterian preacher, seemed as mild a man as her own brother John.

'And will the two children also be accommodated here?'

'Yes, they do not believe in sending babies out to nurse. Dear Philippa attends to her own feeding.'

Sarah did not allow Nicholas to remain long at Vinelands. Philip's treatment of his three children followed that of his father Stephen's towards him, except that he was even more critical of their behaviour. They were allowed to speak only when addressed, made to move as silently as possible and every evening to confess their sins. If they could recollect none, they were instantly beaten for pride and arrogance. Even three-year-old James did not escape his wrath and the house seemed to be constantly filled with the sound of children's screams and for Sarah the even more depressing repetition of prayers. But when Philip attempted one day to incorporate Nicholas into the regime by insisting that he should kneel for an hour on a stone floor for failing to walk quietly through the hall, Sarah turned on him with a violence that subdued even him.

'You will have no authority whatever over either Nicholas or Sarah Clare,' Sarah said icily. 'These children are in my charge, I am their grandmother and I will not have your interference.'

Philip would have remonstrated, demanded that all children be brought up in the true religion, but he hesitated. He had heard that day that Katherine had suffered a severe stroke, that it was feared she could not last, and he had just returned with the intention of breaking the news to Sarah.

So he said mildly, 'Madam, it is for the good of their own souls. The true faith cannot be taught too early.'

'Nicholas is a weakly child,' Sarah replied. 'He shall not be treated thus.'

'Madam,' Philip said. 'I fear I have other news for you.'

'What?' Sarah frowned in apprehension. All news now seemed to be undesirable.

'I have to say that my dear aunt Katherine is seriously ill.'

'Katherine! Why did you not inform me?'

'Madam, I have received the news only within this hour. I have come instantly.'

Sarah grabbed Nicholas and Sarah Clare and called for the coach. She shouted at the coachman to gallop faster, faster, down the drive, over the hills to Greenhayes. She dashed up the steps, into the hall and straight up the stairs, clutching Sarah Clare in her arms. Suddenly, she stopped and turned. Nicholas was trying to keep up with her, his cheeks flushed with the effort.

'Carry the boy,' she said to a servant. 'Bring him up.'

William was just leaving Katherine's chamber as Sarah rushed along the corridor. She looked at him questioningly but he seemed to look through her without comprehension.

'Oh, William, am I too late?'

She set the child down and William put his arms round her, his body shaking with emotion.

'It's so sudden, Sarah.'

Sarah burst into tears and the children began to cry, frightened by the behaviour of their elders. Sarah took the children's hands.

'There,' she said comfortingly. 'It's all right. Give them some refreshment,' she said to a servant, then followed William into Katherine's chamber.

'She knew nothing,' William said. 'She did not regain any awareness.'

Sarah looked at Katherine through her tears. She looked smaller in death, neat and quiet in a way she had never looked in life.

'She was never still,' Sarah said. 'She was never meant to die.'

'Oh, Sarah,' William said brokenly. 'It is like the end of my life.'

Pictures flickered across Sarah's mind of Katherine in a thousand situations, from the moment when she came into the library in her green gown on that first day at Vinelands, talking in her garden bower at Vinelands, laughing, dancing, sad, desperate, but always filled with that warmth that only she possessed.

'And now she is cold,' Sarah said to herself.

The funeral was quiet and simple, the great processions of the past were no longer allowed. But there was a large congregation at St Saviour's, not only of the many members of the family, but of the citizens of Dartmouth. Katherine's son Richard and his wife Judith came from their home in Dorset but her daughter Elizabeth and husband Edward could not risk returning from Paris. The persecution of the royalists had not abated and many had now emigrated to the Continent.

John Kerswill conducted the service and Philip gave a long sermon about the dangers of pride and arrogance and the need constantly to examine one's soul to seek out the devil within. Afterwards they all returned to their own homes and the following day Sarah went to Cornwall with Sarah Clare. Penelope welcomed her eagerly, saying that she must remain until Nicholas returned in a few days' time. He had only gone to London on business.

'I am happy enough to be away from Vinelands,' Sarah admitted. 'Perhaps the past can never be retrieved.'

'Would you not prefer to remain here with us?' Penelope suggested. 'You would have Sarah Clare to entertain you.'

'Perhaps, but I cannot leave Vinelands. I feel that I cannot forsake that place. And dear William is much in need of comfort. Though Richard is a devoted son and visits frequently.'

When Nicholas returned he brought with him a young man whom Sarah did not recognise. Auburn hair, a serious countenance.

'I was but a child when last we met,' he said.

'Yet,' she said, smiling uncertainly, 'there is something about you. Who was your father?'

'I am Adam's son, Robert. I have come from Thė O'Connell.'

'Ah,' her face lit up with joy. 'You are so welcome and I long for news of everyone.'

'It is not happy,' he said slowly. 'I fear that Ireland is no more. It is given over to bloodshed and violence; the Irish have come to the end of their existence.'

'But what of Robert, your stepfather, and Sean? And surely The O'Connell cannot be defeated,' Sarah protested.

'Come,' Penelope interrupted. 'Let us first repair to the dining hall, where food awaits us.'

Sarah ate little as she listened to Robert's painful story. Yet he spoke in a strangely quiet and even voice, as though he were devoid of anger and resentment. Perhaps he was beyond such emotions.

'After the slaughter of Drogheda,' he said, 'I went to search for my mother and stepfather. My mother had insisted on remaining in the besieged town with him. When the attack came and the army broke down the walls and gained entry, the women fought as fiercely as the men. In death, they still held their weapons; pickaxes, forks.'

'Mama,' Nicholas said. 'Do you wish to hear this sad story?'

'Yes,' Sarah and Penelope replied together.

'I think this story must be told,' Robert said, 'though I would spare you much of its horror. I found my mother.'

574

He paused. Sarah waited, unable to look at him. 'She was pierced through the heart.'

In the silence that followed, Sarah tried to look straight at the meaning of his words. It would be an insult to Margaret to refuse to face that final, ghastly event.

'I took her away,' Robert continued. 'She is buried within the grounds of her home, in an unmarked grave.' He cleared his throat. 'I went back to search for my stepfather. He was not then to be found but at least here was one of the miracles of war. When he was wounded, one of his soldiers dragged him to the cellar of a house. There he was tended by a woman who at night took him out of the town to a farmhouse that he might recover to return to fight. But by that time, the battle was over.'

'And then?' Sarah asked.

'After some months, he appeared at the home of my grandfather, O'Connell.'

Sarah sighed with relief.

'At least, Robert survived,' she said. 'And what of them now?'

'The terrible retribution continued,' Robert said. 'The massed armies of Scots and English have taken everything. The new Act for the Settlement of Ireland has meant that every Irishman has been dispossessed. They are all betrayed, Catholic and Protestant alike, even the Old English who were loyal always to the Crown. All who had allegiance to the Irish cause must forfeit part of their estates to the invaders.'

'And The O'Connell?' Sarah asked. 'He was surely beyond the age for battle.'

Robert smiled.

'He will never be that but now all Irish are commanded to move into Connaught or Clare. There they are given a portion of land equivalent to that which they might have retained in their own county. Their own properties are taken over by officers of the English and Scots armies.'

'And what of Sean?' Sarah asked quietly. She glanced at her son. Nicholas had never known of that episode; at the time he was away on the high seas with Gabriel.

'Sean has been our hope, he still is,' Robert replied. 'He has fought in so many battles yet miraculously survived almost unscathed. In fact, he boasts a sword wound about his neck which would have severed any lesser man's head from his shoulders.'

At that moment, Sarah Clare danced into the dining hall to bid her parents goodnight.

Sarah picked her up and kissed her.

'What problems are we preparing for our grandchildren and future generations?' she said. 'What wickedness is being perpetrated in the name of England?'

'When can we go to another fair, Grandmama?' the child asked.

'Soon,' Sarah promised. 'When one occurs, I will come for you.'

As Sarah Clare was led away by her nurse, Nicholas observed, 'Soon even the fairs will be banned as lascivious and immoral.'

'But Sean,' Sarah went on, 'you were telling us, Robert.'

'Yes. He now has emigration plans. He and O'Connell are to sell what little they have retained and go to the New World. Thousands of Irish soldiers are leaving their native soil to escape not only the English troops but also the famine and disease which rages in Ireland. In the New World, they will be free.'

'Would that I could see them before they depart,' Sarah said ruefully, 'yet it is scarcely possible. But what of you, Robert? Do you go also?'

Robert smiled. 'No. I have work to do in Ireland.'

'Work?' Nicholas queried. 'There is surely little enough remaining for you.'

'I am a priest,' Robert said quietly. 'I cannot leave my people.'

'Oh, no,' Sarah said in a hopeless voice.

Her life seemed to have been dominated by the terrible persecution of Catholics, the hiding of priests, the treatment of recusants, the laws and taxes, the trials and executions, and the situation seemed ever to deteriorate.

'It is my choice,' Robert said. 'And perhaps it is not as fearful as you dread. The Irish are quite segregated from the occupiers of our country. The invaders may perhaps show more toleration, or at least display little interest, in our spiritual affairs.'

'And what do you here in England?' Nicholas asked.

'I have much business to attend to in this country. Then I go to the Continent, though not for many months, to endeavour to raise some assistance for the poor Irish. It is to be hoped that the Queen will listen sympathetically to our plight.'

'I have a mind to accompany you thence, Robert,' Sarah said thoughtfully.

'Mama,' Nicholas protested, 'it is a hazardous journey in these times and for what purpose? And you have always protested that you cannot leave Vinelands.'

'No. I would not wish to. Yet since dear Katherine's death, I have longed to visit Elizabeth and Edward. The nature of their parting was most sad and it must have caused her much pain not to attend her mother's funeral. And as I pass through Dorset, I can visit upon Richard and Judith.'

There was much argument but Sarah was adamant.

'It will mean that I also escape from the confines of Vinelands for a period,' she said.

Early in the new year, she departed with Robert for Paris. As they travelled up through the damaged countryside, through Dorset and Wiltshire with its desecrated churches and war-ravaged villages and dark-clothed citizens, its strange dispirited atmosphere, she began to feel an increasing excitement that she was leaving these shores. When she went to the New World with Gabriel, she had not felt this sense of hope; at that time, she had been too fearful and anxious.

They took the boat at Gravesend, Robert acting as her servant and protector, and when she stepped on to French soil she felt a wild joy, a release from what seemed to be a bottomless abyss into which England was descending.

'It is like suddenly being on a mountain,' she laughed to Robert, 'as though we had suddenly been transported to the clouds.'

Robert smiled and sighed also with relief.

As they travelled on an uncomfortable coach to Paris, she looked out on the French countryside, at the flat landscape slowly changing to wooded hills and gentle slopes.

'It truly looks no more prosperous than England,' she observed. 'Yet there is not that dread in the countenances of the people.'

Elizabeth, alerted to her coming, greeted them as the coach travelled up the short drive to her town house near the Louvre where Queen Henrietta Maria, widow of Charles I, resided. Sarah followed her into the vividly papered drawing room, with its ornate furnishings and heavy red velvet draperies.

'Oh, Elizabeth,' Sarah said, 'what a delight to see you, and to stand in such a room once more.'

Elizabeth embraced her eagerly.

'Dear, dear aunt. Oh, I cannot tell you how we have anticipated your visit.'

'And Robert, your cousin,' Sarah said turning to him. 'You will not even remember each other.'

Robert took Elizabeth's hand and she said, 'And what business have you here, sir? We must be of help to you.'

'I am a priest,' he said. 'I come to gather help for my countrymen.'

Sarah looked round anxiously, but Elizabeth laughed.

'It is not a matter for concern, dear aunt. Catholics here

do not go in fear of their lives. A priest is an honoured person.'

'I just cannot imagine it,' Sarah replied. 'All my life . . . It seems impossible.'

Then Edward came in, wearing the elegant attire of a French courtier, to greet them and inform them that that evening they would attend a ball to be given by the Marquise d'Avignon.

Robert demurred but when Edward heard the purpose of his visit, he said, 'The priesthood in this country do not retreat from these events, sir. It would be wise for you to attend. Prince Charles, who is at St Germaine, is likely to be present and also his mother. It is from the Queen that you may get assistance.'

'I have no gowns for such an event,' Sarah said. 'In England, such finery would be deplored.'

'Come,' Elizabeth said. 'Let us go to my chamber. You will find much to please you.' She looked appraisingly at Sarah. 'It is quite absurd,' she said, laughing, 'you look more like my sister than my aunt.'

As she held up the silk and satin gowns for inspection, Sarah said, 'It is strange, Elizabeth. Dear Katherine, your mother, once did this same thing when I first arrived at Vinelands. It is as though I were a waif all over again.'

Elizabeth sat down on the edge of her bed.

'Tell me about her. Oh, Sarah, it has been so hard,' she suddenly said tearfully.

'Yes, I know,' Sarah said comfortingly. 'But she was not unhappy, dear Elizabeth. Your father loved her dearly and they gave much support to each other.'

Sarah sat down beside her and the afternoon passed to evening as she told her of all the events in England, the births and marriages and deaths, the tears and laughter and the Puritan behaviour of Philip and Isobel and of how one day, when all this was over, she would regain Vinelands and all would be happy again.

'Ah, I would that I shared your hope,' Elizabeth said.

'The English here speak in the same way. They are convinced that one day Charles will return as King. Yet that seems a distant prospect.'

'I know that it will come about,' Sarah said firmly, 'though sometimes it is hard to be patient.'

They went in Edward's carriage to the ball, which was held in a great mansion on the other side of Paris. Golden chandeliers hung from the ceiling, the walls were festooned with silk tassels designed in the shape of crowns and coronets, huge mirrors reflected the lights from a thousand candles standing in tall silver stands.

Sarah entered behind Edward and Elizabeth. She wore an ice blue gown cut low at the back with the skirt open at one side to reveal the trimmings of her blue lace petticoats. On her head was a small jewelled coronet. As she entered, all eyes turned to inspect this new arrival. She was presented to the Marquise and later to the Queen, who came in with Harry Jermyn, purported to be her lover for many years.

'I thought this coronet which you suggested might be over-extravagant,' she confided to Elizabeth. 'But now I see you were right. I have never seen such magnificence in the houses of England.'

'No,' Elizabeth agreed. 'There is much wealth here and these events occur in Paris almost nightly.'

Sarah looked round at the dancers. There seemed to be as many English people present as French; all those royalists who had escaped at the end of the civil war now congregated in this city.

She spent the next few weeks with Elizabeth in a whirl of dinners, theatre visits, balls and entertainments. There were also gatherings of the English aristocrats, discussing the future of England, planning and scheming for the return of Charles to the throne.

The months passed; Christmas came and went and England had begun to seem a distant and dismal place. Sarah found herself wondering how the English in France managed to retain that enthusiasm and hope that they all displayed. Early in sixteen hundred and fifty-three, she decided to return.

'If I stay longer,' she confided to Elizabeth, 'I might find it difficult to return at all.'

'You are so welcome to stay,' Elizabeth said. 'You could return when victory has been achieved.'

'No,' Sarah said. 'I feel that I must be at Vinelands. There is always the fear that it might finally be taken from me totally.'

Robert had already departed to the shores of Ireland and she returned to England alone. Her first sight of the coast made her feel cold and tired and as she travelled back to Dartmouth she could think only of that gay and carefree life she had left behind in Paris.

That year, the gloom became more intense. Military rule was established by Cromwell and the Model Army officers, the Independents took over in parliament and ran the country and Oliver Cromwell set himself up as the Protector. Restrictions increased as the Puritans gained complete power and those who did not agree with their religious ideas were deprived of their livings. The Puritan form of service was instituted in all churches. The observance of Christmas Day was prohibited and the Saints' Days, which had meant a holiday for the labourers and poor, were abolished. Any hint of popishness was savagely persecuted and repressed.

Sarah feared constantly for the safety of John and Urith and dear Catherine and Reginald. But she realized that strangely it was Philip and Isobel who felt isolated and alone. Far away from the rigid religion and politics of London, the people of Devon wanted only peace and prosperity. Only a minority had any inclination for the extreme Puritan ethic.

Yet during the next two years, Sarah began to notice a change in the attitude of the people of Dartmouth. For over a century, the country had been governed first by a Catholic queen, then a Protestant one, followed by a Scotsman who had faced them with his own brand of the reformed faith. Then Charles had presented them with his own autocratic rule and a high church run by bishops and the Lords.

But the present ruler had turned out to be as autocratic. Under the grim regime of censorious Puritanism, the country began to tire of all confrontation and extremism. The majority of the citizens of Dartmouth watched in fear and dismay the frenzied antics of the fanatics, the peremptory trials of Anglicans and royalists, the dismissal of uncooperative judges, the revival of witch-hunts, the pious and violent pronouncements of those who perceived themselves to be righteous. The Barebones parliament selected by Army leaders in sixteen hundred and fifty-three was dissolved. Power was then handed back to the Army. Parliament met again in September but was dissolved by Cromwell in the following January. Another royalist uprising in the spring of sixteen hundred and fifty-five led to more total military rule, when eleven major generals were each given power over an area of England.

At that time, Sarah was staying with Katherine's son Richard and his wife Judith in Dorset after the birth of their second child, Ursula.

'She will be another Katherine,' Sarah said. 'She has her black hair and already that eager little face. I would that she could have seen her.'

'Mama was not much addicted to infants,' Richard observed.

'No,' Sarah admitted. 'Yet she would surely have warmed to this little creature.'

When Sarah returned to Vinelands on a July afternoon, rumbling slowly up the drive in the old coach that had long been in need of repair, looking out across the fields, passing John's farm, crossing the bridge, to stop finally at the steps of the house, she had a strange feeling that instead of arriving she was saying farewell. She stood looking towards the stables and then to the sweep of the hills beyond.

'This place,' she thought, 'is in my soul. Yet will the moment come, as Richard believes, and Elizabeth and Edward in Paris, when the world will return to what we once knew?'

She climbed the steps slowly. As she passed through the door, Philip came towards her in the company of two men.

'Madam,' Philip said quietly. 'We have awaited your return.'

Sarah looked at them questioningly.

One of the men bowed.

'It has come to our intelligence that you have been involved in a conspiracy to harm our Lord Protector.'

Sarah laughed.

'I have no interest in such pursuits,' she said sarcastically, 'I leave such activities to better persons than myself.'

Philip said, 'It is their desire that you shall accompany them to Exeter, there to be examined by the magistrates.'

'Examined!'

Then Sarah looked at them in silence. She had a vivid picture of visiting Gabriel in the Tower all those years ago, the judges, the court. She had dealt with them then, she could do so again.

'Come,' she said calmly. 'Let us depart, that you may have your little entertainment.'

It was she who led them, out into the July sunshine.

39

Sarah looked down through the windows of her cell on the snow-covered courtyard below. Guards were leading in another group of prisoners. Their arrest must have been one of the usual dawn raids, because one of them was dressed still in his night attire, with only a flimsy cloak across his shoulders. Another man wore a wooden crucifix around his neck and Sarah felt a pang of anxiety. Ever since she bade farewell to Robert in Paris, she had feared his apprehension and arrest. But word came that he had reached Ireland safely.

She turned away, shivering, as the prisoners disappeared into the building and she pulled her woollen cloak closer round her body. Her thin shoes could not keep out the cold of the stone floor and the only warmth was provided by a candle which lit her gloomy cell.

She straightened the coverlet on the wooden bed and sat down. Food would not be brought for an hour yet, perhaps two, and the bread was likely to be too dry and hard to consume. Perhaps she was fortunate that her early childhood had been so deprived: at least she could endure the pangs of hunger with a kind of indifference which those of the other aristocratic prisoners found impossible. She stood up when the door was suddenly unlocked.

A gaoler entered.

'I have permitted a special visit,' he said peremptorily and looked at her meaningfully.

In spite of the excitement she felt, she looked at him

indifferently, felt in the purse attached inside her gown and handed him some money. He took it without a word and went out again and then William stood before her.

'Dear Sarah,' he said, embracing her eagerly. 'Ah, you are cold. What a wretched place this is.'

'But what brings you?' Sarah asked anxiously.

William smiled grimly. 'Yes, it is only bad news which permits a special visit.'

Sarah sat down on her bed, indicating a chair before the small wooden table which was her only furniture. She began to cough, taking great gasps of breath.

'Sarah, your cough worsens.'

'It is only the cold of this place,' she said, 'and the only air I get is in that uncongenial yard below. I will recover quickly enough when I leave here. But William, what news?'

'Urith died but two days ago of a congestion on her lungs.'

Sarah sighed heavily.

'Dear, patient Urith. And poor John. How can he manage without her?'

'Catherine and Reginald stay with him at the moment, but it will be hard for him to run the farm alone.'

'I will write a letter that you may take with you. And how are Richard and Judith?'

'They are well, Sarah, though Richard finds the court work hard under this regime. But I have also a letter for you from Elizabeth and Edward. They remain in Paris but say that the time cannot be long delayed till their return.'

Sarah put the letter in her bodice.

'May that be so,' she said. 'I will read it later. It gives me some comfort.'

'There is some good news,' William said. 'O'Connell and his grandson Edward and his family have reached the Jamestown settlement with Margaret's two other children, Louise and Cavendish.'

Sarah smiled.

'Good news indeed. Perhaps they will find peace at last.'

'But to other matters, Sarah. How fare you here?'

Sarah made a face.

'Each week I come before the magistrates. They ask the same absurd questions. What did I do in Paris? With what royalists did I consort? Who are the traitors in this country? I repeat the same answers, declaring my ignorance. They threaten me with all manner of violence which so far they have failed to administer.'

William shook his head unhappily.

'I make representations on your behalf weekly but the Army has a dire influence and everyone fears to cross it.'

'I am sure your efforts have protected me so far,' Sarah said, 'be not disheartened, dear William.'

'It is not I who should be discouraged, but you. You show much fortitude in these circumstances.'

'I would not allow these contemptible creatures to defeat me,' Sarah said, 'and I have also had in here much time for reflection.'

Suddenly the door was opened and the gaoler indicated that it was time for William to depart.

'Catherine and Reginald will visit you shortly,' William said, 'if we have not previously gained your release.'

He passed the gaoler some coins and said, 'You will permit the daughter of Viscountess Hooper Humphreys to pass when she comes.'

The man did not reply but half-nodded.

When William had gone, Sarah opened the letter from Elizabeth. She said that in spite of the departure of Charles and his court, Paris saw the constant arrival of royalists from England. They deplored the depressed state of England, the decline in trade, the desecration of churches and Cromwell's latest proclamation that no member of the Church of England was allowed to preach.

'As a Catholic nation,' Elizabeth reported, 'the French are appalled at such fearsome laws.'

When Catherine and Reginald visited her two months later, they told of churches being raided by soldiers, of vicars being imprisoned and threatened, with muskets held against their heads, that they would be shot.

Reginald looked at Sarah with concern.

'You cannot remain in this place,' he said angrily. 'You will waste away and your cough is worse. I will see the magistrates again.'

Sarah said slowly, 'I have had much time to reflect, dear Reginald. It is now clear to me that I am not held because of any suspicions they have of me.'

'What mean you, Mama?' Catherine asked.

'The only person who can benefit from my incarceration, the only one who could desire it, is Philip.'

Reginald frowned. 'Could he be thus depraved?'

'He must fear my wish to retain Vinelands. If he can be rid of me, he can keep this property as his own. I think he sees me as a constant challenge to his ownership.'

'But Mama,' Catherine said hopelessly, 'if this be true, make a deed to his permanent ownership. It matters not. Any member of the family would be willing enough to forego his inheritance if it means your freedom.'

'No.' Sarah's eyes flashed angrily. 'It will never be relinquished to such a creature.'

Reginald and Catherine looked at each other.

'Pray, do nothing to facilitate such a thing,' Sarah said.

She asked them about the progress of John and Gabriel, now at Cambridge, and Reginald also reported that young Nicholas had improved in health. Nicholas and Penelope sent their love and Sarah Clare had sent Sarah a miniature of herself.

When they left, she said, 'Do not worry about me. I shall be more comfortable in these warm clothes you have brought though I hope soon there will be warmer weather. And give my love to the dear children. But I worry much about young Nicholas.'

587

'Believe me, dear mother, he is greatly improved,' Reginald assured her but Sarah only smiled sadly.

As the months passed she felt herself more and more remote from the outside world. She began to look upon that faraway place called Vinelands as though it were a picture in her mind. She saw all the events over the years, the people who had come and gone, the feelings of love and hate and anger and joy as though they were each isolated into separate cubicles, without connection with each other or with her now.

Could she ever return to that life? Was she really meant to remain for ever on the hills like Granny Lott, an outcast from this life? Perhaps the happiest years of her life had been those with Gabriel in the New World, when no Vinelands intruded.

At last, was she free of the need for that security? In a way, though Gabriel had loved the place, he had always been free, always able to walk out and leave. Perhaps, she thought, soon I will join him.

Sarah was permitted visits every two or three months and although all her family made constant representations for her release, the months passed into years. She saw two more springs dawn, two more summers fade away, before Nicholas came to see her one September day to report that Cromwell had died.

Sarah felt a great surge of hope.

'Does it mean the King will return?'

Nicholas shook his head.

'His son, Richard, has been appointed as Protector, but at last I believe events will change. I think he cannot last.'

He told her also that John had died, unable to live without the beloved Urith who had sustained him.

Sarah wept bitterly at the news, as she had for Katherine and Adam. They had been the real part of her childhood, they had been there for ever.

'And what of the farm?' she asked when she had recovered herself.

'Philip has agreed that John's son, Thomas, shall take it over. As he is now a good follower of the Puritan faith, he can have no objection.' Nicholas sighed and added, 'Mama, William has been to the magistrates again this week. They say they refer your case once more to the higher authorities.'

After Nicholas had gone, Sarah's thoughts returned to John and Urith. They had led such a quiet, uneventful life, immersed in the farm and each other; and their religion, she reflected. It was as though they had never been a part of those dramatic events taking place in the country. Perhaps theirs had been true love, she thought ironically.

Then she thought of Vinelands. Now that John was gone, she tried to persuade herself that there could be no problems about the inheritance. Nicholas would inherit it, as she intended. Although she had always been determined about that, she felt a great relief that it was settled.

The next day she was called again before the authorities. The gaoler led her through the cold passages past the cells, some crowded with prisoners, some in which there was an individual silent and alone, and up the stairs to the examining room. The magistrates sat before her, three sombre men in black cloaks, a heavy bible on the bench before them.

The central figure looked at her quizzically. He had a long thin face and his eyes looked half-veiled. Like a vulture, she thought.

'It would be well, madam, if you admitted your implication in the plot to overthrow the Protector.'

'The late Protector,' Sarah corrected.

'His son now reigns in his stead.'

Sarah merely smiled contemptuously.

'We have knowledge that when you journeyed to Paris, you were in the company of a Jesuit priest.'

Sarah looked at them without expression, concealing her concern that they had this information. Had Robert been

589

seized in Ireland? No. They had got this knowledge from an informer.

'You allow your imagination to run riot,' she said.

The chief magistrate blushed with anger.

'Madam, this creature will be brought to justice as you have been.'

Sarah breathed a sigh of relief. Robert had not been captured.

'You waste your time, sir. I have performed no treasonable act.'

'You fought on the royalist side.'

'As did many. My house is now given over to one of your Puritan brethren.'

A second man leaned forward.

'Madam, if you will sign the declaration rejecting all royalist connections and condemning all Catholic activities, your release might be obtained.'

Sarah looked at each of them in turn; they shuffled their papers. She had no sure knowledge of what was happening in the country, yet these three men now exhibited an aura of uncertainty previously foreign to them.

'Gentlemen,' she said suddenly, once again looking at each of them in turn, 'I have an intuition that you yourselves are in a precarious situation.'

'Madam,' the chief official began, but she interrupted boldly, 'Sirs, be not misled. That Sir Philip Kerswill for whom you act will not protect you in your hour of need.'

They all stared at her in astonishment. One of them stood up in indignation.

'Ah, I see it is the truth,' she said triumphantly. 'And I see, too, that your day of judgment cannot be far hence. Soon the country will rise against you. Do you suppose that Sir Philip will then admit to his involvement? He will betray you as he has betrayed me.'

The chief magistrate called for the gaoler.

'Return her to the cell,' he said.

Sarah was grabbed by the gaoler, but she added calmly,

'You would be advised to consult that gentleman. It is he who will one day be named as a traitor.'

Two weeks later, Philip came. Sarah received him coldly.

'Madam,' he said, 'in view of your age and the connections of our birth, I have pleaded with the magistrates for your release.'

Sarah smiled sardonically.

'I must owe you gratitude,' she said. 'And have you been successful?'

'You are permitted to leave this place in my company. We shall depart to Vinelands tonight.'

'What becomes of you, Philip,' Sarah said, 'when your masters are defeated?'

Philip looked at her in astonishment.

'Madam, pray do not address me thus. Your freedom lies within my hands.'

'Sir,' she said icily and she looked at him with a long, cold glare, 'there is nothing that you can do that can disturb me. Let us be away.'

She felt a great strength inside her. At last, she knew it was not Vinelands that could give her identity. Power lay within herself. She knew now that she had no fear of anything. The future could never again hold any terror for her.

She walked from the cell before him and Philip followed in silence.

591

40

Sarah returned to a different world from the one she had been taken from over two years before.

As she rode in silence with Philip down through Totnes to Dartmouth she sensed a new attitude of defiance. She observed people walking in the town pushing past the Puritans, recognizable by their plain black garb, the unstarched ruffs about their necks and their short, severe haircuts. On one occasion, she even saw one Puritan gentleman facing four elegantly attired young men who would not give way for him. Eventually, he stepped into the road and they let him pass.

Sarah smiled and glanced at Philip. He also had seen the incident and he frowned in distaste.

'I have not seen these fashions for some time past,' she said in approval.

'The country becomes dissolute with the indecisions of government,' Philip said curtly. 'The restraints and modest behaviour of our beliefs are everywhere challenged.'

Sarah smiled again.

'Oh,' she said, 'you fill me with much hope.'

'Pray remember, madam, that you are much dependent upon my goodwill and protection. When this parliament is regularized, dissidents will be routed out and dealt with.'

'I fancy,' she said, 'that we shall not again be cursed with civil war.'

'I pray not, madam.'

'There would be no-one who could be persuaded to fight upon the government side,' she retorted.

As they passed through the gates of the estate and went up the long drive, the workers in the fields turned to wave to her and when they halted at the house, the coachman came to help her down the step and said softly, 'Welcome home, m'lady.'

If Philip heard the remark, he gave no indication but marched up the steps in front of her. As they entered the Great Hall, they were greeted by a crowd of servants, all waving and laughing with delight.

Philip shouted at them to be silent, to desist from this unseemly behaviour, but they ignored him as though he did not exist. Yet when Sarah began to speak, there was instant silence.

'Thank you,' she said shakily. 'I am overcome. Let us now prepare for that day when this shall truly be our home once again.'

There were cheers and shouts and suddenly Isobel appeared on the stairs.

She slowly descended and said sharply to Philip, 'How do you permit this effrontery, Philip? Do you not control this impertinence?'

Philip blushed.

'Isobel, the times are difficult and uncertain. We do not need to increase that chaos.'

She stopped and looked at him in bewilderment.

'Have you taken leave of your senses?' she said angrily. 'You are the master here. You belong with the government of this country. Who would dare to defy you?'

The whole assembly stood, looking expressionlessly at her and then at Philip.

Sarah turned to him. 'Tell them,' she said, 'give them your orders.'

He looked at her with hatred and said shortly, 'I have no orders at the moment,' then walked quickly from the hall. Isobel turned and ran back up the stairs.

Sarah nodded to them all meaningfully and they turned away quietly to return to their labours.

Sarah went up to her chamber and Emily came in, exclaiming with distress how pale and weak she had become.

'Ah, dear Emily,' Sarah said, embracing her eagerly, 'how long it has been.'

'You must rest, m'lady. You are in need of victuals.'

'I do not need rest. I have had enough of that. Now I am back, I shall be well. But let me see in the looking-glass. I have been denied one for so long.'

She looked quietly at the image before her.

'Yes,' she said. 'My sojourn has done me much harm. Perhaps I have lost my looks for ever.'

Emily smiled. 'You will never lose those, m'lady. In a few weeks, you will recover.'

And indeed over the next few months, the colour returned to her cheeks, the round contours returned to her figure and even her cough seemed to disappear.

When Catherine and Reginald came, Reginald expressed satisfaction with her progress.

'We feared at one time we would lose you for ever,' Catherine said. 'I went to London myself to speak with the government officials. But they denied any involvement in the affair.'

'Perhaps they spoke the truth,' Sarah said. 'It is perhaps as I feared and only Philip can be blamed.'

Now they visited her regularly, bringing the children with them. Young Nicholas seemed to have recovered somewhat from his malady, but Sarah could never efface the image of Gilbert. So often she had convinced herself that he had improved and so like him young Nicholas seemed to be.

During the summer, Nicholas and Penelope came from Cornwall with Sarah Clare and the other two children, Frances and Cicely. At twelve, Sarah Clare seemed to be a replica of herself at that age, with her long golden

594

hair and distant expression. Only her brown eyes were different. She loved to listen to Sarah's stories of her own childhood, of her life on the hills and then her sudden arrival at Vinelands. They walked round the estate, over the hills to where the old shack had been and down to Jawbones and the harbour below. Sarah told her about the house, the history of the old priory and the castle above. One day, she told her about the hidden chapel and the priests who had lived there.

Meanwhile, there was growing anarchy in the country. By October, the split in the government between the army and the more moderate element had reduced the country to chaos. Rumours reached Dartmouth that the King had returned to Scotland and that soon he would return south as King.

As Sarah's hopes rose, Philip and Isobel became more and more distraught and she came upon them constantly in quiet corners of the house, anxiously whispering to each other.

There were frequent attempts for parliament to meet, only to be dissolved. The Army generals wanted military government, the City of London and parliament refused to cooperate. Richard Cromwell was unable to control events and he was finally overtaken by supporters of the King. General Monck, the commander of the army in Scotland, where Charles had been crowned King in 1651, came south but did not reveal his plans until he reached London early the following year. Parliament, once more asserting itself, gave him orders to arrest the leading members of the government. He then negotiated for the return of the King. It was an event which had come to appear as inevitable to the whole country. Philip made visits to London, seeming to be more and more uncertain whether to support the Army generals or parliament.

A few days after such a visit, a messenger arrived. A steward received the document.

'It comes from London, m'lady, for Sir Philip,' he said to Sarah. 'It has the seal of government upon it.'

Sarah took it from the silver salver.

'I will take it to him,' she said.

She entered the library. Philip stood at the window.

'Sir,' she said, 'do I find you inactive at moments of such crisis?'

He did not reply and she passed him the packet.

'Perhaps it is good news from London,' she said.

Philip opened and read it and glanced at Sarah. He was about to place it in his doublet, then he shrugged and passed it to her. It reported that members of the government had been arrested in London. She read the news with a thrill of delight.

'It is about an adjacent matter that I come to speak with you.'

He raised his eyebrows in enquiry.

'It would be convenient if you depart from this place forthwith. We have no need of you here.'

'What mean you?' he shouted angrily. 'I do not intend to depart. This house is made over to myself as a Puritan, as a supporter of that government which will be soon restored to its proper place.'

'No,' Sarah said. 'There are rumours that the King is already on his way. You must leave immediately.'

'Madam, I shall remain.'

'Sir, your occupation was but a temporary measure. If you should try to retain this property, I shall see that you are thrown into gaol.'

'Madam, I refuse.'

'Then, sir, I must expose your crime to the world.'

'What crime?'

'That you did murder that Commander Welbeck who fought for the Puritan army, out of petty revenge for his attacking Vinelands.'

'Madam, it was on your evidence that he did wantonly demolish this place.'

'Sir,' Sarah said incredulously, 'you are mistaken. I have made no such accusation. I have many persons in this house who will guarantee my words. But I have heard that Commander Welbeck was killed at your command.'

Philip came towards her, trembling with anger.

Sarah stepped back.

'Sir,' she said, 'it cannot be wise for you to behave with further immoderation. Pray consider the matter.' She moved hastily to the door. 'Tomorrow will be a suitable day for your departure,' she said as she left.

So, on the morrow, she assisted Isobel and Philip and the three children to their coach. Their few possessions were piled on the roof and as they began to move off down the drive, the servants all came out cheering and waving lustily and dancing up and down the steps.

'Let this be a holiday,' Sarah said. 'For all of you.'

Sarah watched the coach disappear, feeling a strange sense of anticlimax. After all the violence and anxieties and changes of the past years, the end had come so suddenly. It was all so simple, now that it had happened. She turned back into the house. Now it could be restored, the chapel would be reopened, the hidden treasures retrieved.

But it was too late now. Vinelands had been returned to her, but it would be for future generations, Nicholas and then dear Sarah Clare, to whom she had bequeathed it in trust, to bring it back to life.

The thought of Vinelands jerked her mind sharply back to the present. Now she had one more task to fulfil which might, she feared, be more difficult than all the problems of the Civil War, of imprisonment, even the terrible events in Ireland.

She went up to her chamber and took a document from her bureau. Then she walked down to the farm. 'Thomas and Harriet were busy in the cowsheds and she watched them as they proceeded to lay down straw. It seemed to her a complete mystery that these two, who had inherited an enormous fortune from Urith, should be content with

597

this humble life. They behaved just as John and Urith had done before them. Her fears reasserted themselves. Were they content with this because they knew that one day Vinelands would also be theirs? Were they merely permitting her, as Gabriel's widow, to remain there during her lifetime, only to assert their rights as soon as she was gone?

When they saw her, they came over, looking welcoming.

'Dear Sarah, come into the house. We will take some refreshment,' Harriet said.

She followed them into the farmhouse.

'Philip and his family have just departed,' Sarah said. 'We are free at last.'

Thomas's face lit up eagerly. 'Ah. What a delight. Vinelands is returned to its rightful owner. This calls for celebration. Come.' He led them into the parlour. 'Let us arrange a great party at Vinelands.'

Sarah smiled doubtfully, her suspicions growing.

'Yes,' she said. 'I will do that.'

'But we must assist you,' Harriet said instantly. 'It will be a great homecoming for all the family.'

Sarah took the wine that Thomas offered to her. 'It is about Vinelands that I have come to see you,' she said slowly.

Thomas and Harriet sat down, facing her.

'It much concerns me about its inheritance when I die,' she said.

They looked at each other doubtfully.

'But surely that has been settled,' Thomas said.

Sarah frowned.

'Yet it has not been spoken of. I have here a document, Thomas, signed by your father John, relinquishing all right to the property in favour of Nicholas.'

'Yes,' Thomas said instantly, 'I have it.'

'What mean you? I have it here.'

'My father made also another copy which he gave to me on my grandfather's death.'

598

'Oh.' Sarah looked at them in bewilderment. 'But you said nothing.'

'No.' Thomas smiled.

Then Harriet said, 'Sarah, it was agreed between John and Gabriel that the will should not be altered. It might have caused complications at the time with Gabriel's other relatives. But it was understood that this document is inviolable.'

'Oh.' Sarah felt even more uncomprehending. 'But do you accept this?'

'Sarah,' Thomas said quietly. 'It was my father's wish. I believe he felt that in his youth he had caused my grandfather much sorrow. He was clear that this was his intention, because his father desired it.'

'But do you accept it?' Sarah persisted. 'What of your own children?'

'I have inherited much,' Harriet replied. 'Thomas and I have but simple needs and they will get much land and wealth when they grow up.'

Sarah sighed. 'I think I have cared about Vinelands more than anything in the world. Even more than Gabriel did.'

'And Gabriel would want only what you do,' Thomas said quietly.

Sarah walked slowly back to the house, knowing that at last it was all settled, that there could be no more problem about Vinelands.

As everyone expected, a few months later news came that the King would soon set foot on English soil. Windsor Castle was being repaired in readiness for him.

'There will be great celebrations in the capital,' Sarah said to Catherine and when Nicholas and Penelope arrived from Cornwall, she decided that they should all go there with the children.

As they passed through Exeter and Salisbury on their way to London they saw much festivity, and when they reached the capital they found the streets were filled with delighted revellers. They went to William's house and waited there for the arrival of the King. The next day, they heard news that he and his entourage were entering the capital and they all set out for Westminster.

The streets around White Hall were thronged with people and when Charles arrived in a coach there were loud cheers and music echoed all around them. Other coaches followed, bringing those royalists who had been in exile with him, and it was in one of these that Sarah caught sight of Elizabeth and Edward.

They almost failed to see her in the crowds but Nicholas dashed forward and their coach was halted. They all embraced each other eagerly and the crowds around them cheered, delighted to get so close to the royal party.

'Come,' Elizabeth said, 'we all go to a great banquet at White Hall.'

Sarah and the children were all bundled into the coach, while the other adults said they would walk the short distance along the street.

The Great Hall was decorated and festooned with flowers. Long tables were filled with food, music echoed from the galleries and Sarah sat down on a couch with her family around her.

The King sat on a dais at the end of the hall, looking pale and tired but silence was called for and he made a short speech, thanking all those persons who had supported him so faithfully and expressing the hope that England might soon return to peace and prosperity.

Sarah looked at her family, gathered around her. Catherine and Reginald and their children, tall John, who already spoke of voyaging round the world; Gabriel who was to become an actor and playwright, and dear Nicholas whose health still concerned her. At seventeen he had an indefinable air of remoteness. Sarah always had the agonizing feeling that he would not live to manhood.

Then she smiled at Nicholas and Penelope, at young Frances and Cicely and she took Sarah Clare's hand.

'Come,' she said, 'Elizabeth and Edward beckon us.'

Nicholas put his arm round her and led her forward and they walked to the dais where Edward and the other exiles were seated around the King.

Edward presented Sarah and her family and they all bowed and curtseyed. As they returned down the hall, they were given goblets of wine and they all drank to the King and to peace.

Sarah sat on a blue velvet couch, surrounded by her family. Around them were most of the nobility of England, all those people who had supported the King during the long years of exile.

'Ah,' Sarah said, 'it is such a delight to see once again those beautiful gowns and the elegant cloaks and doublets of the men. All those lovely colours.'

She glanced back to the dais. The King had thick black hair, which hung in waves down to his wide elaborately embroidered collar. His white ermine cape hung in folds around him. As she watched, his gaze turned towards her, a smile came to his lips and he raised his hand slightly and gave her a small gesture of acknowledgment.

Edward was watching and turned to Sarah, smiling.

'He is a rebel,' Sarah said. 'A man after my own heart.'

She glanced back at the King. He was standing now. There was a cool arrogance about him that reminded her of Gabriel.

'He has almost the bearing of Gabriel,' she said, 'but not quite.'

She looked around at her family. 'My happiness is complete with all of you. I have no further desires. Now I know that Vinelands is secured for you, dear Nicholas, and for future generations.'

At the same moment, she gasped, sharply drawing in her breath.

'Mama, what is it?' Catherine asked anxiously.

'I have a strange pain,' Sarah said.

'We must call a physician,' Nicholas said, waving quickly to a servant.

601

'No,' Sarah said. 'Let me rest.'

She was carried into an ante-room and they stood around her, their fears growing as the colour drained from her cheeks. A physician was hastily summoned but before he could arrive, she had raised herself on the couch and said softly, 'Life has been so beautiful. Now I return from whence I came,' and she closed her eyes.

* * *

They brought her back to Vinelands and she was buried, as she requested in her will, in a secluded and solitary place above Dartmouth. No stone marked the spot.

Great crowds lined the streets of Dartmouth on that June morning, pouring up over the hills, above Crowthers Hill and Jawbones where they had first seen her half a century earlier. A thousand flowers covered the earth and grass above her.

When the family returned to Vinelands, they all gathered in the library, Sarah's children and grandchildren. The portraits of Gabriel, Frances, and their offspring and of the generations before them, all hidden during the occupation with the other treasures, had been replaced on the walls. Above the fireplace, Sarah once again looked down at them serenely, her green eyes giving future hope in their present grief, her gentle smile giving them comfort.